The Year's Best
Fantasy and Horror

ALSO EDITED BY ELLEN DATLOW AND TERRI WINDLING

The Year's Best Fantasy: First Annual Collection
The Year's Best Fantasy: Second Annual Collection
The Year's Best Fantasy and Horror: Third Annual Collection
The Year's Best Fantasy and Horror: Fourth Annual Collection
The Year's Best Fantasy and Horror: Fifth Annual Collection
The Year's Best Fantasy and Horror: Sixth Annual Collection
The Year's Best Fantasy and Horror: Seventh Annual Collection
The Year's Best Fantasy and Horror: Eighth Annual Collection
Snow White, Blood Red
Black Thorn, White Rose
Ruby Slippers, Golden Tears

The Year's Best Fantasy and Horror

NINTH ANNUAL COLLECTION

Edited by Ellen Datlow
and Terri Windling

ST. MARTIN'S GRIFFIN ❧ NEW YORK

This volume is dedicated to
the memory of Ian Ballantine, and to Betty Ballantine.
By their example of innovative, daring, and dauntless publishing,
they have inspired generations of editors and publishers
to find new ways to publish good books, reminding us
never to accept less than our own best ideas and
most creative ways to publish and sell
good books for all.

THE YEAR'S BEST FANTASY AND HORROR: NINTH ANNUAL COLLECTION.
Copyright © 1996 by James Frenkel & Associates.
Summation 1995: Fantasy copyright © 1996 by Terri Windling—The Endicott Studio.
Summation 1995: Horror copyright © 1996 by Ellen Datlow.
Horror and Fantasy in the Media: 1995 copyright © 1996 by Edward Bryant.
All rights reserved.
Printed in the United States of America. No part of this book may be used or reproduced in any manner whatsoever without written permission except in the case of brief quotations embodied in critical articles or reviews. For information, address St. Martin's Press, 175 Fifth Avenue, New York, N.Y. 10010.

Library of Congress Catalog Card Number: 91-659320

Paperback ISBN 0-312-14450-4
Hardcover ISBN 0-312-14449-0

First St. Martin's Griffin Edition: July 1996

10 9 8 7 6 5 4 3 2 1

A Blue Cows–Mad City production.

This page constitutes an extension of the copyright page:

"Home for Christmas" by Nina Kiriki Hoffman. Copyright © 1995 by Nina Kiriki Hoffman. First published in *The Magazine of Fantasy & Science Fiction*, January 1995. Reprinted by permission of the author.

"Heartfires" by Charles de Lint. Copyright © 1994 by Charles de Lint. First published as a Triskell Press chapbook. Reprinted by permission of the author.

"Screens" by Terry Lamsley. Copyright © 1995 by Terry Lamsley. First published in *Dark Terrors: The Gollancz Book of Horror* edited by Stephen Jones and David Sutton; Victor Gollancz, Ltd. Reprinted by permission of the author.

"King of Crows" by Midori Snyder. Copyright © 1995 by Midori Snyder. First published in *Xanadu 3* edited by Jane Yolen; Tor Books. Reprinted by permission of the author.

"Professor Gottesman and the Indian Rhinoceros" by Peter S. Beagle. Copyright © 1995 by Peter S. Beagle. First published in *Peter S. Beagle's Immortal Unicorn* edited by Peter S. Beagle and Janet Berliner; A HarperPrism Book. Reprinted by permission of the author.

"The Hunt of the Unicorn" by Ellen Kushner. Copyright © 1995 by Ellen Kushner. First published in *Peter S. Beagle's Immortal Unicorn* edited by Peter S. Beagle and Janet Berliner; A HarperPrism Book. Reprinted by permission of the author.

"More Tomorrow" by Michael Marshall Smith. Copyright © 1995 by Michael Marshall Smith. First published in *Dark Terrors: The Gollancz Book of Horror* edited by Stephen Jones and David Sutton; Victor Gollancz, Ltd. Reprinted by permission of the author.

"Penguins for Lunch" by Scott Bradfield. Copyright © 1995 by Scott Bradfield. First published in *TriQuarterly 93*. Reprinted by permission of the author.

"Ether OR" by Ursula K. Le Guin. Copyright © 1995 by Ursula K. Le Guin. First published in *Asimov's Science Fiction*, November 1995. Reprinted by permission of the author, and the author's agent, Virginia Kidd Agency, Inc.

"Paper Lantern" by Stuart Dybek. Copyright © 1995 by Stuart Dybek. First published in *The New Yorker*, November 27, 1995. Reprinted by permission of the author and the author's agents, International Creative Management, Inc.

"Lunch at the Gotham Café" by Stephen King. Copyright © 1995 by Stephen King. First published in *Dark Love* edited by Nancy A. Collins, Edward E. Kramer, and Martin H. Greenberg; Roc. Reprinted by permission of the author.

"Queen of Knives" by Neil Gaiman. Copyright © 1995 by Neil Gaiman. First published in *Tombs* edited by Peter Crowther and Edward E. Kramer; White Wolf Publishing. Reprinted by permission of the author.

"Dragon-Rain" by Eileen Kernaghan. Copyright © 1995 by Eileen Kernaghan. First published in *MAGIC: A Collection of the Fantastical* edited by David and Morgan Kopaska-Merkel; Stone Lightning Press. Reprinted by permission of the author.

"Llantos de La Llorona: Warnings from the Wailer" by Pat Mora. Copyright © 1995 by Pat Mora. First published in *Agua Santa/Holy Water* by Pat Mora; Beacon Press. Reprinted by permission of Beacon Press, Boston.

"Too Short a Death" by Peter Crowther. Copyright © 1995 by Peter Crowther. First published in

Celebrity Vampires edited by Martin H. Greenberg; DAW Books, Inc. Reprinted by permission of the author.

"The James Dean Garage Band" by Rick Moody. Copyright © 1995 by Rick Moody. First published in *Esquire*, July 1995. Reprinted from *The Ring of Brightest Angels Among Heaven* by Rick Moody; Little, Brown & Company. Reprinted by permission of Little, Brown & Company.

"Because of Dust" by Christopher Kenworthy. Copyright © 1995 by Christopher Kenworthy. First published in *The Third Alternative #7*, Summer 1995. Reprinted by permission of the author.

"Loop" by Douglas E. Winter. Copyright © 1995 by Douglas E. Winter. First published in *Dark Love* edited by Nancy A. Collins, Edward E. Kramer, and Martin H. Greenberg; Roc. Reprinted by permission of the author.

"La Loma, La Luna" by Sue Kepros Hartman. Copyright © 1995 by Sue Kepros Hartman. First published under the byline Sue Kepros in *High Fantastic* edited by Steve Rasnic Tem; Ocean View Press. Reprinted by permission by the author.

"Women's Stories" by Jane Yolen. Copyright © 1995 by Jane Yolen. First published in *Sisters in Fantasy* edited by Susan Shwartz and Martin H. Greenberg; NAL/Dutton. Reprinted by permission of the author, and the author's agent, Curtis Brown, Ltd.

"Swan/Princess" by Jane Yolen. Copyright © 1995 by Jane Yolen. First published in *Xanadu 3* edited by Jane Yolen; Tor Books. Reprinted by permission of the author, and the author's agent, Curtis Brown, Ltd.

"Switch" by Lucy Taylor. Copyright © 1995 by Lucy Taylor. First published in *David Copperfield's Tales of the Impossible* edited by David Copperfield and Janet Berliner; HarperPrism. Reprinted by permission of the author, and the author's agents, Ralph M. Vicinanza Literary Agency.

"Scaring the Train" by Terry Dowling. Copyright © 1994 by Terry Dowling. First published in *The Man Who Lost Red* by Terry Dowling; MirrorDanse Books. Reprinted by permission of the author.

"Blood Knot" by Steve Rasnic Tem. Copyright © 1995 by Steve Rasnic Tem. First published in *Forbidden Acts* edited by Nancy A. Collins and Edward E. Kramer; Avon Books. Reprinted by permission of the author.

"The Girl Who Married the Reindeer" by Eiléan ní Chuilleanáin. Copyright © 1995 by Eiléan ní Chuilleanáin. First published in *The Southern Review*, Autumn 1995. Reprinted by permission of the author.

"The Otter Woman" by Mary O'Malley. Copyright © 1995 by Mary O'Malley. First published in *The Southern Review*, Autumn 1995. Reprinted by permission of the author.

"Resolve and Resistance" by S. N. Dyer. Copyright © 1995 by Sharon N. Farber. First published in *Omni*, April 1995. Reprinted by permission of the author.

"La Dame" by Tanith Lee. Copyright © 1995 by Tanith Lee. First published in *Sisters of the Night* edited by Barbara Hambly and Martin H. Greenberg; Warner Aspect. Reprinted by permission of the author.

"Circe's Power" from *Meadowlands* by Louise Glück. Copyright © 1996 by Louise Glück. Published by the Ecco Press in 1996. Reprinted by permission. "Circe's Power" first appeared in *The New Yorker*.

"Dragon's Fin Soup" by S. P. Somtow. Copyright © 1995 by S. P. Somtow. First published in *The Ultimate Dragon* edited by Byron Preiss, John Betancourt, and Keith R. A. DeCandido; A Byron Preiss Book, A Dell Trade Paperback. Reprinted by permission of the author.

"The Granddaughter" by Vivian Vande Velde. Copyright © 1995 by Vivian Vande Velde. First published in *Tales from the Brothers Grimm and the Sisters Weird*; Jane Yolen Books, Harcourt Brace & Company. Reprinted by permission of Harcourt Brace & Company.

"Daphne and Laura and So Forth" by Margaret Atwood from *Morning in the Burned House*. Copyright © 1995 by Margaret Atwood. Reprinted by permission of Houghton Mifflin Company. All rights reserved.

"A Lamia in the Cévennes" by A. S. Byatt. Copyright © 1995 by A. S. Byatt. First published in *The Atlantic Monthly*, July 1995. Reprinted by permission of the author, and the author's agent, Peters Fraser & Dunlop Group, Ltd.

"The Guilty Party" by Susan Moody. Copyright © 1995 by Susan Moody. First published in *NO ALIBI: The Best New Crime Fiction* edited by Maxim Jakubowski; Ringpull Press. Reprinted by permission of the author.

"She's Not There" by Pat Cadigan. Copyright © 1995 by Pat Cadigan. First published in *Killing Me Softly, Erotic Tales of Unearthly Love* edited by Gardner Dozois; HarperPrism. Reprinted by permission of the author.

"The White Road" by Neil Gaiman. Copyright © 1995 by Neil Gaiman. First published in *Ruby Slippers, Golden Tears* edited by Ellen Datlow and Terri Windling; An AvoNova Book, William Morrow and Company. Reprinted by permission of the author.

"Refrigerator Heaven" by David J. Schow. Copyright © 1995 by David J. Schow. First published in *Dark Love* edited by Nancy A. Collins, Edward E. Kramer, and Martin H. Greenberg; Roc. Reprinted by permission of the author.

"After the Elephant Ballet" by Gary A. Braunbeck. Copyright © 1995 by Gary A. Braunbeck. First published in *Heaven Sent: 18 Glorious Tales of the Angels* edited by Peter Crowther; DAW Books, Inc. Reprinted by permission of the author.

"Henry V, Part 2" by Marcia Guthridge. Copyright © 1995 by Marcia Guthridge. First published in *The Paris Review*, Fall 1995. Reprinted by permission of the author.

"Mrs. Greasy" by Robert Reed. Copyright © 1995 by Robert Reed. First published in *Tomorrow: Speculative Fiction*, No. 18, December 1995. Reprinted by permission of the author.

"███████" by Joyce Carol Oates. Copyright © 1995 by The Ontario Review, Inc. First published in *Fear Itself* edited by Jeff Gelb; Warner Aspect. Reprinted by permission of the author and the author's agent, John Hawkins & Associates, Inc.

"The Printer's Daughter" by Delia Sherman. Copyright © 1995 by Delia Sherman. First published in *Ruby Slippers, Golden Tears* edited by Ellen Datlow and Terri Windling; An AvoNova Book, William Morrow and Company. Reprinted by permission of the author.

"Prayer" from *Among Angels*, copyright © 1995 by Nancy Willard, reprinted by permission of Harcourt Brace & Company.

"Jacob and the Angel" from *Among Angels*, copyright © 1995 by Jane Yolen, reprinted by permission of Harcourt Brace & Company.

"The Lion and the Lark" by Patricia A. McKillip. Copyright © 1995 by Patricia A. McKillip. First published in *The Armless Maiden and Other Tales for Childhood's Survivors* edited by Terri Windling; Tor Books. Reprinted by permission of the author.

CONTENTS

Acknowledgments xi
    Summation 1995: Fantasy Terri Windling xiii
    Summation 1995: Horror Ellen Datlow xxix
    Horror and Fantasy in the Media: 1995 Edward Bryant lxxi
    Obituaries James Frenkel lxxxiii

HOME FOR CHRISTMAS Nina Kiriki Hoffman 1
HEARTFIRES Charles de Lint 21
SCREENS Terry Lamsley 31
KING OF CROWS Midori Snyder 49
PROFESSOR GOTTESMAN AND THE INDIAN RHINOCEROS Peter S. Beagle 59
THE HUNT OF THE UNICORN Ellen Kushner 74
MORE TOMORROW Michael Marshall Smith 86
PENGUINS FOR LUNCH Scott Bradfield 108
ETHER OR Ursula K. Le Guin 125
PAPER LANTERN Stuart Dybek 142
LUNCH AT THE GOTHAM CAFÉ Stephen King 151
QUEEN OF KNIVES (poem) Neil Gaiman 175
DRAGON-RAIN Eileen Kernaghan 183
LLANTOS DE LA LLORONA: WARNINGS FROM THE WAILER (poem)
    Pat Mora 198
TOO SHORT A DEATH Peter Crowther 201
THE JAMES DEAN GARAGE BAND Rick Moody 218
BECAUSE OF DUST Christopher Kenworthy 233
LOOP Douglas E. Winter 243
LA LOMA, LA LUNA Sue Kepros Hartman 256
WOMEN'S STORIES (poem) Jane Yolen 270
SWAN/PRINCESS (poem) Jane Yolen 272
SWITCH Lucy Taylor 273
SCARING THE TRAIN Terry Dowling 285
BLOOD KNOT Steve Rasnic Tem 308
THE GIRL WHO MARRIED THE REINDEER (poem)
    Eiléan Ní Chuilleanáin 313
THE OTTER WOMAN (poem) Mary O'Malley 315
RESOLVE AND RESISTANCE S. N. Dyer 317
LA DAME Tanith Lee 332
CIRCE'S POWER (poem) Louise Glück 341
DRAGON'S FIN SOUP S. P. Somtow 343
THE GRANDDAUGHTER Vivian Vande Velde 362
DAPHNE AND LAURA AND SO FORTH (poem) Margaret Atwood 367
A LAMIA IN THE CÉVENNES A. S. Byatt 369
THE GUILTY PARTY Susan Moody 380
SHE'S NOT THERE Pat Cadigan 387

x   Contents

THE WHITE ROAD (poem)   Neil Gaiman   404
REFRIGERATOR HEAVEN   David J. Schow   413
AFTER THE ELEPHANT BALLET   Gary A. Braunbeck   422
HENRY V, PART 2   Marcia Guthridge   440
MRS. GREASY   Robert Reed   455
████████   Joyce Carol Oates   473
THE PRINTER'S DAUGHTER   Delia Sherman   485
PRAYER (poem)   Nancy Willard   500
JACOB AND THE ANGEL (poem)   Jane Yolen   501
THE LION AND THE LARK   Patricia A. McKillip   502

Honorable Mentions: 1995   517

Acknowledgments

I would like to thank William Congreve, Lawrence Schimel, Kathe Koja, David G. Hartwell, Jeff VanderMeer, Kent Robinson, Linda Marotta, and Gardner Dozois for their recommendations. I'd like to thank my interns for their help: Heather Adams, Joanna Smith, Ayesha Randolph, Michael Epshteyn. Thank you to the writers, editors, and publishers who sent me material for this volume.

And I would particularly like to thank James Frenkel, Jim Minz, Corin See, and Gordon Van Gelder. Thanks goes to Thomas Canty for another beautiful cover art and design. And finally a special thanks to my co-editor Terri Windling for keeping it fun.

(Please note: It's difficult to cover all nongenre sources of short horror, so should readers see a story or poem from such a source, I would appreciate it being brought to my attention. Drop me a line c/o *Omni* magazine, General Media International, 277 Park Avenue, 4th floor, New York, NY 10172-0003.)

I have used the following publications as sources throughout the Summation: *Locus* magazine, published and edited by Charles N. Brown: $43 for 12 issues (2nd class) and $53 for 12 issues (first class) payable to Locus Publications, P.O. Box 13305, Oakland, CA 94661; *Science Fiction Chronicle* published and edited by Andrew I. Porter: $35 for 12 issues (second class) and $42 for first class payable to Science Fiction Chronicle, P.O. Box 022730, Brooklyn, NY 11202-0056.

I would also like to acknowledge the following catalogs, all of which enabled me to write capsule descriptions of titles not seen by me as well as being excellent sources for ordering genre material by mail: The Overlook Connection, P.O. Box 526, Woodstock, GA 30188; Mark V. Ziesing, P.O. Box 76, Shingletown, CA 96088; and DreamHaven Books and Comics, 912 West Lake Street, Minneapolis, MN 55408.

A note of caution: when ordering books by mail, if no postage costs are mentioned it may mean the information was not made available—inquire of the publisher before ordering.

—Ellen Datlow

It takes a lot of people to put together a book like this one. As a result, I am grateful to all the publishers, editors, writers, artists, booksellers, and readers who sent material and shared their thoughts on the year in fantasy publishing with me. *Locus*, *PW*, *The Hungry Mind Review*, and *Folk Roots* magazines have been invaluable reference sources throughout.

I am most grateful to Bill Murphy, my invaluable editorial assistant on the fantasy half of this volume; to Ellen Kushner and Charles de Lint for music recommendations; and to Paul Petrie-Ritchie for all the coffee and support during the deadline crunch. Thanks are also due to: Ellen Steiber, Beth Meacham & Tappan King, Elisabeth Roberts, Patrick Nielsen Hayden, Delia Sherman, Jane Yolen, John Douglas, Christopher Schelling, Peter Stampfel, and Lawrence Schimel. Special thanks go to our St. Martin's editor, Gordon Van Gelder; to our series creator/packager, Jim Frenkel, and his assistant, Jim Minz; to our cover artist Thomas Canty; and to my editorial partner Ellen Datlow.

—Terri Windling

Heartfelt thanks to Ellen Datlow and Terri Windling for their thorough and inspired selections; and to Ed Bryant for his trenchant commentary on the media. Thanks to all those who make this annual project a little easier: the University of Wisconsin Memorial Library Reference Desk, an invaluable resource; Insty Prints, our reliable and indefatigable copy shop; our interns: Amy Fuchs, Jodi Hess, Seth Johnson, Melanie Orpen, Kimberly Vanderheiden, and Paul Wiesner, all of whom contributed in ways large and small to the successful completion of the work, to Joshua Frenkel, for some eleventh-hour fact-checking, and lastly to my assistant, James Minz, who executed most of the permissions paperwork, and heroically fought through a dreadful cold during crunch time to make sure the manuscript was finished on time.

—James Frenkel

Summation 1995: Fantasy
by Terry Windling

Readers familiar with the field of fantasy literature, and with this anthology series in particular, need no explanation of the mission we have set ourselves in compiling the fat volume that follows. For those new to either, however, a brief introduction is in order.

In this book we have gathered together a wide assortment of the best fantasy fiction published in the English language in 1995, drawing our material from the bright dreams of traditional fantasy, the dark nightmares of horror, and the vast, fecund area of storytelling that falls between these two poles. Fantasy and horror are sister fields of literature that overlap, inform, and enrich each other. Our definitions of what makes a "fantasy" or "horror" story tend to be broad and inclusive, not exclusive, ignoring the genre demarcations so beloved by American publishing companies. My co-editor and I have searched for the stories and poems that follow not only in the abundant genre sources (magazines, anthologies, small press 'zines, and single author collections), but anywhere magical, mythical, surrealistic, and horrific fiction might be found: mainstream magazines and anthologies, foreign works in translation, literary quarterlies, poetry reviews, and the parallel field of children's fiction. Each year our task becomes more daunting as more and more short fantasy fiction is published in all of these places. It would take a volume at least twice this size and an army of editors reading here and overseas to provide a truly definitive "best of the year" volume; but in the pages that follow you'll find a broad and representative selection of the very best that our field has to offer. The stories herein are reprinted from *The New Yorker, Esquire, The Paris* and *Southern Reviews, Omni,* and *The Magazine of Fantasy & Science Fiction,* as well as various other magazines, anthologies, and small press publications. They are set in America, England, France, China, Thailand, the frigid North Pole, the historic past, the urban present, and the landscapes of Once Upon a Time.

In general, 1995 was a very strong year for short fantasy fiction. Within the genre, several newsstand magazines now provide a solid market for fantasy stories—although one of the best of them, *Omni* magazine, stopped newsstand publication at the end of the year. (This is sad news indeed, for despite its general science fiction thrust, *Omni* could also be counted on for highly literary works of contemporary fantasy.) A rather astonishing number of fantasy anthologies were published in 1995 (largely "theme" anthologies of original stories), despite genre publishers' continual complaint that readers don't buy short fiction. Mainstream publishers, I'm happy to report, are no longer decrying the short fiction form. Mainstream story collections have begun to sell in record numbers from the large and small press publishers alike, leading some critics to label this "the renaissance of the American short story." Because of the influence of Latin American and European magic realism, good fantasy fiction is a solid part of the mainstream short story revival—particularly in the areas of Chicano, Native American, and Black American fiction.

On the other hand, 1995 was not at all the best of years for novel-length fantasy. The number of titles published in the field did not seem to go down appreciably, but there were only a handful of books this year about which one could get really excited. Reliable pros like Patricia A. McKillip, Tanith Lee, and Orson Scott Card brightened the genre lists; Gabriel García Márquez, Alice Hoffman, and A. A. Attanasio published excellent magical work in the literary mainstream. But by and large I'm sorry to report that it was a rather lackluster year in terms of literary quality—particularly after being spoiled by several years in which publishers' lists were chock full of excellent reads. As a result, the list of recommended titles below is, regrettably, a bit shorter than usual (although there *were* a few gems in 1995). If, however, your taste runs to the young-royal-in-disguise-battles-against-overwhelming-Evil type of fantasy, you are in luck; it remains as overstocked in the big chain bookstores as ever.

In general, publishers of fantasy are reporting strong hardcover and trade paperback sales, and a sluggish market for the standard "mass market" size paperbacks that used to be the backbone of the genre. Big Name authors and media- and game-related books have stronger sales than ever; but most writers are struggling to make a living. This is where I must, once again, make my plea to you, the readers, to protect the lively diversity we have come to enjoy in the fantasy field by supporting our lesser-known authors in the most direct way we can: by buying their books, reading them, recommending them to other readers. We've a whole new generation of talented writers coming into publication in the 1990s: newcomers like Jane Lindskold, Sean Stewart, Susanna Clarke, Susan Wade, Felicity Savage, Stephen Grundy, Elizabeth Wein, Ellen Steiber, Sharon Shinn, and Micole Sudberg. These are writers to watch and encourage—writers who will bring the fantasy field into the new century ahead.

Now to the specifics of the 1995 publishing year. Once again, I won't claim that I've managed to obtain *every* work of fantasy, magic realism, and surrealism published in this country and abroad—but in addition to my own wide reading I have culled recommendations from the community of fantasy writers, editors, and publishers across the United States and England in order to compile the lists below. The following is a Baker's Dozen of the best novels published in 1995, which no fantasy lover should overlook:

In alphabetical order . . .

Reservation Blues by Sherman Alexie (Atlantic Monthly Press). Alexie has made a name for himself with short fiction (collected in *The Lone Ranger and Tonto Fistfight in Heaven*) and several excellent collections of poetry. Now this immensely talented Native American writer has published his first novel—and it, too, is a winner. The story, about a rock-and-roll band on an Indian reservation, has strong magical realist elements and is, by turns, hilarious and sobering.

The Dragon and the Unicorn by A. A. Attanasio (Hodder and Stoughton UK). When a writer as wildly imaginative as A. A. Attanasio takes on the Matter of Britain, one can be sure that the result will be unpredictable . . . to say the least. Attanasio mixes Arthurian lore with Norse gods, modern physics, and sundry faerie creatures in this literary, peculiar, and passionate novel. There has been nothing else quite like it.

Animal Planet by Scott Bradfield (Picador–U. S.). Another wild mainstream publication, the latest work from the author of *The History of Luminous Motion* is a hilarious satiric piece about a modern animal rebellion. Bradford's homage to Orwell's *Animal Farm* is wickedly clever, skillfully written, and enormously engaging.

Alvin Journeyman by Orson Scott Card (Tor Books). Card is creating a masterwork of American fantasy in "The Tales of Alvin Maker," of which this is Volume IV. These are historical novels set in an altered America, blending the homespun magics of frontier folks with wilder magics drawn from the landscape of the vast New World they inhabit. This latest novel in the series crosses from the New World to the Old and back again. Card's thoughtful, entertaining books are among the very best the fantasy genre has to offer.

The Memory Cathedral by Jack Dann (Bantam). This exuberant historical novel explores the alchemical magic of the Italian Renaissance, and the myths surrounding the lost year in the life of Leonardo da Vinci. Dann is a terrific writer and *The Memory Cathedral* is his best work to date. He beautifully evokes the world of Renaissance Florence while creating a suspenseful and mysterious tale.

Practical Magic by Alice Hoffman (G. P. Putnam). This enchanting and exquisitely written American fantasy has my vote as the best book of the year. Hoffman is a mainstream writer who has developed a loyal following of readers within the fantasy genre for books that seem to become increasingly magical by the year. Her latest, about a murder and a family of witches living in contemporary New England, is a romantic yet nonsentimental look at men, women, and the magic of love.

The Silent Strength of Stones by Nina Kiriki Hoffman (AvoNova). Over the last several years, this prolific author has quietly established herself as one of the best contemporary writers in the fantasy field. (See "Home for Christmas," published in this volume.) Loosely connected to *The Thread that Binds the Bones*, Hoffman's new novel is also set in modern Oregon and explores the magic that pervades the daily lives of two rather awkward teenagers. This is more than a "coming-of-age" book, however; it is a moving and skillfully penned American fantasy tale.

When Fox Is a Thousand by Larissa Lai (Press Gang Publishers, Canada). This mainstream historical murder mystery tells the stories of a ninth-century Chinese nun/poet and of a contemporary Asian-American woman, weaving them together with Chinese myths of shape-shifters and fox-women. It is beautifully written, dark, unusual, and thoroughly haunting.

Reigning Cats and Dogs by Tanith Lee (Headline–UK). At her best, British writer Tanith Lee rivals Angela Carter for gorgeous dark fantasy imagery—and this is one of her best. Set in a Dickensian world that is not quite Victorian London, Lee's dark, sensual, and magical novel ranges from the crystalline images of folklore to the phantastes of an opium dream.

Of Love and Other Demons by Gabriel García Márquez (Knopf). Márquez, of course, is the greatest living writer of Latin American magical realism; his work has had a profound influence on contemporary fantasists both in the genre and in the mainstream. The author's storytelling abilities are as transcendent as ever in this new volume, inspired by a strange event he witnessed almost fifty years ago. Highly recommended.

The Book of Atrix Wolfe by Patricia A. McKillip (Ace). This may be the best one yet from this consummate prose stylist—an adult fairy tale, both poetric and engaging, about wolves, magicians, and the lost daughter of the Queen of the Wood. McKillip's writing style is positively luminous, and it is criminal that her work is not as well known as, say, Alice Hoffman's among literary readers. Fantasy genre readers, however, have known for years what a rare treasure we have in McKillip.

The Blind God Is Watching by Nancy Springer (Silver Salamander). Published in a limited small press edition, this dark, harrowing, and spendidly written short novel deserves wider attention than it has received thus far. Springer's story of the monstrous Frog Boy, his carny father, and a lonely adolescent girl is both a modern fairy tale and a hardhitting work of contemporary literature. Absolutely unforgettable.

Resurrection Man by Sean Stewart (Ace). I erroneously mentioned this book last year; it is actually a 1995 release. The publisher is calling it fantasy although it's one of those impossible-to-classify novels, weaving traditional fantasy, alternate history, SF, horror, and mainstream elements together into a powerful story set in contemporary America (albeit a magically altered one). Strong character developments put this novel a cut above the rest, and I'm glad to have the opportunity to recommend it once again.

First Novels:
The best first novel of the year is *Red Earth and Pouring Rain* by Vikram Chandra (Little, Brown). This rich, gorgeous novel by an East Indian American author is an extraordinary piece of contemporary fantasy and absolutely should not be missed.

The runner-up for best first novel was in a more traditional vein: *The Shape-Changer's Wife* by Sharon Shinn (Ace). This is a modest, magical, and enchanting work—a traditional "imaginary world" fantasy novel that reminds you just how good such novels can be when told with simplicity, honesty, and imagination.

Other runners-up are *Pawn's Dream* by Eric Nyland (AvoNova) and *The Baker's Boy* by J. V. Jones (Warner). Both are traditional fantasies with no real suprises, but each has flashes of originality. These are writers to watch.

Oddities:
The "Best Peculiar Book" distinction for 1995 goes to *The Lighthouse at the End of the World* by Stephen Marlowe (Dutton), a bizarre, fragmented, intelligent, and ultimately compelling work of dark fantasy that explores an alternate history of the life of Edgar Allan Poe.

The runner-up is *The Tough Guide to Fantasyland* by Diana Wynne Jones (Gollancz–UK). This peculiar little book is a takeoff on the "Rough Guide" travelers' guidebook series, escorting the reader on a wickedly humorous tour through the world of fantasy novels. Jones doesn't pull any punches here when it comes to the clichés of the genre. And more power to her.

Imaginary World Fantasy:
After the McKillip and Shinn novels listed above, *Royal Assassin* by Robin Hobb (Bantam) is the best of the imaginary world fantasy novels I read this year. This caused me to go back and read the first book in Hobb's series, *Assassin's Apprentice*, which I regret missing before. Strong characterizations give these works a freshness lacking in too many high fantasy novels these days. This is another new writer to watch. Other books of note:

Nobody's Son by Sean Stewart (Maxwell Macmillan, Canada). Like Hobb, Stewart works with familiar material in this young-man-on-a-quest story, but breathes freshness into the formula with clear prose and complex character development, creating a memorable tale.

Fortress in the Eye of Time by C. J. Cherryh (HarperPrism Books). A dark, brooding, ultimately powerful traditional fantasy by one of the field's best writers. This is not a major work, yet it's a thoroughly engrossing one. Cherryh is another writer who demonstrates how good this form of fantasy can be when written with maturity and skill.

Caliban's Hour by Tad Williams (HarperPrism). Williams is a talented and popular writer who seems to get better with each fat novel. His latest is a delight: a romantic mystery tale involving Shakespeare's Caliban and Miranda.

A Sorcerer and a Gentleman by Elizabeth Willey (Tor). This second novel is the prequel to Willey's medieval fantasy, *The Well-Favored Man*. Arch, intelligent, and entertaining.

Kingdoms of the Night by Allan Cole and Chris Bunch (Del Rey Books). This rollicking fantasy adventure novel is a definite cut above the rest. A solid, fast-paced romp.

The Moon and the Thorn by Teresa Edgerton (Ace). Edgerton is one of the better writers working in the "series fantasy" format; her work is lyrical, gentle, romantic. This is Celtic fantasy, the final volume in Edgerton's *Celydonn Trilogy*.

Beyond Ragnorak by Mickey Zucker Reichert (DAW Books). For swords-and-sorcery lovers, Reichert's suspenseful, muscular fantasies are among the best in the form.

Mirror of Destiny by Andre Norton (William Morrow). A light but entertaining piece of work (about a young apprentice-healer) by this Grand Dame of the fantasy genre. It's not published as a Young Adult title, but is perfect for younger readers.

Phantastes: A Faerie Romance for Men and Women by George McDonald (Johannesen–UK). A reprint edition of the nineteenth-century English fantasy novel that remains one of the classics of the field. McDonald's *Lilith* is also available from the same publisher in an interesting edition that includes the text of McDonald's first draft alongside his published draft.

Mythic and Historical Fantasy:
After the Dann, Card, and Lee books listed above, the best historical fantasy published this year was *The Steampunk Trilogy* by Paul Di Filippo (Four Walls Eight Windows). This terrific volume collects three novels set in a wildly alternate nineteenth century, and is highly recommended. Other notable titles:

Electricity by Victoria Glendinning (Little, Brown). This English novel explores Victorian culture, science, and spiritualism (the latter being its slight fantasy element). Glendinning is a Whitbread Prize winner; her latest is particularly recommended to those readers interested in Victoriana.

The Kingdom of Fanes by Connie Prantera (Bloomsbury–UK). This novel, inspired by Italian folktales, is set in an imaginary country, but otherwise the world is roughly our own. It's a lovely work of medieval fantasy.

Dance of the Snow Dragon by Eileen Kernaghan (Thistledown Press, Neville Books, 7793 Royal Oak Avenue, Burnaby, BC V5J 4K2 Canada). A lyrical, beautifully penned story set in eighteenth-century Bhutan.

Pillar of Fire by Judith Tarr (Tor). Both scholarly and entertaining, this is a magical historical novel set in ancient Egypt.

The Lions of Al-Rassan by Guy Gavriel Kay (HarperPrism). An historical fantasy set in eleventh-century Spain, inspired by the legends of El Cid. It's rather nice to see someone working with this material.

To Build Jerusalem by John Whitbourn (Gollancz). Set in an interesting alternate England (where the Reformation failed) in the near future, this novel (sequel to last year's *A Dangerous Energy*) falls on the line between fantasy and SF.

The Psalms of Herod by Esther Friesner (White Wolf). Friesner's unusual novel also falls somewhere between SF and dark fantasy, making use of historical elements and the symbols of Judaic myth. The writer is better known for light, comic works; this dark, complex, and serious tale makes for interesting reading.

Power Dreamers: The Jocasta Complex by Ursule Molinaro (McPherson & Co.). Molinaro explores the story of Oedipus from a female point of view in this bizarre, intriguing novel from an award-winning mainstream writer.

Contemporary and Urban Fantasy:
1995 was not a particularly strong year for the area of the genre known as "urban fantasy," although Stewart's *Resurrection Man*, recommended above, might as easily fall under that label as any other. Otherwise, the best of the lot is an omnibus reprint volume from one of the writers who invented the form: *Jack of Kinrowan* by Charles de Lint (Tor). This trade paperback volume contains two interrelated urban fantasy novels inspired by "Jack" folktales: *Jack the Giant Killer* and *Drink Down the Moon*.

Also of note, *Dreamseeker's Road* by Tom Dietz (AvoNova) is a light but entertaining fantasy that brings the Celtic "Wild Hunt" to modern Georgia.

Fantasy in the Mainstream:
In addition to the mainstream titles listed in the Baker's Dozen above, the best mainstream fantasy in 1995 was *The Chess Garden* by Brooks Hansen (Farrar, Straus & Giroux), an odd

contemporary fantasy involving the game of chess and containing tales within tales within tales.... Other notable titles:

The Hundred Secret Senses by Amy Tan (Putnam). Although primarily a contemporary realist novel about an Asian-American woman and her Chinese half-sister, this novel contains a delicious ghost story at its core. The novel expands upon material from Tan's short story "Young Girl's Wish," published in *The New Yorker* magazine.

Wicked: The Life and Times of the Wicked Witch of the West by Gregory Maguire (Harper-Collins). This is a dark, intense adult fantasy set in the land of Oz (recognizably the movie version of Oz, rather than L. Frank Baum's). More fantastic in conception than Geoff Ryman's *Was* (an excellent book in its own right), Maguire's new novel is equally harrowing in passages.

Jane's Bad Hare Day by Carol Ann Sima (Dalkey Archive Press). A peculiar but rather adorable first novel; an homage to *Alice in Wonderland* (and the movie *Harvey* perhaps?) in which a woman is accosted by a six-foot rabbit in modern Manhattan.

Phosphor in Dreamland by Rikki Ducornet (Dalkey Archive). The publisher bills this epistolary novel as "Jonathan Swift meets Angela Carter via Jorge Luis Borges." That's not a bad description. Set on an imaginary Carribean island, the story is dark, exotic, phantasmagoric, erotic ... and memorable.

Be I Whole by Alyce Miller (MacMurray and Beck). This lovely novel uses the diction of oral storytelling—mixing myths, dreams, and parables into an uneven but engaging narrative—to create the portrait of a West Indian community in Detroit in the 1950s.

Water from the Well by Myra McLarey (Atlantic Monthly Press). Like the Miller book above, this novel uses delicate magical realist touches to color the many-faceted stories of overlapping black and white communities.

Solar Storms by Linda Hogan (Charles Scribner Sons). The latest novel by this talented Chickasaw writer beautifully explores the relationships between several generations of women. It has slight mythic elements in the evocation of the oral storytelling that permeates women's history in Native American cultures.

The Book of Color by Julia Blackburn (Pantheon Books). An interesting but rather grim, dark tale about a nineteenth-century missionary (on an island in the Indian Ocean) who passes a curse on to his son, an English minister and poet.

Portrait of the Artist as a Young Ape by Michael Butor (Dalkey Archive). First published in France, this is a peculiar alchemical tale about a young man who dreams of becoming an ape....

Briefly Noted:

The following fantasy novels were best-sellers in 1995, beloved by large numbers of readers in this country and abroad: *Witches' Brew* by Terry Brooks (Del Rey), *Belgarath the Sorcerer* by David and Leigh Eddings (Del Rey), *Rise of the Merchant Prince* by Raymond E. Feist (Morrow), *Stone of Tears* by Terry Goodkind (Tor), *Lord of Chaos* by Robert Jordan (Tor), *The Bastard Prince* by Katherine Kurtz (Del Rey), and *Storm Rising* and *The Fire Rose* by Mercedes Lackey (DAW).

In the fields of science fiction and horror, there were several good works with magical elements that fantasy readers should be sure to take a look at: *Amnesia Moon* by Jonathan Lethem (Harcourt Brace), *Blood* by Michael Moorcock (Millennium–UK), *All the Bells on Earth* by James P. Blaylock (Ace), *Expiration Date* by Tim Powers (Tor), *Zod Wallop* by William Browning Spencer (St. Martin's Press), *Humility Garden* by Felicity Savage (Roc), *The Off Season* by Jack Cady (St. Martin's), and *The Unusual Life of Tristram Smith* by Peter Carey (Knopf). Also of note is *Jasmine Nights* (St. Martin's), a fictionalized memoir by fantasy/horror writer S. P. Somtow—a moving, haunting, and occasionally hilarious work about a lonely, extremely literate young man growing up in Thailand and Europe.

Young Adult Fantasy:

The best Young Adult fantasy I read this year was *Journey Through Llandor*, the first book in a trilogy by Louise Lawrence (Collins–UK). Although it has a fairly standard imaginary world fantasy plot, Lawrence is a such a skillful writer that she easily turns such stories to gold. Other notable Young Adult fantasy novels:

Baby Be-Bop by Francesca Lia Block (HarperCollins). This is a prequel (of sorts) to the wild *Weetzie Bat* by a terrific and iconclastic writer.

Billy's Drift by Charles Ashton (Walker–UK). A dark and ghostly mystery tale about a boy named Billy and a dog named Drift. This one is beautifully written and packs a punch.

Emperor Mage by Tamora Pierce (Atheneum). Volume III in Pierce's "Immortals" series, this is entertaining imaginary world fantasy full of insufferable gods and wild talking animals. Kids love it.

Deersnake by Lucy Sussex (Hodder Headline Australia). An Australian Young Adult novel in which the use of LSD opens the doors into the faery world. An interesting, if not entirely successful, work of contemporary fantasy.

Sabriel by Garth Nix (HarperCollins Australia). Another fantasy from Down Under, this one is a fairly predictable "Magician's Apprentice" tale, but enjoyable nonetheless. A writer to watch.

The Bellmaker by Brian Jacques (Hutchinson–UK). This is the umpteenth volume in Jacques's talking animal series—and yet it remains as fresh, arch, and wonderful as ever.

Elfsong by Ann Turner (Jane Yolen Books/Harcourt Brace). A delightful little story full of magic and cats, for younger readers.

Hatchling by Midori Snyder (Random House). A charming, moving children's story (by an author well known to adult fantasy readers) set in the world of "Dinotopia," created by artist James Gurney.

Brian Boru by Morgan Llywelyn (Tor). A solid Young Adult historical novel about the first High King of Ireland.

The Wild Hunt by Jane Yolen (Harcourt Brace). This is a very short novel, with a lyrical, fairy tale quality. Based on the Wild Hunts of Celtic myth, it is gorgeously written, as one would expect from this author.

Anthologies:

The best anthology of 1995 is undoubtably *The Penguin Book of Modern Fantasy by Women*, edited by Susan A. Williams and Richard Glyn Jones (Viking), a collection of (primarily reprint) stories by thirty-eight authors from the 1940s to the present. The U.K. edition, with cover art by the surrealist painter/author Leonora Carrington, is particularly handsome. The best of the rest are:

Peter S. Beagle's *Immortal Unicorn*, edited by Peter S. Beagle and Janet Berliner (Harper-Prism). This is a terrific, solid collection of stories, transcending the potentially saccharine unicorn theme. The best are by Karen Joy Fowler, Ellen Kushner, and Beagle himself.

Xanadu 3, edited by Jane Yolen (Tor). This is, sadly, the last of Yolen's collections of all-original short fiction and poetry, mixing interesting work by new writers with good pieces from those established in various fields. Quite a few of the stories in this volume ended up on our Honorable Mentions list; the best are by Midori Snyder, Nancy Etchemendy, Micole Sudberg, and Yolen herself.

The Merlin Chronicles, edited by Mike Ashley (Carroll & Graf). An excellent Arthurian collection of twenty-two stories on the subject of Merlin. It mixes reprint material with original work, including good stories by Tanith Lee, Phyllis Ann Karr, Jessica Amanda Salmonson, and a very strong piece from Robert Holdstock.

David Copperfield's Tales of the Impossible, edited by David Copperfield and Janet Berliner (HarperPrism). This collection of fantasy stories, co-edited by a world famous magician, is slickly produced . . . and rather better than I'd expected. It contains particularly good stories by Ray Bradbury, Lisa Mason, Joyce Carol Oates, Dave Smeds, and S. P. Somtow.

High Fantastic, edited by Steve Rasnic Tem (Ocean View Press). This small press collection of speculative stories from Colorado contains some beautiful works of fantasy by Sue Kepros, Edward Bryant, and other Rocky Mountain writers. The entire collection is engrossing, and strongly recommended.

Full Spectrum 5, edited by Jennifer Hershey, Tom Dupree, and Janna Silverstein (Bantam Spectra). This biannual volume contains much more SF than fantasy in 1995, but the stories are all of such a high quality that I recommend it highly nonetheless. Take a look at the Richard Bowes and Karen Joy Fowler stories in particular.

Dante's Disciples, edited by Peter Crowther and Edward E. Kramer (White Wolf). This collection of tales about "the demonic gateways to the Netherworld" contains primarily horror stories, as might be expected—but there are a few fantasy/dark fantasy pieces worth noting, particularly the Storm Constantine story.

Ruby Slippers, Golden Tears, edited by Ellen Datlow and Terri Windling (AvoNova). This collection of orginal adult fairy tales (Volume III in a series inspired by the fairy tale work of the late Angela Carter) is, of course, one of my favorites of the year; you'll have to decide for yourself if it is one of yours. The writers therein include Tanith Lee, Howard Waldrop, and Joyce Carol Oates.

The Armless Maiden and Other Tales for Childhood's Survivors, edited by Terri Windling (Tor). This is a theme anthology on the subject of childhood and its darker passages; it is also a charity volume to benefit an organization working with homeless and abused children. Original fantasy material includes works by Midori Snyder, Tanith Lee, Ellen Kushner, Charles de Lint, and Jane Yolen.

For those interested in fantasy adventure tales with female protagonists, the best collection of the year was *Sisters in Fantasy*, edited by Susan Shwartz and Martin H. Greenberg (DAW). You might also take a look at *Ancient Enchantresses*, edited by Kathleen M. Massie-Ferch, Martin H. Greenberg, and Richard Gilliam (DAW); *Swords & Sorceress XII*, edited by Marion Zimmer Bradley (DAW); *Chicks in Chainmail*, edited by Esther M. Friesner (Baen); and (for younger readers) *Girls to the Rescue: Tales of Clever, Courageous Girls from Around the World*, edited by Bruce Lansky (Meadowbrook Press).

The Myth of the World: Volume 2 of the Dedalus Book of Surrealism, edited by Michael Richardson (Dedalus) is, like its predecessor, a fascinating volume collecting work from several languages and many different countries on the themes of surrealism and myth. The entries in this volume range from classic pieces by André Breton and Antonin Artaud to works by Rikki Ducornet, Alain Joubert, and Jean Malrieu. Also from Dedalus: *The Grin of the Gargoyle: The Dedalus Book of Medieval Literature*, edited by Brian Murdoch. I can't possibly describe this book better than the publisher: "Texts translated from the prose, chronicles, and verse of the period, such as the *Trials of Gilles de Rais*, Boccaccio's *Decameron*, *I Have a Gentil Cok*, *A Black Mass* and *Metrical Verses on the Subject of his Prick*, reveal the wilder aspects of medieval man."

Other anthologies of interest, briefly noted:

Camelot, edited by Jane Yolen (Philomel). A very nice collection of ten original fantasy stories for children.

Dread and Delight: A Century of Children's Ghost Stories, edited by Phillipa Pearce (Oxford University Press). A solid reprint volume.

Magic, edited by David C. Kopaska-Merkel and Morgan L. Kopaska-Merkel (Stone Lightening Press, 1300 Kicker Rd., Tuscaloosa, AL 35404). A small press collection of original fantasy stories.

Fantastic Alice, edited with an introduction by Margaret Weis (Ace). Original tales inspired by Lewis Carroll's *Alice in Wonderland*.

The Ultimate Dragon, edited by Byron Preiss, John Betancourt, and Keith R.A. DeCandido (BPVP/Dell). Original tales on a dragon theme.

The Book of Kings, edited by Richard Gilliam and Martin H. Greenberg (Roc). Original fantasy stories about kings and kingdoms.

Tales of the Knights Templar, edited by Katherine Kurtz (Warner Aspect). Original fantasy stories about the historical Knights Templar.

Warriors of Blood and Dream, edited by Roger Zelazny (AvoNova). Original stories about the martial arts.

The Best of Weird Tales, edited by John Betancourt (Barnes & Noble). Stories drawn from the pages of *Weird Tales* magazine between 1988 and 1994, containing some dark fantasy works, but primarily horror.

Single Author Collections:

The best collection of the year was a posthumous one: *Burning Your Boats* by Angela Carter (Chatto & Windus–UK), containing all the short fiction of this superb English writer who has had a strong impact on the fantasy field. Highly recommended. Other short fiction collections of note:

The Panic Hand by Jonathan Carroll (HarperCollins–UK). A collection of dark fantasy stories (eighteen reprints, one original) by this quirky and extraordinary writer.

The Ivory and the Horn by Charles de Lint (Tor). This is de Lint's second collection of "urban fantasy" stories set in the imaginary contemporary city of Newford. Recommended.

A Flush of Shadows by Kate Wilhelm (St. Martin's). This collection of five novellas about Wilhelm's pair of sleuths falls in the cracks between fantasy, SF, and mainstream—but the quality of Wilhelm's prose makes this recommended reading nonetheless.

Everard's Ride by Diana Wynne Jones (NESFA Press, PO Box 809, Framingham, MA 01701). A lovely collection of eight stories (and some nonfiction) by one of England's very best fantasy writers, with an introduction by Patricia C. Wrede.

Here There Be Witches by Jane Yolen (Harcourt Brace). This volume, published as an illustrated children's edition, contains magical stories and poetry by one of America's very best fantasy writers.

An Intimate Knowledge of the Night by Terry Dowling (Aphelion Publications, 3 Pepper Tree Lane, N. Adelaide, South Australia, 5006). This beautiful collection of tales by one of Australia's best writers crosses between fantasy, horror, and SF.

Seven Tales and a Fable by Gwyneth Jones (Edgewood Press). The collected adult fairy tales of this gifted British writer, presented in a handsome small press edition.

Truly Grimm Tales by Priscilla Galloway (Delacorte). An uneven collection of original fairy tale retellings, dark in tone.

Dr. Clock's Last Case by Ruth Fainlight (Virago Press). A mainstream collection that contains some good contemporary fantasy and ghost tales, by a writer better known for her poetry.

The Dreaming Child and Other Stories by Isak Dinesen (Penguin "Minibooks"). A reprint volume of three strange, wonderful tales.

Five Letters from an Unknown Empire by Alasdair Gray (Penguin "Minibooks"). A wild and strange reprint fantasy story.

The Birds of the Moon: A Traveller's Tale by Michael Moorcock (Jayde Design, 45 St. Mary's Mansions, St. Mary's Terrace, London W2 1SH). This terrific short fantasy piece, published in a small press edition, is part of Moorcock's "Von Bek & the Holy Grail" sequence, set in Glastonbury.

Lunching With the Antichrist by Michael Moorcock (Ziesing). A handsome small-press collection that includes excellent impossible-to-classify stories that could be considered fantasy.

The Miracle Shed by Philip MacCann (Faber & Faber). There are some magic realist elements in this collection of dark, rather sinister stories by a mainstream writer better known in England.

The Ultimate Egoist by Theodore Sturgeon (North Atlantic Books, PO Box 12327, Berkeley, CA 94712). The first of a projected ten-volume set, collecting the complete works of this master storyteller.

Slewfoot Sally and the Flying Mule and Other Tales from Cotton Country by Ardath Mayhar (Blue Lantern, PO Box 5833, Kingwood, TX 77325). Stories based on the folklore and tall tales of Texas, by a writer known for her adult and YA fantasy novels.

Fairy Tales: Traditional Stories Retold for Gay Men by Peter Cashorali (HarperSan Francisco). Uneven in quality, but heartfelt.

Women Who Wear the Breeches: Delicious and Dangerous Tales by Shahrukh Husain (Virago UK). This collection of original adult fairy tales about women, men, and cross-dressing is interesting in conception and rather purple in execution—but certainly worth taking a look at. The author is from Pakistan; the stories are based on traditional tales from around the world.

Tree of Dreams: Ten Tales from the Garden of Night by Lawrence Yep (BridgeWater). Ten original young adult stories inspired by traditional tales from around the world. Yep, as always, is a wonderful writer.

Tales from the Brothers Grimm and the Sisters Weird by Vivien Vande Velde (Jane Yolen Books/Harcourt Brace). A quirky collection of fractured fairy tales for young readers.

The Complete Fairy Tales of Herman Hesse (Bantam). These works are beautifully translated by Jack Zipes, a noted scholar in the fairy tale field.

The Dragon Path: The Collected Tales of Kenneth Morris (Tor). A reprint collection of forty tales from this historically important fantasy writer (early twentieth century); with an introduction by Douglas A. Anderson.

The Portent and Other Stories by George MacDonald (Johannesen). A reprint edition of enchanting stories from this nineteenth-century English fantasist.

Trudging to Eden by Kim Antieau (Silver Salamander Press, Blue Moon Books, 360 W. 1st, Eugene, OR 97401). A small press collection of twelve stories, with an introduction by Charles de Lint.

Short Fiction in the Magazines:

The best sources for magical stories on the newsstands are *The Magazine of Fantasy & Science Fiction, Asimov's Science Fiction Magazine, Omni,* and *Realms of Fantasy.* Of these, *F & SF* (under the editorial direction of Kristine Kathryn Rusch) publishes the greatest number of good fantasy stories annually. *Realms of Fantasy* (edited by Shawna McCarthy) is notable as the only magazine dedicated exclusively to fantasy fiction; this popular magazine includes columns on genre books, media, games, art, and folklore and offers an abundance of magical fiction on a bimonthly basis, but shies away from the high end of literary fantasy. *RoF's* coverage of magical art is quite good, however, which is an area the other magazines tend to miss.

The New Yorker, Esquire, Harper's, Playboy, and various literary reviews continue to run the occasional fantasy piece—*The New Yorker* and *The Paris Review* seem to be particularly open to the form, bless them. The speculative fiction field now has its own small literary magazine, *Century,* which is an absolute treasure chest of excellent work, handsomely produced by editor Robert K.J. Killheffer and publisher Meg Hamel. I heartily urge all lovers of good fantasy literature to support it; let's not lose this one. (Subscriptions: PO Box 9270, Madison, WI 53715-0270.) Other small press 'zines you may want to take a look at:

Crank!, edited by Bryan Cholfin, Broken Mirrors Press, PO Box 380473, Cambridge, MA 02238 (This quarterly remains the best of the lot. Recommended.)

The Urbanite, edited by Marc McLaughlin, PO Box 4737, Davenport, IA 52808. (Quirky urban surrealism.)

The Silver Web, edited by Ann Kennedy, Buzzcity Press, Box 38190, Tallahassee, FL 32315. (A nice little semipro 'zine, attractively produced.)

Pirate Writings, edited by Edward J. McFadden, 53 Whitman Ave., Islip, NY 11751. (Fantasy/SF/mystery stories.)

Marion Zimmer Bradley's Fantasy Magazine, edited by M. Z. Bradley, PO Box 249, Berkeley, CA 94701. (Primarily swords-and-sorcery.)

After Hours, Sirius Visions, Strange Plasma and *Pulphouse* are all small magazines that discontinued publication in 1995.

Poetry:
Nineteen ninety-five was an amazing year for fantastical poetry, but to find it one had to dig through quite a variety of sources. In this volume we've reprinted several magical pieces culled from magazines, journals, and collections. I'd suggest taking a look at the following three poetry collections in particular:

Among Angels by Nancy Willard and Jane Yolen (Harcourt Brace). This is a book all lovers of fine poetry and art should own. The poems, on the theme of angels, were ones Willard and Yolen wrote back and forth to each other over a period of several years. This is not a "cash in on the popularity of angels" gimmick book, but a rich and thoughtful collection. The luminous, painterly art by S. Saelig Gallagher is worth the cover price alone.

Morning in the Burned House by Margaret Atwood (Houghton Mifflin). This author's extraordinary new collection of poems contains several with potent imagery drawn from myth and folklore.

Agua Santa/Holy Water by Pat Mora (Beacon Press). This Chicana writer's work is stunning. A number of poems in the collection work with Mexican folkloric motifs.

Nonfiction and Folklore:
Last year I recommended the U.K. edition of *From the Beast to the Blonde: On Fairy Tales and Their Tellers* by Marina Warner (Farrar, Straus & Giroux). The 1995 U.S. edition gives me the chance to say once again that no fantasy lover's bookshelf should be without this superb look at the roots of storytelling, by one of England's finest writers. Other nonfiction and folklore collections of note:

The Arabian Nights: A Companion by Robert Irwin (Allen Lane/The Penguin Press). This rich treasure of a book is a wonderful guide to the fascinating material surrounding the classic Oriental fantasy. I highly recommend it to anyone interested in folklore, Oriental or otherwise.

Family of Earth and Sky by John Elder and Hertha D. Wong (Beacon Press). A beautiful collection of indigenous tales about nature from around the world. Recommended.

Sun Stories: Tales from Around the World to Illuminate the Days and Nights of Our Lives by Carolyn McVickar Edwards (HarperSan Francisco). Despite the somewhat smarmy title, this is a good, solid collection of multicultural myths about the sun.

Walking Words by Edward Galeano (W. W. Norton). An excellent compilation of Latin American folktales retold by this acclaimed writer from Uruguay, with woodcut illustrations by José Fancisco Borges, a *cordel* artist from rural Brazil.

The Ch'i-Lin Purse by Linda Fang (Farrar, Straus & Giroux). Nine Chinese tales nicely retold by a well-known oral storyteller; illustrated by Jeanne M. Lee.

The Cat and the Cook and Other Fables of Krylov (Greenwillow). Ethel Heins retells twelve stories by Krylov, a Russian fabulist (1768–1844), with exuberant illustrations by Anita Lobel.

Aboriginal Mythology by Mudrooroo (Thorsons/HarperCollins). A rare and useful exploration of native Australian myth.

Asian-Pacific Folktales and Legends, edited by Jeannette L. Faurot (Touchstone). A good reference volume on the subject.

Goddesses, Heroes and Shamans (Kingfisher). This is a nicely illustrated introduction to world mythology, aimed at "young people."

Pandora's Box by Sara Maitland (Duncan Baird). A three-dimensional introduction to Greek mythology combining a pop-up book, a board game, masks, and other bits and pieces, illustrated by Cristos Kondeatis.

Where Bigfoot Walks: Crossing the Dark Divide by Robert Michael Pyle (Houghton Mifflin). Pyle, a Yale-educated ecologist, received a Guggenheim fellowship to study Bigfoot, and this volume is the result. The author does not attempt to prove or disprove the creature's existence, but examines the Bigfoot legend in history, contemporary society, pop culture, modern fiction . . . and out in the field. A fascinating work.

A War of Witches by Timothy J. Knab (Harper San Francisco). A harrowing personal narrative of the author's exploration of contemporary Aztec culture.

Passing the Time in Ballymenone by Henry Glassie (Indiana University Press). Glassie's work is an absorbing study of the life, work, art, and folklore of a rural community in Northern Ireland, brought back into print in this small press edition. Highly recommended to anyone interested in Celtic folklore.

Deerdancer: The Shapeshifter Archetype in Story and Trance by Michele Jamal (Arkana/Penguin). An unusual exploration of shapeshifter myths in Native American and other cultures.

The Passion of Isis and Osiris by Jean Houston (Random House). A thoughtful study of the romantic themes running through ancient Egyptian story and myth.

The Druids by Peter Berresford Ellis (Eerdmans). A readable yet thorough scholarly volume from a leading Celtic historian who also writes fiction under the pen name of Peter Tremayne.

Robert Graves: Life on the Edge by Miranda Seymour (Henry Holt). A new biography of this poet and author of the mythological study, *The White Goddess*.

Women of the Golden Dawn by Mary K. Greer (Park Street Press, Vermont). A biographical look at the women involved in the mystical order of "The Golden Dawn" in Ireland (at the time of Yeats and Shaw): activist Maud Gonne, psychic Moina Bergson Mathers, theatrical producer Annie Horniman, and actress Florence Farr.

Lord Dunsany: Master of the Anglo-Irish Imagination by S. T. Joshi (Greenwood). A critical look at the work of this important Irish fantasist.

Inventing Wonderland: The Lives and Fantasies of Lewis Carroll, Edward Lear, J. M. Barrie, Kenneth Grahame and A. A. Milne by Jackie Wullschlager (Methuen–UK). A rather pointed examination of the peculiar lives of five important children's fantasy writers, lavishly illustrated.

The Brothers Grimm and Their Critics: Folktales and the Quest for Meaning by Christa Kamenetsky (Ohio University Press). This book is a response to critical works about the folktales of the Brothers Grimm (such as those of Bettelheim and Zipes); it makes for interesting reading, but a familiarity with the academic folklore field is recommended.

Modes of the Fantastic: Selected Essays from the 12th International Conference on the Fantastic in the Arts, edited by Robert A. Latham and Robert A. Collins (Greenwood Press, 88 Post Road W., Box 5007, Westport, CT 06881). A collection of twenty-five essays from the annual academic conference held in Florida.

It's Down the Slippery Cellar Stairs by R. A. Lafferty (Borgo Press, PO Box 2845, San Bernardino, CA 92406). A collection of essays and speeches on fantastic literature (expanded from its first edition) by this iconoclastic fiction writer.

Gulliver's Travels by Jonathan Swift, edited by Christopher Fox (St. Martin's). This volume contains Swift's text, five original critical essays on the subject, and exhaustive bibliographic information.

Coyote v. Acme by Ian Frazier (Farrar, Straus & Giroux). This hilarious collection of essays contains the superlative title piece (reprinted in a previous volume of *Year's Best*) about Wile E. Coyote's product liability suit against the Acme Company. This alone is worth the price of the book.

Children's Books:
Children's picture books are an excellent source of magical tales and magical artwork. The following recommendations are not only for children, but for adult collectors of fine fantasy as well:

My favorite book of 1995 was *Runaway Opposites* by Richard Wilbur (Harcourt Brace). Wilbur's quirky poems are turned into something wild and special by Henrik Drescher's wry, bizarre illustrations. Drescher does extraordinary things to the notions of page layout and design with his completely mad collages. Definitely check this one out.

Another best of the year was *Her Stories: African American Folktales, Fairy Tales and True Tales* by Virgina Hamilton (Scholastic/Blue Sky). An absolute treasure of a book by this master storyteller—one of America's very best writers for young people. The illustrations by Leo and Diane Dillon are also a delight.

Kashtanka by Anton Chekov, translated by Ronald Meyer (Gulliver Books) is a tale of a dog and the Russian circus beautifully illustrated by Gennardy Spirin, a Russian master of the art. *The Frog Princess* by Patrick Lewis (Dial Press Books for Young Readers), also illustrated by Gennardy Spirin, is likewise one of the year's very best.

The Ballad of the Pirate Queens by Jane Yolen (Harcourt Brace) is a terrific romp, with vivid illustrations by David Shannon.

Ian Penny's Book of Fairy Tales (Harry F. Abrams Books) is a lushly illustrated volume of traditional tales. Not quite as wonderful as his *Book of Nursery Rhymes*, but worth taking a look at.

The Rainbow Bridge by Audry Wood (Harcourt Brace) retells a lovely Chumash tribal story, with illustrations by Robert Florczak.

The Girl, the Fish and the Crown by Merilee Heyer (Viking Press) retells a Spanish folk story, with charming illustrations by the author.

Princess Prunella and the Purple Peanut by Margaret Atwood (Workman) is a humorous fantasy tale by this acclaimed Canadian author, with illustrations by Mary Ann Lovalski.

Gutenberg's Gift by Nancy Willard (Harcourt Brace). Willard's poem about the father of the printing industry has been turned into a pop-up book by Bryan Leister, a talented illustrator and historian of Renaissance art. This is a charming piece.

Other art publications of note:
Despite the commercial constraints that limit artists working in the field of book cover illustration, there were exceptional works that stood out from the rest in 1995. To mention just a few of the innovative cover treatments for which fantasy illustrators (and art directors) deserve special commendation: J. K. Potter's animistic photography for Nancy A. Collins' *Walking Wolf* (Ziesing); Phil Hale's wild and painterly cover for Michael Moorock's *Lunching with the Antichrist* (Ziesing), Mel Odom's Grecian art for Shwartz and Greenberg's *Sisters in Fantasy* (DAW); Kinuko Y. Craft's lavishly magical painting for Patricia A. McKillip's *The Book of Atrix Wolfe* (Ace); Charles Vess's lyrical interpretation of Elizabeth's Willey's *A Sorcerer and a Gentleman* (Tor); John Howe's Celtic dreamworld for Robin Hobb's *Royal Assassin* (Bantam), Thomas Canty's elegant Pre-Raphaelism for Gwyneth Jones's *Seven Tales and a Fable* (Edgewood Press), Jacek Yerka's Polish surrealism on Theodore Sturgeon's *The Ultimate Egoist* (North Atlantic Books), and Leonora Carrington's Mexican surrealism on the British edition of Williams and Jones's *The Penguin Book of Modern Fantasy by Women* (Viking). *Century* magazine has featured striking covers by Polish artist Jacek Yerka and Arizonan children's book artist David Christiana in their 1995 issues. *Realms of Fantasy* magazine seems to be wedded to dragon imagery for their covers, but their

Gallery feature has showcased excellent art by Brian Froud, J. K. Potter, Thomas Canty, and others.

For a thorough overview of the year in fantasy illustration, I recommend *Spectrum 2: The Best in Contemporary Fantastic Art*, edited by Cathy Burnett, Arnie Fenner, and Jim Loehr (Underwood Books). This annual volume includes more than two hundred pieces of jury-selected works by the above artists and many others, including fantasy genre favorites like Michael Whelan, David Cherry, and Don Maitz. This year's annual has a terrific punky cover piece by Boston artist Rick Berry.

I also recommend taking a look at *Latin American Women Artists*, edited by Eileen Wright and Polly Scott (Milwaukee Art Museum Press). The collected art of thirty-five painters from eleven Latin American countries, it includes important surrealist works. This is a beautiful and magical book.

Abrams has published a handsome new collection of art by the pre-Raphaelite painter/poet Dante Gabriel Rossetti, with text by Russel Ash. And Houghton Mifflin has released *J.R.R. Tolkien: Artist and Illustrator*, an informative, thorough collection of the fantasy writer's charming and childlike drawings and watercolors.

Music Releases of Note:

Traditional folk music is of interest to many fantasy lovers because the old folk ballads (most particularly in the Celtic folk tradition) are often based on the same folk- or fairy-tale roots as many fantasy stories. Contemporary "worldbeat" can be considered the musical equivalent of contemporary mythic fantasy: these musicians are taking ancient folkloric themes and updating them for our time.

My favorite release of the year was an instrumental one, from Irish accordion player Sharon Shannon, who mixes various cultural influences (skank, reggae, blues, trad folk) into one heady musical brew. Her latest is *Out of the Gap*. Also from Ireland: Pat Kilbride (*Loose Cannon*) and Niamh Parsons (*Loosely Connected*) are two singers at the forefront of progressive Irish music. Moving Cloud is another band that crosses effortlessly over the boundaries of multicultural influences in their new release, *Moving Cloud*. My favorite Irish band these days has to be The Saw Doctors, with original music that falls somewhere between that of the Pogues, the Waterboys, and the early Beatles. The Saw Doctors have two releases out now: *All the Way From Tuam* and *If This Is Rock and Roll I Want My Old Job Back*.

Edward II is an absolutely terrific small band from Manchester, mixing reggae and Celtic tunes into a completely infectious combination. Their first release is *Wicked Men*; it's a delight, but they are even better live. Baka Beyond comes from the west of England with *Spirit Forest*, mixing Celtic rhythms with those of the African Congo into extraordinary, spirit-filled dance music. Boukan Ginen is a young roots band from Haiti, playing a modern take on Haitian music, including voodoo chanting. Their debut album is *Jou a Rive*. John Santos and the Machete Ensemble mix jazz, Yoruban chants, Latin rhythms, and Caribbean drumming on *Machete*. *Las Seis Tentaciones* is the second release from La Musgana, who play indiginous Spanish/Moorish folk music (some of it quite Celtic in sound) on a mix of modern and traditional instruments. Vartinna is a modern Finnish band that is wildly popular throughout Europe for their exotic mix of rock and trad and soaring vocal harmonies. Their latest is *Aitara*.

On our own shores, Peter Kater and R. Carlos Nakai have released *How The West Was Lost, Vol. II*, a gorgeous CD of Native American music originally compiled for the film documentary of that name; they have also collaborated on *Natives: An Improvisational Exploration and Expression of the Seven Directions*. *Skeleton Woman* by Flesh and Bone (keyboardist Peter Kater with vocalist Chris White) is a musical exploration of an Hispanic folk story. *Curandero* (which is the Spanish name for a folk healer) is a CD by Miquel Espinoza and Ty Burrhoe, containing "healing" music combining Indian and Spanish influences. Best of all is *Sacred Common Ground*, the last album by the late jazz pianist

Don Pullen. Pullen and his band (the African Brazilian Connection) have collaborated with Native American singers and drummers, and the result is absolutely unforgettable.

Fantasy novelist Ellen Kushner is known to public radio listeners across the U.S. as the host/writer/producer of eclectic music shows, so I've asked her opinion of the musical year's best. "I'm not sure I have a favorite album of the year," she says, "but my very favorite song of 1995 is on the debut album by a woman named Dar Williams, *The Honesty Room*. 'When I Was a Boy' explores the restrictions of gender with poignant compassion. It utterly won my heart with the opening lines: 'I won't forget when Peter Pan/Came to my house, took my hand/I said I was a boy, I'm glad he didn't check.' " *Sound & Spirit*, Kushner's new weekly series for Public Radio International, will be of particular interest to readers of fantasy and myth. Dubbed "Joseph Campbell meets Ellen's record collection" by its co-producers at WGBH, Boston, the series explores music and ideas that celebrate the human experience. "*Sound & Spirit* gives me the chance to put all the music I love together into one coherent hour of radio—a single show might contain Medieval chant, Nigerian drumming, Native American flute, and a Shaker hymn—while I indulge my passion for exploring myth, spirituality, and systems of belief." (Call your local public radio station to see if it is airing near you, or E-mail the show at SPIRIT@EMAIL.PRI.ORG.) Kushner also helped to produce *Warning: Contains Language*, a 2-CD set by Neil Gaiman, author of *The Sandman* and other fine dark fantasy comics and stories. "We went into the studio and recorded Neil reading fiction and poetry from his collection, *Angels and Visitations*, and then got British artist and musician Dave McKean to create a soundtrack. Not every writer is blessed with a beautiful voice and an infallible sense of dramatic timing. But it's worth crossing more than the street to hear Neil read aloud."

Fantasy novelist Emma Bull is half of the musical duo The Flash Girls (Lorraine Garland is the other half). They released their lively, quirky second CD in 1995, *Maurice and I*, which contains a mix of traditional music and songs by Bull, Garland, Neil Gaiman, Jane Yolen, and others. The legendary Minneapolis Celtic/worldbeat/rock-and-reel band Boiled in Lead released *The Gypsy*, a CD-Rom album (which also plays on regular CD players) of songs based on Steven Brust and Megan Lindholm's urban fantasy novel *The Gypsy*. This is an unusual and fascinating musical collaboration. Fantasy novelist Charles de Lint is also a professional musician, specializing in Celtic music. Two excellent 1995 releases pointed out by de Lint are: *Kate Rusby and Kathryn Roberts*, the debut album by two terrific singers of Celtic ballads (and other songs) á là *Silly Sisters*; and Grace Under Pressure's *Three Sheets to the Wind*, a collection of traditional songs beautifully harmonized by three women singers from Canada.

If "worldbeat" music is new to you, I recommend trying the following compilation CDs: Green Linnet Records' *Heart of the Gaels* and Narada Records' *Celtic Odyssey* (for Celtic music); Rhino's *The Best of World Music* and Xenophile's *Music for a Changing World* (for a world music mix).

Literary Conventions and Conferences:

The World Fantasy Convention (an annual professional gathering of writers, illustrators, publishers, and readers of both fantasy and horror fiction) was held in Baltimore, Maryland, this year, October 27–29. The Guests of Honor were: Terry Bisson, Lucius Shepard, Howard Waldrop, writers; Rick Berry, artist; Lloyd Arthur Eschbach, special guest; Edward Bryant, toastmaster. The World Fantasy Awards were presented at the convention. Winners (for work published in 1994) were as follows: *Towing Jehovah* by James Morrow for Best Novel; "Last Summer at Mars Hill" by Elizabeth Hand for Best Novella; "The Man in the Black Suit" by Stephen King for Best Short Fiction; *Little Deaths*, edited by Ellen Datlow, for Best Anthology; *The Calvin Coolidge Home for Dead Comedians* and *A Conflagration Artist* by Bradley Denton for Best Collection; Jacek Yerka for Best Artist; editor Ellen Datlow for Special Award/Professional; Broken Mirrors Press publisher Bryan Cholfin for Special Award/

Non-professional; Ursula K. Le Guin for Life Achievement. Judges for the awards were: Terry Bisson, Jean-Daniel Breque, Jane Johnson, Kathe Koja, and Brian Stableford. For more information on the next World Fantasy Convention, to be held in October of 1996 in Chicago, write: P. O. Box 423, Oak Forest, IL 60452.

The Fourth Street Fantasy Convention (an annual literary convention devoted specifically to fantasy) was held, as always, in Minneapolis in July. For more information on the 1996 convention, write: David Dyer-Bennet, 4242 Minnehaha Avenue S., Minneapolis, MN 55406.

Mythcon (a scholarly convention sponsored by the Mythopoeic Society and devoted to fantasy) was held Aug. 4–7, in Berkeley, CA. Guests of Honor were Tim Powers and Michael R. Collings.

The Sixteenth International Conference on the Fantastic in the Arts (an academic conference on all areas of speculative fiction) was held, as always, in Ft. Lauderdale, Florida (March 22–26). The Guests of Honor were Joe Haldeman and Douglas E. Winter. For information on the 1996 convention, write: IAFA, College of Humanities, 500 NW 20th, HU 50 BA, Florida Atlantic University, Boca Raton, FL 33431.

That's a brief summation of the year in fantasy. Now on to the fiction itself.

As usual, there are some stories (particularly lengthy ones) that we are unable to include even in an anthology as fat as this one. I consider the following dozen tales to be among the year's best along with the stories and poems reprinted in this volume. If you haven't come across them already, I strongly recommend seeking them out:

In alphabetical order . . .

"There Are No Dead," by Terry Bisson, *Omni*, Jan.
"Fountains in Summer," by Richard Bowes, *Full Spectrum 5*.
"The Rose Girl," by Melissa Hardy, *The Malahat Review*, Fall.
"Infantasm," by Robert Holdstock, *The Merlin Chronicles*.
"Wolf's Heart," by Tappan King, *The Armless Maiden*.
"Water Off a Black Dog's Back," by Kelly Link, *Century #3*.
"The Noonday Pool," by Ian R. MacLeod, *F&SF*, May.
"Every Mystery Unexplained," by Lisa Mason, *David Copperfield's Tales of the Impossible*.
"Below Baghdad," by Gerald Pearce, *Century #3*.
"The Fox Wife," by Ellen Steiber, *Ruby Slippers, Golden Tears*.
"Young Girl's Wish" by Amy Tan, *The New Yorker*, Oct. 2.
"The Bone-Carver's Tale," by Jeff Vandermeer, *Asimov's*, April.
"Occam's Ducks," by Howard Waldrop, *Omni*, Feb.

I also heartily recommend "Eyes of Zapata" by Sandra Cisneros from *Daughters of the Fifth Sun*, a collection of Latina fiction edited by Bryce Milligan, Mary Guerrero Milligan, and Angela de Hoyos (Riverhead Books). It was the best short piece of Latin American magic realism I read in 1995, and I wish we'd been able to include it here.

I hope you will enjoy the stories and poems that follow as much as I did. Many thanks to the authors and publishers who allowed us to reprint them in this volume of the year's very best.

—T. W.
Devon/Tucson/New York

Summation 1995: Horror
by Ellen Datlow

The State of the Field:
There has been a great deal of discussion about the state of the horror field and where it's going. Superficially, things may appear somewhat dim. The disillusioned and worried note that there is no regularly published professional fiction magazine in the field. There are no longer any book publishers who have a regular horror line. There is no horror news magazine. People point out the failure of the Dell Abyss line once its founder, Jeanne Cavelos, departed. Abyss had good intentions but not a very consistent vision. The books ranged from brilliant experiments introducing fresh voices, to material that could have been published on any horror list. To separate horror into its own category, thus ghettoizing it, was probably a mistake—as several respected critics/commentators on the field have pointed out. Horror came out of literature and perhaps should be published there once more.

There *is* horror being published and it's being published on a fairly regular basis. The interested reader just has to be more assiduous to find it. Possibly it's a reviewer's responsibility to point out horror literature in unlikely places. Carroll & Graf, Tor, St. Martin's Press, Berkley, and Pocket Books in the United States and Robinson and Gollancz in the U.K. all publish horror. Ask the book dealers you respect, and the booksellers. In most bookstores (even the superstores) there is usually someone who is an aficionado of one genre or another. Ask for their recommendations.

News of the Year:
The German media conglomerate, Holtzbrinck, acquired a 70 percent interest in the U.K.'s Macmillan Publishers, Ltd., parent company of St. Martin's Press and its subsidiary, Tor. Macmillan's U.K. operations include Macmillan General Books, Pan, Picador, Sidgwick & Jackson, and Papermac. Holtzbrinck already owns the U.S. publishing companies Henry Holt and Farrar, Straus & Giroux. It has been the conglomerate's tradition to give its subsidiaries a great deal of autonomy. Terms of the deal were not disclosed but London publishing observers thought the price tag around $320 million.

Liz Perle McKenna, vice president and publisher of Hearst Books, resigned less than nine months after taking the job. In early June, William M. Wright, COO at Random House for the previous two and a half years, was named president and CEO of the Hearst Book Group, including Morrow and Avon, replacing Howard Kaminsky, who resigned in April 1994. Wright told *Publishers Weekly* that his top priority "is to make the company a house of choice again for submissions." By August, Michael Greenstein, formerly Executive Vice President of Avon, was promoted to President of Avon Books and Lou Aronica, most recently Senior Vice President and Publisher of the Berkley Publishing Group, was hired as Senior Vice President and Publisher of Avon Books, bringing Jennifer Hershey of Bantam Spectra with him as Executive Editor. Aronica's mandate is to start a hardcover imprint, with the first books to appear by Fall 1996. Bantam Spectra was left floundering with only two editors. By the end of 1995 Bantam's commitment to its science fiction line was being questioned as there was still no move to hire a replacement for Hershey.

Christopher Schelling, Executive Editor at HarperPrism, left for health reasons but continues to work with some of his authors. Schelling, along with John Silbersack, was instrumental in starting the Roc line at New American Library. In late November, John Douglas, of AvoNova, took Schelling's position as Executive Editor and Jennifer Brehl, formerly General Fiction Editor at Doubleday (working on some SF), joined Avon as Senior Editor in charge of science fiction. Aronica announced at that time that hardcover science fiction will be published as Avon SF instead of as Morrow/AvoNova Books. The trade paperbacks will keep the AvoNova imprint.

Penguin USA acquired Donald I. Fine, Inc., which is to function as a separate imprint. Fine was founder of Arbor House, subsequently acquired by William Morrow, which kept him on in an executive position for a while and later severed the connection. Fine, unable to use the name Arbor House, basically had begun again from scratch to form Donald I. Fine, Inc.

The cofounders of Four Walls Eight Windows, a small New York company that started publishing in 1986, agreed to split up effective January 1. John Oakes continues as publisher of Four Walls, and Dan Simons plans to start publishing new books in spring 1996 under the name Seven Stories. Quite successful (they published MacArthur Fellowship–winning science fiction writer Octavia E. Butler's novel *Parable of the Sower* and her collection *Bloodchild*), both men agreed that differences in temperament and business styles led to the breakup.

It was announced in the spring that *Omni* magazine would be offered in monthly online editions while the print magazine went quarterly after the April 1995 issue. The first quarterly issue came out in September with three pieces of fiction and was only sold on the newsstand. In early November the entire General Media corporation was downsized by about one-third. A second quarterly print issue was published in the winter of 95/96 with four pieces of fiction, but in February 1996 it was announced that the print edition of *Omni* would be discontinued and that the magazine would only publish online.

In mid-February of 1996, *Pulphouse* publisher Dean Wesley Smith announced that the entire *Pulphouse* operation was closing down, magazines and books. His time has increasingly been taken up by writing. The last two issues were Issue 18, guest-edited by Damon Knight, and Issue 19, edited by Smith. And with that 19th issue *Pulphouse* officially ceased publication. *Aboriginal Science Fiction*, edited and published by Charles Ryan, suspended publication, pending sale of the magazine and/or its subscription liabilities, or new arrangements that will allow it to resume publication. The magazine, originally published bimonthly, went quarterly for the last few years. *Afraid*, the Horror newsletter edited by Mike Baker, ceased publication with its 33rd issue, and his fiction magazine, *Skull*, also ceased publication; *Thin Ice*, edited by Kathleen Jurgens, ceased publication; *Dementia 13*, edited by Pam Creais out of Kent-UK, ceased publication with its 14th issue; *Heliocentric Net*, edited by Lisa Jean Bothell, ceased publication with its 16th issue. Bothell plans to edited a yearly anthology starting July 1996 and from then on coincide publication of the anthology with the World Horror Convention held in March; *Random Realities*, edited by Jeff Dennis, ceased publication; *Black Tears* and *Violent Spectres*, both edited by Adam Bradley, ceased publication with issues #10 and #4 respectively; *Horror*, the horror news magazine edited by John and Kim Betancourt, was discontinued with issue #6 and various other Wildside Press projects will be delayed or cancelled. They were adversely affected by the bankruptcy of the Inland Book Company, a small press wholesaler; Bryan Cholfin, publisher of Broken Mirrors Press, was also adversely affected by the Inland debacle and has ceased publishing books. This will not, however, affect his World Fantasy Award–winning magazine *CRANK!*; *After Hours*, edited by William Raley, ceased publishing with issue #25. It was notable for publishing early stories by some writers who subsequently have broken out of the small press. A report in the November 15 issue of *Folio*, the trade journal about magazine publishing, said that the Dell magazines (including crossword and puzzle magazines, *Analog Fiction and Fact*, *Asimov's Science Fiction Magazine*, *Ellery Queen's Mystery Magazine*, and *Alfred Hitchcock Mystery Magazine*) were for sale because the division was a poor fit for its book publishing (Bantam Doubleday Dell). The report was a surprise to the editorial staff as they were in the process of revamping the magazines, due to rising paper and postage costs. George Richter, president of the magazine division, then backtracked a bit, saying sale was not imminent and the SF magazines were not in trouble despite a drop in circulation for 1995.

Starting with the March 1996 issues, the frequency of both magazines will be cut to ten regular issues plus one "double," which will be on sale for two months. They will also be cut back by one 16-page signature (the same as *The Magazine of Fantasy & Science Fiction*). The same will happen with the two mystery magazines. And just after the New Year, rumors that the magazine division was sold to Penny Press, a company owning puzzle and crossword magazines, were stronger than ever.

Stephen King sold a six-part novel, *The Green Mile*, to Penguin U.S.A. and U.K. for publication in 1996 by Signet Books as a monthly series of original 96-page paperbacks at $2.99 a book. The first installment appears in March 1996.

The Stoker Awards, given by The Horror Writers Association, were revamped by the new, incoming administration. The "Other Media" category (under which the graphic novel, *Jonah Hex: Two Gun Mojo* by Joe R. Lansdale won in 1994) is not allowed under the current bylaws. In addition, as per the rules, eligibility of book-length works is determined by copyright date, rather than date of publication, and collections are defined as being over 60,000 words.

The organization held its annual meeting and banquet at the Warwick Hotel in New York City over the weekend of June 10 and 11. The Bram Stoker Awards for Superior Achievement were won by the following: Novel: *Dead in the Water* by Nancy Holder (Dell Abyss); First Novel: *Grave Markings* by Michael Arnzen (Dell Abyss); Long Story: "A Scent of Vinegar," by Robert Bloch (*Dark Destiny*); Short Story (tie): "Cafe Endless: Spring Rain," by Nancy Holder (*Love in Vein*) and "The Box," by Jack Ketchum (*Cemetery Dance*); Collection: *The Early Fears* by Robert Bloch (Fedogen and Bremer); no award was given for nonfiction because there were not enough nominations. Life Achievement: Christopher Lee.

The winners of the 1995 British Fantasy Awards are: Novel—Michael Marshall Smith, *Only Forward* (HarperCollins-UK); Short Story—Paul J. McAuley, "The Temptation of Dr. Stein" (*The Mammoth Book of Frankenstein*); Anthology/Collection—Joel Lane, *The Earth Wire* (Egerton Press); Small-Press Publication—*Necrofile*, eds. Stefan Dziemianowicz, S. T. Joshi, and Michael A. Morrison; Artist—Martin McKenna; Best Newcomer—Maggie Furey; Special Award—John Jarrold, editor of Legend. The awards were presented at the horror/fantasy convention, Welcome to My Nightmare, Sunday, October 29, at the Forte Hotel in Swansea, Wales.

The first International Horror Critics Guild Awards were presented at the 1995 World Horror Convention in Atlanta by HCG founder Nancy A. Collins in the following categories: Best Novel: *Anno Dracula* by Kim Newman; Best First Novel: *Grave Markings* by Michael Arnzen; Best Short Form/Chapbook: *Black Sun* by Douglas E. Winter; Best Short Story: "The Safety of Unknown Cities" by Lucy Taylor; Best Collection: *Angels and Visitations* by Neil Gaiman; Best Anthology: *Love in Vein* edited by Poppy Z. Brite; Best Graphic Novel: *Jonah Hex: Two Gun Mojo* by Joe R. Lansdale and Tim Truman; Best Artist: Alan M. Clark; Best Film: *Interview With the Vampire*; Best Publication: *Answer Me!* Edited by Jim and Debbie Goad; Living Legend Award: Harlan Ellison. Winners received a gargoyle statuette technically known as the Florentine Watchdog. Collins notes her group was created to "acknowledge the achievements of those in the Horror/Dark Fantasy field without being linked with a writers' association." Though this year the winners were chosen through ballots attached to the convention's second progress report, next year separate ballots will be sent out.

Also at the World Horror Convention, *Deathrealm* publishers Malicious Press announced the winners of the Deathrealm Awards. Best Novel: *Strange Angels* by Kathe Koja; Best Short Fiction: "Driftglider" by Jeffrey Osier; Best Single-Author Collection: *Bibliomen* by Gene Wolfe; Best Anthology: *Year's Best Horror XXII*, edited by Karl Edward Wagner; Best Fiction Magazine: *Terminal Fright*, edited by Ken Abner; Best Nonfiction Magazine: *The Scream Factory*, edited by Peter Enfantino and Robert Morrish; Best Artist: Alan M. Clark.

Stephen King's "The Man in the Black Suit" won the O. Henry Award for best short fiction of 1994 and will appear in *Prize Stories: The O. Henry Award*. Salman Rushdie won the 1995 Whitbread Award for best novel with *The Moor's Last Sigh*. The award comes with a £2,000 cash prize.

From England: *Dark Voices: The Pan Book of Horror*, the longest-running original horror anthology series, moved from Pan to Gollancz and was retitled *Dark Terrors*. The current editors are David Sutton and Stephen Jones, who took over the series in 1990 from editor Clarence Paget, who had followed in the footsteps of the original editor Herbert Van Thal (1959–1983). The series was originally called *The Pan Book of Horror*. The first Gollancz volume appeared in hardcover around Halloween. Previously, the annual has appeared in mass market format exclusively. Stephen Jones has decided not to renew his editorial contract with Raven Books. The London-based mail order company Delectus Books moved into publishing with the release of Charles Nodier's *Lord Ruthven and the Vampires*, translated from the 1820 edition by Paul Buck and Alfred H. Bill's *The Wolf in the Garden*, a facsimile of the 1931 original. Ringpull Press, the small British publisher that came out of nowhere and with Jeff Noon's novel, *Vurt* (which won the Arthur C. Clarke Award), went into receivership due to inability to pay its printing bills. Ringpull's problems stemmed mainly from the forced withdrawal of a non-SF title, *La Philosophie de Cantona*, which occurred when Hodder Headline and the soccer team Manchester United claimed the book infringed upon copyrighted material. In June, it was announced that Ringpull was joining Fourth Estate in Manchester and taking "a number of Ringpull authors, including Jeff Noon." But by the end of the year, with only three new titles published (including a second novel by Noon), Ringpull and Fourth Estate parted ways. Fourth Estate will be publishing the remaining Ringpull inventory as Fourth Estate Books. Macmillan-UK restructured in October, cutting 20 jobs from a staff of 130. Peter Straus, who had headed Picador, was named to the new job of Editor-In-Chief for all the imprints. Maria Rejt was named Publisher of Macmillan and Sidgwick & Jackson, Suzanne Baboneau Executive Editor, fiction, and Georgina Morely Editorial Director, nonfiction; Peter Lavery was named publisher at Pan. In November, "disappointing results" for Penguin-UK led to a round of 75 staff cuts, in addition to the earlier 40 in July. This culminated in the resignation of longtime managing director Trevor Glover.

Censorship issues: Writer Brian Evenson, author of the horrific collection *Altmann's Tongue*, was teaching at Brigham Young University in Salt Lake City, Utah. Soon after learning he was the recipient of a Creative Writing Fellowship from the National Endowment of the Arts, he was told by BYU administrators that if he allowed his second book of stories to be published as written, it would probably guarantee his departure from the faculty. He took another teaching job before this could happen; Magistrate Michael L. Orenstein of the Federal District Court in Uniondale, Long Island, determined that Nassau County's three-year-old law making it a misdemeanor (punishable by up to a year and a $1,000 fine) to sell to minors trading cards depicting a "heinous crime, an element of a heinous crime, or a heinous criminal which is harmful to minors" was an "unconstitutional restriction on the distribution of free speech." The finding was issued October 6. The Nassau County action followed a wave of protests by victims' rights and parents groups after Eclipse Enterprises of Forestville, California, (which has since gone out of business) produced a series of "true crime" trading cards in 1992 that included pictures and information on such killers as Charles Manson, Jeffrey Dahmer, Ted Bundy, John Wayne Gacy, and others. The ordinance was not enforced while Eclipse's suit against the ruling was pending. The magistrate held that "a card which would depict and tell the story of Cain slaying Abel comes within the law's purview, as does a card which would depict the Holocaust"; Salman Rushdie's Booker Prize shortlisted novel, *The Moor's Last Sigh*, was banned by Customs officials in India.

Please note: Many of the hard-to-get items mentioned below can be ordered through various excellent mail order booksellers including DreamHaven Books and Comics, 912 West Lake Street, Minneapolis, MN 55408; Mark Ziesing, PO Box 76, Shingletown, CA 96088; The Overlook Connection, PO Box 526, Woodstock, GA 30188, and in the United Kingdom, Cold Tonnage Books, 22 Kings Lane, Windlesham, Surrey, GU20 6JQ, England.

Novels:
A completely biased reading list for 1995:

Freak by Mark Burnell (New English Library-UK) is about how an ordinary man's life changes abruptly after he interrupts a vicious attack in an underground carpark and miraculously heals the dying victim by his touch. Terrified and confused, he tries to ignore what happened while trying to understand it. Some want to exploit him, others want to kill him, including a fanatic who believes this reluctant healer to be the Antichrist. An entertaining and well-written novel about people trying to cope with the miraculous, in the tradition of the novel *Cold Heaven* by Brian Moore and the movie, *Resurrection* (with Ellen Burstyn). Vividly drawn characters.

Waking the Moon by Elizabeth Hand (HarperPrism) is a fine literate horror novel by the author of three science fiction novels and short stories in both genres. On her first day at the strange University of the Archangels and St. John the Divine, in Washington, D.C., Katherine Sweeney becomes friends with two fellow students who will change her life—the androgynous, fey (and possibly mad) Oliver and the unearthly beautiful and willful Angelica. The three seem untouched by ordinary worries until they become involved in a battle for the soul of the Earth. Oliver crashes and burns, Angelica disappears, and Sweeney is expelled. Conspiracy, goddess cults, patriarchal control, the mysteries, and ancient history make for a rich stew. The British edition, published in 1994, was nominated for the World Fantasy Award.

The Priest by Thomas M. Disch (Alfred A. Knopf) is satire, but barely—it's terrifying in its nearness to reality. This story of pedophile priests and decades-long cover-ups by the diocese, anti-abortion extremism, irrationality, and hypocrisy in the Catholic Church is almost a contemporary social history of the Church. This is Disch's most accessible and satisfying novel in a while.

Relic by Douglas Preston and Lincoln Child (Forge) is a well-done SF/horror thriller taking place mostly in New York's Museum of Natural History. It's not enough that the rain forest is threatening us with more and more virulent viruses but now we have to worry about monsters from the Amazon as well. A dinosaurlike creature haunts the basement of the museum, occasionally making forays onto higher floors and picking off visitors and workers just before a gala opening on "superstition." I hated the ending but it's still fast-moving, slick entertainment.

The Weatherman by Steven Thayer (Viking) is a suspenseful serial killer novel that takes place in the Minneapolis area. The TV weatherman may be a bit strange but he gets great ratings because of his deadly accurate, almost prescient weather forecasts. He becomes a suspect in a series of murders seemingly linked to the seasons. Tornadoes, murder, politics, and the death penalty make for a highly entertaining read, despite a few loose ends. Excellent characterizations, inobtrusive detail, and a subtle anti–capital punishment stance raise this above most serial killer novels.

The Unnatural by David Prill (St. Martin's Press) is a picaresque novel about the American way of death. A young boy with a talent to create art from death aspires to break the United States embalming record. Unfortunately, the once honorable field of undertaking is changing rapidly and he's faced with unexpected obstacles. Although the last third of the novel loses its madcap tone and becomes too serious, on the whole it's great fun.

The perfect complement to the above is William Browning Spencer's clever *Résumé With Monsters* (The Permanent Press). Philip Kenan follows his ex-girlfriend to Austin, Texas, to win her back and protect her from the Lovecraftian monsters who plague them both (he thinks). There has been some disagreement as to whether the novel is fantasy or not—the reader can judge for herself whether Philip is merely crazy or a hero (or both). Not very frightening but charming, fun, and a quick read. Highly recommended.

Where Does Kissing End? by Kate Pullinger (Serpent's Tail) is a wonderfully hip short novel on relationships and vampirism. Mother and daughter Lucy and Mina Savage's names are not coincidences. Both are born illegitimate, both seem doomed to unhappy love lives until Mina meets Stephen Smith, who falls irrevocably in love with her. Cool, obsessive, vampiric. "Where does biting start? Where does kissing end?—H. J. Stenning," reads the epigraph. Came out in the U.K. in 1992 and I missed it until now.

The Lighthouse at the End of the World by Stephen Marlowe (E.P. Dutton) is framed by the week before the death of Edgar Allan Poe, at which time he disappears only to turn up, dying, in a mental hospital. This ingenious and affecting novel interweaves Poe's sad life, his writings, and the possibilities of what happened to him during that "missing" week into a charming, tragic, mysterious fantasy. Poe's famous fictional detective, August Dupin, plays a major role. Not horror but a historical fantasy about one of the first and certainly one of the major purveyors of the short horror tale.

The Torturer by Jim Ballantyne (Victor Gollancz-UK) is a disturbing and grisly combination psycho killer/supernatural thriller. It's lucky Matt Trace has a focus for his vice. Possessing no human feeling whatsoever, he will for a very high price torture victims to order and send the videotape to his employer. Then he makes a mistake, and the supernatural enters the picture. Trace, as a character, isn't all that interesting but the police detectives who hunt him are likable. The book has too many loose ends to be fully satisfying, which is frustrating because with another fifty pages and some care Ballantyne (a pseudonym of a well-known London crime writer) could have created a classic of its type. Not for the squeamish.

The Trial of Elizabeth Cree by Peter Ackroyd (Doubleday/Nan A. Talese) is another tour de force by the author of *Chatterton* and *Hawsmoor*. The novel takes place in Victorian times when the Limehouse Golem, a fiendish, possibly supernatural serial killer, is at large in London. Elizabeth Cree, born in poverty and hopelessness, works her way into an uneasy respectability after a colorful life in the theatre, portrayed beautifully by Ackroyd. She marries well yet ends up on trial for the poisoning of her husband. The combination of John Cree's diaries, Liz's reminiscences of her life, and third-person narrative makes this fascinating and dark reading.

From Potter's Field by Patricia Cornwell (Scribner) is the sixth crime novel focusing on chief medical examiner of Virginia, Kay Scarpetta. A body is found in New York City's Central Park on Christmas Eve, nude and mutilated in ways that indicate the work of serial killer Temple Gault. Characterization and attention to forensic detail are Cornwell's hallmark. And this page-turner has enough darkness and gore to appeal to horror readers. A spellbinder.

Burning Angel by James Lee Burke (Hyperion) captures the atmosphere of Louisiana so well you can feel and taste the swamps. Detective Dave Robicheaux is asked by an old black lady to prove that the piece of land she and her family has been living on for generations was given to them by the family's former masters. The past is never dead; it haunts the living. Black/white relations in the Deep South and the slave legacy continue to have repercussions. Like *Confederacy of the Dead*, a ghost story. Highly recommended.

In the Cut by Susanna Moore (Alfred A. Knopf) is a tense erotic New York City mystery. A young woman is murdered. Another woman, a language scholar, might have seen the murderer. The best thing about this novel (the third by Moore) is the fascinating, troubling character of the teacher. She reminds me of Smilla in *Smilla's Sense of Snow* in that she (and one gets the feeling it *is* her, not the author) makes it difficult for the reader to understand/get her. There is something fierce about her and her relationships—a police detective assigned to the case, an old platonic friend, and a young student. This is a novel for those who want intellectual stimulation along with the more physical kind as it's about sexual politics as much as anything else. Highly recommended.

City of Dreadful Night by Lee Siegel (University of Chicago Press) is a brilliant, odd, and frightening book. Siegel, a professor of religion, traveled to India in order to research horror and the macabre and its relationship to Indian religion and culture. Siegel's seemingly futile search for a legendary itinerant storyteller becomes intertwined with the life of the storyteller himself. The reality of India's past and present political and social upheavals mingle with tales within tales of ghosts, zombies, Dracula, and ghouls. A mixture of fiction and nonfiction.

The Off Season by Jack Cady (St. Martin's) is an utterly charming ghost story about Point Vestal, a town in which time is fluid, a parsonage moves itself around town, a cat named Obed dances and speaks in several languages, and Victorian ghosts act out their passions and pain with great regularity.

The Safety of Unknown Cities by Lucy Taylor (Darkside Press) is the first novel by a writer best known for her erotic horror stories. The novel doesn't disappoint. The erotic and horrific story follows Val Petrillo in her search for the ultimate in sexual excitement. Introduction by Edward Bryant and frontispiece by Alan M. Clark. Four hundred copies of the signed and numbered leather-bound book were offered for sale for $60 and fifty-two copies lettered for $150 payable to Darkside Press, c/o Blue Moon Books, 360 West First, Eugene, OR 97401.

Novel listings:
The Three Imposters by Arthur Machen, edited by David Trotter (J.M. Dent/Orion), a centenary reprint of this classic horror/thriller with tales within tales; *The Two-Bear Mambo* by Joe R. Lansdale (Warner/Mysterious Press); *Red, Red Robin* by Stephen Gallagher (Ballantine); *Pinocchio's Sister* by Jan Slepian (Philomel); *Angel* by Nicholas Guild (Carroll & Graf); *Zombie* by Joyce Carol Oates (Dutton); *Blood Crazy* by Simon Clark (New English Library); *Dry Skull Dreams* by Michael Green (Pocket); *The Manuscript Found in Saragossa* by Jan Potocki (Viking) was written in French sometime between 1797 and 1815 and this new translation by Ian Maclean makes the full text available in English for the first time; *No Night Is Too Long* by Barbara Vine (Harmony Books); *My Education: A Book of Dreams* by William S. Burroughs (Viking); *Ghost of Chance* by William S. Burroughs (High Risk); *12 Monkeys* by Elizabeth Hand (HarperPrism); *Dark Dominion* by Bentley Little (Headline-UK); *Psychoville* by Christopher Fowler (Warner-UK); *The Resurrectionist* by Thomas F. Monteleone (Warner); *Daemonic* by Stephen Laws (Hodder & Stoughton-UK); *Gilray's Ghost* by John Gordon (Walker Books); *The Blood Countess* by Andre Codrescu (Simon & Schuster); *The Secret Laboratory Journals of Dr. Victor Frankenstein* by Jeremy Kay (Overlook Press); *The Prestige* by Christopher Priest (Simon & Schuster-UK); *The Island of the Day Before* by Umberto Eco (Harcourt, Brace); *The Children's Hour* by Douglas Clegg (Dell); *The Blue Manor* by Jenny Jones (Gollancz-UK); *The Between* by Tananarive Due (HarperCollins); *The Six Messiahs* by Mark Frost (William Morrow); *The Golem* by Gustav Meyrink (Dedalus-UK), a classic horror novel originally published in German in 1915, newly translated by Mike Mitchell with a new introduction and chronology by Robert Irwin; *Expiration Date* by Tim Powers (HarperCollins-UK); *The Boiling Pool* by Gary Brandner (Severn House-UK); *Vivia* by Tanith Lee (Little, Brown-UK); *Diary of a Vampire* by Gary Bowen (Masquerade); *Darkness, I* by Tanith Lee (St. Martin's); *A Ring in a Case* by Yuz Aleshkovsky, translated by Jane Anne Miller (Northwestern University Press/Hydra); *Now You See It* by Richard Matheson (Tor); *The Memoirs of Elizabeth Frankenstein* by Theodore Roszak (Random House); *Ancestral Hungers* by Scott Baker (Tor), a revision of *Dhampire*, originally published several years ago; *Pandora's Clock* by John J. Nance (Doubleday); *The Matrix* by Jonathan Aycliffe (HarperCollins); *Requiem* by Graham Joyce (Creed-UK); *Nightrider* by Sheila Holligon (Creed-UK); *Night Hunter* by Michael Reaves (Tor); *Black Lightning* by John Saul (Columbine); *The Vampyre: Being the True Pilgrimage of George Gordon, Sixth*

Lord Byron by Tom Holland (Little, Brown-UK); *Caravan of Shadows* by Richard Lee Byers (White Wolf); *Rose Madder* by Stephen King (Viking); *Bone Deep* by David Wiltse (G.P. Putnam's Sons); *Bloodsucking Fiends: A Love Story* by Christopher Moore (Simon & Schuster); *To Build Jerusalem* by John Whitbourn (Gollancz-UK); *Frank's World* by George Mangels (St. Martin's); *Intensity* by Dean Koontz (Alfred A. Knopf); *The Cold One* by Christopher Pike (Hodder & Stoughton-UK); *Jackals* by Charles L. Grant (NEL-UK); *Memnoch the Devil* by Anne Rice (Alfred A. Knopf); *Host* by Peter James (Villard Books); *Deathwalker* by R. Patrick Gates (Dell/Abyss); *The Ghosts of Sleath* by James Herbert (HarperPrism); *You Can't Catch Me* by Rosamund Smith (Dutton/A William Abrahams Book); *The Perfect Child* by Tom Hyman (Onyx); *Children of the Vampire* by Jeanne Kalogridis (Delacorte Press); *Nailed by the Heart* by Simon Clark (NEL-UK); *The Bloody Red Baron* by Kim Newman (Simon & Schuster-UK/Carroll & Graf); *Bone Music* by Alan Rodgers (Longmeadow Press); *Paint It Black* by Nancy A. Collins (NEL-UK); *The Blood of the Covenant* by Brent Monahan (St. Martin's); *The Wendigo Border* by Catherine Montrose (Tor); *California Gothic* by Dennis Etchison (Dreamhaven, Dell/Abyss); *Spirit* by Graham Masterton (Heinemann-UK); *Tap Tap* by David Martin (Random House); *Frankenstein's Bride* by Hilary Bailey (Simon & Schuster); *All the Bells on Earth* by James P. Blaylock (Ace); *The Psalms of Herod* by Esther M. Friesner (White Wolf/Borealis); *The Death Prayer* by David Bowker (Gollancz-UK); *Graven Images* by Jane Waterhouse (Putnam); *The Flower Man* by Donna Anders (Pocket Books); *Midnight Blue: The Sonja Blue Collection*, an omnibus of Nancy A. Collins' novels *Sunglasses After Dark*, *In the Blood*, and *Paint It Black* (White Wolf); *The Basement* by Bari Wood (William Morrow); *The Night School* by Bentley Little (Headline-UK); *University* by Bentley Little (Signet); *December* by Phil Rickman (Macmillan-UK); *Candlenight* by Phil Rickman (Jove); *Zod Wallop* by William Browning Spencer (St. Martin's); *Dragonfly* by John Farris (Forge); *Passive Intruder* by Michael Upchurch (Norton); *Bleeding in the Eye of a Brainstorm* by George C. Chesbro (Simon & Schuster); *Slow Fuse* by Masako Togawa (Pantheon); *Topping from Below* by Laura Reese (St. Martin's); *Wicked: The Life and Times of the Wicked Witch of the West* by Gregory Maguire (HarperCollins); *Uninvited* by James Gabriel Berman (Warner); *Lizard* by Banana Yoshimoto (Grove Atlantic); *The Tattooed Map* by Barbara Hodgson (Chronicle); *Vanishing Act* by Thomas Perry (Random House); *Interstate* by Stephen Dixon (Henry Holt); *H* by Elizabeth Shepard (Viking); *Into the Deep* by Ken Grimwood (William Morrow); *Restraint* by Sherry Sonnett (Simon & Schuster); *Desmodus* by Melanie Tem (Dell/Abyss); *Only Child* by Jack Ketchum (Headline-UK); *Head and Tales* by Susan Price (Faber & Faber-UK); *Gone Tomorrow* by Gary Indiana (High Risk); *Resurrection Man* by Eoin McNamee (Picador); *Night Magic* by Tom Tryon (Simon & Schuster); *Companions of the Night* by Vivian Vande Velde (Harcourt Brace); *Coin Locker Babies* by Ryu Murakami (Kodansha International); *Night Vision* by Ronald Munson (Dutton); *The Trickster* by Muriel Gray (Doubleday); *The Changeling Garden* by Winifred Elze (A Wyatt Book for St. Martin's); *Whit* by Iain Banks (Little, Brown-UK); *Sick* by Jay Bonansinga (Warner); *Soul Catcher* by Colin Kersey (St. Martin's); *Madeline's Ghost* by Robert Girardi (Delacorte); *Stranglehold* and *Joyride* by Jack Ketchum (Berkley); *Deadrush* by Yvonne Navarro (Bantam); *Sacrifice* by Richard Kinnion (Zebra); *Widow* by Billie Sue Mosiman (Berkley); *Blood Ties* by Karen E. Taylor (Zebra); *Virus* by Graham Watkins (Carroll & Graf); *Bloodwar* and *Unholy Allies* by Robert Weinberg (White Wolf); *Human Resources* by Floyd Kemske (Catbird Press).

Anthologies:

The anthology market continues to thrive, mostly on theme anthologies, many cross-genre. Something that truly bothers me as a reader/editor is when editors use their own fiction in their anthologies. I feel this is unprofessional and improper. I estimate that at least half of the anthologies below edited by writer/editors use a story by the editor. Now not being a fiction writer myself I cannot say what compels writers to add their own stories—

pride? inability to fill the anthology? publisher pressure? I realize that if the editor has a "name" the publisher is very likely to exert pressure for the editor to use her own material, but nonetheless I feel editors should resist.

Seeds of Fear: The Hot Blood Series, edited by Jeff Gelb and Michael Garrett (Pocket), is about the same as the last four in this series. A few good stories but mostly thick-headed, obvious variations on the theme of erotic horror. Introduction by "scream queen" Brinke Stevens. And *Stranger by Night: The Hot Blood Series*, edited by Jeff Gelb and Michael Garrett (Pocket), is the worst in the batch, with only a handful of stories that will be remembered five minutes after reading them. A trudge through the dross to find the few gems. If you're looking for "cutting edge" fiction don't expect to find it in this series.

Ghosts, edited by Peter Straub (Pocket/Borderlands Press), is the Horror Writers Association–sponsored annual anthology. This one is substantially more of a showcase for the membership than in the past, probably because of the broader theme, but I still feel this annual should be a nonthematic anthology. The Borderlands hardcover has a striking cover by Rick Lieder. This is a 350-copy signed, numbered, slip-cased limited edition. $65 payable to Borderlands Press, Box 146, Brooklandville, MD 21022.

Fear Itself, edited by Jeff Gelb (Warner Aspect), is meant to be an anthology about the personal fears of the contributors. Unfortunately, while most anthologies can get away with "stretching" their themes, a high concept anthology like this one suffers if a story doesn't ring true to the proposed intent of the book. Most of the stories in *Fear Itself* are varied and some *do* seem very personal to the authors. Others seem utterly out of place—which could have been remedied by editorial direction if the afterwords or the author bios explained how the story connected to the contributor's own fear. Only occasionally is this done. Despite this problem there are some very good stories. My favorite is by Joyce Carol Oates.

Tombs, edited by Peter Crowther and Edward E. Kramer (White Wolf), has an execrable, incomprehensible introduction by Forrest J. Ackerman. The book is a classic example of overdesigning, with impossible-to-read vertical type for titles and contributor names. And the author bios are inconsistent in *their* design. Despite this, the stories in the anthology are a varied lot, with one poem by Neil Gaiman.

Heaven Sent, edited by Peter Crowther with Martin H. Greenberg (the latter credited only on the copyright page) (DAW), is a good mix of fantasy and dark fantasy on the subject of angels. The introduction is by Storm Constantine. Some very strong stories, particularly one by Gary A. Braunbeck.

Love Bites, edited by Amarantha Knight (A Richard Kasak Book), is another entry in the erotic vampire sweepstakes. It's not bad but if you're looking for subtlety there's little to be had in this volume.

Vampire Detectives, edited by Martin H. Greenberg (DAW), is better than its title suggests—surprisingly varied, with only a few lapses into the obvious. However, at least four of the stories have no detectives in them at all.

Ruby Slippers, Golden Tears, edited by Ellen Datlow and Terri Windling (AvoNova), is the third volume of the ongoing series of retold fairy tales. The stories range from light and dark fantasy to at least one SF story (by Jane Yolen) and horror. This volume on the whole is darker than the first two.

Xanadu 3, edited by Jane Yolen (Tor), is the third and last volume in this series of original fantasy short stories and poems. This literate and intelligent anthology contains a wide range of fantasy and dark fantasy of different types—historical, high fantasy, dark fantasy, veering into horror. Some lovely stories and poems.

Dark Love, edited by Nancy A. Collins, Edward E. Kramer, and Martin H. Greenberg (Roc), is a terrific anthology that's meant to revolve around dark, obsessive love (I think). Relatively few of the stories are actually written on that theme (it's more like obsession) but I'm willing to let this pass as so many of the stories were top-notch, probably making this the best original purely horror anthology of the year. Introduction by T. E. D. Klein. Highly recommended.

Forbidden Acts, edited by Nancy A. Collins and Edward E. Kramer (Avon), is curiously (considering it's edited by the same editorial team) a far less successful anthology. As much as I tried, I never felt they got a handle on the theme—it's meant to be about breaking taboos. There's a lot of violence in general and sexual violence in particular. Too many of the stories are shallow or obvious with glittery surfaces and no depth; I'm afraid those overwhelm the few excellent stories.

Sisters of the Night, edited by Barbara Hambly and Martin H. Greenberg (Warner Aspect), has the female vampire as its theme. Some excellent variations and only one complete miss.

Dark Terrors: The Gollancz Book of Horror, edited by Stephen Jones and David Sutton (Gollancz-UK), is the old *Pan Book of Horror* and more recently, *Dark Voices*. This volume is the best since Jones and Sutton took over the series. The series has always had extreme highs and lows—with this volume the lows are more moderate while the highs remain very high indeed. The best stories here are by Michael Marshall Smith, Terry Lamsley, and Graham Masterton. Highly recommended.

More Phobias, edited by Wendy Webb, Richard Gilliam, Edward E. Kramer, and Martin Greenberg (Pocket), is the follow-up to *Phobias*—literate and readable, with a variety of stories and tones.

Killing Me Softly edited by Gardner Dozois (HarperPrism) is a fine half original-half reprint anthology that seems to be about love and ghosts. Billed by the publisher as "erotic," it isn't, and unfortunately readers looking for that kind of thrill will be disappointed. But for readers interested in literate ghost stories by writers not usually associated with the horror field (most are better known as SF writers) this is a treat.

Celebrity Vampires, edited by Martin H. Greenberg (DAW), is a mixed bag of subtlety and silliness. One danger of using well-known *real* people as characters is that the reader will easily spot any falseness of characterization. This works *against* the freshness or the believability of the story. The more obscure the celebrity, the more effective the story—at least from my point of view.

Desire Burn, edited by Janet Berliner (Carroll & Graf), is another entry in the women's sexual fantasy sweepstakes, containing mostly reprints with originals by Melanie Tem, Marina Fitch, P. D. Cacek, Nancy Holder, and a few others including two stories by the editor. It's a pretty good mix of SF, fantasy, horror, and mainstream writers. Nothing earth-shaking, but entertaining.

Adventures in the Twilight Zone, edited by Carol Serling (Martin H. Greenberg on copyright page) (DAW), is the third in this series of original stories based on the concept of Rod Serling's eerie TV program. As such, this volume is the most successful of the three, with some excellent ghost stories.

Werewolves, edited by Martin H. Greenberg (DAW), is an all-original anthology of werewolf stories. The stories are not as varied as they could be, but there are a few very good contributions. Copyright is in Ed Gorman's name as well as Greenberg's, but otherwise Gorman is not credited.

Two massive instant remainders from Barnes & Noble provide some fun for browsers in search of mostly light entertainment: *100 Wicked Little Witch Stories*, edited by Stefan Dziemianowicz, Robert Weinberg, and Martin H. Greenberg, and *100 Vicious Little Vampire Stories*, edited by Robert Weinberg, Stefan Dziemianowicz, and Martin H. Greenberg (Barnes & Noble Books), are pleasant trifles to dip into. A few short sharp shocks, but not many of the stories stay with the reader for any period of time.

Dark House, edited by Gary Crew (Reed Books-Australia), is a good anthology of haunted house stories. Little here is brilliant but the majority of the stories are entertaining. The writers hail from Australia and they're all new to me.

Northern Frights 3, edited by Don Hutchison (Mosaic Press-Canada), doesn't quite have the highs of last year's volume but is a strong anthology of horror fiction set in Canada. $16.95 including shipping payable to Mosaic Press, 85 River Rock Drive, Suite 202, Buffalo, NY 14207.

Cold Cuts III, edited by Paul Lewis and Steven Lockley (Alun Books-UK), is a solid, well-written anthology mixing psychological and supernatural horror. The first volume focused on stories about Wales, the second volume contained psychological horror exclusively. This one has no such strictures.

Point Horror 13 Again, edited by A. Finnis (Scholastic), is an odd anthology for young adults. At least two of the stories are about relationships from hell—not exactly great models for impressionable kids. On the whole, though, this is the best of the books in this series.

Made in Goatswood: New Tales of Horror in the Severn Valley is a celebration of Ramsey Campbell, edited by Scott David Aniolowski (Chaosium Fiction). The stories on the whole are quite enjoyable, although few break new ground in approach or style; also, from Chaosium comes *The Azathoth Cycle: Tales of the Blind Idiot God*, edited by Robert M. Price. It's half reprints and half originals with most of the new stories predictable and/or dull. Only a few stood out as more than "homages" to Lovecraft.

Palace Corbie Six, edited by Wayne Edwards (Merrimack Books), is a cross-genre anthology with a few good horror stories in it. There's some good writing but too many of the stories are a bit short on plot. $9.95 payable to Merrimack Books, PO Box 83514, Lincoln, NE 68501-3514.

Great Writers & Kids Write Spooky Stories, edited by Martin H. Greenberg, Jill M. Morgan, and Robert Weinberg (Random House), is a wonderful anthology for children and young adults. The gimmick is that all the stories are written by writers with their children or grandchildren. The stories are all good and some are even better than that. Icing the cake are Gahan Wilson's gloriously macabre illustrations throughout. Some of the authors included are John Jakes, Anne McCaffrey, Peter Straub, and Jane Yolen.

Blood Muse, edited by Esther M. Friesner and Martin H. Greenberg (Donald I. Fine), combines vampires with the arts to disappointing effect. There's far too much of the expected with only a few good jolts.

Once Upon a Midnight . . . , edited by Jame A. Riley, Michael N. Langford, and Thomas E. Fuller (Unnameable Press), is an excellent anthology of seventy-five pieces of dark poetry commemorating the 150th anniversary of Poe's "The Raven." Some of the poets included are Lee Ballantine, James S. Dorr, Fred Chappell, Robert Frazier, Neil Gaiman, S. P. Somtow, Steve Rasnic Tem, Thomas Wiloch, and Jane Yolen. The trade paperback is published in an edition of 750. $10.95 plus $1 postage payable to Unnameable Press, PO Box 11689, Atlanta, GA 30355-1689.

Tales From Tartarus, edited by R. B. Russell and Rosalie Parker (Tartarus Press), is a worthwhile anthology from England with some admirable "weird tales" and ghost stories and a great-looking package with a classy black dust jacket with gold type and design. £14.95. Tartarus Press, 5 Birch Terrace, Hangingbirch Lane, Horum, East Sussex, UK.

Strange Fruit: Tales of the Unexpected edited by Paul Collins (Penguin-Australia) is a trade paperback horror/dark fantasy anthology of reprints and originals from Australia, which are a nice representation of the genre worth ordering through mail-order booksellers.

Other anthologies with some good horror stories: *Still More Bone-Chilling Tales of Fright*, anonymous editor (Lowell House juvenile), seven YA horror stories; *Peter S. Beagle's Immortal Unicorn*, edited by Peter S. Beagle and Janet Berliner (HarperPrism), is a consistently well-written, nicely varied fantasy anthology with a few bits of horror. A tough subject to make fresh but enough of the contributors run with the theme to make it interesting. The Beagle story is a gem; *Witch Fantastic*, edited by Mike Resnick and Martin H. Greenberg (DAW), contains only a dollop of horror but some of the darker stories are fine; *Flesh Fantastic*, edited by Amarantha Knight (Rhinoceros), is mostly SF erotica with a few darker stories by Brian McNaughton, Lucy Taylor, and other writers associated with horror; *Sisters in Fantasy*, edited by Susan Shwartz and Martin H. Greenberg (Roc), is a literate fantasy anthology with a few darker stories. The long introduction argues the need for an all-female contributor fantasy anthology. I, for one, was not convinced; *Bruce Coville's Book of Nightmares*, edited by Bruce Coville (Scholastic/Apple), is a YA anthology of horror stories—surprisingly, many deal with death; *The Armless Maiden and Other Tales for Childhood's Survivors*, edited by Terri Windling (Tor), is a ground-breaking anthology of reprints and originals in which writers use the fairy tale form as a means of healing and transformation. Varied in style and form, it has little that can be considered in the horror genre, but many painful and dark experiences are explored fictionally. This is a volume to be read a little at a time. Its intensity and denseness demands this; *David Copperfield's Tales of the Impossible*, edited by David Copperfield and Janet Berliner (HarperPrism), is a beautifully produced original anthology. There are lovely woodcuts by Cathie Bleck subtly illustrating each story; also, a surprisingly charming and well-crafted opener by Copperfield himself, gracious introductions by him to each story, and a nice mix of fantasy and dark fantasy using magic and about magic. Although there's very little horror in it, this anthology is a must for fantasy readers; *The Haunted House*, edited by Jane Yolen and Martin H. Greenberg (HarperCollins), is an original anthology of seven children's stories all about the same haunted house. Includes stories by Yolen and Bruce Coville; *The Splendour Falls: A Changeling: The Dreaming Anthology*, edited by Erin E. Kelly (White Wolf); *Wheel of Fortune*, edited by Roger Zelazny (Martin H. Greenberg on copyright page) (Avon), is an anthology of gambling stories with a few good darker stories, particularly the collaboration by Kathe Koja and Barry N. Malzberg; *Warriors of Blood and Dream*, edited by Roger Zelazny (Greenberg on copyright page) (Avon), is a martial arts anthology with a couple of dark stories; *Full Spectrum 5*, edited by Jennifer Hershey, Tom Dupree, and Janna Silverstein (Bantam Spectra), had excellent fiction but only a smattering of horrific tales; *The Book of Kings*, edited by Richard Gilliam and Martin H. Greenberg (Roc), anthologizes stories of kings and kingdoms—it has an excellent Stephen Donaldson story; *No Alibi*, edited by Maxim Jakubowski (Ringpull-UK), is a mostly original crime anthology with some solidly dark fiction; *Out for Blood: Tales of Mystery and Suspense by Women*, edited by Victoria A. Brownworth (Third Side Press), has a few well-wrought darker suspense stories; *The Ultimate Dragon*, edited by Byron Preiss, John Betancourt, and Keith R. A. DeCandido (Bryon Preiss Book/Dell Trade Paperback), has a couple of good dark stories and one excellent fantasy by S. P. Somtow; *Rat Tales*, edited by Jon Gustafson (Pulphouse), has a copyright of 1994 but I didn't see it until 1995. The intriguing premise is that each story begins with the line: "There were rats in the soufflé again." Surprisingly this device produced some fine stories of fantasy, SF, and minimal horror; *Green Echo*, edited by Gary Bowen (Obelesk Books), collects three "ecological SF & f" tales; *Enchanted Forests*, edited by Katharine Kerr and Martin H. Greenberg (DAW), has some good fantasy and dark fantasy; *New Tales of Lovecraft Country: Four Tales of Dread and Darkness* (Chaosium); *Midnight Journeys*, edited by Davi Dee and Bill Allen (Ozark Triangle Press—not seen), an anthology of twenty-one horror vignettes, seven original, the rest published in the small press; *Strangers in the Night* by Anne Stuart, Chelsea Quinn Yarbro, and Maggie Shayne (Silhouette), an original anthology of three supernatural love stories; *The Merlin Chronicles*, edited by Mike Ashley (Raven), is an anthology of twenty-two stories and novel excerpts, nine original, about Merlin and King Arthur; *Dark Destiny: Proprietors of Fate*, edited by Edward E. Kramer (White Wolf), is based on this gaming publisher's *World of Darkness*. This is the second in this series and it isn't bad for a shared world; *Dark Angels*, edited by Pam Keesey (Cleis), follows up *Daughters of Darkness* with a mix of original and reprinted erotic vampire stories. This is definitely steamy but I fear that those searching for horror will be disappointed; *A Crimson Kind of Evil*, edited by S. G. Johnson (Obelesk Books), is a mini-paperback anthology of six horror stories. $7 payable to Obelesk Books, PO 1118, Elkton, MD 21922-1118. Also from Obelesk and edited by

Johnson is a series of "shared world" gothic romance/horror novellas called *Dominion of the Ghosts* about a rather dysfunctional family. $6.00.

Reprint Anthologies:

Splatterpunks II: Over the Edge, edited by Paul M. Sammon (Tor), is an attractive package of twenty-six stories, eighteen of which are reprints, and essays by Anya Martin and Martin Amis. Why another splatterpunk anthology? If, as the editor states in his introduction, it's to give the women a chance, then why are only *half* the stories by women? Oh, they're *about* women this time. . . . You mean unlike the first volume where the female characters are mostly victims? But at least eleven of the stories in *Splat II* feature women as victims of torture, degradation, and/or murder.

Many of the reprints are excellent and stood out in their original venues; some of the originals are very good and would impress in "other company," but putting them all together as representative of "splatterpunk" seems to prove exactly what many readers have perceived all along—whether the stories are by women or men, what is being called "splatterpunk" is for the most part violent, brutal, ugly fiction treating women as victims; *Tales of Terror from Blackwood's Magazine,* edited and with an introduction by Robert Morrison and Chris Baldick (Oxford University Press); *Demons of the Night: Tales of the Fantastic, Madness, and the Supernatural from Nineteenth-Century France,* edited by Joan C. Kessler (University of Chicago), is an anthology of thirteen stories by authors such as Balzac, Jules Verne, Guy de Maupassant. Edited, with notes to each story by Kessler, who translated nine of the stories and wrote a 51-page critical introduction; *The Giant Book of Myths and Legends,* edited by Mike Ashley (Parragon-UK-instant remainder) has fifty-one stories, told by authors ranging from William Morris and Nathaniel Hawthorne to Peter Tremayne and Jessica Amanda Salmonson; *Murder Most Medical,* edited by Cathleen Jordan and Cynthia Manson (Carroll & Graf), collects stories from *Alfred Hitchcock Mystery Magazine* and *Ellery Queen's Mystery Magazine* by such writers as Dorothy Sayers, Arthur Conan Doyle, and Lawrence Block; *The Penguin Book of Modern Fantasy by Women,* with an introduction by Joanna Russ and edited by A. Susan Williams and Richard Glyn Jones (Viking-UK), is a massive volume of over 550 pages and collects thirty-eight short stories by women ranging from Elizabeth Bowen (Ireland, 1941) to Lucy Sussex (Australia, 1994). The word "fantasy" is used quite broadly, encompassing the science fiction of Octavia E. Butler and James Tiptree, Jr. and the mystery writing of P. D. James as well as what most readers consider fantasy by Tanith Lee, Angela Carter, and Joyce Carol Oates. Two original stories by Ann Oakley and Lynda Rajan; *The Best New Horror VI,* edited by Stephen Jones (Robinson-UK/Carroll & Graf), contained an overview of 1994 and a necrology, along with twenty-two stories and novellas. Only two stories overlapped with *The Year's Best Fantasy and Horror: Eighth Annual Collection,* those by Charles L. Grant and M. John Harrison; *The Mammoth Book of Victorian and Edwardian Ghost Stories: Classic tales from the masters of the macabre,* edited by Richard Dalby (Robinson-UK), includes stories by Charles Dickens, Sheridan Le Fanu, Henry James, William Hope Hodgson, Edith Nesbit, and Harriet Beecher Stowe; *Shivers for Christmas,* edited by Richard Dalby (Michael O'Mara-UK), contains stories by Jessica Amanda Salmonson, Terry Lamsley, and others; *Bad Behavior,* edited by Mary Higgins Clark in conjunction with the International Association of Crime Writers (Gulliver/Harcourt, Brace), is a YA mystery anthology with eight original stories, some dark; *Murder by the Glass,* edited by Peter Haining (Pocket-UK), seems to be about drinking and includes classics by Ruth Rendell, Roald Dahl, Edgar Allan Poe, Joan Aiken, and others; *The Year's Best Mystery and Suspense Stories,* edited by Edwad D. Hoch (Walker and Company), picks stories from the obvious venues, including *Alfred Hitchcock Mystery Magazine, Ellery Queen's Mystery Magazine,* and anthologies such as *The Mysterious West, Deadly Allies,* and *London Noir.* But it also contains a necrology, list of the year's awards, and a bibliography of mystery/suspense material published during the year 1994; *The Year's 25 Finest Crime & Mystery Stories: Fourth Annual Edition,* edited by the staff of *Mystery Scene* and with an introduction by Jon L. Breen (Carroll & Graf), overlaps the Walker volume with five stories. It's missing the Robert L. Fish Award winner by Batya Swift Yasgur but it does reprint the wonderful novella "Porkpie Hat" by Peter Straub; *Between Time and Terror*, edited by Robert Weinberg, Stefan Dziemianowicz, and Martin H. Greenberg (Roc), is an anthology of SF horror stories by H. P. Lovecraft, Arthur C. Clarke, Ray Bradbury, Dan Simmons, John Shirley, and others; *Mystery Cats 3*, edited by Cynthia Manson (Signet), reprints stories by Patricia Highsmith, Lillian Jackson Braun, Manly Wade Wellman, Theodore Sturgeon, and Edward Pangborn from *Ellery Queen's Mystery Magazine* and *Alfred Hitchcock Mystery Magazine*; *Best of Weird Tales*, edited by John Betancourt (Barnes & Noble-instant remainder edition), collects twenty-seven horror and dark fantasy tales published between 1988 and 1994; *The Eyes Still Have It*, edited by Robert Randisi (Dutton), collects twelve stories that have won the award for Best Short Story given by the Private Eye Writers of America. Stories by Lawrence Block, Loren Estleman, Marcia Muller; *Tales From the Rogue's Gallery*, edited by Peter Haining (Warner), reprints horror stories by Angela Carter, Ray Bradbury, Anthony Boucher, Ruth Rendell, and others; *The Haunted Hour*, edited by Cynthia Manson and Constance Scarborough (Berkley Prime Crime), reprints twenty stories from *Ellery Queen's Mystery Magazine* and *Alfred Hitchcock Mystery Magazine*, including works by Ray Bradbury, Richard Matheson, Robert Bloch, and others; *Dream Police: Selected Poems, 1969–1993* by Dennis Cooper (Grove Press) are erotic, obsessive, and disturbing like his novels and short stories; *Mondo Marilyn: An Anthology of Fiction and Poetry*, edited by Richard Peabody and Lucinda Ebersole (St. Martin's), reprints Barker's "Son of Celluloid"; *Tomorrow Bites*, edited by Greg Cox and T. K. F. Weisskopf (Baen), reprints eleven scientific werewolf stories ranging from James Blish's "There Shall Be No Darkness," published in 1950, to Rod Garcia's "Werewolves of Luna," published in 1994; *The Screaming Skull: and Other Great American Ghost Stories*, edited by David G. Hartwell (Tor), reprints stories by Edgar Allan Poe, Nathanial Hawthorne, Mark Twain, Edith Wharton, Willa Cather, and others. The book would have been well served by an introduction placing the stories in a thematic context—for example, how does the American ghost story differ from the classic British ghost story? and why?; *Dread and Delight: A Century of Children's Ghost Stories*, edited by Philippa Pearce (Oxford University Press), has an informative introduction by Pearce on the history of ghost tales for children and makes a noteworthy attempt to define her terms. She states that despite all her research she could not find any ghost stories written specifically for children before 1900. There are stories by M. R. James, Arthur Machen, R. Chetwynd-Hayes, Joan Aiken, Isaac Bashevis Singer, Penelope Lively, Vivian Alcock, Robert Westall, and Tim Wynne-Jones among the forty authors; *Cthulhu 2000: A Lovecraftian Anthology*, edited by James Turner, reprints three stories from the out-of-print *New Tales of the Cthulhu Mythos*, plus fifteen stories that show Lovecraft's influence on writers such as F. Paul Wilson, Michael Shea, Esther Friesner, Poppy Z. Brite, Kim Newman, Gene Wolfe, and others. Dust jacket by Bob Eggleton. $24.95 from Arkham House Publishers, Box 546, Sauk City, WI 53583; Andy Cox, editor of the cross-genre magazine, *The Third Alternative*, published *Last Rites & Resurrections: Stories from The Third Alternative: Volume One*, with sixteen stories from the first eight issues of the magazine. Cover artwork by David Checkley with stories by Rick Cadger, Nicholas Royle, Joel Lane, Chris Kenworthy, Mike O'Driscoll, Conrad Williams, Julie Travis, and others; *Creepy Stories*, ed. Anonymous (Bracken Books-UK), is a compendium including stories from the anthologies *The Black Cap*, *The Ghost Book*, *Shudders*, and *When Churchyards Yawn*, all edited by Cynthia Asquith. This edition adds an introduction by Fred Urquhart but omits twenty-three of the stories; *The Puffin Book of Horror Stories*, edited by Anthony Horowitz (Viking-UK), is a YA anthology of eight reprints, one original, and an extract from *Dracula*; *Ghost Movies: Famous Supernatural Films*, edited by Peter Haining (Severn House-UK), has twelve stories and an excerpt; *Horror Stories*, edited by Susan Price (Kingfisher), is a YA anthology of twenty-four stories, ranging from Poe, Dickens, and Blackwood to Philip K. Dick, T. H. White, and Stephen King; *The Vampire Omnibus*, edited by Peter Haining (Orion-UK), is meant to show representative examples of vampire stories that appeared before Stoker's *Dracula* as well as the films that took the tradition into a new medium, and a cross-selection of some of the stories written in the past fifty years; *On Spec: The First Five Years*, edited by the *On Spec* Editorial Collective (Tesseract), is an anthology of twenty-two stories from this generally excellent Canadian cross-genre magazine. Introduction by editor Barry Hammond. $9.95 ppd (paperback), $23.95 ppd (hardcover). Available from Tesseract Books/The Books Collective, 214-21 10405 Jasper Avenue, Edmonton, Alberta, Canada T5J 3S2; *Isaac Asimov's Ghosts*, edited by Gardner Dozois and Sheila Williams (Ace), includes twelve stories that originally appeared in *Asimov's Science Fiction Magazine*; *Classic Vampire Stories*, edited by Leslie Shepard (Citadel), includes stories by Stoker, Crawford, and E. F. Benson; *Thrillers: True Crimes and Dark Mysteries from the City by the Bay*, edited by John Miller and Tim Smith (Chronicle), and with an introduction by Martin Cruz Smith, is a very attractive trade paperback package with b&w photographs by Francis Bruguiére and thirteen noir stories by such as Dashiell Hammett, Jim Thompson, Alfred Hitchcock, and Mark Twain; *Doubles, Dummies, and Dolls*, edited by Leonard Wolf (Newmarket Press), is a wonderful theme for a reprint anthology, there being a long tradition of this sort of tale in the mainstream and horror fields. Wolf provides a solid introduction ruminating on why we find these replicas of human beings so disturbing and such a spur to the creative imagination. Odd though that he mentions the episode of the Zulu warrior menacing Karen Black in the made-for-TV *Trilogy of Terror* but neglects to reprint (let alone credit) the Richard Matheson story it's based upon.

Nonfiction:

Not all of these books were seen by me. Some of the descriptions are taken from *Psychotronic Video*, *Locus*, and *Science Fiction Chronicle*, and *Filmfax* and the DreamHaven and Mark Ziesing catalogs.

Our Vampires, Ourselves by Nina Auerbach (The University of Chicago Press) is a historical/cultural study of vampires and vampirism in text and film ranging from Byron, Polidari, and Stoker through the vampires of Fred Saberhagen, Chelsea Quinn Yarbro, Suzy McKee Charnas, Anne Rice, Brian Stableford, and Kim Newman to the movies *Lost Boys* and Kathryn Bigelow's *Near Dark*. It's a bit academic in spots but should be of interest to anyone enamored of the subject. Auerbach traces the cultural influences on the depiction of the undead and although she occasionally misinterprets text (e.g., proclaiming that the ending of Whitley Streiber's novel *The Hunger* is an example of "love conquers all"—huh?) Auerbach's done a good job on the whole. Her feminist readings of *Near Dark* and other books/movies are dead on.

The Knife and Gun Club by Eugene Richards (Atlantic Monthly Press) is a reissue in trade paperback from the original 1989 publication. Photojournalist Richards was assigned by a magazine to do a piece on what goes on in an urban emergency room. He chose Denver Hospital, and emotionally recuperating from the death by cancer of his wife, he asked to stay on. This document (I don't know over what period of time this takes place) is a harrowing account of men and women striving to save the wounded, maimed, and dying and puts the reader in the middle of life-threatening situations. Surprisingly, the photographs aren't as powerful as the words of the paramedics, doctors and nurses, orderlies, aides, etc., as they go about their work. A visceral view of life on the edge.

Ed Gein Psycho by Paul Anthony Woods (St. Martin's Griffin) is a "faction" book about the cannibalistic serial killer who inspired Robert Bloch's novel and Alfred Hitchcock's movie *Psycho*. After recounting Gein's life and crimes (occasionally putting words in the mouths of folk from the late 1800s), Woods goes on to pay homage to Gein's "children," the fictional serial killers who came after.

Classic Horror Writers, edited by Harold Bloom, is from the *Writers of English: Lives and* Works series published by Chelsea House. Bloom introduces each volume, which has biographical, critical, and bibliographical information on the twelve writers he deems the most significant of the late eighteenth to late nineteenth century. He includes most of those one would expect: Poe, Henry James, Stoker, Bierce, Radcliffe, and Mary Shelley. Then there is a series of critical extracts taken from each writer's lifetime up to the contemporary, in chronological order. A superficial but useful survey for the beginner.

Immoral Tales: European Sex and Horror Movies 1956–1984 by Cathal Tohill and Pete Tombs (St. Martin's Griffin) is an oversize trade paperback with 16 pages of color photos, hundreds of b&w stills, and interviews with filmmakers. According to this book, in the 1960s and 1970s the European horror film created a new type of cinema that combined sex with terror. The book covers such, ahem, classics as *The Nude Vampire*, *The Living Dead Girl*, and *Sadomania*.

Filmmaking on the Fringe: The Good, the Bad, and the Deviant Directors by Maitland McDonagh (A Citadel Press Book) is an interesting and invaluable source of information about makers of comtemporary exploitation movies. These, according to one critic, are "Films made with little or no attention to quality or artistic merit but with an eye to profit usually via high pressure sales and promotion techniques emphasizing some sensational aspect of the product." McDonagh interviews and writes about fifteen directors and their films and adds over thirty pages of capsule bios/filmographies of other notable exploitation moviemakers.

Inside Teradome: An Illustrated History of Freak Film by Jack Hunter (Creation Books-UK) is another informative and entertaining film book. This one provides a historical overview of teratology, freaks in myth and medicine, and a history of freak shows before moving on to the influence of sideshows on cinema, the use of human anomalies in cinema, and bizarre cinema: mutilation and other fetishes. Hunter uses Tod Browning's *Freaks* as the starting point for his illustrated guide to the roots and development of this genre.

Suspended Animation: Six Essays on the Preservation of Bodily Parts by F. Gonzalez-Crussi with photographs by Rosamund Purcell (Harcourt Brace) is an elegantly written series of meditations on the human body and mortality by the author of *The Day of the Dead*. From visits to a medical school in Madrid and the Anatomical Cabinet in Bologna, and essays on the development of wax modeling and the "history of teratology" (the study of monsters), Gonzalez-Crussi makes it all fascinating and somehow beautiful.

Hitchcock on Hitchcock, Selected Writings and Interviews, edited by Sidney Gottlieb (University of California Press), includes a piece by Hitchcock on the "Enjoyment of Fear" written for *Good Housekeeping* in 1949; an explanation for the term the "MacGuffin"—which Hitchcock claims as having invented—interviews, and interestingly a "dialogue" originally published in *Redbook*, with Dr. Frederic Wertham. Highly recommended; and fans of Hitchcock will also enjoy *Psycho: Behind the Scenes of the Classic Thriller* by Janet Leigh with Christopher Nickens (Harmony Books), an entertaining memoir of the making of the movie that still thrills after thirty-five years. Leigh is a good storyteller and the book gives credit where it's due—to Robert Bloch, to the screenwriter, and especially to Hitchcock.

Flesh and Blood: The National Society of Film Critics on Sex, Violence, and Censorship, edited by Peter Keough, (Mercury House) collects essays by American film critics on movies from Buñuel's *Belle de Jour* through Tarantino's *Pulp Fiction*, addressing such topics as voyeurism, slasher films, women as aggressors, and issues of exploitation. An important and fascinating book for film-lovers; *They Went Thataway: Redefining Film Genres*, edited by Richard T. Jamison, is from the same series. It examines the movies that have defined their genres and those that have transcended genre conventions, such as *The Crying Game*, *Unforgiven*, and *The Silence of the Lambs*.

And then there's *Ed Wood* by Scott Alexander and Larry Karaszewski (Faber & Faber), the screenplay of the movie with an introduction by the authors about the genesis of the project.

Burton on Burton, edited by Mark Salisbury (Faber & Faber), brings the reader into the world of Tim Burton, creator of *Beetlejuice, Edward Scissorhands, Batman,* and *Ed Wood*. The darkness inherent in much of his artistic vision gives Burton's work an edge appreciated by horror fans. This is the first book-length work on him and his oeuvre. His sketches seem to be influenced by Edward Gorey and Ronald Searles.

Freaks, Geeks & Strange Girls: Sideshow Banners of the Great American Midway by Randy Johnson, Jim Secreto, and Teddy Varndell (Hardy Marks Publications) are now considered folk art but in their heyday they documented a part of life that makes us uncomfortable today—the exploitation of genetic freaks and self-created freaks. While this book is prolifically illustrated with banners, it's more than an art book. The authors place the art in a historical and sociological context. This is a fascinating look at Americana.

Imagining Monsters by Dennis Todd (The University of Chicago Press) examines a hoax perpetrated by an illiterate woman in Surrey, England, in 1726 who announced that she had given birth to seventeen rabbits. Todd tells the story of the incident and shows how it illuminates eighteenth-century beliefs about the power of imagination and the problems of personal identity. It was a common belief that the imagination of a pregnant woman could deform her fetus, creating a monster within her.

The Female Thermometer by Terry Castle (Oxford University Press) interestingly has as its cover art the same painting of a woman giving birth to rabbits as is inside the previous volume. This book collects Castle's essays on phantasmagoria in eighteenth-century literature and culture. The "female thermometer" is an imaginary instrument invented by eighteenth-century satirists to measure levels of female sexual arousal. She writes extensively about Freud's essay on "The Uncanny."

The Violence of Our Lives: Interviews with American Murderers by Tony Parker (Henry Holt) is told completely in their own voices and is separated into several sections: released men, released women, men serving life sentences, imprisoned women, and victims.

Dark Carnival: The Secret World of Tod Browning, Hollywood's Master of the Macabre by David J. Skal and Elias Savada (Doubleday) is the first full-length biography of the director of *Dracula, The Unholy Three,* and the notorious movie *Freaks,* the failure and condemnation of which effectively destroyed Browning's career.

Nonfiction Listings:

P. T. Barnum: America's Greatest Showman is an illustrated biography by Philip B. Kunhardt Jr., Philip B. Kunhardt III, and Peter W. Kundhardt (Alfred A. Knopf) with over 500 photographs, engravings, and other color lithographs, it sets the record straight on the man who apparently did *not* say "there's a sucker born every minute"; *From the Beast to the Blonde: On Fairy Tales and Their Tellers* by Marina Warner (Farrar, Straus & Giroux); *Madame Blavatsky's Baboon: A History of the Mystics, Mediums, and Misfits Who Brought Spiritualism to America* by Peter Washington (Schocken); *Man and Microbes: Disease and Plagues in History and Modern Times* by Arno Karlen (Tarcher/Putnam); *Mind Hunter: Inside the FBI's Elite Serial Crime Unit* by John Douglas and Mark Olshaker (Scribner); *Secret Life* by Michael Ryan (Pantheon) is a memoir of psychosexual addition and predation, by an exellent poet; *Dictionary of Symbolic and Mythological Animals* by J. C. Cooper (Thorsons); *The Complete Book of Superstition, Prophecy and Luck* by Leonard R. N. Ashley and *The Complete Book of Magic and Witchcraft* also by Ashley (both from Barricade Books); *The Stephen King Companion* by George Beahm (Andrews & McMeel) is a revised edition that claims to contain 80 percent more material, including extensive photographs, and a chronological overview of King's books through *Insomnia* by Michael R. Collings; *The Essential Dr. Jekyll and Mr. Hyde: The Definitive Annotated Edition of Robert Louis Stevenson's Classic Novel,* edited by Leonard Wolf (Penguin/Plume), includes the complete text of the novel, with commentary from fans past and present, contemporary reviews, a selection of Stevenson's short fiction, filmography, photographs, and a detailed introduction. Interior illustrations by Michael Lank. Curiously, the book has no table of contents or running heads. *When the Music's Over: My Journey into Schizophrenia* by Ross David Burke, edited by Richard Gates and Robin Hammond (Basic Books); *The Lucifer Principle: A Scientific Expedition into the Forces of History* by Howard Bloom (The Atlantic Monthly Press); *Where the Ghosts Are: The Ultimate Guide to Haunted Houses* by Hans Holzer (Carol); *Return to Derleth: Selected Essays, Volume Two*, edited by James P. Roberts (White Hawk Press), collects seven critical essays on the works of August Derleth, with an introduction by the editor and illustrations by Eugene Gryniewicz and Frank Utpatel. $7 trade paperback from White Hawk Press, 950 Jenifer Street, Madison, WI 53703-3522; *A Delusion of Satan: The Full Story of the Salem Witch Trials* by Frances Hill (Doubleday); *An Encyclopedia of Lies, Frauds, and Hoaxes of the Occult and Supernatural Exposed* by James Randi, introduction by Arthur C. Clarke (St. Martin's); *Dark Prisms: Occultism in Hispanic Drama* by Robert Lima (University Press of Kentucky); *J. Sheridan Le Fanu: A Bio-Bibliography* by Gary Williams Crawford (Greenwood Press) is an annotated bibliography of works by and about Le Fanu; *Fantasies of Love and Death in Life and Art: A Psychoanalytic Study of the Normal and the Pathological* by Helen K. Gediman (New York University Press); *Encyclopedia Cthulhiana* (Chaosium); *Lord Dunsany: Master of the Anglo-Irish Imagination* by S. T. Joshi (Greenwood Press); *Speaking of Horror: Interviews with Writers of the Supernatural* by Darrell Schweitzer (Borgo Press, 1994); *Permanent Italians: An Illustrated Guide to the Cemeteries of Italy* by Judi Culbertson and Tom Randall (Walker and Company); *Daddy Was the Black Dahlia Killer* by Janice Knowlton with Mike Newton (Pocket Books); *The Turn of the Screw by Henry James*, edited by Peter G. Beidler (St. Martin's/Bedford), has complete text and five new critical essays examining the work from different contemporary viewpoints. Also, biographical and historical contexts, and a survey of major critical response over time; *The Mysterious Death of Mary Rogers: Sex and Culture in Nineteenth Century New York* by Amy Gilman Srebnick (Oxford University Press) is the real-life story behind the fictionalized Edgar Allan Poe's "The Mystery of Marie Roget"; *The Monsters in the Mind* by Frank Cawson (The Book Guild) is a study of the monster through history, using texts such as Jane Austen, the Marquis de Sade, and Thomas Harris, to demonstrate how the face of evil has been shaped by social attitudes and psychological needs; *Lewis Carroll: A Biography* by Morton N. Cohen (Knopf); *The R'Lyeh Text*, edited by Robert Turner (Skoob Books), is the companion text to the *Necronomicon*, "deciphering, as promised, the rest of the hidden mss." Introduction by Colin Wilson; *The Flesh Eaters: True Stories of Cannibals and Blood Drinkers* by Peter Haining (Boxtree); *The Supernatural Index: A Listing of Fantasy, Supernatural, Occult, Weird, and Horror Anthologies* by Mike Ashley and William G. Contento (Greenwood) is an index to 2,100 fantasy, supernatural, occult, weird, and horror anthologies and their contents published between 1813 and 1994; *New England's Gothic Literature: History of Folklore of the Supernatural from the Seventeenth Through the Twentieth Centuries* by Faye Ringel (The Edwin Mellen Press); *A War of Witches: A Journey into the Underworld of the Contemporary Aztecs* by Timothy Knab (HarperCollins) is "an account of a world of magic and sorcery that echoes the deepest roots of Aztec mysticism"; *Dust: A Creation Books Reader* (Creation Press) gathers pieces from some of their authors including Kathy Acker, Alan Moore, and others. Creation Press has published some very weird and definitely horrific books, including last year's *Killing for Culture; The World's Most Dangerous Places* by Robert Young Pelton and Coskun Aral (Fielding) is a travel guide that provides the usual travel guide information plus advice on how to stay out of trouble in such hot spots as Chechnya, Rwanda, Iraq, Lebanon, etc.; *Ghosts of the Air: True Stories of Aerial Hauntings* by Martin Caidin (Galde) collects accounts of the supernatural by the pilots who experienced them; *Dreams, Myths, & Fairy Tales in Japan* by Hayao Kawai (Daimon) is a look at Japanese culture by way of examining myths; *Monsters of Weimer* (author unknown) (Nemesis) is the story of Fritz Haarmann and Peter Kurten, two serial killers in Germany just prior to WWII; *Selected Letters by the Marquis de Sade* (Owen); *Apparitions of Things* to Come: Tales of Mystery and Imagination by Edward Bellamy (Kerr), a reissue of a volume that has not been available in a popular edition since the First World War; *The Unexplained: 347 Strange Sightings, Incredible Occurrences, and Puzzling Physical Phenomena* by Jerome Clark (Visible Ink) includes stuff on cattle mutilations, reptile men, monsters, fireballs, dinosaurs, werewolves, etc. (Mark Ziesing recommends it so it can't be all bad); *The Supernatural and English Fiction* by Glen Cavaliero discusses all the principal English writers who have handled the subject, including Ann Radcliffe, M. R. James, William Golding, Iris Murdoch, Muriel Spark, and Peter Ackroyd, among others (Oxford University Press): *Roald Dahl: From the Gremlins to the Chocolate Factory* by Alan Warren (Borgo Press); *Selected Letters of Mary Wollstonecraft Shelley* (Johns Hopkins University Press) is a selection of 230 letters from the three-volume *Complete Letters of Mary Wollstonecraft Shelley*; *Stern Fathers 'Neath the Mould: The Lovecraft Family in Rochester* by Richard D. Squires (Necronomican Press); *Science Fiction, Fantasy, and Horror Writers* by Marie J. McNee (Gale Research) is a YA reference work in two volumes, with eighty biographical entries, each with photos and a recommended reading list that includes plot outlines; *Anatomy of Wonder, Fourth Edition*, edited by Neil Barron (R.R. Bowker), is a major one-volume reference work on SF, its history, major authors, etc. Almost 2,000 books are critically annotated; *Vital Mummies: Performance Design for the Show-Window Mannequin* by Sara K. Schneider (Yale University Press) is disappointing for two reasons: not enough photographs and not enough digging into the psyche of the few display directors Schneider manages to interview; *Daemonic Reality: A Field Guide to the Otherworld* by Patrick Harpur (Viking) is an utterly credulous account of supposed sightings of apparitions, crop circles, mysterious beasts, and the like.

Nonfiction (movie-related):
Hollywood Cauldron: Thirteen Horror Films from the Genre's Golden Age by Gregory William Mark (McFarland & Company, Inc., Publishers, Box 611, Jefferson, NC 28640); *Christopher Lee and Peter Cushing and Horror Cinema* by Mark A. Miller (McFarland); *Fearing in the Dark—The Val Lewton Career* by Edmund G. Bansak (McFarland); *House of Horror: The Hammer Films Story*, edited by Jack Hunter (Creation/Lorrimer-UK); *Final Curtain: Deaths of Noted Movie and TV Personalities* by Everett G. Jarvis (Carol); *Dissecting Aliens: Terror in Space* by John Flynn (Boxtree) is a comprehensive behind-the-scenes look at the film series; *More Gore Score: Brave New Horrors* by Chas. Balun (Fantasma Books, 419 Amelia Street, Key West, FL 33040) is more than 100 pages, indexed, and has reviews, ratings, and information on newer horror movies; *Sleaze Creatures: An Illustrated Guide to Obscure Hollywood Horror Movies 1956–1959* by D. Earl Worth (Fantasma) is a large trade paperback with more than 250 indexed pages; *Nightwalkers: Gothic Horror Movies, the Modern Era* by Bruce Wright (Taylor) is an indexed and illustrated 170-page trade paperback; *The Creatures Features Movie Guide Strikes Again: Fourth Revised Edition* by John Stanley is a guide to 5,600 SF, fantasy, and horror movies with notations, cross-references, and over 230 photographs. Available as a deluxe hardcover edition with full-color dust jacket, signed by Stanley for $50 or as a trade paperback for $20 payable to Creatures at Large Press, Box 687, 1082 Grand Teton Drive, Pacifica, CA 94044; *The Monster Magazine & Fanzine Collector's Guide: 1995* edited by Michael W. Pierce (Monsters Among Us); *They Fought in the Creature Features* by Tom Weaver (McFarland) covers twenty-one actors and others involved in moviemaking. Most of the original interviews were in *Starlog* but they are more complete here; *Vincent Price: Actor and Art Collector* (no author given) is a series of previously unpublished interviews with Price to coincide with a 1982 museum show of his movies and some of his rare art. Movie stills and photos of his art including Mayan sculptures and a signed James Thurber cartoon. $13 ppd to Riverside Museum Press, 3720 Orange Street, Riverside, CA 92501; *Film, Horror, and the Body Fantastic* by Linda Badley (Greenwood Press) is a critical look at horror in films, drawing on feminist critical theory, psychoanalytic theory, cultural criticism, and gender studies; *Film into Books: An Analytical Bibliography*

of Film Novelizations, Movie and TV Tie-Ins by Randall D. Larson (Scarecrow Press) is a critical examination of the subgenre, with interviews with more than fifty authors who share their perspectives on the hows and whys of tie-ins. Authors mentioned include Isaac Asimov, Ramsey Campbell, Chelsea Quinn Yarbro, and Robert Bloch. $69.50 from the University Press of America, 4720 Boston Way, Lanham, MD 20706; *Midnight Marquee Actors Series: Bela Lugosi*, various authors, edited by Gary J. and Susan Svehla (Midnight Marquee Press, Inc.), 9721 Britinay Lane, Baltimore, MD 21234; *The Complete Films of Vincent Price* by Lucy Chase Williams (Citadel Film series); *The Sleaze Merchants: Adventures in Exploitation Filmmaking* by John McCarty (St. Martin's Press); *Cult Science Fiction Films* by Welch Everman (Citadel Press) is a large trade paperback arranged in alphabetical order covering movies from *Bride of the Monster* to *THX 1138*; and *Outposts: A Catalog of Rare and Disturbing Alternative Information* by Russ Kick (Carroll & Graf). Also, it has an appendix with general book catalogs and book publishers that carry this material (including Mark Ziesing).

Collections:
One of the most important and certainly longest-awaited collections of the year is Jonathan Carroll's first collection in English, *The Panic Hand* (HarperCollins-UK). Originally published in Germany, it collects nineteen stories, including one original and one published for the first time in English. If you haven't read anything by this master fantasist, shame on you. His short fiction, like his work at longer lengths, makes the unlikely possible on the strength of his characterizations.

Another important collection was that of the late fantasist Angela Carter's fiction, *Burning Your Boats: Collected Short Stories* (Chatto & Windus-UK), supposedly an omnibus of every short story from her four collections plus one original. However, the book, according to one source, seems to be missing one story, "The Bridegroom." Introduction by Salman Rushdie.

The Lepers by Frank Weissenborn (86 Publishing-Australia) collects surreal, horrific, and science fiction stories by this Australian writer. Three stories are reprinted from Australian magazines. Finely rendered illustrations throughout by Guy Browning. Includes a bizarre hard-boiled almost-parody of an American noir story. In general, there's some very effective material, some painfully pretentious prose, and a disappointing un-Australian flavor.

A Flush of Shadows by Kate Wilhelm (St. Martin's Press) collects five novellas centering around Constance Leidl and Charlie Meiklejohn, a married couple who often become involved in detecting puzzling (occasionally, seemingly supernatural) cases. Kate Wilhelm has had a distinguished and varied career writing science fiction, fantasy, mainstream, and mystery short stories and novels. Her writing is always crisp and her characters believable. Two excellent original novellas.

The Ivory and the Horn (Tor) is Charles de Lint's second collection of short fiction about the fictional city of Newford. The stories originally appeared in such magazines as *Worlds of Fantasy and Horror* and *Thunder's Shadow*, and various anthologies, chapbooks, or small press limited editions. De Lint has created a magical world in which harsh reality is usually tempered with grace. One original.

Michael Moorcock's *Fabulous Harbours* (Millennium) collects nine stories that first appeared in various U.S. and U.K. anthologies, with some characters overlapping with *Blood*.

Peter Carey, author of *Bliss, Illywhacker, Oscar and Lucinda, The Tax Inspector*, and *The Unusual Life of Tristan Smith*, has a third collection out: *Collected Stories* (Faber & Faber), which contains twenty-seven stories, some from his earlier collections *The Fat Man in History* and *War Crimes*, and newly collects four stories that originally appeared in magazines and anthologies.

Kim Newman's second collection, *Famous Monsters* (Pocket), collects fourteen reprints and one original story. Newman's fantasy, science fiction, and horror is reprinted from such venues as *Interzone, Fantasy Tales, Fear,* and a multitude of anthologies. Paul McAuley has written the appreciative introduction.

Tor published two collections by one of the Grand Masters of Science Fiction and Fantasy, Richard Matheson: *I Am Legend,* containing the eponymous classic short novel plus nine short stories (including "Prey," which was made into one of a trilogy of horror episodes starring Karen Black). And *The Incredible Shrinking Man,* collecting that short novel with another nine stories, including "Duel," upon which Spielberg's first film, a made-for-TV movie, is based and the story on which the classic *Twilight Zone* episode starring William Shatner, "Nightmare at 20,000 Feet," is based.

Severn House released *Faces of Fear* and *Flights of Fear,* two collections by Graham Masterton, and, as usual, omits first publication data. However, each collection contains recent reprints with a few originals. Masterton is an excellent short story writer, creating believable characters who earn the reader's empathy even if they don't always behave well.

MacArthur Fellowship–winning author Octavia E. Butler's rare short fiction is collected in a lovely little hardcover volume published by Four Walls Eight Windows. *Bloodchild and other stories* collects, along with the multi–award-winning title SF/horror story, Butler's first published story, her only non-SF story, two other science fiction stories, and two autobiographical essays.

The Second Wish by Brian Lumley (NEL-UK) is a third volume of Lumley's stories of the macabre. His thirteen story introductions give insight into the inspiration and some of the circumstances surrounding their writing.

In addition to being a writer and a talented artist, Clive Barker is a playwright. *Incarnations: Three Plays by Clive Barker* (HarperPrism) collects *Colossus, Frankenstein in Love,* and *The History of the Devil* in one volume with an introduction by the playwright.

British writer Christopher Fowler has a fifth collection of mostly original horror stories. *Flesh Wounds* (Warner-UK) mixes contemporary urban settings and some historical grotesqueries for an eclectic and entertaining mix.

R. Chetwynd-Hayes's new collection, *Shudders and Shivers* (Robert Hale-UK), is of the traditional British school, and many of the stories deal with hauntings of various types.

Ed Gorman's new collection, *Cages* (Deadline Press), has five new stories as well as reprints that do a fine job of demonstrating his range in the thriller and horror tale. It's hard edges all around; there's a particularly good, moving SF horror story called "Survival." Introduction by F. Paul Wilson, afterword by Marcia Muller, and unusual cover art by the talented new artist Carlos Batts. A limited edition of 500 copies signed by Ed Gorman and F. Paul Wilson for $35 plus $3 shipping, payable to Deadline Press, PO Box 2808, Apache Junction, AZ 85217.

Close to the Bone by Mark Morris (Piatkus-UK), the first collection by this popular new writer from Great Britain, contains two good originals and nine reprints from British magazines and anthologies. Morris is author of the novels *Toady, Stitch, The Immaculate,* and *The Secret of Anatomy.*

CD Publications published William F. Nolan's *Night Shapes,* a collection of twenty-five horror stories (one original) with an introduction by Peter Straub and an afterword by Robert Bloch. The cover is by Alan M. Clark. A signed (by Nolan and Straub), limited, slipcased edition of 500 is $50 from CD Publications, PO Box 18433, Baltimore, MD 21237.

The Man Who Lost Red by Terry Dowling is a limited (500 copies) two-story collection from Australia's Mirrordanse Books. Although the copyright date for the book is 1994, the book actually came out in January 1995. It contains "Scaring the Train," a very creepy tale. It's a lovely little perfect-bound paperback illustrated by Shaun Tan and with a foreword by artist Nick Stathopoulos. A more extensive 1995 collection of Dowling's horror stories can be found in Aphelion's paperback volume *An Intimate Knowledge of the Night.* The unifying conceit is a series of increasingly bizarre phone calls from a troubled friend who becomes more nutty as they continue. Some of the stories included are "The Daemon Street Ghost-

Trap" and "Scaring the Train." *The Man Who Lost Red* is just about out of print but might still be available from specialty book dealers. *An Intimate Knowledge of the Night* can be bought for $10 through Mark V. Ziesing (for address, see acknowledgment).

Worming the Harpy and Other Bitter Pills is an excellent collection of sixteen tales of fantasy, horror, and surrealism by Rhys Hughes. Published by the U.K.'s Tartarus Press in an attractive hardcover (same design as *Tales from Tartarus*) edition of 226 copies; 26 lettered and signed by the author, and 200 numbered copies. £14.95 payable to Tartarus Press (address under anthologies).

Unbearable! More Bizarre Stories by Paul Jennings has clever, sometimes scary stories. But a second book in the series, *Undone! More Bad Endings*, is terrific, the perfect book for children who like a good scare. It's clever, well-written, with wonderful characterizations of boys and girls (and adults), and doesn't always have happy endings. Highly recommended. Both are Viking Children's Books.

Macabre, Inc., published two perfect-bound paperbacks: Brian A. Hopkins's *Something Haunts Us All* collects seven stories from small press sources and two originals. Introduction by William G. Raley (publisher of the defunct magazine *After Hours*) and illustrated by Donald W. Schank; *The Fall of the House of Escher and Other Illusions* by David Niall Wilson collects two reprints (one of which made Karl Edward Wagner's *Year's Best Horror*) and five originals. One is an excellent Cthulhu mythos story. Introduction by Hugh B. Cave, attractive illustrations by Michael Grilla, and a good cover by H. E. Fassl. Both limited to 500 copies. $5.95 payable to Macabre, Inc., 454 Munden Avenue, Norfolk, VA 23505.

Crib Death and Other Bedtime Stories by Clifford Lawrence Meth (Aardwolf Publishing) is a perfect-bound collection of six stories with great illustrations by Rob Orzechowski, Paul Abrams, Dave Cockrum, Marie Severin, Paty, and Mike Witherby and cover by Michael Linsner. $7.95 payable to Aardwolf Publishing, 45 Park Place South, Suite 270, Morristown, NJ 07960.

Michael Hemmingson's *Nice Little Stories Jam-Packed With Depraved Sex & Violence* is more or less truth in advertising. Some of the six stories (two are reprints) are simply ugly and gross set pieces—for those looking at trends in horror, I notice necrophilia cropping up far too often. "Skull-Fuck" is the perfect companion piece to Edward Lee's "Headers." But a couple of the pieces actually work as stories. It's an attractive little perfect-bound book with illustrations by Jim Bob Cook and Paul Schiola. More varied and subtle is Sue Storm's collection of SF, fantasy, and horror called *Star Bones Weep the Blood of Angels*. Introduction by Edward Lee and illustrated by Karen Harris. Both have teeny tiny type. $5.00 plus $1.50 postage payable to Jasmine Sailing, Cyber-Psycho's A.O.D. PO Box 581, Denver, CO 80201.

Basil Copper's *The Recollections of Solar Pons* (Fedogan & Bremer) collects four novellas featuring the Sherlockian detective created by August Derleth. Three are original and the fourth is a restored version of the original, modified publication. Illustrated by Stefanie K. Hawks. A 100-copy limited edition is available for $75 and a trade edition for $25. F&B also published Hugh B. Caves's collection of seventeen horror stories from the "weird menace" pulps, *Death Stalks the Night*. The cover is by Alan M. Clark and there's a foreword by Cave and an introduction by Karl Edward Wagner. The trade edition is $25 and a limited is $90. Both from Fedogan & Bremer, 603 Washington Avenue SE #77, Minneapolis, MN 55414-2950.

Here There Be Witches by Jane Yolen (Harcourt Brace) with lovely, expressive illustrations by David Wilgus is a charming collection of short stories and poems about witches. Meant for children, the book is probably too tame for most adult horror readers. It's a good companion volume to *Here There Be Dragons* and *Here There Be Unicorns*.

Wordcraft of Oregon published *The Eleventh Jaguarundi*, collecting fourteen of Jessica Amanda Salmonson's surreal/fantastic pieces. Cover and illustrations by Thomas Wiloch;

there's also an introduction on surrealism by the author. Signed limited edition of 250 copies in trade paperback. $8.95. Also from the same publisher under the "Jazz Police" imprint, Thomas Wiloch's *Mr. Templeton's Toyshop*, a collection of forty-five "prose poems" with illustrations by the author for $9.95. Payable to Wordcraft of Oregon, PO Box 3235, La Grande, OR 97850.

Bambada Press (publisher of the Australian horror magazine, *Bloodsongs*) has begun to publish books. The first is a collection of five reprints and two original stories called *Skin Tight* by Bryce Stevens. The book looks good with illustrations by Kurt Stone. Introduction by Christopher Sequeira. Limited to 300 signed copies. $6.95 payable to Bambada Press, PO Box 7530, St. Kilda Road, Melbourne Vic 3004 Australia.

Pentacle by Tom Piccirilli (Pirate Writings Publishing) collects the four necromancer and "self" stories that *Terminal Fright* published during 1995 and adds one original to the volume. These are strong, well-plotted stories. Jack Cady wrote the introduction and Keith Minnion and David Lee Ingersoll did the interior illustrations. Highly recommended. $5.99 payable to Pirate Writings, 543 Whitman Avenue, Islip, NY 11715.

The talented SF/fantasy/horror writer Cherry Wilder's short fiction has been collected in *Dealers in Light and Darkness* by Edgewood Press. Her stories have appeared everywhere from the Australian anthologies *Distant Worlds* and *Alien Worlds*, *Twenty Houses of the Zodiac*, to the magazines *Strange Attractors*, *Interzone*, *Omni*, *Strange Plasma*, and *Asimov's Science Fiction*. With a neat cover by Nick Stathopoulos. $9 payable to Edgewood Press, PO Box 380264, Cambridge, MA 02238.

A *Creepy Company* by Joan Aiken (Dell Yearling) is a YA collection of ten ghost stories, eight of the ten reprinted from the U.K. edition of 1993, with two later stories.

Cemetery Dance Press brought out Dean Koontz's collection, *Strange Highways*, in a signed limited (750) edition in slipcase. Dust jacket art by Phil Parks plus fifteen interior illustrations. $150. The collection features the eponymously titled short novel, a second novel called *Chase*, revised, and twelve short stories and novellas, plus ten pages of new "story notes." Trade edition published by Warner Books.

Ghost Story Press published Dermot Chesson Spence's *Little Red Shoes, and Other Tales of the Odd and Unseen*, originally published in 1937. The book contains sixteen stories and two poems with a reminiscence of Dermot Spence by his son, Keith Spence. Full-color dust jacket artwork by Steven Stapleton. GSP also published H. D. Everett's *The Death Mask, and Other Ghosts*. This celebrates the 75th anniversary of this supernatural collection. Introduction by Richard Dalby and full-color dust jacket artwork by Steven Stapleton. Both books are limited to 400 copies and cost £24. £5 airmail postage to the United States, U.S. payment acceptable by prior arrangement. Payment to Ghost Story Press, BM Wound, London WC1N 3XX, England. Another, *Master of Fallen Years: The Complete Supernatural Stories of Vincent O'Sullivan*, edited by and with an introduction by Jessica Amanda Salmonson, collects fourteen of his largely uncollected works of prose and poetry. O'Sullivan was a poet, essayist, novelist, short story writer, and close friend of Oscar Wilde and Aubrey Beardsley. This is a limited edition of 300 hardcover copies. £24 plus £6.50 airmail postage.

Ash-Tree Press brought out *They Return at Evening* by H. R. Wakefield, a landmark collection of supernatural stories republished for the first time since 1928. It's the first volume in what will be a uniform series assembling all of Wakefield's known supernatural fiction. Case-bound in dust jacket, with an illustration by Paul Lowe and an introduction by Barbara Roden. Numbered limited edition of 300 copies. $31 plus $8 (air), $4.25 (sea); *The Five Jars*, a fantasy novel by M. R. James reprinted from 1922, has a new introduction by Rosemary Pardoe. *The Alabaster Hand and Other Ghost Stories* by A. N. L. Munby is a reprint of a ghost story collection from 1949. It has a foreword by Barbara and Christopher Roden and an introduction by Michael Cox. The cover of this hardcover is by Rachel Crittenden. Both are $27 plus $8.50 (air), $4.40 (sea); *Intruders: New Weird Tales* by A. M. Burrage is a hardcover with cover by Douglas Walters collecting twenty-six previously uncollected ghost stories, most unreprinted since their original publication. Edited and with an introduction by Jack Adrian. $35 plus $8.50 (air), $4.40 (sea); also *Nine Ghosts* by R. H. Malden. This collection, by a friend of M. R. James, is Malden's only collection of supernatural fiction. The stories were a tribute to James's memory. Introduction by David G. Rowlands and new cover illustration by Rachel A. Crittenden. $29 plus $8 airmail, $4.50 seamail, payable to Ash-Tree Press, Ashcroft, 2 Abbottsford Drive, Penyffordd, Chester CH4 OJG, United Kingdom.

A. F. Kidd published the booklet *Wraiths & Ringers*, which collects ten supernatural stories by this author. $5 payable to A. F. Kidd, 113 Clyfford Road, Ruislip Gardens, Middlesex HA4 6PX, England.

Weird Family Tales II by Ken Wisman has been combined with volume I in a nice trade paperback edition. Each volume is introduced by Peter Crowther. There is reportedly a signed and limited edition. Dark Regions Press published it at $6.95; also from Dark Regions Press's The Selected Works Series comes *Sensuous Debris: Selected Poems 1970–1995* by SF/fantasy poet Bruce Boston. This is an important collection for anyone interested in genre poetry. It includes poems from various magazines and anthologies, including those reprinted in *The Year's Best Fantasy and Horror* and *The Year's Best Horror*. Cover and interior illustrations by Thomas Wiloch and an introduction by t. Winter-Damon. Two editions, both signed and limited: $6.95 plus $1.05 postage for the trade paperback and $40 for the hardcover (ppd); and *Eonian Variations, the Collected Poetry of Marge Simon* was brought out in an edition of 125 signed by the poet and artist John Borkowski. The poetry, some of it nominated for the Rhysling Award, is reprinted from such magazines as *Deathrealm, Amazing, Thin Ice, Eldritch Tales,* and *Tales of the Unanticipated*. $4.95. All payable to Dark Region Press, Box 6301, Concord, CA 94524.

Ganglion & Other Stories by Wayne Wightman from Tachyon Publications collects ten stories (SF, often with dark overtones) reprinted from *The Magazine of Fantasy & Science Fiction, Asimov's Science Fiction,* and *Thirteenth Moon*. Introduction by Elinor Mavor, former editor of *Amazing Stories*. A signed and limited hardcover edition of 674 copies is priced at $23 (postage included) and a special deluxe, leather-bound edition, signed and lettered, A–Z for $37 (postage included), payable to Tachyon Publications, 1459 18th Street #139, San Francisco, CA 94107.

Necropolitan Press published Jeffrey Thomas's *The Bones of the Old Ones and Other Lovecraftian Tales*. Five original stories and two poems make up this nice little volume, illustrated by Allen Koszowski, Doug Ferrin, and Thomas himself. $4.00 payable to Jeffrey Thomas, 63 South Street, Westborough, MA 01581.

Fragrant Sorrows collects four stories by Thomas S. Roche in a handsome chapbook with an edition of 100. $3 payable to Thomas S. Roche, PO Box 210429, San Francisco, CA 94121. A signed statement of age is required.

Necronomicon Press published *Tales of the Lovecraftian Collectors* by Kenneth W. Faig Jr., a collection of four stories about Lovecraft collectors, supposedly from the diary of a (fictional) collector. Cover by Jason C. Eckhardt. $5.95; also Clark Ashton Smith's *Tales of Zothique*, edited by Will Murray and Steve Behrends. This trade paperback collects all of the Zothique cycle, including surviving fragments and a play. $11.95 from Necronomican Press, PO Box 1304, West Warwick, RI 02893.

Rhoda Broughton's Ghost Stories and Other Tales of Mystery and Suspense was published by Paul Watkins. This is a new, complete edition of Broughton's short stories, including seven previously uncollected tales, all of which have been totally neglected (according to Richard Dalby) for more than a century since their original appearances, plus five better-known pieces collected in 1873, 1879, and 1947. £7.95 payable to Paul Watkins, 18 Adelaide Street, Stamford, Lincolnshire PE9 2EN England.

And a few mainstream collections that might be of interest to horror readers: *Fresh Girls and Other Stories* by Evelyn Lau (Hyperion) are short stories from the seamy side of life—

the world of loveless sex populated by dominatrixes and prostitutes. Told from the point of view of the women, the stories chronicle their hopes, aspirations, and illusions. Written by a twenty-four-year-old Chinese-Canadian who lived the life, and at seventeen wrote a memoir of her years on the street in *Runaway*. Lau has also written two poetry collections, one of which was nominated for a Canadian literary prize; Ben Marcus's *The Age of Wire and String* (Alfred A. Knopf) is utterly different, with quirky and clever vignettes, surreal juxtapositions, and inventive definitions (like playing Fictionary); *While the Messiah Tarries* by Melvin Jules Bukiet (Harcourt Brace) concerns itself with Jewish themes but the stories are varied and inviting to readers of all faiths. A bit of dark fantasy and some darker realistic material: *The Acid House* by Irvine Welsh (Norton) is an interesting Scottish collection, mostly mainstream with some fantastic and horrific material: *Despair: and Other Stories of Ottawa* by André Alexis (Coach House) collects strange, surreal stories by a Canadian of Trinidadan birth. Several of the stories are original to the volume, the rest were published in small literary presses; *The Sadness of Sex* by Barry Yougrau (Delta Fiction) is a collection of short-shorts that are more surreal than horrific.

Other collections:
Robert Bloch: Appreciations of the Master (Tor) collects thirty tributes to and twenty stories by Bloch, plus an excerpt from his screenplay for *Earthman's Burden*. Contributors include Peter Straub, Gahan Wilson, Harlan Ellison, and Andre Norton; *Fairy Tales of Hans Christian Andersen*, illustrated by Isabelle Brent (Viking), with a new translation by Neil Philip. Brent's vivid illustrations re-create the effects of illuminated manuscripts; *The Fairy Tales of Herman Hesse*, translated and with an introduction by Jack Zipes (Bantam), with woodcut illustrations by David Frampton. Zipes maintains that although Hesse's fairy tales often followed traditional form, he also experimented "with science fiction, the grotesque and macabre, romantic realism, and dreams, thereby generating his own unique form and style"; *Wormwood* by Poppy Z. Brite (Dell) is the first paperback edition of the collection originally called *Swamp Foetus*; *The Scarlet Plague and Other Stories by Jack London* (Alan Sutton) collects six stories, two mainstream, led by the title novel; *Jonathan Kellerman's ABC of Weird Creatures* by Jonathan Kellerman (A.S.A.P.) is a children's picture book, a collection of poems illustrated by the author. A signed limited hardcover (150 copies) is available for $50, and a trade paperback edition is available for $25 payable to A.S.A.P. Publishing, 23852, Via Navarra, Mission Vieja, CA 92691. *Behind the Mask: The Unknown Thrillers of Louisa May Alcott*, edited by Madeleine Stern (William Morrow), is a reissue of a collection originally published in 1975. Described as "gruesome, passionate . . . blood and thunder tales"; *Disney's Enter If You Dare!: Scary Tales from the Haunted Mansion* by Nicholas Stephens is a YA collection of six horror stories; *Scary Stories for Stormy Nights* by R. C. Welch (Lowell House juvenile) collects ten YA horror stories; *The Dream Cycle of H. P. Lovecraft: Dreams of Terror and Death* (Del Rey) reprints twenty-five horror stories about dreams. Introduction by Neil Gaiman; *The Eye above the Mantel and Other Stories* by Frank Belknap Long, edited by Perry M. Grayson (Tsathoggua Press, 6442 Pat Avenue, West Hills, CA 91307), collects four stories. 26-page trade paperback $5; *The Language of Fear* by Del James (Dell Abyss); *Winter of the Soul* by Gary Bowen (Obelesk Books); Kim Elizabeth is the author of *Netherworld* (Ghost Girl Graphix), a collection of poetry and prose; Delacorte Press's children's division published Priscilla Galloway's *Truly Grim Tales*, a series of retold fairy tales; *Rats in the Attic and Other Stories to Make Your Skin Crawl* by G. E. Stanley (Avon Flare) is a YA collection of twenty horror stories; the trade paperback edition of Thomas Ligotti's *The Agonizing Resurrection of Victor Frankenstein and Other Gothic Tales* (Silver Salamander Press); *The Siege of 318: Thirteen Mystical Stories* by Davis Grubb (Back Fork); and *Beer Fear* by Jeff Gilbert, the author of last year's *Two Werewolves, a Six-Pack, and Elvis*. This trade paperback contains nineteen new stories, most seemingly written for adolescent boys (Hairball Press).

Nonfiction Magazines:

Mystery Scene, edited by Joe W. Gorman, occasionally has something of interest to the horror reader. #46 had a piece about the 35th anniversary of Robert Bloch's classic novel, *Psycho*, and Jack Ketchum writing about his new novel, *Joyride*. #47 had an article on John Farris and an interview with Ramsey Campbell, and #48 had an interview with Richard Laymon.

Scarlet Street, edited by Richard Valley, on the other hand, veered sharply into horror with its seventeenth issue covering the film version of Robert Bloch's short story, "The Skull of the Marquis de Sade," an excellent piece on the underrated (according to George Hatch) Sal Mineo movie, *Who Killed Teddy Bear?*, and the musical collaborations between Ray Harryhausen and Bernard Herrman on *The Seventh Voyage of Sinbad*, *Mysterious Island*, *Jason and the Argonauts*, and other genre movies. Also, a piece on *Demon Knight*. #20 had some good material on *The Innocents* and interviews with Deborah Kerr and Martin Stephens about their roles. Also, a piece on *The Haunting* and another on Shirley Jackson, her life and work.

Fangoria, edited by Anthony Timpone, is the old reliable gorezine that covers all the studio genre films with lots of colorful gore and splat. There are a few excellent reviewers and the always entertaining David J. Schow, who unfortunately is taking his "Raving and Drooling" column on hiatus.

Psychotronic Video®, edited by Michael J. Weldon, is a great source for information on exploitation movies—sex, violence, horror, SF, you name it. It features interviews with the stars and character actors of yesteryear; also, an extensive obituaries column. The magazine is always fun to read. A six-issue subscription to this quarterly is $22 ($45 airmail) payable to *Psychotronic*®, 3309 Route 97, Narrowsburg, NY 12764-6803.

Video Watchdog, edited by Tim Lucas, with its detailed reviews of new releases is a *must* for genre movie watchers. The magazine describes acutely the variations between different versions of the same movie. Although most of the videos are not ones I'm familiar with, the comparison of two laserdisc versions of *The Silence of the Lambs* amply demonstrates Lucas's expertise and eagle eye.

Filmfax: The Magazine of Unusual Film & Television, edited by Michael Stein and Ted Okuda, is an excellent bimonthly magazine specializing in classic low budget horror and SF films. The May/June issue is #50. Best for its entertaining and informative interviews with film- and TV-makers, such as Robert Wise, Samuel Fuller, George Baxt, the interviewers actually get their subjects going. (Better, for example, than *Scarlet Street*'s, which sometimes feel canned.) Issue #52 contains a moving profile of the late Anthony Perkins. Subscriptions are $30 (six) payable to *Filmfax* subscriptions, PO Box 1900, Evanston, IL 60204.

Outré is a new quarterly magazine from the same people who create *Filmfax*, only this magazine focuses less on genre films and more on pop culture. Early issues include profiles of Jayne Mansfield, Bettie Page, and Edd "Kookie" Byrnes. A four-issue subscription is $20, payable to *Filmfax* at the address above.

Cinefantastique, edited by Frederick S. Clarke, covers the mainstream Hollywood horror and SF films but covers them well, for example, the feud between designer/artist H. R. Giger and MGM on the final version of Sil, the alien in *Species*. Apparently Giger fought very hard (but unsuccessfully) to prevent *Species* from regurgitating elements of the *Alien* series.

SFX: The Science Fiction Magazine, edited by Matt Bielby, is a big bright oversize glossy, chock full of book, movie, comic, toy, and video reviews. A lot of media material. Often slops over into horror. It's pretty pricey for U.S. subscribers—14 issues for £92 (about $130). Or you might try a back issue for £5.50. Payable to *SFX* Subscriptions, Future Publishing, Somerton, Somerset TA11 6TB, United Kingdom.

Tangent, edited by David Truesdale, is a critical magazine specializing in short science fiction, fantasy, and horror. It uses several different reviewers and covers the professional magazines, some small press magazines, and anthologies. For the most part, the reviews are thoughtful and useful, making the magazine an invaluable addition to the field for its coverage of short fiction But then there are the Paul Riddell rants. A good rant can focus attention on the particular bugaboo of the ranter but is difficult to take seriously when the facts are wrong. Riddell attacks Charles N. Brown, publisher and editor of *Locus*, in one such rant and buried under the anger, hyperbole, and insults is some valid criticism. In the next issue Riddell was far more restrained in a thoughtful critique of the horror field. One-year subscription (four issues) is $20 payable to David A. Truesdale, 5779 Norfleet, Raytown, MO 64133.

Necrofile, the best critical horror magazine being published, deservedly won the 1994 British Fantasy Award for Best Small Press Publication. Edited by Stefan Dziemianowicz, S. T. Joshi, and Michael A. Morrison. Reviews, essays, forthcoming book listings, etc. One-year subscription (four issues) $12.00. $15.00 Canada, overseas $17.50 all payable through a U.S. bank to Necronomicon Press. Necronomicon Press also regularly publishes *Lovecraft Studies*, edited by S. T. Joshi, originally founded in 1979 to offer a forum for serious study of Lovecraft's work and *Studies in Weird Fiction*, also edited by Joshi, a journal designed to "promote the criticism of fantasy, horror, and supernatural fiction subsequent to Poe." Both magazines have essays, reviews, and brief notes of import to the genre. $5 each. See address under "Collections."

Scavenger's Newsletter, published by Janet Fox, is a long-running monthly small press market newsletter. It's most useful for those interested in getting into the small press. It features interviews with editors and biannual round-ups of SF, fantasy, horror, and mystery markets. Subscriptions are $19.50 (first class) annually, $9.75 for six months payable to Janet Fox, 519 Ellinwood, Osage City, KS 66523-1329.

Gila Queen's Guide to Markets, published by Kathryn Ptacek, is overall the most valuable regular marketing newsletter for writers. Ptacek often covers specialized markets as well as the more usual, lists contests, runs articles on writing, and has a running column with news of the publishing industry. Was monthly but has drifted a bit. Still excellent. A 12-issue subscription costs $30 (U.S.), $34 (Canada), and $48 (overseas). Cash, check, or money order (U.S. funds) only payable to Kathryn Ptacek, GQHQ, PO Box 97, Newton, NJ 07860-0097.

Heliocentric Network Newsletter, edited by Lisa Jean Bothell, is a useful bimonthly that provides up-to-date information on horror, science fiction, and fantasy. Not a market report, it offers "Information/tips/ideas/announcements/about writers, editors, publishers, poets, artists, the craft and industry, distributors, marketing, polls, interviews, etc., for all writers/artists/editors/publishers of all genres, and of amateur, semipro, and pro ranks." $4 a copy or $7 a year (6 issues) payable to Three-Stones Publications, Ltd., PO Box 68817, Seattle, WA 98168-0817.

The New York Review of Science Fiction, edited by David G. Hartwell et. al., continues to provide intelligent and often provocative criticism of the science fiction and fantasy fields (with the occasional foray into horror). Published monthly. $3.50 per copy. Annual subscription is $31 (U.S.), $36 (Canada), $39 first class, overseas, $44 (via air printed matter) payable to Dragon Press, PO Box 78, Pleasantville, NY 10570.

Tabula Rasa, edited by David Carroll, has been running an excellent history and overview of the horror field for the past two years. With #7, the magazine's first "volume" comes to an end. The magazine is now on hiatus but will return—the next eight issues will take the reader up to Lovecraft. $5 (includes airmail postage) an issue payable to David Carroll, 13/87 Flora Street, Sutherland, NSW 2232, Australia. Carroll says he'd rather "swap" 'zines than take U.S. checks.

Gauntlet: Exploring the Limits of Free Expression, edited by Barry Hoffman, is an invaluable biannual providing a forum for free speech issues. Unfortunately, the occasionally smug and self-satisfied editorial tone can be off-putting. The editorial pat on the back for running a mastectomy-scarred nude on the cover is infuriating in its inaccuracy and naiveté. Calling *Playboy* and *Penthouse* hypocrites for not displaying breasts on their covers shows a lack of knowledge about advertising and distribution realities—it's economic necessity if they want to get into grocery stores. Why not mention the hypocrisy of the movie industry for showing only female frontal nudes for years (although this taboo has recently been broken in *Bad Lieutenant* and *The Crying Game*) and the implication that because the *New York Times* ran their groundbreaking photo in the Sunday Magazine section rather than in the daily paper it "wasn't a risk at all" is, shall we say, "misguided." The Sunday Magazine probably gets a more varied readership (certainly more people outside NYC buy that section) and thereby would be *more* at risk from other parts of the country less liberal than NY. Excellent journalistic piece on the longtime feud between Harlan Ellison, Gary Groth, and Charles Platt. Also an issue on *Sexual Harassment* that questions whether this isn't the new McCarthyism?

The Velvet Vampyre: The Journal of the Vampyre Society is a quarterly edited by Tina Rath, and although already into its 25th issue, this is the first year I've seen the magazine. It's an attractive little magazine with reviews and articles on vampiric subjects and one piece of fiction per issue. In 1995 there were stories by William Meikle and Brian Stableford, and an interesting pictorial on hearses. For information on membership, send a SAE to the Membership Secretary, PO Box 68, Keighley, West Yorkshire, BD22 6RU, England.

Magazines:

Let the buyer beware! Most small press magazines are labors of love run by one or two people. They often do not keep to their stated publication schedules. . . . If in doubt you might consider buying a single copy. Foreign subscriptions are generally somewhat higher than the listed price, so inquire first. An excellent way around this is dealing with Chris Reed's The New Science Fiction Alliance (NSFA), as many of the titles offered (eg. *Back Brain Recluse, Auguries, Dreams from the Strangers' Café, Peeping Tom, Psychotrope, The Third Alternative*, and others) are cheaper than when ordering (from the United States) directly through the publishers. Reed's *Supplementary Catalog* is free; just send a large SAE and $1 or $2 international reply coupons to Chris Reed, PO Box 625, Sheffield, S13 GY, UK.

There were so many magazines publishing at least some horror during 1995 that there isn't enough room to cover them all. I'm going to stick to those I considered the best.

Deathrealm, edited by Mark Stephen Rainey, is one of the best regularly published horror magazines, with consistently readable and entertaining fiction, articles, interviews, and reviews and a highly accomplished stable of artists. It deserves reader support. #23 has the last column by Karl Edward Wagner and what is possibly the last Manly Wade Wellman story. This past year has seen a steady improvement in the mix of fiction. Excellent art by Chad Savage, H. E. Fassl, Susan Kenney, Keith Minnion, Augie Weidemann, Mark Rainey, Wayne Miller, Alan M. Clark, Julia Morgan Scott, and Charles Stevens Hill. A four-issue (one-year) subscription is $15.95 payable to *Deathrealm*, 2210 Wilcox Drive, Greensboro, NC 27405.

Grue Magazine, edited by Peggy Nadramia, is another of the best small press horror magazines. It's perfect bound with a glossy cover and attractive, appropriate interior illustrations by H. E. Fassl, Peter H. Gilmore, Phil Reynolds, Roger Gerberding, Augie Weidemann, Chris Pelletiere, Timothy Patrick Butler, and Christine and Harry O. Morris. It also features overall excellent art direction by Peter H. Gilmore and good fiction. A three-issue subscription (the magazine has not kept to its three-issue-a-year schedule for some time—there was only one issue in 1995) is $13 payable to Hell's Kitchen Productions, Inc., PO Box 370, Times Square Station, New York, NY 10106-0370.

Carnage Hall, edited by David Griffin, published one issue during 1995 and as usual it was a good one with one excellent short story and some very fine poetry and vignettes. Griffin opens the issue with an essay about style and ends with a piece about Edward Gorey. It's an elegant little magazine that I, for one, would love to see more often. $5 for this issue (or to reserve issue #7) payable to David Griffin, PO Box 7, Esopus, NY 12429.

Worlds of Fantasy and Horror, edited by Darrell Schweitzer, published one issue during 1995. The confrontational essay by S. T. Joshi certainly raised a few hackles. This issue showcased Charles de Lint and there was fine fiction by de Lint and other writers, good cover art by Jason Van Hollander, and good interior illustrations by Rodger Gerberding, Allen Koszowski, and Denis Tiani. Single copies $4.95, a one-year (four issues, although only one issue was published during 1995) subscription is $16 payable to Terminus Publishing Co. Inc., 123 Crooked Lane, King of Prussia, PA 19406-2570. $22 elsewhere (U.S. funds).

Bloodsongs, edited by Chris A. Masters and Steve Propisch out of Melbourne, Australia, is a maddingly uneven mix of the professional and the amateur. The interviews and nonfiction articles are generally professional and engaging, yet the editors seems unable to resist challenging—in the most offensive way—*any* criticism in their editorials. And I can't get all that worked up about the fiction—it's mostly the same old ultra violence with minimal depth. Contains probably one of the last interviews with Karl Edward Wagner. It has nice looking covers, sometimes overdesigned interiors; the magazine desperately needs better copyediting and proofreading. $28 for four issues airmail, payable in cash or bank draft from outside of Australia. Bambada Press, PO Box 7530, St. Kilda Road, Melbourne, Vic 3004 Australia.

Aurealis: The Australian Magazine of Fantasy and Science Fiction, edited by Dirk Strasser and Stephen Higgins. Nineteen ninety-five had only a bit of horror fiction but issue #14 did have a brief overview of the past twenty years of Australian horror in magazines, books, and movies. With the 16th issue the magazine has officially decided to accept supernatural horror. Excellent interior art by Shaun Tan and Ian Gunn. A four-issue subscription is $43 (Australian) airmail and all checks and money orders must be paid in Australian dollars. Credit cards accepted. Payable to Chimaera Publications, PO Box 2164, Mount Waverly Victoria 3149 Australia.

Skintomb, edited by Rod Williams, is an erratically published horror magazine from Australia. Only one issue was published in 1995. In it Williams gives an illuminating "tour" of some exceptional twentieth-century artists who work in horror territory: H. R. Giger, J. K. Potter, Tom Vigil, Clive Barker, Virgil Finley, Dave Carson, Allen Koszowski, Dave Seagrove, and Margret Brundage. Reviews of novels, graphic novels, other magazines, an important update on censorship, and a bit of fiction. More noteworthy for its nonfiction. No subscriptions but readers can buy single issues for $4.00 (U.S. cash or overseas check or money order or 'zine swap) plus one international reply coupon for each dollar spent. Payable to Rod Williams, PO Box 166, Roma Street, Brisbane Q 4003 Australia.

Dreams and Nightmares, edited by David C. Kopaska-Merkel, is a long-running poetry magazine that publishes SF, fantasy, and horror. The 45th issue has excellent art. A six-issue subscription is $10. 1300 Kicker Road, Tuscaloosa, AL 35404.

Tomorrow: Speculative Fiction, edited by Algis Budrys, has, since its inception, published a certain amount of horror. In 1995 Budrys published some top-notch horror material, particularly Robert Reed's "Mrs. Greasy." The excellent interior illustrations are not shown to advantage with the pulp paper used for the magazine. A bimonthly, it costs $20 a year (six issues) payable to *Tomorrow Speculative Fiction*, The Unifont Company, Inc., Box 6038, Evanston, IL 60204.

The Magazine of Fantasy & Science Fiction, edited by Kristine Kathryn Rusch, is not generally known for horror but when it does publish it, it's usually very good. This is a magazine horror readers should keep an eye out for. *Ellery Queen's Mystery Magazine*, edited by Janet Hutchings, specializes in mystery but often has dark stories of interest to the horror reader; *Alfred Hitchcock Mystery Magazine*, edited by Cathleen Jordan, while not generally as dark as its sister magazine, *Queen*, had a nice selection of dark fiction in 1995.

Peeping Tom, edited by Stuart Hughes, published four good issues with very good art by Alan Casey and Andrew Haigh. Peter Tennant addressed the continuing problems of censorship in the U.K. in a guest editorial. A four-issue subscription is £7.50. Checks payable to *Peeping Tom*, c/o David Bell (publisher), Yew Tree House, 15 Nottingham Road, Ashby-de-la-Zouch, Leicstershire, LE65 1DJ, UK. Recommended.

Realms of Fantasy, edited by Shawna McCarthy, has some pretty standard fantasy art on its slick covers and rarely publishes dark fantasy or horror. Regular features include Terri Windling's erudite column on the history of fairy tales and portfolios of fantasy/dark fantasy artists. These have included work by J. K. Potter and Thomas Canty. *Realms of Fantasy*, PO Box 736, Mount Morris, IL 61054-8130. One year (six issues), $14.95.

Beyond (Fantasy & Science Fiction), edited by David Riley, is a new British magazine that's worth a look. The first issue had original stories by Ramsey Campbell, Karl Edward Wagner, Stephen Law, Rick Kennett, and Alex Stewart. Also interviews, essays, and reviews. Two issues out in 1995. The second had Stephen Gallagher giving advice on writing screenplays and one of the last Roger Zelazny interviews. $45 for 12 issues payable to *Beyond*, Parallel Universe Publications, 130 Union Road, Oswaldtwistle, Lancashire, BB5 3DR, U.K.

Grotesque, edited by David Logan, is a consistently literate horror magazine out of Northern Ireland. It just changed over to triquarterly from quarterly with its 8th issue. I'm not sure you can actually buy a copy from the States although you might be able to order it through Cold Tonnage Books, *Grotesque*, 39 Brook Avenue (off Barn Road), Carrickfergus, CO Antrim, N. Ireland BT38 7TE.

Not One of Us, edited by John Benson, published two good issues in 1995 with excellent art by John Borkowski, Alan Casey, and Augie Wiedemann. Single copies $4.50 (including p&h), a three-issue subscription is $10.50, and a one-shot magazine, *Good News Bad News*, with three stories and two poems, was published in October and had some good fiction and effective art by Casey, Wiedemann, and Richard Dahlstrom. $3.50 (including p&h) payable to John Benson, 12 Curtis Road, Natick, MA 01760.

Terminal Fright: The Journal of Traditional Haunts and Horrors, edited by Ken Abner, has kept to its quarterly schedule for two years and publishes a variety of horror. Particularly noteworthy is Tom Piccirilli's "Self" series. Single issue is $6, a one-year subscription (four issues) is $22.00 payable to Terminal Fright Publications, PO Box 100, Black River, NY 13612-0100. Recommended.

Weirdbook 29, edited by W. Paul Ganley, is the first issue in two years of this long-running magazine and the wait's been worth it. The new issue is an excellent venue for more traditional types of horror and ghost stories. Ganley hasn't been idle during this time but has been continuously publishing books. (More on them in the small press section.) $7.35 for issue #29 (includes p&h) in the United States and Canada, $7.60 elsewhere. Seven issues for $25 ($30 outside the U.S.) payable to W. Paul Ganley: Publisher, P.O. Box 149, Buffalo, NY 14226-0149.

Rictus, edited by Mary E. Spock, was unfamiliar to me until I saw issues #5 and #6 in 1995. There's enough good fiction to make it worth a look. The interior art, which is quite good, shows what can be done on the cheap by someone with a good eye and a computer. $4.25 per issue payable to *Rictus*, 2712 Wisconsin Avenue, NW, #408, Washington, DC 20007.

Funeral Party, edited by David Fox, Marlene Leach, Michael Rorro, and Shade Rupe, is a very attractive one-shot (at least for now), with excellent art direction and design, good articles (one about the Grand-Guignol of Paris), a piece on the (H. R.) Gigerbar in Switzerland (there's one in Tokyo, too), and interviews with low-budget horror producers and screenwriters, artists, and performance artists. The six pieces of fiction are the least impressive aspect of the magazine. $15 payable to Shade Rupe, 511 6th Avenue, #325, New York, NY 10011.

Ghosts & Scholars, edited by Rosemary Pardoe, is dedicated to M. R. Jamesian tales and matters. The aficionado can always count on excellent fiction and critical articles and reviews. Excellent art by Douglas Walters. Highly recommended for Jamesian enthusiasts. Subscriptions cost $20 seamail, $30 airmail, which entitles the subscriber to receive everything at a 20 percent discount on the full price. Please say whether you want "G&S only" or "all Haunted Library publications," e.g., of earlier Haunted Library items: *The Greater Arcana*—three stories in the M. R. James tradition by Ron Weighell, *Supernatural Pursuits*, three parodies by William Read, and *The Reluctant Ghost-Hunter*, three ghost stories by Rick Kennett. U.S. payment for individual copies ($6) payable to Richard Fawcett, 61 Teecomwas Drive, Uncasville, CT 06382. Subscription (cash only) to Rosemary Pardoe, Flat One, 36 Hamilton Street, Hoole, Chester CH2 3JQ, UK.

All Hallows, edited by Barbara and Christopher Roden, is *The Journal of the Ghost Story Society*. This excellent journal is published thrice-yearly in February, June, and October. Issue #8 celebrates macabre illustrator Edward Gorey on his seventieth birthday and has some fine illustrations. It generally publishes interesting fiction.

The Ghost Story Society was formed in 1989 to provide admirers of the classic ghost story with an outlet for their interest. There are now over 200 members worldwide. The society publishes regular publications and has occasional meetings, and has held two ghost story writing competitions. Membership costs $30 (airmail) and $24 (seamail) with checks made payable to The Ghost Story Society. Canadian membership is several dollars more. See address under "Collections." In addition to *All Hallows*, the society has been publishing other volumes. And for fans of August Derleth, writer and founder of Arkham House, he has his own society. Formed in 1978, the August Derleth Society, based in the writer's home state of Wisconsin, publishes a quarterly newsletter. For information, write to ADS, Box 481, Sauk City, WI 53583.

Lore, edited by Rod Heather, is a quarterly that published three issues in 1995. The first two issues were disappointing (despite a story by Harlan Ellison in the first) but with #3 the magazine seemed to blossom, with an excellent cover and interior art by Richard Corben, Sean O'Leary, Roddy Williams, and Jeffrey Thomas, and fiction generally head and shoulders above that in the first two issues. $4 an issue payable to Rod Heather, PO Box 672, Middletown, NJ 07748.

Crypt of Cthulhu, edited by Robert M. Price, is a must for Lovecraft fans. This quarterly carries articles, fiction, and poetry. $5.95 payable to Necronomicon Press (address under "Collections").

There are a handful of cross-genre magazines that specialize in blurring the boundaries between genre and the mainstream. This is an admirable but risky goal. At the worst you have the formlessness and often ultimate meaninglessness of dreams. The best, of course, can (and should) transcend the paralysis/stasis of stream-of-consciousness writing. Some of the best are below.

Century, edited by Robert K. J. Killheffer, made an auspicious debut with a literate mix of science fiction, fantasy, and horror—highly recommended as an example of the best the convergence of fantastic literature has to offer. Bimonthly. A one-year subscription is $27, but single copies can be purchased for $5.95 and a special three-issue starter subscription is $15 payable to *Century*, PO Box 9270, Madison, WI 53715-0270. Overseas orders $1 more per issue.

The Third Alternative, edited by Andy Cox, is continuing to publish an excellent mix of SF, fantasy, and horror. Includes a concise news column and a lively letter column. Always literate and a pleasure to look at with fine art and covers by Dave Mooring, Dave Checkley, Roddy Williams, and Alan Casey. A four-issue subscription costs $22 or a single issue is $6 payable to *The Third Alternative*, 5 Martin's Lane, Witcham, Ely, Cambs, CB6 2LB, UK. One of the best and a good one to support.

The Urbanite, edited by Mark McLaughlin, came out with two theme issues in 1995:

Strange Relationships and *Strange Fascinations*. The magazine looks attractive and publishes some interesting SF, fantasy, and horror. $5 per issue payable to Urban Legend Press, PO Box 4737, Davenport, IA 52808.

Transversions, the ambitious, little (literally, in size) Canadian cross-genre magazine edited by Dale. L. Sproule and Sally McBride, brought out three issues in 1995. Some good mixed genre fiction, but there was only a bit of horror this year. $18 for four issues, or $4.95 (Canadian or U.S.) a copy payable to Island Specialty Reports, 1019 Colville Road, Victoria, BC, Canada V9A 4PS.

On Spec: The Canadian Magazine of Speculative Writing, edited by a rotating board—members of the Copper Pig Society, a writer's collective—always has fine writing in whatever genre it's showcasing. The art is also consistently excellent. Covers in 1995 were by Adrian Kleinbergen, W. B. Johnston, Lynne Taylor Fahnestalk, and Sylvie Nadeau. Fine art portfolios by Peter Francis and W. B. Johnston. Digest size, perfect bound, and designed for readibility. One-year subscription is $18 (U.S.) payable to *On Spec*, PO Box 4727, Edmonton, Alberta, T6E 5GE, Canada. Highly recommended.

Psychotrope, edited by Mark Beech, published some solid stories with fine interior illustrations by Alan Casey and an Alfred Jarry woodcut on one cover. A four-issue subscription is $20 payable to Psychotrope, Flat 6, 17 Droitwich Road, Barbourne, Worcester WR3 7LG, UK.

Cyber-Psycho's A.O.D., edited by Jasmine Sailing, is a weird and interesting quarterly mix of fiction, interviews, and reviews of music and books. It's invaluable for its small press reviews, but the eensie-teensie type is hard on the eyes. A four-issue subscription is available for $15 payable to Jasmine Sailing, PO Box 581, Denver, CO 80201.

The Silver Web, edited by Ann Kennedy, is an excellent cross-genre magazine that is generally literate and entertaining. Issue #12 had some good horror fiction and poetry and some very fine art by Carlos Batts, Phil Reynolds (a portfolio of this important newcomer), H. E. Fassl, Michael Betancourt, Alan M. Clark, Scott Eagle, Barrett John Erickson, Kenneth W. McCool, Thalia Ragsdale, Eric Turnmire, and Alan Casey. The magazine appears semiannually. A one-year subscription is $10 payable to *The Silver Web*, PO Box 38190, Tallahassee, FL 32315. New subscribers were offered a special edition 11" by 15" Phil Reynolds poster as long as supplies lasted.

Space & Time, edited by Gordon Linzner, is probably the longest-running small press magazine around. Over the past few years it's looked better and better with excellent art and perfect-bound covers. The fiction and poetry is a mix of speculative fiction, fantasy, and horror. A one-year subscription (two issues) is $10, payable to G. Linzner, 138 W. 70th Street (4B), New York, NY 10023–4432.

Eidolon: The Journal of Australian Science Fiction and Fantasy, edited by Jonathan Strahan, Jeremy G. Byrne, and Richard Scriven, is an important purveyor of SF and fantasy. Its fiction is varied and its nonfiction concentrates on Australian SF. Shaun Tan's art direction is uniformly excellent with excellent interior illustrations by Tan, Petri Sinda, and terrific cover and back cover illustrations by Marc McBride. *Eidolon* 17/18 was the fifth-anniversary issue and showcased a variety of Australian SF and a couple of cranky (which is not to say inaccurate) essays by George Turner and Greg Egan. The cover is by Nick Stathopoulos. The spring issue actually appeared in October. One year's subscription (quarterly, though only three issues came out in 1995). A$45 airmail ($30 American) A$35 seamail ($22 American).

Other magazines that published some good horror stories:

Interzone, edited by David Pringle, generally publishes more science fiction than horror, but there was some excellent crossover SF/horror by Brian Stableford and others in the latter half of the year. The cover art and interior illustrations are always good. One year's subscription is $56 payable by check (or by Visa, Mastercard, or Eurocard) to *Interzone*, 217 Preston

Drive, Brighton BN1 6FL, UK. An exceptionally worthy magazine that deserves reader support. *Playboy* fiction, edited by Alice K. Turner; *New Mystery*, edited by Charles Raisch; *Asimov's Science Fiction Magazine*, edited by Gardner Dozois; *Pulp Fiction*, edited by Clancy O'Hara; *Pirate Writings*, edited by Edward J. McFadden; *Premonitions*, edited by Tony Lee; *Eldritch Tales*, edited by Crispin Burnham; *Aberrations*, edited by Michael Andre-Druissi; *Urges*, edited by Ian Hunter, a new Scottish quarterly of "erotic tales of fantasy and horror"; *Footsteps*, also edited by Hunter, specializes in "quiet horror." Each magazine is £2.50 an issue payable to Ian Hunter, Huntiegouke Press, c/o 32 Caneluk Avenue, Carluke, ML8 4LZ Scotland; *Crossroads*, edited by Pat Nielson; *Symphonie's Gift*, edited by Bryan Lindenberger; *Kimota*, edited by Graeme Hurry; *Psychosis: Tales of Madness from the Whetstone Group*, published in Manitoba, Canada; *White Knuckles*, edited by John R. Platt, a promising new quarterly. $4 per issue or a year's subscription $15 payable to John Platt, PO Box 973, New Providence, NJ 07974-0973; *Dead of Night*, edited by Lin Stein, was starting to run better fiction when it went on hiatus. Stein plans to return in the autumn of 1996, 100+ pages, four-color cover, new typeface, etc. Stay tuned; *Tales of the Unanticipated*, edited by Eric M. Heideman; *Into the Darkness: The Magazine of Extreme Horror*, edited by David Barnett, has a lot of grisly, body-invasive stories. *Dark Regions*, edited by Joe Morey. Volume 3 issue #1 is combined with *The Year's Best Fantastic Fiction* volume 1 issue #1, edited by Morey and Mike Olson, which is meant to be a small press version of the *Year's Best*. It includes stories from *Analog* and *Asimov's* and *Worlds of Fantasy and Horror*, hardly small press publications. $14 annually (four issues) payable to Dark Regions Press, PO Box 6301, Concord, CA 94524; *Haunts: Tales of Unexpected Horror and the Supernatural*, edited by Joseph Cherkes, has been publishing for ten years on an irregular schedule. Only one issue was published in 1995. Two issues for $9 payable to Nightshade Publications, PO Box 8068, Dept. SC, Cranston, RI 02920-0068; *Phantasm: A Horror Fiction Magazine*, edited by J. F. Gonzales. Volume 1, #2 is the reincarnation of *Iniquities*, this time all fiction. Only one issue came out in 1995.

Chapbooks:

The Sixth Dog by Jane Rice (Necronomicon Press) is an original, with well-rendered characters and an excellent mise en scene, but the story itself is utterly predictable. Cover and frontispiece art by Jason Eckhardt. $4.95 to Necronomicon Press. And also from Necronomicon Press comes *The Final Diary Entry of Kees Huijgens*, transcribed and edited by Jozef P. Janszoon, translated into English by D. E. LeRoss, an excellent tale of mysterious and sinister architecture that takes off from de Stijl and goes off to woo-woo land. *Twisted Images* by Don D'Ammassa is published by Necronomicon Press with nice-looking cover and frontispiece by Robert H. Knox. $4.95 payable to Necronomicon Press. Address under "Collections." $4.95. Orders up to $20 pay $1.50 p&h (U.S.), $2.50 Canadian or U.S. currency.

The Free Way by Lisa Morton is an ambitious story by a newer writer with a great deal of potential. Introduction by Roberta Lannes. Illustrations by Rick Pickman. The chapbook is a first effort by Fools Press. It has a major typo in the second word of the first sentence. Signed by author and illustrator and limited to 250 copies of which 200 numbered are for sale. $6.95 USA/$8.00 foreign payable to Fool's Press, 11671 Ohio Avenue, West Los Angeles, CA 90025.

Header by Edward Lee from Necro Publications. Having a "header" is the ultimate revenge against those who offend the hillfolk. A truly disgusting perversion. One may not like what Lee writes about but he certainly gets his dialect down. Gleefully repulsive. $5.95 payable to Necro Publications, PO Box 677205, Orlando, FL 32867-7205. Signed and numbered edition of 500 copies in a slick-covered paperback with introduction by Lucy Taylor.

Tooth & Nail: Two Stories by Pamela Briggs are two reprints by a newcomer to watch. It's a bargain at $2 payable to Urban Legend Press, PO Box 4737, Davenport, IA 52808.

The Bars on Satan's Jailhouse by Norman Partridge has the feeling of a traditional American folktale. A young Chinese mail-order bride, the black man who is her escort, and her would-be groom represent three diverse cultures that coexisted (uneasily) in the Old West. Add a dollop of the supernatural and you've got a very entertaining story. The effective illustrations are by Melissa Sherman. $7 plus $1 shipping payable to Roadkill Press, Little Bookshop of Horrors, 10380 Ralston Road, Arvada, CO 80004.

Common Threads by Nina Kiriki Hoffman was brought out by Hypatia Press. It collects her dark fantasy novel *The Thread that Binds the Bones* with fourteen short stories. Introduction by P. C. Hodgell and illustrations by Alan M. Clark. $35 payable to Hypatia Press. See address for ordering (Blue Moon Books) under "Novels."

Edgewood Press brought out a collection of eight fairy tales by Gwyneth Jones called *Seven Tales and a Fable*. Three are previously unpublished. Cover by Thomas Canty. $8 payable to Edgewood Press, PO Box 380264, Cambridge, MA 02238.

Subterranean Press debuted with two attractive bargains: *Spyder*, a reprinted story by Norman Partridge about James Dean and his car; cover art by Timothy Standish. And a creepy little psychological horror tale by Ed Gorman called "Out There in the Darkness." Cover by Martin McKenna. Both are limited to 500 signed and numbered copies and cost $8 postpaid.

The British Fantasy Society published a collaborative ghost story by Simon Clark and Stephen Laws called "Annabelle Says." Limited to 500 signed copies, of which 400 were sent to BFS members as part of their membership package. $8 ppd airmail. The two-color cover is by David J. Howe. 2 Harwood Street, Stockport, SK4 1JJ, UK. Annual membership is $35.

P. D. Cacek's short story "Ancient One" is a little chiller with a nice buildup about several generations of a family with a strange guardian. $5 for a signed, limited edition of 100 from Paper Moon Books, 360 West First, Eugene, OR 97401.

Small Press:
Arkham House, which has generally been moving away from horror and more into SF in the past few years, is still occasionally an important source for horror material. This year, for example, Arkham House published *Miscellaneous Writings by H. P. Lovecraft*, edited by S. T. Joshi. Included are several early fiction pieces and a history of the Necronomicon. The bulk of material consists of essays, travelogues, letters, reviews, and political statements. $29.95. See address under "Anthologies."

Tippi N. Blevins's poetry is collected in two lovely $2 chapbooks: *Strange Angels* (120 copies) and *The Divine Heretic* (100 copies) published by Night Sky Publications, PO Box 1511, Pasadena, TX 77501-1511.

Bambada Press (publisher of the horror magazine *Bloodsongs*) put out a chapbook by Francis Payne called *Olympia*. The story is a gruesome one about a school of torture. Attractively produced book limited to 300 signed copies. It's a buy for $6.95, if you like that sort of thing. The single blurb (by the publisher) on the back cover seems inappropriate. See address under collections.

The Tartarus Press published *The Secret of the Sangraal: A Collection of Writings by Arthur Machen*, edited by R. B. Russell. This is a collection of thirty-nine rare essays, including the title essay on the grail myth, "The Strange Tale of Mount Nephin," a true account of a girl's brief disappearance on an Irish mountain in 1929, a retelling of "Guinevere and Lancelot," his essay, "A Note on Poetry," and notes on his writings. Limited to 250 numbered copies. £22.50 payable to The Tartarus Press.

Gauntlet Press brought out a signed, limited, and slipcased edition (500) of Peter Straub's *Shadowland*. Preface by Peter Straub, introduction by Ramsey Campbell, and afterword by Thomas Tessier. Dust jacket art by Harry O. Morris. $60. Also, *I Am Legend*, the 40th-anniversary edition of the classic Richard Matheson novel, is a 500-copy signed and numbered and slipcased edition. It contains an interview with Matheson, introduction by Dan Simmons, and afterword by George Clayton Johnson. $75 plus $4.50 postage payable to Gauntlet Publications, 309 Powell Road, Springfield, PA 10964.

Lucius Shepard's horror novella "The Last Time," one of the dropped stories in the American version of *Little Deaths*, was published in an attractive signed, limited hardcover edition of 150 copies. The white-on-red leather front and rear covers are by Phil Parks. Color photograph of Shepard as a frontispiece plus a numbered print of the cover signed by Shepard and Parks. Boxed in an acrylic slipcase. Introduction by James P. Blaylock, an essay by Shepard collector Tom Joyce, and an American and British bibliography. $95 payable to A.S.A.P. Publishing, 23852 Via Navarra, Mission Viejo, CA 92691. 26 collector's copies were also available as were 10 pc collector's copies.

DreamHaven published a 750-copy signed, numbered edition of *California Gothic* by Dennis Etchison. The wraparound dust jacket and interior art are by J. K. Potter. $28 through DreamHaven Books (see address on Acknowledgment page).

Mark Ziesing published Nancy A. Collins's western horror novel, *Walking Wolf*. Color dust jacket by J. K. Potter. Available in a $60 signed, slipcased first edition or as a $25 trade edition (see Mark Ziesing address on Acknowledgment page).

Maclay & Associates brought out a new suspense novel by Rex Miller, *Saint Louis Blues*, limited to 500 copies autographed by the author for $40 payable to John Maclay & Associates, Publishers, PO Box 16253, Baltimore, MD 21210.

W. Paul Ganley brought out a hardcover reprint of Brian Lumley's fourth in his "Cthulhu Mythos" series. *Spawn of the Winds*, illustrated by Linda Michaels, was published in a $26.50 trade edition and a deluxe, signed, and numbered edition of 300 for $42.50. Also, the fifth in the series, *In the Moons of Borea*, for $27.50 and $45 for the signed and numbered limited edition of 300. Illustrations by Jim Pianfetti. Payable to W. Paul Ganley. Address under "Magazines."

The City on the Edge of Forever is the complete edition of the award-winning *Star Trek* script by Harlan Ellison. Published by Borderlands Press, it comes in a 1,000-copy limited edition, numbered with dust jacket. It contains the original script, an essay by Ellison, and afterwords by Peter David, David Gerrold, Walter Koenig, George Takei, D.C. Fontana, DeForest Kelley, Melinda Snodgrass, and Leonard Nimoy. $75 payable to Borderlands Press. See address under "Anthologies."

Crossroads Press published the first American hardcover edition of Joe R. Lansdale's western/horror novel, *Dead in the West*. This is a signed limited slipcased edition of 300 copies with a new introduction by Lansdale, a foreword by Neal Barrett Jr., and interior illustrations by Stephen R. Bissette. Somewhat rewritten and corrected, it is the author's preferred text. $55 plus $5 postage payable to Thomas Crouss, Crossroads Press, PO Box 10433, Holyoke, MA 01089-1706. May no longer be available—check first.

Cobblestone Books published a graphic adaptation of Lansdale's short story, "My Dead Dog, Bobby." Illustrated by Joe Vigil with an introduction by Norman Partridge. Not much to it but a collectable for Lansdale fans. Signed and numbered edition limited to 750 copies. $14 plus $4 postage payable to Cobblestone Books, 5111 College Oak Drive, Sacramento, CA 95841.

Transylvania Press published *Vanitas*, S. P. Somtow's third novel in the *Valentine* trilogy, in a signed, limited edition of 500. The cover is by Val Lakey-Lindahn. This is the first edition of the author's preferred text. $65 payable to Transylvania Press, PO Box 75012-WRPS, White Rock, BC Canada V4A 9M4.

Graphic Novels:

Taboo #8, edited by Stephen R. Bissette (Kitchen Sink Press), is back after a few years. As usual some great stuff, including another installment of Tim Lucas's series (made into a novel), *Throat Sprockets*, illustrated by David Lloyd; a creepy piece by Jack Butterworth and Greg Capullo; and Jeff Nicholson's nasty *Cat Lover. Taboo #9*, the last issue, was published in the Fall. Some excellent work by Jon Neruda and Allen Stevens, Chet Williamson and Tim Truman, and two excellent pieces by Philip Hester.

Give It Up! and Other Short Stories by Franz Kafka, illustrated by Peter Kuper (NBM) with an introduction by Jules Feiffer. Artist and writer are a perfect match. Nine fables/stories by Kafka, including "The Hunger Artist" and the title story. The least successful pieces are those that are barely classifiable even as vignettes. But Kuper's mordant and witty b&w illustrations bring out the black humor in the text.

The Tell Tale Heart: Stories and Poems by Edgar Allan Poe, illustrated by Bill D. Fountain (Mojo Press), is enjoyable and Fountain generally does a fine job matching illustration to text—particularly in "Hop Frog" and "The Cask of Amontillado." But the series of "Poe Bytes" and the heavy-handed rendition of "Annabel Lee" fall flat. $4.95 payable to Mojo Press, PO Box 140005, Austin, TX 78714.

One of the major events of 1995 was the *Harlan Ellison's Dream Corridor* series from Dark Horse. Under Ellison's close supervision, DH produced five 32-page books with stories, vignettes, graphic novels, and Ellison himself as a character leading you through his tongue-in-cheek "place where he gets his ideas." Wonderful concept, even better execution. Reprints of "On the Slab," "Catman," and the classic "I Have No Mouth and I Must Scream," as well as a western and a hard-boiled story. And also a new story per issue by Ellison. Excellent art by John Byrne, Leo and Diane Dillon, newcomer Eric White, and others. Adaptations by Nancy A. Collins and others. Highly recommended.

Industrial Gothic by Ted McKeever (DC-Vertigo) looks to be an interesting series. The first five issues take an odd couple—Nickel has no arms and legs so Pencil carries her on his back—on the run into postindustrial ruins of the United States, searching for a mysterious aluminum tower; also from Vertigo comes the two-issue *The Horrorist* by Jamie Delano and David Lloyd, featuring *Hellblazer*'s John Constantine tracking down a mysterious woman who, emanating the despair, ugliness, and violence from around the world, brings it all home to the U.S.A. An honest effort but too preachy.

Weird Business, edited by Joe R. Lansdale and Richard Klaw, from the newly started Mojo Press, is a hardcover anthology of twenty-three adapted classics and originals: Poppy Z. Brite and Miran Kim's text and art are perfectly matched to create the violent yet beautiful expressionistic "Becoming the Monster." Also, great renditions of Lansdale's revenge story "The Steel Valentine," illustrated by Marc Erickson; the goofy "Stranger," by Brian Biggs; Robert Bloch's Hugo Award–winning classic "That Hell-Bound Train," adapted by Neal Barrett Jr. and illustrated by Philip Hester, Ande Parks, and Andrew Walls; "Coccyx," a grotesque little sexual fantasy by John Bergin; other writers include Charles de Lint, F. Paul Wilson, Howard Waldrop, Michael Moorcock, Roger Zelazny, and Nancy A. Collins. Nice lineup. $29.95 plus $2.05 postage payable to Mojo Press.

Voodoo Child: The Illustrated Legend of Jimi Hendrix, created and produced by Martin I. Green and illustrated by Bill Sienkewicz (Penguin Studio), with an unreleased CD, "celebrates the life and genius" of the great musician. This is worth the price just for the illustrations.

If you enjoy Kaz's raucous and raw comic strips in the *New York Press* and elsewhere you'll love his new book *Underworld: Cruel and Unusual Comics* (Fantagraphics Books) with a foreword by Mark Leyner.

The Big Book of Death by Bronwyn Carlton and sixty-seven comic artists, with an introduction by Luc Sante, and *The Big Book of Weirdos* by Carl Posey and sixty-seven comic artists, with an introduction by Gahan Wilson, both from Paradox Press/DC Comics, are oversize trade paperbacks with lots of wonderful comics.

Family Man by Jerome Charyn and Joe Staton (Paradox Mystery) is a three-volume futuristic noir graphic novel. Charyn is one of the most underrated suspense novelists around. He's good in whatever media he's writing for.

Oink: Heaven's Butcher by John Mueller (Kitchen Sink) is a new series that looks like a vicious little parable about pigs. Definitely not a *Babe*, these porkers are mean and out for vengeance. Looks promising.

Other interesting-looking graphic novels: *God Flesh* collects two very violent graphic novels: *Flickering Flesh* by Bill Yukish and John Lucas and *The God That Failed* by Bill Yukish and Hart D. Fisher (Boneyard Press); a strange new work by Charles Burns called *Black Hole* (Kitchen Sink); Al Columbia's *Biologic Show* (Fantagraphics); a new anthology series called *Death Rattle* (Kitchen Sink), written and drawn by various artists.

Children's Books:

Triangle, Square, Circle and *1,2,3*, both by William Wegman (Hyperion Books for Children) using the famous wiemaraner Fay and her family, are both charming ways of teaching young children.

An Alphabet of Dinosaurs by Peter Dodson and paintings by Wayne D. Barlowe (Scholastic) makes a good introduction to dinosaurs for children. The book is graced by Barlowe's pink and green otherworldly creatures (as odd as any "aliens") and Dobson's text, both of which update what is known about dinosaurs.

The House that Drac Built by Judy Sierra and illustrated by Will Hillenbrand (Gulliver/Harcourt Brace) is a clever retelling of "The House That Jack Built" with charming illustrations of mummies, manticores, zombies, and other creatures of the night. Strictly for the kids.

The Pelican Chorus by Edward Lear, illustrated by Fred Marcellino (Scholastic), is a treat with amusing new artistic interpretations of the title nonsense rhyme and two others, "The New Vestment," and "The Owl and the Pussycat." Marcellino is at his best here, having more interesting text to work with than with his last two children's books, using unembellished, traditional texts of "Puss in Boots" and "The Steadfast Tin Soldier."

I Know an Old Lady, illustrated by G. Brian Karas (Scholastic), is another goody, with funnier than usual renderings of the old lady and her story told from the point of view of the little boy who is her next-door neighbor and spies her swallowing that fly and everything else.

Unwrap the Mummy by Ian Dicks and David Hawcock (Random House) makes a clever and fun tool for teaching children. Kind of a pop-up book, the mummy's parts pull out and underneath is information on "how to make a mummy" and mummy lore.

Math Curse by Jon Scieszka and Lane Smith (Viking)—okay, I love it because of the art. And it's clever. Kid goes to school, his teacher says, "you can think of everything as a math problem," and the kid does, making the kid's life miserable. Well, since I hate math, it would make me miserable, too. Not sure kids will really appreciate this one.

Art Books:

The Iron Woman by Ted Hughes, with engravings by Barry Moser (Dial Books), is the companion to last year's *The Iron Man*. The story itself is a simplistic antipollution morality tale but I recommend the book for collectors of Moser.

Julie Taymor: Playing with Fire by Eileen Blumenthal and Julie Taymor (Harry N. Abrams) is a gorgeous coffee-table book. Taymor grew up in Newton, Massachusetts, and was already putting on plays in her backyard at age seven. Her early travels to India and Sri Lanka profoundly influenced her artistry, and she became interested in Far Eastern art forms of puppetry and masks. The book traces her evolution as an artist/director in text and with over 100 color photographs of her sketches, designs, and finished productions. While living in Indonesia for four years, she wrote, directed, and designed the play *Tirai*, set in Bali and produced in Java, Sumatra, and Bali in the late 1970s and then, in a new version, was produced in New York in 1981. She made the puppets for Stravinksy's opera *Oedipus Rex*, and staged and directed Shakespeare's *Titus Andronicus* after studying Joel-Peter Witkin's photographic images, various artistic interpretations of *The Rape of the Sabine Women*, and the crucifixion. She made a one-hour movie of Poe's story "Hop-Frog" called *Fool's Fire*, using grotesque puppetry for all but "Hop-Frog" and his lady love.

The World of Peter Greenaway by Leon Steinmetz and Peter Greenaway (Journey Editions) is a stunning coffee-table book for fans of Greenaway's strange, surreal, and often grotesque movies. The creator of *The Draughtman's Contract*, *A Zed and Two Noughts*, *Drowning by Numbers*, and *The Cook, the Thief, His Wife and Her Lover*, Greenaway is an artist first and most of the ideas for his movies come from an image he has seen and/or painted. Steinmetz, himself an artist, writes about the work (paintings, collages, and still photographs from the films throughout) as does Greenaway. Some of the text is quite illuminating as to the filmmaker's intentions and themes.

The Alien World of Wayne Barlowe (Morpheus International) is written and illustrated by Barlowe, creator of *Barlowe's Guide to Extraterrestrials*. This volume is a treat, showcasing Barlowe's talent as an illustrator of aliens and dinosaurs. His style ranges from the lush and sensuous paintings he created for the covers of novels by Tanith Lee, Paul Monette, and Octavia E. Butler to finely detailed demons and lost souls for his work-in-progress, *A Pilgrimage to Hell*. Includes sketches, experiments, doodlings, and commentary by Barlowe on his techniques and inspirations; The new H. R. Giger book, *Species Design*, also comes from Morpheus. This fascinating look behind the scenes of *Species* can even be enjoyed by those who haven't seen the movie. It opens with writer/producer Dennis Feldman's written "pitch" for what he originally called "The Message" and has running commentary by Giger about his work on the alien, Sil. But this is also a heavy-duty art book with sketches, constructions, and photographs of the design and construction of Sil and stills of her transformations. For fans of fantastic/grotesque art.

The Pain Doctors of Suture Self General by The Bovine Smoke Society, with illustrations by Alan M. Clark (Arts Nova Press), is a delicious nightmare that reminds one of the really icky parts of Lindsay Anderson's movie, *O Lucky Man*, with Malcolm McDowell as the bewildered and beleaguered everyman. World Fantasy Award–winning artist Clark painted *Blasted Femurs, a Sack o' Religion* in 1993 and the painting inspired a short story by the artists who regularly meet at his home. Thirteen illustrations and page decorations by Clark, and the introduction by writer/doctor F. Paul Wilson is a nice touch. This is a 550-copy signed, limited edition. Highly recommended and highly collectable. $50.00 hardcover available from Blue Moon Books. See address under "Novels."

Spectrum 2: The Best in Contemporary Art, edited by Cathy Burnett, Arnie Fenner, and Jim Loehr (Underwood Books), is the second in a series of juried yearbooks of professional fantasy art. This is a beautiful book and shows the spectrum from fantasy to horror in illustration. $34.95 hardcover and $22.96 trade paperback available from Underwood Books, PO Box 1607, Grass Valley, CA 95945.

Joel-Peter Witkin's much-delayed first major book since 1989's *Gods of Heaven and Earth* came out in time to coincide with a show of his work at the Guggenheim Museum in New York City. The book, published by Scalo and simply titled *Witkin*, is introduced by an illuminating essay by Germano Celant, translated from the Italian by Stephen Sartarelli, and includes another essay by Witkin himself.

Untitled by Diane Arbus (Aperture) is the third volume of Arbus's work and the only one devoted totally to her photographic work at residences for the mentally retarded between 1969 and 1971. Most of the photographs have never been seen before and the afterword by Doon Arbus, the daughter of the photographer, brings an additional dimension to the work. Simply designed to show the photographs with no commentary, this is a major addition to Arbus's photographic work. Highly recommended.

Going into Darkness: Fantastic Coffins from Africa by Thierry Secretan (Thames & Hudson) is a colorful book about the folk art of coffin-building among the Ga, the dominant people of Accra and the surrounding region of Ghana. From fish and birds to buses and Mercedes-Benzes, the coffins reflect the occupation, character, or status of the deceased.

Truths and Fictions by Pedro Meyer (Aperture) is an odd but beautiful book. Moving from his stark b&w images of the United States during the Reagan years into the phantasmagoric color images in his native Mexico, Meyer uses digital photography to manipulate reality. Introduction by Joan Fontcuberta. It's strange seeing *how* he does it, and yes, frightening, that reality *can* be so easily changed.

A *Small Book of Black and White Lies* by Dave McKean (Allen Spiegel Fine Arts and Hourglass) is a beautiful collection of photographs by one of the major artists of the fantasy field. McKean does the covers of the *Sandman* graphic novels and has collaborated with Neil Gaiman on *Violent Cases* and *Mr. Punch*. Introduction by Bill Laswell. The sepia-toned photographs are mysteries and each one might tell a story. A must-have for those who love McKean's work. He also created the *Vertigo Tarot* (DC/Vertigo) in collaboration with Rachel Pollack, who wrote the text. Introduction by Neil Gaiman. It comes with a hardcover guide by McKean and Pollack and seventy-eight full-color Tarot cards illustrated by McKean.

Odds and Ends:

Mr. Wilson's Cabinet of Wonder by Lawrence Weschler (Pantheon) is the gift book of the year. The Museum of Jurassic Technology is a storefront museum in Los Angeles, California, created and run by David Wilson. In it are "pronged ants, horned humans, mice on toast, and other marvels of Jurassic technology." Moving from the real to the surreal, Wilson's exhibits challenge, amuse, and puzzle the visitor. A joke yet not a joke. Some of the oddities are indeed real. The challenge for Weschler was to find out which are. In addition, the book (like the museum itself) is a meditation on the tradition of wonder cabinets and the nature and use and meaning of museums. A smallish hardcover with a neat design and gorgeous endpapers. This book is sheer wonder and delight. Nominated for the National Book Critics Circle Award in nonfiction. Charming and highly recommended.

Vampire Diary: The Embrace by Robert Weinberg, Mark Rein, and Hagen (White Wolf) is a clever package—it's published as a diary with lock and key. The text itself is a so-so novella about an L.A. guy who is seduced (not very interestingly) into vampirism.

Open All Night by Ken Miller with text by William T. Vollmann (The Overlook Press) will be a collectable item for Vollmann fans, with snippets of excerpts from his novels and stories used as commentary on Miller's b&w photographs of skinheads, junkies, prostitutes, alkies, and other outsiders. The most fascinating thing about this book is the thought that if you put all these people in one room they'd probably end up killing each other.

Night: Night Life, Night Language, Sleep, and Dreams by A. Alvarez (Norton) combines personal experiences—his fear of the dark, a venture out on the night with NYC police officers—with an analysis of the physiology of sleep and the interpretation of dreams.

Strange Ritual by David Byrne (Chronicle) is a very attractive and beautifully designed collection of Byrne's (Talking Heads) photographs with some text. Saturated color photos of religious artifacts, dolls, furniture, advertising, books, bathroom fixtures, and other objects that are the focus of Byrne's obsession. Somehow sacred objects. Nothing particularly profound but a hell of a lot more entertaining than the David Lynch coffee-table book fiasco of 1994.

Saving Graces by David Robinson (W.W. Norton) collects b&w photographic images of statues of women adorning mostly nineteenth-century graves in European cemeteries. Robinson calls these sensuous, often skimpily (if at all) clad, weeping young marble women the Saving Graces. His afterword provides insight as he attempts to explain their raison d'etre. Foreword by Joyce Carol Oates. A lovely gift book.

After the Funeral: The Posthumous Adventures of Famous Corpses by Edwin Murphy (Citadel Press) lets you know just where it stands as soon as you read the table of contents, which handily categorizes the book into: Heads, Hearts, Bodies, and Miscellaneous. So you can learn how Haydn lost his head (after he was dead), how Cardinal Richelieu's head was stolen, and how labor activist Joe Hill's cremated ashes were mailed to labor organizations all over the world. A lively, entertaining, and informative read.

Who Lies Where: A Guide to Famous Graves by Michael Kerrigan (Fourth Estate-UK) is *the* book for tourists to the United Kingdom who enjoy searching cemeteries for the famous dead. Organized county by county and utterly straight-faced, the book is a bit dry but in it you can learn where Roald Dahl, Boris Karloff, Pocohontas, and Macbeth are buried.

The Magic Box, edited by Mel Gooding, designed by Julian Rothenstein, and compiled by Daniel Stashower (Shambhala Publications) is a wow! Introduced by Will Self and with two new postcards by Glen Baxter, you can't go wrong. Included is a pamphlet on how to be a contortionist, one booklet about *Charles Dickens: Conjuror*, one on "conjuring for smokers," and reproductions of old postcards providing instruction on conjuring tricks. Great for gifts, fun for yourself. And from the same publisher, *The Moon Box: Legends, Mystery, and Lore from Luna* another perfect gift edited by John Miller and Tim Smith. Four small hardcover books in a box: a mini-anthology of SF stories about trips to the moon; a book of werewolf stories; one on the subject of women's mystical connection to the moon; a collection of poems, chants, fables, parlor games, and curses about the moon.

Dragons: A Natural History by Dr. Karl Shuker (S&S) is profusely and colorfully illustrated with dragons of all varieties and cultures, including serpents, wyverns, orms, and guivres—French, British, and Chinese. Shuker seems an expert dracontologist and tells the reader all about these strange creatures.

Encyclopedia of Signs, Omens, and Superstitions by Zolar (Citadel) is an entertaining and useful compendium. E.g.: Do *you* know where the expression "abracadabra" comes from? Would you like to know all the superstitions related to horseshoes, bears, apples, and shoes? Then read this book.

And if you want to know more about shoes, and specifically, perhaps a bit about shoe fetishism, try *Female Fetishism* by Lorraine Gamman and Merja Makinen (NYU Press). They argue, basically, that women haven't been getting a fair shake when it comes to the study of fetishism. Somewhat on the dry side and a wee bit defensive, it nonetheless looks to be a useful companion to *Female Peversions*, reviewed here a couple of years ago.

Valerie Steele's *Fetish: Fashion, Sex, and Power* (Oxford University Press) is much more lively in its approach and inviting to read. Color and b&w illustrations and photographs throughout the book. Steele explores the historical relationship between fashion and fetishism and discusses how the iconography of sexual fetishism has been increasingly assimilated into popular culture.

How would you like to protect your newly polished shoes during the rush-hour commute with steel-spiked toe guards? Or slab butter on your toast with a butterstick? Or perhaps you feel your cats need to help around the house more? Now you can buy them dust dislodging footsocks. These are only a sampling of the devices illustrated and written about in *101 Unuseless Japanese Inventions* by Kenji Kawakami (Norton), a wonderfully witty little book featuring the best inventions and devices of Kawakami, famous in Japan for his creation and promotion of "chindogu"—the art of "the unuseless idea." You really *need* this book.

Although Pamela Ditchoff's *The Mirror or Monsters and Prodigies* (Coffee House Press) is called a novel, it's more of a fictionalized series of interconnected vignettes about human oddities. Each entry is written in the flavor of the period in which it takes place, so there's an interesting mix of tone and language from 2,500 B.C. Egypt to New Orleans, Louisiana, in the 1970s.

Walk on the Wild Side by Jeannette Jones (Barricade Books) is a coffee-table book of b&w

photographs of tranvestites in drag and transsexuals. Some of them are quite beautiful. Not much commentary.

Dining with Headhunters by Richard Sterling (The Crossing Press) is a goofy travelogue/cookbook. Sterling's search for black pepper (as a seaman with the navy) leads him to Borneo, the largest of the Spice Islands, while on leave. Here he eats ants and other bugs with his hosts. Sprinkled with the history of spices, recipes, and adventures (including those erotic), Sterling seems a bit like an innocent abroad.

Legal Limit is a quarterly catalog and 'zine published through DreamHaven, the SF and fantasy store and mail-order business, in addition to their regular monthly catalog. *Legal Limit* is edited by Peter Larsen with assistance from Steve Matuszak. It lists and describes adult "fringe books" (you must give an age statement [18] upon ordering some of the material). One issue talks about the First Amendment, citing the Mike Diana case (mentioned in a previous volume of the *Year's Best* and in *Gauntlet*) and reviews books such as a recent William Burroughs biography and a recent book of essays by Pat Califia.

The 1995 Lovecraftian Horror Calendar is a b&w illustrated calendar with Mythos art by Allen Koszowski, H. E. Fassl, Phil Reynolds, Dave Carson, and others with text selections by H. P. Lovecraft, Thomas Ligotti, T. E. D. Klein, Ramsey Campbell, Robert Bloch, and others. $9.95 ppd, payable to Kevin Ross ($3 extra for overseas), Artefact publications, 1210 Greene Street, Suite 4, Boone, IA 50036.

The 1996 Mütter Museum Calendar, put out by The College of Physicians of Philadelphia, continues to teach, fascinate, and repulse with its collection of photographs of items from the famous medical collection. Photographs by Max Aguilera-Hellweg, Steven E. Katzman, Scott Lindgren, Olivia Parker, Rosamund Purcell, Arne Svenson, and Gwen Akin and Allan Ludwig. This year some of the photographs are of an "anatomical preparation of the skull, showing nerves and the arteries photographs . . . with dried dahlias"; "eight foetal skeletons, which is part of a series showing the development of the foetal skeleton, second-month gestation to postpartum"; and "a tumor of the face, plaster model." The calendar is usually available in some bookstores for $14.95. Information from The College of Physicians of Philadelphia, 19 South 22nd Street, Philadelphia, PA 19103. Bad news. The 1996 calendar is the last they will put out.

Morpheus Calendar of Fantastic Art 1996 has stunning reproductions of art by H. R. Giger, Ernst Fuchs, Robert Venosa, Jacek Yerka, and others. This is a useful and attractive sampler of some excellent fantasy art from this fine art publisher.

Dark Delicacies (a bookstore) and Fool's Press (the new publisher that put out the Lisa Morton chapbook) has published *Dark Progress*—a very attractive and fun 1996 Horror Writers Calendar, featuring California horror writers such as Clive Barker, Robert Lannes, Dennis Etchison, Nancy Holder, Chelsea Quinn Yarbro, etc. There is a b&w photograph of each author with their bio, bibliography, and their greatest phobia. Cover art by Barker. Notable dates in horror are marked appropriately on the calendar. The 1996 calendar costs $16.96 plus $2 shipping ($2 donated to HWA) 3725 Magnolia Blvd., Burbank, CA 91505.

Limited edition photographic portfolios of Greg Weber's "cuddly abominations" are available, signed and numbered in an attractive handmade box. This second series set contains fourteen color prints for $20 including postage. Greg Weber, 163 Cook Avenue, Pasadena, CA 91107. Photographs of his grotesque sculptures have run in *Deathrealm* (I've even bought a few for my own delectation). Great stuff.

The Pain Doctors of Suture Self General greeting cards by Alan M. Clark (Blue Moon), full-color set of six cards and envelopes (goes with the book); Postcards from Night Sky has two sets designed: by Chad Savage ($3 per set of 12) and Tippi N. Blevins ($2.50 per set of 12) on gray granite card stock. Payable to T. Blevins, PO Box 1511, Pasadena, TX 77501.

Insomnia: A Portfolio of Paintings by Phil Hale (Glimmer Graphics) is a limited portfolio of 400 sets, signed and numbered by Phil Hale and Stephen King. Six full-color plates, including the original version of the cover, which has not been previously produced, and one plate of a new painting exclusive to this set. $85 plus $5 postage payable to Glimmer Graphics, 137 Fulton Street, Trenton, NJ 08611.

Dope Fiends trading cards (Kitchen Sink), compiled and annotated by Doug Aanes, collects thirty-six color reproductions of vintage paperbacks of the 1950s and 1960s by such as Evan Hunter writing as Ed McBain and others. Nice commentary on each card, too.

Horror and Fantasy in the Media: 1995
by Edward Bryant

Film

Here are a few financial figures to ponder, courtesy of Frank M. Robinson's most excellent (though, after this year, sadly defunct—send Frank civil, well-reasoned cards, letters, faxes, and E-mail in care of his editor) cinema summary in *Locus*. Although all the numbers are still not in, the approximate United States total box office grosses for 1995 are in the $5.4 billion range. Of this amount, roughly 28 percent, a bit more than a billion and a quarter, is generated by genre films ranging from *Batman Forever* ($184 million) to *Nadja* ($175 thousand).

While those sums can be subdivided into ticket prices ranging from bargain amounts at the twilight shows to full-price evening admissions, the real money is probably a much larger amount generated from the theaters' refreshment stands. Did you pay attention the last time you bought a family-size tub o' popcorn, a large diet Coke, some Junior Mints, a hotdog, and a couple Bromo Seltzer tablets? And if you took a date or, worse, voracious children, the tariff was even worse. It used to be it was only perverts who wore long trenchcoats to the movies; now it's budget-conscious yuppies who hide shopping bags full of home-prepared air-popped corn beneath their London Fogs.

As ever, gross ticket sales do not necessarily reflect the whole story—and certainly not in terms of the salient points of the films in question. Take the economic high and low points Frank Robinson listed. Get out your calculator to check my Old Math. If you go by the criteria of figures alone, was the latest *Batman* movie really more than a thousand times (1051.43 to be precise) better than the low-budget vampire art movie, *Nadja*? Nope.

Tickets sold are rarely a sound argument for esthetic judgments. But then you knew that. When Joel Schumacher took the helm of the Batman mega-hits from Tim Burton, he changed the core of the *Dark Knight* from quirky to slick, from askew to mainstream. Not that it ruined the whole thing—it simply suggested that the folks fronting the money wanted to make sure the franchise didn't stray too far into the commercially unconventional. That money also bought star power:

Val Kilmer replacing Michael Keaton as the Caped Crusader, Chris O'Donnell debuting as Robin, Tommy Lee Jones going postal as Two Face, Nicole Kidman slinking in gorgeously as psychiatrist Dr. Chase Meridian, and Jim Carrey going over the top as the Riddler. So was this movie great? Well . . . no. But it made the grade as basic fun. The real saving grace was Carrey, whose over-the-top approach (adored him in *The Mask*; hated him in *Ace Ventura*), made him the salvation of *Batman Forever*.

Nadja, on the other hand, was a very low-budget, black-and-white, grainy—indeed, gritty—urban close encounter with the Dracula myth, set in a contemporary big city. It's elegant, sensual, and moody. The film must have played for all of about two days in art houses in about six cities. Peter Fonda appears to have had a blast in a dual role both as Dracula (shot at a distance, thoroughly caped, looking a bit like Bela Lugosi's double in *Plan 9*), and with long hair and a manic attitude as Van Helsing. As Dracula's daughter, the eponymous vampire is played by the luminous Elina Lowensohn. The film uses an old Fisher-Price Pixelvision camera for vampire's-eye-view scenes maybe a little too much, but that's a small indulgence. *Nadja*'s one of those tiny films produced with enormous ingenuity, patience, and sacrifice that doesn't compromise, and will reward those few dedicated fans who seek it out.

Now then. What all was the cream? What rose to the top? I think the year's finest serious fantasy feature film was John Sayles's *The Secret of Roan Inish*. This is a magical tale, set in the late 1940s, on and just off the coast of western Ireland. A ten-year-old girl (Jeni Courtney) is sent from the economically depressed mainland back to the island from which her father moved (her mother died in childbirth). Living with her grandparents, Courtney becomes convinced that her youngest brother, who drifted out to sea years before in a marvelously constructed cradle, is still somehow alive. Intertwined with this is the legend of the Selkies, the were-seals who can strip off their skins and appear as fully human. Susan Lynch takes a sublimely eerie turn as a Selkie. As ever, Sayles directs magnificently. The script is based on Rosalie K. Fry's 1957 novella, "The Secret of the Ron Mor Skerry," and is the sort of adaptation any prose writer should be happy with. Haskell Wexler's (*Medium Cool*) cinematography elegantly and eloquently captures both the primal power of the sea and the moody Irish coastal landscapes. Best of all, John Sayles touches the heart of magical realism, telling a story in which all the characters accept the element of magic as a real element of the mundane world.

For a close second, though, I'd have to nominate the talking pig movie. Yes, *that* talking pig movie. I must admit I was prepared to dislike *Babe*, both on general principles because it was alleged to be a cutesy talking-animal kids' show, and because public adoration was reaching a fevered pitch by the time I got around to seeing it. On the other hand, I figured a movie produced and cowritten by George Miller (*Road Warrior*) couldn't be all sugar and fluff.

I was right. From the initial sequence wherein we meet the young pig of the title, an exceedingly dark view of porcine metaphysics that echoes humankind's own boundless capacity for rationalization, *Babe* is a movie about nature in which death and devouring is an ever-present reality. True, Babe comes to live on a decently run farm in scenic New South Wales where he eventually gets a shot at realizing his ambition of becoming a sheep dog, but it's no utopia for either animals or humans. The script by Miller and director Chris Noonan, adapted from the Dick King-Smith book, is sharp and funny. Perhaps the standout in the cast is the survival-obsessed duck Ferdinand, voiced by Danny Mann. What's orchestrated exceedingly well are the special effects, merging live animals, puppets, and animatronic constructions. Jim Henson's Creature Shop receives (and deserves) considerable credit. From start to finish, from plot to characters to camerawork, *Babe* is a movie that satisfies; but more, it charms. And that's the bottom line for any good fantasy work.

For anybody under thirty, and perhaps for a few people above that age, *Apollo 13* might well have been a cool science fiction space adventure. (Let's face it—a substantial percentage of older Americans still have the paranoid belief that the government completely faked the space program through the use of Hollywood effects, and young Americans don't remember anything before the fall of disco, and consequently see Oliver Stone's *JFK* as a historical documentary.) Ron Howard's spectacular adaptation of astronaut James Lovell and Jeffrey Kluger's *Lost Moon*, the story of the ill-fated 1970 lunar mission, took minor liberties with literal truth, but that's a minor cavil beside the major achievement of this picture. Sure, we mostly all knew how the story would end, but then we also knew the ending of *Schindler's List* going in. The script by William Broyles Jr. and Al Reinert, Ron Howard's direction, and the acting by Tom Hanks, Bill Paxton, Kevin Bacon, and Gary Sinise (as astronauts Lovell, Haise, Swigert, and Mattingly), and Ed Harris, a standout as flight director Gene Kranz, all melded together in the sort of involving drama that reenergized American public interest in the space program. I think my favorite factoid from the film's production notes had to do with the filming done in a NASA KC-135; the plane would loop in a parabola to simulate zero-gee conditions for about twenty-five seconds at a time. All told, the cast and crew flew 612 parabolas for a total of three hours and fifty-four minutes of weightlessness. But all the nifty tricks and techniques only ornamented the innately gripping story of one of America's most courageous and nearly tragic dramas of human exploration.

In terms of what everyone would agree truly was a science fiction film, the best of the year was Terry Gilliam's *12 Monkeys*. Inspired by French director Chris Marker's 1960s' experimental time travel piece, *La Jetée*, Gilliam took the material into wonderful new realms. With some of the look reminiscent of *Brazil*, *12 Monkeys*, ironically enough, was backed by Universal. But it's a new regime now, and the studio heads against whom Gilliam went to the mat are now departed. Gilliam's triumph here was to fuse solid SF ideas with equally solid engaging characters and imaginative staging. When tech-wonks in the future send Bruce Willis back to the '90s, it's not to get engaged in some sort of simple-minded attempt to risk paradoxes and stop the plague that's wiped out most of the world's population decades hence; rather, it's simply to secure useful information. But the time travel process is a little haywire—and Willis finds himself in a mental hospital, making the acquaintance of an extraordinarily manic Brad Pitt. A fine chemistry builds between Willis and his shrink, Madeleine Stowe. Everything builds—and builds. One hesitates to label anything a likely classic so close to its inception, but I'd go out on that proverbial limb for *12 Monkeys*.

The best SF movie that didn't succeed at all in the immediate marketplace was Kathryn Bigelow's *Strange Days*. I think a major problem was that its studio never figured out how to market it. I talked to any number of people who, having seen the trailer on TV, dismissively assumed it was just another *Blade Runner* ripoff. That was not the case. Directed from a script by James Cameron and Jay Cocks, *Strange Days* is set just a few years from now in an increasingly desperate L.A. about to face the massive party marking the change of centuries and millennia. Ralph Fiennes plays an ex-cop loser now making his living selling illegal memory chips that allow the user vicariously to relive the exact memories of the donor. Fiennes has his own private stash, well-used, that records peak experiences with his ex-lover, Juliette Lewis. Lewis has gone on to an involvement with a very dangerous man. Though the movie suffers from writer Cameron's infatuation with using nifty visuals to the exclusion of any real concern with character (*The Abyss* being the fine exception), the script occasionally allows the classic science fictional issue of how technology affects people and their relationships. There's an affecting scene when Angela Bassett, Fiennes's long-suffering friend and ally, chews him out for not dumping his old memory chips and simply getting on with life. It's spot on, but there's not nearly enough of this sort of material to balance all the hyperkinetic spectacle. Still, if there's one SF movie to catch on video this year, *Strange Days* is it. It deserved so much more than it got.

My favorite dark fantasy of the year, with no hesitation at all, was *The Prophecy*. A low budget didn't stop writer/director Gregory Widen from gathering a cast that included Christopher Walken, Elias Koteas, Virginia Madsen, Amanda Plummer, Viggo Mortensen, and Eric Stoltz. The time is the present, and the earth is both a chessboard and a battleground for God's minions and those of Satan. For heaven's sake, it's a melodrama about angels. And it works! The film's major saving grace is in treating the angels as the sort of heavenly host, whether fallen or still Up There, who clearly hail from the Old Testament. No cutesy, fluffy-feathered angels here, no sirree. These angels kick butt. *The Prophecy* is perhaps the perfect antidote to all the New Age diluters of the good old-fashioned angelic image—the one with the flaming sword.

One of the niftiest echoes from the past this last year was the art-house rerelease of a restored print of Henri-Georges Clouzot's 1955 French hit, *Diabolique*. Clouzot's also the director of that incredible 1952 epic of suspense, *Wages of Fear* (and if you didn't see the restored full-length cut of that stunner two years ago, then you missed a major movie experience).

Clouzot was a director with a gift for creating films that just have not dated at all. At any rate, *Diabolique*'s a creepy Hitchcockian melodrama about a real prick of a boarding school headmaster who gets bumped off in the tub by his wife and mistress. The women (Simone Signoret and Vera Clouzot) then discover that something may have gone horribly awry with their murder plan. Has their victim become a revenant? The last twenty minutes are purely wonderful for their tension. Your fingers and toes wouldn't begin to comprise the number of modern suspense films that have ripped off Clouzot's plot gimmicks. You might as well see and appreciate the original. There was a Hollywood remake released in early 1996. Be afraid; be very afraid.

One of the few contemporary dark suspense films that doesn't steal shamelessly from Henri-Georges Clouzot is Atom Egoyan's *Exotica*. This Canadian production centers around the strip club of the title, a baroquely gussied up version of the sort of place where the dancers perform table dances for a little extra (as best one can estimate these things, Canadian table dances are a lot more bargain-priced than similar club options down in the lower forty-eight). Egoyan's an art-house favorite Miramax is trying to break into the commercial mainstream. Folks looking for an erotic thriller will find it, but they'll have to be patient about accumulating their kicks.

Egoyan's script allows the film to disclose its many, many revelations in a deliberate but inevitable, onion-peeling style. There's an ensemble cast and they're all good. The tone is something reminiscent of David Lynch by way of Robert Altman. And the return of Leonard Cohen crooning a sinister ballad on the soundtrack is an added treat.

Speaking of sinister, the surprise hit over in the dark suspense corridor was also the career comeback of the year for director David Fincher. Fincher, you'll recall, was the British music video director who helmed the not immensely likable $Alien^3$. He went from there to the strange and intriguing, filmed on location in Namibia, cut to ribbons by its distributor, dark fantasy film, *Dust Devil*. In 1995 he gave us *Seven*. Filmed primarily in shadow and night, *Seven* featured Brad Pitt and Morgan Freeman as homicide detectives on the trail of a serial killer (an unbilled Kevin Spacey—be sure to catch him as well in Bryan Singer's cleverly *noir*ish *The Usual Suspects*) doing his best to cast his victims in living (and dying) tableaus of the seven deadly sins. I loved the occasional ultra-violent humor in Andrew Kevin Walker's script—there's a nifty visual joke in one scene where the cops are searching an apartment empty save for a now-dead victim who was confined there for a year. The spaces are festooned with hundreds of pine-tree air fresheners dangling in the darkness. Perhaps the most surprising thing about *Seven* is that it became such a huge hit at all, since it ends with the kind of Arctic chilly downer that usually turns off the Saturday night date crowd. Go figure.

I thought *Jumanji* was pretty cool, but then I'm a great fan of Chris Van Allsburg, the artist and writer whose books bring true strangeness, offbeat wonder, and occasionally twisted humor into the world of children's literature. Robin Williams does well starring as a kid who gets sucked into a magic board game a quarter century ago, and is stuck in some kind of mystical time-warp jungle growing older until a contemporary boy and girl play the game and rescue him in 1995. *Jumanji* functioned as, I frequently hope, good all-ages-but-aimed-primarily-at-kids movies do. It didn't condescend, betrayed a surreal intelligence, and didn't compromise. The digitally imaged elephants stomping cars and the rhinos rushing down an upstairs hallway in an old house were certainly striking. Director Joe Johnston helmed the project well.

Toy Story was something of a surprise hit—and hit it was, making only $30 million less than *Batman Forever*. This mega-success drove computer animation house Pixar's stock through the roof. Or at least made Steve Jobs a somewhat richer man. The animation was superb state-of-the-art work. The story, a collaborative effort by about a gazillion writers, still somehow managed to work. This tale of forgotten toys coming to life, and of the generation gap between old and new toys, appealed for a variety of reasons to all ages.

You want horror? *Crumb* is a documentary, a nonfiction portrait of the underground comics artist R. Crumb that really feels like it needs to be listed here. Terry Zwigoff's film portrait is completely riveting and absolutely terrifying. R. Crumb and his supremely dysfunctional family present a disturbing image of artistic brilliance balanced on a knife-edge only about an Angstom Unit separated from complete madness. The story of Robert, his mom, and his two brothers is all the darker and more disturbing for its reality. This

Horror and Fantasy in the Media: 1995   lxxv

should go on the required viewing list for everyone aspiring to become any sort of professional in the arts.

My greatest cinematic disappointment last year was probably *Johnny Mnemonic*, scripted by William Gibson from his short story and directed by Robert Longo. There were plenty of cyberpunk pictures in 1995, and this should have been the best. Filmed inexpensively in Canada with first-rate effects, the film boasted a wonderful supporting cast: Ice-T, the incredible Henry Rollins, and Dolph Lundgren looking not at all like himself as a psychotic, bearded preacher-cum-assassin. I think the major casting problem came with Keanu Reeves as the title character, the burned-out courier carrying invaluable information uploaded into his brain, trying to avoid the Bad Guys who want to cut off his head and eventually extract the stolen info. Reeves just didn't get the character. Too bad. There were other problems, but I won't list them. Suffice it to say that *Johnny Mnemonic* was so close, so damned close.

I was also troubled that Clive Barker's *Lord of Illusion* didn't work all that well either. Directed and scripted by Barker from his Harry D'Amour tale, "The Last Illusion," the cast didn't work out much better than in the Gibson picture. Scott Bakula, as Harry, just seemed to lack the weight to carry the role—and I'm not talking physical poundage. Famke Janssen, as the Love Interest, was gorgeous. The supporting villains were great. But the whole production never seemed quite to jell. There were some good grisly moments; and a wonderfully mounted scene that parodied David Copperfield's extravagant stage productions; but the entirety never came together. I hate to put it this way, but this movie driven by dark magic was never, itself, quite magical enough.

I was sorry that Rachel Talalay's *Tank Girl*, starring Lori Petty as the comic book heroine, didn't do better at the box office. Set in a wasted future where an authoritarian bureaucracy, the insidious Bureau of Water and Power, keeps an iron grip on natural resources, the movie's a quick, smart, amusing take on rebellion. Nothing too deep, but it is entertaining. Ice-T's in here, along with Malcolm McDowell as the entirely too pragmatic head of the BWP.

John Carpenter's *In the Mouth of Madness* was a Lovecraftian melodrama that unfortunately fell short. Sam Neill plays an insurance guy dispatched to locate the most famous horror novelist in the world, one Sutter Kane. He travels to a small and isolated New England town where it's obvious that all is not exactly right. Turns out that Kane's work can have an all too literal effect on the real world, and not in the essentially benign sense of an *Uncle Tom's Cabin*. The Great Old Ones are coming back, and it's not that they're pissed—they're hungry. Unfortunately, Michael Di Luca's script doesn't hang together as tightly as one might wish.

John Carpenter's other movie this year was *Village of the Damned*, the remake of the 1960s minor classic, directed by Wolf Rilla, scripted by Stirling Silliphant with others, and based on John Wyndham's *The Midwich Cuckoos*. This is a remake that would, in theory, seem ideal for another go. In the Carpenter version, the small English village of Midwich has been removed to northern California. The film effectively and chillingly has the town isolated from all human contact for six hours one sunny morning. Every inhabitant, human or animal, falls unconscious. When they awake, one poor guy's been barbecued on a cookout burger grill, and ten women are mysteriously impregnated. Naturally each is shocked and chagrined, but no one opts for an abortion. Nine months later, all give birth simultaneously. Nine babies are delivered alive; one is stillborn. Government scientist Kirstie Alley steals the body of the dead infant. Local sawbones Christopher Reeve loses his wife after their daughter (the most mean and nasty of the little moppets with platinum hair) develops strangely glowing eyes that can control human beings, and first orders Mom to stick her arm into a boiling pot, then orders the woman to jump off a seaside cliff. Linda Koslowski, on the other hand, is mother to the runt of the litter, a little boy who learns a few basic human qualities—such as empathy.

And that's why this plot shouldn't date. What better premise for the 1990s than to examine the prospect of the bright new generation, Gen X, as Homo superior, growing to adulthood without any human empathy? Unfortunately this kernel tends to get largely overlooked in the melodramatic grain bin.

Casper the friendly ghost first appeared a half century ago as a screen cartoon character. The audience was not wild. Some cultural pundits have speculated that our culture doesn't respond well to funny bits about the shades of dead children. Too harsh. The cartoons and the comic books, not to mention the 1950s TV series, gradually accumulated a dedicated following. *Casper*, the 1995 big-screen special effects extravaganza, was not a mega-hit, but it still had its points. First-time feature director Brad Silberling and first-time feature writers Sherri Stoner and Deanna Oliver had the advantage of a first-rate cast. Newcomer Malachi Pearson did fine as the voice for the title character. Christina Ricci, so splendid in the Addams Family films, did well here too as Casper's newfound object of affection. Ditto Bill Pullman as an "afterlife therapist" and Cathy Moriarty and Monty Python's Eric Idle as the villains. This Spielberg production utilized some forty minutes of computer animation, far more than the 6.5 onscreen minutes of the dinosaurs in *Jurassic Park*. Shenanigans of the "Ghostly Trio" weren't nearly as scary as either the T Rex or the velociraptors, but Casper carried its moments.

Everything was big about Universal's *Waterworld*. The budget was immense—in excess, it is said, of $150 million. The ego battle between director Kevin Reynolds and star Kevin Costner was rumored to be epic. Unfortunately, big doesn't necessarily mean better. Reynolds was no George Miller. Costner was no Mel Gibson. And *Waterworld* very much smacked of being an aquatic recycled *Road Warrior*. Set a ways in the future, the ice caps have melted and all land, apparently, has been submerged. Never mind that here in the real world the ice caps melting would raise the ocean levels only fourteen feet or so, rather than the thousands of feet needed to submerge the Himalayas.

For the purposes of the movie, all surviving humankind is living in a variety of recycled and ramshackle marine craft. But rumors have generated of dry land existing somewhere. Then mutant (he has delicate little gills and can breathe underwater) Kevin Costner happens upon Helen (Jeanne Tripplehorn) and her young ward Enola (Tina Majorino). The girl has an enigmatic tattoo of a map. That map is obsessively desired by an over-the-top Dennis Hopper playing the Deacon, the crazed leader of 5,000 heavy smokers and drinkers who dwell on the rusted and barely afloat supertanker, the Exxon Valdez (apparently they needed a craft this large to hold centuries of tobacco and liquor supplies). Nobody's terribly charismatic in the cast. The stage tends to be hogged and the eye caught by the nifty life-size sets of things like entire oceanic colonies. All very well and good, but the story, in the form of Peter Rader and David Twohy's script, is just plain inadequate. I must hasten to submit that this is not a *bad* action-adventure movie; it's just not as good as one would hope for the immense amount of resources invested. *Waterworld*'s the world's most expensive B movie.

Tales from the Crypt Presents Demon Knight is the first of at least three projected films spinning off from the cable series and the old EC Comics. Directed by Ernest Dickerson from a script by Ethan Reiff, Cyrus Voris, and Mark Bishop, *Demon Knight* featured William Sadler as a mysterious good guy trying first to escape a mysterious pursuer, then to protect the inhabitants of an isolated hotel from Billy Zane (remember him in *Dead Calm*?). Billy, it turns out, is a person of some peculiarly demonic (and demon-raising) talents. Jada Pinkett ably holds down a role as one of the hotel's terrified denizens. As with so much of *Tales from the Crypt* material, the movie's nastily bright, splashy, hyperkinetic, and amusing.

Species? Well, the H. R. Giger designs were, as ever, gorgeous in an intensely and viscerally creepy way. Natasha Henstridge, the actress who played Sil, the genetically accelerated hybrid of human and alien DNA, was quite attractive. Ben Kingsley, playing the first-contact project leader, seemed to be a fugitive from a different movie. The presumed horrific suspense never really gripped.

However, for *really* disappointing suspense, there was the biological thriller, *Outbreak*. Starring Dustin Hoffman, Renee Russo, and Morgan Freeman, this was essentially an exploitation of Richard Preston's nonfiction best-seller, *The Hot Zone*, intended to beat Ridley Scott's never-filmed version of the Preston book to the gate. What resulted was an amazingly fumble-fingered melodrama of government paranoia and the outbreak of an African plague right here in River City. Gee, there seems to be no particular explanation for a Hollywood production that opts to thoroughly vitiate the effect of a melodrama about Ebola Fever. Imagine a series of victims who never display the symptoms of hemorrhagic fever. You don't see Hollywood opting for restraint all that frequently. This probably shouldn't have been the time.

Then there was *A Vampire in Brooklyn*, Eddie Murphy's ill-fated comeback vehicle. It indeed had its moments, including casting the always impressive Angela Bassett as the one rational character in the script. Unfortunately there wasn't a whole lot of genuine fun in this production; and what there was, was easily overlooked if the viewer knew about the tragic and stupid accident that claimed the life of Bassett's stunt double.

I think it's time to change tone. Frank Marshall's *Congo* was a little dumb and almost universally reviled by critics, but this adaptation of one of Michael Crichton's less-noticed novels pulled its plow. It's a mélange of high-tech need for a mysterious crystal found only in Africa, an Africa presented as one last truly mysterious continent, a lost city and a vanished people, a tribe of previously unknown gray gorillas who function as savage security guards until wiped out by our heroes' automatic weapons and a providentially exploding volcano, and the issue of ape-human communication. Silly? Yes. Fun? I thought so.

Ditto for Tobe Hooper's *The Mangler*, a modest but entertaining version of Stephen King's short story. Set atmospherically in Maine, utilizing the great set piece of an old steam laundry's huge mangle, this horror film of machinery gone thoroughly possessed, amok, and absolutely mad delivers proper recompense for the time spent watching it. Ted Levine's a properly stalwart protagonist; and Robert Englund does very well as the aging, gimpy, crusty owner of the cleaning plant.

Mortal Kombat? Well, it had Christopher Lambert as a mystical authority figure. Then there was *Mighty Morphin Power Rangers*. Think of this one as Jackie Chan for kiddies. *Virtuosity* featured Denzel Washington in a cyber-melodrama that unsuccessfully tried to blend VR programs with AI creatures, along with instant cloned bodies. Brett Leonard directed, achieving more (though not a whole lot, ultimately) than he did with his earlier 1995 movie, an absolute hash of an adaptation of Dean Koontz's *Hideaway*.

Two of the other cyberpunkish thrillers last year were *The Net* and *Hackers*. The former had the always charming Sandra Bullock as the endangered protagonist, and the latter featured Fisher Stevens as the not-terribly-menacing bad guy with a crazed plan to capsize large numbers of supertankers and cause an ecological disaster. The primary technical interest of these two movies was to figure out how to make something visually interesting out of characters basically just sitting around and typing into computers. Clearly it's a technical and esthetic problem that has yet to be solved.

And, of course, there was the debacle of Sylvester Stallone in *Judge Dredd*. Danny Cannon directed this expensive version of the British comic book about a ruined future in which mega-cities are governed by the judges, men and women who have the power to investigate crime, arrest, try, convict, judge, and execute, all in one handy power-fantasy package. The look of the film is impeccable. Visually, it's a wonderfully realized image of the original art. But for god knows what reason, Stallone seems to have a difficult time acting the part of a comic book hero. Strange. On the other hand, Armand Assante looks quite convincing, playing Stallone's Evil Twin.

For lush, romantic, perhaps a touch florid, historical fantasy, I'll recommend *First Knight*. How can you lose with Sean Connery playing the aging Arthur? Richard Gere as Lancelot and Julia Ormond as Guinevere did fine. Ben Cross didn't get nearly enough credit for being a thoughtfully swinish Mordred. Every once in a while, Jerry Zucker's direction and staging seemed to bog down in the deeply rutted paths of historical epics gone by, but then the visuals (including Connery) would rise and save the day.

Finally I've got to say that the best bad movie of the year is *The Scarlet Letter*, directed by Roland Joffe, written by (a card in the credits says this was "freely adapted" from Nathaniel Hawthorne) Douglas Day Stewart, starring Demi Moore, Gary Oldman, and Robert Duvall. You've all heard the snide jokes, no doubt chuckled at the critical derision. But did you actually see this unbelievably flightless bird? You should. Think of it as bizarre fantasy, on one hand a parody of everything Hollywood and big budgets can do wrong; on the other, picture this as a magnificent *Monty Python* send-up—but without a single punch line. You haven't lived until you've stared, amazed, at the scene where the mystic black serving wench Tituba sits in the antique Puritan hot tub in Hester Prynne's kitchen, enjoying vicarious psychic sexual fantasies as a dyed scarlet bird shuttles to the barn where Hester and the Reverend Dimmesdale are (literally) having a roll in the hay. Now that's show-biz. But I doubt even that would have lessened the drop-out rate if the Hollywood version were the edition of Hawthorne's classic that was taught in high school. Oh yeah, and don't miss the close-ups of Puritan Hester's multiply pierced ears. She was ahead of her time. But the film isn't. Great trashy fun.

B Movies

Once upon a time, B movies were called that because they were the cheap quickies ground out by the studios to fill the B side of double bills in first standard movie houses, then in drive-ins. Well, there aren't many double features anymore, a practice killed by simple scheduling economics. And there are about as many drive-in theaters still functioning. That's too bad, but that's also another topic for a different venue.

These days the equivalent of B movies is the inexpensive feature film fabricated for cable or for the direct-to-video market. Low budgets and unknown casts don't necessarily predicate a wretched product. A good script, a dedicated talent, an obsessive vision can sometimes lead to absolutely wonderful gems hiding in the gravel of abbreviated late-night program guide listings or garish and indistinguishable one-from-the-other cassette cases on endless racks in video stores.

A lot of movies end up in these venues. No human being can ferret them all out, then watch and winnow them—not and keep both sanity and some semblance of a life. I see some. And I depend on tips from friends with both good sensibilities and more stamina.

Let me offer an example of what a person interested in low-budget films of the fantastic has to slog through. Gary Jonas, writer and video counter manager, kept a log of 1995 new releases for me. Here's a sampling: *Castle Freak* (a troubled family moves into the Italian castle they've inherited, only to find the place haunted by a sadistic and malevolent creature), *Children of the Corn III: Urban Harvest* ("a reign of mind-numbing terror"—absolutely apt, though I'm tempted to strike "terror"), *Android Affair*, *Embrace of the Vampire*, *Jacko* (with Brinke Stevens and Linnea Quigley), *The Fear* ("a wooden demon named Monty"), *The Howling: New Moon Rising*, *Ice Cream Man* (Clint Howard and Sandahl Bergman star as the character of the title, "dispenses bone-chilling terror along with frozen treats containing horrific surprises"), *Leprechaun 3* (in which the estimable Warwick Davis, dressed all in green and in fangs, makes it to Las Vegas), *Carnosaur 2*, *Darkman II: Return of Durant* (which at least featured Arnold Vosloo, along with Larry Drake), *Relative Fear* ("Is murder in the child's blood?"), *Witchboard: The Possession*, *Sorceress* ("Combine black magic and the pleasures of the flesh"—Linda Blair starred), *Sleepstalker: The Sandman's Last Rites* ("As a boy, a reporter witnesses the death of his parents by a serial killer who is caught and put to death, only to have him reborn as a supernatural executioner"), *Witchcraft 7: Judgment Hour* ("An attorney . . . battles an evil as old as mankind—a coven of vampires!"—no comment, my bro's a lawyer), *Voodoo* ("A sinister and evil presence lies deep in the heart of L.A."—again, no comment).

Want more? There's *Attack of the 60 Foot Centerfold, Automatic, 8 Man, Biohazard: The Alien Force, Deadlock-2, Cosmic Slop, The Companion, Dragon Fury, Digital Man, Death Machine, Dark Future, Cybertracker 2, Evolver, Expect No Mercy, Cyberzone, Cyborg 3—The Recycler, Galaxis, Hologram Man, Heatseeker, Harrison Bergeron, Nightscare, Nemesis 2, Mutant Species, Project Metalbeast-DNA Overload, Project Shadowchaser 3000, Nightscare, Timemaster, Solar Force, T-Force*, and on and on.

So are they all bad? Of course not. On the other hand, I had hopes when I tuned in Stella Stevens playing a tough old lady who comes back from the dead to give what-for to her greedy relatives in *The Granny*. I hope she had fun appearing in this feature. I didn't have much fun watching it.

And then there was the Showtime feature film of *Fist of the North Star*, a futuristic adventure based on Japanese manga. It even had people like Chris Penn and Costas Mandylor in it. I couldn't finish—and I have the patience to watch almost anything. It was essentially *Road Warrior* with nice production values and some metaphysics thrown in. But my god, was it dull for an action picture. Clint Howard overacted well, however.

There are the occasional rays of light. Harlan Ellison, someone I wouldn't expect to spend a whole lot of time soaking up cheap late-night horror films, told me, "Bryant, you gotta see a little movie called *Shrunken Heads*." So I did. Hey, it's not perfect, but it's sure entertaining. Richard Elfman directed from the mostly smart script by Matthew Bright— maybe you can figure out how the main theme of this Full Moon production was written by famed musical talent, Danny Elfman. It's set in a digitized city that brings Tim Burton settings to mind. Three teenaged boys get into trouble with the local gang and are shot to death for their insolence. Julius Harris, playing Mr. Sumatra, the proprietor of the neighborhood newsstand, saws their heads off and uses his finely honed vodoun talents (he was a Tonton Macoute officer and a magician back in Haiti) to bring them to life. Our young lads find themselves as mostly disembodied superheroes with strange superpowers. In a film full of bizarre touches, perhaps the most amazing is Meg Foster, playing the local crime boss, a woman named Big Mo. Costumed and made up to look something like Michael Jackson on steroids, Foster deadpans as a lesbian lout with a blonde bimbo girlfriend and a voice right out of Damon Runyon. I suspect she did have a great deal of fun. As do we in the audience. *Shrunken Heads* isn't a perfect fantasy by any means, but it's so much fun, you won't notice. So yes, there's always a pony in there somewhere.

If you want to see a strange but engaging literary attempt to recapture some of the oddball and occasionally wondrous flavor of 1950s and 1960s B movie and drive-in pop culture, check out *It Came from the Drive-In* (DAW Books), edited by Norman Partridge and Martin H. Greenberg. Here are eighteen brand-new stories that take a variety of approaches in terms of bringing back the Hollywood sensibilities that made Roger Corman rich, powerful, and successful. There are everything from J.D./Tarzan hybrids to weird westerns, disgusto invaders from space, haunted bikers, sensitive teenaged blobs, giant bugs and bigger women, and mutants up the wazoo. It's a hoot.

Movies on TV

Fans of *Alien Nation* got a treat with a full-length TV movie called *Body and Soul*. The interstellar slavers find out where their escaped and stranded cargo have sought sanctuary. Naturally they want their property back. Most of the original cast is back, too, so the drama works just fine. The attraction of *Alien Nation* has always been centered in the characterization lent by the quality of writing and the level of acting. Even with the series' checkered production life, that involving quality has not been lost. Will it return as a new series? Not likely. But the occasional movies well may.

The Invaders returned as a spiffed up, two-part miniseries. The expansionist humanoid villains are still bent on taking our world away from us, though they've apparently used genetic reprogramming to fix the stiff-pinky syndrome that tipped folks off back when Roy

Thinnes was fighting them a couple decades ago. (Thinnes, by the way, returns in a nice cameo in this version.) Fortunately you can still tell the invaders by the fact that they smoke more, eat more red meat, and wear tackier clothing than most of the general public. Also they carry guns that shoot death rays. That's a dead giveaway. Comic Richard Belzer did yeoman service in a deadpan portrayal of a scuzzy radio talk-show host who may or may not be one of the creepozoids from outer space.

If there ever was a Stephen King novella that commended itself as a B movie project, it was *The Langoliers*. And so it came to pass, as a two-part miniseries. I'm just not sure the cast was up to it. The acting was hardly memorable. And the eponymous phenomena, the scary eating machines, the ravening meta-sharks that devour the very fabric of reality, suffered from being depicted through computer animation, alas. Sometimes literalness works against what was a wonderfully realized image in printed fiction, thanks to the active imagination.

Lifetime adapted Sherry Gottlieb's contemporary vampire novel *Love Bite* as *Deadly Love*. Susan Dey starred. This is one I didn't see. As one who read and greatly enjoyed the novel, I've been told that perhaps I shouldn't catch the rerun.

Television Series

The small screen (or the large screen, depending on your affluence and your dedication to setting up a complete home theater in your mingy East Village efficiency flat) actually saw an enormous amount of SF, fantasy, and horror programming.

Fox, of course, got most of the notice for the third and most successful season of *The X-Files*. This somewhat unpredictable mélange of science fiction, political paranoia, UFO conspiracy, dark suspense, and the supenatural continues to gather a healthy audience with spendable income. It also seems to be gathering viewers from the right-wing fringers who devoutly believe the U.S. government is a lot more adept at coordinating massive conspiratorial plots than it's probably capable of in reality. The advertisers continue to become ever more upscale. More important, Chris Carter's series continues to keep the carefully tensed-up relationship between the credulous FBI agent (David Duchovny) and the skeptical one (Gillian Anderson) vital, believable, and involving. While some of the plots don't work equally well (I was not enamored of the story that included invisible elephants . . .), others ride high with the help of wonderfully wacko details (Agent Mulder, watching a video about an alien autopsy, makes snide comments about Fox's alien autopsy special right after the station break where Fox's promo for their "documentary" aired).

Fox aired a noble experiment with *VR-5*, a virtual reality conspiracy melodrama with Lori Singer as a shy, alienated, repressed but still sexual, bright, competent technogeek protagonist. Great special effects and an intriguing story line. John Shirley worked as story editor. This one really did deserve a longer trial and more support from both network and audience. Young American females could use more pop culture role models who clearly have both brains and pluck, and who, once established as having these qualities, don't turn off the guys around them.

X-Files producer/writer alumni James Wong and Glen Morgan launched the Fox SF adventure series, *Space: Above and Beyond*. This is solid interstellar action adventure set in a not-too-distant future when U.S. Marine Corps space aviators battle the alien chigs. It's not as gritty as the space combat you get in Heinlein's *Starship Troopers* or Haldeman's *The Forever War*, but it is still pretty damn visual, with spectacular digital effects from Area 51. There's an ensemble cast of young characters who are at least competent. There are occasional touches that do well what print SF has always prided itself on doing in terms of cultural commentary. The Marine pilots are all races both genders. In an early episode Nathan (Morgan Weisser) takes his fellow space jockey Shane (Kristen Cloke) back home on leave to see the folks. Nathan's parents, without reaction or comment, treat her as she is, his military buddy. In a later episode centering around the issue of mainstream human prejudice against "tanks," the in vitro strain of humanity first bred as slave labor, then recently emancipated, it is a black crewman who is the most virulent racist. The irony is lost on all but the viewers. Cool stuff; a show with great promise.

The syndicated *Babylon 5* soared into its third season, continuing to pick up steam, verve, even better digital effects, increased excitement, a wider canvas for stories, and improved acting from the cast. J. Michael Straczynski's dream SF extravaganza is blasting toward its projected five-year story arc with panache. This story of interstellar war and politics holds escalating interest as alliances form and crumble, battles are won and lost. A recent episode showed the eerie and disturbingly alien shadow ships being excavated from ancient graves on Mars and Ganymede. There's a mysterious conspiracy to keep the ships as a hideously unstable secret weapon for certain forces on earth. There's a space battle culminating in Jupiter's gravity well. Great stuff— the kind of sense-of-wonder material that drew me to science fiction when I was a kid and kept me glued to the imagery. *Babylon 5's* really coming into its own.

Back at Star Fleet HQ, *Star Trek: Voyager* and *Deep Space 9* are still cranking along. The weather report from Trekkers seems to be that while *DS9* is finally getting more adventurous, *Voyager* is still lurching and staggering after a shaky launch. Too bad. Human space needs more competent female top officers like Kate Mulgrew.

I had some (admittedly slim) hopes for the retooling of NBC's *SeaQuest*. Roy Scheider left the boat and was replaced as captain by the wonderful Michael Ironside. In the first episode we got to see the submarine returned from interstellar space (don't ask) and plunked down in the midst of a cornfield near Bettendorf, Iowa. We also got to see Michael York as the oversexed bad guy, the leader of a future expansionist Australian empire. Things never got any better and the series went belly up.

Fox launched *Sliders*, a parallel worlds series in which the (mostly) young cast traveled each week to a different time track based on one or another slim premise: women rule and need men badly; a deadly lottery is used to control overpopulation, etc. Simplistic. The series died. I've got to admit I much preferred George R. R. Martin's earlier, more complex, vastly more sophisticated version of this premise, *Doorways*, done as an unsold pilot for ABC.

Series proliferated, thanks to syndication and cable. *Hercules: The Legendary Journeys* and *Xena: Warrior Princess* both gave viewers a healthy portion of Conanesque sword and sorcery. Kevin Sorbo plays the Big Dude, Lucy Lawless, the Tough Dudette. The action's good; the deliberate humor's even better.

Fox's *Strange Luck*, adventures in synchronicity, started up well and with some positive audience response. *Nowhere Man* is a contemporary adventure series that tries to build on *The Prisoner*, but doesn't have the courage of its convictions. The truly surreal is not welcome here. Swords are still crossed and human heads collected, as an increasingly lengthy list of immortals duke it out in the continuing *Highlander: The Series*. The syndicated vampires of *Forever Knight* can still be found haunting late-night optical fibers and sucking up pixels. *Lois and Clark* continue the adventures of Lois Lane and Superman on ABC. The comedic aliens-among-us *Third Rock from the Sun* started up boasting John Lithgow in the lead, but not too much else.

The Simpsons remain the favored animated family on Fox. Warner's *Animaniacs* are still alive, as it were, and transfusing enormous hilarity to this needy presidential election year. Spun off from *Animaniacs*, *Pinky and the Brain* gives us two escaped lab mice, one of whom is amiable and a little slow; the other has an enormous forebrain and has a new scheme each week to Take Over The World. Funny stuff. Not Kotzwinkle's *Dr. Rat*, but hey, if it were, it wouldn't be funny at all.

Showtime continued its revival of *Outer Limits*, with earlier episodes rerun on Fox. The quality level is incredibly unpredictable. For every solid episode, there's another that is flat-out dumb. Known names such as Alan Brennert and David Schow appear occasionally on the writing credits.

CBS did a fine and brave thing by launching Shaun Cassidy's *American Gothic*, an absolutely terrific contemporary dark fantasy serial set in the small town of Trinity, South

Carolina. Then the network seemed at a loss in figuring out what to do with this intense, imaginative landscape set somewhere a little right of *Twin Peaks* and just left of *Picket Fences*. Gary Cole, late of *The Brady Bunch Movie*, plays Sheriff Lucas Buck who, if he's not the Devil, certainly has a favorable service contract with Old Scratch. Prime time hasn't seen such an engaging antihero in a demon's age. *American Gothic* may need some satanic intervention if it's going to survive.

Music

Hey, I love doing this whole column, but my favorite niche to explore is mentioning what's happening with the wonderful world of imaginative storytelling in country music. Admittedly I don't usually have a lot to report. This year is no exception. At least last year I could steer you toward Doug Supernaw's exuberant tune about a stalker and Joe Diffie's exploration of chaos theory. This year there's . . . well . . . the man Kinky Friedman calls the Anti-Hank. I speak of Garth Brooks, the self-described chubby guy in the black hat. On Brooks's latest album, *Fresh Horses*, there's a really nice ballad called "The Beaches of Cheyenne." It's a tough lyric about a woman who tells her man not to come back if he rides the rodeo again. Naturally he heads out to Cheyenne Frontier Days anyhow, draws "the bull no man could ride," and proceeds to die. The woman blames herself (that's where the psychology of superstition comes in), screams a lot, and smashes up the house, then runs into the ocean. Does she die? Probably. But people keep seeing her on the beach at sunset and still see her footprints in the sand. A lot more subtle a ghost story than, say, Alan Jackson's "Midnight in Montgomery" or Concrete Blonde's "Ghost of a Texas Lady's Man," "Beaches" manages to be both tuneful and eerie.

Tattered Cover Bookstore staffer Siobhan Keleher reminded me I had managed to overlook Lyle Lovett's western/southern gothic "Creeps Like Me" from his '94 album, *I Love Everybody* (Curb/MCA). Lots of nice touches such as good old Uncle Leon in the closet and that delicate matter of Grandmother's tooth of gold and her ring, two items stolen by the song's nasty narrator. Warren Zevon's not the only first-class performer to let endearingly swinish characters narrate their songs.

Horror writer and rock drummer Trey Barker offered some catholic suggestions spanning the gulf from Broadway to strange rock. In the former category he notes the advent on the Great White Way of *Honky Tonk Highway*, a "cheesy country and western musical" about one Clint Colby, deceased C&W singer. On the first anniversary of Clint's death, his band gets together and passes his battered Stetson around from hand to hand. Whoever wears the hat is possessed by Clint's ghost and proceeds to speak and sing in the dead man's persona. Standard country songs, says Trey, but great fun. The music is by Robert Nassif-Lindsey; the book is by Richard Berg.

Barker also mentioned all new musical versions of *Cinderella* and *A Christmas Carol*, the latter re-done by Alan Menken.

Some rock suggestions from 1995: Soul Asylum's "String of Pearls" made for a good murder-driven tune. Then U2 got together with Brian Eno and, as Passengers, recorded *Original Soundtracks I* (Island). A variety of surprise visitors such as Luciano Pavarotti appear on the album. Songs such as "United Colors of Plutonium" and "Plot 180" are funky little surreal things-are-not-as-they-seem, end-of-the-world type pieces. Sting fans noted that the Police produced a *Live* album (A&M) with new mixes of classics such as "Wrapped Around Your Finger" (that archetypal Faustian bargain song) and "Every Breath You Take" (stalking at its most melodious).

Coming Attractions

By now most of you will have seen *From Dusk Til Dawn*, *Mary Reilly*, *Screamers*, and many of the other promised treasures of the new year. Perhaps even the animated version of *The Thief of Forever*. I hope you all found a proper reward.

Obituaries
by James Frenkel

Death claimed a number of fine creative talents in 1995, none more important to literature of the imagination than a man who was neither author nor artist, yet who had more influence over the course of the field than perhaps any other single person in the twentieth century. **Ian Ballantine**, 79, was nothing less than the most innovative, important publishing executive of this century. In the course of his extraordinary career, and working from the start with his wife, Betty, who was editor for many of the books they published, Ballantine started three publishing companies: Penguin Books (in the United States), Bantam Books, and Ballantine Books. In these and other ventures he was always trying things that hadn't been done before. Perhaps his most enduring contribution was what he did for fantasy publishing when Ballantine Books published "authorized" editions of *The Lord of the Rings* by J. R. R. Tolkien, after Ace Books published unauthorized editions. Ace was within the law to publish their editions, because of a loophole in the copyright law of the time, but Ballantine's editions forced Ace's off the shelves. Ballantine promoted the trilogy with a vigor and flair previously unknown to fantasy books; with an ongoing campaign for Tolkien and the subsequent establishment of Ballantine's Adult Fantasy program, Ian Ballantine did more to put fantasy on the publishing map than anyone else before or since. Ballantine's publishing innovations extended well beyond paperbacks into trade publishing and art books. As an independent editor he was largely responsible for the publication of the coffee-table illustrated books *Faeries* and *Gnomes*, both of which were best-sellers; also, under his Peacock Press imprint in the 1970s, he published trade paperback art books that were very successful; he also created the concept and published the first "mass-market hardcovers," books with enough commercial appeal to be million-copy best-sellers in hardcover, such as Chuck Yeager's autobiography and Lee Iacocca's as well. A full list of Ian Ballantine's accomplishments would take page upon page of space, but suffice it to say that he was beloved and respected by his publishing peers, his authors, and readers who knew what he did. There will never be another like him, but his legacy lives on in those whose lives he touched, including this editor's.

Among the authors who died in 1995, undoubtedly the most important to the field was **Roger Zelazny**, 58, winner of multiple Hugo and Nebula Awards for various imaginative works. His novel *Lord of Light* shook up the SF/fantasy establishment with its hip, knowing mix of fantasy, science fiction, and Eastern philosophy. It won both Hugo and Nebula Awards; his short fiction blazed new paths in the mid-1960s, striking out in many directions within a period of several years of sustained and brilliant creative energy. His most popular work was the series of novels *The Chronicles of Amber*. He collaborated with a number of other writers, including Philip K. Dick (*Deus Irae*, 1976), Fred Saberhagen (*Coils*, 1982), and Robert Sheckley. Other noteworthy works include the novels *Doorways in the Sand*, *Jack of Shadows*, and the short novel "This Immortal," which won the Hugo Award. Zelazny also edited several anthologies in the last years of his life. He was by no means finished when he died. His untimely death was a blow to all who knew him or his work. He had never stopped trying to find new ways to express his visions.

Also an important figure, in a completely different literary vein, was **Jack Finney**, 84, who was best known for two novels, *Time and Again* and *The Body Snatchers*. The latter novel was adapted for the screen three times, twice as *Invasion of the Body Snatchers*. Finney wrote fantasy and contemporary fiction, always with a marvelous gift for character and establishing a sense of place. He wrote a number of quietly effective short stories, many of which possessed a sense of the spirit of a place, which is also evident in his novel *The*

Woodrow Wilson Dime. He wrote a sequel to *Time and Again*, titled *Time After Time*, in 1995. He also wrote thrillers, including the notable *Five Against the House*.

Charles Monteith, 74, was a noted British publisher who was instrumental in the publishing careers of fine writers of diverse talents, among them William Golding. He also was the first British publisher, when he was at Faber & Faber, to recognize the potential of and support the publishing of science fiction and fantasy, in the 1950s.

Robertson Davies, 82, was a prize-winning novelist, playwright, critic, and academic whose novels brought him a measure of critical acclaim and financial success. His works were intensely spiritual in a decidedly unorthodox sense, concerned with the magic and transcendence of life. Among his best known works of fiction are *The Manticore* (1972) and *The Lyre of Orpheus* (1989). **Terry Southern**, 71, was a satiric novelist and screenwriter. His novel, *The Magic Christian*, became a film with a cult following in the late 1960s. His adaptation of the cold war novel *Red Alert* became Stanley Kubrick's brilliantly trenchant satire *Dr. Strangelove; or, How I Learned to Stop Worrying and Love the Bomb* (1963). He also wrote the screenplay for the adaptation of the comic *Barbarella*, a wildly unbridled sexual space fantasy that embodied the contradictions of the mid-1960s American cultural gestalt, and *Easy Rider* (1969), the famous road movie that brought Jack Nicholson to prominence and spawned a rash of youth exploitation films. **John Brunner**, 60, was best known for his science fiction writing, but was also the author of the fine existential fantasy cycle of stories collected in *The Compleat Traveler in Black* (1986), and a number of other trenchant, compelling stories. This British author, always pushing the limits of his range and abilities, wrote novels that tackled some of the most complex and difficult sociopolitical issues of the day. His early works were mainly adventures, but held seeds of his later, more mature works. In his most effective novels he sustained narratives that had a seriousness seldom seen in genre fiction. Winner of the Hugo Award for his spectacular tour de force *Stand on Zanzibar*, Brunner also was the recipient of the British Fantasy Award, the Prix Apollo, and other awards. In the later 1970s and the 1980s his work lost some of its fire, but he was an entertaining and thought-provoking author to the end, which came too soon for one of the field's major intellects.

Edward Whittemore, 62, was the author of the unique and fascinating literary tetralogy, *The Jerusalem Quartet*. Essentially works of fantasy, the four novels are extraordinary in the depth of their passion and the sweep of their imaginative scope. **Michael Ende**, 65, was the internationally acclaimed author of children's and adult fantasies. His best known work was *The Neverending Story* (1983). Translated into many languages, it was produced as a film in 1984. Other books include *Momo, The Gray Gentleman* (1974), and *The Night of Wishes* (1992), among others.

Donald Pleasence, 75, was a serious and versatile British actor of stage, screen, and television who created many memorable character roles, including that of the villain Blofeld in *You Only Live Twice* (1967). **Woody Strode**, 80, was a character actor for over forty years. He was one of the first black professional football players, and appeared in many action films and a number of fantasy and horror films, as well as many television shows. **Peter Cook**, 57, the British actor and comedian, was a major talent in the world of comedy in the 1960s and 1970s. Paired with Dudley Moore for many years, Cook was the tall one. Together they were half of the creative team of the revue "Beyond the Fringe," and appeared in a number of films, including the wonderful comic Victorian romp *The Wrong Box*, and others. **Severn Darden**, 65, was an actor and improvisational comedian who worked in theater, film, and television. He was a founder of Chicago's Second City troupe, the source of dozens of today's most talented comics. He appeared in a number of episodes of *The Twilight Zone* and other television shows, as well as film fantasies such as *The President's Analyst*.

Patricia Highsmith, 74, was best known as a mystery writer. Her novel *Strangers on a Train* was adapted for the famous Alfred Hitchcock film. She won the Silver Dagger and other awards in her long and varied career. In addition to her marvelous work in the mystery field, she wrote fantasy and horror, including the novel *Edith's Diary* (1977), as well as some superlative fantastical short fiction. **Edith Pargeter**, 82, also known as **Ellis Peters**, was best known for her *Brother Cadfael* medieval mysteries under the latter name. She also wrote fantasies under her own name, including *The City Lies Four-Square* (1939), *By Firelight* (1947), published in the United States as *By This Strange Fire* in 1948, and a collection, *The Lily Hand and Other Stories*. She received the Mystery Writers of America Award and the Crime Writers' Association Silver Dagger for her mysteries. Her mysteries were marked by sharp characterization and strong period flavor. **Andrew Nelson Lytle**, 92, was a writer and teacher who wrote the novel *A Name for Evil* (1947), a psychological ghost story. He had a distinguished career as a creative writing professor at the University of the South and the University of Florida. His most famous student was Flannery O'Connor.

Isidore "Friz" Freling, 95, was an animator who worked for Disney when he started out, then did "Krazy Kat," and finally found bliss at Warner Bros., where he was an animator and director for three decades. When Warner stopped making cartoons, he formed a company and produced Pink Panther cartoons. He was one of the leading lights of the Warner production group that made that studio world-famous for its inventive, madcap cartoons.

Ida Lupino, 77, was a noted actress and director. She was honored for a number of fine performances on stage and screen in the 1940s and 1950s. She was also well regarded for her direction of a number of low budget but finely produced films. She became well known for her numerous appearances in *Four Star Playhouse* on television from 1952 to 1956, and for the situation comedy she produced in which she and her third husband, Howard Duff, costarred, *Mr. Adams and Eve*.

David Wayne, 81, was an actor who played in innumerable television productions, many films, and on Broadway, where he won the first Tony Award, for playing a leprechaun in *Finian's Rainbow*. His face was very familiar to television viewers of the sixties and seventies when he was extremely busy. He played the Mad Hatter in the 1960s *Batman* series.

Miklos Rozsa, 88, was an Oscar-winning composer who composed the scores for many film classics, including such fantasies as *A Thief of Baghdad* (1940), and *Spellbound* (1940). He won the Acadamy Award for the latter score. **Michael Hordern**, 83, was a stage actor who also did a considerable amount of screen work as a character actor in a great variety of British and American films, including *Young Sherlock Holmes* (1985) and other fantasy and horror films. **Elizabeth Montgomery**, 62, was an actress whose greatest work was done on television in films and series. She is best known for her long-running series *Bewitched*. **Jack Clayton**, 73, was a British director of many documentaries and feature films, including *Something Wicked This Way Comes* (1982). **Ed Flanders**, 60, was a Tony and Emmy Award–winning actor best known for his continuing role on the television series *St. Elsewhere*. Among his film credits are roles in *Salem's Lot* (1979) and *The Exorcist III* (1990). He committed suicide. **Lana Turner**, 75, was a Hollywood star, glamorous and always in the eye of publicity. She became a star in *Dr. Jekyll and Mr. Hyde* (1941), and starred in a number of films in the 1950s. Her private life became notoriously public when her daughter stabbed to death Turner's gangster lover, Johnny Stompanato, in 1958. **Tony Azito**, 46, was a stage actor who appeared in a number of Broadway and Off-Broadway productions, as well as in some film and television productions. His most memorable role was probably as the leader of the Keystone Kops in the 1981 New York Shakespeare production of *The Pirates of Penzance*.

Howard W. Koch, 93, was an Oscar Award–winning screenwriter, creator of such screenplays as *Casablanca* and *The Best Years of Our Lives*. He also wrote the radio script for *War of the Worlds*, which Orson Welles produced in 1938, creating a famous Halloween panic. He was blacklisted in the 1950s, along with many other fine creative people in the film business, because he was suspected of having Communist ties. He produced various low budget films in the late 1950s, including two with Boris Karloff in starring roles.

Obituaries

Brigid Brophy, 66, was a noted literary author and social activist. Her novel, *Palace without Chairs* (1978), was her one fantasy. She wrote a number of other works, including four plays, six other novels, and fourteen other books. Among the social causes she worked for was the British law giving authors royalty payments based on the frequency with which their books are checked out from libraries. **(Walter) Ryerson "Johnny" Johnson**, 94, was a pulp fiction writer who wrote in all the pulp genres, including Doc Savage's adventures, under the house name, Kenneth Robeson. Later in his career he also wrote a number of children's books. **Margaret St. Clair**, 84, was a writer of science fiction and fantasy. Writing under the name Idris Seabright as well as her own, she wrote a number of novels in the pulps, and many short stories. **Elleston Trevor**, 75, was a British author of thrillers and other novels, including novels of supernatural horror and children's fantasies. His most successful books were the *Quiller* spy series written under the name Adam Hall, especially *The Quiller Memorandum*, which was made into a very effective film.

Charlotte Franke, 60, was a German author, translator, and editor who wrote at least ten novels, published mostly under her maiden name, Charlotte Winheller, and translated a number of issues of *The Magazine of Fantasy & Science Fiction*. She was active in the Milford SF Writers Conference for many years. She was married to the well known German SF writer, Dr. Herbert W. Franke. They were divorced. **Diane Cleaver**, 53, was an editor, literary agent, and writer. She worked with Lawrence Ashmead when he was at Doubleday, and became an editor there. She was the editor of the Science Fiction Book Club for a time, before going into agenting and writing. **Stanley D. McNail**, 77, was a poet, editor, and publisher. His poetry tended toward horror and the macabre. His works were collected in various volumes, including *Something Breathing* (1965), and *Tea in the Mortuary*. He founded the journal *Galley Sail Review*. **G. C. Edmondson**, 72, was a writer of fantasy, science fiction, and adventures and thrillers in many other genres. He wrote both solo and collaborative works, including the fantasy *The Black Magician* (with C. M. Kortlan). **May Sarton**, 83, was best known for her poetry. She was the author of the cat fantasy *The Fur Person* (1957). **Nigel D. Findley**, 35, was a prolific and popular author of fantasy games and novels. **Janice Elliott**, 63, was a British author who wrote some twenty-three novels and several children's books, including the Young Adult fantasies *The King Awakes* (1987) and *The Empty Throne* (1988).

Cy Endfield, 81, was a screenwriter and director. He wrote the screenplay for *Mysterious Island*, adapted from Jules Verne's novel, and various other films, fantasy and otherwise. His best directorial effort was undoubtedly *Zulu* (1964). **William H. D. Cotrell Jr.**, 89, worked for Disney for many years, as a cameraman and animation director, and then as head of the division that designed and built Disneyland. He worked on such classic films as *Alice in Wonderland* and *Pinocchio*. **Al Adamson**, 66, was a director of many low budget horror films, including *Satan's Sadists* and *Blood of Dracula's Castle*. He was murdered, his body found buried under his house. **Sidney Sion**, 84, was a radio scriptwriter for a number of shows in the golden age of radio, including *The Shadow*.

Patsy Ruth Miller, 91, was a film actress. She played the gypsy girl Esmeralda in Lon Chaney's 1923 silent film version of *The Hunchback of Notre Dame*. **Cecil H. Roy**, 94, was an actor who voiced many animated characters, including Casper the Friendly Ghost. British ballet dancer **Prudence Hyman**, 81, was also an actress, playing the title role in Hammer Films' *The Gorgon* (1964). **Iris Adrian**, 81, was a dancer who started out in the Ziegfeld Follies and acted in over 150 films, including *Mighty Joe Young*. **Derek Ford**, 62, was a British screenwriter and director. He cowrote, with his brother Donald, the horror films *A Study in Terror* and *Corruption*; on his own he wrote *The House that Vanished* and *Don't Open Till Christmas*. British actor **Patric Knowles**, 84, appeared in many films, including a number of 1940s horror classics. **Derek Meddings**, 64, was a British special effects director whose credits included *Superman* and several "James Bond" films. Mexican film director **Raphael Portillo**, 79, directed over fifty features, including *The Aztec Mummy* (1957) and other horror and fantasy films. British actor **John Van Eyssen,** 73, was best known for the role of Jonathan Harker in the 1958 *Horror of Dracula*. He appeared in various other films. **Robert Emhardt,** 80, was a character actor who played tall, cold villains. He was in numerous film and television productions, including the TV series *Alfred Hitchcock Presents*. **Martha Raye,** 78, was a vaudevillian and comedienne in radio and films. She appeared in dozens of films, including *Alice in Wonderland* (1985).

And finally, **Mickey Mantle,** 63, wasn't a creator of fantasy in the conventional sense, but in a very real way he lived a life that for millions of baseball fans young and old represented the ultimate fantasy. He was the quintessential baseball hero for a generation, the successor to the previous New York Yankees icon in center field, Joe DiMaggio, capable of clouting mighty home runs, fielding his position well, hitting for both power and average, often best in the clutch. He also was a tragic figure, raised dirt-poor in Oklahoma, groomed by his father for baseball, cursed to inherit his father's degenerative muscle disease, and ultimately victim to his own drinking. Idolized by fans, the Mick, as he was known, never realized how his drinking and partying hurt his career and ultimately brought his doom, until it was far too late. He was a true-life tragic folk hero.

HOME FOR CHRISTMAS
Nina Kiriki Hoffman

Nina Kiriki Hoffman has earned a reputation as one of the best of the new generation of speculative fiction writers, with work that ranges from fantasy (like the following story) to darker stories of pure horror. Hoffman lives in Eugene, Oregon, and has published many stories in magazines and anthologies over the last few years. Her dark fantasy novel, *The Thread that Binds the Bones*, set in modern-day Oregon, is highly recommended, as is its sequel, *The Silent Strength of Stones*.

"Home for Christmas" is a poignant tale of contemporary magic, and Hoffman's young heroine is a character who lingers in the mind long after the story is done. It comes from the January issue of *The Magazine of Fantasy & Science Fiction*.

—T.W.

Matt spread the contents of the wallet on the orange shag rug in front of her, looking at each item. Three oil company charge cards; an auto club card, an auto insurance card; a driver's license that identified the wallet's owner as James Plainfield, thirty-eight, with an address bearing an apartment number in one of the buildings downtown; a gold MasterCard with a hologram of the world on it; a gold AmEx card; six hundred and twenty-three dollars, mostly in fifties; a phone credit card; a laminated library card; five tan business cards with "James Plainfield, Architect" and a phone number embossed on them in brown ink; receipts from a deli, a bookstore, an art supply store; a ticket stub from a horror movie; and two scuffed color photographs, one of a smiling woman and the other of a sullen teenage girl.

The wallet, a soft camel-brown calfskin, was feeling distress.—He's lost without me—it cried,—he needs me; he could be dead by now. Without me in his back pocket he's only half himself.—

Matt patted it and yawned. She had been planning to walk the frozen streets later that night while people were falling asleep, getting her fill of Christmas Eve dreams for another year, feeding the hunger in her that only quieted when she was so exhausted she fell asleep herself. But her feet were wet and she was tired enough to sleep now. She was going to try an experiment: this year, hole up, drink cocoa, and remember all her favorite dreams from Christmas Eves past. If that worked, maybe she could change her lifestyle, stay someplace long enough to . . . to . . .

she wasn't sure. She hadn't stayed in any one place for more than a month in years.

"We'll go find him tomorrow morning," she said to the wallet. Although tomorrow was Christmas. Maybe he would have things to do, and be hard to find.

—Now!—cried the wallet.

Matt sighed and leaned against the water heater. Her present home was the basement of somebody's house; the people were gone for the Christmas holidays and the house, lonely, had invited her in when she was looking through its garbage cans a day after its inhabitants had driven off in an overloaded station wagon.

—He'll starve,—moaned the wallet,—he'll run out of gas and be stranded. The police will stop him and arrest him because he doesn't have identification. We have to rescue him *now*.—

Matt had cruised town all day, listening to canned Christmas music piped to the freezing outdoors by stores, watching street-corner Santas ringing bells, cars fighting for parking spaces, shoppers whisking in and out of stores, their faces tense; occasionally she saw bright dreams, a parent imagining a child's joy at the unwrapping of the asked-for toy, a man thinking about what his wife's face would look like when she saw the diamond he had bought for her, a girl finding the perfect book for her best friend. There were the dreams of despair, too: grief because five dollars would not stretch far enough, grief because the one request was impossible to fill, grief because weariness made it too hard to go on.

She had wandered, wrapped in her big olive-drab army coat, never standing still long enough for anyone to wonder or object, occasionally ducking into stores and soaking up warmth before heading out into the cold again, sometimes stalling at store windows to stare at things she had never imagined needing until she saw them, then laughing that feeling away. She didn't need anything she didn't have.

She had stumbled over the wallet on her way home. She wouldn't have found it—it had slipped down a grate—except that it was broadcasting distress. The grate gapped its bars and let her reach down to get the wallet; the grate was tired of listening to the wallet's whining.

—Now,—the wallet said again.

She loaded all the things back into the wallet, getting the gas cards in the wrong place at first, until the wallet scolded her and told her where they belonged. "So," Matt said, slipping the wallet into her army jacket pocket, "if he's lost, stranded, and starving, how are we going to find him?"

—He's probably at the Time-Out. The bartender lets him run a tab sometimes. He might not have noticed I'm gone yet.—

She knew the Time-Out, a neighborhood bar not far from the corner where James Plainfield's apartment building stood. Two miles from the suburb where her temporary basement home was. She sighed, pulled still-damp socks from their perch on a heating duct, and stuffed her freezing feet into them, then laced up the combat boots. She could always put the wallet outside for the night so she could get some sleep; but what if someone else found it? It would suffer agonies; few people understood nonhuman things the way she did, and fewer still went along with the wishes of inanimate objects.

Anyway, there was a church on the way to downtown, and she always liked to see a piece of the midnight service, when a whole bunch of people got all excited about a baby being born, believing for a little while that a thing like that could actually change the world. If she spent enough time searching this guy out, maybe she'd get to church this year.

She slipped out through the kitchen, suggesting that the back door lock itself behind her. Then she headed downtown, trying to avoid the dirty slush piles on the sidewalk.

"Hey," said the bartender as she slipped into the Time-Out. "You got I.D., kid?"

Matt shrugged. "I didn't come in to order anything." She wasn't sure how old she was, but she knew it was more than twenty-one. Her close-cut hair, mid-range voice, and slight, sexless figure led people to mistake her for a teenage boy, a notion she usually encouraged. No one had formally identified her since her senior year of high school, years and years ago. "I just came to find a James Plainfield. He here?"

A man seated at the bar looked up. He was dressed in a dark suit, but his tie was emerald green, and his brown hair was a little longer than business-length. He didn't look like his driver's license picture, but then, who did? "Whatcha want?" he said.

"Wanted to give you your wallet. I found it in the street."

"Wha?" He leaned forward, squinting at her.

She walked to the bar and set his wallet in front of him, then turned to go.

"Hey!" he said, grabbing her arm. She decided maybe architecture built up muscles more than she had suspected. "You pick my pocket, you little thief?"

"Sure, that's why I searched you out to return your wallet. Put it in your pocket, Bud. The other pocket. I think you got a hole in your regular wallet pocket. The wallet doesn't like being out in the open."

His eyes narrowed. "Just a second," he said, keeping his grip on her arm. With his free hand he opened the wallet and checked the bulging currency compartment, then looked at the credit cards. His eyebrows rose. He released her. "Thanks, kid. Sorry. I'd really be in trouble without this."

"Yeah, that's what it said."

"What do you mean?"

She shrugged, giving him a narrow grin and stuffing her hands deep into her pockets. He studied her, looking at the soaked shoulders of her jacket, glancing down at her battered boots, their laces knotted in places other than the ends.

"Hey," he said softly. "Hey. How long since you ate?"

"Lunch," she said. With all the people shopping, the trash cans in back of downtown restaurants had been full of leftovers after the lunch rush.

He frowned at his watch. "It's after nine. Does your family know where you are?"

"Not lately," she said. She yawned, covering it with her hand. Then she glanced at the wallet. "This the guy?"

—Yes, oh yes, oh yes, oh joy.—

"Good. 'Bye, Bud. Got to be getting home."

"Wait. There's a reward." He pulled out two fifties and handed them to her. "And you let me take you to dinner? And drive you home afterwards? Unless you have your own car."

She folded the fifties, slipped them into the battered leather card case she used as a wallet, and thought about this odd proposition. She squinted at the empty glass on the bar. "Which number are you," she muttered to it, "and what were you?"

—I cradled an old-fashioned,—said the glass,—and from the taste of his lips, it was not his first.—

"You talking to my drink?" Amusement quirked the corner of his mouth.

Matt smiled, and took a peek at his dreamscape. She couldn't read thoughts, but she could usually see what people were imagining. Not with Plainfield, though. Instead of images, she saw lists and blueprints, the writing on them too small and stylized for her to read.

He said, "Look, there's a restaurant right around the corner. We can walk to it, if you're worried about my driving."

"Okay," she said.

He left some cash on the bar, waved at the bartender, and walked out, leaving Matt to follow.

The restaurant was a greasy spoon; the tables in the booths were topped with red linoleum and the menus bore traces of previous meals. At nine on Christmas Eve, there weren't many people there, but the waitress seemed cheery when she came by with coffee mugs and silverware. Plainfield drank a whole mugful of coffee while Matt was still warming her hands. His eyes were slightly bloodshot.

"So," he said as he set his coffee mug down.

Matt added cream and sugar, lots of it, stirred, then sipped.

"So," said Plainfield again.

"So," Matt said.

"So did you learn all my deep dark secrets from my wallet? You did look through it, right?"

"Had to find out who owned it."

"What else did you find out?"

"You carry a lot of cash. Your credit's good. You're real worried about your car, and you're an architect. There's two women in your life."

"So do we have anything in common?"

"No. I got no cash,—'cept what you gave me—no credit, no car, no relationships, and I don't build anything." She studied the menu. She wondered if he liked young boys. This could be a pickup, she supposed, if he was the sort of man who took advantage of chance opportunities.

The waitress came by and Matt ordered a big breakfast, two of everything, eggs, bacon, sausages, pancakes, ham slices, and biscuits in gravy. Christmas Eve dinner. What the hell. She glanced at Plainfield, saw him grimacing. She grinned, and ordered a large orange juice. Plainfield ordered a side of dry wheat toast.

"What do you want with me, anyway?" Matt asked.

He blinked. "I . . . I thought you must be an amazing person, returning a wallet like mine intact, and I wanted to find out more about you."

"Why?"

"You are a kid, aren't you?"

She stared at him, keeping her face blank.

"Sorry," he said. He looked out the window at the night street for a moment, then turned back. "My wife has my daughter this Christmas, and I . . ." He frowned. "You know how when you lose a tooth, your tongue keeps feeling the hollow space?"

"You really don't know anything about me."

"Except that you're down on your luck but still honest. That says a lot to me."

"I'm not your daughter."

He lowered his eyes to stare at his coffee mug. "I know. I know. It's just that Christmas used to be such a big deal. Corey and I, when we first got together, we decided we'd give each other the Christmases we never had as kids, and we built it all up, tree, stockings, turkey, music, cookies, toasting the year behind and the year ahead and each other. Then when we had Linda it was even better; we could plan and buy and wrap and have secrets just for her, and she loved it. Now the apartment's empty and I don't want to go home."

Matt had spent last Christmas in a shelter. She had enjoyed it. Toy drives had supplied presents for all the kids, and food drives had given everybody real food. They had been without so much for so long that they could taste how good everything was. Dreams came true, even if only for one day.

This year. . . . She sat for a moment and remembered one of the dreams she'd seen a couple of years ago. A ten-year-old girl thinking about the loving she'd give a baby doll, just the perfect baby doll, if she found it under the tree tomorrow. Matt could almost feel the hugs. Mm. Still as strong a dream as when she had first collected it. Yes! She had them inside her, and they still felt fresh.

Food arrived and Matt ate, dipping her bacon in the egg yolks and the syrup, loving the citrus bite of the orange juice after the sopping, pillowy texture and maple sweetness of the pancakes. It was nice having first choice of something on a restaurant plate.

"Good appetite," said Plainfield. He picked out a grape jelly from an assortment the waitress had brought with Matt's breakfast and slathered some on his dry toast, took a bite, frowned. "Guess I'm not really hungry."

Matt smiled around a mouthful of biscuits and gravy.

"So," Plainfield said when Matt had eaten everything and was back to sipping coffee.

"So," said Matt.

"So would you come home with me?"

She peeked at his dreamscape, found herself frustrated again by graphs instead of pictures. "Exactly what did you have in mind, Bud?"

He blinked, then set his coffee cup down. His pupils flicked wide, staining his gray eyes black. "Oh. That sounds bad. What I really want, I guess, is not to be alone on Christmas, but I don't mean that in a sexual way. Didn't occur to me a kid would hear it like that."

"Hey," said Matt. Could anybody be this naive?

"You could go straight to sleep if that's what you want. What I miss most is just the sense that someone else is in the apartment while I'm falling asleep. I come from a big family, and living alone just doesn't feel right, especially on Christmas."

"Do you know how stupid this is? I could have a disease, I could be the thief of the century, I could smoke in bed and burn your playhouse down. I could just be really annoying."

"I don't care," he said.

She said, "Bud, you're asking to get taken." Desperation like his was something she usually stayed away from.

"Jim. The name's Jim."

"And how am I supposed to know whether you're one of these Dahmer dudes, keep kids' heads in your fridge?" She didn't seriously consider him a risk, but she would have felt better if she could have gotten a fix on his dreams. She had met some real psychos—their dreams gave them away—and when she closed dream-eyes, they looked almost more like everybody else than everybody else did.

He stared down at his coffee mug, his shoulders slumped. "I guess there is no way to know anymore, is there?"

"Oh, what the hell," she said.

He looked at her, a slow smile surfacing. "You mean it?"

"I've done some stupid things in my time. I tell you, though . . ." she began, then touched her lips. She had been about to threaten him. She never threatened people. Relax. Give the guy a Christmas present of the appearance of trust. "Never mind. This was one great dinner. Let's go."

He dropped a big tip on the table, then headed for the cash register. She followed. "You have any . . . luggage or anything?"

"Not with me." She thought of her belongings, stowed safely in the basement two miles away.

"There's a drugstore right next to my building. We could pick up a toothbrush and whatever else you need there."

Smiling, she shook her head in disbelief. "Okay."

The drugstore was only three blocks from the restaurant; they walked. Plainfield bought Matt an expensive boar-bristle toothbrush, asking her what color she wanted. When she told him purple, he found a purple one, then said, "You want a magazine? Go take a look." Shaking her head again, she headed over to the magazine rack and watched him in the shoplifting mirror. He was sneaking around the aisles of the store looking at things. Incredible. He was going to play Santa, and buy her a present. Kee-rist. Maybe she should get him something.

She looked at school supplies, found a pen and pencil set (the best thing she could think of for someone who thought in graphs), wondered how to get them to the cash register without him seeing them. Then she realized there was a cash register at both doors, so she went to the other one.

By the time he finished skulking around she was back studying the magazines. It had been years since she had looked at magazines. There were magazines about wrestlers, about boys on skateboards, about muscle cars, about pumping iron, about house blueprints, men's fashions, skinny women. In the middle of one of the thick women's fashion magazines she found an article about a murder in a small town, and found herself sucked down into the story, another thing she hadn't experienced in a long time. She didn't read often; too many other things to look at.

"You want that one?"

"What? No." She put the magazine back, glanced at the shopping bag he was carrying. It was bulging and bigger than a breadbox. "You must of needed a lot of bathroom stuff," she said.

He nodded. "Ready?"

"Sure."

On the way into his fifth-floor apartment, she leaned against the front door and thought,—Are you friendly?—

—I do my job. I keep Our Things safe inside and keep other harmful things out.—

—I'm not really one of Our Things—Matt thought.—I have an invitation, though.—

—I understand that.—

—If I need to leave right away, will you let me out, even if Jim doesn't want me to leave?—

The door mulled this over, then said,—All right.—

—Thanks.—She stroked the wood, then turned to look at the apartment.

She had known he had money—those gold cards, that cash. She liked the way it manifested. The air was tinted with faint scents of lemon furniture polish and evergreen. The couch was long but looked comfortable, upholstered in a geometric pattern of soft, intense lavenders, indigos, grays. The round carpet on the hardwood floor was deep and slate blue; the coffee table was old wood, scarred here and there. A black metal spiral plant-stand supported green, healthy philodendrons and Rabbit Track Marantas. Everything looked lived-in or lived-with.

To the left was a dining nook. A little Christmas tree decorated with white lights, tinsel, and paper angels stood on the dining table.

"I thought Linda was going to come," Plainfield said, looking at the tree. There were presents under it. "Corey didn't tell me until last night that they were going out of state. You like cocoa?"

"Sure," said Matt, thinking about her Christmas Eve dream, cocoa and other peoples' memories.

"Uh—what would you like me to call you?"

"Matt," said Matt.

"Matt," he said, and nodded. "Kitchen's through there." He gestured toward the dining nook. "I make instant cocoa, but it's pretty good."

Matt looked at him a moment, then headed for the kitchen.

"Be there in a sec," said Jim, heading toward a dark hallway to the right.

—Cocoa?—she thought in the kitchen. Honey-pale wooden cupboard doors wore carved wooden handles in the shape of fancy goldfish, with inlaid gem eyes. White tiles with a lavender border covered the counters; white linoleum tiles inset with random squares of sky blue, rose, and violet surfaced the floor. A pale spring green refrigerator stood by the window, and a small green card table sat near it, with three yellow-cushioned chairs around it. Just looking at the room made Matt smile.

—Who are you?—asked the refrigerator as it hummed.

—A visitor.—

—Where's the little-girl-one who stands there and holds my door open and lets my cold out?—

—I don't think she's coming,—Matt said. She wasn't sure if a refrigerator had a time sense, but decided to ask.—How often is she here?—

—Every time Man puts ice cream in my coldest part. There's ice cream there now.—

Ah ha, Matt thought. She went to the stove, found a modern aqua-enameled teakettle.—May I use you to heat water?—she thought at it.

—Yes yes yes!—Its imagination glowed with the pleasurable anticipation of heat and simmer and expansion.

She ran water into it, greeted the stove as she set the teakettle on the gas burner, then asked the kitchen about mugs. A cupboard creaked open. She patted the door and reached inside for two off-white crockery mugs. A drawer opened to offer her spoons. The whole kitchen was giggling to itself. It had never before occurred to the kitchen that it could move things through its own choice.

—Cocoa?—thought Matt. The cupboard above the refrigerator eased open, and she could see jars of instant coffee and a round tin of instant cocoa inside, but it was out of her reach. She glanced at one of the chairs. She could bring it over—

—Hey!—cried the cocoa tin. She looked up to see it balanced on the edge of the refrigerator. She held out her hands and it dropped heavily into them, the cupboard door closing behind it.

"What?" Jim's voice sounded startled behind her.

She turned, clutching the cocoa, wondering what would happen now. Though she couldn't be sure, she got no sense of threat from him at all, and she was still in the heightened state of awareness she thought of as Company Manners. "Cocoa," she said, displaying the tin on her palms as though it were an award.

"Yeah, but—" He looked up at the cupboard, down at her hands. "But—"

The teakettle whistled—a warbling whistle, like a bird call. The burner turned itself off just as Jim glanced toward it. His eyes widened.

—Chill,—Matt thought at the kitchen.

—Want warmth?—A baseboard heater made clicking sounds as its knob turned clockwise and it kicked into action.

—No! I mean, stop acting on your own, please. Do you want to upset Jim?—

—But this is—!—The concept it showed her was delirious joy.—We never knew we could do this!—

Matt sucked on her lower lip. She'd never seen a room respond to her this way. Some things were wide awake when she met them, and leading secret lives when no one was around to see. Other things woke up and discovered they could choose movement when they talked to her, but never before so joyfully or actively.

"What—" Jim said again.

Matt walked over to the counter by the stove, popped the cocoa tin's top with a spoon.

"Uh," said Matt.

"Can you—uh, make things move around without touching them?" His voice was thin.

"No," she said.

He blinked. Looked at the cupboard over the refrigerator, at the burner control, at the baseboard heater. He shook his head. "I'm seeing things?"

"No," said Matt, spooning cocoa into the mugs. She reached for the teakettle, but before she could touch it, a pot holder jumped off a hook above the stove, gliding to land on the handle.

"Design flaw in the kettle," Jim said in a hollow voice. "Handle gets hot too."

"Oh. Thanks," she said, gripping the pot holder and the kettle and pouring hot water into the mugs. The spoon she had left in one mug lifted itself and started to stir. "Hey," she said, grabbing it.

—Let me. Let me!—

She let it go, feeling fatalistic, and the other spoon lying on the counter rattled against the tiles until she picked it up and put it in the other mug. The sight of both of them stirring in unison was almost hypnotic.

"I've been reading science fiction for years," Jim said, his voice still coming out warped, "maybe to prepare myself for this day. Telekinesis?"

"Huh?" said Matt as she set the teakettle back on the stove and hung up the pot holder.

"You move things with mind power?"

"No," she said.

"But—" The spoons still danced, crushing lumps of cocoa against the sides of the mugs, making a metal and ceramic clatter.

"I'm not doing it. They are."

"What?"

"Your kitchen," she said, "is very happy."

Cupboards clapped and drawers opened and shut. Somehow the sound of it all resembled laughter.

After a moment, Jim said, "I don't understand. I'm starting to think I must be asleep on the couch and I'm dreaming all this."

—Done,—said the spoons. Matt fished them out of the cocoa and rinsed them off.

"Okay," she said to Jim, handing him a mug.

"Okay what?"

"It's only a dream."—Thanks,—she thought to the kitchen, and headed out to the living room.

Jim followed her. She found coasters stacked on a side table and laid a couple on the coffee table, set her cocoa on one, then shrugged out of her coat and sat on the couch.

"It's only a dream?" Jim said, settling beside her.

"If that makes it easier."

He sipped cocoa. "I don't want easy. I want the truth."

"On Christmas Eve?"

He raised his eyebrows. "Are you one of Santa's elves, or something?"

She laughed.

"For an elf, you look like you could use a shower," he said.

"Even for a human I could."

He fished the toothbrush out of his breast pocket and handed it to her. "Magic wand," he said.

"Thanks." She laid it on the table and drank some cocoa. She was so full from dinner that she wasn't hungry anymore, but the chocolate was enticing.

"All those things were really moving around in the kitchen, weren't they?" he said.

"Yes," she said.

"Is the kitchen haunted?"

"Kind of."

"I never noticed it before."

She drank more cocoa. Didn't need other peoples' memories at the moment; making one of her own. She wasn't sure yet whether she'd want to keep this one or not.

Jim said, "Can you point to something and make it do what you want?"

"No."

"Just try it. I dare you. Point to that cane and make it dance." He waved toward a tall vase standing by the front door. It held several umbrellas and a wooden cane carved with a serpent twisting along its length.

"That's silly," she said.

"I've always, always wished I could move things around with my mind. It's been my secret dream since I was ten. Please do it."

"But I—" Frustrated, she set her mug on the table, but not before the coaster slid beneath it.

"See, look!" He lifted his mug, put it down somewhere else. His coaster didn't seem to care.

"But I—oh, what the hell."—Cane? Do you want to dance?—

The cane quivered in the vase. Then it leapt up out of the vase and spun in the air like a propellor. It landed on the welcome mat, did some staggering spirals, flipped, then lay on the ground and rolled back and forth.

"That's so—that's so—"

She looked at him. His face was pale; his eyes sparkled.

"It's doing it because it wants to," she said.

"But it never wanted to before."

"Maybe it did, but it just didn't know it could."

He looked at the cane. It lifted itself and did some flips, then started tapdancing on the hardwood, somewhat muted by its rubber tip. "If everything knew what it could do—" he said. "Does everything *want* to do stuff like this?"

"I don't know," said Matt. "I've never seen things act like your things." She cocked her head and looked at him sideways.

With one loud tap from its head, the cane jumped back into the big vase and settled quietly among the umbrellas.

"I was wondering how you get things to stop," he whispered.

"Me too," she whispered back. "Usually things act mostly like things when I talk to them. They just act thing ways. Doors open, but they do that anyway. You know?"

"Doors open?" he said. His eyebrows rose.

She could almost see his thoughts. So: that's how this kid gets along. Doors open. She met his gaze without wavering. It had been a long time since she'd told anyone about talking to things, and other times she'd revealed it hadn't always worked out well.

"Doors open, and locks unlock," she said.

"Wow," he said.

"So," she said, "second thoughts about having me stay the night?"

"No! This is like the best Christmas wish I ever had, barring having Linda here."

Matt felt something melt in her chest, sending warmth all through her. She laughed.

He stared at her. "You're a girl," he said after a moment.

She grinned at him and set her mug on the coaster. "Could you loan me some soap and towels and stuff? I sure could use a shower now."

"You're a girl?"

"Mmm. How old do you have to be not to be a girl?"

"Eighteen," he said.

"I'm beyond girl."

"You're an elf," he said.

She grinned. "Could I borrow something clean to sleep in?"

He blinked, shook his head. "Linda's got clothes here, in her old room. She's actually a little bigger than you now." He put his mug down and stood up. "I'll show you," he said.

She grabbed her new toothbrush and followed him down the little hall. He opened a linen closet, loaded her arms with a big fluffy towel and a washrag, then led her into a bedroom.

—Hello,—she thought to the room. It smelled faintly of vanished perfume, a flowery teen scent. All the furniture was soft varnished honey wood. The built-in bed against the far wall had wide dresser drawers below it and a mini-blind–covered window above. A desk held a small portable typewriter; bookshelves cradled staggering rows of paperbacks, and a big wooden dresser with chartreuse drawers supported about twenty stuffed animals in various stages of being loved to pieces. On the wall hung a framed photographic poster of pink ballerina shoes with ribbons; another framed poster showed different kinds of owls. Ice green wall-to-wall deep pile carpet covered the floor.

—You're not the one,—said the room.

—No, I'm not. The one isn't coming tonight. May I stay here instead? I won't hurt anything.—

—You can't have his heart,—said the room.

—All right,—said Matt. This room was not happy like the kitchen.

It relaxed, though.

—Thanks,—Matt thought.

Jim walked to the dresser and opened a drawer. "How do you feel about flannel?" he said, lifting out a nightgown. The drawer slammed shut, almost catching his hand, and successfully gripping the hem of the nightgown. "Hey!" he said.

—*Our* things,—said the room.

Matt thought about the sullen teenager she had seen in the photo in Jim's wallet. Afraid of losing things, holding them tight; Matt had learned instead to let go.

"Maybe you better put that back," she said. "I can rinse out my T-shirt."

Jim touched the drawer and it opened. He dropped the nightgown back in and the drawer snapped shut again. "I've got pajamas you can use. Actually, my girlfriend left some women's things in my closet. . . ."

"Pajamas would be good," Matt said.

He showed her the bathroom, which was spacious and handsome and spotless, black, white, and red tile, fluffy white carpet, combination whirlpool tub and shower, and a small stacked washer-dryer combination. "Wait a sec, I'll get you some pajamas. You want to do laundry?"

"Yeah," she said. "That'd be great." She wished she had the rest of her clothes with her, but they were still in the basement of that suburban house, two miles away. Oh well. You did what you could when the opportunity arrived.

He disappeared, returned with red satin pajamas and a black terrycloth robe.

"Thanks," she said, wondering what else he had in his closet. She hadn't figured him for a red satin kind of guy. She took a long hot shower without talking to anything in the bathroom, using soap and shampoo liberally and several times. The soap smelled clean; the shampoo smelled like apples. His pajamas and robe were huge on her. She hitched everything up and bound it with the robe's belt so she could walk without tripping on the pantlegs or the robe's hem. She brushed her teeth, then started a load of laundry, all her layers, except the coat, which she had left in the living room: T-shirt, long johns top and bottom, work shirt, acrylic sweater, jeans, two pairs of socks, even the wide Ace bandages she bound her chest with. Leaving the mirror steamed behind her, she emerged, flushed and clean and feeling very tired but contented.

"I can't believe I ever thought you were a boy," Jim said, putting down a magazine and sitting up on the couch. Christmas carols played softly on the stereo. The mugs had disappeared.

"Very useful, that," said Matt.

"Yes," he said. She sat down at the other end of the couch from him. Sleep was waiting to welcome her; she wasn't sure how long she could keep her eyes open.

After a minute he said, "I went in the kitchen and nothing moved."

Matt frowned.

"Was it a dream?"

"Was what a dream?" she asked, before she could stop herself.

"Please," he said, pain bright in his voice.

"Do you want things dancing? Drawers closing on you?"

He stared at her, then relaxed a little. "Yes," he said, "at least tonight I do."

She pulled her knees up to her chest and huddled, bare feet on the couch, all of her deep in the night clothes he had given her. She thought about it. "What happens is I talk to things," she said. "And things talk back. Like, I asked the kitchen where the cocoa was. Usually a thing would just say, this cupboard over here. In your kitchen, the cupboard opened itself and the cocoa came out. I don't know why that is, or why other people don't seem to do it."

"Like if I said, Hey, sofa, do you wanna dance?" He patted the seat cushions next to him.

—Sofa, do you want to dance?—Matt thought.

The couch laughed and said,—I'm too heavy to get around much. Floor and I like me where I am. I could. . . .—And the cushions bounced up and down, bumping Matt and Jim like a trampoline.

Jim grinned and gripped the cushion he was sitting on. The couch stopped after a couple minutes. "But you did that, didn't you?" he said. "My saying it out loud didn't do anything."

"I guess not," Matt said.

"And things actually talk back to you?"

"Yeah," she said.

"Like my wallet."

"It kept whining about how you would die or at least be arrested without it. It really cares about you." She yawned against the back of her hand.

He fished his wallet out of his back pocket and stared at it for a minute, then stroked it, held it between his hands. "This is very weird," he said. "I mean, I keep this in my back pants pocket, and . . ." He flipped his wallet open and closed. He pressed it to his chest. "I have to think about this." He glanced at the clock on the VCR. "Let's go to sleep. It's already Christmas."

Matt squinted at the glowing amber digits. Yep, after midnight.

"Will you be okay in Linda's room?" Jim asked.

"As long as I don't steal your heart," Matt said and yawned again. Her eyes drifted shut.

"Steal my heart?" Jim muttered.

Matt's breathing slowed. She was perfectly comfortable on the couch, which was adjusting its cushions to fit around her and support her; but she felt Jim's arms lift her. She fell asleep before he ever let go.

She woke up and stared at a barred ceiling.—Where is this?—she asked. Then she rolled her head and glanced toward the door, saw the ballerina toe shoes picture, and remembered: Linda. Jim.

The mini-blinds at the window above the bed were angled to aim slitted daylight at the ceiling. Matt could tell it was morning by the quality of the light. She sat up amid a welter of blankets, sheets, and quilt, and stretched. When she reached skyward, the satin pajama sleeves slid down her arms to her shoulders. She wasn't sure she liked being inside such slippery stuff, but she had been comfortable enough while asleep.

She reached up for the mini-blinds' rod and twisted it until she could see out the window. Jim's apartment was on the fifth floor. Across the street stood another apartment building, brick-faced, its windows mostly shuttered with mini-blinds and curtains, keeping its secrets.

She put her hand against the wall below the window.—Building, hello.—

—Hello, Parasite,—said the building, a deeper structure that housed all the apartments, all the rooms in the apartments, all the things in the rooms, all the common areas, and all the secret systems of wiring and plumbing, heating and cooling, the skeleton of board and girders and beams, the skin of stucco and the eyes of glass-lidded windows.

Parasite, thought Matt. Not a promising opening. But the building sounded cheerful.—How are you?—she thought.

—Warm, snug inside,—thought the building.—Freezing outside. Quiet. It won't last.—

—Oh, well, just wanted to say hi,—thought Matt.

—All right,—thought the building. She felt its attention turning away from her.

—Aren't you getting up now?—asked Linda's room. It sounded grumpy.—It's Christmas morning!—

—Oh. Right.—Matt slipped out of bed, pulled the big black robe around her, and ventured out into the hall, heading for the bathroom. Not a creature was stirring. She finished in the bathroom, then crept into the living room to check the clock on the VCR; it was around 7:30 A.M., a little later than her usual waking time. She peeked at the Christmas tree on the table in the dining nook. Its white lights still twinkled, and there were a couple more presents under it.

—Coat?—she thought. It occurred to her that she had never talked to her own clothes before. Too intimate. Her clothes touched her all the time, and she wasn't comfortable talking to things that touched her anywhere but her hands and feet. If her clothes talked back, achieved self-will, could do whatever they wanted—she clutched the lapels of the black robe, keeping it closed around her. She would have to think about this. It wasn't fair to her clothes.—Coat, where are you?—she thought.

A narrow closet door in the hall slid open. Looking in, she saw that Jim had hung her coat on a hanger. She put out a hand and stroked the stained army-drab. Coat had been with her through all kinds of weather, kept her warm and dry as well as it could, hidden her from too close an inspection, carried all kinds of things for her. She felt an upwelling of gratitude. She hugged the coat, pressing her cheek against its breast, breathing its atmosphere of weather, dirt, Matt, and fried chicken (she had carried some foil-wrapped chicken in a pocket yesterday). After a moment warmth glowed from the coat; its arms slid flat and empty around her shoulders. She closed her eyes and stood for a long moment letting the coat know how much she appreciated it, and hearing from the coat that it liked her. Then she reached into the inside breast pocket and fished out the pen-and-pencil set she had bought the night before. With a final pat on its lapel, she slid out of the coat's embrace.

—Anybody know where I could find some wrapping paper and tape?—she asked the world in general.

The kitchen called to her, and she went in. A low, deep drawer near the refrigerator slid open, offering her a big selection of wrapping paper for all occasions and even some spools of fancy ribbons. Another drawer higher up opened; it held miscellaneous useful objects, including rubber bands, paperclips, pens, chewing gum, scissors, and a tape dispenser.

—Thanks,—she said. She chose a red paper covered with small green Christmas trees, sat at the card table with it and the tape, and wrapped up the writing set after she peeled the price sticker off it. Silver ribbon snaked across the floor and climbed up the table leg, then lifted its end at her and danced, until she laughed and grabbed it. It wound around her package, tied itself, formed a starburst of loops on top. She patted it and it rustled against her hand.

She put everything away and set her present under the tree, then went back to Linda's room and lay on the bed, yawning. The bed tipped up until she fell out.

—It's Christmas morning—it said crossly as she felt the back of her head; falling, she'd bumped it, and it hurt.—The one never comes back to bed until she's opened her presents!—

—I'm not the one,—Matt thought.—Thanks for the night.—She left the room, got her coat out of the closet, and lay on the couch with her coat spread over her. The couch cradled her, shifting the cushions until her body lay comfortable and embraced. She fell asleep right away.

The smell of coffee woke her. She sighed and peered over at the VCR. It was an hour later. A white porcelain mug of coffee steamed gently on a coaster on the table. She blinked and sat up, saw Jim sitting in a chair nearby. He wore a gray robe over blue pajamas. He smiled at her. "Merry Christmas."

"Merry Christmas," Matt said. She reached for the coffee, sipped. It was full of cream and sugar, the way she'd fixed it in the restaurant the night before. "Room service," she said. "Thanks."

"Elf pick-me-up." He had a mug of his own. He drank. "What are you doing out here?"

"The room and I had a little disagreement. It said it was time for me to wake up and open presents, like Linda, and I hadn't slept long enough for me."

He gazed into the distance. "Linda's always real anxious to get to the gifts," he said slowly. "She used to wake me and Corey up around six. Of course, we always used to wait to hide the presents until Christmas Eve. We used to get a full-sized tree and set it up over there—" he pointed to a space in a corner of the room between bookshelves on one wall and the entertainment center on the other—"and we wouldn't decorate it until after she'd gone to sleep. So it was as if everything was transformed overnight. God, that was great."

"Magic," said Matt, nodding.

Jim smiled. Matt peeked at his dreamscape, and this time she could see the tree in his imagination, tall enough to brush the ceiling, glowing with twinkling colored lights, tinsel, gleaming glass balls, and Keepsake ornaments—little animals, little Santas, little children doing Christmas things with great good cheer—and here and there, old, much-loved ornaments, each different, clearly treasures from his and Corey's pasts. Beneath the tree, mounds of presents in green, gold, red, silver foil wrap, kissed with stick-on bows. Linda, young and not sullen, walking from the hall, her face alight as she looked at the tree, all of her beaming with wonder and anticipation so that for that brief moment she was the perfect creature, excited about the next moment and expecting to be happy.

"Beautiful," Matt murmured.

"What?" Jim blinked at her and the vision vanished.

Matt sat quiet. She sipped coffee.

"Matt?" said Jim.

Matt considered. At last she said, "The way you saw it. Beautiful. Did Corey take the ornaments?"

"Matt," whispered Jim.

"The old ones, and the ones with mice stringing popcorn, and Santa riding a surfboard, and the little angel sleeping on the cloud?"

He stared at her for a long moment. He leaned back, his shoulders slumping. "She took them," he said. "She's the custodial parent. She took our past."

"It's in your brain," Matt said.

He closed his eyes, leaned his head against the seat back. "Can you see inside my brain?"

"Not usually. Just when you're looking out at stuff, like the tree. And Linda. And I'm not sorry I saw those things, because they're great."

He opened his eyes again and peered at her, his head still back. "They are great," he said. "I didn't know I remembered in such detail. Having it in my brain isn't the same as being able to touch it, though."

"Well, of course not." She thought about all the dreams she had seen since she first woke to them years before. Sometimes people imagined worse than the worst: horrible huge monsters, horrible huge wounds and mistakes and shame. Sometimes they imagined beautiful things, a kiss, a sharing, a hundred musicians making music so thick she felt she could walk on it up to the stars, a sunset that painted the whole world the colors of fire, visions of the world very different from what she saw when she looked with her day-eyes. Sometimes they just dreamed things that had happened, or things that would happen, or things they wished would happen. Sometimes people fantasized about things that made her sick; then she was glad that she could close her dream-eyes when she liked.

All the time, people carried visions and wishes and fears with them. Somehow Matt found in that a reason to go on; her life had crystallized out of wandering without destination or purpose into a quest to watch peoples' dreams, and the dreams of things shaped by people. She never reported back to anyone about what she saw, but the hunger to see more never lessened.

She had to know. She wasn't sure what, or why.

"In a way, ideas and memories are stronger than things you can touch," she said. "For one thing, much more portable. And people can't steal them or destroy them—at least, not very easily."

"I could lose them. I'm always afraid that I'm losing memories. Like a slow leak. Others come along and displace them."

"How many do you need?"

He frowned at her.

She set down her coffee and rubbed her eyes. "I guess I'm asking myself: how many do I need? I always feel like I need more of them. I'm not even sure how to use the ones I've got. I just keep collecting."

"Like you have mine now?"

"My seeing it didn't take it away from you, though."

"No," he said. He straightened. "Actually it looked a lot clearer. I don't usually think in pictures."

"Mostly graphs and blueprints," Matt said.

He tilted his head and looked at her.

"And small print I can't read."

"Good," he said. After a moment's silence, he said, "I would rather you didn't look at what I'm thinking."

"Okay," she said. For the first time it occurred to her that what she did was spy on people. It hadn't mattered much; she almost never talked to people she dreamwatched, so it was an invasion they would never know about. "I do it to survive," she said.

"Dahmer dudes," he said, and nodded.

"Right. But I won't do it to you anymore."

"Thanks. How about a pixie dust breakfast?"

"Huh?"

"Does the kitchen know how to cook?"

She laughed and they went to the kitchen, where he produced cheese omelets, sprinking red paprika and green parsley on them in honor of Christmas. He had to open the fridge, turn on the stove, fetch the fry-pan himself, but drawers opened for Matt as she set the table, offering her silver and napkins, and a pitcher jumped out of a cupboard when she got frozen orange juice concentrate out of the freezer, its top opening to eat the concentrate and the cans of water. She had never before met such a cooperative and happy room. Her own grin lighted her from inside.

Jim's plates were egg-shell white ceramic with a pastel geometric border. He slid the omelets onto them and brought breakfast to the table. She poured orange juice into square red glass tumblers, fetched more coffee from the coffee-maker's half-full pot, and sat down at the green table.

"I'm so glad you're here," Jim said.

"Me too," said Matt.

"Makes a much better Christmas than me quietly moping and maybe drinking all day."

Matt smiled and ate a bite of omelet. Hot fluffy egg, cheese, spices greeted her mouth. "Great," she said after she swallowed.

Jim finished his omelet one bite behind Matt. She sat back, hands folded on her stomach, and grinned at him until he smiled back.

"Presents," she said.

"That was my line. Also I wanted to say having you here is the best present I can think of, because all my life I've wanted to see things move without being touched. It makes me so happy I don't have words for it."

"Did you design this kitchen?"

He glanced around, smiled. "Yeah. I don't do many interiors, but I chose everything in here, since I like to cook. Corey did the living room and our bedroom."

"This kitchen moves more than any other place I've ever been. I think it was almost ready to move all by itself. I bet your buildings would like to take a walk. I wonder if they're happy. I bet they are."

He sat back and beamed at her. Then he reached for his coffee mug and it slid into his hand. His eyes widened. "Matt. . . ."

She shook her head.

"Gosh. You *are* an elf." He sipped coffee, held the mug in front of him, staring at it. He stroked his fingers along its smooth glaze. He looked up at Matt. "It's beautiful," he said.

"Yeah," she said. "Everything is."

For a long time they stared at each other, their breathing slow and deep. At last he put the mug down, but then curled his fingers around it as though he couldn't bear to let go.

"Everything?" he said.

"Mmm," she said. For a moment she thought of ugly dreams, and sad dreams, and wondered if she believed what she had just said. Some things hurt so much she couldn't look at them for long. Still, she wanted to see them all. Without every part, the balance was missing. Jim's image of a Christmas Linda was intensified by how much he missed her. Cocoa tasted much better on a really cold day, and a hug after a nightmare could save a life. . . .

After a moment, she said, "I got you something." She stood up. He stood up too, and followed her into the dining nook. She picked up the parcel she had wrapped that morning and offered it to him. "I had to, uh, borrow the paper."

"How could you get me anything?" he said, perplexed. "These are for you." He handed her three packages. "I didn't know what to get you." He shrugged.

"Dinner, cocoa, conversation, a shower, laundry, a place to sleep, coffee, breakfast," she said. She grinned and took her packages to the couch, where she shoved her coat over and sat next to it. "Thanks," she said.

He joined her.

She opened the first present, uncovered a card with five die-cast metal microcars attached, all painted skateboard colors: hot rods with working wheels. Delighted, she freed them from their plastic and set them on the coffee table, where they growled and raced with each other and acted like demented traffic without ever going over the edge.

Jim sat gripping his present, watching the cars with fierce concentration. "I got them for the teenage boy," he said in a hushed voice after a moment. Two of the cars seemed to like each other; they moved in parallel courses, looping and reversing. One of the others parked. The two remaining were locked bumper to bumper, growling at each other, neither giving an inch.

Matt laughed. "They're great! They can live in my pocket." She patted her coat. "Open yours."

He touched the ribbon on his package and it shimmered with activity, then dropped off the package and slithered from his lap to the couch, where it lifted one end as if watching. Eyebrows up, he slid a fingernail under the paper, pulled off the wrapping. He grinned at the pen and pencil, which were coated with hologram diffraction grating in magenta and teal, gold and silver. "The office isn't going to know what hit it," he said. "Thanks."

"I bought 'em for the architect with a green tie. Not a whole lot of selection in that store."

"Yeah," he said, tucking them into the pocket of his robe. "Go on." He gestured toward the other two presents.

She opened the first one and found a purple knit hat. The second held a pair of black leather gloves. She slid her hands into them; they fit, and the inner lining felt soft against her palms. "Thanks," she said, her voice a little tight, her heart warm and hurt, knowing he had bought them for the homeless person. She smiled and leaned her cheek against the back of her gloved hand. "Best presents I've gotten in years."

"Me too," he said, holding out a hand to the silver ribbon. It reached up and coiled around his wrist. He breathed deep and stroked the ribbon. "God!"

Matt tucked the hat and gloves into a coat pocket, patted the coat, held out a hand to the little cars. They raced over and climbed up onto her palm. "Look," she said, turning over her coat. "Here's your new garage." She laid the coat open and lifted the inner breast pocket so darkness gaped. The cars popped wheelies off her hand and zipped into the cave. One peeked out again, then vanished. She laughed. She had laughed more in the last twelve hours than she had in a whole month.

The phone rang, and Matt jumped. Jim picked up a sleek curved tan thing from a table beside the couch and said, "Merry Christmas" into it.

Then, "Oh, hi, Corey!"

Hugging her coat to her, Matt stood up. She could go in the other room and change while he talked to his ex-wife. Jim patted the couch and smiled at her and she sat down again, curious, as ever, about the details of other peoples' lives.

"Nope. I'm not drunk. I'm not hungover. I'm fine. Missing Linda, that's all. . . . Okay, thanks."

He waited a moment, his eyes staring at a distance, one hand holding the phone to his ear and the other stroking the silver ribbon around the phone-hand's wrist. "Hi, Hon. Merry Christmas! You having fun?"

A moment.

"I miss you too. Don't worry, your presents are waiting. When you get home we can have a mini-Christmas. I hope you're someplace with snow in it. I know how much you like that . . . oh, you are? Great! Snow angels, of course. What'd your mom get for you?"

Matt thought about family Christmases, other peoples' and then, at last, one of her own—she hadn't visited her own memories in a long long time. Her older sister, Pammy, sneaking into her room before dawn, holding out a tiny wrapped parcel. "Don't tell anybody, Mattie. This is just for you," Pammy had said, and crept into bed beside her and kissed her. Matt opened the package and found inside it a heart-shaped locket. Inside, a picture of her as a baby, and a picture of Pammy. Matt had seen the locket before—Pammy had been wearing it ever since their mother gave it to her on her tenth birthday, four years earlier. Only, originally, it had had pictures of Mom and Dad in it.

"I'll never tell," Matt had whispered, pressing the locket against her heart.

"It's supposed to keep you safe," Pammy said, her voice low and tight. "That's what Mom told me. It didn't work for me but maybe it will for you. Anyway, I just want you to know . . . you have my heart."

And Matt had cried the kind of crying you do without sound but with tears, and she didn't even know why, not until several years later.

"That's great," Jim said, smiling, his eyes misty. "That's great, Honey. Will you sing one for me when you get home? Yeah, I know it will feel funny to sing a carol after Christmas is over, but we're doing a little time warp, remember? Saving a piece of Christmas for later . . ."

"Me? I thought I was going to miss you so much I wasn't going to have any fun, but I found a friend, and she gave me a couple presents. No, not Josie! You know she's at her folks'. I know you don't like it if she's here when you come, so we set it up before I knew you weren't . . ." He glanced at Matt and frowned, shrugged. "No, this is a kid. Actually, an elf."

He smiled again. "I wish you could have been here. She made the kitchen dance and the couch dance. I gave her these little cars, because I thought she was a boy, and she made them run all over the coffee table even though they don't have motors in them. I think she works for Santa Claus."

Matt slipped her hand into a coat pocket and touched the hat he had given her. It was soft like cashmere. Maybe *he* worked for Santa Claus. It had been a long time since she had had a Christmas of her own instead of borrowing other peoples', and this was the first one she could remember where she was actually really happy.

"You're too old to believe in Santa?" he said. He sighed. "I thought I was, too, but I'm not anymore." He listened, then laughed. "Okay, call me silly if you like. I'm glad you're having a good Christmas. I love you. I'll see you when you get back." He laid the phone down with a faint click.

Matt grinned at him. She liked thinking of herself as an elf and an agent of Christmas. Better than thinking she must be some kind of charity project for Jim, the way she had been at first.

Stranger still to realize she was having a no-peek Christmas, alone in her own head.

She thought of families, and, at long last, of her sister, Pammy. How many years had it been? She didn't even know if Pam were still alive, still married to her first husband, if she had kids. . . .

"Can I use that?" she said. He handed the phone to her. She dialed information.

"What city?"

"Seattle," she said. "Do you have a listing for Pam Sternbach?"

There was a number. She dialed it.

"Merry Christmas," said a voice she had not heard since she had lived at home, half a life ago.

"Pam?"

"Mattie! Mattie? Omigod, I thought you were dead! Where are you? What have you been doing? Omigod! Are you all right?"

For a moment she felt very strange, fever and chills shifting back and forth through her. She had reached out to her past and now it was touching her back.

She had put so much distance between it and herself. She had walked it away, stamped it into a thousand streets, shed the skin of it a thousand times, overlaid it with new thoughts and other lives and memories until she had thousands to choose from. What was she doing?

"Mattie?"

"I'm fine," she said. "How are you?"

"How am I? Good God, Mattie! Where have you been all these years?"

"Pretty much everywhere." She reached into the coat's breast pocket and fished out one of the little cars, watched it race back and forth across her palm. She was connecting to her past, but she hadn't lost her present doing it. She drew in a deep breath, let it out in a huge sigh, smiled at Jim, and snuggled down to talk.

HEARTFIRES
Charles de Lint

Each year, Charles de Lint's name winds up on the list of authors of the year's best fantasy tales—usually with a story set in "Newford," his imaginary city where myths and folklore come to life on modern urban streets. This year is no exception, for de Lint continues to turn out a rather astonishing number of memorable stories in addition to very popular novels (the latest of which is *Memory and Dream*). His first collection of Newford fiction, *Dreams Underfoot*, was nominated for the World Fantasy Award. In 1995, he published a second volume, *The Ivory and the Horn*. The following unusual tale, however, comes from a small chapbook published in Canada by Triskell Press.

—T.W.

Dance is the breath-of-life made visible.
—seen on a T-shirt
on 4th Avenue, Tucson, AZ

1

Nobody tells you the really important stuff so in the end you have to imagine it for yourself. It's like how things connect. A thing is just a thing until you have the story that goes with it. Without the story, there's nothing to hold on to, nothing to relate this mysterious new thing to who you are—you know, to make it a part of your own history. So if you're like me, you make something up and the funny thing is, lots of times, once you tell the story, it comes true. Not *poof*, hocus-pocus, magic it comes true, but sure, why not, and after it gets repeated often enough, you and everybody else end up believing it.

It's like quarks. They're neither positive nor negative until the research scientists look at them. Right up until that moment of observation they hold the possibility of being one or the other. It's the *looking* that makes them what they are. Which is like making up a story for them, right?

The world's full of riddles like that.

The lady or the tiger.

Did she jump, or was she pushed?

The door standing by itself in the middle of the field—does it lead to somewhere, or from somewhere?

Or the locked room we found one night down in Old City, the part of it that runs under the Tombs. A ten-by-ten-foot room, stone walls, stone floor and ceiling, with a door in one wall that fits so snugly you wouldn't even know it was there except for the bolts—a set on either side of the door, big old iron fittings, rusted, but still solid. The air in that room is dry, touched with the taste of old spices and sagegrass. And the place is clean. No dust. No dirt. Only these scratches on that weird door, long gouges cut into the stone like something was clawing at it, both sides of the door, inside and out.

So what was it for? Before the 'quake dropped the building into the ground, that room was still below street level. Somebody from the long ago built that room, hid it away in the cellar of what must have been a seriously tall building in those days—seven stories high. Except for the top floor, it's all underground now. We didn't even know the building was there until Bear fell through a hole in the roof, landing on his ass in a pile of rubble, which, luckily for him, was only a few feet down. Most of that top floor was filled with broken stone and crap, like someone had bulldozed another tumbled-down building inside it and overtop of it, pretty much blocking any way in and turning that top floor into a small mountain covered with metal junk and weeds and every kind of trash you can imagine. It was a fluke we ever found our way in, it was that well hidden.

But why was it hidden? Because the building couldn't be salvaged, so cover it up, make it safe? Or because of that room?

That room. Was it to lock something in? Or keep something out?

Did our going into it make it be one or the other? Or was it the story we found in its stone confines?

We told that story to each other, taking turns like we usually do, and when we were done, we remembered what that room was. We'd never been in it before, not that room, in that place, but we remembered.

2

Devil's Night, October 30th. It's not even nine o'clock and they've already got fires burning all over the Tombs: sparks flying, grass fires in the empty lots, trash fires in metal drums, the guts of derelict tenements and factory buildings going up like so much kindling. The sky overhead fills with an evil glow, like an aura gone bad, gone way bad. The smoke from the fires rises in streaming columns. It cuts through the orange glare hanging over that square mile or so of lost hopes and despair the way ink spreads in water.

The streets are choked with refuse and abandoned cars, but that doesn't stop the revelers from their fun, the flickering light of the fires playing across their features as they lift their heads and howl at the devil's glow. Does stop the fire department, though. This year they don't even bother to try to get their trucks in. You can almost hear the mayor telling the chiefs: "Let it burn."

Hell, it's only the Tombs. Nobody living here but squatters and hoboes, junkies and bikers. These are the inhabitants of the night side of the city—the side you only see out of the corner of your eye until the sun goes down and suddenly they're all over the streets, in your face, instead of back in the shadows where they belong. They're not citizens. They don't even vote.

And they're having some fun tonight. Not the kind of recreation you or I might look for, but a desperate fun, the kind that's born out of knowing you've got nowhere to go but down and you're already at the bottom. I'm not making excuses for them. I just understand them a little better than most citizens might.

See, I've run with them. I've slept in those abandoned buildings, scrabbled for food in Dumpsters over by Williamson Street, trying to get there before the rats and feral dogs. I've looked for oblivion in the bottom of a bottle or at the end of a needle.

No, don't go feeling sorry for me. I had me some hard times, sure, but everybody does. But I'll tell you, I never torched buildings. Even in the long ago. When I'm looking to set a fire, I want it to burn in the heart.

3

I'm an old crow, but I still know a few tricks. I'm looking rough, maybe even used up, but I'm not yet so old I'm useless. You can't fool me, but I fool most everyone, wearing clothes, hiding my feathers, walking around on my hind legs like a man, upright, not hunched over, moving pretty fast, considering.

There were four of us in those days, ran together from time to time. Old spirits, wandering the world, stopped awhile in this place before we went on. We're always moving on, restless, looking for change so that things'll stay the same. There was me, Crazy Crow, looking sharp with my flat-brimmed hat and pointy-toed boots. Alberta the Dancer with those antlers poking up out of her red hair, you know how to look, you can see them. Bear, he was so big you felt like the sky had gone dark when he stood by you. And then there was Jolene.

She was just a kid that Devil's Night. She gets like that. One year she's about knee-high to a skinny moment and you can't stop her from tomfooling around, another year she's so fat even Bear feels small around her. We go way back, Jolene and me, knew each other pretty good, we met so often.

Me and Alberta were together that year. We took Jolene in like she was our daughter, Bear her uncle. Moving on the wheel like a family. We're dark-skinned—we're old spirits, got to be the way we are before the European look got so popular—but not so dark as fur and feathers. Crow, grizzly, deer. We lose some color when we wear clothes, walking on our hind legs all the time.

Sometimes we lose other things, too. Like who we really are and what we're doing here.

4

"Hey, 'bo."

I look up to see it's a brother calling to me. We're standing around an oil drum, warming our hands, and he comes walking out of the shadows like he's a piece of them, got free somehow, comes walking right up to me like he thinks I'm in charge. Alberta smiles. Bear lights a smoke, takes a couple of drags, then offers it to the brother.

"Bad night for fires," he says after he takes a drag. He gives the cigarette a funny look, tasting the sweetgrass mixed in with the tobacco. Not much, just enough.

"Devil's Night," Jolene says, grinning like it's a good thing. She's a little too fond of fires this year for my taste. Next thing you know she'll be wanting to tame metal, build herself a machine and wouldn't that be something?

"Nothing to smile about," the brother tells her. "Lot of people get hurt, Devil's Night. Gets out of hand. Gets to where people think it's funny, maybe set a few of us 'boes on fire, you hear what I'm saying?"

"Times are always hard," I say.

He shrugs, takes another drag of the cigarette, then hands it back to Bear.

"Good night for a walk," he says finally. "A body might walk clear out of the Tombs on a night like this, come back when things are a little more settled down."

We all just look at him.

"Got my boy waiting on me," he says. "Going for that walk. You all take care of yourselves now."

We never saw the boy, standing there in the shadows, waiting on his pa, except maybe Jolene. There's not much she misses. I wait until the shadow's almost swallowed the brother before I call after him.

"Appreciate the caution," I tell him.

He looks back, tips a finger to his brow, then he's gone, part of the shadows again.

"Are we looking for trouble?" Bear asks.

"Uh-huh," Jolene pipes up, but I shake my head.

"Like he said," I tell them, jerking a thumb to where the brother walked away.

Bear leads the way out, heading east, taking a direct route and avoiding the fires we can see springing up all around us now. The dark doesn't bother us; we can see pretty much the same, doesn't matter if it's night or day. We follow Bear up a hillside of rubble. He gets to the top before us and starts dancing around, stamping his feet, singing, "Wa-hey, look at me. I'm the king of the mountain."

And then he disappears between one stamp and the next, and that's how we find the room.

5

I don't know why we slide down to where Bear's standing instead of him climbing back up. Curious, I guess. Smelling spirit mischief and we just have to see where it leads us, down, down, till we're standing on a dark street, way underground.

"Old City," Alberta says.

"Walked right out of the Tombs we did," Jolene says, then she shoots Bear a look and giggles. "Or maybe slid right out of it on our asses'd be a better way to put it."

Bear gives her a friendly whack on the back of the head but it doesn't budge a hair. Jolene's not looking like much this year, standing about halfway to nothing, but she's always solidly built, doesn't much matter what skin she's wearing.

"Let's take that walk," I say, but Bear catches hold of my arm.

"I smell something old," he tells me.

"It's an old place," I tell him. "Fell down here a long time ago and stood above ground even longer."

Bear shakes his head. "No. I'm smelling something older than that. And lower down."

We're on an underground street, I'm thinking. Way down. Can't get much lower than this. But Bear's looking back at the building we just came out of and I know what's on his mind. Basements. They're too much like caves for him to pass one by, especially when it's got an old smell. I look at the others. Jolene's game, but then she's always game when she's wearing this skin. Alberta shrugs.

"When I want to dance," she says, "you all dance with me, so I'm going to say no when Bear wants to try out a new step?"

I can't remember the last time we all danced, but I can't find any argument with what she's saying.

"What about you, Crazy Crow?" Bear asks.

"You know me," I tell him. "I'm like Jolene, I'm always game."

So we go back inside, following Bear who's following his nose, and he leads us right up to the door of that empty stone room down in the cellar. He grabs hold of the iron bolt, shoves it to one side, hauls the door open, rubs his hand on his jeans to brush off the specks of rust that got caught up on his palm.

"Something tried hard to get out," Alberta says.

I'm thinking of the other side of the door. "And in," I add.

Jolene's spinning around in the middle of the room, arms spread wide.

"Old, old, old," she sings.

We can all smell it now. I get the feeling that the building grew out of this room, that it was built to hold it. Or hide it.

"No ghosts," Bear says. "No spirits here."

Jolene stops spinning. "Just us," she says.

"Just us," Bear agrees.

He sits down on the clean stone floor, cross-legged, rolls himself a smoke. We all join him, sitting in a circle, like we're dancing, except it's only our breathing that's making the steps. We each take a drag of the cigarette, then Bear sets the butt down in the middle of the circle. We watch the smoke curl up from it, tobacco with that pinch of sweetgrass. It makes a long curling journey up to the ceiling, thickens there like a small storm cloud, pregnant with grandfather thunders.

Somewhere up above us, where the moon can see it, there's smoke rising, too, Devil's Night fires filling the hollow of the sky with pillars of silent thunder.

Bear takes a shotgun cartridge out of his pocket, brass and red cardboard, twelve-gauge, and puts it down on the stone beside the smoldering butt, stands it on end, brass side down.

"Guess we need a story," he says. He looks at me. "So we can understand this place."

We all nod. We'll take turns, talking until one of us gets it right.

"Me first," Jolene says.

She picks up the cartridge and rolls it back and forth on that small dark palm of hers and we listen.

6

Jolene says:

It's like that pan-girl, always cooking something up, you know the one. You can smell the wild onion on her breath a mile away. She's got that box that she can't look in, tin box with a lock on it that rattles against the side of the box when she gives it a shake, trying to guess what's inside. There's all these scratches on the tin, inside and out, something trying to get out, something trying to get in.

That's this place, the pan-girl's box. You know she opened that box, let all that stuff out that makes the world more interesting. She can't get it back in, and I'm thinking why try?

Anyway, she throws that box away. It's a hollow now, a hollow place, can be any size you want it to be, any shape, any color, same box. Now we're sitting in it, stone version. Close that door and maybe we can't get out. Got to wait until another pan-girl comes along, takes a break from all that cooking, takes a peek at what's inside. That big eye of hers'll fill the door and ya-hey, here we'll be, looking right back at her, rushing past her, she's swatting her hands at us trying to keep us in, but we're already gone, gone running back out into the world to make everything a little more interesting again.

7

Bear says:

Stone. You can't get much older than stone. First house was stone. Not like this room, not perfectly square, not flat, but stone all the same. Found places, those caves, just like we found this place. Old smell in them. Sometimes bear. Sometimes lion. Sometimes snake. Sometimes the ones that went before.

All gone when we come. All that's left is their messages painted or scratched on the walls. Stories. Information. Things they know we have to figure out, things that they could have told us if they were still around. Only way to tell us now is to leave the messages.

This place is a hollow, like Jolene said, but not why she said it. It's hollow because there's no messages. This is the place we have to leave our messages so that when we go on we'll know that the ones to follow will be able to figure things out.

8

Alberta says:

Inside and out, same thing. The wheel doesn't change, only the way we see it. Door opens either way. Both sides in, both sides out. Trouble is, we're always on the wrong side, always want the thing we haven't got, makes no difference who we are. Restless spirits want life, living people look for something better to come. Nobody *here*. Nobody content with what they got. And the reason for that's to keep the wheel turning. That simple. Wheel stops turning, there's nothing left.

It's like the woman who feels the cage of her bones, those ribs they're a prison for her. She's clawing, clawing at those bone bars, making herself sick. Inside, where you can't see it, but outside, too.

So she goes to see the Lady of the White Deer—looks just like you, Jolene, the way you were last year. Big woman. Big as a tree. Got dark, dark eyes you could get lost in. But she's smiling, always smiling. Smiling as she listens, smiling when she speaks. Like a mother smiles, seen it all, heard it all, but still patient, still kind, still understanding.

"That's just living," she tells the caged woman. "Those aren't bars, they're the bones that hold you together. You keep clawing at them, you make yourself so sick you're going to die for sure."

"I can't breathe in here," the caged woman says.

"You're not paying attention," the Lady of the White Deer says. "All you're doing is breathing. Stop breathing and you'll be clawing at those same bones, trying to get back in."

"You don't understand," the caged woman tells her and she walks away.

So she goes to see the Old Man of the Mountains—looks just like you, Bear. Same face, same hair. A big old bear, sitting up there on the top of the mountain, looking out at everything below. Doesn't smile so much, but understands how everybody's got a secret dark place sits way deep down there inside, hidden but wanting to get out. Understands how you can be happy but not happy at the same time. Understands that sometimes you feel you got to go all the way out to get back in, but if you do, you can't. There's no way back in.

So not smiling so much, but maybe understanding a little more, he lets the woman talk and he listens.

"We all got a place inside us, feels like a prison," he tells her. "It's darker in some people than others, that's all. Thing is, you got to balance what's there with what's around you or you'll find yourself on a road that's got no end. Got no beginning and goes nowhere. It's just always this same thing, never grows, never changes, only gets darker and darker, like that candle blowing in the wind. Looks real nice till the wind blows it out—you hear what I'm saying?"

"I can't breathe in here," the woman tells him.

That Old Man of the Mountain he shakes his head. "You're breathing," he says. "You're just not paying attention to it. You're looking inside, looking inside, forgetting what's outside. You're making friends with that darkness inside you and that's not good. You better stop your scratching and clawing or you're going to let it out."

"You don't understand either," the caged woman says and she walks away.

So finally she goes to see the Old Man of the Desert—looks like you, Crazy Crow. Got the same sharp features, the same laughing eyes. Likes to collect things. Keeps a pocket full of shiny mementos that used to belong to other people, things they threw away. Holds onto them until they want them back and then makes a trade. He'd give them away, but he knows what everybody thinks: all you get for nothing is nothing. Got to put a price on a thing to give it any worth.

He doesn't smile at all when he sees her coming. He puts his hand in his pocket and plays with something while she talks. Doesn't say anything when she's done, just sits there, looking at her.

"Aren't you going to help me?" she asks.

"You don't want my help," the Old Man of the Desert says. "You just want me to agree with you. You just want me to say, aw, that's bad, really bad. You've got it bad. Everybody else in the world is doing fine, except for you, because you got it so hard and bad."

The caged woman looks at him. She's got tears starting in her eyes.

"Why are you being so mean to me?" she asks.

"The truth only sounds mean," he tells her. "You look at it from another side and maybe you see it as kindness. All depends where you're looking, what you want to see."

"But I can't breathe," she says.

"You're breathing just fine," he says right back to her. "The thing is, you're not thinking so good. Got clouds in your head. Makes it hard to see straight. Makes it hard to hear what you don't want to hear anyway. Makes it hard to accept that the rest of the world's not out of step on the wheel, only you are. Work on that and you'll start feeling a little better. Remember who you are instead of always crying after what you think you want to be."

"You don't understand either," she says.

But before she can walk away, the Old Man of the Desert takes that thing out of his pocket, that thing he's been playing with, and she sees it's her dancing. He's got it all rolled up in a ball of beads and cowrie shells and feathers and mud, wrapped around with a rope of braided sweetgrass. Her dancing. Been a long time since she's seen that dancing. She thought it was lost in the long ago. Thought it disappeared with her breathing.

"Where'd you get that dancing?" she asks.

"Found it in the trash. You'd be amazed what people will throw out—every kind of piece of themselves."

She puts her hand out to take it, but the Old Man of the Desert shakes his head and holds it out of her reach.

"That's mine," she says. "I lost that in the long ago."

"You never lost it," the Old Man of the Desert tells her. "You threw it away."

"But I want it back now."

"You got to trade for it," he says.

The caged woman lowers her head. "I got nothing to trade for it."

"Give me your prison," the Old Man of the Desert says.

She looks up at him. "Now you're making fun of me," she says. "I give you my prison, I'm going to die. Dancing's not much use to the dead."

"Depends," he says. "Dancing can honor the dead. Lets them breathe in the faraway. Puts a fire in their cold chests. Warms their bone prisons for a time."

"What are you saying?" the caged woman asks. "I give you my life and you'll dance for me?"

The Old Man of the Desert smiles and that smile scares her because it's not kind or understanding. It's sharp and cuts deep. It cuts like a knife, slips in through the skin, slips past the ribs of her bone prison.

"What you got caging you is the idea of a prison," he says. "That's what I want from you."

"You want some kind of . . . story?"

He shakes his head. "I'm not in a bartering mood—not about this kind of thing."

"I don't know how to give you my prison," she says. "I don't know if I can."

"All you got to do is say yes," he tells her.

She looks at that dancing in his hand and it's all she wants now. There's little sparks coming off it, the smell of smudge-sticks and licorice and gasoline. There's a warmth burning in it that she knows will drive the cold away. That cold. She's been holding that cold for so long she doesn't hardly remember what it feels like to be warm anymore.

She's looking, she's reaching. She says yes and the Old Man of the Desert gives her back her dancing. And it's warm and familiar, lying there in her hand, but she doesn't feel any different. She doesn't know what to do with it, now she's got it. She wants to ask him what to do, but he's not paying attention to her anymore.

What's he doing? He's picking up dirt and he's spitting on it, spitting and spitting and working the dirt until it's like clay. And he makes a box out of it and in one side of the box he puts a door. And he digs a hole in the dirt and he puts the box in it. And he covers it up again. And then he looks at her.

"One day you're going to find yourself in that box again," he says, "but this time you'll remember and you won't get locked up again."

She doesn't understand what he's talking about, doesn't care. She's got other things on her mind. She holds up her dancing, holds it in the air between them.

"I don't know what to do with this," she says. "I don't know how to make it work."

The Old Man of the Desert stands up. He gives her a hand up. He takes the dancing from her and throws it on the ground, throws it hard, throws it so hard it breaks. He starts shuffling his feet, keeping time with a clicking sound in the back of his throat. The dust rises up from the ground and she breathes it in and then she remembers what it was like and who she was and why she danced.

It was to honor the bone prison that holds her breathing for this turn of the wheel. It was to honor the gift of the world underfoot. It was to celebrate what's always changing: the stories. The dance of our lives. The wheel of the world and the sky spinning above it and our place in it.

The bones of her prison weren't there to keep her from getting out. They were there to keep her together.

9

I'm holding the cartridge now, but there's no need for me to speak. The story's done. Somewhere up above us, the skies over the Tombs are still full of smoke, the Devil's Night fires are still burning. Here in the hollow of this stone room, we've got a fire of our own.

Alberta looks across the circle at me.

"I remember," she says.

"That was the first time we met," Jolene says. "I remember, too. Not the end, but the beginning. I was there at the beginning and then later, too. For the dancing."

Bear nods. He takes the cartridge from my fingers and puts it back into his pocket. Out of another pocket he takes packets of color, ground pigments. Red and yellow and blue. Black and white. He puts them on the floor, takes a pinch of color out of one of the packets and lays it in the palm of his hand. Spits into his palm. Dips a finger in. He gets up, that Old Man of the Mountain, and he crosses over to one of the walls. Starts to painting. Starts to leave a message for the ones to follow.

Those colors, they're like dancing. Once someone starts, you can't help but twitch and turn and fidget until you're doing it, too. Next thing you know, we're all spitting into our palms, we're all dancing the color across the walls.

Remembering.

Because that's what the stories are for.

Even for old spirits like us.

We lock ourselves up in bone prisons same as everybody else. Forget who we are, why we are, where we're going. Till one day we come across a story we left for ourselves and remember why we're wearing these skins. Remember why we're dancing.

SCREENS
Terry Lamsley

Terry Lamsley came out of nowhere in 1993 with a self-published collection of brilliant ghost stories called *Under the Crust*. The volume was subsequently nominated for the World Fantasy Award, and the title novella **won** that award and was picked by Karl Edward Wagner for *The Years's Best Horror XXII*. Since then, Lamsley has had stories published in *Ghosts & Scholars* and has sold a story to my upcoming "revenge" anthology. A new collection of his stories will be published by Ash-Tree Press in 1996. He is working on a novel.

"Screens" is one of those stories that "got away." Originally sent to Steve Jones for *Dark Voices: The Pan Book of Horror*, that series was canceled and the story was sent to me. I read it, loved it, and wanted it immediately for my "revenge" anthology. The day Lamsley received my letter saying I wanted the story, he heard from Jones that Gollancz was taking over the original anthology series as *Dark Terrors* and therefore he (Jones) would indeed be able to publish the story. It's a good thing Steve and I are friends. . . . The next best thing I could do was reprint this creepy and not quite traditional ghost story herewith.

—E.D.

SCREEN. 1. To hide from view as with a screen. 2. To project (a lantern-slide, cinematograph picture, etc.).

—O.U.D.

"Of course," said Mrs. Ashe, pausing over the task of wrapping his wedge of Blue Stilton and leering up at him over her spectacles without raising from her customary stoop, "if you've been abroad for the last few weeks, you won't have heard . . . " and she let the last word hang in the air like a baited hook.

Andrew realized he had set himself up. To pass the time while she encased his cheese in layers of cellophane and paper, and because something about her always made him slightly nervous, he had asked if anything had happened in the village while he had been away, expecting the usual bland response. Instead, he could tell, she had something juicy for a change, some not-very-good news *he* in particular was not going to welcome. He wished he had kept quiet. He wanted the conversation to drop, but Mrs. Ashe wasn't going to let it. She stood immobile over her task, demanding a response, as though trapped in an enchantment that only a word from him could break.

"Heard what?" he said flatly, trying to sound disinterested.

Mrs. Ashe slipped the cheese into a bag with his other purchases.

"About your friend," she said slyly, "Mrs. Shaster."

Kate Shaster was his next-door neighbor, and his only friend in the village. They occupied two tiny detached but adjacent cottages on the edge of Longton, in a position of comparative isolation. Because they were both single (Kate a widow, he divorced) and recent incomers to the community, and they spent quite a lot of time together, visiting each other's homes, and escorting each other to the local pub, rumors of a romantic attachment between them had naturally grown and flourished. There was, however, no truth in this: Kate and Andrew were just the "good friends" of the cliche and sometimes Andrew wondered if they were even that. The joke between them was that she was too ancient and he was too ugly, and they were doomed to stay single forever. Kate, at forty-one, was seven years older than Andrew, whose face had been disfigured slightly in a hang-gliding accident.

"Has something happened to Kate?" he said, noting that Mrs. Ashe's eyes widened slightly at his use of the Christian name.

"Oh, no, duck." She shook her head and showed her dentures behind a cranky smile. "Not as far as we know. But she's not been out; we've not seen her about." She raised the bag of shopping from the counter and moved it slightly towards him. "Young Darrel noticed she hadn't used her milk. The pints he'd delivered for two days hadn't been taken in. He told his dad, and Mr. Lomax called at her house. She wasn't dressed, Mr. Lomax said, when she came to the door at one in the afternoon, so he knew something was wrong."

"What do you mean, 'She wasn't dressed'?"

"She was in her dressing gown. Mr. Lomax said her hair was all over her face, as though she'd just got out of bed." Mrs. Ashe clearly relished this detail.

Kate was fussy about her appearance. Andrew could not imagine her answering the door looking anything but her best. Perhaps she *was* in trouble.

"Was she sick? Has she seen a doctor?"

"Mr. Lomax offered to get one, but she wouldn't have it. Said she wasn't ill, and there was nothing wrong."

Andrew reached out, removed his groceries from the shopkeeper's weakly grasping hand, and stepped back towards the door.

"I'll call round now," he said. "See how she is."

"You better had, duck," said Mrs. Ashe officiously. "I expect you'll be able to sort her out," and she winked at him, as though they were joined together in some naughty complicity. "She'll listen to you," she added.

As Andrew went out onto the street and the brass bell above the door jangled, she called, "Are you back for a while now, Mr. Colvin? Shall I tell Darrel to start delivering your milk again?"

"Yes," said Andrew. "Thanks. I won't be going away again for some months."

It was when he came back to it after a spell away that Andrew noticed how deserted the village seemed to be. Except at weekends when, at all seasons, there were booted tourists trudging through on their way from one beauty spot to another,

Longton looked an empty, forsaken place. People kept to themselves and their houses to a degree that was downright morbid. Nothing moved for hours on end, and nothing changed except the weather and the gardens, where things sprouted and grew unnoticed for the most part, though they must have been tended by someone, since they were invariably kept in neat good-order.

It had been a wet afternoon and the darkening effect of the damp on the stone walls of the houses gave them a drab, self-effacing uniformity. The sky beyond the not-so-distant horizon was scarred by columns of sooty clouds that seemed to rise up vertically, and sweep along behind the crests of the hills like a line of megaliths on the march.

Andrew was startled when a girl of about fourteen in a long green coat, her face wedge-shaped in a high, turned-up collar, stepped out of a gate onto the road ahead of him. She had a dog on a lead. She stood and watched without expression as he drove past, leaning back to resist the tug of the big, impatient Alsatian. Andrew saw in the driving mirror that she remained watching his car for some seconds before turning and running off in the opposite direction, and felt obscurely uncomfortable. It was odd how even such a brief and remote encounter with a resident of Longton could make him feel unwelcome.

He parked by his front door, unpacked the luggage from the boot, and dropped it in the tiny hall. He took a brief turn round the house to check all was as he had left it, then looked out of his first-floor window at Kate's house, about twenty yards away from his. All seemed normal. There was no milk on the step by the side door, where Darrel, the delivery boy, always put it. The curtains were drawn back, and a fuzz of smoke drifted out of the chimney.

Probably Old Farmer Lomax was making a lot out of little, Andrew decided. It was the man's way. For all his size and lumpish manner, he was a gossip at heart, quite capable of embroidering a tiny tale into an epic to amuse himself and entertain his friends, especially if it was about the "incomers."

Nevertheless, Andrew felt a need to visit Kate to put his mind at rest. If she had seen or heard him return, she might think it strange if he went round at once, without pausing to wash or eat, so he did those things quickly, making a meal of the Stilton and fresh bread. Then he remembered he had an excuse to call on his neighbor anyway; he had a present for her.

Moments later, with the gift in its fancy wrapping under his arm, he tapped on the stained-glass sunset on her door. She was a long time in answering, and opened the door just as he knocked a second time. He saw at once she had been expecting him, was, at the very least, disturbed about something, and was going to try to conceal that fact from him. She smiled with her mouth, but her eyes had a different look, suggesting her mind was on whatever it was that troubled her, something serious and mysterious. Her sharp-featured, expressive face always betrayed her thoughts to some extent.

She reached up to kiss his forehead. He pecked her cheek in return, and handed her her present. She pushed him ahead into the comfortable, overfurnished parlor at the back of the cottage, murmuring what he took to be the usual words of gratitude. After handing him a bottle and glass, and instructing him to help himself, she unwrapped the gift. Her movements were uncharacteristically violent. She tugged at the tape round the box without trying to unfasten the simple bow he had tied, and tore at the paper clumsily. She seemed to be trying to regain the self-possession she had unaccountably lost, and to be aware that she was not succeeding.

He pointedly looked away from her toward the television. The screen was mostly dark, but formless, off-white, slithering shapes that he could not identify drifted languorously across it from time to time. He couldn't make out what was going on. He leaned forward and squinted. The volume was low; he was unable to understand a word of the whispered commentary.

When she saw what he was doing Kate pointed the remote control at the set and touched a button. The picture shrank and sank. There was a whirr and a click, and Andrew realized that he been watching a video.

He turned back to Kate, expecting some explanation as to why she had abruptly censored his viewing, but did not get one. She glanced at him, and their eyes met. She looked away at once, to the gift on her lap. She praised it hurriedly and overmuch, but without conviction. Words tumbled out of her as though they had been cramped away in some tight place and were glad to be free at last, then she suddenly shut up, and looked annoyed with herself. He beamed with pleasure in her apparent satisfaction, and poured a drink for himself. He asked if she wanted one, knowing that she hardly ever drank at home, or at all. After a brief, frozen pause, when her face opened wide like a window, and he could see her thoughts spinning, she nodded emphatically.

Surprised, he went to fetch her a glass.

In the kitchen, he was brought up short. The room was a mess. Empty cans and packages and half-eaten meals were spread about the work surfaces, and dirty dishes stuck out of greasy water in the sink. A box of cereal had spilt onto the floor and its contents crunched and crackled under foot. The food cupboard doors were open and the shelves inside were almost empty.

After some searching he found and rinsed a glass, half filled it with Smirnoff, added a drip of lime, and went and handed it to her. He hoped the spirit might loosen her tongue.

As she reached for the drink, she gave him a smile that got strangled at birth, and only increased his rising discomfort.

"How have things been?" he said. "In Longton, I mean," he added, as she looked at him slightly askance. "Anything interesting happen?"

"It never does," she said, "does it?"

"Not when I'm here. Not so far, anyway."

She shook her head cynically. "Nothing changes."

"You've been keeping okay?"

She sipped her vodka, pursed her lips, and nodded.

"Good," he said.

And thought, End of conversation! Christ, have I come to the wrong house? Or is this Kate's dozy twin sister that she's never told me about, and always kept hidden? It was as though she'd fixed a dimmer switch to her personality and turned it to minimum, or taken some numbing narcotic.

That's it, he thought, drugs!

He took a good look at what he could see of her eyes, but they were just dull and lifeless, not high and crazy, or pained and anxious from withdrawal. Something seemed to have been taken out of her, not inhaled or injected in. Something was missing.

He started to tell her about his time away, to give himself time to think. It had been just another dull business trip to Scandinavia, and he was hard pressed to come up with something amusing. She smirked at his attempts at wit, and smiled wanly at his trite tales about a lost-luggage crisis and the price of restaurant meals in Stockholm. After a few minutes, he gave up.

"By the way," he ventured, "is your car running again?"

"I had it fixed weeks ago. It's fine."

"Only I noticed you don't have much food in, so I wondered if you were off the road?"

She didn't react. He was still waiting for some comment when he suddenly noticed something else.

"Where's Bruckner?" he said. The dog usually gave him a warm but dignified welcome, being one of the rare ones of its race that was able to exercise self-control when a visitor came through its owner's front door. Now, there was no sign of it.

"He's gone." She sounded irritable, almost resentful.

"He's dead?"

"Probably. He just went. I let him out, and he didn't come back."

"That's odd. You looked for him?"

"Of course."

"You must really miss him."

"Yes; well, I did at first." She sounded as though she was finding it hard to remember how she had felt about her pet's disappearance.

Andrew couldn't believe it. Bruckner and Kate had been very close. She had never been silly about him, or treated him like a surrogate child, and they seemed to have developed a relationship based on respect. Bruckner had a steady nature, though he was prepared to look fierce for strangers when Kate required him to. He'd been a good dog. Now he was gone, and she hardly seemed to care.

He noticed her glass was empty. He'd hardly touched his drink. How long had he been holding it? Surely no more than a minute or two?

He drained his glass. Perhaps it's me, he thought. Jet lag, stress, something like that. He'd been traveling for almost twenty-four hours. He didn't feel too bad; a bit bleak and hazy, but not overtired.

Still, he didn't trust himself to wrestle with Kate's problems just then.

He'd sleep on his impressions, he decided, and consider them again in the morning.

When he got up to go, Kate didn't try to detain him, something that, out of affection or politeness, she usually made some small show of doing.

As he passed the front of her house he noticed, behind the net curtains, the glow of her TV set. She must have turned it back on the instant he was out of the room! He remembered the whitish smudges drifting through the cloudy depths of the screen. What had they been? Faces, perhaps, blurred and distorted?

Something, anyway, that she had not wanted him to see.

He spent the next morning unpacking and freshening up the cottage. Then he drove seven miles into Buxton to pick up supplies from a supermarket. He thought to ask Kate if she wanted anything, but couldn't bring himself to do so. He had been wondering restlessly about their relationship. He had thought they were, on many levels, quite close, but he had never been sure of Kate's friendship. Frequently, what seemed to be affection on her part had an artificial, warmed-over flavor, like fast food. Her amity sometimes had a false edge, but Andrew had not let this bother him. After all, they were neighbors, brought together by chance. On the whole, on the surface, they got on remarkably well.

But he was full of mixed feelings about his visit to her the previous evening. On one hand he had an impression that he may have been treated rather shabbily by her. On the other, he feared that he may have blundered in on Kate when she had been vulnerable and unhappy, and he had not been sensitive enough to appreciate the situation and react accordingly. He shouldn't have rushed round and thrust his gift at her as though it were an invitation to a party at her place. He should have ignored the siren warnings of trouble-stirring Mrs. Ashe and waited for a more appropriate time to visit.

His worst fear was that the loss of Bruckner explained Kate's obviously disturbed state, and he'd been crass enough to go on about the bloody dog, probably the one subject she did not want to think about. Still, there was no way he could have known that the creature was dead, and he tried to shrug off the wisps of guilt that lingered in his conscience.

He had lunch in Buxton and got back to his cottage just before three in the afternoon. He glanced across at Kate's house as he motored up his drive, and saw that her curtains were closed.

He watched part of a football match on TV but, at halftime, couldn't resist going upstairs and looking across at Kate's house. An unclaimed bottle of milk stood by her door.

I'm getting worse than Mrs. Ashe and the rest of the villagers, he thought. It's none of my business how Kate spends her days. I'm worrying about nothing. I saw her less than a day ago, and she was okay. Off color perhaps, but aren't we all sometimes? So what if she's tired? If she spends a day in bed?

Then an obvious explanation occurred to him. She had a *lover*. He was in there with her. She's having a wild affair!

The possibility made him feel worse than ever about his intrusion.

The theory would account for a lot: the disorder in the kitchen that, on reflection, was merely untidy (no time or energy for housework); Kate's distant, slightly nervous demeanor, and her lack of genuine enthusiasm to see him back.

As he half watched the last half of the match he searched inside himself to see if his speculations engendered any jealousy. They did. Not specifically sexual jealousy, though there was an element of that; more a nagging, resentful envy that was surprisingly painful. He would surely miss Kate's company.

But he felt he had been dumped abruptly, unceremoniously. She should have told him, given him some explanation, and not left him to puzzle things out himself. It *was* shabby. He was surprised at her for acting so covertly, as though she were ashamed. It was just not like her.

He wondered what sort of man was capable of causing her to behave so uncharacteristically and tried to picture him.

Then he realized that he had made the whole thing up out of almost nothing. There was not a scrap of real evidence to support his fanciful theory! There were a dozen equally plausible explanations.

The football petered out in a draw. The faces of the exhausted, frustrated players as they walked off the pitch brought the afternoon to a depressing anticlimax. Andrew switched off the TV.

He put on his boots, Gortex jacket, and waterproof trousers, and went for a long walk in the pouring rain.

He got back late.

The light was on in Kate's parlour. All looked normal. He peered over the hedge that divided their gardens. The milk had been taken in.

I'm an idiot, he thought, and Mrs. Ashe is a bloody witch.

Sunday started well. He was up early. He made a lot of coffee and drank it slowly as he read the papers, filling his mind with national scandals and despairs that he had missed while abroad. This took him to almost midday, when he had arranged to drive to Ashbourne to visit friends. He was running a bath and pulling the pins out of a new shirt when there was a knock at the door.

He thought, Kate!

He realized that he was unwashed and in his dressing gown, much as Mrs. Ashe had said Kate had been when Farmer Lomax had paid her a call. The thought amused him. He would point it out to her. He should have mentioned to her that Mrs. Ashe had spoken to him about her. It would be easy to make a joke of the whole affair, and perhaps clear the air a bit.

Andrew found a tired, rather aged policeman standing on his step when he opened his front door. The man stepped forward, took off his helmet awkwardly, and pushed a lick of long dark hair back over a bald spot with the palm of his free hand. At the same time he said, "Sorry to disturb you on the day of rest, sir, but we're making enquiries about a child who's been missing from her home in the village for two nights. You might know her: Linda Morris? The family lives at this end of the village."

Andrew shook his head.

"It's got serious," the PC continued. "She took her dog out for exercise Friday evening and didn't come back. The dog turned up at the house last night, badly injured, so we're fearing the worst."

"That's terrible."

"Yes. Have you seen a child, or anyone unusual about?"

Andrew was about to answer in the negative when he remembered the girl with a dog he had seen from his car.

"Perhaps," he said. "How was she dressed. Was she wearing a green coat?"

"She was. You've seen her?"

Andrew described the tiny encounter while the PC took notes. He was aware that the man was taking in his untidy, unwashed state, and watching his face closely.

"You didn't by any chance give her a lift, did you, sir?" the policeman asked.

"Of course not. Why should I?"

"It was a raw evening, last Friday."

"She didn't need a lift from me or anyone."

"You asked her then, sir?"

"No." Andrew was beginning to feel the thin edge of anger. "I didn't stop. She looked in no kind of trouble. Anyway, she was with that enormous dog."

"Was that the only reason why you didn't offer her a lift, sir? Because of the dog?"

"I'm not sure what you're getting at. I've told you what happened, what I saw, which was nothing much."

"But you said she was looking at you?"

"She seemed to be, yes."

"That's a bit strange, if you don't know her, isn't it?"

"Not really. She probably recognized me."

"Why would she?"

"I'm an 'incomer.' I've lived here little more than a year; I'm still a stranger."

"And very likely you always will be, sir," the policeman said dourly. "What time would you say you saw the missing girl?"

"About five forty-five."

"And you went next door to see your neighbor about an hour later?"

"That's right."

"So you were on your own during that period," the policeman stated pointedly.

"Correct," Andrew snapped. "And I've been alone since I left my neighbor's house on Friday evening, if it's of any interest."

"You stayed in your cottage all that time, did you?"

"I shopped in Buxton yesterday morning, and went for a walk last night."

The policeman looked amazed. "You must be a keen hiker. It was pissing down yesterday evening."

"I like walking in the rain," Andrew said, almost petulantly, perhaps because it was a lie. He had not enjoyed the walk at all, in any normal sense, and had only persevered with it because of some grim, urgent, masochistic need, the memory of which now embarrassed and disturbed him.

The policeman told Andrew he would be required to make a statement.

Andrew explained he was going to see some friends. The policeman looked doubtful at this, thought about it, then smiled and said Andrew had been very helpful. He would be contacted later. Meanwhile, if he remembered anything else however small . . .

The bathwater was chilly when Andrew stepped into it. He poured in more hot. He sat shivering and thinking about what he had said to the policeman. He wished that he *had* gone straight round to see Kate when he had got home on Friday evening. Because he hadn't done so, and had no alibi for the hour immediately after his return, he knew that the police would look upon him as a suspect. He would be investigated.

But I'm innocent! he thought anxiously as, later, he pulled the crisp new shirt down over his cold, damp body.

Then, for some reason, he found himself thinking about Kate's absent dog, Bruckner.

He got back from Ashbourne at about nine-thirty, went straight round to Kate's house, and rapped on the door. There was a tradition that they went together to the Magnus Arms for the last hour on Sunday night, and he had decided he was going to try to keep her to it. He would do his best to persuade her, if she proved reluctant to go. He had not been able to enjoy his Ashbourne friends' company because his mind had been on Kate, the lost girl, and his interview with the policeman. He had not felt able to discuss anything with his friends, though they heard on TV that a murder hunt was on for a child was missing from the village where Andrew lived, and had asked him about it. A feeling of totally unwarranted guilt made him reluctant to relate his slight knowledge of the subject, though his thoughts were of nothing else. Except Kate.

He decided he needed to talk to her at once.

The cottage seemed in darkness as he strode up her drive but, when he was close to the parlor window, he saw the cold glow of the TV behind the curtains. He banged on the door, waited, then banged harder. He stepped back a few paces and saw that the light from the TV was no longer showing. She'd turned it off. She was in there, knowing he was outside, and she was not going to let him in!

He couldn't believe it.

He felt a surge of rage, picked up a pebble, tapped loudly on her window, and called her name. The house responded with a powerful silence, like an ancient, empty ruin, and he felt like a desecrater, a hooligan bent on mischief. His voice sounded wild and peevish. He called again, deliberately deepening his tone.

No answer.

His anger, with nothing to center on, seeped away, giving place to confusion and hurt irritation.

"Well, sod you too," he muttered, then was ashamed of himself.

He strode round the side of the house into the chaotic back garden. He was aware, as he passed, of the squat black shape of his own cottage hanging, like a reflection of Kate's, on his right. The night was dark, with only a thin shell of moon to light the autumn sky, but his eyes were adjusting well, and he picked his way through the disorder of untrimmed bushes and collapsing outhouses without stumbling. He found at one point that he was walking on loose earth, as though Kate had been doing some digging. If so, it was the first heavy gardening he had ever known her to do.

Looking round, he could see no sign of life anywhere at the rear of the cottage. Feeling puzzled and let down, he was about to retreat to his own home when he sensed a movement directly behind him and something pressed hard across his shoulders. Shocked, he leapt forward, turning as he did so. He lost his balance, fell on one knee, but scrambled up quickly, ready to defend himself. Whatever had blundered against him had not been friendly.

Then, out of the silhouette of a collapsed greenhouse that sheltered a dim confusion of moon-bathed broken glass, struts of peeling, white-painted wood, and dark overgrown plant shapes, something rose up and floated towards him.

At first he wondered if he was at the receiving end of an elaborate, foolish joke. He thought someone was waving a shrunken balloon or a partly inflated paper bag at him on the end of a stick. Briefly, the pallid form hovered close in front of him, at a height a little greater than his own. Then he began to get a better idea what confronted him. He realized that the blunt-ended, ash grey, slightly luminous shape that seemed to be inspecting him, but that had no eyes, was nothing he could account for. It was outside of his experience. It inspired not just fear, but a sensation of awe, of chilling reverence.

The dull, dumb, faceless thing that still seemed to be somehow solemn regarding him then drifted backwards with a silky, dancing motion, swaying like an enchanted snake.

He got the impression that it was hollow, empty, a husk. Its movements had no weight.

As it drew away he saw that the pale blob was a head attached to an impossibly scrawny body dressed in some kind of loose, dark suit. It stepped carefully back on naked, shriveled, possibly human feet and edged its way silently down into the ruins of the greenhouse, like a crab tucking itself under weed in a rock pool.

When the thing had gone, Andrew remained for some moments, paralyzed and hardly breathing, in the position into which he had stumbled when he had first caught sight of it. He was overwhelmingly grateful to it for going away. He had been afraid, when it had been close to him, that his heart had stopped beating, and that he had pitched into some afterlife from which there was no escape.

Moments later, when he could think more freely, he realized that, though the thing had retreated into the greenhouse, it had risen out of the freshly dug earth that he had walked over seconds before it had appeared. He had disturbed it. It had come to find out who or what he was.

And now it knew.

He was not aware of returning to his own cottage but, half an hour later, he was in his tiny kitchen when the phone rang. It was the police wanting his statement.

A car with a flashing light came to drive him to Buxton. He thought, They don't trust me to drive there myself. Why not?

In a bleak room at the police station he was asked a lot more questions. Hard questions. Some of them he couldn't understand. He was confused. The thing he had seen hung in his mind, as earlier it had hovered close to his face, disturbing his thoughts. He had an urge to mention it, but dared not do so.

His hands were trembling when he was asked to sign his statement. The pen shook. Three policemen watched him without pity, their critical faces expressing a mixture of unfriendly emotions.

He was returned home in silence, alone in the back of the car. The driver sniffed from time to time and half turned his head, as though he detected a nasty odor somewhere behind him. He didn't answer when Andrew wished him good night.

Andrew had been awake for hours when his alarm went off at seven the next morning. He had decided to go to his office early, to throw himself into the backlog of work he expected to find there.

He felt awful, drained and anxious. He made coffee, and found he had no milk. He couldn't drink coffee black.

Darrel, the milkman, delivered to the cottage at seven twenty-five every morning precisely. A minute after that time Andrew opened his side door and reached down in the dark for his bottle. It wasn't there. Then he remembered he had heard no bottles clinking. Darrel was a punctual boy, but clumsy and noisy. He was late.

As he retreated back through the door Andrew noticed a dim light from Kate's house opposite. He peered over the scruffy hedge that divided their gardens.

The door corresponding to the one he was standing in was open. A figure stood there with its back to Andrew. Its arms were flung wide, as though it had been crucified against the wall on either side above the door. The two hands remained fixed in place, but the body writhed and reached back, as though it was trying to withdraw from a source of pain. Andrew recognized at once that the figure, dressed in a blue nylon jacket and trousers, was Darrel. Just beyond the boy, inches from him, he could see someone else, facing him. Kate. She was holding her hands up on either side of her face, her fingers outstretched. Her head was tilted back. Her eyes, as far as he could tell, were shut, but her mouth was open wide, as though she were screaming. She was quite silent.

Behind her, in the dark, and obscured by the two closer figures, stood someone else. Andrew could see no details, but he thought whoever it was was male. As he watched the man seemed to reach round the right side of Kate and stab at Darrel's chest. Andrew thought he saw the glint of glass or a knife. Darrel's back convulsed, and Kate brought her hands together on the boy's face, as though to smother or silence him. Nevertheless, Darrel made a terrible sound. He sank away from Kate, who let go of his head, bent down, and appeared to kiss his chest. It was a long, lover's kiss. It was audible to Andrew. Sickeningly so.

Darrel was handicapped. At eighteen he had a mental age of eight. He had been born badly; his body was unsymmetrical; he walked with a jolting, ungainly stride. His head was huge, and lolled from side to side. Kate had always liked him. She enjoyed his simplicity and his odd, childish sense of fun. She thought his father treated him harshly, so she made a fuss of him on his birthdays and at Christmas, giving him generous tips. She had been sisterly and kind towards him. Nothing more. Nothing else.

Now she suddenly drew back from the boy's chest as though the man behind had wrenched her away. She retreated quickly into the cottage, sliding along the wall to allow the other past to take her place. She left a smear of something along the wallpaper.

Briefly, Andrew got a glimpse of the third member of the group. He recognized the long, almost tubular bare oval of the head and the sharp, yet sinuous movements, as those of the being he had encountered the previous evening. But it had changed. It now had a mouth, and two livid eyes glared out of bluish patches above a sharp, canine nose.

Andrew knew it had seen him. He felt the thing's eyes lock onto his own for one terrible second. The face seemed to sneer at him. It tipped contemptuously back, and remained poised in that position for a moment. Then the wide stretched jaws lunged down on Darrel's shoulder. The boy jerked, as though he had been kicked, and howled softly, piteously.

Andrew jumped back into his house. He pushed the glass and plywood door away from him into its frame slowly, as though it were huge and heavy, as though by doing so he was protecting and distancing himself from all he had seen. He stumbled round the house in the almost dark like a thief searching for a way out. He tripped over a coffee table, tipping the things he had prepared for breakfast across the floor, and fell onto the resulting mess. Uncomfortable as he was, he wanted to lie there for the rest of the day, but his curiosity wouldn't let him. It drove him to a window overlooking Kate's house where he stood and gazed across at the open door, fascinated but horrified, and hoping he could not be seen.

As Andrew watched, Darrel broke free, or was released. He seemed to almost bounce away. Unable to run, he seesawed from side to side, wildly trying to make haste on his unequal legs. There were bloodstains on his shirt emanating from above his heart where there was a darker patch, like an open wound.

As Darrel disappeared down Kate's front path the lights in her cottage went out and the side door closed. Andrew watched for a while, but nothing more happened.

He worried frantically about Darrel, and would have gone out to him, but he was worried even more about Kate. He was also aghast at the scene he had witnessed, and was limp with fear and incredulity. He leaned against the wall by the window with his eyes shut, trying to make sense of it all for perhaps an hour, then sat on the floor hugging his knees for as long again.

Then he called his office and told them he was sick.

Just before midday he had a further visit from the police. It was the constable who had first called, this time with a WPC as company. They explained that the lost child had still not been found and that they were searching all houses and outbuildings in the area. The policeman was even less friendly than before, Andrew thought, realizing that yet again he was unshaven and in his dressing gown and must be creating an odd impression. The WPC was nicer, but unnerving. She kept staring at a point above his nose as she spoke, shaking her head slightly and slowly, as though reading words printed on his forehead.

He told them to search where they liked, and wandered out into his garden. He tried to see over into Kate's, looking for the newly dug patch, but everything was too overgrown; he could see nothing but unpruned roses choking in a jungle of giant, gone-to-seed weeds.

On returning to the house he found his visitors had switched on his television. The screen was a jitter of static fuzz. The WPC was fiddling buttons, trying to get a picture. She explained that they wanted the news as they might be in it. They had been filmed earlier searching local fields. Andrew was gratified to see she was pink with embarrassment as she moved aside to make room for him.

"Something wrong with the set?" she asked.

Andrew shook his head. "You must have pushed the wrong button."

"I don't think so," she insisted. "Mine's the same model."

Andrew made no comment. The set *was* acting strange. No picture on any channel, and he couldn't get more than a whisper on the sound. Irritated, he pushed buttons at random. The screen went milky, then filled with monochromatic swirling eddies, like simmering oil.

Dim shapes rose out of this slick. One of them reached up and grew big, like a deep-sea creature approaching and peering into a diver's helmet. It almost filled the screen. To Andrew, it resembled a bare bald head, encased in tight opal flesh that looked ready to split and peel. Its mouth was a pale, straight gash. It had sharp eyes like black diamonds that seemed to be searching for something or someone out beyond the screen.

Andrew thought he knew what it was, and who it was looking for.

He swore, and switched off the set with an angry motion.

"You were getting something then!" the policeman said, apparently undisturbed by the images he had seen.

"Not the news," Andrew snapped.

"You should have stayed with it," the WPC protested. "It'll be on in a moment."

"I don't think so." Andrew slipped the remote control into the pocket of his dressing gown. The woman looked cross and disappointed. "You're right," Andrew added. "It's not working properly. It needs fixing."

The policeman watched him curiously, as though he suspected he was drunk or crazy and might shortly need restraining. Andrew scratched the scar tissue left by the hang-gliding injury on the side of his face. It itched when he was stressed or nervous. It was not a pleasant action to watch as it made one side of his face look like Lon Chaney in profile. The Phantom of the Opera! The WPC stopped reading the lines on his forehead and looked away. Perhaps to change the subject or to distract herself she said, "That was a terrible accident this morning. The boy was badly injured. He may not survive."

Andrew gaped. "What accident? What boy?"

"The delivery boy. He drove his milk-float into a lorry. Head-on. He's in intensive care."

Andrew felt himself swaying. "Darrel? The milk boy?"

"That's him."

Andrew dropped into a chair, his face white, and slapped his brow like a ham actor. He felt the two pairs of eyes watching him closely, and realized the constables must think he was wildly overreacting.

"Friend of yours, was he?" the man asked, with a hint of sympathy.

"No," Andrew said sharply, rejecting the idea. Then, shaking his head confusedly, "Not really. But I knew him, of course."

"Lots of things happening in Longton all of a sudden," the man observed. "Strange, isn't it?"

Satisfied that they had made a thorough search of the cottage, the two constables went into Andrew's long back garden and began stalking carefully through it. It was not nearly as chaotic as his neighbor's, but weeds had begun to take over during his absence. They'd spent five minutes poking about there when they were suddenly called away. They seemed reluctant to go, and promised to return later that day, with lights if necessary, as it would soon start to get dark.

As soon as they were out of sight Andrew went and banged on Kate's doors. There was no response. He leaned on the side door, then hit it with his knee just below the lock. It gave a bit, but not enough. He went home, found a large screwdriver, and attacked the door with that. He chipped away at the wood, and kicked it viciously. It slammed back against an inner wall.

The first thing Andrew noticed as he stepped inside was the long red smudge along the opposite wall, like the path of a bloody comet, that he had seen Kate make that morning.

He edged into the silent house and called Kate's name. There was no reply, but the beams over his head creaked once, as though something on the first floor had shifted weight.

He went into the parlor and found Kate in the same seat she had occupied when he had last spoken to her, nearly seventy hours ago. The lower half of her body was covered with a blanket that she clutched with both thin hands above her stomach, in a frail, old-womanish gesture. She was watching the TV. On screen the pallid, washed-out, floating shapes he was familiar with drifted in and out of background of metamorphosing gray masses, to an accompaniment of small, almost inaudible sounds.

Kate started to move as he entered the room. She lifted and turned her head slowly, as though it weighed heavy. She nodded blankly at him, accepting rather than greeting him, and watched as he drew a chair closer to hers.

He couldn't help staring at her. She looked terribly frail. Her frizzy blond hair was a mess. She had aged years. Her half-closed eyes were dull, even against the smudges of bruised skin on her upper cheeks. Her face, always thin, was now sharply bony. Her lips were almost invisible, and her nostrils wide and dark. Andrew thought again of drugs, then dismissed the idea, knowing her problems were worse than that.

She said something, probably his name, then coughed to clear her throat. He said hello, his voice faltering.

"You shouldn't be here," she stated wearily. "Be careful. For now, he needs you, but you're next."

Andrew's brow creased uncomprehendingly. "What do you mean, Kate?" he asked gently, and leaned out of his seat towards her.

She shook her head fretfully, said, "It's probably too late; there's nothing you can do," and turned her face back to the TV screen, as though no further explanation were necessary or possible.

Andrew followed her gaze for a while, then said, "What *is* this that you're watching, Kate?"

"A video. It belonged to my husband. I found it, and others like it, among some of his belongings a few weeks ago.

"I thought I had destroyed everything of his," she added, with a whining note of anger, "but somehow a few things survived. They always do. I should have known."

"What's it about?" Andrew insisted. "What does it represent?"

Kate's razor-thin lips stretched, perhaps in a smile. "It represents my husband," she said. "It's a film that was made just before he died, over three years ago. He went away for a while and returned with this, and other things. You could say it was his holiday snapshots; something like that."

"I don't understand you, Kate," Andrew said uneasily, not sure if she was intending to be humorous.

She turned to him again, her head moving with greater ease now. "Don't you?" she said. "Are you sure? When I first found the videos (he was alive then, and I watched them without telling him), *I* understood them at once. Mind you, I had some reason to suspect. . . ."

Andrew waited for her to continue then; when she didn't, said, "I'm getting those pictures, or something like them, on my set. I know it's not possible, but I am."

"Then he's got to you," she said. "I was right. It *is* too late."

"For what? And who's 'he'?"

"Don't pretend," Kate said almost scornfully. "I know you were watching from your door the other morning when there was an . . . incident. So does he. And he won't forget."

She became rigid in her chair, with her eyes half closed and an intense expression on her face, as though she were reviewing or reliving the grotesque events he had witnessed.

"You never told me much about your husband," Andrew observed, seemingly somewhat obliquely, after a period of strained silence, "just that he was dead."

"Oh yes, he died at last, there's no doubt about that. I *know* he was dead; I made sure of it."

"How did he die?"

"Violently. Very violently. He was a powerful man. It took a lot to kill him. I learned that lesson a few weeks before his life finally ended. He seemed to have died *then*, but I was wrong; somehow, he survived, and came back for me."

"You mean, 'to you'?"

"I mean what I say," she insisted. "Anyway, I eluded him then; I escaped: he didn't get me. He died, undoubtedly he died, and I thought I was free of him."

"The trouble is," she added bitterly, "I'd locked him up, but I forgot to throw away the key."

She clutched with both hands at the arm of the chair as though to lift herself, but failed to rise up. Andrew wondered if she had the strength to get to her feet. He thought not.

He stood up himself and, without asking, poured two big drinks. Kate took the one he offered without comment. She drank half at once. He drank all of his.

He said, "The police are searching the area for a girl who's gone missing. They're looking everywhere. They've been through my house, and almost finished my garden. They'll come to you next. I wanted to warn you."

She shrugged. "They came before to ask me questions. They could see me through the window. I think they thought that *I* was dead. I had to let them in or they would have knocked the door in, as you have done. But I had nothing to tell them. I know nothing about a lost girl."

"No, perhaps not," Andrew said uncertainly, "but is there anyone else here with you now?"

Kate's eyes automatically flickered up towards the ceiling. "If the police do come, and insist on searching the house, then they will have to deal with whatever they find in their own way, if they can. It could be interesting."

"Interesting? Christ! I can't believe you can be so indifferent to your situation, Kate," Andrew said impatiently. "The boy who was involved in your 'incident' was in a serious accident immediately after he left here. Our houses are the last on the edge of the village, and yours was the last delivery he made. The police are bound to question you about him, as a matter of course. You can't say you don't know about *that*."

"You're wrong," Kate replied shortly. "I know nothing about the accident. It's the first I've heard of it."

Andrew noticed she expressed no anxiety about Darrel or his condition, and felt a stab of repugnance that made him wonder if he was beginning to hate her. He remembered her indifference to the loss of Bruckner, her dog. That was bad, but Bruckner was only a pet; Darrel was a friend who was probably going to die, and Kate seemed unmoved. She didn't even seem to find it "interesting."

On the floor above, something stirred. There were heavy footfalls, and a long scraping sound, as though a weighty object were being shoved into place. Perhaps it's barricading itself in, Andrew thought, with no inclination to go and investigate the truth of his speculation. Kate ignored, or did not notice, the noises.

Andrew was worried that the police would be returning soon. He did not want to be with Kate when they did. He was not sure quite what he thought they would find but, whatever it was, he did not want to be associated with it or with Kate.

She must have detected his anxiety to get away, because she said, "You may as well leave. There's nothing you can do to help."

"But are you sure? What will you do?"

She shook her head slightly, a tiny movement. "Nothing much. I'm very tired; I shall probably sleep."

"I'll call round tomorrow, to see how you are," he said dutifully.

"No you won't," she murmured, sinking deeper into her chair. "Don't bother. I'll come to you, when I'm ready. That may not be for some time, but I will come."

Her voice was so low, it was almost inaudible. As he left the room, he thought he heard her say, as she tumbled into sleep:

"Don't forget; I told you; you're next."

He didn't like it because he didn't understand it, but it sounded like a threat.

The police returned half an hour later. Lots of them.

Andrew stood at the back of his home in the autumn twilight, and watched as they combed through his garden, finding nothing.

They marched next door to Kate's cottage. They got no answer from the front, then found that the side door had been forced. They got quite excited about this discovery. A small but senior-looking man, an officer in a flat hat, was instantly called up from somewhere. He took charge. He carefully pushed the door open and took half a step inside.

Then there was a vivid flash, bright as lightning, that hurt Andrew's eyes, blinding him for seconds. When he could see again, the air was full of tiny fragments of black ash and the smell of burning.

The officer who had tried to enter the building was screaming. The front of his body looked like burnt toast, his face had turned to cinders that were beginning to ooze blood. Two other men who had been close behind him were writhing on the ground, similarly injured.

Andrew noticed that there was no fire raging, and no smoke. He ran through the hedge into Kate's garden, shouting that she was in the building.

As he got near he could see, through the open door, she could not have survived. The inside of the house looked as though someone had gone through it with a flame-thrower. Nothing had moved, but the surface of everything had been charred black by a flash-fire of intense heat.

A policewoman ordered Andrew back into his house. Someone shouted to him to call the fire brigade, which he did, though there was no fire to put out. He spent a confused hour with people running in and out of his house.

Kate's house was searched, then it was declared safe. Two corpses were found. Kate was dead in her chair. The second was discovered in an upper room. From snatches of half-heard conversation, Andrew got the impression that there was something strange about it, something that disturbed and disgusted those who came across it.

Then the plot of freshly dug earth at the rear of Kate's cottage was spotted, sparking off another round of activity. Men started digging down into it carefully with spades. Something was dug out and taken away. Lights were brought from somewhere, and the site was hidden away behind walls of thick plastic sheeting.

Later, other, bigger finds were made.

At first, the police merely put out the information that Kate had died in a gas explosion. Later, when they revealed what they had discovered in her garden, this explanation was widely questioned, but no more satisfactory cause for the gutting of the cottage was forthcoming, though it was assumed that she and the . . . other person had committed suicide.

The contents of the pit, that turned out to have been a grave, were:

First, not far beneath the surface, the remains of part of a large dog, later more or less identified as Bruckner, Kate's lost pet. It had been there some weeks. Its head and heart were missing, and never were found.

Five feet below Bruckner was the body of a young girl. She was lying facedown and was fully dressed. There were tooth marks and a deep wound above her left breast. Her green coat and her blouse and sweater were torn above this injury, as though someone (or thing) had bitten right through them. The injury was not the cause of her death. She had suffocated. Her mouth and throat were full of dirt, as though she had somehow died down there, under the earth.

It was what was found *under her* that totally mystified everyone—with the single exception of Andrew—however. This was the corpse of a man who had been dead for three or more years. He was lying on his back below the girl and, most strangely, had his arms around her back as though he were hugging her, or so the men who did the digging insisted, though few believed them. But the most singular thing of all was the fact that the male corpse was headless.

The head was found—between the man's feet. It had been buried in a crudely constructed wooden box that was a tight fit. Two dozen eight-inch nails had been driven through the box into the skull on all six sides, creating quite a puzzle for the police surgeon whose task it was to sort the whole thing out.

But sort it out he did. He was even able to identify the corpse. It was Kate's husband, a man who, it transpired, the police had been wanting to question about a number of murders and mysterious disappearances at the time of *his* disappearance, at what was now understood to be also the time of his death.

As soon as he was able to do so, Andrew went abroad for six weeks, to get away from the press and police.

His time of absence from Longton did not do him much good. He hated the place when he returned, and decided to move out as soon as he could.

On his first day back he wandered into the Magnus Arms at lunchtime in the hope of learning what had occurred while he had been away. People were not particularly friendly towards him; but then, they never had been. They were noticeably reluctant to talk to him, even when he bought them drinks. Nevertheless, he realized that the village had quickly settled back into its normal somnolence.

He drank too much in the pub, and tottered home with a couple of tins of lager, intending to watch football on TV. He had not turned the set on since before Kate's death and had forgotten that it had seemed to have something wrong with it.

He opened a tin, slumped into his chair, and thumbed the remote. The screen filled with ugly, oily, swirling shapes. Familiar shapes. They filled him with dread. He swore at them. Feeling his flesh creep, he lurched towards the TV and tried to turn it off.

He hit the off switch, but nothing happened. The pictures wouldn't go away. The shapes seemed to get clearer and more active, if anything.

Kneeling down with his face close to the set, he could clearly hear the soft sounds that it was making. He put his ear close to the speaker and listened, trying to make sense of the nagging noises.

After a while, he thought he could, just. Under the babble and clatter he could hear another sound that reoccurred from time to time.

It was a human voice, a woman's voice.

It was Kate's voice, and she was repeating the same two words over and over again:

"You're next—you're next—you're next."

He got very frightened then.

He went to the wall and pulled the TV plug out of its socket.

Again, nothing happened. The picture didn't waver. The sounds even got louder.

Then he made a big mistake.

He kicked the screen.

It collapsed into fragments, releasing all that was inside of it, all the things that had come across to him from Kate's house the moment it had burned, and had been impatiently waiting for him to return to free them. They swirled around him triumphantly, terrifyingly.

He saw Kate and her husband among them.

The man smiled.

Kate smiled. She held out her arms to Andrew.

"You're next," she said.

And he believed her.

KING OF CROWS
Midori Snyder

Midori Snyder has written five well-received magical novels, as well as short fiction for both children and adults. Her most recent works are *The Flight of Michael McBride*, an Irish-American fantasy novel set on the old Texas frontier, and a children's book set in the world of James Gurney's *Dinotopia*. She is currently at work on a novel based on Italian myths and history. Snyder is the daughter of French poet Emile Snyder; she grew up in the U.S. and Africa. She recently returned to the U.S. after spending a year living in Milan.

The story that follows, of music and crows, has a beautiful folkloric quality. It comes from *Xanadu 3*, edited by Jane Yolen.

—T.W.

The day had been hot and dusty, the sky a wide bowl of blue overhead when Johnny Fahey walked into the canyon. The sudden sweet taste of water in the air opened his parched lips in surprise. Along the high walls of the canyon, the wind whistled in the deepening crevasses and scattered drifts of pink sandstone. Johnny smiled and then he sighed, his exhalation a dry puff.

He'd walked much of that day and the day before; always on the lookout for the mining camp, the lonely settler, and the small towns with their weddings and wakes. Johnny Fahey had left home many years since, left the green of his own country to wander across the sun-bleached West, the dry flat roads of the plains, and the dark rugged mountains. But no matter where he traveled, stranger though he was, he was never at a loss for words, for he needed none. The music of his fiddle spoke for him and it was welcomed wherever he went. Doors opened at its sound, a place was made by a campfire, and food and drink appeared. It was a free life, one that chased forward like the sprinkle of notes, each connected for an instant but not remaining.

In a patch of long grass, Johnny Fahey sat down to rest in the shade. He leaned his back companionably against the rocks and took off his hat. The wind played through his damp blond hair and cooled his forehead. At thirty-odd years, Johnny had the face of a child with china-blue eyes and an easy smile. His cheeks had reddened beneath the sun's glare, but the skin of his forehead, protected by his hat, was white and no lines creased his smooth brow beneath the straight fine hair.

He took from his pack a small canteen, shaking it first to hear the splash of its contents. Not much left, came the echoing reply. He opened its lid and drained the last few sips of water. The canyon would provide more. If there was grass, there must be a spring or a stream, he reasoned, somewhere in the heart of the canyon. Johnny closed his eyes and rested, feeling his limbs sink into the yielding grass. It was peaceful after a day's walk.

But he didn't rest long. The wind that tugged at his hair brought with it sounds.

Johnny opened his eyes and cocked his head to the wind. There it was again, a sharp, shrill calling. A bark, he guessed, imagining the coyotes taking their pleasure like himself in the unexpected grass. No, he thought again as the wind brought the sound closer. Not a bark, but the harsh cawing of crows, their raucous voices rising from the hidden basin of the canyon.

Johnny stood up and, shouldering his pack and fiddle, walked deeper into the canyon. The road twisted and turned through high-walled corridors until at last the canyon opened into a wide grassy field. Spread across the field were crows, fanning their black wings over the grass. He stopped, awed at the sight of so many, their necks thrown back as they called to one another. The swirling flocks settled themselves uneasily, stalking through the long grass, their heads reared to catch the sunlight. And with a common cry, they shook their feathers, beaks breaking and limbs stretching until they had shaped themselves into the semblance of human form. Now standing before him were men and women striding over the green, their wings changed into cloaks of black velvet.

And among them was one who caught Johnny's gaze. Her face was moon-white in the night sweep of her long hair. Across her forehead the black eyebrows arched over two eyes of glittering jet and the pouting lips were a stained mulberry. A black velvet ribbon fluttered at her white throat. The black cloak draped over her rounded shoulders that perched above small breasts and a slender waist. As Johnny Fahey gazed at her, music burst in his head into a loud and joyous peal; the reels tripping over the stately waltzes, the fast jigs into the slow airs, and the more the music tumbled, the more his heart felt driven by the girl with the black eyes and the moon-white skin. He had no fear of the strange assembly, for the music coursing in his veins chased it out and, without another thought, he walked into the green field where the crows stood arguing in the rough shouts of human speech.

"The King must name his successor!" cried a man whose black cloak carried a border of gray diamonds. "Before it's too late!"

"He has a daughter!" cried out a woman, her hands curled tightly around the billowing folds of a rebellious cloak.

"But she must have a mate! The law requires it. And she refuses!"

"Do you blame her?" a younger woman cackled loudly to her companion. "Not one among them would I choose if it were up to me."

"It isn't up to you anyway," the second snipped in return.

"But who would you pick?"

"The one with the loudest voice, who else? To be heard over this!" the companion answered, shaking the folds of her light cape.

"Rilka has to choose among us!" came a new chorus. "She must marry! There must be a new King crowned before the end of the season."

Johnny Fahey felt the earth tremble beneath his feet as he approached the court of crows. The whistled wind was hushed beneath their loud cries and the crickets silent between the rocks. Johnny bowed his head, the sounds of their rising arguments clashing in his ears. They did not listen to each other but each voice shouted more loudly until they merged into a single cacophony of discontent.

The crows parted at Johnny's approach, some turning astonished faces at his unexpected presence, but never stopping in their loud cries. It wasn't until Johnny Fahey stood before the girl with white skin and black hair that the violent arguments subsided into grumbles and then at last into an uneasy silence. The girl stared at him with curiosity, her head tilted to one side as the glittering eyes fastened on his face. A smile crooked the edges of her mouth and the arched brows drew together in a challenge.

"Who are you?" she asked, her voice sharp as a scythe.

"No one as grand as you," he answered softly.

She lifted her chin proudly, the sweep of her black hair flowing into the curve of her back. Opals sparkled in her earlobes like tiny stars, and around her slender waist she wore a belt of freshwater pearls.

"What are you?" she demanded, and her shoulders hunched, her face thrust forward.

"A musician," he said simply, arms resting at his side.

The cloaks of the crows fluttered in the rising wind with a dry chaffing noise.

"Play for us," she ordered.

"Rilka, we've no time for it!" a man snapped. Johnny Fahey turned to the man, hearing immediately the authority in his voice. A singular voice amongst so much discord. The man was old, the plumage on his cloak speckled at the breast and dull and ragged along the hem. But circling his forehead was a narrow crown of silver, set with turquoise. There was still power in his carriage, the heavy body leaning over his hips, his shoulders arched back. In one hand he held a scepter made from a fresh stalk of corn that gleamed as bright as minted gold. Johnny Fahey had no doubt but that this was the King of Crows. He looked back at the girl called Rilka and the music in his heart stumbled as he realized that the girl with the moon-white skin and black hair was his daughter. No chance for you, the sad chords played, no chance this haughty creature could be charmed by the fiddle or the song.

"I want to hear it, Father," the girl demanded, "if only to hear something other than their bickering," and she tossed her head toward the line of men who stood glowering at the quiet figure of Johnny Fahey.

The King rolled his eyes to the blue bowl sky.

"Spoiled bitch," came a nasty whisper followed by snickering.

"Play then!" the King roared, turning on the restless court to silence them.

Rilka lowered her face, the shadow of her hair on her cheek not quite hiding the angry blush. Johnny Fahey winced seeing how the insult cut her pride to the quick. But he took out his fiddle and tucked it under his chin. He rested the bow over the strings and waited a moment more to hear what the wind would bring him. A tune came from listening, knowing what was already playing in the hearts of those gathered. He thought he could well guess at the tunes a crow might wish; something wild, with the harsh rasp of double-stops. Then Rilka raised her face and he saw in the dark eyes an unexpected yolk of gentleness.

The soft whisper of her sigh touched him and without intending to, he lowered his fiddle again and began to sing slowly in a clear tenor voice.

> *I met a fairy woman*
> *At the river's eddy.*
> *And I asked her*
> *Would anything unlock love?*
> *She said to me in whispered words,*
> *When it enters the heart*
> *It will never be released.*

There followed a silence, filled only with the rise and hollow of the wind in the grass. Johnny Fahey heard the slow beat of his filled heart. Abruptly he put the fiddle beneath his chin again and played a reel as fast as his singing was slow, the notes scraping against a sudden ache. He might gain her, they sang, but how could he keep her? He might lose her now, but she would be forever in his thoughts. Amber rosin smoked over the strings and the white hairs of his bow broke like the strands of a clinging web. He drove the tune, as if to empty the sight of her face from his heart, and yet as he finished the last notes he looked up and her glittering eyes snared him.

"Teach me to do that!" she demanded.

Johnny gave a weary smile. "To play the fiddle?" he asked. "It's not that easily done."

"No, not the fiddle," she answered, shaking her head, and in the sunlight the black hair glimmered blue. "Teach me to sing."

The King, silent until now, threw back his head and roared with laughter. Around him the court followed suit, their strident cries glancing off the stones and circling the air. Rilka's white face flamed and she turned angrily to the King, her fists clenched.

"Laugh if you want, but I won't choose a mate until I have learned to sing!" she proclaimed.

"You already sing well enough!"

"No, not like that. A sweet voice, that's what I want."

"No!" the King protested. "You're my daughter, a crow, and must call with a crow's voice."

"I'll learn to sing, or I'll not be married!" Rilka cried again, stamping her foot.

The King frowned, his expression sour, but his daughter crossed her arms over her chest and stood stubbornly facing him, the flaming cheeks adamant.

Johnny Fahey gave a slight smile. "I'll teach your daughter to sing," he said quietly. "But on one condition."

"A waste of time!" the King said gruffly.

"I'm in no hurry," Johnny replied.

"What's your condition?" Rilka asked, eagerly.

"That if I succeed, I be made the King of Crows," Johnny answered, surprised by his own boldness. But how else to gain her? he thought.

The King laughed again and the court followed in a clamoring chorus. The King's cloak snapped fitfully in the rising wind and he lunged toward Johnny Fahey. A gnarled fist grabbed Johnny around the collar of his old shirt, and lifted him up on his toes. The King peered deeply into Johnny's face, the black eyes as piercing as daggers.

"You think she's a woman. Make no mistake, musician, she's a crow. And harsh though her call, she'll be no other thing but what she is. Your offer is foolish and has the mark of a man stupid enough to love a creature beyond his reach."

"And still I make the offer," Johnny said calmly, though his heart was pounding. The King released his hold slowly and Johnny felt the soles of his feet returning to the earth.

"Fair enough. You have until the end of summer. If you succeed, I will relinquish this crown to you, though I've no fear that will happen. And when he fails," the King turned to his daughter with a jutting chin, "I'll choose your mate and the matter will be settled once and for all."

Rilka opened her mouth to speak but the King's upraised hand commanded silence. "Think well on it, daughter. You're a crow, the daughter of the King of Crows, and there's no musician that can change that truth."

"I'll learn to sing!" Rilka said tartly.

"And then what?" the King said sharply. "Who will you sing for? For us?" He opened wide his arms to the court of crows.

"I'll sing for myself."

"Then you'll sing alone, my daughter," the King answered. "But so be it; you'll learn the hard way that you are a crow." The King looked over his restless court and exclaimed, "I am done here."

All around him the waiting court burst into noise, the shrill cawing and harsh scraping of their voices breaking the spell that held their forms. Their cloaks flapped wildly, lifting the dust from between the bladed grass and in the swirling clouds, they gave themselves over to flight. Johnny held his hand over his face to protect it from the seething dust, glimpsing in the distance the turquoise sky stippled with black veins at their parting. And then the winds quieted, the dust was exhaled back to earth, and the sky shone clear again. Johnny Fahey found himself alone with Rilka, daughter of the King of Crows.

"What are you called?" she demanded.

"Johnny Fahey."

"What sort of name is that?" she asked, her head cocked back as she looked up at him with her sharp eyes.

"One without shame," he answered with a light shrug.

"And where did you learn to sing?"

Johnny smiled, remembering. "It was all around me. I had only to listen. My mother—"

"—Just listen?" Rilka interrupted. "That doesn't sound right. Surely there were people who taught you, gave the know-how so you didn't make a fool of yourself. That's what my father always says. You have to get the way of it from someone that knows how, otherwise you're stuck, flying in a circle with one wing. Have you ever seen the deserts from up high? No, of course you haven't. You can't fly. Well I have and let me tell you—"

And on she went, not stopping for a breath or pause, scarcely even caring whether he answered her rapid questions or not. Johnny's face turned slowly to stone, the constant rattle of her voice hammering against his ear. It amazed him on the one hand, for as a crow she had seen a great deal of the world and was only too willing to talk and talk and talk about it. In small spoonfuls it might have even been interesting. But the words poured from her in a deluge as if all her life she had stored them up, waiting for this moment to release them.

The sun rose higher in the sky, tinting the green grass to a fallow gold, and still Rilka talked. It was only when the sun had reached the lip of the high canyon wall that Johnny Fahey stuttered to life and caught the girl by the shoulders.

"That's enough for today's lesson," he blurted out, exhausted.

"But you didn't do anything!" she said peevishly. "I didn't do anything!"

"You did quite a bit," Johnny said. "And now it's time to end. Tomorrow I'll try again." Johnny stumbled wearily to where his pack lay and made camp for the night. Rilka watched him and with a flurry of angry wings transformed herself and flew away.

That night as he lay beside his fire, listening to the sound of the dry wood sigh itself into ash, Johnny Fahey wondered how he was going to reach beyond Rilka's chatter. She talks, he thought, because among the crows listening is not valued. She talks, he thought, because no one has ever listened to her. Until now. Did he have the patience, he wondered, to listen while she talked until she emptied herself of all the words she needed to say before she could begin to listen? He would have to teach her how to listen without words. He stirred the fire and in the black coals rimmed with white hot flames, saw her cheek against her black hair. He chuckled, knowing himself to be smitten, and for that, he knew he would listen a long time. And maybe, there were small things, gestures that might gentle her tongue, and make her settle into quiet. Only then would she be able to hear the songs that waited inside her voice.

When he woke in the morning, Rilka was beside him, stirring up the campfire. He got up from his blankets, shyly, and she laughed at his hair that stuck out over his head like so much thistledown. He combed it with his fingers good-naturedly and offered her coffee. She nodded yes and began again to talk. She chattered on about the world, about the tops of the mountains, the sea, the stupidity of the court, even about her own beauty. The morning sun caught her face and the white skin glowed. And in Johnny Fahey's heart, the day began.

Johnny said not one word, but did his work, moving slowly round her, where she sat on a stone by the fire. He mixed the dough for biscuits, he ground the coffee beans in their burlap sack between two stones and set them in a pot of water to boil. He soaked the beans and bacon in a second pot and set them over the fire. He hummed as he worked, his voice a subtle background to the constant prattle of her voice. He touched her hand from time to time, putting a cup in it, a biscuit, every gesture in the rhythm of his hummed tune. The flow of Rilka's words broke and stumbled with the touch, but just as quick returned. Only Johnny Fahey heard the moment her speech began to flow with the rhythm of his tune. She smiled now as she spoke, almost without realizing that his song carried her along, changed the harsh tone of her chatter into a sweeter babble. But babble it still was, and Johnny was glad when they ate, for it gave him a moment's respite from all her talk.

And so it went throughout that day and the next and the next; Johnny saying little, only a nod, a murmured reply between the softly whistled tune to show that he still heard her. He wondered that it didn't drive him away, so much empty talk. But something in the soft yolk of her eyes, in the need to speak so much, stayed him. And gradually, he heard the compulsion in her to talk begin to exhaust itself. Passages of silence broke like sunlight sparkling in a cloud break at the end of a long storm. One day she sighed, folded her hands into her lap, and said nothing for a long time.

"Is it done, you are?" Johnny asked, taking out his fiddle.

Rilka gave a nod of her head.

Johnny smiled and put the fiddle beneath his chin. He played a sweet air, as soft as the new grass and as sad as the bent bough. Rilka heard it, and tears swam in her eyes. Johnny stopped playing and put away his fiddle.

"Come on," he said, giving her his hand. "Walk a ways with me."

They walked through the canyon walls, and then climbed the back of the high escarpments. Along the rim of the canyon, Johnny whistled a shrill tune and far in the distance, coyotes yipped.

"Can you hear it?" he asked her, the flow of sound touching him. A jig, he thought, to shape the barks of the coyotes.

"Hear what?" Rilka asked, puzzled.

Johnny Fahey turned to her and touched her softly, a finger tracing the outline of her ear. "It's there," he whispered.

She raised her face to him, waiting. And then her eyes hardened. "I hear nothing."

"It'll come," he promised, and let his hand hold her chin. Her upturned mouth was so close to his that he felt himself lean in to kiss her.

She pulled her head free from his hand and bristled angrily. "But I want to sing. Make me sing!"

"Rilka," he said, softly stepping back from her. "You will sing, but first you must learn to hear."

"That's stupid! I'm sure I hear well enough!" she replied hotly.

"If you can hear the tune, then you can sing it."

"Is that all there is to it?" Rilka threw back her head, her white throat to the sun, and opened her mouth to sing. But out came only the harsh cries of a crow, and the harder she tried to sweeten her voice, the louder she croaked and cawed. At last, stamping her feet in frustration, she leapt from the canyon wall, and in the open air, transformed into a crow. But Johnny saw her face just before the black feathers hid it and it was sad and hurt.

"Well," he muttered to himself as she flew away, "you've unraveled that." And he walked slowly down the trail to the camp.

He couldn't bring himself to leave the canyon just yet. He'd enough food and water, so he remained there, one eye glancing hopefully at the horizon for the sight of her. Almost a month passed before Rilka returned again. She came one morning early, walking through the grass, the dew sparkling on her hem. Her face was pensive, her hands clasped together.

Johnny nodded in greeting and quietly set about making coffee. He mixed the dough for biscuits and set the beans on to boil. And when it was done, he held her hands lightly before he gave her the coffee cup and touched her on her shoulder when he handed her the biscuits. She sighed deeply.

And then she talked again, her voice hard-edged but not hurried as it had once been. She talked about the court, about her father's wish to end his reign, and about the life that was being shaped for her among the court of crows.

Johnny heard the dull pitch of sorrow in her voice. He wanted to hold her and shelter her from whatever sadness had brought her to him now. She was proud, but her pride had bowed before defeat. There was no eagerness or arrogance in her speech, and she sat hunched, her arms folded close to her chest.

"I am to be married," she declared at last. "For I sing like a crow and will never be anything other. Or at least my father has told me. I don't like the mate he has chosen, but he has a strong voice and will be heard over the racket of the others," she added bitterly.

Johnny Fahey trembled as he took her hands between his. "No," he said, "no, give it more time. Give yourself another chance yet. At least until the end of summer."

She turned her sharp eyes on him. "It would be a waste of time. I learned that on the cliffs."

"No, that isn't true. Listen to me, Rilka."

She stiffened, pulling her hands free of his grasp. "No. I couldn't hear it then, and I won't hear it now," she said angrily.

She started to stand but Johnny held her by the shoulders and kissed her on the mouth.

On his tongue her soft lips tasted of elderberries and her skin smelled of sage. At first Rilka didn't move, startled by Johnny's boldness. And then she leaned into the kiss, her face tilted up to meet his. Her hands circled his neck and Johnny felt her cool fingers lace through his hair. He embraced her, bringing her body close to his chest to hear the rapid beating of her pulse and the soft murmured sighs.

It was a long kiss, and when they broke apart, there were no words to match its intensity. He stroked her cheek, his eyes never leaving her face. She held him by the waist, and only smiled.

They stayed together that day, wandering through the canyon, and marking the slow passage of the sun. In the night Rilka lay beside Johnny and in the moonlight the length of her body flashed white as a comet beneath the black velvet cloak. He called her name over and over until it carried a tune all its own. She answered and the words breathed from her mouth into his and back again until it was all one song. And late in the night, when both grew weary, Johnny laid his head against her white breasts and slept, hearing the wind shiver through the long grass.

He woke in the morning to find himself alone. He sat up confused, not knowing when she had left him. He walked through the grass, following a trail of dew-damp footprints until they disappeared abruptly. He searched the pale morning sky and knew, by the utter silence, that she was gone.

He stayed another week, stubbornly refusing to believe that she had returned to the court of crows. But the wind shifted, growing colder, and he felt the summer come to a close. If he remained much longer in the canyon, hoping against hope to see her again, he would be trapped when the winter came with its unexpected snowstorms. Reluctantly he repacked his dwindling food supplies. He filled his canteen at the spring, and with slow, heavy steps he left the canyon.

On the following day the court of crows returned. They flapped their wide black wings in the air, descending into the grass with shrill caws. Once transformed into human form, they continued bickering, tugging at wedding gifts and challenging each other for the right to stand beside the bride and groom.

The groom preened himself, stopping now and again to crack out orders to his attending men. He was tall and stood erect, his black hair slicked down over his proud head. He shook out his cloak, straightened the fine embroidered vest, and glanced occasionally where his bride stood, silent among the noisy throng. He frowned at her, wishing she'd more to say for herself.

Rilka looked around her in the canyon. She had not thought to see any signs of Johnny Fahey and yet his absence pained her terribly. She knew now how much she had silently hoped for another sight of him. Her arms felt heavy at her sides, her hands empty. She raised her hands and remembered with a smile that he was always putting a cup into them, or a biscuit. Always giving her something of himself without a word. And she heard in her ear like the sudden lilt of the thrush the constant tune he had hummed. She shook her head, the black veil rustling, and even this she heard as music. He had taught her to listen not by words but in his deeds and in his touch. Her constant chatter had deafened her to his message and she had fled, humiliated by her own ugly voice. She had blamed him for her failure until that last day when she had come to see him once more. In a single day, he had given everything of himself to her. But she had held back, fearing the ugliness of her crow's voice. It was her vanity that made her leave him in the morning and not return.

Her serving women crackled and groused, pulling her dress into place, lowering the black veil, and smoothing the train behind her. But all Rilka could hear now was the sorrow in her heart. Her vanity had cost her the man she loved. It had made her deaf to the music. And now she would marry a man like herself: a crow, sharp-tongued and loud. Johnny Fahey's smile came into her mind and she touched her lips with her fingers, remembering the softness of his mouth against hers, the breath that even as he kissed her carried a tune. And as Rilka swallowed, her throat was filled with the thick sweet taste of wild honey.

"Wait!" she cried to the assembled court.

"For what?" demanded the groom.

"I will sing," she said softly.

"Rilka, enough of your foolishness," the King of Crows declared. But already the summer had aged him and his voice that once was so powerful was subdued.

"I will sing, Father, and we will see who is the King of Crows."

Rilka lifted her veil and brushed it back from her face. She gazed up into the sky, blue as Johnny Fahey's eyes, and started to sing. She knew at once the words and the tune; it was his song. He had sung it often to her when they had sat together by the fire or walked along the rim of the canyon, though she had scarce heard it through her chatter. Now it was in her ear as clear as the sharp piping of crickets.

Her voice rose in her chest and traveled the length of her honey-coated throat until it issued forth beyond her lips. Not a crow's voice at all but a low hollow sound, sad and haunting, as she continued to sing. The long black veil faded into a fine white lace of pale silk and the black wedding dress softened into a smoky shadow. Rilka let the song change her, bleed the color from her shining black hair and her jet black eyes until her cloak was a dull gray and her eyes red with weeping.

And before the astonished court she shuddered out of her human form and took to the air as a dove. She flew over the high walls of the canyon, and her mournful cry was carried aloft by the wind.

The court of crows disbanded, for according to the King's own bargain, Johnny Fahey was the rightful King of Crows and he could not be found. The crows searched but every time they met, they scrabbled and fought and news that might have aided their search was dropped like useless scraps.

Johnny Fahey made his way through the mountains until he came to a small farmhouse nestled in a grove of cedar trees. There he met a woman with hair the color of wheat and an easy grace. He married her and the children came, one, two, and three. He played his fiddle for the weddings and the wakes and in the winter months he played it for his family.

But always in the spring, when the birds returned to the cedar grove, Johnny Fahey would find himself alone late at night standing on the porch of his house. His wife and children asleep, he would listen to the sad song of the mourning dove hidden among the fragrant cedars and without knowing why, he would lower his head and the tears would come.

PROFESSOR GOTTESMAN AND THE INDIAN RHINOCEROS
Peter S. Beagle

In the 1960s, Peter S. Beagle published two gentle fantasy novels that influenced a generation of writers and became modern classics of the field: *The Last Unicorn* and *A Fine and Private Place*. Since then, he has published *The Folk of the Air*, *The Innkeeper's Song*, a collection of short fiction, five books of nonfiction, and the libretto for an opera. He is also a musician and a screenwriter (his credits include Ralph Bakshi's animated *The Lord of the Rings* and an animated version of his own *The Last Unicorn*). Born in New York, Beagle now lives in northern California.

The story that follows contains the author's distinctive blend of whimsy and wisdom. It comes from *Peter S. Beagle's Immortal Unicorn*, an anthology he coedited with Janet Berliner.

—T.W.

Professor Gustave Gottesman went to a zoo for the first time when he was thirty-four years old. There is an excellent zoo in Zurich, which was Professor Gottesman's birthplace, and where his sister still lived, but Professor Gottesman had never been there. From an early age he had determined on the study of philosophy as his life's work; and for any true philosopher this world is zoo enough, complete with cages, feeding times, breeding programs, and earnest docents, of which he was wise enough to know that he was one. Thus, the first zoo he ever saw was the one in the middle-sized Midwestern American city where he worked at a middle-sized university, teaching comparative philosophy in comparative contentment. He was tall and rather thin, with a round, undistinguished face, a snub nose, a random assortment of sandyish hair, and a pair of very intense and very distinguished brown eyes that always seemed to be looking a little deeper than they meant to, embarrassing the face around them no end. His students and colleagues were quite fond of him, in an indulgent sort of way.

And how did the good Professor Gottesman happen at last to visit a zoo? It came about in this way: his older sister Edith came from Zurich to stay with him for several weeks, and she brought her daughter, his niece, Nathalie, along with her. Nathalie was seven, both in years and in the number of her that there sometimes seemed to be, for the Professor had never been used to children even when he was one. She was a generally pleasant little girl, though, as far as he could tell; so when his sister besought him to spend one of his free afternoons with Nathalie while she went to lunch and a gallery opening with an old friend, the Professor graciously consented. And Nathalie wanted very much to go to the zoo and see tigers.

"So you shall," her uncle announced gallantly. "Just as soon as I find out exactly where the zoo is." He consulted with his best friend, a fat, cheerful, harmonica-playing professor of medieval Italian poetry named Sally Lowry, who had known him long and well enough (she was the only person in the world who called him Gus) to draw an elaborate two-colored map of the route, write out very precise directions beneath it, and make several copies of this document, in case of accidents. Thus equipped, and accompanied by Charles, Nathalie's stuffed bedtime tiger, whom she desired to introduce to his grand cousins, they set off together for the zoo on a gray, cool spring afternoon. Professor Gottesman quoted Thomas Hardy to Nathalie, improvising a German translation for her benefit as he went along.

> *This is the weather the cuckoo likes,*
>   *And so do I;*
> *When showers betumble the chestnut spikes,*
>   *And nestlings fly.*

"Charles likes it too," Nathalie said. "It makes his fur feel all sweet."

They reached the zoo without incident, thanks to Professor Lowry's excellent map, and Professor Gottesman bought Nathalie a bag of something sticky, unhealthy, and forbidden, and took her straight off to see the tigers. Their hot, meaty smell and their lightning-colored eyes were a bit too much for him, and so he sat on a bench nearby and watched Nathalie perform the introductions for Charles. When she came back to Professor Gottesman, she told him that Charles had been very well behaved, as had all the tigers but one, who was rudely indifferent. "He was probably just visiting," she said. "A tourist or something."

The Professor was still marvelling at the amount of contempt one small girl could infuse into the word *tourist*, when he heard a voice, sounding almost at his shoulder, say, "Why, Professor Gottesman—how nice to see you at last." It was a low voice, a bit hoarse, with excellent diction, speaking good Zurich German with a very slight, unplaceable accent.

Professor Gottesman turned quickly, half expecting to see some old acquaintance from home, whose name he would inevitably have forgotten. Such embarrassments were altogether too common in his gently preoccupied life. His friend Sally Lowry once observed, "We see each other just about every day, Gus, and I'm still not sure you really recognize me. If I wanted to hide from you, I'd just change my hairstyle."

There was no one at all behind him. The only thing he saw was the rutted, muddy rhinoceros yard, for some reason placed directly across from the big cats' cages. The one rhinoceros in residence was standing by the fence, torpidly mumbling a mouthful of moldy-looking hay. It was an Indian rhinoceros, according to the placard on the gate: as big as the Professor's compact car, and the approximate color of old cement. The creaking slabs of its skin smelled of stale urine, and it had only one horn, caked with sticky mud. Flies buzzed around its small, heavy-lidded eyes, which regarded Professor Gottesman with immense, ancient unconcern. But there was no other person in the vicinity who might have addressed him.

Professor Gottesman shook his head, scratched it, shook it again, and turned back to the tigers. But the voice came again. "Professor, it was indeed I who spoke. Come and talk to me, if you please."

No need, surely, to go into Professor Gottesman's reaction: to describe in detail how he gasped, turned pale, and looked wildly around for any corroborative witness. It is worth mentioning, however, that at no time did he bother to splutter the requisite splutter in such cases: "My God, I'm either dreaming, drunk, or crazy." If he was indeed just as classically absentminded and impractical as everyone who knew him agreed, he was also more of a realist than many of them. This is generally true of philosophers, who tend, as a group, to be on terms of mutual respect with the impossible. Therefore, Professor Gottesman did the only proper thing under the circumstances. He introduced his niece Nathalie to the rhinoceros.

Nathalie, for all her virtues, was not a philosopher, and could not hear the rhinoceros's gracious greeting. She was, however, seven years old, and a well-brought-up seven-year-old has no difficulty with the notion that a rhinoceros—or a goldfish, or a coffee table—might be able to talk; nor in accepting that some people can hear coffee-table speech and some people cannot. She said a polite hello to the rhinoceros, and then became involved in her own conversation with stuffed Charles, who apparently had a good deal to say himself about tigers.

"A mannerly child," the rhinoceros commented. "One sees so few here. Most of them throw things."

His mouth dry, and his voice shaky but contained, Professor Gottesman asked carefully, "Tell me, if you will—can all rhinoceri speak, or only the Indian species?" He wished furiously that he had thought to bring along his notebook.

"I have no idea," the rhinoceros answered him candidly. "I, myself, as it happens, am a unicorn."

Professor Gottesman wiped his balding forehead. "Please," he said earnestly. "Please. A rhinoceros, even a rhinoceros that speaks, is as real a creature as I. A unicorn, on the other hand, is a being of pure fantasy, like mermaids, or dragons, or the chimera. I consider very little in this universe as absolutely, indisputably certain, but I would feel so much better if you could see your way to being merely a talking rhinoceros. For my sake, if not your own."

It seemed to the Professor that the rhinoceros chuckled slightly, but it might only have been a ruminant's rumbling stomach. "My Latin designation is *Rhinoceros unicornis*," the great animal remarked. "You may have noticed it on the sign."

Professor Gottesman dismissed the statement as brusquely as he would have if the rhinoceros had delivered it in class. "Yes, yes, yes, and the manatee, which suckles its young erect in the water and so gave rise to the myth of the mermaid, is assigned to the order *sirenia*. Classification is not proof."

"And proof," came the musing response, "is not necessarily truth. You look at me and see a rhinoceros, because I am not white, not graceful, far from beautiful, and my horn is no elegant spiral but a bludgeon of matted hair. But suppose that you had grown up expecting a unicorn to look and behave and smell exactly as I do—would not the rhinoceros then be the legend? Suppose that everything you believed about unicorns—everything except the way they look—were true of me? Consider the possibilities, Professor, while you push the remains of that bun under the gate."

Professor Gottesman found a stick and poked the grimy bit of pastry—about the same shade as the rhinoceros, it was—where the creature could wrap a prehensile upper lip around it. He said, somewhat tentatively, "Very well. The unicorn's horn was supposed to be an infallible guide to detecting poisons."

"The most popular poisons of the Middle Ages and Renaissance," replied the rhinoceros, "were alkaloids. Pour one of those into a goblet made of compressed hair, and see what happens." It belched resoundingly, and Nathalie giggled.

Professor Gottesman, who was always invigorated by a good argument with anyone, whether colleague, student, or rhinoceros, announced, "Isidore of Seville wrote in the seventh century that the unicorn was a cruel beast, that it would seek out elephants and lions to fight with them. Rhinoceri are equally known for their fierce, aggressive nature, which often leads them to attack anything that moves in their shortsighted vision. What have you to say to that?"

"Isidore of Seville," said the rhinoceros thoughtfully, "was a most learned man, much like your estimable self, who never saw a rhinoceros in his life, or an elephant either, being mainly preoccupied with church history and canon law. I believe he did see a lion at some point. If your charming niece is quite done with her snack?"

"She is not," Professor Gottesman answered, "and do not change the subject. If you are indeed a unicorn, what are you doing scavenging dirty buns and candy in this public establishment? It is an article of faith that a unicorn can only be taken by a virgin, in whose innocent embrace the ferocious creature becomes meek and docile. Are you prepared to tell me that you were captured under such circumstances?"

The rhinoceros was silent for some little while before it spoke again. "I cannot," it said judiciously, "vouch for the sexual history of the gentleman in the baseball cap who fired a tranquilizer dart into my left shoulder. I would, however, like to point out that the young of our species on occasion become trapped in vines and slender branches which entangle their horns—and that the Latin for such branches is *virge*. What Isidore of Seville made of all this . . ." It shrugged, which is difficult for a rhinoceros, and a remarkable thing to see.

"Sophistry," said the Professor, sounding unpleasantly beleaguered even in his own ears. "Casuistry. Semantics. Chop-logic. The fact remains, a rhinoceros is and a unicorn isn't." This last sounds much more impressive in German. "You will excuse me," he went on, "but we have other specimens to visit, do we not, Nathalie?"

"No," Nathalie said. "Charles and I just wanted to see the tigers."

"Well, we have seen the tigers," Professor Gottesman said through his teeth. "And I believe it is beginning to rain, so we will go home now." He took Nathalie's hand firmly and stood up, as that obliging child snuggled Charles firmly under her arm and bobbed a demure European curtsy to the rhinoceros. It bent its head to her, the mud-thick horn almost brushing the ground. Professor Gottesman, mildest of men, snatched her away.

"Good-bye, Professor," came the hoarse, placid voice behind him. "I look forward to our next meeting." The words were somewhat muffled, because Nathalie had tossed the remainder of her sticky snack into the yard as her uncle hustled her off. Professor Gottesman did not turn his head.

Driving home through the rain—which had indeed begun to fall, though very lightly—the Professor began to have an indefinably uneasy feeling that caused him to spend more time peering at the rearview mirror than in looking properly ahead.

Finally he asked Nathalie, "Please, would you and—ah—you and Charles climb into the backseat and see whether we are being followed?"

Nathalie was thrilled. "Like in the spy movies?" She jumped to obey, but reported after a few minutes of crouching on the seat that she could detect nothing out of the ordinary. "I saw a helicopter," she told him, attempting the English word. "Charles thinks they might be following us that way, but I don't know. Who is spying on us, Uncle Gustave?"

"No one, no one," Professor Gottesman answered. "Never mind, child, I am getting silly in America. It happens, never mind." But a few moments later the curious apprehension was with him again, and Nathalie was happily occupied for the rest of the trip home in scanning the traffic behind them through an imaginary periscope, yipping "It's that one!" from time to time, and being invariably disappointed when another prime suspect turned off down a side street. When they reached Professor Gottesman's house, she sprang out of the car immediately, ignoring her mother's welcome until she had checked under all four fenders for possible homing devices. "Bugs," she explained importantly to the two adults. "That was Charles's idea. Charles would make a good spy, I think."

She ran inside, leaving Edith to raise her fine eyebrows at her brother. Professor Gottesman said heavily, "We had a nice time. Don't ask." And Edith, being a wise older sister, left it at that.

The rest of the visit was enjoyably uneventful. The Professor went to work according to his regular routine, while his sister and his niece explored the city, practiced their English together, and cooked Swiss-German specialties to surprise him when he came home. Nathalie never asked to go to the zoo again—stuffed Charles having lately shown an interest in international intrigue—nor did she ever mention that her uncle had formally introduced her to a rhinoceros and spent part of an afternoon sitting on a bench arguing with it. Professor Gottesman was genuinely sorry when she and Edith left for Zurich, which rather surprised him. He hardly ever missed people, or thought much about anyone who was not actually present.

It rained again on the evening that they went to the airport. Returning alone, the Professor was startled, and a bit disquieted, to see large muddy footprints on his walkway and his front steps. They were, as nearly as he could make out, the marks of a three-toed foot, having a distinct resemblance to the ace of clubs in a deck of cards. The door was locked and bolted, as he had left it, and there was no indication of any attempt to force an entry. Professor Gottesman hesitated, looked quickly around him, and went inside.

The rhinoceros was in the living room, lying peacefully on its side before the artificial fireplace—which was lit—like a very large dog. It opened one eye as he entered and greeted him politely. "Welcome home, Professor. You will excuse me, I hope, if I do not rise?"

Professor Gottesman's legs grew weak under him. He groped blindly for a chair, found it, fell into it, his face white and freezing cold. He managed to ask, "How—how did you get in here?" in a small, faraway voice.

"The same way I got out of the zoo," the rhinoceros answered him. "I would have come sooner, but with your sister and your niece already here, I thought my presence might make things perhaps a little too crowded for you. I do hope their departure went well." It yawned widely and contentedly, showing blunt, fist-sized teeth and a gray-pink tongue like a fish fillet.

"I must telephone the zoo," Professor Gottesman whispered. "Yes, of course, I will call the zoo." But he did not move from the chair.

The rhinoceros shook its head as well as it could in a prone position. "Oh, I wouldn't bother with that, truly. It will only distress them if anyone learns that they have mislaid a creature as large as I am. And they will never believe that I am in your house. Take my word for it, there will be no mention of my having left their custody. I have some experience in these matters." It yawned again and closed its eyes. "Excellent fireplace you have," it murmured drowsily. "I think I shall lie exactly here every night. Yes, I do think so."

And it was asleep, snoring with the rhythmic roar and fading whistle of a fast freight crossing a railroad bridge. Professor Gottesman sat staring in his chair for a long time before he managed to stagger to the telephone in the kitchen.

Sally Lowry came over early the next morning, as she had promised several times before the Professor would let her off the phone. She took one quick look at him as she entered and said briskly, "Well, whatever came to dinner, you look as though it got the bed and you slept on the living room floor."

"I did not sleep at all," Professor Gottesman informed her grimly. "Come with me, please, Sally, and you shall see why."

But the rhinoceros was not in front of the fireplace, where it had still been lying when the Professor came downstairs. He looked around for it, increasingly frantic, saying over and over, "It was just here, it has been here all night. Wait, wait, Sally, I will show you. Wait only a moment."

For he had suddenly heard the unmistakable gurgle of water in the pipes overhead. He rushed up the narrow hairpin stairs (his house was, as the real-estate agent had put it, "an old charmer") and burst into his bathroom, blinking through clouds of steam to find the rhinoceros lolling blissfully in the tub, its nose barely above water and its hind legs awkwardly sticking straight up in the air. There were puddles all over the floor.

"Good morning," the rhinoceros greeted Professor Gottesman. "I could wish your facilities a bit larger, but the hot water is splendid, pure luxury. We never had hot baths at the zoo."

"Get out of my tub!" the Professor gabbled, coughing and wiping his face. "You will get out of my tub this instant!"

The rhinoceros remained unruffled. "I am not sure I can. Not just like that. It's rather a complicated affair."

"Get out exactly the way you got in!" shouted Professor Gottesman. "How did you get up here at all? I never heard you on the stairs."

"I tried not to disturb you," the rhinoceros said meekly. "Unicorns can move very quietly when we need to."

"*Out!*" the Professor thundered. He had never thundered before, and it made his throat hurt. "Out of my bathtub, out of my house! And clean up that floor before you go!"

He stormed back down the stairs to meet a slightly anxious Sally Lowry waiting at the bottom. "What was all that yelling about?" she wanted to know. "You're absolutely pink—it's sort of sweet, actually. Are you all right?"

"Come up with me," Professor Gottesman demanded. "Come right now." He seized his friend by the wrist and practically dragged her into his bathroom, where there was no sign of the rhinoceros. The tub was empty and dry, the floor was spotlessly clean; the air smelled faintly of tile cleaner. Professor Gottesman stood gaping in the doorway, muttering over and over, "But it was here. It was in the tub."

"What was in the tub?" Sally asked. The Professor took a long, deep breath and turned to face her.

"A rhinoceros," he said. "It says it's a unicorn, but it is nothing but an Indian rhinoceros." Sally's mouth opened, but no sound came out. Professor Gottesman said, "It followed me home."

Fortunately, Sally Lowry was no more concerned with the usual splutters of denial and disbelief than was the Professor himself. She closed her mouth, caught her own breath, and said, "Well, any rhinoceros that could handle those stairs, wedge itself into that skinny tub of yours, and tidy up afterwards would have to be a unicorn. Obvious. Gus, I don't care what time it is, I think you need a drink."

Professor Gottesman recounted his visit to the zoo with Nathalie, and all that had happened thereafter, while Sally rummaged through his minimally stocked liquor cabinet and mixed what she called a "Lowry Land Mine." It calmed the Professor only somewhat, but it did at least restore his coherency. He said earnestly, "Sally, I don't know how it talks. I do not know how it escaped from the zoo, or found its way here, or how it got into my house and my bathtub, and I am afraid to imagine where it is now. But the creature is an Indian rhinoceros, the sign said so. It is simply not possible—not possible—that it could be a unicorn."

"Sounds like *Harvey*," Sally mused. Professor Gottesman stared at her. "You know, the play about the guy who's buddies with an invisible white rabbit. A big white rabbit."

"But this one is not invisible!" the Professor cried. "People at the zoo, they saw it—Nathalie saw it. It bowed to her, quite courteously."

"Um," Sally said. "Well, I haven't seen it yet, but I live in hope. Meanwhile, you've got a class, and I've got office hours. Want me to make you another Land Mine?"

Professor Gottesman shuddered slightly. "I think not. We are discussing today how Fichte and von Schelling's work leads us to Hegel, and I need my wits about me. Thank you for coming to my house, Sally. You are a good friend. Perhaps I really am suffering from delusions, after all. I think I would almost prefer it so."

"Not me," Sally said. "I'm getting a unicorn out of this, if it's the last thing I do." She patted his arm. "You're more fun than a barrel of MFA candidates, Gus, and you're also the only gentleman I've ever met. I don't know what I'd do for company around here without you."

Professor Gottesman arrived early for his seminar on "The Heirs of Kant." There was no one in the classroom when he entered, except for the rhinoceros. It had plainly already attempted to sit on one of the chairs, which lay in splinters on the floor. Now it was warily eyeing a ragged hassock near the coffee machine.

"What are you doing here?" Professor Gottesman fairly screamed at it.

"Only auditing," the rhinoceros answered. "I thought it might be rewarding to see you at work. I promise not to say a word."

Professor Gottesman pointed to the door. He had opened his mouth to order the rhinoceros, once and for all, out of his life, when two of his students walked into the room. The Professor closed his mouth, gulped, greeted his students, and ostentatiously began to examine his lecture notes, mumbling professorial mumbles to himself, while the rhinoceros, unnoticed, negotiated a kind of armed truce with the hassock. True to its word, it listened in attentive silence all through the seminar, though Professor Gottesman had an uneasy moment when it seemed about to be drawn into a heated debate over the precise nature of von Schelling's intellectual debt to the von Schlegel brothers. He was so desperately careful not to let the rhinoceros catch his eye that he never noticed until the last student had left that the beast was gone, too. None of the class had even once commented on its presence; except for the shattered chair, there was no indication that it had ever been there.

Professor Gottesman drove slowly home in a disorderly state of mind. On the one hand, he wished devoutly never to see the rhinoceros again; on the other, he could not help wondering exactly when it had left the classroom. "Was it displeased with my summation of the *Ideas for a Philosophy of Nature?*" he said aloud in the car. "Or perhaps it was something I said during the argument about *Die Weltalter*. Granted, I have never been entirely comfortable with that book, but I do not recall saying anything exceptionable." Hearing himself justifying his interpretations to a rhinoceros, he slapped his own cheek very hard and drove the rest of the way with the car radio tuned to the loudest, ugliest music he could find.

The rhinoceros was dozing before the fireplace as before, but lumbered clumsily to a sitting position as soon as he entered the living room. "Bravo, Professor!" it cried in plainly genuine enthusiasm. "You were absolutely splendid. It was an honor to be present at your seminar."

The Professor was furious to realize that he was blushing; yet it was impossible to respond to such praise with an eviction notice. There was nothing for him to do but reply, a trifle stiffly, "Thank you, most gratifying." But the rhinoceros was clearly waiting for something more, and Professor Gottesman was, as his friend Sally had said, a gentleman. He went on. "You are welcome to audit the class again, if you like. We will be considering Rousseau next week, and then proceed through the romantic philosophers to Nietzsche and Schopenhauer."

"With a little time to spare for the American Transcendentalists, I should hope," suggested the rhinoceros. Professor Gottesman, being some distance past surprised, nodded. The rhinoceros said reflectively, "I think I should prefer to hear you on Comte and John Stuart Mill. The romantics always struck me as fundamentally unsound."

This position agreed so much with the Professor's own opinion that he found himself, despite himself, gradually warming toward the rhinoceros. Still formal, he asked, "May I perhaps offer you a drink? Some coffee or tea?"

"Tea would be very nice," the rhinoceros answered, "if you should happen to have a bucket." Professor Gottesman did not, and the rhinoceros told him not to worry about it. It settled back down before the fire, and the Professor drew up a rocking chair. The rhinoceros said, "I must admit, I do wish I could hear you speak on the scholastic philosophers. That's really my period, after all."

"I will be giving such a course next year," the Professor said, a little shyly. "It is to be a series of lectures on medieval Christian thought, beginning with St. Augustine and the Neoplatonists and ending with William of Occam. Possibly you could attend some of those talks."

The rhinoceros's obvious pleasure at the invitation touched Professor Gottesman surprisingly deeply. Even Sally Lowry, who often dropped in on his classes unannounced, did so, as he knew, out of affection for him, and not from any serious interest in epistemology or the Milesian School. He was beginning to wonder whether there might be a way to permit the rhinoceros to sample the cream sherry he kept aside for company, when the creature added, with a wheezy chuckle, "Of course, Augustine and the rest never did quite come to terms with such pagan survivals as unicorns. The best they could do was to associate us with the Virgin Mary, and to suggest that our horns somehow represented the unity of Christ and his church. Bernard of Trèves even went so far as to identify Christ directly with the unicorn, but it was never a comfortable union. Spiral peg in square hole, so to speak."

Professor Gottesman was no more at ease with the issue than St. Augustine had been. But he was an honest person—only among philosophers is this considered part of the job description—and so he felt it his duty to say, "While I respect your intelligence and your obvious intellectual curiosity, none of this yet persuades me that you are in fact a unicorn. I still must regard you as an exceedingly learned and well-mannered Indian rhinoceros."

The rhinoceros took this in good part, saying, "Well, well, we will agree to disagree on that point for the time being. Although I certainly hope that you will let me know if you should need your drinking water purified." As before, and as so often thereafter, Professor Gottesman could not be completely sure that the rhinoceros was joking. Dismissing the subject, it went on to ask, "But about the Scholastics—do you plan to discuss the later Thomist reformers at all? Saint Cajetan rather dominates the movement, to my mind; if he had any real equals, I'm afraid I can't recall them."

"Ah," said the Professor. They were up until five in the morning, and it was the rhinoceros who dozed off first.

The question of the rhinoceros's leaving Professor Gottesman's house never came up again. It continued to sleep in the living room, for the most part, though on warm summer nights it had a fondness for the young willow tree that had been a Christmas present from Sally. Professor Gottesman never learned whether it was male or female, nor how it nourished its massive, noisy body, nor how it managed for toilet facilities—a reticent man himself, he respected reticence in others. As a houseguest, the rhinoceros's only serious fault was a continuing predilection for hot baths (with Epsom salts, when it could get them). But it always cleaned up after itself, and was extremely conscientious about not tracking mud into the house; and it can be safely said that none of the Professor's visitors—even the rare ones who spent a night or two under his roof—ever remotely suspected that they were sharing living quarters with a rhinoceros. All in all, it proved to be a most discreet and modest beast.

The Professor had few friends, apart from Sally, and none whom he would have called on in a moment of bewildering crisis, as he had called her. He avoided whatever social or academic gatherings he could reasonably avoid; as a consequence his evenings had generally been lonely ones, though he might not have called them so. Even if he had admitted the term, he would surely have insisted that there was nothing necessarily wrong with loneliness, in and of itself. "*I think,*" he would have said—did often say, in fact, to Sally Lowry. "There are people, you know, for whom thinking is company, thinking is entertainment, parties, dancing even. The others, other people, they absolutely will not believe this."

"You're right," Sally said. "One thing about you, Gus, when you're right, you're really right."

Now, however, the Professor could hardly wait for the time of day when, after a cursory dinner (he was an indifferent, impatient eater, and truly tasted little difference between a frozen dish and one that had taken half a day to prepare), he would pour himself a glass of wine and sit down in the living room to debate philosophy with a huge mortar-colored beast that always smelled vaguely incontinent, no matter how many baths it had taken that afternoon. Looking eagerly forward all day to anything was a new experience for him. It appeared to be the same for the rhinoceros.

As the animal had foretold, there was never the slightest suggestion in the papers or on television that the local zoo was missing one of its larger odd-toed ungulates. The Professor went there once or twice in great trepidation, convinced that he would be recognized and accused immediately of conspiracy in the rhinoceros's escape. But nothing of the sort happened. The yard where the rhinoceros had been kept was now occupied by a pair of despondent-looking African elephants; when Professor Gottesman made a timid inquiry of a guard, he was curtly informed that the zoo had never possessed a rhinoceros of any species. "Endangered species," the guard told him. "Too much red tape you have to go through to get one these days. Just not worth the trouble, mean as they are."

Professor Gottesman grew placidly old with the rhinoceros—that is to say, the Professor grew old, while the rhinoceros never changed in any way that he could observe. Granted, he was not the most observant of men, nor the most sensitive to change, except when threatened by it. Nor was he in the least ambitious: promotions and pay raises happened, when they happened, somewhere in the same cloudily benign middle distance as did those departmental meetings that he actually had to sit through. The companionship of the rhinoceros, while increasingly his truest delight, also became as much of a cozily reassuring habit as his classes, his office hours, the occasional dinner and movie or museum excursion with Sally Lowry, and the books on French and German philosophy that he occasionally published through the university press over the years. They were indifferently reviewed, and sold poorly.

"Which is undoubtedly as it should be," Professor Gottesman frequently told Sally when dropping her off at her house, well across town from his own. "I think I am a good teacher—that, yes—but I am decidedly not an original thinker, and I was never much of a writer even in German. It does no harm to say that I am not an exceptional man, Sally. It does not hurt me."

"I don't know what exceptional means to you or anyone else," Sally would answer stubbornly. "To me it means being unique, one of a kind, and that's definitely you, old Gus. I never thought you belonged in this town, or this university, or probably this century. But I'm surely glad you've been here."

Once in a while she might ask him casually how his unicorn was getting on these days. The Professor, who had long since accepted the fact that no one ever saw the rhinoceros unless it chose to be seen, invariably rose to the bait, saying, "It is no more a unicorn than it ever was, Sally, you know that." He would sip his latté in mild indignation, and eventually add, "Well, we will clearly never see eye to eye on the Vienna Circle, or the logical positivists in general—it is a very conservative creature, in some ways. But we did come to a tentative agreement about Bergson, last Thursday it was, so I would have to say that we are going along quite amiably."

Sally rarely pressed him further. Sharp-tongued, solitary, and profoundly irreverent, only with Professor Gottesman did she bother to know when to leave things alone. Most often, she would take out her battered harmonica and play one or another of his favorite tunes—"Sweet Georgia Brown" or "Hurry On Down." He never sang along, but he always hummed and grunted and thumped his bony knees. Once he mentioned diffidently that the rhinoceros appeared to have a peculiar fondness for "Slow Boat to China." Sally pretended not to hear him.

In the appointed fullness of time, the university retired Professor Gottesman in a formal ceremony, attended by, among others, Sally Lowry, his sister Edith, all the way from Zurich, and the rhinoceros—the latter having spent all that day in the bathtub, in anxious preparation. Each of them assured him that he looked immensely distinguished as he was invested with the rank of *emeritus*, which allowed him to lecture as many as four times a year, and to be available to counsel promising graduate students when he chose. In addition, a special chair with his name on it was reserved exclusively for his use at the Faculty Club. He was quite proud of never once having sat in it.

"Strange, I am like a movie star now," he said to the rhinoceros. "You should see. Now I walk across the campus and the students line up, they line up to watch me totter past. I can hear their whispers—'Here he comes!' 'There he goes!' Exactly the same ones they are who used to cut my classes because I bored them so. Completely absurd."

"Enjoy it as your due," the rhinoceros proposed. "You were entitled to their respect then—take pleasure in it now, however misplaced it may seem to you." But the Professor shook his head, smiling wryly.

"Do you know what kind of star I am really like?" he asked. "I am like the old, old star that died so long ago, so far away, that its last light is only reaching our eyes today. They fall in on themselves, you know, those dead stars, they go cold and invisible, even though we think we are seeing them in the night sky. That is just how I would be, if not for you. And for Sally, of course."

In fact, Professor Gottesman found little difficulty in making his peace with age and retirement. His needs were simple, his pension and savings adequate to meet them, and his health as sturdy as generations of Swiss peasant ancestors could make it. For the most part he continued to live as he always had, the one difference being that he now had more time for study, and could stay up as late as he chose arguing about structuralism with the rhinoceros, or listening to Sally Lowry reading her new translation of Cavalcanti or Frescobaldi. At first he attended every conference of philosophers to which he was invited, feeling a certain vague obligation to keep abreast of new thought in his field. This compulsion passed quickly, however, leaving him perfectly satisfied to have as little as possible to do with academic life, except when he needed to use the library. Sally once met him there for lunch to find him feverishly rifling the ten Loeb Classic volumes of Philo Judaeus. "We were debating the concept of the logos last night," he explained to her, "and then the impossible beast rampaged off on a tangent involving Philo's locating the roots of Greek philosophy in the Torah. Forgive me, Sally, but I may be here for awhile." Sally lunched alone that day.

The Professor's sister Edith died younger than she should have. He grieved for her, and took much comfort in the fact that Nathalie never failed to visit him when she came to America. The last few times, she had brought a husband and two children with her—the youngest hugging a ragged but indomitable tiger named Charles under his arm. They most often swept him off for the evening; and it was on one such occasion, just after they had brought him home and said their goodbyes, and their rented car had rounded the corner, that the mugging occurred.

Professor Gottesman was never quite sure himself about what actually took place. He remembered a light scuffle of footfalls, remembered a savage blow on the side of his head, then another impact as his cheek and forehead hit the ground. There were hands clawing through his pockets, low voices so distorted by obscene viciousness that he lost English completely, becoming for the first time in fifty years a terrified immigrant, once more unable to cry out for help in this new and dreadful country. A faceless figure billowed over him, grabbing his collar, pulling him close, mouthing words he could not understand. It was brandishing something menacingly in its free hand.

Then it vanished abruptly, as though blasted away by the sidewalk—shaking bellow of rage that was Professor Gottesman's last clear memory until he woke in a strange bed, with Sally Lowry, Nathalie, and several policemen bending over him. The next day's newspapers ran the marvelous story of a retired philosophy professor, properly frail and elderly, not only fighting off a pair of brutal muggers but beating them so badly that they had to be hospitalized themselves before they could be arraigned. Sally impishly kept the incident on the front pages for some days by confiding to reporters that Professor Gottesman was a practitioner of a long-forgotten martial-arts discipline, practiced only in ancient Sumer and Babylonia. "Plain childishness," she said apologetically, after the fuss had died down. "Pure self-indulgence. I'm sorry, Gus."

"Do not be," the Professor replied. "If we were to tell them the truth, I would immediately be placed in an institution." He looked sideways at his friend, who smiled and said, "What, about the rhinoceros rescuing you? I'll never tell, I swear. They could pull out my fingernails."

Professor Gottesman said, "Sally, those boys had been *trampled*, practically stamped flat. One of them had been *gored*, I saw him. Do you really think I could have done all that?"

"Remember, I've seen you in your wrath," Sally answered lightly and untruthfully. What she had in fact seen was one of the ace-of-clubs footprints she remembered in crusted mud on the Professor's front steps long ago. She said, "Gus. How old am I?"

The Professor's response was off by a number of years, as it always was. Sally said, "You've frozen me at a certain age, because you don't want me getting any older. Fine, I happen to be the same way about that rhinoceros of yours. There are one or two things I just don't want to know about that damn rhinoceros, Gus. If that's all right with you."

"Yes, Sally," Professor Gottesman answered. "That is all right."

The rhinoceros itself had very little to say about the whole incident. "I chanced to be awake, watching a lecture about Bulgarian icons on the Learning Channel.

I heard the noise outside." Beyond that, it sidestepped all questions, pointedly concerning itself only with the Professor's recuperation from his injuries and shock. In fact, he recovered much faster than might reasonably have been expected from a gentleman of his years. The doctor commented on it.

The occurrence made Professor Gottesman even more of an icon himself on campus; as a direct consequence, he spent even less time there than before, except when the rhinoceros requested a particular book. Nathalie, writing from Zurich, never stopped urging him to take in a housemate, for company and safety, but she would have been utterly dumbfounded if he had accepted her suggestion. "Something looks out for him," she said to her husband. "I always knew that, I couldn't tell you why. Uncle Gustave is *somebody's* dear stuffed Charles."

Sally Lowry did grow old, despite Professor Gottesman's best efforts. The university gave her a retirement ceremony too, but she never showed up for it. "Too damn depressing," she told Professor Gottesman, as he helped her into her coat for their regular Wednesday walk. "It's all right for you, Gus, you'll be around forever. Me, I drink, I still smoke, I still eat all kinds of stuff they tell me not to eat—I don't even floss, for God's sake. My circulation works like the post office, and even my cholesterol has arthritis. Only reason I've lasted this long is I had this stupid job teaching beautiful, useless stuff to idiots. Now that's it. Now I'm a goner."

"Nonsense, nonsense, Sally," Professor Gottesman assured her vigorously. "You have always told me you are too mean and spiteful to die. I am holding you to this."

"Pickled in vinegar only lasts just so long," Sally said. "One cheery note, anyway—it'll be the heart that goes. Always is, in my family. That's good; I couldn't hack cancer. I'd be a shameless, screaming disgrace, absolutely no dignity at all. I'm really grateful it'll be the heart."

The Professor was very quiet while they walked all the way down to the little local park, and back again. They had reached the apartment complex where she lived, when he suddenly gripped her by the arms, looked straight into her face, and said loudly, "That is the best heart I ever knew, yours. I will not *let* anything happen to that heart."

"Go home, Gus," Sally told him harshly. "Get out of here, go home. Christ, the only sentimental Switzer in the whole world, and I get him. Wouldn't you just know?"

Professor Gottesman actually awoke just before the telephone call came, as sometimes happens. He had dozed off in his favorite chair during a minor intellectual skirmish with the rhinoceros over Spinoza's ethics. The rhinoceros itself was sprawled in its accustomed spot, snoring authoritatively, and the kitchen clock was still striking three when the phone rang. He picked it up slowly. Sally's barely audible voice whispered, "Gus. The heart. Told you." He heard the receiver fall from her hand.

Professor Gottesman had no memory of stumbling coatless out of the house, let alone finding his car parked on the street—he was just suddenly standing by it, his hands trembling so badly as he tried to unlock the door that he dropped his keys into the gutter. How long his frantic fumbling in the darkness went on, he could never say; but at some point he became aware of a deeper darkness over him, and looked up on hands and knees to see the rhinoceros.

"On my back," it said, and no more. The Professor had barely scrambled up its warty, unyielding flanks and heaved himself precariously over the spine his legs could not straddle when there came a surge like the sea under him as the great beast leaped forward. He cried out in terror.

He would have expected, had he had wit enough at the moment to expect anything, that the rhinoceros would move at a ponderous trot, farting and rumbling, gradually building up a certain clumsy momentum. Instead, he felt himself flying, truly flying, as children know flying, flowing with the night sky, melting into the jeweled wind. If the rhinoceros's huge, flat, three-toed feet touched the ground, he never felt it: nothing existed, or ever had existed, but the sky that he was and the bodiless power that he had become—he himself, the once and foolish old Professor Gustave Gottesman, his eyes full of the light of lost stars. He even forgot Sally Lowry, only for a moment, only for the least little time.

Then he was standing in the courtyard before her house, shouting and banging maniacally on the door, pressing every button under his hand. The rhinoceros was nowhere to be seen. The building door finally buzzed open, and the Professor leaped up the stairs like a young man, calling Sally's name. Her own door was unlocked; she often left it so absentmindedly, no matter how much he scolded her about it. She was in her bedroom, half-wedged between the side of the bed and the night table, with the telephone receiver dangling by her head. Professor Gottesman touched her cheek and felt the fading warmth.

"Ah, Sally," he said. "Sally, my dear." She was very heavy, but somehow it was easy for him to lift her back onto the bed and make a place for her among the books and papers that littered the quilt, as always. He found her harmonica on the floor, and closed her fingers around it. When there was nothing more for him to do, he sat beside her, still holding her hand, until the room began to grow light. At last he said aloud, "No, the sentimental Switzer will not cry, my dear Sally," and picked up the telephone.

The rhinoceros did not return for many days after Sally Lowry's death. Professor Gottesman missed it greatly when he thought about it at all, but it was a strange, confused time. He stayed at home, hardly eating, sleeping on his feet, opening books and closing them. He never answered the telephone, and he never changed his clothes. Sometimes he wandered endlessly upstairs and down through every room in his house; sometimes he stood in one place for an hour or more at a time, staring at nothing. Occasionally the doorbell rang, and worried voices outside called his name. It was late autumn, and then winter, and the house grew cold at night, because he had forgotten to turn on the furnace. Professor Gottesman was perfectly aware of this, and other things, somewhere.

One evening, or perhaps it was early one morning, he heard the sound of water running in the bathtub upstairs. He remembered the sound, and presently he moved to his living room chair to listen to it better. For the first time in some while, he fell asleep, and woke only when he felt the rhinoceros standing over him. In the darkness he saw it only as a huge, still shadow, but it smelled unmistakably like a rhinoceros that has just had a bath. The Professor said quietly, "I wondered where you had gone."

"We unicorns mourn alone," the rhinoceros replied. "I thought it might be the same for you."

"Ah," Professor Gottesman said. "Yes, most considerate. Thank you."

He said nothing further, but sat staring into the shadow until it appeared to fold gently around him. The rhinoceros said, "We were speaking of Spinoza."

Professor Gottesman did not answer. The rhinoceros went on. "I was very interested in the comparison you drew between Spinoza and Thomas Hobbes. I would enjoy continuing our discussion."

"I do not think I can," the Professor said at last. "I do not think I want to talk anymore."

It seemed to him that the rhinoceros's eyes had become larger and brighter in its own shadow, and its horn a trifle less hulking. But its stomach rumbled as majestically as ever as it said, "In that case, perhaps we should be on our way."

"Where are we going?" Professor Gottesman asked. He was feeling oddly peaceful and disinclined to leave his chair. The rhinoceros moved closer, and for the first time that the Professor could remember its huge, hairy muzzle touched his shoulder, light as a butterfly.

"I have lived in your house for a long time," it said. "We have talked together, days and nights on end, about ways of being in this world, ways of considering it, ways of imagining it as a part of some greater imagining. Now has come the time for silence. Now I think you should come and live with me."

They were outside, on the sidewalk, in the night. Professor Gottesman had forgotten to take his coat, but he was not at all cold. He turned to look back at his house, watching it recede, its lights still burning, like a ship leaving him at his destination. He said to the rhinoceros, "What is your house like?"

"Comfortable," the rhinoceros answered. "In honesty, I would not call the hot water as superbly lavish as yours, but there is rather more room to maneuver. Especially on the stairs."

"You are walking a bit too rapidly for me," said the Professor. "May I climb on your back once more?"

The rhinoceros halted immediately, saying, "By all means, please do excuse me." Professor Gottesman found it notably easier to mount this time, the massive sides having plainly grown somewhat trimmer and smoother during the rhinoceros's absence, and easier to grip with his legs. It started on briskly when he was properly settled, though not at the rapturous pace that had once married the Professor to the night wind. For some while he could hear the clopping of cloven hooves far below him, but then they seemed to fade away. He leaned forward and said into the rhinoceros's pointed silken ear, "I should tell you that I have long since come to the conclusion that you are not after all an Indian rhinoceros, but a hitherto unknown species, somehow misclassified. I hope this will not make a difference in our relationship."

"No difference, good Professor," came the gently laughing answer all around him. "No difference in the world."

For Joe Mazo

THE HUNT OF THE UNICORN
Ellen Kushner

Ellen Kushner is a novelist and public radio personality in Boston, Massachusetts. She has hosted many popular music shows for WGBH Boston, as well as various shows heard nationally, including three award-winning Jewish Holiday specials, which she also wrote and produced. She is currently the host, coproducer, and writer of *Sound and Spirit*, a weekly series from Public Radio International. She has published short fiction, children's fiction, and two excellent novels: *Swordspoint: A Melodrama of Manners* and *Thomas the Rhymer*. The later book won the 1991 World Fantasy Award.

"The Hunt of the Unicorn" is sensual, stylish, intricate, and arch—which is precisely the kind of tale readers have come to expect from Kushner's pen. The story draws on imagery from the medieval Unicorn Tapestries, and was published in *Peter S. Beagle's Immortal Unicorn*, edited by Peter S. Beagle and Janet Berliner.

—T.W.

> . . . *Berowne also is here in Nantes, examining rugs newly off the vessels from Turkey. His family could well hire an agent to do this foreign collecting for them, to furnish the walls and tables of their houses at Hastings, Ardmere, Little River . . . not to mention his own apartments at court. Perhaps they assign him such tasks as consolation for the real work already being accomplished by his elder brother, whose movements I know you concern yourself with. What, after all, can the young Berowne do but occupy himself with ornament, being himself nothing but an ornament currying grace and favor at the court of the Baseborn Queen? My lord, you shall be kept well aware of his movements here, and those of all the rest of your countrymen as they touch these shores, to the greater future of our noble enterprise, which cannot fail to thrive.*
>
> *As for our Quarry, I have several reports to hand, but none of good repute. Your servant while I live—.*

Lord Thomas Berowne was indeed in Nantes, though not at the moment examining anything particularly beautiful. He was in a dockside tavern where even the beer was stale to match the air. He wore a heavy cloak to hide the splendor of his clothes. It was much too hot. With one gloved hand he cracked a vent in its folds for air, and received a warning glare from his manservant, Jenkin. Lord Thomas sighed, and looked around again for the stranger who earlier that day had offered him a chance at a rare carving. Berowne was on time for the rendezvous, and the stranger was not—unless he'd managed to disguise himself as a redheaded barmaid with a squint, or a one-legged sailor with a greasy beard. Over by the poor excuse for a fire, two men sat playing cards. One, with his back to the light, was nothing but a shape, and that not the shape of the antiquities dealer; the other was a heavy-built fellow who seemed to be mostly voice: he was on a losing streak, and as his cries of annoyance grew louder, other taverners emerged from the shadows to watch the fun.

"Yer an imp!" the loser roared. "Foreign devil, magicking away a sailor's good money, yer not a man at all!" This provoked predictable comments from the watchers that drowned out his opponent's answer. The loser was drinking heavily, and Jenkin muttered that there might be a fight toward, and perhaps they'd better go now?

Berowne cast another annoyed look toward the door. Still no sign of the stranger and his Hermaphrodite Venus.

"Yes, all right, Jenkin." But as the disguised nobleman rose, so did the drunken cardplayer, stumbling back from his bench, and holding up a glittering knife. The spectators drew back, the winning cardplayer drew his sword—or tried to.

Thomas could see the other now. He was a study in black and white with his dark clothes and pale skin, pale hair. Only the low glow of the fire created a faint flush along his right side, running along his emerging blade, while above it his ivory fingers were sketched in charcoal, and his eyes a smear of shadow over high, wide-set cheekbones. Even the swordsman's movements were like the most graceful poses imaginable—and that was the problem: he moved as if he were in a court ballet, slow, deliberate, beautiful, and at about half the speed required for him to survive the encounter.

"Draw!" Lord Thomas ordered his servant; "I know this man!"

At the sight of two outsiders taking an interest in his quarrel, the drunken sailor turned tail and fled, stumbling and cursing his way out of the tavern.

The swordsman turned his head slowly to look at his rescuers. His eyes widened.

"Oh, no," he said.

But they managed to get him out of the smoky tavern and into the sharp night air. Jenkin lit their way down several streets, always away from the wharves. At length they stopped under a cooper's sign, leaning against the shuttered windows of his shop.

"I am not drunk," the beautiful swordsman explained meticulously. "Drink does not affect me. My hands are perfectly steady, and I know exactly where I am."

"Yes, yes." Berowne was delighted to wrap him in the heavy cloak. "I've heard this before, remember? When you were in my rooms at court, drinking my claret and beating us all at cards. You weren't well then, either, though I agree your hands were perfectly steady."

"I am perfectly all right."

"No you're not. You're white as a sheet, and you keep looking at your own hands as though you're not sure whether they're flesh or marble. Which they might well be; Carrara, I think, with the blue veining . . ."

"Ahem," said Jenkin.

"Yes." With an effort, the fair man moved his hand slowly down out of his sight. "Thank you, I must go now."

"I don't think you'll get very far," Berowne said patiently. "Besides, that sailor might have friends. You'd best come home with me."

And so Lazarus Merridon awoke the next morning in an enormous curtained bed, the kind he had slept in during his days at court, and in his master's house. The bed-hangings were brocade, patterned with doves and ivy intertwined; he pulled them back and found a vase of white roses by the bed, a pitcher of water flavored with rosemary, and a blue silk bedgown hung over a chair.

His own clothes were nowhere in sight, which was a pity; he couldn't leave the house clad only in silk, nor yet without his sword. Jenkin was no doubt washing and brushing the clothes; perhaps he was polishing the sword as well? Lazarus rose easily from the bed. He felt fresh and whole again. The tavern had been a regrettable mistake; most regrettable, now. He had thought no one from his past would find him there. A whim of fate had brought the young nobleman. For which he supposed he should be grateful, considering what a fool he had been, drinking more even than he could handle. He wished he were like other men, to whom strong drink brought the mercies of folly and forgetting.

He was thirsty, and drank nearly all the water that was in the pitcher. From the courtyard below his window, women's voices drifted up, laughing and bantering. He went to the casement, and looked out through the cloudy diamond panes. He saw the women as bright spots of color, fetching water at the well. He knew that their lives were not carefree, but in this moment they were happy in the day, in their task, in one another's company. He wished that he might join them then; but that choice had been lost to him.

"Ah, good! You're up."

Lord Thomas Berowne stood in the doorway, neat in brown satin modishly piped with velvet and trimmed with pearls.

Lazarus was wearing nothing. The nobleman was staring. In the moment when he realized it, Thomas turned to the roses and busied himself with rearranging them. The fair man crossed the room, and slipped the blue silk robe over his naked body. If he looked now like a Knight of Love resting between bouts, at least he resembled less a pagan god new-minted in flesh.

"Good morning," he said smoothly to his host. "I slept very well. I'm sorry I disturbed your household. If I might disturb them once more to the tune of my sorry possessions, I'll quit all disturbance hereafter."

"No, no." Thomas broke off a rose, occupied himself pinning it to his doublet. Lazarus couldn't help smiling, to see the young lord again with his floral hallmark. Last winter at court the nobleman had seldom been seen without his precious blossoms out of season, just as Lazarus had seldom been seen without his lute. Thomas smiled back. "Your linen is drying, and you must be starving. Stay at least for a meal. This cook does a very nice omelette, and the rolls are fresh; I just tried one."

Lazarus nearly laughed at the man's disingenuousness. Instead, he set his teeth. "I will not strain your courtesy."

"Strain my—? No, it's no trouble; I'll be eating myself."

It was the fair man's turn to stare. "You are very bold, Lord Thomas. Stay me with omelettes, comfort me with apples if you will; I do trust that while you so stay me your hospitality does not extend to finding me better lodgings on a prison ship bound back for home, but only that you take some weird joy in dining with a traitor."

Lord Thomas looked evenly at his guest, all mirth gone from his round and pleasant face. "Are you a traitor, Master Merridon?"

"I loved the queen, it is well known."

"As do we all."

"No." With one hard word Lazarus froze the practiced courtesy. "As no one else did."

"That is not treason. You served her majesty's pleasure," Thomas said quietly. "As do we all."

"And when she took sick, and like to die, I fled the court."

"That was unhappy."

"Poison was spoken of."

Berowne shrugged. "Strange if it had not been. But she will not hear of it in the same breath as your name."

At that, the fair man's composure faltered; but only for an instant, while he drew a breath and closed his hands tightly on nothing.

The nobleman said carefully, "It was a wonderful winter for many, when you were there."

"If my love had been her death, you would not say so."

"I watched you all last year, and heard you play your music. The queen has many enemies. I never thought that you were one of them."

Lazarus turned away from his steady gaze. "Thank you."

"You're welcome."

"And yet," Lazarus Merridon turned his eyes full upon Thomas, "you do not know me at all." His eyes were wide, fringed with heavy lashes, the blue almost silver. Thomas met them, although it was not easy to look into them and speak at the same time.

"I would like to know you. I would like to be your friend."

"Would you?" Agitated, he paced the room, trying to keep his anger away from this generous man. "Because I play the lute, and sing, and can dance, and handle a sword, read Latin and some Greek; in short, play the gentleman in each and every part?"

Lord Thomas smiled fondly. "No, you fool. Because I like you."

"You—*like* me?" Even poised on the edge of confusion, head cocked, brow furled, hands taut, Merridon looked only as if he were performing some complicated dance turn. "What kind of reason is that?"

"The only reason. The very best."

Lazarus let the robe fall open. "Come, know me, then."

Berowne's face paled to match his own, then flushed. "Is this what you want?" he asked hoarsely. "I hadn't thought . . ."

"Come," said Lazarus Merridon, and sighed once as he felt the white rose being crushed between their two breasts.

My lord I dispatch this in haste only to tell you that the Quarry is Sighted.

They awoke in the late afternoon sun, amid a tangle of sweaty sheets.

Thomas sighed. "I did not think that I could be so happy."

"You've had other lovers, surely."

"But none like you."

Lazarus smiled wryly. "Certainly none like me."

Thomas looked at his own well-tended hand; it seemed brown, even coarse against the man's pale, soft skin. "You are so beautiful. It's almost hard to believe that you are real."

"Let me help you to believe it." Lazarus kissed him, and they spoke no more until the sun was set.

A discreet tap at the door woke them only from their contemplation of one another.

"Yes?" answered Thomas, because it was his house.

Jenkin's rusty head appeared around the doorframe. "My lord, I wondered if you wanted supper. And if the gentleman wanted his clothes."

"Yes," said one voice, and "No," said the other.

Jenkin understood them perfectly.

There was bread, and cheese, and sausage, and white wine to wash them down with, stony and cold. Because they had slept enough, they lit the candles and they talked.

"I wish that I had known you all my life," said Thomas. "Come, tell me: what were you like as a little boy?"

"I don't remember," Lazarus answered.

"I was rather pious." Thomas rested on his lover's chest. "I like for people to like me, and most of the people I knew were adults. Even my brother, Stephen—he's always been very grown-up. He's virtuous and brave, like an old-fashioned knight: he's studied fighting, and tactics, and history and all. He is the heir, and a good thing, too. I am only a second son—a fifth, actually, but I'm the one that lived. Have you brothers and sisters?"

"No. I was hatched. From an egg—or maybe an alembic. I was an experiment."

Thomas laughed. "Of course. Your patron, Lord Andreas, always liked to dabble in the weird sciences." Lazarus shuddered. "Quite," said his friend. "Something about all those rings, crammed on his puffy fingers . . ."

"Oh, Thomas. You dislike him only because he is not beautiful!"

"Well, I am sure that there are many other reasons to dislike him." Thomas rolled over, and wrapped his arms around his companion. "You let me talk and talk, and you don't say a word. You are so brilliant, so accomplished; is there not one good memory for you to share? Some piece of music heard for the first time; a kindly tutor; a lover; a warm spring night?"

Lazarus pressed his knuckles to his eyes, as though he would squeeze tears out of them. "Oh, do not ask me. Be my friend and do not ask me that."

> *Of ships in the harbor here, full xiv are provisioning to the benefit of our enterprise under pretext of an Eastern Expedition, and idle men are easy come by to man them; expecting one profit, they will rejoice to find another!*
> *. . . . Meanwhile, I will make it my business to create the occasion for some idle conversation with the Quarry, to know which way his mind*

tends concerning our affairs. That he is skillful and clever I well believe, since he contrived to elude me for so long. I will do all I can not to start him into further flight, knowing his value to yr ldshp.

They woke to midmorning sunlight. The curtains were drawn, the roses were fresh, and Lazarus's clothes lay neatly folded on a chest. Even his sword had been polished.

Thomas Berowne said, "It's funny, how much more interested I was in Turkey carpets two days ago. But I suppose I had better finish my dealings, since I've begun. Dress and come with me; you can tell me which ones to buy."

But Lazarus shook his head. "I think that would be unwise."

"Why? You have excellent taste."

The fair man smiled. "Thank you. But I will stay here."

"Ashamed to be seen with me, are you?" Berowne teased. "Afraid we'll fall to it in the street, is that it?"

"That is exactly it."

"Oh, come, you're a model of self-control; I've seen you at court, where the thing is truly tested."

Lazarus sighed, laughing. "Oh, Thomas . . . ! Just because you think me blameless doesn't mean others do. Shall I spell it out? People are looking for me."

"But the queen has called off the search; I was there."

"Enemies of the queen, then."

"And you, the great swordsman that you are, to fear them!"

"Much service I would do her, being taken up for quarreling and murder in a foreign country."

"I can protect you, Lazarus. I promised."

"But who will protect you?"

Thomas raised his eyebrows. "You?"

"And there you have it," Lazarus nodded; "a perfectly closed system. Pretty in two places only: philosophy and bed. Go on; be off with you and buy your carpets. I will be here when you get back."

Lord Thomas looked at him gravely. "Will you?"

"Yes, I will. I like it here."

Welcome, my lord, to these shores, blessed by our most sovereign lady. I rejoice in your deliverance from the realm of the Baseborn Queen, and hope you will return there soon in triumph at the side of our gracious lady, her sister, whose true right to the throne of her father is incontestible.

It was late that night under a full moon when Lord Thomas returned to their room. What he saw made him catch his breath: a man seated on the windowseat, fair head bent over a lute, all silvered by moonlight, the strings shimmering like liquid as they were plucked.

He stood still, listening to the music, wishing it could go on and on; but Lazarus looked up, and set the lute aside. "There you are. I went back to my old lodgings to rescue a few things."

Around his neck a gold chain gleamed. Thomas approached, and lifted from his chest a jewel, a heavy pendant of a unicorn crusted with gemstones and pearls.

"The queen's jewel. You have it still."

"I was thinking of pawning it."

"But you did not."

"No." Lazarus laced his fingers with Thomas's, closed together around the gaudy unicorn. For a long time, he looked at them. He opened his mouth, closed it, then wet his lips and said, "Tell me—how is she?"

"Truly? She is sad. She reads philosophy, and speaks no more of masques, nor yet of love."

"Poor lady."

"Her younger sister, the Gallish queen, has an eye to her kingdom as well; rumors of invasion are common as starlings in June. Because the Gallish woman has sons, and in her pride seeks kingdoms for them all, while our sweet lady sits alone—"

"And will not wed. I know."

Thomas's fingers tightened around them both. "She still wants you. My family serves her, and always has," he said earnestly. "Lazarus, I can—I can arrange certain things. A passage. A pardon. You might return to her."

"No. It would kill her."

Thomas knelt at his feet, to look up into his moonsilver eyes. "Sweet, why do you say so? I know you are a good man. You may not love her, but you value her happiness, as I do. You would never seek to harm her."

Lazarus looked back at his friend. His pupils were huge and dark. "It has to do with Andreas. With my guardian, my patron."

"He is no longer your patron. He cast you off when you fled."

"No. He did not," Lazarus said bitterly. "Never mind what he told the court. He did not cast me off and never will."

"Sweet, what is it? Are you his son?"

The fair man barked a laugh. "God, no! I made a bargain."

"It can be broken. Whether you are bound by money, honor, duty—Lord Andreas is a rotten man, and a greedy one; it is not right for such as you to owe him anything! Tell me, only tell me, and I will see to it; I am not so very unworldly that I cannot do that for you."

"No. This bargain cannot be broken. And if it were to be, you would not like it." Lazarus smiled thinly. "I promise you that."

"Riddles, my love." Thomas unknit his fingers from the overwrought jewel, and smoothed his hand like a kitten, or a rumpled sheet. "I wish that you could tell me. I wish that I could help. . . ."

"You do." Lazarus's voice was muffled by Thomas's shirt. "Oh, you do. But there are things I cannot say—I cannot *tell* you, Thomas!"

Thomas kissed the back of his neck, where the fine hair grew like down. "What is it? What is so terrible? Are you a murderer? An adulterer? Father of a hundred bastards?" Lazarus laughed against his chest. "I know you do not kick small children in the street. What is this terrible thing you cannot tell?"

But the glib-tongued man was silent.

"Let me ask you questions, then. These painful secrets, kept too long, will fester, and, like old worms, begin to feed on that which is their home. I will ask, and you will answer as you may." He felt the fair man stiffen in his arms. "Right. Then cut straight to the heart. Lazarus, why did you flee the court?"

"For the harm I did the queen."

"What harm is that?"

"I did not mean to—I did not know—and when I knew, I fled."

"What did you do?"

He turned his head away. "I poisoned her."

"You did. And by what means?" Thomas asked patiently.

Lazarus swallowed, and in a muffled voice said, "It is my love. My love that poisons."

Thomas nearly shook him, but wrapped his arms around him tighter instead. "Nonsense! People have only told you that . . . angry people, people you've hurt who want to hurt you. But you mustn't listen to them," he soothed; "they are wrong, it isn't true—"

Lazarus wrenched himself from his lover's grasp. His face was nothing but eyes and hollow angles, unnatural and lovely, like cut glass. "But it is true, Thomas. This is not some quaint conceit—or maybe that is exactly what I am: the poetic *love that kills* made flesh, walking the earth. A lover's song incarnate."

"How is that possible?"

"To be a dream made flesh? I do not know. Ask Andreas and his alchemical friends. But I am perfect, am I not? You have said so yourself. Created for a queen to be her death. And maybe I will be yours as well."

"How?" Lord Thomas only stared. "I do not understand."

"Because you do not want to understand! Look at me, Thomas, only look at me and think. I have no past, no childhood, no store of memories but dreams. I cannot get drunk, I cannot be killed, by poison or by the sword—instead of getting drunk, I go to sleep; my wounds close up as soon as they are made. I am not a man, Thomas, so do not waste your sympathy and your kind understanding on me. I'm not a man like you, or Jenkin, or the beggar in the street!"

Thomas sat, impassive. "And the queen?"

"I carry poison in my flesh. For others, not for me."

"I see." Thomas nodded. "Yes."

Moonlight flashed across his lover's body as he paced back and forth between the shadows and the window.

"But you were mortal once?"

"Of course. Only God can make a human soul from nothing," Lazarus said scornfully. "Do not ask me what I was before; it comes to me in dreams, but that is all."

Thomas said slowly, "I've taken no harm of you thus far."

"Neither did the queen, at first."

"Yes."

Lazarus stopped his pacing. He stood in the shadows, watching Thomas in the moonlight. Thomas rose, and turned from him, pressing his forehead to the moon-washed glass, hands raised above his head against the panes.

"There," Lazarus said. "You asked, and now you know." Lord Thomas's eyes were closed, his face washed blue, like someone in a tomb. "You will not want to see me, now. It is disgusting, I know."

"No," Thomas spoke, his cheek against the cold glass. "Oddly enough, that isn't true. I've heard all that you have said, and I think that I believe it. But I find I do not care. It makes no difference. And that surprises me."

"Ah," said Lazarus with a bravado he did not feel. "I have frightened you at last."

Lord Thomas smiled. "Oh, no, my dear; you do not frighten me." His face was warm enough to melt the coldness of the glass; but still he stood where he was, cheek pressed to the night.

Lazarus came to him, slowly and gently, and turned him in his arms, and sat him down, and laid his head in Thomas's lap.

> *It is a wonderful thing, how Berowne scarcely ventures from his house, and yet he is not ill, save with that disease common to bridegrooms and green girls! Neither do any come in to him, and so yr ldshp's thought that he might be passing and receiving information under cover of his collecting may be disproved. Let him do our work for us the whiles, for as a Keeper he does excel any that Art or Nature could provide!*

They had flowers and wine, music and conversation, darkness and light, and the warmth of one another's breath in the silences in between action and talk; they had all that they needed to make them happy.

In the dark, they talked of everything that came to them, or ever had. Thomas yearned to know the rhythms of his lover's body, his breathing and his silences; when he needed comfort, when passion; when he might be taken, and when it was necessary to give.

Lazarus, too, learned to see without eyes, and to make music for one person only. *Pretty fool*, Thomas called him; and, knowing he could outmatch Thomas at anything but love, Lazarus found he liked that.

Thomas tended his love like a garden. He pulled the weeds out from among the fragile shoots, careful not to tangle with their roots. Thomas asked, "Is it true you cannot die?"

Lazarus shrugged. "Only time will tell. It adds a certain spice to life. I think that I cannot be killed—except, perhaps," he frowned, "by those who made me. My making was expensive; they told me so many times. They are unlikely to waste their labor by undoing me."

Thomas stroked the length of his body, infinitely precious now in light and dark. "I would like to think no one can touch you now."

Lazarus laughed gently. "No one but you."

> *My lord has in the past had the kindness to credit me with some good sense, and so will not think me derelict or negligent, particularly when the good resolution of our enterprise is so very near, that I have not contrived, by accident or by design, to meet with and hold some conversation with the Quarry. And yr ldshp's warnings about his prodigious skills at arms and clever speech have not made me timid, nor lax to do yr bidding, but only cautious not to betray my interest lest some word of this come to Berowne. After all, the thing now is underway, and cannot be stopped, least of all by two such inward-turning fellows. Yr ldshp's concern that the Quarry not return to his Baseborn love, lest he in his great gifts should prove of service against us, I think unfounded. Your further uses for him you may achieve when you sit at the hand of the True*

> Queen, whose enterprise will surely thrive. Meanwhile, so long as he remains the chief toy and jewel of the young lord, and they do content themselves with one another, then why not trust the words of the old adage, and "Let sleeping dogs lie"?

But the end came, as it so often does, with news of the outside world. They were at breakfast, a meal of honey and golden sunlight, both making golden patches on their skin, and oranges, and country butter on rolls hot from the oven.

Thomas wiped a trickle of honey from the other's chin, and regarded him critically. "Hmm," he said; "you are, if possible, even paler than before. Fresh air is what you need, and if you must go out disguised, it won't be in that ridiculous black-hooded cloak."

"I must not be recognized with you—"

". . . too dangerous, I know, I know. We must find some way of altering your looks that does no lasting harm—a wig? A wig. . . ." The nobleman's smile stretched into a gloat of pure mischief. "Certainly a wig; a nice long one, and a veil, and paint to your eyes, and a lovely gown, green, I think!"

"Oh, excellent!" His friend's hilarity held a note of near-hysteria. "Disguise me as that I am!"

"Well you're hardly a courtesan, my dear, though some might call you my mistress—"

"My lord."

Jenkin stood holding a folded parchment bound about with tape and wax. "This is new come off the boat for you, my lord. A man waits below for your reply."

Thomas broke open the heavy seals. Lazarus knew the device stamped into them; the family crest was on Berowne's dagger, his goblets, his plate. He waited quietly across the room, until Thomas lifted a drawn face to him.

"My father—my brother—it seems I must come home."

"Are they ill?"

"No, no. But this is not a time for me to be abroad." Lord Thomas glanced down at the letter, and forced a smile. "They like the rugs I chose."

Lazarus felt it then, the hard-edged border between what he was to Berowne, and what a man's family was: the loyalties held, the confidences understood. "Well," he said. "You will close up this house?"

"I must." Thomas walked around the room, rapping at things with the parchment: the wall, a chair, a chest, the bed. "From what they say, I will not be back soon."

Lazarus felt his stomach lurch with understanding. "Good. I'll send you some music."

"Music?!" Thomas looked at him with amazement. "What music?"

"For the procession. The banquet." With pride, Lazarus noted that his own voice held light and steady. "It will be a gift between us."

"My dear, what on earth are you talking about?"

"Now that your family has found you a bride."

"A—oh!" Thomas laughed with his fingers spread over his face. "Oh, no. I wish it were that simple, that would be easy."

Lazarus saw that he was not laughing after all. He knelt at his side. "My dear, tell me—what is it?"

Thomas handed him the letter. Skimming over the salutations, the family news, Lazarus Merridon read:

". . . that Her Majesty's sister plans invasion is now certain, and the time will be soon. Although we could wish you safely away, your place is here."

> Berowne is closing his house up very suddenly. Doubtless he returns home to join ranks with the Baseborn Queen. Should the Quarry seek to accompany him thither, I will take those measures yr ldshp instructed me in.

"Come with me," said Thomas; "please come."

"I will be more use to you here. Hidden in the taverns, I can collect reports—"

"I do not care for use! I want you by me."

In the dark, Lazarus put his fingers to his lover's mouth, stilling the words on his lips. "I dare not come. I dare not. If the queen sees me—or anyone thinks I've hurt her—if those who made me find me . . ."

"Come under my protection—come disguised—do you mean to live an exile all your life?"

"An exile? You speak as though I had a home."

"In love, you do. In love and honor."

"Oh, Thomas . . . ! I am not a man of honor. I am not noble, as you are, in any sense of the word."

"You are loyal, to those you love. You would not suffer the queen to be harmed through you."

"Pride," Lazarus dismissed it. "I would not be used. If I go back, they will try to use me to harm—to harm those around me."

"You will not let them. You know now that you did not know before. You're strong, my love, and true."

The slender fingers clenched in upon themselves, biting half-moons in his perfect flesh. "*I do not know what I will do.* You must understand, Thomas, try—I do not know fully what I am. My limits or my strength. Andreas knows. I am afraid, Tom: afraid of him, afraid to let him find me."

"My dear, how long must you live thus?"

"I need time, I must have time to find out what I am in truth."

"I will kill Andreas when I see him! He is a traitor, and a pig besides. He never told you, he and his friends, what you were made of?"

"They gave me what they promised me."

"Lazarus—what did they promise you? What did you trade yourself away for?"

"It was to be that which I am. The form, the grace, the gifts, the skills—all of it. I desired it above all things," the beautiful man said with bleak defiance. "I thought I would be happy."

"Poor Lazarus!" He heard the smile in Thomas's voice, but the man's warm hands were all comfort and affection. "You may not be mortal, but I fear that you are human after all."

Lazarus rolled in his lover's arms. And where one held the other and where one was held was a thing indistinguishable as hair from hair in a braided coronet, or the interlaced twining of vines in the bower.

Lazarus spoke at last. "Go home and do what you must do. If it is done well, I will be free to return. If ill—then you will come to me, and we will go adventuring together the wide world over."

The Quarry is fled. The trail is cold. I rejoice in your victory, and that of our most Sovereign Lady.

In a tavern in another harbor town, Lazarus Merridon heard of the fall of the crown, and the death and attainder of many of its noble supporters. Among the dead, the Berowne heir; the parents fled to friends across the sea. And their surviving son, attainted traitor, awaiting now the new prince's judgment in a little room behind the thick walls of a tower, encircled with woven rushes in a field of flowers.

MORE TOMORROW
Michael Marshall Smith

Michael Marshall Smith was born in Knutsford, Cheshire, England, and grew up in the United States, South Africa, and Australia. He now lives in North London with his girlfriend, Paula, two cats, and "enough computer equipment to launch a space shuttle." His short fiction has been published in *Omni, Peeping Tom, Chills, Dark Voices, Shadows Over Innsmouth, The Anthology of Fantasy and the Supernatural,* both *Darkland* anthologies, *Best New Horror,* and *The Year's Best Fantasy and Horror.* He has won the British Fantasy Award for short fiction twice and the August Derleth Award for his critically acclaimed first novel *Only Forward.* His second novel *Spares* will be published in October 1996 by HarperCollins U.K. He is currently scriptwriting the miniseries adaptation of Clive Barker's *Weaveworld* and is working on other projects as a partner in the Smith & Jones production company.

There are stories whose endings have the inevitability of an oncoming wreck. In this kind of story it doesn't matter that you might suspect or even know what's going to happen at the conclusion; it's the getting there that's important. You keep reading in morbid fascination/repulsion because you must. "More Tomorrow" is one of those stories. It was first published in *Dark Terrors* (formerly Pan's *Dark Voices* series), edited by Stephen Jones and David Sutton.

—E.D.

I got a new job a couple of weeks ago. It's pretty much the same as my old job, but at a much nicer company. What I do is troubleshoot computers and their software, and yes, I know that sounds dull. People tell me so all the time. Not in words, exactly, but in their glassy smiles and their awkward "let's be nice to the drone" demeanor.

It's a strange phenomenon, really, the whole "computer people are losers" mentality. All round the world, in every office in every building, people are using computers day in, day out. Every now and then, these machines go wrong. They're bound to: they're complex systems, like a human body, or society. When someone gets hurt, you call in a doctor. When a riot breaks out, it's the police that—for once—you want to see on your doorstep. Similarly, if your word processor starts dumping files or your hard disk goes nonlinear, it's someone like me you need.

Someone who actually *understands* the box of magic that sits on your desk, and can make it all lovely again.

But do we get any thanks, any kudos for being the emergency services of the late twentieth century? Do we fuck.

I can understand it to a degree. There are enough nerds and geeks around to make it seem like a losing way of life. But there are plenty of pretty random earthlings doing all the other jobs too, and no one expects them to turn up for work in a pinwheel hat and a T-shirt saying "Programmers do it recursively." For the record, I play reasonable blues guitar, I've been out with a girl, and have worked undercover for the CIA. The last bit isn't true, of course, but you get the general idea.

Up until recently I worked for a computer company, which was full of very perfunctory human beings. When people started passing around jokes that were written in C++, I decided it was time to go. One of the other advantages of knowing about computers is that unemployment isn't going to be a problem until the damn things start fixing themselves, and so I called a few contacts, posted a CV up on the Internet, and within twenty-four hours had seven opportunities to choose from. Most of them were other computer businesses, which I was kind of keen to avoid, and in the end I decided to have a crack at a company called the VCA. I put on my pinwheel hat, rubbed pizza on my shirt, and strolled along for all interview.

The VCA, it transpired, was a nonprofit organization dedicated to promoting effective business communication. The suave but shifty chief executive who interviewed me seemed a little vague as to what this actually entailed, and in the end I let it go. The company was situated in tidy new offices right in the center of town, and seemed to be doing good trade at whatever it was they did. The reason they needed someone like me was they wanted to upgrade their system, computers, software, and all. It was a month's contract work, at a very decent rate, and I said yes without a second thought.

Whitehead, the guy in charge, took me for a gloating tour round the office. It looked the same as they always do, only emptier, because everyone was out at lunch. Then I settled down with their spreadsheet-basher to find out what kind of system they could afford. His name was Egerton, and he wasn't out at lunch because he was clearly one of those people who see working nine-hour days as worthy of some form of admiration. Personally I view it as worthy of pity, at most. He seemed amiable enough, in a curly-haired, irritating sort of way, and within half an hour we'd thrashed out the necessary. I made some calls, arranged to come back in a few days, and spent the rest of the afternoon helping build a hospital in Rwanda. Well, actually, I spent it listening to loud music and catching up on my Internet newsgroups, but I could have done the other had I been so inclined.

The Internet is one of those things that more and more people have heard of without having any real idea of what it means. It's actually very simple. A while back a group of universities and government organizations experimented with a way of linking up all their computers so they could share resources, send little messages, and play *Star Trek* games with each other. After a time this network started to take on a momentum of its own, with everyone from Pentagon heavies to pinwheeling wireheads taking it upon themselves to find new ways of connecting things up and making more information available. Just about every major computer on the planet is now connected, and if you've got a modem and a phone line, you can get on there too. I can tell you can hardly wait.

What you find when you're there almost qualifies as a parallel universe. There are thousands of pieces of software, probably millions of text files. You can check the records of the New York Public Library, send a message to someone in Japan that will arrive within minutes, download a picture of the far side of Jupiter, and monitor how many cans of Dr Pepper there are in a particular soda machine in the computer science labs of American universities. A lot of this stuff is fairly chaotically organized, but there are a few systems that span the net as a whole. One of these is the newsgroups.

There are about ten thousand of these groups now, covering anything from computers to fine art, science fiction to tastelessness, the books of Stephen King to quirky sexual preferences. If it's not outright illegal, out there on the information superhighway people will be yakking about it twenty-four hours a day, every day of the year. Either that or posting images: there are paintings and animals, NASA archives and abstract art, and in the alt.billaries.pictures.tasteless group you can find anything from close-up shots of roadkills to people with acid burns on their faces. Not very nice, but trust me, it's a minority interest.

Basically the groups are little discussion centers that stick to their own specific topic. People read each other's messages and reply, or forward their own pronouncements or questions. Some groups have computer files, like software or pictures, other just have text messages. Now that I think of it, there's some illegal stuff too (drugs, mainly): there's a system by which you can send untraceable and anonymous messages, though I've never bothered to check it out.

No one, however sad, could hope to keep abreast of all of these groups, and nor would you want to. I personally don't give a toss about recent developments in Multilevel Marketing Businesses or the Nature of Chinchilla Farming in America Today, and have no interest in reading megabytes of mindless burblings about them. So I, like most people, stick to a subset of the groups that carry stuff I'm interested in—Mac computers, guitar music, cats, and the like.

So now you know.

The following Tuesday I got up bright and early and made my way to the VCA for my first morning's work. England was doing its best to be summery, which, as always, meant that it was humid without being hot, bright without being sunny, and every third commuter on the hellish Underground was intermittently pebble-dashing nearby passengers with hayfever sneezes. I emerged moist and irritable from the tube, more determined than ever to find a way of working that meant never having to leave my apartment. The walk from the station to the VCA was better, passing through an attractive square and a selection of interesting sidestreets, and I was feeling chipper again by the time I got there.

My suppliers had done their work, and the main area of the VCA's open-plan office was piled high with exciting boxes. When I walked in, just about all the staff were standing round the pile, coffee mugs in hand, regarding it with a wary enthusiasm as if they were simple country folk and it was a recently landed UFO. There was a slightly toe-curling five minutes of introductions, embarrassing merely because I don't enjoy that kind of thing. Only one person, John, seemed to view me with the sniffy disdain of someone greeting an underling whose services are, unfortunately, in the ascendant. Everybody else seemed nice, some very much so.

Whitehead eventually oiled out of his office and dispensed a few weak jokes, which had the—possibly intentional—effect of scattering everyone back to their desks to get on with their work. I took off my jacket, rolled up my sleeves, and got on with it.

I spent the morning cabling like a wild thing, placing the hardware of the network itself. As this involved a certain amount of disrupting everyone in turn by drilling, pulling up carpet, and moving their desks, I was soon on apologetic grinning terms with most of them. I guess I could have done the wire-up over the weekend when nobody was there, but I like my weekends as they are. John gave me the invisibility routine that people once used on servants, but everyone else was fairly cool about it. One of the girls, Jeanette, actually engaged me in conversation while I worked nearby, and seemed genuinely interested in understanding what I was doing. When I broke it to her that it was actually fairly dull, she smiled.

The wiring took a little longer than I was expecting, and I stayed on after everybody else had gone. Everyone but Egerton, that was, who stayed, probably to make sure that I didn't run off with their spoons, or database, or plants. Either that or to get some brownie points with whoever it is he thought cared about people putting in long hours. The invoicing supremo was in expansive mood, and chuntered endlessly about his adventures in computing, which were, to be honest, of slender interest to me. In the end he got bored with my monosyllabic grunts from beneath desks, and left me with some keys instead.

The next day was pretty much the same, except I was setting up the computers themselves. This involved taking things out of boxes and installing interminable pieces of software on the server. This isn't quite such a sociable activity as disturbing people, and I spent most of the day in the affable but distant company of Sarah, their PR person. At the end of the day everyone gathered in the main room and then left together, apparently for a meal to celebrate someone's birthday. I thought I caught Jeanette casting a glance in my direction at one point, maybe embarrassed at the division between me and them. It didn't bother me much, so I just got my head down and got on with swopping floppy disks in and out of the machines.

Well, it did bother me a little, to be honest. It wasn't their fault—there was no reason why they should make the effort to include someone they didn't know, who wasn't really a part of their group. People seldom do. You have to be a little thick-skinned about that kind of thing if you work freelance. There are still tribes, you know, everywhere you go. They owe their allegiance to shared time, if they're friends, or to an organization, if they're colleagues: but they're tribes just as much as if they'd tilled the same patch of desert for centuries. As a freelancer, especially in the cyber-areas, you tend to spend a lot of time wandering between them, occasionally being granted access to their watering hole, but never being one of the real people. Sometimes it can get on your nerves. That's all.

I finished up, locked the building carefully—I'm a complete anal-retentive about such things—and went home. I used my mobile to call for a pizza while I was on route, and it arrived two minutes after I got out of the shower. A perfect piece of timing, which sadly no one was on hand to appreciate. My last experiment with living with someone did not end well, mainly because she was a touchy and irritable woman who needed her own space twenty-three-and-a-half hours a day. Well it was more complicated than that, of course, but that was the main impression I took away with me. I mulled over those times as I sat and munched my "everything on it, and then a few more things as well" pizza, vague-eyed in front of white-noise television, and ended up feeling rather grim.

Food event over, I made a jug of coffee and settled down in front of the Mac. I tweaked my invoicing database for a while, exciting young man that I am, and then wrote a letter to my sister in Australia. She doesn't have access to Internet E-mail, unfortunately, otherwise she'd hear from me a lot more often. Write letter, print letter, put it in envelope, get stamps, get it to a post office. A chain of admin of that magnitude usually takes me about two weeks to get through, and it's a hit primitive, really, compared to "write letter, press button, there in five minutes."

I called my friend Nick, who's a freelance sub-editor on a trendy magazine, but he was chasing a deadline and not disposed to chat. I tried the television, but it was still outputting someone else's idea of entertainment. By nine o'clock I was very bored, and so I logged on to the net.

Probably because I was bored, and feeling a bit isolated, after I'd done my usual groups I found myself checking out alt.binaries.pictures.erotica. "alt" means the group is an unofficial one; "binaries" means it holds computer files rather than just messages; "pictures" means those files are images. As for the last word, I'm prepared to be educational about this but you're going to have to work that one out for yourself.

The media has the impression that the minute you're in cyberspace, countless pictures of this type come flooding at you down the phone, pouring like ravening hordes onto your hard disk and leaping out of the screen to take over your mind. This is not the case, and all of you worried about your little Timmy's soul can afford to relax a little. You need a computer, a modem, access to a phone line, and a credit card to pay for your Internet feed. You need to find the right newsgroup, and download about three segments for each picture. You require several bits of software to piece them together, convert the result, and display it.

The naughty pictures don't come and get you, and if you see one, it ain't an accident. If your little Timmy has the kit, finance, and inclination to go looking, then maybe it's you who needs the talking to. In fact, maybe you should be grounded.

The flipside of that, of course, is the implication that I have the inclination to go looking, which I guess I occasionally do. Not very often—honest—but I do. I don't know how defensive to feel about that fact. Men of all shapes and sizes, ages and creeds, and states of marital or relationship bliss enjoy, every now and then, the sight of a woman with no clothes on. It's just as well we do, you know, otherwise there'd be no new little earthlings, would there? If you want to call that oppression or sexism or the commodification of the female body, then go right ahead, but don't expect me to talk to you at dinner parties. I prefer to call it sexual attraction, but then I'm a sad fuck who spends half his life in front of a computer, so what the hell do I know?

Still, it's not something that people feel great about, and I'm not going to defend it too hard. Especially not to women, because that would be a waste of everyone's time. Women have a little bit of their brain missing, which means they cannot understand the attraction of pornography. I'm not saying that's a *bad* thing, just that it's true. On the other hand they understand the attraction of babies, shoe shops, and the details of other people's lives, so I guess it's swings and roundabouts.

I've talked about it for too long now, and you're going to think I'm some Neanderthal with his tongue hanging to the ground who goes round looking up people's skirts. I'm not. Yes, there are rude pictures to be found on the net, and yes, I sometimes find them. What can I say? I'm a bloke.

Anyway, I scouted round for a while, but in the end didn't even download anything. From the descriptions of the files they seemed to be the same endless permutations of badly lit mad people, which is ultimately a bit tedious. Also, bullish talk notwithstanding, I don't feel great about looking at that kind of thing. I don't think it reflects very well upon one, and you only have to read a few other people's slaverings to make you decide it is too sad to be a part of.

So in the end I played the guitar for a while and went to bed.

The next few days at the VCA passed pretty easily. I installed and configured, configured and installed. The birthday meal went pretty well, I gathered, and featured amongst other highlights the secretary Tanya literally sliding under the table through drunkenness. That was her story, at least. By the Monday of the following week everyone was calling me by name, and I was being included in the coffee-making rounds. England had called its doomed attempt at summer off, or at least called time out, and had settled for a much more bearable cross between spring and autumn instead. All in all, things were going fairly well.

And as the week progressed, slightly better even than that. The reason for this was a person. Jeanette, to be precise.

I began, without even noticing at first, to find myself veering towards the computer nearest her when I needed to do some testing. I also found that I was slightly more likely to offer to go and make a round of coffees in the kitchen when she was already standing there, smoking one of her hourly cigarettes. Initially it was just because she was the politest and most approachable of the staff, and it was a couple of days before I realized that I was looking out for her return from lunch, trying to be less dull when she was around, and noticing what she wore.

It was almost as if I was I beginning to fancy her, for heaven's sake.

By the beginning of the next week I passed a kind of watershed, and went from undirected, subconscious behavior to actually facing the fact that I was attracted to her. I did this with a faint feeling of dread, coupled with occasional, mournful tinges of melancholy. It was like being back at school. It's awful, when you're grown-up, to be reminded of what it was like when a word from someone, a glance, even just their presence can be like the sun coming out from behind clouds. While it's nice, in a lyric, romantic novel sort of way, it also complicates things. Suddenly it matters if other people come into the kitchen when you're talking to them, and the way they interact with other people becomes more important. You start trying to engineer things, trying to be near them, and it all gets just a bit weird.

Especially if the other person hasn't a clue what's going on in your head and you've no intention of telling them. I'm no good at that, the telling part. Ten years ago I carried a letter round with me for two weeks, trying to pluck up the courage to give it to someone. It was a girl who was part of the same crowd at college, who I knew well as a friend, and who had just split up from someone else. The letter was a very carefully worded and tentative description of how I felt about her, ending with an invitation for a drink. Several times I was on the brink, I swear, but somehow I didn't give it to her. I just didn't have what it took.

The computer stuff was going OK, if you're interested. By the middle of the week the system was pretty much in place, and people were happily sending pop-up messages to each other. Egerton, in particular, thought it was just fab that he could boss people around from the comfort of his own den. Even John was bucked up by seeing how the new system was going to ease the progress of whatever dull task it was he performed, and all in all my stock at the VCA was rising high.

It was time, finally, to get down to the nitty-gritty of developing their new databases. I tend to enjoy that part more than the wireheading, because it's more of a challenge, gives scope for design and creativity, and I don't have to keep getting up from my chair. When I settled down to it on Thursday morning, I realized that it was going to have an additional benefit. Jeanette was the VCA's events organizer, and most of the databases they needed concerned various aspects of her job. In other words, it was her I genuinely had to talk to about them, and at some length.

We sat side by side at her desk, me keeping a respectful distance, and I asked her the kind of questions I had to ask. She answered them concisely and quickly, didn't pipe up with a lot of damn fool questions, and came up with some reasonable requests. It was rather a nice day outside, and sunlight that was for once not hazy and obstructive angled through the window to pick out the lighter hues amongst her chestnut hair, which was long, and wavy, and as far as I could see, entirely beautiful. Her hands played carelessly with a Biro as we talked, the fingers long and purposeful, the forearms a pleasing shade of skin color. I hate people who go sprinting out into parks at the first sign of summer, to lie with insectile patience or brainlessness in the desperate quest for a tan. As far as I was concerned, the fact that she clearly hadn't done so—in contrast to Tanya, for example, who already looked like a hazelnut (and probably thought with the same fluency as one)—was just another thing to like her for.

It was a nice morning. Relaxed, and pleasant. Over the last week we'd started to speak more and more, and were ready for a period of actually having to converse with each other at length. I enjoyed it, but didn't get overexcited. Despite my losing status as a technodrone, I am wise in the ways of relationships. Just being able to get on with her, and have her look as if she didn't mind being with me—that was more than enough for the time being. I wasn't going to try for anything more. Or so I thought.

Then, at half-past twelve, I did something entirely unexpected. We were in the middle of an in-depth and speculative wrangle on the projected nature of their hotel-booking database, when I realized that we were approaching the time at which Jeanette generally took her lunch. Smoothly, and with a nonchalance that I found frankly impressive, I lofted the idea that we go grab a sandwich somewhere and continue the discussion outside. As the sentences slipped from my mouth I experienced an out-of-body sensation, as if I was watching myself from about three feet away, cowering behind a chair. Not bad, I found myself thinking, incredulously. Clearly she'll say no, but that was a good, businesslike way of putting it.

Bizarrely, instead of shrieking with horror or poking my eye out with a ruler, she said yes. We rose together, I grabbed my jacket, and we left the office, me trying not to smirk like some recently ennobled businessman who'd done a lot of work for charity. We took the lift down to the lobby and stepped outside, and I chattered inanely to avoid coming to terms with the fact that I was now standing with her *outside* work, beyond our usual frame of reference.

She knew a snack bar around the corner, and within ten minutes we found ourselves at a table outside, plowing through sandwiches. She even ate attractively, as if she was a genuine human taking on sustenance rather than someone appearing in amateur dramatics. I audibly mulled over the database for a while, to give myself time to settle down, and before long we'd pretty much done the subject.

Luckily, as we each smoked a cigarette, she pointed out with distaste a couple of blokes walking down the street, both of whom had taken their shirts off, and whose paunches were hanging over their jeans.

"Summer," she said, with a sigh, and I was away. There are few people with a larger internal stock of complaints to make about summer than me, and I let myself rip.

Why, I asked her, did everyone think it was so nice? What were supposed to be the benefits? One of the worst things about summer, I maintained hotly, as she smiled and ordered us coffee, was the constant pressure to enjoy oneself in ways that are considerably less fun than death.

Barbecues, for example. Now I don't mind barbies, especially, except that *my* friends never have them. If I end up at a barbeque, it's because I've been dragged there by my partner, to stand round in someone else's scraggy back garden as the sky threatens rain, watching drunken blokes teasing a nasty barking dog, and girls I don't know standing in clumps gossiping about people I've never heard of, while trying to eat badly cooked food that I could have bought for £2.50 in McDonald's *and* had somewhere to sit as well. That washed-out, exhausted, and depressed feeling that comes from getting not quite drunk enough in the afternoon while standing up and either trying to make conversation with people I'll never see again, or putting up with them doing the same to me.

And going and sitting in parks. I hate it, as you may have gathered. Why? Because it's fucking *horrible*, that's why. Sitting on grass that is both papery and damp, surrounded by middle-class men with beards teaching their kids to unicycle, the air rent by the sound of some asshole torturing a guitar to the delight of his fourteen-year-old hippy girlfriend. Drinking lukewarm soft drinks out of overpriced cans, and all the time being repetitively told how nice it all is, as if by some process of brainwashing you'll actually start to enjoy it.

Worst of all, the constant pressure to *go outside*. "What are you doing inside on a day like this? You want to go outside, you do, get some fresh air. You want to go outside." No. Wrong. I don't want to go outside. For a start, I like it inside. It's nice there. There are sofas, drinks, cigarettes, books. There is shade. Outside there's nothing but the sun, the mindless drudgery of suntan cultivation, and the perpetual sound of droning voices, yapping dogs, and convention shouting at you to enjoy yourself.

And always the constant refrain from everyone you meet, drumming on your mind like torrential rain on a tin roof: "Isn't it a beautiful day?," "Isn't it a beautiful day?," "Isn't it a beautiful day?," "Isn't it a beautiful day?"

No, say I. No, it fucking *isn't*.

There was all that, and some more, but I'm sure you get the drift. By halfway through Jeanette was laughing, partly at what I was saying, and partly—I'm sure— at the fact that I was getting quite so worked up about it. But she was with me, and chipped in some valuable observations about the horrors of sitting outside dull country pubs surrounded by red-faced career girls and loud-mouthed estate agents in shorts, deafened by the sound of open-topped cars being revved by people who clearly had no right to live. We banged on happily for quite a while, had another cup of coffee, and then were both surprised to realize that we'd gone into overtime on lunch. I paid, telling her she could get the next one, and although that sounds like a terrible line, it came out pretty much perfect and she didn't stab me or anything. We strode quickly back to the office, still chatting, and the rest of the afternoon passed in a hazy blur of contentment.

I could have chosen to leave at the same time as her, and walked to whichever station she used, but I elected not to. I judged that enough had happened for one day, and I didn't want to push my luck. Instead I went home alone, hung out by myself, and went to sleep with, I suspect, a small smile upon my face.

Next day I sprang out of bed with an enthusiasm that is utterly unlike me, and as I struggled to balance the recalcitrant taps of my shower, I was already plotting my next moves. Part of my mind was sitting back with folded arms and watching me with indulgent amusement, but in general I just felt really quite happy and excited.

For most of the morning I quizzed Jeanette further on her database needs. She was lunching with a friend, I knew, so I wasn't expecting anything there. Instead I wandered vaguely round a couple of bookshops, wondering if there was any book I could legitimately buy for Jeanette. It would have to be something very specific, relevant to a conversation we'd had—and sufficiently inexpensive that it looked like a throwaway gift—and in the end I came away empty-handed. Which was probably just as well. Buying her a present was a ridiculous idea, out of proportion to the current situation. As I walked back to the office I told myself to be careful. I was in danger of getting carried away and disturbing the careful equilibrium of my life and mind.

Then, in the afternoon, something happened that made my heart sing. I was off the databases for a while, trying to work out why Jeanette's computer was behaving rather strangely. Tanya wandered up to ask Jeanette about something, and before she went, reminded her that there'd been talk of everyone going out for a drink that evening. Jeanette hummed and ha-ed for a moment, and I bent further over the keyboard, giving them a chance to ignore me. Then, as from nowhere, Tanya said the magic words.

Why, she suggested, didn't I come too?

Careful to be nonchalant and cavalier, pausing as if sorting through my myriad other options, I said yes, why the hell not. Jeanette then said yes, she could probably make it, and for a moment I saw all the locks and chains around my life fall away, as if a cage had collapsed around me, leaving only the open road.

For a moment it was like that, and then suddenly it wasn't.

"I'll have to check with Chris, though," Jeanette added, and I realized she had a boyfriend.

I spent the rest of the afternoon violently but silently cursing and trying to calm myself down. I should have known that someone like her would already be taken—after all, they always are. Of course, that didn't mean it was a no-go area. People sometimes leave their partners. I know; I've done it myself. But suddenly it had changed, changed from something that might—in my dreams, at least—have developed smoothly into a nice thing. It had changed into a miasma of potential grief that was unlikely even to start.

For about half an hour I was furious, with what I don't know. With myself, for letting my feelings grow and complicate. With her, for having a boyfriend. With life, for always being that bit more disappointing than it absolutely has to be. Then, because I'm an old hand at dealing with my inner conditions, I talked myself around. It didn't matter. Jeanette could simply become a nice thing about a month-long contract, someone I could chat to. Then the job would end, I'd move on, and none of it would matter. I had to nail that conclusion down on myself pretty hard, but thought I could make it stick.

I decided that I might as well go out for the drink anyway. There was another party I could go to but it would involve trekking halfway across town. Nick was busy. I might as well be sociable, now that they'd made the offer.

So I went, and I wish I hadn't.

The evening was OK, in the way that they always are when people from the same office get together to drink and complain about their boss. Whitehead wasn't there, thankfully, and Egerton quickly got sufficiently drunk that he didn't qualify as a Whitehead substitute. The evening was fine, for everyone else. It was just me who didn't have a good time.

Jeanette disappeared just before we left the office, and I found myself walking to the pub with the rest of them. I sat drinking Budweisers and making conversation with John and Sarah, wondering where she was. She'd said she'd meet everyone there. So where was she?

At about half past eight the question was answered. She walked into the pub and I started to get up, a smile of greeting on my face. Then I noticed she looked different somehow, and I noticed the man standing behind her.

The man was Chris Ayer. He was her boyfriend. He was also the nastiest man I've met in quite some time. That sounds like sour grapes, but it's not. He was perfectly presentable, in that he was good-looking and could talk to people, but everything else about him was wrong. There was something odd about the way he looked at people, something both arrogant and closed off. There was an air of restrained violence about him that I found unsettling, and his sense of his possession of Jeanette was complete. She sat at his side, hands in her lap, and said very little throughout the evening. I couldn't get over how different she looked to the funny and confident woman I'd had lunch with the day before, but nobody else seemed to notice it. After all, she joined in the office banter as usual, and smiled with her lips quite often. Nobody apart from me was looking for any more than that.

As the evening wore on I found myself feeling more and more uncomfortable. I exchanged a few tight words with Ayer, mainly concerning a new computer he'd bought, but wasn't bothered when he turned to talk to someone else. The group from the office seemed to be closing in on itself, leaning over the table to shout jokes that they understood and I didn't. Ayer's harsh laugh cut across the smoke to me, and I felt impotently angry that someone like him should be able to sit with his arm around someone like Jeanette.

I drank another couple of beers and then abruptly decided that I simply wasn't having a good enough time. I stood up and took my leave, and was mildly touched when Tanya and Sarah tried to get me to stay. Jeanette didn't say anything, and when Ayer's eyes swept vaguely over me I saw that for him I didn't exist. I backed out of the pub smiling, and then turned and stalked miserably down the road.

By Sunday evening I was fine. I met my ex-girlfriend-before-last for lunch on Saturday, and we had a riotous time bitching and gossiping about most of the people we knew. In the evening I went to a restaurant that served food only from a particular four-square-mile region of Nepal, or so Nick claimed, such venues being his specialty. It tasted just like Indian to me, and I didn't see any sherpas, but the food was good. I spent Sunday doing my kind of thing, wandering round town and sitting in cafés to read. I called my folks in the evening, and they were on good form, and then I watched a horror film before going to bed when I felt like it. The kind of weekend that only happily single people can have, in other words, and it suited me just fine.

Monday was OK too. I was regaled with various tales of drunkenness from Friday night, as if for the first time I had a right to know. I had all the information I needed from Jeanette for the time being, so I did most of my work at a different machine. We had a quick chat in the kitchen while I made some coffee, and it was more or less the same as it had been the week before. Because she'd always known she had a boyfriend, of course. I caught myself dipping a couple of times on the afternoon, but bullied my mood into holding up. In a way it was kind of a relief, not to have to care.

The evening was warm and light, and I took my time walking home. Then I rustled myself up a chef's salad, which is my only claim to culinary skill. It has iceberg lettuce, black olives, grated cheese, julienned ham (that's "sliced," to you and me), diced tomato, and two types of homemade dressing: which is more than enough ingredients to count as cooking in my book. When I was sufficiently gorged on roughage I sat in front of the computer and fooled around, and by the time it was dark outside found myself cruising around the net.

And, after a while, I found myself accessing alt.binaries.pictures.erotica. I was in a funny sort of mood, I guess. I scrolled through the list of files, not knowing what I was after, and round the usual stuff, like "-TH2xx.GIF-{m/f}-hot sex!" Hot sex wasn't really what I was looking for, especially if it had an exclamation mark after it. Of all the people who access the group, I suspect it's less than about five percent who actually put pictures up there in the first place. It seems to be a matter of intense pride with them, and they compete with each other on the volume and "quality" of their postings. Their tragically sad bickering is often more entertaining than the pictures themselves.

It's complete pot luck what is available at any given time, and no file stays on there for more than about two days. The servers that hold the information have only limited space, and files get rolled off the end pretty quickly in the high-volume groups. I was about to give up when suddenly something caught my attention.

"j1.gif-{f}-"Young woman__fully clothed__(part ⅓)."

Fuck me, I thought: that's a bit weird. The group caters for a wide spectrum of human sexuality, and I'd seen titles that promised fat couples, skinny girls, interracial bonding, and light S&M. What I'd never come across was something as perverted as a woman with all her clothes *on*. Intrigued, I did the necessary to download the picture's three segments onto my hard disk.

By the time I'd made a cup of coffee they were there, and I severed the net connection and stitched the three files together. Until they were converted, they were just text files, which is one of the weird things about the net. Absolutely anything, from programs to articles to pictures, is up there as plain text. Without the appropriate decoders it just looks like nonsense, which I guess is as good a metaphor as any for the net as a whole. Or indeed for life.

When the file was ready, I loaded up a graphics package and opened it. I was doing so with only half an eye, not really expecting anything very interesting. But when, after a few seconds of whirring, the image popped onto the screen, I dropped my cup of coffee and it teetered on the desk before falling to shatter on the floor.

It was Jeanette.

The image quality was not fantastically good, and looked as if it had been taken with some small automatic camera. But the girl in the picture was Jeanette, without a shadow of a doubt. She was perched on the arm of an anonymous armchair, and with a lurch I realized it was probably taken in her flat. She was, as advertised, fully clothed, wearing a shortish skirt and a short-sleeved top that buttoned up at the front. She was looking in the general direction of the camera, and her expression was unreadable. She looked beautiful, as always, and somehow much, much more appealing than any of the buck-naked women who cavorted through the usual pictures to be found on the net.

After I'd got over my jaw-dropped surprise, I found I was feeling something else. Annoyance, possibly. I know I'm biased, but I didn't think it right that a picture of her was plastered up in cyberspace for everyone to gawk at, even if she was fully clothed. I realize that's hypocritical in the face of all the other women up there, but I can't help it. It was different.

Because I knew her.

I was also angry because I could think of only one way it could have got there. I'd mentioned a few net-related things in Jeanette's presence at work, and she'd shown no sign of recognition. It was a hell of a coincidence that I'd seen the picture at all, and I wasn't prepared to speculate about stray photos of her falling into unknown people's hands. There was only one person who was likely to have uploaded it. Her boyfriend.

The usual women (and men) in the pictures are getting paid for it. It's their job. Jeanette wasn't, and might not even know the picture was there.

I quickly logged back on to the net and found the original file. I extricated the uploader information and pulled it onto the screen, and then swore.

Remember a while back I said it was possible to hide yourself when posting up to the net? Well, that's what he'd done. The E-mail address of the person who'd uploaded the picture was listed as "anon99989@penet.fi." That meant that rather than posting it up in his real name, he'd routed the mail through an anonymity server in Finland called PENET. This server strips the journey information out of the posting and assigns a random address that is held on an encrypted database. I couldn't tell anything from it at all. Feeling my lip curl with distaste, I quit out.

By the time I got to work the next day I knew there wasn't anything I could say about it. I could hardly pipe up with "Hey! Saw your pic on the Internet porn board last night!" And after all, it was only a picture, the kind that people have plastic folders stuffed full of. The question was whether Jeanette knew Ayer had posted it up. If she did, well, it just went to show that you didn't know much about people just because you worked with them. If she didn't, then I think she had a right both to know, and to be annoyed.

I dropped a few net references into the conversations we had, but nothing came of them. I even mentioned the newsgroups, but got mild interest and nothing more. It was fairly clear she hadn't heard of them. In the end I sort of mentally shrugged. So her unpleasant boyfriend had posted up a picture. There was nothing I could do about it, except bury still further any feelings I might have entertained for her. She already had a life with someone else, and I had no business interfering.

In the evening I met up with Nick again, and we went and got quietly hammered in a small drinking club we frequented. I successfully fought off his ideas on going and getting some food, doubtless the cuisine of one particular village on the top of Kilimanjaro, and so by the end of the evening we were pretty far gone. I stumbled out of a cab, flolloped up the stairs, and mainlined coffee for a while, in the hope of avoiding a hangover the next day. And it was as I sat, weaving slightly, on the sofa, that I conceived the idea of checking a certain newsgroup.

Once the notion had taken hold, I couldn't seem to dislodge it. Most of my body and soul was engaged in remedial work, trying to save what brain cells they could from the onslaught of alcohol, and the idea was free to romp and run as it pleased. So I found myself slumped at my desk, listening to my hard disk doing its thing, and muttering quietly to myself. I don't know what I was saying. I think it was probably a verbal equivalent of that letter I never gave to someone, an explanation of how much better off Jeanette would be with me. I can get very maudlin when I'm drunk.

When the newsgroup appeared in front of me I blearily ran my eye over the list. The group had seen serious action in the last twenty-four hours, and there were over three hundred titles to contend with. I was beginning to lose heart and interest when I saw something about two-thirds of the way down the list.

"j2.gif-{f}-'Young___woman,' " one line said, and it was followed by "j3.gif-{f}-'Young___woman.' "

These two titles started immediately to do what half a pint of coffee hadn't: sober me up. At a glance I could tell that there were two differences from the description of the first picture of Jeanette I'd seen. The numerals after the 'j' were different, implying they were not the same picture. Also, there were two words missing at the end of the title: the words 'fully clothed.'

I called the first few lines of the first file onto the screen, and saw that it too had come from "anon99989@penet.fi." Then, reaching shakily for a cigarette, I downloaded the rest. When my connection was over I slowly stitched the text files together and then booted up the viewer.

It was Jeanette again. Wincing slightly, hating myself for having access to photos of her under these circumstances, when I had no right to know what they might show, I looked briefly at first one and then the other.

j2.gif looked as if it had been taken immediately after the first I'd seen. It showed Jeanette, still sitting on the arm of the chair. She was undoing the front of her top, and had got as far as the third button. Her head was down, and I couldn't see her face. Trembling slightly from a combination of emotions, I looked at j3.gif. Her top was now off, showing a flat stomach and a dark blue lacy bra. She was steadying herself on the chair with one arm, and her position looked uncomfortable. She was looking off to one side, away from the camera, and when I saw her face I thought I had the answer to at least one question. She didn't look very happy. She didn't look as if she was having fun.

She didn't look as if she wanted to be doing this at all.

I stood up suddenly and paced round the room, unsure of what to do. If she hadn't been especially enthralled about having the photos taken in the first place, I couldn't believe that Jeanette condoned or even knew about their presence on the net. Quite apart from anything else, she wasn't that type of girl, if that type of girl indeed existed at all.

This constituted some very clear kind of invasion by her boyfriend, something that negated any rights he may have felt he had upon her. But what could I do about it?

I copied the two files on to a floppy, along with j1.gif, and threw them off my hard disk. It may seem like a small distinction to you, but I didn't want them on my main machine. It would have seemed like collusion.

I got up the next morning with no more than a mild headache, and before I left for work decided to quickly log on to the net. There were no more pictures, but there was something that made me very angry indeed. Someone had posted up a message whose total text was the following.

"Re: j-pictures {f}: EXCELLENT! More pleeze!"

In other words, the pictures had struck a chord with some nameless net-pervert, and they wanted to see some more.

I spent the whole morning trying to work out what to do. The only way I could think of broaching the subject would involve mentioning the alt.binaries.pictures.erotica group itself, which would be a bit of a nasty moment. I hardly got a chance to talk to her all morning anyway, because she was busy on the phone. She also seemed a little tired, and little disposed to chat on the two occasions we found ourselves in the kitchen together.

It felt as if parts of my mind were straining against each other, pulling in different directions. If she didn't know about it, it was wrong, and she should be put in the picture. If I did so, however, she'd never think the same of me again. There was a chance, of course, that the problem might go away: despite the net-loser's request, the expression on Jeanette's face in j3.gif made it seem unlikely there *were* any more pictures. And ultimately the whole situation probably wasn't any of my business, however much it felt like it was.

In the event, I missed the boat. About half past four I emerged from a long and vicious argument with the server software to discover that Jeanette had left for the day. "A doctor's appointment." In most of the places I've worked, that phrase translates directly to "a couple of hours off from work, *obviously* not spent at the doctor's," but that didn't seem to be the general impression at the VCA. She'd probably just gone to the doctor's. Either way, she was no longer in the office, and I was slightly ashamed to find myself relaxing now that I could no longer talk to her.

At half past eight that evening, after my second salad of the week, I logged on and checked the group again. There was nothing there. I fretted and fidgeted around the apartment for a few hours, and then tried again at eleven o'clock. This time I found something. Two things: j4.gif, and j5.gif, both from the anonymous address.

In the first picture Jeanette was standing. She was no longer wearing her skirt, and her long legs led up to underwear that matched the bra I'd already seen. She wasn't posing for the picture. Her hands were on her hips, and she looked angry. In j5 she was leaning back against the arm of the chair, and no longer wearing her bra. Her face was blank.

I stared at the second picture for a long time, mind completely split in two. If you ignored the expression on her face, she looked gorgeous. Her breasts were small but perfectly shaped, exactly in proportion to her long, slender body. It was, undeniably, an erotic picture. Except for her face, and the fact that she obviously didn't want to be photographed, and the fact that someone was doing it anyway. Not only that, but broadcasting it to the planet.

I decided that enough was enough, and that I had to do something. After a while I came up with the best that I could. I loaded up my E-mail package, and sent a message to anon99989@penet.fi. The double-blind principle the server operated on meant that the recipient wouldn't know where it had come from, and that was fine by me. The message was this:

"I know who you are."

It wasn't much, but it was something. The idea that someone out there on the information superhighway could know his identity *might* be enough to stop him. It was only a stop-gap measure, anyway. I now knew I had to do something about the situation. It simply wasn't on.

And I had to do it soon. When I checked the next morning there were no more pictures, but two messages from people who'd downloaded them. "Keep 'em cumming!" one wit from Japan had written. Some slob from Texas had posted in similar vein, but added a small request: "Great, but pick up the pace a little. I want to see more FLESH!"

All the way to work I geared myself up to talking to Jeanette, and I nearly punched the wall when I heard she was out at a venue meeting for the whole morning and half the afternoon. I got rid of the morning by concentrating hard on one of her databases, wanting to bring at least something positive into her life. I know it's not much, but all I know is computers, and that's the best that I could do.

At last three o'clock rolled round, and Jeanette reappeared in the office. She seemed tired and a little preoccupied, and sat straight down at her desk to work. I loitered in the main office area, willing people to fuck off out of it so hard my head started to ache. I couldn't get anywhere near the topic if there were other people around. It would be hard enough if we were alone.

Finally, bloody, *finally* she got up from her desk and went into the kitchen. I got up and followed her in. She smiled faintly and vaguely on seeing me, and, seeing that she had a bandage on her right forearm, I used that to start a conversation. A small mole, apparently, hence the visit to the doctor. I let her finish that topic, keeping half an eye out to make sure that no one was approaching the kitchen.

"I bought a camera today," I blurted, as cheerily as I could. It wasn't great, but I wanted to start slowly. She didn't respond for a moment, and then looked up, her face expressionless.

"Oh yes?" she said, eventually. "What are you going to photograph?"

"Oh, you know, buildings, landscapes. Black and white, that kind of thing." She nodded distantly, and I ran out of things to say.

I ran out because, in retrospect, the topic didn't lead anywhere, but I stopped for another reason too. I stopped because as she turned to pick up the kettle, the look on her face knocked the wind out of me. The combination of unhappiness and loneliness, the sense of helplessness. It struck me again that despite the anger in her face in j4, in j5 she had not only taken her bra off but looked resigned and defeated. Suddenly I didn't care how it looked, didn't care what she thought of me.

"Jeanette," I said, firmly, and she turned to look at me again. "I saw a pict—"

"Hello, boys and girls. Having a little tea party, are we?"

At the sound of Whitehead's voice I wanted to turn round and smash his face in. Jeanette laughed prettily at her employer's sally, and moved out of the way to allow him access to the kettle. Whitehead asked me some balls-achingly dull questions about the computer system, obviously keen to sound as if he had the faintest conception of what it all meant. By the time I'd finished answering him, Jeanette was back at her desk.

The next hour was one of the longest of my life. I'd gone over, crossed the line. I knew I was going to talk to her about what I'd seen. More than that, I'd realized that it didn't have to be as difficult as I'd assumed.

The first picture, j1.gif, simply showed a pretty girl sitting on a chair. It wasn't pornographic, and could have been posted up in any number of places on the net. All I had to do was say I'd seen *that* picture. It wouldn't implicate me, and she would know what her boyfriend was up to.

I hovered round the main office, ready to be after her the minute she looked like leaving, having decided that I'd walk with her to the tube and tell her then. So long as she didn't leave with anyone else, it would be perfect. While I hovered I watched her work, her eyes blank and isolated. About quarter to five she got a phone call. She listened for a moment, said "Yes, all right" in a dull tone of voice, and then put the phone down. There was nothing else to distract me from the constant cycling of draft statements in my head.

At five she started tidying her desk, and I slipped out and got my jacket. I waited in the hallway until I could hear her coming, and then went out and got in the lift. I walked through the lobby as slowly as I could, and then went and stood outside the building. My hands were sweating and I felt wired and frightened, but I knew I was going to go through with it. A moment later she came out.

"Hi," I said, and she smiled warily, surprised to see me, I suppose. "Look, Jeanette, I need to talk to you about something."

She stared at me, looked around, and then asked what.

"I've seen pictures of you." In my nervousness I blew it, and used the plural rather than singular.

"Where?" she said, immediately. She knew what I was talking about. From the speed with which she latched on, I realized that whatever fun and games were going on between her and Ayer were at the forefront of her mind.

"The Internet. It's . . ."

"I know what it is," she said. "What have you seen?"

"Five so far," I said. "Look, if there's anything I can do . . ."

"Like what?" she said, and laughed harshly, her eyes beginning to blur. "Like what?"

"Well, anything. Look, let's go talk about it. I could . . ."

"There's no use," she said hurriedly, and started to pull away. I followed her, bewildered. How could she not want to do anything about it? I mean, all right, I may not have been much of a prospect, but surely some help was better than none.

"Jeanette..."

"Let's talk tomorrow," she hissed, and suddenly I realized what was happening. Her boyfriend had come to pick her up. She walked towards the curb where a white car was coming to a halt, and I rapidly about-faced and started striding the other way. It wasn't fear, not purely. I also didn't want to get her in trouble.

As I walked up the road, I felt as if the back of my neck was burning, and at the last moment I glanced to the side. The white car was just passing, and I could see Jeanette sitting bolt upright in the passenger seat. Her boyfriend was looking out of the side window. At me. Then he accelerated and the car sped away.

That night brought another two photographs. j6 had Jeanette naked, sitting in the chair with her legs slightly apart. Her face was stony. In j7 she was on all fours, photographed from behind. As I sat in my chair, filled with impotent fury, I noticed something in both pictures, and blew them up with the magnifier tool. In j6 one side of her face looked a little red, and when I looked carefully at j7 I could see that there was a trickle of blood running from a small gash on her right forearm.

And suddenly I realized, with help from memories of watching her hands and arms as she worked, that there had never been a mole on her arm. She hadn't got the bandage because of the doctor.

She had it because of him.

I hardly slept that night. I stayed up until three, keeping an eye on the newsgroup. Its denizens were certainly becoming fans of the j pictures, and I saw five requests for some more. As far as they knew, all this involved was a bit more scanning originals from some magazine. They didn't realize that someone was having them taken against her will. I considered trying to do something within the group, like posting a message telling what I knew. While its frequenters are a bit sad, they tend to have a strong moral stance about such things. It's not like the alt.binaries.pictures.tasteless group, where anything goes, the sicker the better. If the a.b.p.erotica crowd were convinced the pictures were being taken under coercion, there was a strong chance they might mailbomb Ayer off the net. It would be a big war to start, however, and one with potentially damaging consequences. The mailbombing would have to go through the anonymity server, and would probably crash it. While I couldn't give a fuck about that, it would draw the attention of all manner of people. In any event, because of the anonymity, nothing would happen directly to Ayer apart from some inconvenience.

I decided to put the idea on hold, in case talking to Jeanette tomorrow made it unnecessary. Eventually I went to bed, where I thrashed and turned for hours. Some time just before dawn I drifted off, and dreamed about a cat being caught in a lawnmower.

I was up at seven, there being no point in me staying in bed. I checked the group, but there were no new files. On an afterthought I checked my E-mail, realizing that I'd been so out of it that I hadn't done so for days. There were about thirty messages for me, some from friends, the rest from a variety of virtual acquaintances around the world. I scanned through them quickly, to see if any needed urgent attention, and then, slap in the middle, I noticed one from a particular address.

anon99989@penet.fi.

Heart thumping, I opened the E-mail. In the convention of such things, he'd quoted my message back at me, with a comment. The entire text of the mail read:
>I know who you are.
>Maybe. But I know where you live.

When I got to work, on the dot of nine, I discovered Jeanette wasn't there. She'd left a message at half-past eight announcing she was taking the day off. Sarah was a bit sniffy about this, though she claimed to be great pals with Jeanette. I left her debating the morality of such cavalier leave-taking with Tanya in the kitchen, as I walked slowly out to sit at Jeanette's desk to work. After five minutes' thought I went back to the kitchen and asked Sarah for Jeanette's number, claiming I had to ask her about the database. Sarah seemed only too pleased to provide the means of contacting a friend having a day off. I grabbed my jacket, muttered something about buying cigarettes, and left the office.

Round the corner I found a public phone box and called her number. As I listened to the phone ring I glanced at the prostitute cards that liberally covered the walls, but soon looked away. I didn't find their representation of the female form amusing anymore. After six rings an answering machine cut in. A man's voice, Ayer's, announced that—they were out. I rang again, with the same result, and then left the phone box and stood aimlessly on the pavement.

There was nothing I could do.

I went back to work. I worked. I ran home.

At half-past six I logged on for the first time, and the next two pictures were already there. I could tell immediately that something had changed. The wall behind her was a different color, for a start. The focus of the action seemed to have moved, to the bedroom, presumably, and the pictures were getting worse. j8 showed Jeanette spread-eagle on her back. Her legs were very wide open, and both her hands and feet were out of shot. j9 was much the same, except you could see that her hands were tied. You could also see her face, with its hopeless defiance and fear. As I erased the picture from my disk I felt my neck spasming, and tears coming to my eyes.

Too late I realized that what I should have done was get Jeanette's address while I was at work. It would have been difficult, and viewed with suspicion, but I might have been able to do it. Now I couldn't. I didn't know the home numbers of anyone else from the VCA, and couldn't trace her address from her number. The operator wouldn't give it to me. If I'd had the address, I could have gone round. Maybe I would have found myself in the worst situation of my life, but it would have been something to try. The idea of her being in trouble somewhere in London, and me not knowing where, was almost too much to bear.

Suddenly I decided that I had to do the one small thing I could. I logged back on to the erotica group and prepared to start a flame war. The classic knee-jerk reaction that people on the net use to express their displeasure is known as "flaming." Basically it involves bombarding the offender with massive mail messages until their virtual mailbox collapses under the load. This generally comes to the attention of the administrator of their site, and they get chucked off the net. What I had to do was post a message providing sufficient reason for the good citizens of pornville to dump on anon99989@penet.fi.

So it might cause some trouble. I didn't fucking care.

I had a mail slip open and my hands poised over the keyboard before I noticed something that stopped me in my tracks.

There were two more files. Already. The slob from Texas was getting his wish: the pace was being picked up.

In j10 Jeanette was on her knees on a dirty mattress. Her hands appeared to be tied behind her, and her head was bowed. j11 showed her lying awkwardly on her side, as if she'd been pushed over. She was glaring at the camera, and when I magnified the left side of the image I could see a thin trickle of blood from her right nostril.

I leaped up from the keyboard, shouting. I don't know what I was saying. It wasn't coherent. Jeanette's face stared up at me from the computer and I leaned wildly across and hit the switch to turn the screen off. Just quitting out didn't seem enough. Then I realized that the image was still there, even though I couldn't see it. The computer was still sending the information to the screen, and the minute I turned it back on, it would be there. So I hard-stopped the computer by just turning it off at the mains. Suddenly what had always been my domain felt like the outpost of someone very twisted and evil, and I didn't want anything to do with it.

Then, like a stone through glass, two ideas crashed into each other in my head.

Gospel Oak.

Police.

From nowhere came a faint half memory, so tenuous that it might be illusory, of Jeanette mentioning Gospel Oak Station. In other words, the rail station in Gospel Oak. I knew where that was.

An operator wouldn't give me an address from a phone number. But the police would be able to get it.

I couldn't think of anything else.

I rang the police. I told them I had reason to believe that someone was in danger, and that she lived at the house with this phone number. They wanted to know who I was and all manner of other shit, but I rang off quickly, grabbed my coat, and hit the street.

Gospel Oak is a small area, filling up the gap between Highgate, Chalk Farm, and Hampstead. I knew it well because Nick and I used to go play pool at a pub on Mansfield Road, which runs straight through it. I knew the entrance and exit points of the area, and I got the cab to drop me off as near to the center as possible. Then I stood on the pavement, hopping from foot to foot and smoking, hoping against hope that this would work.

Ten minutes later a police car turned into Mansfield Road. I was very pleased to see them, and enormously relieved. I hadn't been particularly sure about the Gospel Oak part. I shrank back against the nearest building until it had gone past, and then ran after it as inconspicuously as I could. It took a left into Estelle Road and I slowed at the corner to watch it pull up outside number 6. I slipped into the doorway of the corner shop and watched as two policemen took their own good time about untangling themselves from their car.

They walked up to the front of the house. One leaned hard against the doorbell while the other peered around the front of the house as if taking part in an officiousness competition. The door wasn't answered, which didn't surprise me. Ayer was hardly going to break off from torturing his girlfriend to take social calls. One of the policemen nodded to the other, who visibly sighed, and made his way around the back of the house.

"Oh come on, come *on*," I hissed in the shadows. "Break the fucking door down."

About five minutes passed, and then the policeman reappeared. He shrugged flamboyantly at his colleague, and pressed the doorbell again.

A light suddenly appeared above the door, coming from the hallway behind it. My breath caught in my throat and I edged a little closer. I'm not sure what I was preparing to do. Dash over there and force my way in, past the policemen, to grab Ayer and smash his head against the wall? I really don't know.

The door opened, and I saw it wasn't Ayer or Jeanette. It was an elderly man with a crutch and gray hair that looked like it had seen action in a hurricane. He conversed irritably with the policemen for a moment and then shut the door in their faces. The two cops stared at each other for a moment, clearly considering busting the old tosser, but then turned and made their way back to the car. Still looking up at the house, the first policeman made a report into his radio, and I heard enough to understand why they then got into the car and drove away.

The old guy had told them that the young couple had gone away for the weekend. He'd seen them go on Thursday evening. I was now more than twenty-four hours too late.

When the police car had turned the corner I found myself panting, not knowing what to do. The last two photographs, the ones with the dirty mattress, hadn't been taken here at all. Jeanette was somewhere in the country, but I didn't know where, and there was no way of finding out. The pictures could have been posted from anywhere.

Making a decision, I walked quickly across the road towards the house. The policemen may not have felt they had just cause, but I did, and I carefully made my way around the back of the house. This involved climbing over a gate and wending through the old guy's crowded little garden, and I came perilously close to knocking over a pile of flowerpots. As luck would have it, there was a kind of low wall that led to a complex exterior plumbing fixture, and I quickly clambered on top of it. A slightly precarious upward step took me next to one of the second-floor windows. It was dark, like all the others, but I kept my head bent just in case.

When I was closer to the window I saw that it wasn't fastened at the bottom. They might have gone, and then come back. Ayer could have staged it so the old man saw them go, and then slipped back when he was out.

It was possible, but not likely. But on the other hand, the window was ajar. Maybe they were just careless about such things. I slipped my fingers under the pane and pulled it open. Then I leaned with my ear close to the open space and listened. There was no sound, and so I boosted myself up and quickly in.

I found myself in a bedroom. I didn't turn the light on, but there was enough coming from the moon and streetlights to pick out a couple of pieces of Jeanette's clothing, garments that I recognized, strewn over the floor. She wouldn't have left them like that, not if she'd had any choice in the matter. I walked carefully into the corridor, poking my head into the bathroom and kitchen, which were dead. Then I found myself in the living room.

The big chair stood in front of a wall I recognized, and at the far end a computer sat on a desk next to a picture scanner. Moving as quickly but quietly as possible,

I frantically searched over the desk for anything that might tell me where Ayer had taken her. There was nothing there, and nothing in the rest of the room. I'd broken—well, opened—and entered for no purpose. There were no clues. No sign of where they'd gone. An empty box under the table confirmed what I'd already guessed: Ayer had a laptop computer as well. He could be posting the pictures on to the net from anywhere that had a phone socket. Jeanette would be with him, and I needed to find her. I needed to find her soon.

I paced around the room, trying to pick up speed, trying to work out what I could possibly do. No one at the VCA knew where they'd gone—they hadn't even known Jeanette wasn't going to be in. The old turd downstairs hadn't known. There was nothing in the flat that resembled a phone book or personal organizer, something that would have a friend or family member's number. I was prepared to do anything, call anyone, in the hope of finding where they'd gone. But there was nothing, unless . . .

I sat down at the desk, reached behind the computer, and turned it on. Ayer had a fairly flash deck, together with a scanner and laserprinter. He knew the net. Chances were he was wireheaded enough to keep his phone numbers somewhere on his computer.

As soon as the machine was booted up I went rifling through it, grimly enjoying the intrusion, the computer-rape. His files and programs were spread all over the disk, with no apparent system. Each time I finished looking through a folder, I erased it. It seemed the least I could do.

Then after about five minutes I found something, but not what I was looking for. I found a folder named "j."

There were files called jl2 to jl6 in the folder, in addition to all the others that I'd seen. Wherever Jeanette was, Ayer had come back here to scan the pictures. Presumably that meant they were still in London, for all the good that did me.

I'm not telling you what they were like, except that they showed Jeanette, and in some she was crying, and in jl5 and jl6 there was blood running from the corner of her mouth. A lot of blood. She was twisted and tied, face livid with bruises, and in jl6 she was staring straight at the camera, face slack with terror.

Unthinkingly I slammed my fist down on the desk. There was a noise downstairs and I went absolutely motionless until I was sure the old man had lost interest. Then I turned the computer off, opened up the case, and removed the hard disk. I climbed out the way I'd come and ran out down the street, flagged a taxi by jumping in front of it and headed for home.

I was going to the police, but I needed a computer, something to shove the hard disk into. I was going to show them what I'd found, and fuck the fact it was stolen. If they nicked me, so be it. But they had to do something about it. They had to try and find her. If he'd come back to do his scanning, he had to be keeping her somewhere in London. They'd know where to look, or where to start. They'd know what to do.

They had to. They were the police. It was their job.

I ran up the stairs and into the flat, and then dug in my spares cupboard for enough pieces to hack together a compatible computer. When I'd got them I went over to my desk to call the local police station, and then stopped and turned my computer on. I logged on to the net and kicked up my mail package, and sent a short, useless message.

"I'm coming after you," I said.

It wasn't bravado. I didn't feel brave at all. I just felt furious, and wanted to do anything that might unsettle him, or make him stop. Anything to make him stop.

I logged quickly on to the newsgroups, to see when anon99989@penet.fi had most recently posted. A half hour ago, when I'd been in his apartment, jl2–16 had been posted up. Two people had already responded: one hoping the blood was fake and asking if the group really wanted that kind of picture, the other asking for more. I viciously wished a violent death upon the second person, and was about to log off, having decided not to bother phoning but to just go straight to the cops, when I saw another text-only posting at the end of the list.

"Re: j-series" it said, and it was from anon99989@penet.fi. I opened it.

"End of series," the message said. "Hope you all enjoyed it. Next time, something tasteless."

"And I hope," I shouted at the screen, "that you enjoy it when I ram your hard disk down your fucking throat." Then suddenly my blood ran cold.

"Next time, something tasteless."

I hurriedly closed the group, and opened up alt.binaries.pictures.tasteless. As I scrolled past the titles for roadkills and people crapping I felt the first heavy, cold tear roll out on to my cheek. My hand was shaking uncontrollably, my head full of some dark mist, and when I saw the last entry I knew suddenly and exactly what Jeanette had been looking at when jl6 was taken.

"jl7.gif," it read. "{f} Pretty amputee."

PENGUINS FOR LUNCH
Scott Bradfield

Scott Bradfield divides his time between London, England, and Storrs, Connecticut, where he teaches at the University of Connecticut. He's best known as a mainstream writer, but he occasionally strays into the fantasy field with delightful, acerbic tales like the unusual story that follows. "Penguins for Lunch" (like "Animals Behind Bars!," which we published in last year's volume of The Year's Best Fantasy & Horror), is one of Bradfield's recent animal stories. He is also the author of three novels—The History of Luminous Motion, What's Wrong with America, and Animal Planet—and his most recent short story collection is Greetings from Earth. "Penguins for Lunch" is reprinted from the TriQuarterly journal.

—T.W.

> Though dabbling in all three elements, and indeed
> possessing some rudimentary claims to all, the penguin
> is at home in none. On land it stumps; afloat it
> sculls; in the air it flops. As if ashamed of her
> failure, Nature keeps this ungainly child hidden away
> at the ends of the earth.
>   —Melville, "The Encantadas"

1. THE ICE FLOE BAR AND GRILL

"I'm a high-rolling entrepreneur on the free-market of love," Whistling Pete told his closest friend, Buster Davenport, one sunny afternoon at the Ice Floe Bar and Grill. "You don't blame Mercedes for selling cars, do you? You don't blame McDonald's for frying burgers, or the Japs for peddling cheap cars. Well, what *I've* got just happens to be what the little girlies *want*. And when the little girlies want it, well. I don't mean to sound rude, Buster—but I happen to be *just* the guy that's gonna give it to them."

The Ice Floe Bar and Grill was one of a series of new up-market franchise restaurants that had recently opened all across the tundra. As part of their inaugural promotion campaign, the Ice Floe was offering dollar margaritas during Happy Hour, along with all the free mackerel you could lay your flippers on.

Whistling Pete slid a creamy oyster into his throat and sighed. He patted his firm white belly, as if testing for tone.

"This is the life, Buster," he said philosophically, leaning back in his green vinyl lawn chair and folding his sleek muscular flippers behind his head. He and Buster were sitting on a veranda overlooking the outdoor pool. "Sunny days, starry nights, envelopes of rich fatty tissue to keep our butts warm, and loving spouses to go home to. What more could we ask? What more, that is, than maybe a hasty little frolic in the frost with one of yonder ice-maidens?"

Nodding towards the various lithe Penguinettes sporting themselves seductively around the pool, Whistling Pete clock-clocked his black tongue. His entire body shivered with a slow delicious enthusiasm for itself.

"Yeah, well, I just hope you know what you're doing," Buster said. Buster's gaze was roving back and forth across the restaurant and patio. He kept glancing sheepishly over his shoulders, as if he expected their indignant wives to appear at any moment brandishing blunt objects.

When the waitress came up behind him and said, "How you boys doing?" Buster nearly jumped out of his socks.

"Whoa, there, Buster—relax, old buddy. It's not the *gendarmes*, you know." Whistling Pete cautioned his friend with an upraised flipper and presented the waitress his best award-winning smile. "And how are *you* doing this afternoon, sweetie?"

"If you boys don't need anything," she said, "I'll go check on my other tables."

Buster, slightly out of breath, was still smoothing his ruffled tail feathers. "I guess I'll have another margarita," he said, looking forlornly at his empty white side dish. "And if Happy Hour's still on, could you maybe find us a little more mackerel?"

Whistling Pete unashamedly examined the waitress's fatty deposits.

"Me," Whistling Pete said, "I'll have some of what *she's* having."

He indicated the large commercial advertisement posted behind the bar. The ad featured a lithe, lovely Penguinette scantily clad in a white silk top hat and baggy white fishnet stockings. She was leaning against a sporty red snowmobile and stroking a large icy bottle of Smirnoff's.

The bold black caption exclaimed: IT'S PENGUINIFIC!

While Buster resumed his edgy lookout for wives, Whistling Pete appreciatively watched their waitress waddle back to the bar with their order.

"Vah-vah-vah-*voom!*" he said, and saluted her departing buttocks with the dissolving ice in his glass. Then he tossed down the slush with the last of his oyster sliders. His toes evinced a self-satisfied little wriggle.

"Life's definitely the coolest," Whistling Pete pronounced. "The sun rises, the sun sets. And so do I, Buster, old pal. So do I."

Whistling Pete slammed his glass down on the table with a familiar emphasis.

"Yeah, well." Buster's eyes flicked from entrance to exit, from restroom to window to door. He picked up the extinguished mackerel plate and sadly licked it.

"I just hope you know what you're doing," he said.

Whistling Pete arranged for a clandestine rendezvous with one of his ladies nearly every day at noon, just when the twilight sky was beginning to generate something like phosphorescence. They met unashamedly at the Ice Floe for drinks and quick, light lunches while Pete proffered flowers, compliments, stockings, and chocolates. Then, as fast as their little legs could carry them, they dashed next door to the Crystal Palace Motel where Whistling Pete kept an open account. They ordered caviar and champagne through room service, sported themselves silly across the taut-fitted coverlets, and made the most they could of an hour—sometimes an hour and a half.

"This is the life," Whistling Pete muttered every so often. "This is what the All-Mighty Penguin had in mind when he designed such cute little Penguinettes."

Infidelity took all the knots out of a morning. The bad breakfast with the screaming baby, the frantic rush of late orders at the warehouse where Pete worked, and the sense of blue dissolute formlessness Pete experienced whenever he gazed out his office window at the utterly black sky littered with cold white stars.

"It's the worst weather in the entire universe," Pete regularly complained to his early morning mug of Earl Grey. "Icicles, icebergs, ice-mountains, and ice-rocks. I'm not ashamed to say it. Antarctica really sucks, even for penguins."

Then, looking up, he found himself exchanging a quick, illicit glance with Berenice, an accounts secretary across the hall. A warm amorous pulse filled Whistling Pete's sinuses and face.

After a moment, Berenice smiled and waved. Then, after another moment, Whistling Pete smiled and waved back.

One of these days, Pete reminded himself, I really must go over there and chat up our little Berenice.

The Penguinettes he did chat up were invariably young, impressionable, intelligent, and very quick to please. Some of them worked in Whistling Pete's office at Consolidated Fish, but mostly he met them during Happy Hour at the Ice Floe, or while swimming in the local ponds. They were office girls in a hurry to be young and didn't bother themselves too much about moral imperatives or social graces.

"I just figure we have nice times together," Whistling Pete's favorite girlfriend, Melody Long, frequently explained, usually after her second gin-and-tonic and a quick steamy romp in the Motel Sauna. "So maybe you're married and have a baby—that's cool. I'm not a material girl. I don't need, like, to *own* a boy just because I *like* him."

Then, with a bubbly flirt and a giggle, she pinched Pete's belly with one hand, and soothed his inflated pride with the other.

"Not that we can call our little whistler a *boy* exactly," she reminded him, and began nibbling playfully at a stray chest-feather. "Mr. Pete is more what you'd have to call a dirty old *man*. Isn't that right, cutey? Isn't that right, you big bad boy, you?"

Lunchtime was what Whistling Pete lived for—brightness, intoxication, energy, and truth. Lunchtime was the passion and the glory. Lunchtime was life.

By the time Pete returned to his office he was already subsiding into a post-coital melancholy, which wasn't altogether unpleasant. He felt his mind descend into the sluggish depths of his own body, drifting through continents of ice, landmass, gravity, and weight like a sort of bathysphere. Down here the green, gnarly water was populated by pulsing black shellfish, gigantic cyclopean squid, translucent spiny seaweeds, and dark brooding prehistoric entities squeezed into barnacled caverns and shipwrecked galleons.

"Hey there, bro," Buster said, leaning into the office around four P.M. The day's tentative flare of sunlight was already extinguishing. Weird bright glows and refractions cast themselves across the planes of dazzling white ice like spinning crystal discs. "We hitting Happy Hour today or what?"

Buster was already glancing anxiously over both his shoulders. He was not the sort of penguin who rushed headlong into life's vast hiss and adventure. Instead, he anxiously avoided every bit of life that came rushing after him.

Whistling Pete took his feet off the desk and sat up abruptly in his spring-cocked office chair. He saw the binders and ledgers, the interoffice memos and gray, slimy faxes. This desk, this office. These hours measured by dollars, these dimensions demarcated by ice.

(And somewhere else entirely: Melody, Martha, Trudy, Dallas, Pippa, Dolores, and Joyce.)

Or perhaps, Pete realized, Buster simply pretended not to know.

"Buster, old pal," Pete said finally, and clapped his flippers together with brisk authority, "has the sun stopped shining or the earth ceased to spin? Of *course* we're hitting Happy Hour. And if I recall correctly, I believe it's your turn to pick up the tab."

2. MAKING MARRIAGE WORK

"It's just a phase Pete's going through," Estelle said, and succinctly regurgitated chunky blue broth into a white ceramic bowl. "Ever since he turned forty, he can't seem to sit still anymore. He stares at himself in the bathroom mirror all morning, combing his feathers, and picking his teeth. Every day on his way home from work he forgets to pick things up at the store—milk, bread, mineral water, you name it. He's wandering around in a dream world, Sandy, I swear. I know I should probably be hurt or angry, but I can't help feeling sorry for him. I think he's going through some pretty heavy emotional changes right now."

Estelle dabbed her beak with a pastel cloth napkin. Then she passed the bowl of broth to their six-month old fledgling, who was presently conducting a happy inner symphony with an upraised wooden ladle.

"Fish," Junior exclaimed. "Fish-*fishy*-fish."

Estelle sighed. Then, almost imperceptibly, belched.

"Excuse me," Estelle said.

Buster's wife, Sandy, lit another menthol cigarette and shook out her paper match with bristly impatience.

"For chrissakes, Estelle. Read the writing on the *wall*, will you? Your lousy husband's out fertilizing every yolk in town. What are you—*blind* or something?"

Estelle gazed out the sparkling window and sighed, leaning her beak on one cocked flipper. Sometimes she just wanted to sit in her clean kitchen, watch the thin sunlight, and feel the deep, immanent warmth of her own body. She was so bulked up with raw meat after months of gravid-gorging that she could hardly waddle to the sink and back without falling out of breath. And now Sandy, lean and mean, telling her what to do with her life, as if she were some sort of expert.

"You don't understand, Sandy," Estelle said. "If you want to make a marriage work, then some things just aren't that simple."

"Things *are* that simple, Estelle, and let me tell you how simple they are. Pete's screwing every cow on the island. He's dipping his wick in every candle on the beach. You can either tell him to shape up or move out. Or you can hack him to death with the stainless steel. I'll tell you one thing," Sandy said, punctuating her resolve by flicking a long, intact gray ash onto the checkered tablecloth, "if Buster ever pulled a fast one on me, boy, I'd bite out a long message in his fat butt, that's what I'd do."

Estelle wanted to explain, but she couldn't seem to work up any words from the mulchy depths of her overloaded body. It was strange how flesh could reshape itself around you, as if it possessed mind and intention all its own. Estelle looked at the flaring brightness outside. Then she looked at her six-month-old fledgling, Pete Junior.

Without a second thought, Estelle thumped the side of Junior's high chair.

"Don't *play* with your food, mister," she said.

Caught in midgargle with a bolus of macerated mussel, Junior swallowed abruptly. He looked at his mum with wide eyes and slowly put down his wooden ladle.

"Fish," he said evenly, indicating his chunky broth. "*Mum's fish.*"

Estelle felt the sadness in her body start to rotate.

"Yes, baby," Estelle said. "Mum's fish."

Then, lowering her head to her folded and glistening black flippers, Estelle began to cry. Softly at first, but with a slowly rising intensity, like the sound of distant winter thunderclaps.

Sandy bit off another tiny puff from her menthol cigarette. She looked at Junior and Junior looked at her.

"There there, honey," Sandy said softly. "It'll be all right, honey. There there, there there."

Then, extinguishing her cigarette in the glass ashtray, Sandy leaned over and took Estelle gently in her arms.

Some days Whistling Pete didn't have any patience for family life. Grocery bills, diaper services, overpriced podiatrists, peeling linoleum, and faulty pipes. "Domesticity is for the birds," Pete pronounced solidly, walking home with Buster through the starry night. Atmospheric strobes and opacities wheeled across the high black sky like chapters out of Revelation. "I'm talking the feathery, flighty kind of birds, you know? The ones with their heads in the clouds? Sure, it *sounds* nice and all—big tract houses, gas central heating, indoor plumbing, and all that. Trade, commerce, low-tech industry, certified schools for the kids, community rep, all the bread in one basket, *that* sort of domesticity, *you* know. But basically, man, it's an idea cooked up by the little girlies. Wives, man; females seeking security for their babes. Girlies are home*builders*, but us guys, we're like home*breakers*. It's not our *fault*, Buster, it's just our nature. Girlies like home and hearth, three square meals, new wallpaper for the nursery, church weddings, and matching cutlery. Us guys, however, we're hunters and gatherers. We don't want cornflakes for breakfast—we want the hot blood of the kill in our mouths. We want to venture *beyond* what we already know, and stop remembering the boring old places we've already been. Nature's *cruel*, Buster, just like *us*. Nature's cruel, and *so* are us guys."

The long white road descended into the village, leading Pete towards the smell of yeasty bread baking. He saw yellow light glowing in the windowpanes of his house, and the idea that he was anticipated made him edgy and ungallant. Two strange minds waiting in a house where he didn't belong. They knew he was coming. They knew he was already late.

He put his arm around Buster with a comradely squeeze and gestured downhill. "There it is, buddy. Our little village in the snow, the home our forefathers and foremothers planted in the wilderness. Back in the old days our ancestors waddled around on *rocks*, man. They starved, hunted, mated, and died without proper funerals or mortgage insurance. The only education they got came from the School of Hard Knocks. And who do you think first initiated the idea of *houses*, man? Why, the *ladies*, of course. 'Let's stack a few ice blocks over there as a sort of lean-to,' they told their weary, flatulent old husbands. 'How about four walls, honey? A roof and a floor?' Us guys would have lain out there scratching our lice on that stupid rock forever if *we'd* had the choice, but the choice *wasn't* ours, no way."

Buster, well oiled with budget tequila, was waddling along beside Pete with uncustomary resolution. Instead of glancing over his twitchy shoulders he gazed dreamily into the endlessly illuminated sky. Showers of meteors, swirls of galaxies, planets entrained by moons and whorling dust. Buster loved the night when it got like this: vast, unencompassable, and rinsed with sensation. It was a time when everything, even the universe, seemed at once awesomely complicated and weirdly specific.

"Actually," Buster muttered out loud, "I always kind of dug domesticity. Beds with sheets, down comforters, canned lager, and imported salsa. I like knowing I'll get paid every Friday, week after week, as regular as clockwork. Some days, Sundays especially, I lie in my warm bed and let my mind wander. I don't go anywhere. I just let my imagination loose and I wander."

Pete whistled softly to himself. He wasn't listening to a word Buster said, but then he hadn't been listening to anybody for months now. He was thinking: Melody, Marianne, Gwendolyn, and Jane. Tomorrow at noon and next Wednesday at twelve forty-five. While Pete's body waddled down the steep slope towards the hard, unendurable village, his mind journeyed into different realms altogether. Places with thrill and expectation. Places of slow tongue and undress. Times like this, Pete believed he would never die. Even when the hard village stopped enduring, Whistling Pete wouldn't.

"Men may build the cities," Pete said softly, just before they arrived at his white doorway, his paved driveway, his leaning mailbox, "but believe you me. It's the little girlies who make us live in them."

Despite his protestations to the contrary, Pete arrived home each night aching with apology and self-reproach.

"I *know* I should have called," he told her. "I *know* it's late, and I forgot to buy milk again. And yes I *did* drink too much, and spent too much money, and Little Petey's gone to bed again without kissing Daddy good night. I'm sorry, Estelle, I really am. I'm sorry but I can't seem to explain. Some nights I just have to get away with my buddies, have a few drinks and unwind. No, and I can't say it won't happen again. I wish I could, Estelle, but I can't."

Later, in bed, Estelle pretended to sleep. Pete could feel the slow breath of the hard house around them, the ticking radiators and ruminating clocks. Next door in the nursery, Little Petey, true to his genotype, faintly whistled while he snored.

"I'll try to be better," Whistling Pete told his wife, pretending he believed her when she pretended not to hear. "But that doesn't mean I'm going to. Maybe I can tell you what you want to hear, Estelle. But that doesn't mean I can *be* somebody I'm not."

Then, too tired for remorse, he fell asleep with a hypnagogic little kick. And descended into the dreams he pretended not to know.

"Of *course* I worry about Estelle and Junior," Buster told his wife that night, tossing and turning among the knotted sheets and lumpy pillows. "But Pete's my *friend*, Sandy, and I'm not just going to lie here and listen while you trash him."

"*Trash* him?" Sandy said, in a rising crescendo of disbelief. "*I'm* trashing *him?*"

Buster turned onto his other side and gazed out the bare, glistening window. The full moon glared at him like a primitive mandala; Buster could feel the cold, deep resonance in his bones like a hum.

"What about *Estelle*, huh? Who's trashing *her*, Buster? Who's doing the *serious* emotional trashing in this morbid little scenario of ours? *Me*, or your close *friend*, Whistling Pete?"

Buster submitted with something like relief. Sandy was like a geyser or an earth tremor. He could hear her about to happen all day, charging the dark air with rumor and electricity.

"So I guess poor little Estelle is supposed to grin and bear it—is *that* what you mean? Because if she calls her wonderful husband a liar and a cheat then she's *trashing* him? And if *I* start calling him a *louse*—which is exactly what he *is*, Buster—then *I'm* trashing him *too?* I guess if it's a *man* doing the trashing then that makes it O.K., huh? Is *that* what you're saying, Buster? If *men* trash *women*, then that's the proper order of things, *right?*"

Buster took a long deep breath and sighed.

"That's not what I said, Sandy. That's not what I said and you know it."

Every morning after a fight, breakfast became a ceremony of courtesy and toast. While Sandy brought in bottles of frozen milk from the front porch and thawed them on the stove, Buster took up the sports page and read through yesterday's skating and ice-hockey scores, enjoying the cool comfort of abstractions, a sort of rousing statistical hum. Click, clicka-click-click. Clicka-click-click.

"I'm going shopping," Sandy said flatly, peering at him across her china teacup.

"That's a good idea," Buster said, nervously glancing at the wall clock. In another few minutes he might be able to leave for work without appearing too obvious.

"I'm getting a beak trim and a pedicure at Valerie's. Then I'm meeting Estelle for lunch at the Green Kitchen."

Buster felt the weight of depth charges hidden beneath the surface of Sandy's blithe words. He refused to look up from his paper.

"Have a nice time, honey," he said. "I should be home by dinner."

* * *

Later, traipsing back up the long winding road to the Factory, Buster rehearsed his concern until it resembled indignation. He gestured severely with his red metal lunchpail.

"Enough's enough, buddy," he said. "And believe me—I'm telling you this for your own good. If you want a little fling now and then, that's *cool*. But these daily rallies of yours are getting to be *too much*. Show a little *discretion*, man. What do you think we are—*seals* or something? Happy flappers lying out on the beach all day, mating indiscriminately, barking like morons? No, Pete, we've built something for ourselves out here. Homes and schools and factories and jobs. So if you want to shoot off your mouth about how rotten civilization is and all, well, that's your prerogative. But if you're going to continue *living* here, then you've *got* to start taking responsibility for yourself. I hate to be so hard on you, bro'—believe me, I don't like it any more than you do. But I'm being hard on you because I *care*. And if you don't understand that, well, just forget it. Maybe I've been wasting my time with you all along."

Steaming with resolution, Buster chugged into the factory just as the second whistle blew. Grizzly fishermen were dragging weirs full of squirming carp and tuna from the harbor while the factory gates were rolled open by large, muscly looking penguins in greasy gray overalls.

By the time Buster reached Pete's office he knew he was finally going to do it. He was going to tell Whistling Pete what he thought about him once and for all. The hot energized words carried him up the stairs and down the hall. They carried him through payroll, group insurance, and personnel, past filing cabinets, bulletin boards, and water fountains. Buster was finally going to speak his mind, come hell or high water. Or perhaps he was just going to let the unrestrainable anger in his mind speak for itself.

Inside Pete's office, Nadine, the accounts secretary, was stirring a big pot of tea with a wooden spoon.

"Let me speak to Whistling Pete," Buster told her. "And tell him I mean *muy pronto*."

Nadine took a moment to understand. She looked at Buster, then at the open door to Pete's office. She was smiling faintly, as if she had been expecting this pathetic little display all morning.

"Sorry, Buster," Nadine said, "but your buddy's not around." Then she placed the teapot on a wooden tray alongside four chipped ceramic mugs, one tarnished teaspoon, and a bowl of brown, lumpish sugar. "If there's an emergency, though—and it better be one hell of an emergency—you can always leave a message for him at the Crystal Palace Motel."

3. MORDIDA GIRLS

Spring returned and the squat white sun wouldn't leave, skating round the horizon's meniscus of thinning ice and dripping mountains like a sentry. Time grew increasingly diffuse, gray, and immeasurable.

Not that time mattered to Whistling Pete anymore—only the quick lapse into timelessness he regained every afternoon in the arms of his adorable Penguinettes. Often he trysted two or three of them on a single afternoon, bang bang bang, beginning each session with a few shots of Jack Daniel's and a plate of imported caviar. Often by the third or fourth session he fell rudely asleep and dreamed of white, sandy beaches and tropical heat. Later he awoke in the dim room, saw the windows hung with thick black curtains like a shroud, and heard the hissing radiators. Sometimes his latest Penguinette was sitting in front of the vanity mirror gazing dreamily into the vertex of her own multiple reflections.

Usually, though, Whistling Pete awoke to an empty room laced with perfume and musk. Hotel personnel knocked summarily at the door.

"Maid service," said a woman with a heavy Dutch accent. "Should we clean up, mister? Or you want we should come back later?"

By the time Pete waddled into work it was often as late as three or three-thirty. Fellow administrators and their assistants looked up distantly when Pete skirted through the halls. Back in accounts his assistant, Nadine, was always in a furious temper.

"Mr. Oswald came by from marketing, and Joe Wozniak asked again about your expense receipts. I've *tried* covering for you as far as the sales conference, but I can't do anything if I don't see some retail brochures pretty damn soon. Oh, and your wife and little boy popped round asking for you—you were supposed to take your son fishing today. I think you blew it, Pete."

"Oh shit," Whistling Pete said, and slumped into his swivel chair. He checked both his vest pockets for stray cigarettes but located only twisted bits of tobacco and a small white business card. The card said:

Henrietta Philpott
Public Relations Consultant.

He wondered if he and Henrietta had spent any time together. Or if maybe they were about to.

"I *knew* I'd forgotten something," Whistling Pete said.

He knew but he couldn't quite bring himself to care. He had passed through a barrier of some sort, and was now journeying fearlessly into some primitive wilderness of the mind penguins weren't supposed to know. Cold black spaces where the sun never got to. Huge white polar bears roaming about, cracking shellfish against rocks. Dark hot shapes swooping overhead while strange animals cried in the distance, hungry for fresh meat. When you journeyed this far south, the old rules didn't apply. The only thing you could do was keep moving forward and never look back.

Pete continued making excuses, but they felt more like formalities than contentions.

"But I'm *going* to take Junior fishing," Pete declared, with a forced sincerity even he didn't recognize. "I *want* to help teach him to fish. But I got *delayed* meeting a distributor on the Stroud Islands. What do you want me to do—neglect my job?"

"I sure wouldn't want that," Estelle said emptily, leaning against the kitchen table. She held a mackerel-cracker in front of her face like a cue card. "Obviously, neglecting your job's all you're worried about anymore. So tell that to your year-old son who adores you."

"I'll make it up to you, sport—I really will." Pete paced back and forth in the living room while Junior lay on the floor perusing his geography homework (*Fishing

Routes of Our Polar World, Twelfth Edition). "We'll go camping, that's it. A weekend on the Outer Orkneys. Just you, me, and those mackerel. We'll bring along that new sealskin pup tent we've been meaning to use."

Junior didn't look up. He tapped a pencil against his beak, and turned the page of his textbook. In the last few months since being weaned, Junior's body had grown angular and weirdly composed. It wasn't a body Pete entirely recognized anymore.

"Like, that's *cool*, Dad. It's no big deal or anything. We'll go fishing some other time. When you're not so busy, that is."

"I've *got* the expense receipts," Pete told the executive staff in the factory green room. "Of *course* I've got the expense receipts." The executive directors had called him in during lunch break. They sat around the long black conference table, munching processed-salmon sandwiches and prawn-flavored crisps.

"It's just that, well, payroll screwed up the group finance report, and by the time Nadine and I got that mess straightened out with the commissary it was time for the monthly service catalog, and, well, I *know* it sounds like a bunch of half-assed excuses and all. . . . " A bright cold sweat broke out on Pete's forehead; he tried to shake a little ventilation into his facial feathers and felt a faint dizzying rush, as if he were falling through vortices of warm air. " . . . And of course I'll get the reports to you by Friday, and I don't like to sound like I'm trying to divert blame or anything, right, 'cause of *course* Nadine's a great girl and all, but she *does* have something of a temperament. I'm not trying to cast aspersions or anything but I mean, like, she's always blaming everything on the *system*, right, and the male-dominated patriarchy and all that, and, well, it's sort of hard to get Nadine to cooperate as far as her official responsibilities are concerned. I'm not blaming Nadine for all the screwups, understand. I'm just saying there's only so much I can do, right? I've only got two flippers, you know."

But no matter how hard Whistling Pete expostulated, prevaricated, and fibbed, he knew the game was coming to a rapid conclusion. Even though he'd ordered a new company-account checkbook only two weeks ago, he had already used it all up. He'd paid last month's motel, room service, and bar bills, but now this month's bills were beginning to fall due, and finance wouldn't be forthcoming with another checkbook until May. Pete had purchased a half dozen pearl necklaces, brooches, and earrings, but couldn't even remember which Penguinettes he had distributed them to, or for how much in return. He journeyed through each day in a weird sort of somnambulism, never certain of the time, suffering sinus headaches and blurred vision. He began to avoid his own bloodshot eyes in the bathroom cabinet mirror.

A line from an old Dylan song kept recurring to him: "To live outside the law you must be honest." What Pete decided was: To live outside the law you must work really, really hard. He awoke every day at seven, gulped black coffee, and hurried to the factory where he unsuccessfully tried to catch up with the work he'd been neglecting for weeks. Then he fell asleep at his desk, awoke to Nadine's pottering, and skipped off in a faint anxiety rush to the Crystal Palace Motel, where he encountered the silk-clad bodies of Stella, Ariadne, Velma, and Chloe. Then he returned home each evening through a slow dull daze of incertitude, to be greeted by unpaid utility bills, humming kitchen appliances, and stiff, intricate silences. Estelle in bed with her book. Junior out gallivanting with his friends.

Some nights Pete found the bedroom door bolted shut and he knocked politely like a timid solicitor.

"Estelle?"

"What?"

"Are you in there?"

"Of course I'm in here."

"Can I come in?"

"No you can't."

"I'm really bushed, Estelle. I need to lie down and sleep."

"So sleep on the couch."

"I feel very strange, you know, all run down and everything. I've got stomach pains, my liver's enlarged, there may even be something wrong with my spleen. I've got a rash on my inner thigh that burns like crazy. I'm really beat, Estelle, and I think, well. Maybe we should talk."

"There's nothing to talk about," Estelle said with calm conviction, as if she were slipping a form letter under the door. "I'm afraid the time for talking is over."

Her voice was clipped and regular, like the factory's canning machine. Whistling Pete leaned against the flimsy plywood door. He could detect her warmth in there, like radium or metal. It felt very far away, divided from him by distances more extensive than space.

"Oh Estelle," Pete sighed, feeling his entire body slump into itself like an expiring party balloon. "Maybe you're right, honey. Maybe you're right."

"If you don't mind my saying so, Pete—you're starting to look pretty thin and unraveled lately."

Melody was sitting on the edge of the mattress and pulling on her baggy white fishnet stockings.

"I'll do what I can," Whistling Pete said dreamily. He imagined himself floating downriver on a wide jagged platform of ice. He was gazing up at the white sky, the thin white sun and moon.

Melody gazed distantly at herself in the shimmering vanity mirror. "You're starting to lose a little of your, oh, what do you call it? Your get-up-and-go. I don't mean to sound impolite or anything, baby, because we've had some great times together. But I just don't look forward to seeing you anymore. I mean, when I know we've got a date coming up—oh, how do I say this? Knowing I've got to see you is getting to be a big bummer."

Melody anchored the tops of her stockings to a matching pair of elasticized red-velvet garters. Her body gave off thin, languorous heat and a sense of benign inattention.

"Even General Motors suffers an occasional financial slump," Whistling Pete said, smiling fondly at the clock on the wall. "Even the Japanese experience an occasional recession."

Melody pulled on her short black cocktail skirt with a wriggle. She scowled faintly at herself in the mirror as if she remembered something anterior to her own reflection. Some memory that did not belong to this face, these eyes, this body, this occupied and lonely room.

"I worry about you, Pete. I really do. You used to be *fun*. You used to be a lot of laughs. What happened to the *old* Whistling Pete I *used* to know?"

Drifting in the direction towards which all currents yearned, Pete saw empty planes of ice, tall white mountains, gaping crevasses, rust-red lichen the size of dinner plates. We've lived for thousands and thousands of years, the lichen collectively muttered. And want to know what's happened out here in all that time?

Nothing, man. Nothing nothing nothing nothing.

"I'll be fine," Pete said. He reached for his glass of Smirnoff's. "A bit of the bug, probably. I've been working too hard. I need to relax."

"Yeah, well." Melody got up and brushed herself off. She was wearing a lot of crushed black velvet and pink powdery body-blush. "You take care of yourself, Petey, because I worry about you, I really do. But until you get your act together, I think maybe we shouldn't see each other for a while."

4. THE CRYSTAL PALACE MOTEL

Buster sat at the Ice Floe sipping a strawberry margarita while Al the portly bartender swabbed everything down with a damp dishcloth.

"He's been over there every night," Al said. He shifted a toothpick from one side of his beak to the other, and nodded in the general direction of the Crystal Palace Motel. "Every day and night, actually. And when he comes in here—usually for another bottle of Smirnoff's—he doesn't say hi or anything. He just takes what he needs and leaves."

"No skin off my butt," Buster said, and lit another menthol cigarette. Buster had recently taken up smoking, just to give his hands something to do. "He doesn't need my help with anything. He's got his little girlies to keep him company."

"Little girlies," Al said, and poured himself a soda water from the hand-dispenser. "Little girlies and God knows what else."

Buster sat at the bar and watched Al gaze abstractedly across the empty restaurant. It was three P.M. and Buster had just finished a late lunch of oysters in clam sauce.

"And God knows what else," Al said again. He refused to look at Buster, and there was something in this refusal that Buster took as a reproach.

After lunch and a second margarita Buster tried calling Pete's room at the Crystal Palace Motel but there wasn't any answer. When he stopped by the lobby on his way back to work he found the day clerk playing a new hand-held electronic ice-hockey game. The day clerk swung the beeping computer toy back and forth, as if he were steering a particularly nasty slalom down the rocky hillsides of his imagination.

"Is Whistling Pete still in Room 408?" Buster asked. Buster lit a fresh cigarette off the old one and crushed the old one out in a hip-high, sand-filled aluminum ashtray.

"Ah *shit*," the day clerk said.

The computer beeped its tiny contempt and the day clerk looked up.

"Whistling Pete, huh?" He gave Buster the once-over. "He's not the sort of guy who has many friends. So you must be another customer, right?"

Before he knew what he was doing, Buster was lifting the stroppy, bell-hatted little penguin up over the countertop and slamming him rudely against the clattery ashtray.

"What's *that* supposed to mean, Numb-nuts?"

"Hey, I was just kidding, is all."

Buster heard a tone in his own voice he didn't recognize.

"I'll ask you one more time," he said simply, "and don't give me any more blather. Just tell me where can I find my friend, Whistling Pete?"

By the time Buster found him he wished he hadn't. The day clerk had come clean, and as a result left Buster feeling irredeemably dirty.

"You know what I'm talking about, mister—don't play Baby Innocence with me," the day clerk had replied, hitching up his uniform blue-serge slacks with a pompous little swagger. "I'm talking seals, man. Otters. Big slimy lady walruses with fat blundery arses. It's like the Tart's Grand National around here—them strutting their stuff up and down those stairs day after day. And your pal, Mr. Pete, he doesn't even leave the room at all anymore. You can't *imagine* the sort of disgusting activities that're going on in there. It's sick, that's what it is. There should be a police ordinance or something. Not to mention his hotel tab, which has gotten completely out of hand. In another couple days, your old buddy's going to find himself tossed out on the tundra with the wolves and the polar bears."

Pete's room had recently been relocated to the second-floor servants' quarters. Buster took the service elevator and arrived at a long angular hallway dingy with infrequent lighting, where the linty velour carpets emitted a greasy, unsavory sheen. The entire area smelled of cigarettes and spoiled vegetables.

When Buster knocked at Room 7, he heard a slow slumberous rouse from deep inside.

Buster coughed awkwardly. Then he knocked again.

"Yeah, well, it's not paradise," Pete conceded. "But then, who's looking for paradise, right?" He was sitting on the edge of his frayed, sunken mattress, scratching his genitals through tatty checkered boxer shorts. The room was littered with bottles, newspapers, and fast-food wrappers.

"Why don't you take a shower, Pete? Put on some clean underwear, for godsake. Then I'll take you home to your wife and kid."

"My wife and kid are history, Buster. Estelle took Junior to her sister's on the Fimbul Ice Shelf."

Buster refused to be deterred. If Pete was ever again to have faith in himself, Buster would have to be the one to teach him how.

"First we'll get you squared away," Buster said. "Then we'll go bring her back. She still loves you, Pete. I know she does."

"Bring her back to what?" Pete asked. His voice and eyes were phlegmy and aimless. He picked a white sticky substance from his ear and wiped it on the mottled sheets. "What's left of me ain't exactly a work of art, you know. And you must have heard about the expense money I embezzled. Nadine getting fired for *my* incompetence and graft. The fact that I've lost what little reputation and self-respect I had left—and the funny thing is, I don't give a goddamn. I don't miss any of it. Especially not the self-respect."

Buster, embarrassed by the false assurances he was tempted to offer, looked away. He saw the messy bathroom, the broken dripping toilet, towels on the floor.

"We'll find you a new job," Buster said. The lie echoed hollowly in the filthy room. "With Estelle and Junior's help we'll get you back on your feet again. Hell, buddy—*I* can loan you a few bob till you get yourself straightened out. What are friends for, huh?"

"Oh Buster," Pete sighed. "Wake up and smell the coffee, will you?" Pete indicated his entire body with a small ironic flourish. The high strain of ribs, the frazzled patchy feathers, the haunted and thinning gleam in his eyes. "All my nice sleek body fat has melted away. No job, no family, no savings to speak of. It's quite ironic, really. Because civilization has given me the luxury of thinking, I've had time to disrespect all the civilized comforts that allow me to think."

"Don't," Buster said. He knew he was in trouble if Pete started talking. "Stop it, Pete. Stop winding yourself up."

Pete was on his feet again, waddling back and forth in front of the bed. "But that's the *point*, isn't it? What do you build when you build yourself a civilization? Nice warm houses, nice warm restaurants, nice warm places to go to the bathroom. What does civilization give us, Buster? Temperature. Heat. Oxygen. Light. And what do we do with all this, this *energy*, this year-round fat and reserve? We burn it, pal. We use it to stoke the fire of our bodies all day and all night. Heat and oxygen fuels the brain to think, the loins to procreate, the body to consume. We are burners of hard fuel, Buster, and thinkers of hard thoughts, and we can't ever rest until we die. Civilization doesn't solve problems, Buster. It reminds us of all the problems we haven't yet solved. What we don't have. Who we haven't been. How much we haven't spent. How many little girlies we haven't plugged. It doesn't end, Buster. I keep thinking it *will* end, but it *doesn't* end, not really."

"Don't do this to yourself, buddy," Buster said desperately. "Turn it *off*, man. Give yourself a good swift kick in the backside and shut your damn brain *off*."

Pete came to a sudden halt and he turned. His face was sunken, his eyes lit with a fire that burned itself as much as the things it saw.

"But, Buster," he said, "the only way to turn it off is to stop living. The only way to forget what you know is to pretend not to be."

At which point, Whistling Pete fell to the floor with a terrible crash.

With friends from the Ice Floe Buster managed to transport Pete back to his home, where the atmosphere had grown stale, sluggish, and unreal, almost as bleak as Pete's room at the Crystal Palace. The walls, beds, and furniture were icy with neglect and disuse. The pilot light had extinguished in the furnace, and a shutter in the bedroom had ruptured under the impact of a recent storm, permitting an avalanche of rocky ice and sludge to build up around the dressing table. The only whiff of life remaining in the entire house was exuded by the bowels of the refrigerator, where shriveled vegetables and garlic bulbs blossomed. When they laid Pete out on the cold bed, he tossed and turned in his sleep, muttering against the tide of visions only he could save himself from. Buster wasn't able to reactivate the pilot light in the furnace, but he did manage to get a good blaze started in the fireplace.

"More," Whistling Pete murmured, drifting in the depths of oceans much deeper than sleep. "More yesterdays. More todays. More tomorrows."

"Sleep tight, old buddy," Buster said, posting himself in a cracked wooden chair beside the bed. He had just started a pot of canned soup simmering over the fireplace. "And if you need anything, you know where to find me."

Sandy didn't understand, but Buster never thought she had to.

"Who's your real wife, anyway?" she asked him. "Me or Whistling Pete? And since when did you take up cooking and housecleaning? I never even seen you open a can of beans before."

Buster was wearing one of Estelle's frayed white aprons and scrubbing rusty pans in the sink.

"It's just something I've got to do," Buster said. He felt strangely peaceful and solid. "If you love me, you'll try to understand."

"Try to understand," Sandy said. Suddenly, like a wind snuffing out a candle, all the fight went out of her. "Try to understand."

Buster took his overdue vacation time from the factory and repaired Whistling Pete's window and furnace. Every afternoon, after preparing a lunch of chicken broth and fresh fruit salad, he helped Pete out of bed, walked him around the room a few times, and changed the linen. Whistling Pete's body was all slump and desuetude, his complexion jaundiced and scabby. He was losing feathers all around his skull and under his armpits.

"We'll get you a nice wool cap," Buster promised one day during their exercise session. "The body loses ninety percent of its heat through the old skull, you know. In order to keep the body warm, you gotta keep your lid on—get me?"

"That's why we've got gas fires," Pete said. "That's why we've got central heating."

"Go back to sleep now," Buster said, laying him back in the cool fresh linen. "You don't have anything to worry about for a long, long time."

Usually Whistling Pete drifted off again, but some afternoons, as if driven by the momentum of his own feverish imaginings, he started talking out loud in his sleep.

"I dreamed all night of the white ice," Whistling Pete said. "I was walking south, into a region of thin air and dazzling aurorae. I knew I was heading into the big nothing, but I couldn't seem to stop myself. I knew I had to keep going, not because I wanted to get anywhere specific, but because I couldn't bear to remain anywhere I already was."

The dreams seemed to increase in force and volume, and Buster could never decide whether this was a good omen or a bad one. Sitting beside Pete's bed with his newspaper, Buster watched his friend toss and turn with slow, gathering intensity, like a kettle heating on a stove. Sometimes he cried out or started upright and Buster soothed him with a steaming wet towel.

"Human beings are the next step," Whistling Pete cried out from time to time. "They'll be here any day now. And if human beings don't get here pretty soon, then I'm afraid us penguins won't have a choice. We'll start turning into human beings. You, me, Estelle, Junior, Melody, the girls, the beautiful girls. Big fat hairy human beings with guns, oil, and machinery. We'll start erecting supermarkets and shopping malls. We'll drive like maniacs across the ice on motorbikes and mopeds. We'll start shooting each other in the head, and chewing tobacco, and pissing on our own front stoops. I have seen the future, Buster. I have seen the future and it is us. Animals who can't stop themselves anymore. Animals who always want more than they've already got."

"It's O.K., Pete," Buster said. He shook and repositioned the foam pillows, helping Pete subside back into them. "Stop worrying. Stop thinking and just relax. It'll be O.K.—I promise. I'll stick by you. All you've got to do is get better, Pete. I'll take care of everything."

They buried Whistling Pete beside the pond where he first went fishing with his father. A lid was cut in the ice and Pete's naked body inserted into the frothy, secret currents beneath. The various attending penguins seemed too stunned, disoriented, or angry to look at one another. On the fringes of the small crowd a few lonely, heavily veiled Penguinettes sobbed quietly into black satin handkerchiefs.

When the lid of ice was refitted into place a few words were said by each of Pete's surviving friends and relatives. Usually they offered slow, awkward condolences like, "He will be missed," or, "He was always a hard worker and good provider," with a dull casual flourish, as if they were signing a form letter. The last person to take the mound was Pete's father, who had swum in that morning from his retirement village on Carney Island. (Pete's mother had died two years previously in a freak skiing accident.)

"Whistling Pete was a good boy," his father said in a cracked, halting voice, trying to read from a sheet of foolscap in his trembling hands. He wore a faded gray flannel shirt, a black wool stocking cap, and wire-rim bifocals. "He was always polite to his parents. He always did well in school and helped his mother with the housework. Now maybe he exaggerated the truth every once in a while, but that's just the way he was, I guess. He found the truth a little too boring, so he tried to embellish it a little, it was kind of like generosity. Pete always thought big. He was ambitious and talented. Ever since he learned to swim, he dreamed of going to faraway places and accomplishing great deeds. I remember when he was little, he was such an enthusiastic fisherman. He kept bringing home sacks and sacks of them, more fish than we could possibly eat in one modest household. So then he started giving away all the extra fish he caught to the poor homes and convalescent hospitals. He always gave that little bit extra to everything he did. Maybe some people considered it selfish. But I always thought he gave life everything he had because he loved it so much."

Mr. Pete paused to wipe a frozen teardrop from one eye and continued in a wet, quavering voice. "Maybe he made some mistakes when he grew up. He never visited his mother and me after we retired, but by then he had a family of his own, so I guess he just got too busy. But he was always good to me and his mother when he was little, and that's, that's . . . " Abruptly, Mr. Pete began to sob. A hush fell over the mourners. Even some of the succinctly sobbing black-clad Penguinettes fell respectfully silent.

Buster stepped up and whispered something in Mr. Pete's ear.

"No, no, I'm O.K.," Mr. Pete declared irritably, and shook his sheet of foolscap at Buster as if he were shooing flies. Then he wiped his glasses with the end of his stocking cap, folded the foolscap in half, and slipped it into his vest pocket.

"I just wanted to say that Whistling Pete was always polite to his mother and father when he was little, and that's how I'll always remember him."

5. THE LAND OF THE MIDNIGHT SUN

Estelle and Junior moved back into the house and Whistling Pete's father returned to his retirement village by the sea. With much stern and obvious ceremony, Buster and Sandy began making what they referred to as "a fresh start" together. They exchanged small occasional gifts on personal anniversaries and public holidays, and in the renewed silence of their co-op duplex apartment they cautiously maintained a tender, almost obstinate parity.

"No, sweetheart," Buster would demur, leaning to grant her a kiss behind each ear. "This is my night to do the dishes again. You washed up two nights in a row last week."

They sat in the living room every evening after dinner sipping Darjeeling, nibbling oven-hot gingerbread, and listening to the BBC World Service. Old empires disintegrating in the Baltic, Adriatic, Sahara, South Africa, Taiwan. Currencies crashing and stock markets rocketing. The pose and strut of presidents, businessmen, pretenders, and kings. "Before civilization," Whistling Pete used to say, "we never had time to realize what we didn't have. Now we've got all the time in the world to worry about what we'll never keep." Sitting with Sandy in the recently redecorated living room, Buster often felt Pete's voice sneak up behind him like a physical presence. It was a summons to attend conversations never conducted, a simple memory of resonance.

In the mornings before work Buster took long aimless walks into the wilderness, wrapped tight in his sealskin parkas and scratchy woolen underdrawers. He knew this was the dream Pete had died trying to realize, and that if he tried to realize it himself then he would have to die, too. Not a dream of comfort or plenitude, but a sort of homeless insufficiency, a careless surfeit of the blood's pulse and circuit. Buster ascended mountains and forded rivers. He skated across plains of ice and refraction, hopping from one jaggedy landmass to another. Some mornings he got lost and arrived late for work. He received three warnings and one official reprimand. One more tardy report or no-show, they told him, and he would be fired, no explanations asked.

That night at home, Sandy tried to understand.

"Do you know what you're doing?" she asked. Sandy had lit soft candles and prepared a cheese soufflé. She wore a string of pearls, rubber pedal pushers, and a Dacron shower cap—a combination she knew looked really good on her.

"Not really," Buster said. He sat beside the fireplace and waited. He didn't know what he was waiting for anymore, he only knew it would be here soon. "I try not to worry too much, though. If it happens, it happens. I'll get another job. I'll do the best I can."

"I'll do the shopping again tomorrow if you like. Is there anything special you need?"

Buster thought about this for a moment as if it were an especially tricky parable.

"Not really," he said. "These days it's hard for me to think too much about tomorrow."

ETHER OR
Ursula K. Le Guin

Ursula K. Le Guin has a reputation as one of the finest writers working today, both inside and out of the fantasy genre. The following story shows, once again, that her reputation is well deserved. "Ether OR" is a gorgeous, moving tale of American magical realism. It comes from the November issue of *Asimov's SF Magazine.*

Le Guin has won the American Book Award, the World Fantasy Award, and the Harold D. Vursell Memorial Award from the American Academy and Institute of Arts and Letters. She is the author of numerous books including the "Earthsea" quartet and, more recently, *Four Ways to Forgiveness* and *Unlocking the Air.* Her essay collection, *The Language of the Night,* ought to be required reading for aspiring fantasy writers. Le Guin describes herself as "a feminist, a conservationist, and a western American, passionately involved with West Coast literature, landscape, and life." She lives in Portland, Oregon.

—T.W.

EDNA

I never go in the Two Blue Moons anymore. I thought about that when I was arranging the grocery window today and saw Corrie go in across the street and open up. Never did go into a bar alone in my life. Sook came by for a candy bar and I said that to her, said I wonder if I ought to go have a beer there sometime, see if it tastes different on your own. Sook said Oh Ma you always been on your own. I said I seldom had a moment to myself and four husbands, and she said You know that don't count. Sook's fresh. Breath of fresh air. I saw Needless looking at her with that kind of dog look men get. I was surprised to find it gave me a pang, I don't know what of. I just never saw Needless look that way. What did I expect, Sook is twenty and the man is human. He just always seemed like he did fine on his own. Independent. That's why he's restful. Silvia died years and years and years ago, but I never thought of it before as a long time. I wonder if I have mistaken him. All this time working for him. That would be a strange thing. That was what the pang felt like, like when you know you've made some kind of mistake, been stupid, sewn the seam inside out, left the burner on.

They're all strange, men are. I guess if I understood them I wouldn't find them so interesting. But Toby Walker, of them all he was the strangest. The stranger. I never knew where he was coming from. Roger came out of the desert, Ady came out of the ocean, but Toby came from farther. But he was here when I came. A lovely man, dark all through, dark as forests. I lost my way in him. I loved to lose my way in him. How I wish it was then, not now! Seems like I can't get lost anymore. There's only one way to go. I have to keep plodding along it. I feel like I was walking across Nevada, like the pioneers, carrying a lot of stuff I need, but as I go along I have to keep dropping off things. I had a piano once but it got swamped at a crossing of the Platte. I had a good frypan but it got too heavy and I left it in the Rockies. I had a couple ovaries but they wore out around the time we were in the Carson Sink. I had a good memory but pieces of it keep dropping off, have to leave them scattered around in the sagebrush, on the sand hills. All the kids are still coming along, but I don't have them. I had them, it's not the same as having them. They aren't with me anymore, even Archie and Sook. They're all walking along back where I was years ago. I wonder will they get any nearer than I have to the west side of the mountains, the valleys of the orange groves? They're years behind me.

They're still in Iowa. They haven't even thought about the Sierras yet. I didn't either till I got here. Now I begin to think I'm a member of the Donner Party.

THOS. SUNN

The way you can't count on Ether is a hindrance sometimes, like when I got up in the dark this morning to catch the minus tide and stepped out the door in my rubber boots and plaid jacket with my clam spade and bucket, and overnight she'd gone inland again. The damn desert and the damn sagebrush. All you could dig up there with your damn spade would be a goddamn fossil. Personally I blame it on the Indians. I do not believe that a fully civilized country would allow these kind of irregularities in a town. However as I have lived here since 1949 and could not sell my house and property for chicken feed, I intend to finish up here, like it or not. That should take a few more years, ten or fifteen most likely. Although you can't count on anything these days anywhere let alone a place like this. But I like to look after myself, and I can do it here. There is not so much government meddling and interference and general hindering in Ether as you would find in the cities. This may be because it isn't usually where the government thinks it is, though it is, sometimes.

When I first came here I used to take some interest in a woman, but it is my belief that in the long run a man does better not to. A woman is a worse hindrance to a man than anything else, even the government.

I have read the term *a crusty old bachelor* and would be willing to say that that describes me so long as the crust goes all the way through. I don't like things soft in the center. Softness is no use in this hard world. I am like one of my mother's biscuits.

My mother, Mrs. J.J. Sunn, died in Wichita, Kansas, in 1944, at the age of seventy-nine. She was a fine woman and my experience of women in general does not apply to her in particular.

Since they invented the kind of biscuits that come in a tube that you hit on the edge of the counter and the dough explodes out of it under pressure, that's the kind I buy, and by baking them about one half hour they come out pretty much the way I like them, crust clear through. I used to bake the dough all of a piece, but then discovered that you can break it apart into separate biscuits. I don't hold with reading directions and they are always printed in small, fine print on the damn foil that gets torn when you break open the tube. I use my mother's glasses. They are a good make.

The woman I came here after in 1949 is still here. That was during my brief period of infatuation. Fortunately I can say that she did not get her hooks onto me in the end. Some other men have not been as lucky. She has married or as good as several times and was pregnant and pushing a baby carriage for decades. Sometimes I think everybody under forty in this town is one of Edna's. I had a very narrow escape. I have had a dream about Edna several times. In this dream I am out on the sea fishing for salmon from a small boat, and Edna swims up from the sea waves and tries to climb into the boat. To prevent this I hit her hands with the gutting knife and cut off the fingers, which fall into the water and turn into some kind of little creatures that swim away. I never can tell if they are babies or seals. Then Edna swims after them making a strange noise, and I see that in actuality she is a kind of seal or sea lion, like the big ones in the cave on the south coast, light brown and very large and fat and sleek in the water.

This dream disturbs me, as it is unfair. I am not the kind of man who would do such a thing. It causes me discomfort to remember the strange noise she makes in the dream, when I am in the grocery store and Edna is at the cash register. To make sure she rings it up right and I get the right change, I have to look at her hands opening and shutting the drawers and her fingers working on the keys. What's wrong with women is that you can't count on them. They are not fully civilized.

ROGER HIDDENSTONE

I only come into town sometimes. It's a now-and-then thing. If the road takes me there, fine, but I don't go hunting for it. I run a two-hundred-thousand-acre cattle ranch, which gives me a good deal to do. I'll look up sometimes and the moon is new that I saw full last night. One summer comes after another like steers through a chute. In the winters, though, sometimes the weeks freeze like the creek water, and things hold still for a while. The air can get still and clear in the winter here in the high desert. I have seen the mountain peaks from Baker and Rainier in the north, Hood and Jefferson, Three-Fingered Jack and the Sisters east of here, on south to Shasta and Lassen, all standing up in the sunlight for eight hundred or a thousand miles. That was when I was flying. From the ground you can't see that much of the ground, though you can see the rest of the universe, nights.

I traded in my two-seater Cessna for a quarterhorse mare, and I generally keep a Ford pickup, though at times I've had a Chevrolet. Any one of them will get me into town so long as there isn't more than a couple feet of snow on the road. I like to come in now and then and have a Denver omelette at the cafe for breakfast, and a visit with my wife and son. I have a drink at the Two Blue Moons, and spend the night at the motel. By the next morning I'm ready to go back to the ranch to find out what went wrong while I was gone. It's always something.

Edna was only out to the ranch once while we were married. She spent three weeks. We were so busy in the bed I don't recall much else about it, except the time she tried to learn to ride. I put her on Sally, the cutting horse I traded the

Cessna plus fifteen hundred dollars for, a highly reliable horse and more intelligent than most Republicans. But Edna had that mare morally corrupted within ten minutes. I was trying to explain how she'd interpret what you did with your knees, when Edna started yipping and raking her like a bronc rider. They lit out of the yard and went halfway to Ontario at a dead run. I was riding the old roan gelding and only met them coming back. Sally was unrepentant, but Edna was sore and delicate that evening. She claimed all the love had been jolted out of her. I guess that this was true, in the larger sense, since it wasn't long after that that she asked to go back to Ether. I thought she had quit her job at the grocery, but she had only asked for a month off, and she said Needless would want her for the extra business at Christmas. We drove back to town, finding it a little west of where we had left it, in a very pretty location near the Ochoco Mountains, and we had a happy Christmas season in Edna's house with the children.

I don't know whether Archie was begotten there or at the ranch. I'd like to think it was at the ranch so that there would be that in him drawing him to come back some day. I don't know who to leave all this to. Charlie Echeverria is good with the stock, but can't think ahead two days and couldn't deal with the buyers, let alone the corporations. I don't want the corporations profiting from this place. The hands are nice young fellows, but they don't stay put, or want to. Cowboys don't want land. Land owns you. You have to give in to that. I feel sometimes like all the stones on two hundred thousand acres were weighing on me, and my mind's gone to rimrock. And the beasts wandering and calling across all that land. The cows stand with their young calves in the wind that blows March snow like frozen sand across the flats. Their patience is a thing I try to understand.

GRACIE FANE

I saw that old rancher on Main Street yesterday, Mister Hiddenstone, was married to Edna once. He acted like he knew where he was going, but when the street ran out onto the sea cliff he sure did look foolish. Turned round and came back in those high-heel boots, long legs, putting his feet down like a cat the way cowboys do. He's a skinny old man. He went into the Two Blue Moons. Going to try to drink his way back to Eastern Oregon, I guess. I don't care if this town is east or west. I don't care if it's anywhere. It never is anywhere anyway. I'm going to leave here and go to Portland, to the Intermountain, the big trucking company, and be a truck driver. I learned to drive when I was five on my grandpa's tractor. When I was ten I started driving my dad's Dodge Ram, and I've driven pickups and delivery vans for Mom and Mr. Needless ever since I got my license. Jase gave me lessons on his eighteen-wheeler last summer. I did real good. I'm a natural. Jase said so. I never got to get out onto the I-5 but only once or twice, though. He kept saying I needed more practice pulling over and parking and shifting up and down. I didn't mind practicing, but then when I got her stopped he'd want to get me into this bed thing he fixed up behind the seats and pull my jeans off, and we had to screw some before he'd go on teaching me anything. My own idea would be to drive a long way and learn a lot and then have some sex and coffee and then drive back a different way, maybe on hills where I'd have to practice braking and stuff. But I guess men have different priorities. Even when I was driving he'd have his arm around my back and be petting my boobs. He has these huge hands can reach right across both boobs at once. It felt good, but it interfered with his concentration teaching me. He would say *Oh baby you're so great* and I would think he meant I was driving great but then he'd start making those sort of groaning noises and I'd have to shift down and find a place to pull out and get in the bed thing again. I used to practice changing gears in my mind when we were screwing and it helped. I could shift him right up and down again. I used to yell *Going eighty!* when I got him really shifted up. *Fuzz on your tail!* And make these sireen noises. That's my CB name: Sireen. Jase got his route shifted in August. I made my plans then. I'm driving for the grocery and saving money till I'm seventeen and go to Portland to work for the Intermountain Company. I want to drive the I-5 from Seattle to LA, or get a run to Salt Lake City. Till I can buy my own truck. I got it planned out.

TOBINYE WALKER

The young people all want to get out of Ether. Young Americans in a small town want to get up and go. And some do, and some come to a time when they stop talking about where they're going to go when they go. They have come to where they are. Their problem, if it's a problem, isn't all that different from mine. We have a window of opportunity; it closes. I used to walk across the years as easy as a child here crosses the street, but I went lame, and had to stop walking. So this is my time, my heyday, my floruit.

When I first knew Edna she said a strange thing to me; we had been talking, I don't remember what about, and she stopped and gazed at me. "You have a look on you like an unborn child," she said. "You look at things like an unborn child." I don't know what I answered, and only later did I wonder how she knew how an unborn child looks, and whether she meant a fetus in the womb or a child that never came to be conceived. Maybe she meant a newborn child. But I think she used the word she meant to use.

When I first stopped by here, before my accident, there was no town, of course, no settlement. Several peoples came through and sometimes encamped for a season, but it was a range without boundary, though it had names. At that time people didn't have the expectation of stability they have now; they knew that so long as a river keeps running it's a river. Nobody but the beavers built dams, then. Ether always covered a lot of territory, and it has retained that property. But its property is not continuous.

The people I used to meet coming through generally said they came down Humbug Creek from the river in the mountains, but Ether itself never has been in the Cascades, to my knowledge. Fairly often you can see them to the west of it, though usually it's west of them, and often west of the Coast Range in the timber or the dairy country, sometimes right on the sea. It has a broken range. It's an unusual place. I'd like to go back to the center to tell about it, but I can't walk anymore. I have to do my flourishing here.

J. NEEDLESS

People think there are no Californians. Nobody can come from the promised land. You have to be going to it. Die in the desert, grave by the wayside. I come from California, born there, think about it some. I was born in the Valley of San Arcadio.

Orchards. Like a white bay of orange flowers under bare blue-brown mountains. Sunlight like air, like clear water, something you lived in, an element. Our place was a little farmhouse up in the foothills, looking out over the valley. My father was a manager for one of the companies. Oranges flower white, with a sweet, fine scent. Outskirts of Heaven, my mother said once, one morning when she was hanging out the wash. I remember her saying that. We live on the outskirts of Heaven.

She died when I was six and I don't remember a lot but that about her. Now I have come to realize that my wife has been dead so long that I have lost her too. She died when our daughter Corrie was six. Seemed like there was some meaning in it at the time, but if there was I didn't find it.

Ten years ago when Corrie was twenty-one she said she wanted to go to Disneyland for her birthday. With me. Damn if she didn't drag me down there. Spent a good deal to see people dressed up like mice with water on the brain and places made to look like places they weren't. I guess that is the point there. They clean dirt till it is a sanitary substance and spread it out to look like dirt so you don't have to touch dirt. You and Walt are in control there. You can be in any kind of place, space or the ocean or castles in Spain, all sanitary, no dirt. I would have liked it as a boy, when I thought the idea was to run things. Changed my ideas, settled for a grocery.

Corrie wanted to see where I grew up, so we drove over to San Arcadio. It wasn't there, not what I meant by it. Nothing but roofs, houses, streets, and houses. Smog so thick it hid the mountains and the sun looked green. Goddamn, get me out of here, I said, they have changed the color of the sun. Corrie wanted to look for the house but I was serious. Get me out of here, I said, this is the right place but the wrong year. Walt Disney can get rid of the dirt on his property if he likes, but this is going too far. This is my property.

I felt like that. Like I thought it was something I had, but they scraped all the dirt off and underneath was cement and some electronic wiring. I'd as soon not have seen that. People come through here say how can you stand living in a town that doesn't stay in the same place all the time, but have they been to Los Angeles? It's anywhere you want to say it is.

Well, since I don't have California what have I got? A good enough business. Corrie's still here. Good head on her. Talks a lot. Runs that bar like a bar should be run. Runs her husband pretty well too. What do I mean when I say I had a mother, I had a wife? I mean remembering what orange flowers smell like, whiteness, sunlight. I carry that with me. Corinna and Silvia, I carry their names. But what do I have?

What I don't have is right within hand's reach every day. Every day but Sunday. But I can't reach out my hand. Every man in town gave her a child and all I ever gave her was her week's wages. I know she trusts me. That's the trouble. Too late now. Hell, what would she want me in her bed for, the Medicare benefits?

EMMA BODELY

Everything is serial killers now. They say everyone is naturally fascinated by a man planning and committing one murder after another without the least reason and not even knowing who he kills personally. There was the man up in the city recently who tortured and tormented three tiny little boys and took photographs of them while he tortured them and of their corpses after he killed them. Authorities are talking now about what they ought to do with these photographs. They could make a lot of money from a book of them. He was apprehended by the police as he lured yet another tiny boy to come with him, as in a nightmare. There were men in California and Texas and I believe Chicago who dismembered and buried innumerably. Then of course it goes back in history to Jack the Ripper who killed poor women and was supposed to be a member of the Royal Family of England, and no doubt before his time there were many other serial killers, many of them members of Royal Families or Emperors and Generals who killed thousands and thousands of people. But in wars they kill people more or less simultaneously, not one by one, so that they are mass murderers, not serial killers, but I'm not sure I see the difference, really. Since for the person being murdered it only happens once.

I should be surprised if we had a serial killer in Ether. Most of the men were soldiers in one of the wars, but they would be mass murderers, unless they had desk jobs. I can't think who here would be a serial killer. No doubt I would be the last to find out. I find being invisible works both ways. Often I don't see as much as I used to when I was visible. Being invisible, however, I'm less likely to become a serial victim.

It's odd how the natural fascination they talk about doesn't include the serial victims. I suppose it is because I taught young children for thirty-five years, but perhaps I am unnatural, because I think about those three little boys. They were three or four years old. How strange that their whole life was only a few years, like a cat. In their world suddenly instead of their mother there was a man who told them how he was going to hurt them and then did it, so that there was nothing in their life at all but fear and pain. So they died in fear and pain. But all the reporters tell is the nature of the mutilations and how decomposed they were, and that's all about them. They were little boys not men. They are not fascinating. They are just dead. But the serial killer they tell all about over and over and discuss his psychology and how his parents caused him to be so fascinating, and he lives forever, as witness Jack the Ripper and Hitler the Ripper. Everyone around here certainly remembers the name of the man who serially raped and photographed the tortured little boys before he serially murdered them. He was named Westley Dodd, but what were their names?

Of course we the people murdered him back. That was what he wanted. He wanted us to murder him. I cannot decide if hanging him was a mass murder or a serial murder. We all did it, like a war, so it is a mass murder, but we each did it, democratically, so I suppose it is serial, too. I would as soon be a serial victim as a serial murderer, but I was not given the choice.

My choices have become less. I never had a great many, as my sexual impulses were not appropriate to my position in life, and no one I fell in love with knew it. I am glad when Ether turns up in a different place as it is kind of like a new choice of where to live, only I didn't have to make it. I am capable only of very small choices. What to eat for breakfast, oatmeal or cornflakes, or perhaps only a piece of fruit? Kiwi fruits were fifteen cents apiece at the grocery and I bought half a dozen. A while ago they were the most exotic thing, from New Zealand I think, and a dollar each, and now they raise them all over the Willamette Valley. But then, the Willamette Valley may be quite exotic to a person in New Zealand. I like the way they're cool in your mouth, the same way the flesh of them looks cool, a smooth green you can see into, like jade stone. I still see things like that perfectly clearly. It's only with people that my eyes are more and more transparent, so that I don't always see what they're doing, and so that they can look right through me as if my eyes were air and say, "Hi, Emma, how's life treating you?"

Life's treating me like a serial victim, thank you.

I wonder if she sees me or sees through me. I don't dare look. She is shy and lost in her crystal dreams. If only I could look after her. She needs looking after. A cup of tea. Herbal tea, echinacea maybe, I think her immune system needs strengthening. She is not a practical person. I am a very practical person. Far below her dreams.

Lo still sees me. Of course Lo is a serial killer as far as birds are concerned, and moles, but although it upsets me when the bird's not dead yet it's not the same as the man taking photographs. Mr. Hiddenstone once told me that cats have the instinct to let a mouse or bird stay alive a while in order to take it to the kittens and train them to hunt, so what seems to be cruelty is thoughtfulness. Now I know that some tomcats kill kittens, and I don't think any tom ever raised kittens and trained them thoughtfully to hunt. The queen cat does that. A tomcat is the Jack the Ripper of the Royal Family. But Lo is neutered, so he might behave like a queen or at least like a kind of uncle if there were kittens around, and bring them his birds to hunt. I don't know. He doesn't mix with other cats much. He stays pretty close to home, keeping an eye on the birds and moles and me. I know that my invisibility is not universal when I wake up in the middle of the night and Lo is sitting on the bed right beside my pillow purring and looking very intently at me. It's a strange thing to do, a little uncanny. His eyes wake me, I think. But it's a good waking, knowing that he can see me, even in the dark.

EDNA

All right now, I want an answer. All my life since I was fourteen I have been making my soul. I don't know what else to call it, that's what I called it then, when I was fourteen and came into the possession of my life and the knowledge of my responsibility. Since then I have not had time to find a better name for it. The word *responsible* means that you have to answer. You can't not answer. You'd might rather not answer, but you have to. When you answer you are making your soul, so that it has a shape to it, and size, and some staying power. I understood that, I came into that knowledge, when I was thirteen and early fourteen, that long winter in the Siskiyous. All right, so ever since then, more or less, I have worked according to that understanding. And I have worked. I have done what came into my hands to do, and I've done it the best I could and with all the mind and strength I had to give to it. There have been jobs, waitressing and clerking, but first of all and always the ordinary work of raising the children and keeping the house so that people can live decently and in health and some degree of peace of mind. Then there is responding to the needs of men. That seems like it should come first. People might say I never thought of anything but answering what men asked, pleasing men and pleasing myself, and goodness knows such questions are a joy to answer if asked by a pleasant man. But in the order of my mind, the children come before the fathers of the children. Maybe I see it that way because I was the eldest daughter and there were four younger than me and my father had gone off. Well, all right then, those are my responsibilities as I see them, those are the questions I have tried always to answer: can people live in this house, and how does a child grow up rightly, and how to be trustworthy.

But now I have my own question. I never asked questions, I was so busy answering them, but I am sixty years old this winter and think I should have time for a question. But it's hard to ask. Here it is. It's like all the time I was working keeping house and raising the kids and making love and earning our keep I thought there was going to come a time or there would be someplace where all of it all came together. Like it was words I was saying, all my life, all the kinds of work, just a word here and a word there, but finally all the words would make a sentence, and I could read the sentence. I would have made my soul and know what it was for.

But I have made my soul and I don't know what to do with it. Who wants it? I have lived sixty years. All I'll do from now on is the same as what I have done only less of it, while I get weaker and sicker and smaller all the time, shrinking and shrinking around myself, and die. No matter what I did, or made, or know. The words don't mean anything. I ought to talk with Emma about this. She's the only one who doesn't say stuff like, "You're only as old as you think you are," "Oh Edna, you'll never be old," rubbish like that. Toby Walker wouldn't talk that way either, but he doesn't say much at all anymore. Keeps his sentences to himself. My kids that still live here, Archie and Sook, they don't want to hear anything about it. Nobody young can afford to believe in getting old.

So is all the responsibility you take only useful then, but no use later—disposable? What's the use, then? All the work you did is just gone. It doesn't make anything. But I may be wrong. I hope so, I would like to have more trust in dying. Maybe it's worthwhile, like some kind of answering, coming into another place. Like I felt that winter in the Siskiyous, walking on the snow road between black firs under all the stars, that I was the same size as the universe, the same thing as the universe. And if I kept on walking ahead there was this glory waiting for me. In time I would come into glory. I knew that. So that's what I made my soul for. I made it for glory.

And I have known a good deal of glory. I'm not ungrateful. But it doesn't last. It doesn't come together to make a place where you can live, a house. It's gone and the years go. What's left? Shrinking and forgetting and thinking about aches and acid indigestion and cancers and pulse rates and bunions until the whole world is a room that smells like urine, is that what all the work comes to, is that the end of the babies' kicking legs, the children's eyes, the loving hands, the wild rides, the light on water, the stars over the snow? Somewhere inside it all there has to still be the glory.

ERVIN MUTH

I have been watching Mr. "Toby" Walker for a good while, checking up on things, and if I happened to be called upon to I could state with fair certainty that this "Mr. Walker" is *not an American*. My research has taken me considerably farther afield than that. But there are these "gray areas" or some things, which many people as a rule are unprepared to accept. It takes training.

My attention was drawn to these kind of matters in the first place by scrutinizing the town records on an entirely different subject of research. Suffice it to say that I was checking the title on the Fane place at the point in time when Mrs. Osey Jean Fane put the property into the hands of Ervin Muth, Realtor, of which I am proprietor. There had been a dispute concerning the property line on the east side of the Fane property in 1939 into which, due to being meticulous concerning these kind of detailed responsibilities, I checked. To my surprise I was amazed to discover that the adjoining lot, which had been developed in 1906, had been in the name of Tobinye Walker since that date, 1906! I naturally assumed at that point in time that this "Tobinye Walker" was "Mr. Toby Walker's" father and thought little more about the issue until my researches into another matter, concerning the Essel/Emmer lots, in the town records indicated that the name "Tobinye Walker" was shown as purchaser of a livery stable on that site (on Main St. between Rash St. and Goreman Ave.) in 1880.

While purchasing certain necessaries in the Needless Grocery Store soon after, I encountered Mr. Walker in person. I remarked in a jocular vein that I had been meeting his father and grandfather. This was of course a mere pleasantry. Mr. "Toby" Walker responded in what struck me as a suspicious fashion. There was some taking aback going on. Although with laughter. His exact words, to which I can attest, were the following: "I had no idea that you were capable of traveling in time!"

This was followed by my best efforts to seriously inquire concerning the persons of his same name that my researches in connection with my work as a Realtor had turned up. These were only met with facetious remarks such as, "I've lived here quite a while, you see," and, "Oh, I remember when Lewis and Clark came through," a statement in reference to the celebrated explorers of the Oregon Trail, who I ascertained later to have been in Oregon in 1806.

Soon after Mr. Toby Walker "walked" away, thus ending the conversation.

I am convinced by evidence that "Mr. Walker" is an illegal immigrant from a foreign country who has assumed the name of a Founding Father of this fine community, that is to wit the Tobinye Walker who purchased the livery stable in 1880. I have my reasons.

My research shows conclusively that the Lewis and Clark Expedition sent by President Thomas Jefferson did not pass through any of the localities that our fine community of Ether has occupied over the course of its history. Ether never got that far North.

If Ether is to progress to fulfill its destiny as a Destination Resort on the beautiful Oregon Coast and Desert as I visualize it with a complete downtown entertainment center and entrepreneurial business community, including hub motels, RV facilities, and a theme park, the kind of thing that is represented by "Mr." Walker will have to go. It is the American way to buy and sell houses and properties continually in the course of moving for the sake of upward mobility and self-improvement. Stagnation is the enemy of the American way. The same person owning the same property since 1906 is unnatural and Unamerican. Ether is an American town and moves all the time. That is its destiny. I can call myself an expert.

STARRA WALINOW AMETHYST

I keep practicing love. I was in love with that French actor Gerard but it's really hard to say his last name. Frenchmen attract me. When I watch *Star Trek: The Next Generation* reruns I'm in love with Captain Jean-Luc Picard, but I can't stand Commander Riker. I used to be in love with Heathcliff when I was twelve and Miss Freff gave me *Wuthering Heights* to read. And I was in love with Sting for a while before he got weirder. Sometimes I think I am in love with Lieutenant Worf but that is pretty weird, with all those sort of wrinkles and horns on his forehead, since he's a Klingon, but that's not really what's weird. I mean it's just in the TV that he's an alien. Really he is a human named Michael Dorn. That is so weird to me. I mean I never have seen a real black person except in movies and TV. Everybody in Ether is white. So a black person would actually be an alien here. I thought what it would be like if somebody like that came into like the drugstore, really tall, with that dark brown skin and dark eyes and those very soft lips that look like they could get hurt so easily, and asked for something in that really, really deep voice. Like, "Where would I find the aspirin?" And I would show him where the aspirin kind of stuff is. He would be standing beside me in front of the shelf, really big and tall and dark, and I'd feel warmth coming out of him like out of an iron woodstove. He'd say to me in a very low voice, "I don't belong in this town," and I'd say back, "I don't either," and he'd say, "Do you want to come with me?" only really really nicely, not like a come-on but like two prisoners whispering how to get out of prison together. I'd nod, and he'd say, "Back of the gas station, at dusk."

At dusk.

I love that word. Dusk. It sounds like his voice.

Sometimes I feel weird thinking about him like this. I mean, because he is actually real. If it was just Worf, that's okay, because Worf is just this alien in some old reruns of a show. But there is actually a Michael Dorn. So thinking about him in a sort of story that way makes me uncomfortable sometimes, because it's like I was making him a toy, something I can do anything with, like a doll. That seems like it was unfair to him. And it makes me sort of embarrassed when I think about how he actually has his own life with nothing to do with this dumb girl in some hick town he never heard of. So I try to make up somebody else to make that kind of story about. But it doesn't work.

I really tried this spring to be in love with Morrie Stromberg, but it didn't work. He's really beautiful looking. It was when I saw him shooting baskets that I thought maybe I could be in love with him. His legs and arms are long and smooth and he moves smooth and looks kind of like a mountain lion, with a low forehead and short dark blond hair, tawny colored. But all he ever does is hang out with Joe's crowd and talk about sport scores and cars, and once in class he was talking with Joe about me so I could hear, like "Oh yeah Starra, wow, *she* reads *books*," not really mean, but kind of like I was like an alien from another planet, just totally absolutely strange. Like Worf or Michael Dorn would feel here. Like he meant okay, it's okay to be like that only not here. Somewhere else, okay? As if Ether wasn't already somewhere else. I mean, didn't it use to be the Indians that lived here, and now there aren't any of them either? So who belongs here and where does it belong?

About a month ago Mom told me the reason she left my father. I don't remember anything like that. I don't remember any father. I don't remember anything before Ether. She says we were living in Seattle and they had a store where they sold crystals and oils and New Age stuff, and when she got up one night to go to the bathroom he was in my room holding me. She wanted to tell me everything about how he was holding me and stuff, but I just went, "So, like, he was molesting me." And she went, "Yeah," and I said, "So what did you do?" I thought they would have had a big fight. But she said she didn't say anything, because she was afraid of him. She said, "See, to him it was like he owned me and you. And when I didn't go along with that, he would get real crazy." I think they were into a lot of pot and heavy stuff, she talks about that sometimes. So anyway next day when he went to the store she just took some of the crystals and stuff they kept at home, we still have them, and got some money they kept in a can in the kitchen just like she does here, and got on the bus to Portland with me. Somebody she met there gave us a ride here. I don't remember any of that. It's like I was born here. I asked did he ever try to look for her, and she said she didn't know but if he did he'd have a hard time finding her here. She changed her last name to Amethyst, which is her favorite stone. Walinow was her real name. She says it's Polish.

I don't know what his name was. I don't know what he did. I don't care. It's like nothing happened. I'm never going to belong to anybody.

What I know is this: I am going to love people. They will never know it. But I am going to be a great lover. I know how. I have practiced. It isn't when you belong to somebody or they belong to you or stuff. That's like Chelsey getting married to Tim because she wanted to have the wedding and the husband and a no-wax kitchen floor. She wanted stuff to belong to.

I don't want stuff, but I want practice. Like we live in this shack with no kitchen let alone a no-wax floor, and we cook on a trashburner, with a lot of crystals around, and cat pee from the strays Mom takes in, and Mom does stuff like sweeping out for Myrella's beauty parlor, and gets zits because she eats Hostess Twinkies instead of food. Mom needs to get it together. But I need to give it away.

I thought maybe the way to practice love was to have sex so I had sex with Danny last summer. Mom bought us condoms and made me hold hands with her around a bayberry candle and talk about the Passage Into Womanhood. She wanted Danny to be there too but I talked her out of it. The sex was okay but what I was really trying to do was be in love. It didn't work. Maybe it was the wrong way. He just got used to getting sex and so he kept coming around all fall, going "Hey Starra baby you know you need it." He wouldn't even say that it was him that needed it. If I need it, I can do it a lot better myself than he can. I didn't tell him that. Although I nearly did when he kept not letting me alone after I told him to stop. If he hadn't finally started going with Dana I might would have told him.

I don't know anybody else here I can be in love with. I wish I could practice on Archie but what's the use while there's Gracie Fane? It would just be dumb. I thought about asking Archie's father, Mr. Hiddenstone, if I could work on his ranch, next time we get near it. I could still come see Mom, and maybe there would be like ranch hands or cowboys. Or Archie would come out sometimes and there wouldn't be Gracie. Or actually there's Mr. Hiddenstone. He looks like

Archie. Actually handsomer. But I guess he is too old. He has a face like the desert. I noticed his eyes are the same color as Mom's turquoise ring. But I don't know if he needs a cook or anything and I suppose fifteen is too young.

J. NEEDLESS

Never have figured out where the Hohovars come from. Somebody said White Russia. That figures. They're all big and tall and heavy with hair so blond it's white and those little blue eyes. They don't look at you. Noses like new potatoes. Women don't talk. Kids don't talk. Men talk like, "Vun case yeast peggets, tree case piggle beet." Never say hello, never say good-bye, never say thanks. But honest. Pay right up in cash. When they come in town they're all dressed head to foot, the women in these long dresses with a lot of fancy stuff around the bottom and sleeves, the little girls just the same as the women, even the babies in the same long stiff skirts, all of them with bonnet things that hide their hair. Even the babies don't look up. Men and boys in long pants and shirt and coat even when it's desert here and a hundred and five in July. Something like those Amish folk on the East Coast, I guess. Only the Hohovars have buttons. A lot of buttons. The vest things the women wear have about a thousand buttons. Men's flies the same. Must slow 'em down getting to the action. But everybody says buttons are no problem when they get back to their community. Everything off. Strip naked to go to their church. Tom Sunn swears to it, and Corrie says she used to sneak out there more than once on Sunday with a bunch of other kids to see the Hohovars all going over the hill buck naked, singing in their language. That would be some sight, all those tall, heavy-fleshed, white-skinned, big-ass, big-tit women parading over the hill. Barefoot, too. What the hell they do in church I don't know. Tom says they commit fornication but Tom Sunn don't know shit from a hole in the ground. All talk. Nobody I know has ever been over that hill.

Some Sundays you can hear them singing.

Now religion is a curious thing in America. According to the Christians there is only one of anything. On the contrary there seems to me to be one or more of everything. Even here in Ether we have, that I know of, Baptists of course, Methodists, Church of Christ, Lutheran, Presbyterian, Catholic (though no church in town), a Quaker, a lapsed Jew, a witch, the Hohovars, and the gurus or whatever that lot in the grange are. This is not counting most people, who have no religious affiliation except on impulse.

That is a considerable variety for a town this size. What's more, they try out each other's churches, switch around. Maybe the nature of the town makes us restless. Anyhow people in Ether generally live a long time, though not as long as Toby Walker. We have time to try out different things. My daughter Corrie has been a Baptist as a teenager, a Methodist while in love with Jim Fry, then had a go at the Lutherans. She was married Methodist but is now a Quaker, having read a book. This may change, as lately she has been talking to the witch, Pearl W. Amethyst, and reading another book, called *Crystals And You*.

Edna says the book is all tosh. But Edna has a harder mind than most.

Edna is my religion, I guess. I was converted years ago.

As for the people in the grange, the guru people, they caused some stir when they arrived ten years ago, or is it twenty now? Maybe it was in the sixties. Seems like they've been there a long time when I think about it. My wife was still alive. Anyhow, that's a case of religion mixed up some way with politics, not that it isn't always.

When they came to Ether they had a hell of a lot of money to throw around, though they didn't throw much my way. Bought the old grange and thirty acres of pasture adjacent. Put a fence right round and goddamn if they didn't electrify that fence. I don't mean the little jolt you might run in for steers but a kick would kill an elephant. Remodeled the old grange and built on barns and barracks and even a generator. Everybody inside the fence was to share everything in common with everybody else inside the fence. Though from outside the fence it looked like the Guru shared a lot more of it than the rest of 'em. That was the political part. Socialism. The bubonic socialism. Rats carry it and there is no vaccine. I tell you people here were upset. Thought the whole population behind the Iron Curtain plus all the hippies in California were moving in next Tuesday. Talked about bringing in the national guard to defend the rights of citizens. Personally I'd of preferred the hippies over the national guard. Hippies were unarmed. They killed by smell alone, as people said. But at the time there was a siege mentality here. A siege inside the grange, with their electric fence and their socialism, and a siege outside the grange, with their rights of citizens to be white and not foreign and not share anything with anybody.

At first the guru people would come into the town in their orange color T-shirts, doing a little shopping, talking politely. Young people got invited into the grange. They were calling it the osh rom by then. Corrie told me about the altar with the marigolds and the big photograph of Guru Jaya Jaya Jaya. But they weren't really friendly people and they didn't get friendly treatment. Pretty soon they never came into town, just drove in and out the road gate in their orange Buicks. Sometime along in there the Guru Jaya Jaya Jaya was supposed to come from India to visit the osh rom. Never did. Went to South America instead and founded an osh rom for old Nazis, they say. Old Nazis probably have more money to share with him than young Oregonians do. Or maybe he came to find his osh rom and it wasn't where they told him.

It has been kind of depressing to see the T-shirts fade and the Buicks break down. I don't guess there's more than two Buicks and ten, fifteen people left in the osh rom. They still grow garden truck, eggplants, all kinds of peppers, greens, squash, tomatoes, corn, beans, blue and rasp and straw and marion berries, melons. Good quality stuff. Raising crops takes some skill here where the climate will change overnight. They do beautiful irrigation and don't use poisons. Seen them out there picking bugs off the plants by hand. Made a deal with them some years ago to supply my produce counter and have not regretted it. Seems like Ether is meant to be a self-sufficient place. Every time I'd get a routine set up with a supplier in Cottage Grove or Prineville, we'd switch. Have to call up and say sorry, we're on the other side of the mountains again this week, cancel those cantaloupes. Dealing with the guru people is easier. They switch along with us.

What they believe in aside from organic gardening I don't know. Seems like the Guru Jaya Jaya Jaya would take some strenuous believing, but people can put their faith in anything, I guess. Hell, I believe in Edna.

ARCHIE HIDDENSTONE

Dad got stranded in town again last week. He hung around a while to see if the range would move back east, finally drove his old Ford over to Eugene and up the McKenzie River highway to get back to the ranch. Said he'd like to stay but Charlie Echevarria would be getting into some kind of trouble if he did. He just doesn't like to stay away from the place more than a night or two. It's hard on him when we turn up way over here on the coast like this.

I know he wishes I'd go back with him. I guess I ought to. I ought to live with him. I could see Mama every time Ether was over there. It isn't that. I ought to get it straight in my mind what I want to do. I ought to go to college. I ought to get out of this town. I ought to get away.

I don't think Gracie ever actually has seen me. I don't do anything she can see. I don't drive a semi.

I ought to learn. If I drove a truck she'd see me. I could come through Ether off the I-5 or down from 84, wherever. Like that shit kept coming here last summer she was so crazy about. Used to come into the 7-Eleven all the time for Gatorade. Called me Boy. Hey boy gimme the change in quarters. She'd be sitting up in his eighteen-wheeler playing with the gears. She never came in. Never even looked. I used to think maybe she was sitting there with her jeans off. Bareass on that truck seat. I don't know why I thought that. Maybe she was.

I don't want to drive a goddamn stinking semi or try to feed a bunch of steers in a goddamn desert either or sell goddamn Hostess Twinkies to crazy women with purple hair either. I ought to go to college. Learn something. Drive a sports car. A Miata. Am I going to sell Gatorade to shits all my life? I ought to be somewhere that is somewhere.

I dreamed the moon was paper and I lit a match and set fire to it. It flared up just like a newspaper and started dropping down fire on the roofs, scraps of burning. Mama came out of the grocery and said, "That'll take the ocean." Then I woke up. I heard the ocean where the sagebrush hills had been.

I wish I could make Dad proud of me anywhere but the ranch. But that's the only place he lives. He won't ever ask me to come live there. He knows I can't. I ought to.

EDNA

Oh how my children tug at my soul just as they tugged at my breasts, so that I want to yell, Stop! I'm dry! You drank me dry years ago! Poor sweet stupid Archie. What on earth to do for him. His father found the desert he needed. All Archie's found is a tiny little oasis he's scared to leave.

I dreamed the moon was paper, and Archie came out of the house with a box of matches and tried to set it afire, and I was frightened and ran into the sea.

Ady came out of the sea. There were no tracks on that beach that morning except his, coming up toward me from the breaker line. I keep thinking about the men lately. I keep thinking about Needless. I don't know why. I guess because I never married him. Some of them I wonder why I did, how it came about. There's no reason in it. Who'd ever have thought I'd ever sleep with Tom Sunn? But how could I go on saying no to a need like that? His fly bust every time he saw me across the street. Sleeping with him was like sleeping in a cave. Dark, uncomfortable, echoes, bears farther back in. Bones. But a fire burning. Tom's true soul is that fire burning, but he'll never know it. He starves the fire and smothers it with wet ashes, he makes himself the cave where he sits on cold ground gnawing bones. Women's bones.

But Mollie is a brand snatched from his burning. I miss Mollie. Next time we're over east again I'll go up to Pendleton and see her and the grandbabies. She doesn't come. Never did like the way Ether ranges. She's a stay-putter. Says all the moving around would make the children insecure. It didn't make her insecure in any harmful way that I can see. It's her Eric that would disapprove. He's a snob. Prison clerk. What a job. Walk out of a place every night where the others are all locked in, how's that for a ball and chain? Sink you if you ever tried to swim.

Where did Ady swim up from, I wonder? Somewhere deep. Once he said he was Greek, once he said he worked on an Australian ship, once he said he had lived on an island in the Philippines where they speak a language nobody else anywhere speaks, once he said he was born in a canoe at sea. It could all have been true. Or not. Maybe Archie should go to sea. Join the navy or the coast guard. But no, he'd drown.

Tad knows he'll never drown. He's Ady's son, he can breathe water. I wonder where Tad is now. That is a tugging too, that not knowing, not knowing where the child is, an aching pull you stop noticing because it never stops. But sometimes it turns you, you find you're facing another direction, like your body was caught by the thorn of a blackberry, by an undertow. The way the moon pulls the tides.

I keep thinking about Archie, I keep thinking about Needless. Ever since I saw him look at Sook. I know what it is, it's that other dream I had. Right after the one with Archie. I dreamed something, it's hard to get hold of, something about being on this long, long beach, like I was beached, yes, that's it, I was stranded, and I couldn't move. I was drying up and I couldn't get back to the water. Then I saw somebody walking toward me from way far away down the beach. His tracks in the sand were ahead of him. Each time he stepped in one, in the footprint, it was gone when he lifted his foot. He kept coming straight to me and I knew if he got to me I could get back in the water and be all right. When he got close up I saw it was him. It was Needless. That's an odd dream.

If Archie went to sea he'd drown. He's a drylander, like his father.

Sookie, now, Sook is Toby Walker's daughter. She knows it. She told me, once, I didn't tell her. Sook goes her own way. I don't know if he knows it. I don't think so. She has my eyes and hair. And there were some other possibilities. And I never felt it was the right thing to tell a man unless he asked. Toby didn't ask, because of what he believed about himself. But I knew the night, I knew the moment she was conceived. I felt the child-to-be leap in me like a fish leaping in the sea, a salmon coming up the river, leaping the rocks and rapids, shining. Toby had told me he couldn't have children—"not with any woman born," he said, with a sorrowful look. He came pretty near telling me where he came from, that night. But I didn't ask. Maybe because of what I believe about myself, that I only have the one life and no range, no freedom to walk in the hidden places.

Anyhow, I told him that that didn't matter, because if I felt like it I could conceive by taking thought. And for all I know that's what happened. I thought Sookie and out she came, red as a salmon, quick and shining. She is the most beautiful child, girl, woman. What does she want to stay here in Ether for? Be an old-maid teacher like Emma? Pump gas, give perms, clerk in the grocery? Who'll she meet here? Well God knows I met enough. I like it, she says, I like not knowing where I'll wake up. She's like me. But still there's the tug, the dry longing. Oh, I guess I had too many children. I turn this way, that way, like a compass with forty norths. Yet always going on the same way in the end. Fitting my feet into my footprints that disappear behind me.

It's a long way down from the mountains. My feet hurt.

TOBINYE WALKER

Man is the animal that binds time, they say. I wonder. We're bound by time, bounded by it. We move from a place to another place, but from a time to another time only in memory and intention, dream and prophecy. Yet time travels us. Uses us as its road, going on never stopping always in one direction. No exits off this freeway.

I say we because I am a naturalized citizen. I didn't used to be a citizen at all. Time once was to me what my backyard is to Emma's cat. No fences mattered, no boundaries. But I was forced to stop, to settle, to join. I am an American. I am a castaway. I came to grief.

I admit I've wondered if it's my doing that Ether ranges, doesn't stay put. An effect of my accident. When I lost the power to walk straight, did I impart a twist to the locality? Did it begin to travel because my traveling had ceased? If so, I can't work out the mechanics of it. It's logical, it's neat, yet I don't think it's the fact. Perhaps I'm just dodging my responsibility. But to the best of my memory, ever since Ether was a town it's always been a real American town, a place that isn't where you left it. Even when you live there it isn't where you think it is. It's missing. It's restless. It's off somewhere over the mountains, making up in one dimension what it lacks in another. If it doesn't keep moving the malls will catch it. Nobody's surprised it's gone. The white man's his own burden. And nowhere to lay it down. You can leave town easy enough, but coming back is tricky. You come back to where you left it and there's nothing but the parking lot for the new mall and a giant yellow grinning clown made of balloons. Is that all there was to it? Better not believe it, or that's all you'll ever have: blacktop and cinderblock and a blurred photograph of a little boy smiling. The child was murdered along with many others. There's more to it than that, there is an old glory in it, but it's hard to locate, except by accident. Only Roger Hiddenstone can come back when he wants to, riding his old Ford or his old horse, because Roger owns nothing but the desert and a true heart. And of course wherever Edna is, it is. It's where she lives.

I'll make my prophecy. When Starra and Roger lie in each other's tender arms, she sixteen, he sixty, when Gracie and Archie shake his pickup truck to pieces making love on the mattress in the back on the road out to the Hohovars, when Ervin Muth and Thomas Sunn get drunk with the farmers in the ashram and dance and sing and cry all night, when Emma Bodeley and Pearl Amethyst gaze long into each other's shining eyes among the cats, among the crystals—that same night Needless the grocer will come at last to Edna. To him she will bear no child but joy. And orange trees will blossom in the streets of Ether.

PAPER LANTERN
Stuart Dybek

Stuart Dybek is one of America's finest contemporary fiction writers. He is the author of *The Coast of Chicago, Childhood and Other Neighborhoods,* and *Brass Knuckles;* his short fiction has appeared in *The Atlantic Monthly, Ploughshares, The Iowa Review,* and the O. Henry Prize collections. Dybek lives in Kalamazoo, Michigan, where he teaches at Case Western Reserve University.

"Paper Lantern" is a powerful story exploring the mysterious nature of time. It is one of the finest stories of this or any other year, and it is a great pleasure to be able to include Dybek's work in this collection. The story comes from the November 27 issue of *The New Yorker.*

—T.W.

We were working late on the time machine in the little makeshift lab upstairs. The moon was stuck like the whorl of a frozen fingerprint to the skylight. In the back alley, the breaths left behind by yowling toms converged into a fog slinking out along the streets. Try as we might, our measurements were repeatedly off. In one direction, we'd reached the border at which clairvoyants stand gazing into the future, and in the other we'd gone backward to the zone where the present turns ghostly with memory and yet resists quite becoming the past. We'd been advancing and retreating by smaller and smaller degrees until it had come to seem as if we were measuring the immeasurable. Of course, what we really needed was some new vocabulary of measurement. It was time for a break.

Down the broken escalator, out the blue-lit lobby past the shuttered newsstand, through the frosty fog, hungry as strays we walk, still wearing our lab coats, to the Chinese restaurant around the corner.

It's a restaurant that used to be a Chinese laundry. When customers would come for their freshly laundered bundles, the cooking—wafting from the owner's back kitchen through the warm haze of laundry steam—smelled so good that the customers began asking if they could buy something to eat as well. And so the restaurant was born. It was a carryout place at first, but they've since wedged in a few tables. None of us can read Chinese, so we can't be sure, but since the proprietors never bothered to change the sign, presumably the Chinese characters still say it's a

Chinese laundry. Anyway, that's how the people in the neighborhood refer to it—the Chinese Laundry, as in, "Man, I had a sublime meal at the Chinese Laundry last night." Although they haven't changed the sign, the proprietors have added a large, red-ribbed paper lantern—their only nod to décor—that spreads its opaque glow across the steamy window.

We sit at one of the five Formica tables—our favorite, beside the window—and the waitress immediately brings the menu and tea. Really, in a way, this is the best part: the ruddy glow of the paper lantern like heat on our faces, the tiny, enamelled teacups warming our hands, the hot tea scalding our hunger, and the surprising, welcoming heft of the menu, hand-printed in Chinese characters, with what must be very approximate explanations in English of some of the dishes, also hand-printed, in the black ink of calligraphers. Each time we come here the menu has grown longer. Once a dish has been offered, it is never deleted, and now the menu is pages and pages long, so long that we'll never read through it all, never live long enough, perhaps, to sample all the food in just this one tucked-away, neighborhood Chinese restaurant. The pages are unnumbered, and we can never remember where we left off reading the last time we were here. Was it the chrysanthemum pot, served traditionally in autumn when the flowers are in full bloom, or the almond jelly with lichees and loquats?

"A poet wrote this menu," Tinker says between sips of tea.

"Yes, but if there's a poet in the house, then why doesn't this place have a real name—something like the Red Lantern—instead of merely being called the Chinese Laundry by default?" the Professor replies, wiping the steam from his glasses with a paper napkin from the dispenser on the table.

"I sort of like the Chinese Laundry, myself. It's got a solid, working-class ring. Red Lantern is a cliché—precious chinoiserie," Tinker argues.

They never agree.

"Say, you two, I thought we were here to devour aesthetics, not debate them."

Here, there's nothing of heaven or earth that can't be consumed, nothing they haven't found a way to turn into a delicacy: pine-nut porridge, cassia-blossom buns, fish-fragrance-sauced pigeon, swallow's-nest soup (a soup indigenous to the shore of the South China Sea; nests of predigested seaweed from the beaks of swifts, the gelatinous material hardened to form a small, translucent cup). Sea-urchin roe, pickled jellyfish, tripe with ginger and peppercorns, five-fragrance grouper cheeks, cloud ears, spun-sugar apple, ginkgo nuts and golden needles (which are the buds of lilies), purple seaweed, bitter melon . . .

Nothing of heaven and earth that cannot be combined, transmuted; no borders, in a wok, that can't be crossed. It's instructive. One can't help nourishing the imagination as well as the body.

We order, knowing we won't finish all they'll bring, and that no matter how carefully we ponder our choices we'll be served instead whatever the cook has made today.

After supper, sharing segments of a blood orange and sipping tea, we ceremoniously crack open our fortune cookies and read aloud our fortunes as if consulting the I Ching.

"*Sorrow is born of excessive joy.*"

"Try another."

"*Poverty is the common fate of scholars.*"

"Does that sound like a fortune to you?" Tinker asks.

"I certainly hope not," the Professor says.

"*When a finger points to the moon, the imbecile looks at the finger.*"

"What kind of fortunes are these? These aren't fortune cookies, these are proverb cookies," Tinker says.

"*In the Year of the Rat you will be lucky in love.*"

"Now that's more like it."

"What year is this?"

"The Year of the Dragon, according to the placemat."

"*Fuel alone will not light a fire.*"

"Say, did anyone turn off the Bunsen burner when we left?" The mention of the lab makes us signal for the check. It's time we headed back. A new theory was brewing there when we left, and now, our enthusiasm rekindled, we return in the snow—it has begun to snow—through thick, crumbling flakes mixed with wafting cinders that would pass for snowflakes except for the way the wind is fanning their edges to sparks. A night of white flakes and streaming orange cinders, strange and beautiful until we turn the corner and stare up at our laboratory.

Flames occupy the top floor of the building. Smoke billows out of the skylight, from which the sooty moon has retreated. On the floor below, through radiant, buckling windows, we can see the mannequins from the dressmaker's showroom. Naked, wigs on fire, they appear to gyrate lewdly before they topple. On the next floor down, in the instrument-repair shop, accordions wheeze in the smoke, violins seethe like green kindling, and the saxophones dissolve into a lava of molten brass cascading over a window ledge. While on the ground floor, in the display window, the animals in the taxidermist's shop have begun to hiss and snap as if fire had returned them to life in the wild.

We stare helplessly, still clutching the carryout containers of the food we were unable to finish from the blissfully innocent meal we sat sharing while our apparatus, our theories, our formulas, and years of research—all that people refer to as their "work"—were bursting into flame. Along empty, echoing streets, sirens are screaming like victims.

Already a crowd has gathered.

"Look at that seedy old mother go up," a white kid in dreadlocks says to his girlfriend, who looks like a runaway waif. She answers, "Cool!"

And I remember how, in what now seems another life, I watched fires as a kid—sometimes fires that a gang of us, calling ourselves the Matchheads, had set.

I remember how, later, in another time, if not another life, I once snapped a photograph of a woman I was with as she watched a fire blaze out of control along a river in Chicago. She was still married then. Her husband, whom I'd never met, was in a veteran's hospital—clinically depressed after the war in Vietnam. At least, that's what she told me about him. Thinking back, I sometimes wonder if she even had a husband. She had come to Chicago with me for a fling—her word. I thought at the time that we were just "fooling around"—also her words, words we both used in place of others like "fucking" or "making love" or "adultery." It was more comfortable, and safer, for me to think of things between us as fooling around, but when I offhandedly mentioned that to her she became furious, and instead of fooling around we spent our weekend in Chicago arguing, and ended up having a terrible time. It was a Sunday afternoon in early autumn, probably in the Year of the Rat, and we were sullenly driving out of the city. Along the north branch of the river, a factory was burning. I pulled over and parked, dug a camera out of my duffle, and we walked to a bridge to watch the fire.

But it's not the fire itself that I remember, even though the blaze ultimately spread across the city sky like a dusk that rose from the earth rather than descended. The fire, as I recall it, is merely a backdrop compressed within the boundaries of the photograph I took of her. She has just looked away from the blaze, toward the camera. Her elbows lean against the peeling gray railing of the bridge. She's wearing the black silk blouse that she bought at a secondhand shop on Clark Street the day before. Looking for clothes from the past in secondhand stores was an obsession of hers—"going junking," she called it. A silver Navajo bracelet has slid up her arm over a black silk sleeve. How thin her wrists appear. There's a ring whose gem I know is a moonstone on the index finger of her left hand, and a tarnished silver band around her thumb. She was left-handed, and it pleased her that I was, too, as if we both belonged to the same minority group. Her long hair is a shade of auburn all the more intense for the angle of late-afternoon sunlight. She doesn't look sullen or angry so much as fierce. Although later, studying her face in the photo, I'll come to see that beneath her expression there's a look less recognizable and more desperate: not loneliness, exactly, but *aloneness*—a look I'd seen cross her face more than once but wouldn't have thought to identify if the photo hadn't caught it. Behind her, ominous gray smoke plumes out of a sprawling old brick factory with the soon to be scorched white lettering of "Guttman & Co. Tanners" visible along the side of the building.

Driving back to Iowa in the dark, I'll think that she's asleep, as exhausted as I am from our strained weekend; then she'll break the miles of silence between us to tell me that, disappointing though it was, the trip was worth it if only for the two of us on the bridge, watching the fire together. She loved being part of the excitement, she'll say, loved the spontaneous way we swerved over and parked in order to take advantage of the spectacle—a conflagration the length of a city block, reflected over the greasy water, and a red fireboat, neat as a toy, sirening up the river, spouting white geysers while the flames roared back.

Interstate 80 shoots before us in the length of our racing headlight beams. We're on a stretch between towns, surrounded by flat black fields, and the candlepower of the occasional, distant farmhouse is insufficient to illuminate the enormous horizon lurking in the dark like the drop-off at the edge of the planet. In the speeding car, her voice sounds disembodied, the voice of a shadow, barely above a whisper, yet it's clear, as if the cover of night and the hypnotic momentum of the road have freed her to reveal secrets. There seemed to be so many secrets about her.

She tells me that as the number of strangers attracted by the fire swelled into a crowd she could feel a secret current connecting the two of us, like the current that passed between us in bed the first time we made love, when we came at the same moment as if taken by surprise. It happened only that once.

"Do you remember how, after that, I cried?" she asks.

"Yes."

"You were trying to console me. I know you thought I was feeling terribly guilty, but I was crying because the way we fit together seemed suddenly so familiar, as if there were some old bond between us. I felt flooded with relief, as if I'd been missing you for a long time without quite realizing it, as if you'd returned to me after I thought I'd never see you again. I didn't say any of that, because it sounds like some kind of channeling crap. Anyway, today the same feeling came over me on the bridge, and I was afraid I might start crying again, except this time what would be making me cry was the thought that if we *were* lovers from past lives who had waited lifetimes for the present to bring us back together, then how sad it was to waste the present the way we did this weekend."

I keep my eyes on the road, not daring to glance at her, or even to answer, for fear of interrupting the intimate, almost compulsive way she seems to be speaking.

"I had this sudden awareness," she continues, "of how the moments of our lives go out of existence before we're conscious of having lived them. It's only a relatively few moments that we get to keep and carry with us for the rest of our lives. Those moments *are* our lives. Or maybe it's more like those moments are the dots and what we call our lives are the lines we draw between them, connecting them into imaginary pictures of ourselves. You know? Like those mythical pictures of constellations traced between stars. I remember how, as a kid, I actually expected to be able to look up and see Pegasus spread out against the night, and when I couldn't it seemed like a trick had been played on me, like a fraud. I thought, Hey, if this is all there is to it, then I could reconnect the stars in any shape I wanted. I could create the Ken and Barbie constellations. . . . I'm rambling. . . ."

"I'm following you, go on."

She moves closer to me.

"I realized we can never predict when those few, special moments will occur," she says. "How, if we hadn't met, I wouldn't be standing on a bridge watching a fire, and how there are certain people, not that many, who enter one's life with the power to make those moments happen. Maybe that's what falling in love means—the power to create for each other the moments by which we define ourselves. And there you were, right on cue, taking my picture. I had an impulse to open my blouse, to take off my clothes and pose naked for you. I wanted you. I wanted—not to 'fool around.' I wanted to fuck you like there's no tomorrow against the railing of the bridge. I've been thinking about that ever since, this whole drive back."

I turn to look at her, but she says, "No . . . don't look. . . . Keep driving. . . . Shhh, don't talk. . . . I'm sealing your lips."

I can hear the rustle beside me as she raises her skirt, and a faint smack of moistness, and then, kneeling on the seat, she extends her hand and outlines my lips with her slick fingertips.

I can smell her scent; the car seems filled with it. I can feel the heat of her body radiating beside me, before she slides back along the seat until she's braced against the car door. I can hear each slight adjustment of her body, the rustle of fabric against her skin, the elastic sound of her panties rolled past her hips, the faintly wet, possibly imaginary tick her fingertips are making.

"Oh, baby," she sighs.

I've slowed down to fifty-five, and as semis pull into the passing lane and rumble by us, their headlights sweep through the car and I catch glimpses of her as if she'd been imprinted by lightning on my peripheral vision—dishevelled, her skirt hiked over her slender legs, the fingers of her left hand disappearing into the V of her rolled-down underpants.

"You can watch, if you promise to keep one eye on the road," she says and turns on the radio as if flicking on a night-light that coats her bare legs with its viridescence.

What was playing? The volume was so low I barely heard. A violin from some improperly tuned-in university station, fading in and out until it disappeared into static—banished, perhaps, to those phantom frequencies where Bix Beiderbecke still blew on his cornet. We were almost to Davenport, on the river, the town where Beiderbecke was born, and one station or another there always seemed to be playing his music, as if the syncopated licks of Roaring Twenties jazz, which had burned Bix up so quickly, still resonated over the prairie like his ghost.

"You can't cross I-80 between Iowa and Illinois without going through the Beiderbecke Belt," I had told her when we picked up a station broadcasting a Bix tribute on our way into Chicago. She had never heard of Bix until then and wasn't paying him much attention until the d.j. quoted a remark by Eddie Condon, an old Chicago guitarist, that "Bix's sound came out like a girl saying yes." That was only three days ago, and now we are returning, somehow changed from that couple who set out for a fling.

We cross the Beiderbecke Belt back into Iowa, and as we drive past the Davenport exists the nearly deserted highway is illuminated like an empty ballpark by the bluish overhead lights. Her eyes closed with concentration, she hardly notices as a semi, outlined in red clearance lights, almost sideswipes us. The car shudders in the backdraft as the truck pulls away, its horn bellowing.

"One eye on the road," she cautions.

"That wasn't my fault."

We watch its taillights disappear, and then we're alone in the highway dark again, traveling along my favorite stretch, where, in the summer, the fields are planted with sunflowers as well as corn, and you have to be on the alert for pheasants bolting across the road.

"Baby, take it out," she whispers.

The desire to touch her is growing unbearable, and yet I don't want to stop—don't want the drive to end.

"I'm waiting for you," she says. "I'm right on the edge just waiting for you."

We're barely doing forty when we pass what looks like the same semi, trimmed in red clearance lights, parked along the shoulder. I'm watching her while trying to keep an eye on the road, so I don't notice the truck pulling back onto the highway behind us or its headlights in the rearview mirror, gaining on us fast, until its high beams flash on, streaming through the car with a near-blinding intensity. I steady the wheel, waiting for the whump of the trailer's vacuum as it hurtles by, but the truck stays right on our rear bumper, its enormous radiator grill looming through the rear window, and its headlights reflecting off our mirrors and windshield with a glare that makes us squint. Caught in the high beams, her hair flares like a halo about to burst into flame. She's brushed her skirt down over her legs and looks a little wild.

"What's his problem? Is he stoned on uppers or something?" she shouts over the rumble of his engine, and then he hits his horn, obliterating her voice with a diesel blast.

I stomp on the gas. We're in the right lane, and, since he refuses to pass, I signal and pull into the outside lane to let him go by, but he merely switches lanes, too, hanging on our tail the entire time. The speedometer jitters over ninety, but he stays right behind us, his high beams pinning us like spotlights, his horn bellowing.

"Is he crazy?" she shouts.

I know what's happening. After he came close to sideswiping us outside Davenport, he must have gone on driving down the empty highway with the image of her illuminated by those bluish lights preying on his mind. Maybe he's divorced and lonely, maybe his wife is cheating on him—something's gone terribly wrong for him, and, whatever it is, seeing her exposed like that has revealed his own life as a sorry thing, and that realization has turned to meanness and anger.

There's an exit a mile off, and he sees it, too, and swings his rig back to the inside lane to try and cut me off, but with the pedal to the floor I beat him to the right-hand lane, and I keep it floored, although I know I can't manage a turnoff at this speed. He knows that, too, and stays close behind, ignoring my right-turn signal, laying on his horn as if to warn me not to try slowing down for this exit, that there's no way of stopping sixty thousand pounds of tractor-trailer doing over ninety.

But just before we hit the exit I swerve back into the outside lane, and for a moment he pulls even with us, staying on the inside as we race past the exit so as to keep it blocked. That's when I yell to her, "Hang on!" and pump the brakes, and we screech along the outside lane, fishtailing and burning rubber, while the truck goes barreling by, its air brakes whooshing. The car skids onto the gravel shoulder, kicking up a cloud of dust, smoky in the headlights, but it's never really out of control, and by the time the semi lurches to a stop, I have the car in reverse, veering back to the exit, hoping no one else is speeding toward us down I-80.

It's the Plainview exit, and I gun into a turn, north onto an empty two-lane, racing toward someplace named Long Grove. I keep checking the mirror for his headlights, but the highway behind us stays dark, and finally she says, "Baby, slow down."

The radio is still playing static, and I turn it off.

"Christ!" she says. "At first I thought he was just your everyday flaming asshole, but he was a genuine psychopath."

"A real lunatic, all right," I agree.

"You think he was just waiting there for us in his truck?" she asks. "That's so spooky, especially when you think he's still out there driving west. It makes you wonder how many other guys are out there, driving with their heads full of craziness and rage."

It's a vision of the road at night that I can almost see: men, not necessarily vicious—some just numb or desperately lonely—driving to the whining companionship of country music, their headlights too scattered and isolated for anyone to realize that they're all part of a convoy. We're a part of it, too.

"I was thinking, Oh, no, I can't die now, like this," she says. "It would be too sexually frustrating—like death was the ultimate tease."

"You know what I was afraid of," I tell her. "Dying with my trousers open."

She laughs and continues laughing until there's a hysterical edge to it.

"I think that truck driver was jealous of you. He knows you're a lucky guy tonight," she gasps, winded, and kicks off her sandal in order to slide a bare foot along my leg. "Here we are together, still alive."

I bring her foot to my mouth and kiss it, clasping her leg where it's thinnest, as if my hand were an ankle bracelet, then slide my hand beneath her skirt, along her thigh to the edge of her panties, a crease of surprising heat, from which my finger comes away slick.

"I told you," she moans. "A lucky guy."

I turn onto the next country road. It's unmarked, not that it matters. I know that out here, sooner or later, it will cross a gravel road, and when it does I turn onto the gravel, and after a while turn again at the intersection of a dirt road that winds into fields of an increasingly deeper darkness, fragrant with the rich Iowa earth and resonating with insect choirs amassed for one last Sanctus. I'm not even sure what direction we're traveling in any longer, let alone where we're going, but when my high beams catch a big turtle crossing the road I feel we've arrived. The car rolls to a stop on a narrow plank bridge spanning a culvert. The bridge—not much longer than our car—is veiled on either side by overhanging trees, cottonwoods probably, and flanked by cattails as high as the drying stalks of corn in the acres we've been passing. The turtle, his snapper's jaw unmistakable in the lights, looks mossy and ancient, and we watch him complete his trek across the road and disappear into the reeds before I flick off the headlights. Sitting silently in the dark, we listen to the crinkle of the cooling engine, and to the peepers we've disturbed starting up again from beneath the bridge. When we quietly step out of the car, we can hear frogs plopping into the water. "Look at the stars," she whispers.

"If Pegasus was up there," I say, "you'd see him from here."

"Do you have any idea where we are?" she asks.

"Nope. Totally lost. We can find our way back when it's light."

"The backseat of a car at night, on a country road—adultery has a disconcerting way of turning adults back into teenagers."

We make love, then manage to doze off for a while in the backseat, wrapped together in a checkered tablecloth we'd used once on a picnic, which I still had folded in the trunk.

In the pale, early light I shoot the rest of the film on the roll: a closeup of her, framed in part by the line of the checkered tablecloth, which she's wearing like a shawl around her bare shoulders, and another, closer still, of her face framed by her tangled auburn hair, and out the open window behind her, velvety cattails blurred in the shallow depth of field. A picture of her posing naked outside the car in sunlight that streams through countless rents in the veil of the cottonwoods. A picture of her kneeling on the muddy planks of the little bridge, her hazel eyes glancing up at the camera, her mouth, still a yard from my body, already shaped as if I've stepped to her across that distance.

What's missing is the shot I never snapped—the one the trucker tried to steal, which drove him over whatever edge he was balanced on, and which, perhaps, still has him riding highways, searching each passing car from the perch of his cab for that glimpse he won't get again—her hair disheveled, her body braced against the car door, eyes squeezed closed, lips twisted, skirt hiked up, pelvis rising to her hand.

Years after, she called me out of nowhere. "Do you still have those photos of me?" she asked.

"No," I told her, "I burned them."

"Good," she said, sounding pleased—not relieved so much as flattered—"I just suddenly wondered." Then she hung up.

But I lied. I'd kept them all these years, along with a few letters—part of a bundle of personal papers in a manila envelope that I moved with me from place to place. I had them hidden away in the back of a file cabinet in the laboratory, although certainly they had no business being there. Now what I'd told her was true: they were fueling the flames.

Outlined in firelight, the kid in dreadlocks kisses the waif. His hand glides over the back of her fringed jacket of dirty white buckskin and settles on the torn seat of her faded jeans. She stands on tiptoe on the tops of his gym shoes and hooks her fingers through the empty belt loops of his jeans so that their crotches are aligned. When he boosts her closer and grinds against her she says, "Wow!" and giggles. "I felt it move."

"Fires get me horny," he says.

The roof around the skylight implodes, sending a funnel of sparks into the whirl of snow and the crowd *ahs* collectively as the beakers in the laboratory pop and flare.

Gapers have continued to arrive down side streets, appearing out of the snowfall as if drawn by a great bonfire signaling some secret rite: gangbangers in their jackets engraved with symbols, gorgeous transvestites from Wharf Street, stevedores, and young sailors, their fresh tattoos contracting in the cold. The homeless, layered in overcoats, burlap tied around their feet, have abandoned their burning ashcans in order to gather here, just as the shivering, scantily clad hookers have abandoned their neon corners; as the Guatemalan dishwashers have abandoned their scalding suds; as a baker, his face and hair the ghostly white of flour, has abandoned his oven.

Open hydrants gush into the gutters; the street is seamed with deflated hoses, but the firemen stand as if paired off with the hookers—as if for a moment they've become voyeurs like everyone else, transfixed as the brick walls of our lab blaze suddenly lucent, suspended on a cushion of smoke, and the red-hot skeleton of the time machine begins to radiate from the inside out. A rosy light plays off the upturned faces of the crowd like the glow of an enormous red lantern—a paper lantern that once seemed fragile, almost delicate, but now obliterates the very time and space it once illuminated. A paper lantern raging out of control with nothing but itself left to consume.

"Brrrr." The Professor shivers, wiping his fogged glasses as if to clear away the opaque gleam reflecting off their lenses.

"Goddamn cold, all right," Tinker mutters, stamping his feet.

For once they agree.

The wind gusts, fanning the bitter chill of night even as it fans the flames, and instinctively we all edge closer to the fire.

LUNCH AT THE GOTHAM CAFÉ
Stephen King

Stephen King lives in Maine with his wife, the novelist Tabitha King. Perhaps the most popular writer of our generation, Stephen King is known best for his novels of suspense, both supernatural and psychological. His most recent novels are *Rose Madder* and *Insomnia*. His serial novel, *The Green Mile*, was published in six monthly installments beginning March 1996. King's short stories have been published in venues as diverse as *Omni*, *The New Yorker*, *Cemetery Dance*, *Shock Rock*, *Redbook*, and *The Magazine of Fantasy & Science Fiction*, *The Year's Best Fantasy & Horror*, and *Prize Stories: The O. Henry Awards*. He has published three collections of short stories: *Night Shift*, *Skeleton Crew*, and *Nightmares and Dreamscapes*, and two collections of novellas: *Different Seasons* and *Four Past Midnight*.

"Lunch at the Gotham Café," with its marvelously subtle buildup and deft characterizations, demonstrates King's continuing evolution and experimentation as a writer. It also demonstrates his continued ability to scare the bejeezus out of his readers. The story is reprinted from *Dark Love*, edited by Nancy A. Collins, Edward E. Kramer, and Martin H. Greenberg.

—E.D.

One day I came home from the brokerage house where I worked and found a letter—more of a note, actually—from my wife on the dining room table. It said she was leaving me, that she needed some time alone, and that I would hear from her therapist. I sat on the chair at the kitchen end of the table, reading this communication over and over again, not able to believe it. The only clear thought I remember having in the next half hour or so was *I didn't even know you had a therapist, Diane.*

After a while I got up, went into the bedroom, and looked around. All her clothes were gone (except for a joke sweatshirt someone had given her, with the words RICH BLOND printed on the front in spangly stuff), and the room had a funny dislocated look, as if she had gone through it, looking for something. I checked my stuff to see if she'd taken anything. My hands felt cold and distant while I did this, as if they had been shot full of some numbing drug. As far as I could tell, everything that was supposed to be there was there. I hadn't expected anything different, and yet the room had that funny look, as if she had *pulled* at it, the way she sometimes pulled on the ends of her hair when she felt exasperated.

I went back to the dining room table (which was actually at one end of the living room; it was only a four-room apartment) and read the six sentences she'd left behind over again. It was the same, but looking into the strangely rumpled bedroom and the half-empty closet had started me on the way to believing what it said. It was a chilly piece of work, that note. There was no "Love" or "Good luck" or even "Best" at the bottom of it. "Take care of yourself" was as warm as it got. Just below that she had scratched her name.

Therapist. My eye kept going back to that word. *Therapist.* I supposed I should have been glad it wasn't *lawyer*, but I wasn't. *You will hear from William Humboldt, my therapist.*

"Hear from this, sweetiepie," I told the empty room, and squeezed my crotch. It didn't sound tough and funny, as I'd hoped, and the face I saw in the mirror across the room was as pale as paper.

I walked into the kitchen, poured myself a glass of orange juice, then knocked it onto the floor when I tried to pick it up. The juice sprayed onto the lower cabinets and the glass broke. I knew I would cut myself if I tried to pick up the glass—my hands were shaking—but I picked it up anyway, and I cut myself. Two places, neither deep. I kept thinking that it was a joke, then realizing it wasn't. Diane wasn't much of a joker. But the thing was, I hadn't seen it coming. I didn't have a clue. What therapist? When did she see him? What did she talk about? Well, I supposed I knew what she talked about—me. Probably stuff about how I never remembered to put the ring down again after I finished taking a leak, how I wanted oral sex a tiresome amount of the time (how much was tiresome? I didn't know), how I didn't take enough interest in her job at the publishing company. Another question: how could she talk about the most intimate aspects of her marriage to a man named William Humboldt? He sounded like he should be a physicist at CalTech, or maybe a back-bencher in the House of Lords.

Then there was the Super Bonus Question: why hadn't I known *something* was up? How could I have walked into it like Sonny Liston into Cassius Clay's famous phantom uppercut? Was it stupidity? Insensitivity? As the days passed and I thought about the last six or eight months of our two-year marriage, I decided it had been both.

That night I called her folks in Pound Ridge and asked if Diane was there. "She is, and she doesn't want to talk to you," her mother said. "Don't call back." The phone went dead in my ear.

Two days later I got a call at work from the famous William Humboldt. After ascertaining that he was indeed speaking to Steven Davis, he promptly began calling me Steve. You may find that a trifle hard to believe, but it is nevertheless exactly what happened. Humboldt's voice was soft, small, and intimate. It made me think of a cat purring on a silk pillow.

When I asked after Diane, Humboldt told me that she was "doing as well as expected," and when I asked if I could talk to her, he said he believed that would be "counterproductive to her case at this time." Then, even more unbelievably (to my mind, at least) he asked in a grotesquely solicitous voice how I was doing.

"I'm in the pink," I said. I was sitting at my desk with my head down and my left hand curled around my forehead. My eyes were shut so I wouldn't have to look into the bright gray socket of my computer screen. I'd been crying a lot, and my eyes felt like they were full of sand. "Mr. Humboldt . . . it *is* mister, I take it, and not doctor?"

"I use mister, although I have degrees—"

"Mr. Humboldt, if Diane doesn't want to come home and doesn't want to talk to me, what *does* she want? Why did you call me?"

"Diane would like access to the safe-deposit box," he said in his smooth, purry little voice. "Your *joint* safe-deposit box."

I suddenly understood the punched, rumpled look of the bedroom and felt the first bright stirrings of anger. She had been looking for the key to the box, of course. She hadn't been interested in my little collection of pre–World War II silver dollars or the onyx pinkie ring she'd bought me for our first anniversary (we'd only had two in all) . . . but in the safe deposit box was the diamond necklace I'd given her, and about thirty thousand dollars' worth of negotiable securities. The key was at our little summer cabin in the Adirondacks, I realized. Not on purpose, but out of simple forgetfulness. I'd left it on top of the bureau, pushed way back amid the dust and the mouse turds.

Pain in my left hand. I looked down, saw my hand rolled into a tight fist, and rolled it open. The nails had cut crescents in the pad of the palm.

"Steve?" Humboldt was purring. "Steve, are you there?"

"Yes," I said. "I've got two things for you. Are you ready?"

"Of course," he said in that purry little voice, and for a moment I had a bizarre vision: William Humboldt blasting through the desert on a Harley-Davidson, surrounded by a pack of Hell's Angels. On the back of his leather jacket: BORN TO COMFORT.

Pain in my left hand again. It had closed up again on its own, just like a clam. This time when I unrolled it, two of the four little crescents were oozing blood.

"First," I said, "that box is going to stay closed unless some divorce court judge orders it opened in the presence of Diane's attorney and mine. In the meantime, no one is going to loot it, and that's a promise. Not me, not her." I paused. "Not you, either."

"I think that your hostile attitude is counterproductive," he said. "And if you examine your last few statements, Steve, you may begin to understand why your wife is so emotionally shattered, so—"

"Second," I overrode him (it's something we hostile people are good at), "I find you calling me by my first name patronizing and insensitive. Do it again on the phone and I'll hang up on you. Do it to my face and you'll find out just how hostile my attitude can be."

"Steve . . . Mr. Davis . . . I hardly think—"

I hung up on him. It was the first thing I'd done that gave me any pleasure since finding that note on the dining room table, with her three apartment keys on top of it to hold it down.

That afternoon I talked to a friend in the legal department, and he recommended a friend of his who did divorce work. I didn't want a divorce—I was furious at her, but had not the slightest question that I still loved her and wanted her back—but I didn't like Humboldt. I didn't like the *idea* of Humboldt. He made me nervous, him and his purry little voice. I think I would have preferred some hardball shyster who would have called up and said, *You give us a copy of that lockbox key before the close of business today, Davis, and maybe my client will relent and decide to leave you with something besides two pairs of underwear and your blood donor's card—got it?*

That I could have understood. Humboldt, on the other hand, felt sneaky.

The divorce lawyer was John Ring, and he listened patiently to my tale of woe. I suspect he'd heard most of it before.

"If I was entirely sure she wanted a divorce, I think I'd be easier in my mind," I finished.

"Be entirely sure," Ring said at once. "Humboldt's a stalking horse, Mr. Davis . . . and a potentially damaging witness if this drifts into court. I have no doubt that your wife went to a lawyer first, and when the lawyer found out about the missing lockbox key, he suggested Humboldt. A lawyer couldn't go right to you; that would be unethical. Come across with that key, my friend, and Humboldt will disappear from the picture. Count on it."

Most of this went right past me. I was concentrating on what he'd said first.

"You think she wants a divorce," I said.

"Oh, yes," he replied. "She wants a divorce. Indeed she does. And she doesn't intend to walk away from the marriage empty-handed."

I made an appointment with Ring to sit down and discuss things further the following day. I went home from the office as late as I could, walked back and forth through the apartment for a while, decided to go out to a movie, couldn't find anything I wanted to see, tried the television, couldn't find anything there to look at, either, and did some more walking. And at some point I found myself in the bedroom, standing in front of an open window fourteen floors above the street and chucking out all my cigarettes, even the stale old pack of Viceroys from the very back of my top desk drawer, a pack that had probably been there for ten years or more—since before I had any idea there was such a creature as Diane Coslaw in the world, in other words.

Although I'd been smoking between twenty and forty cigarettes a day for twenty years, I don't remember any sudden decision to quit, or any dissenting interior opinions—not even a mental suggestion that maybe two days after your wife walks out is not the optimum time to quit smoking. I just stuffed the full carton, the half carton, and the two or three half-used packs I found lying around out the window and into the dark. Then I shut the window (it never once crossed my mind that it might have been more efficient to throw the user out instead of the product; it was never *that* kind of situation), lay down on my bed, and closed my eyes.

The next ten days—the time during which I was going through the worst of the physical withdrawal from nicotine—were difficult and often unpleasant, but perhaps not as bad as I had thought they would be. And although I was on the verge of smoking dozens—no, hundreds—of times, I never did. There were moments when I thought I would go insane if I didn't have a cigarette, and when I passed people on the street who were smoking I felt like screaming *Give that to me, motherfucker, that's mine!*, but I didn't.

For me the worst times were late at night. I think (but I'm not sure; all my thought processes from around the time Diane left are very blurry in my mind) I had an idea that I would sleep better if I quit, but I didn't. I lay awake some mornings until three, hands laced together under my pillow, looking up at the ceiling, listening to sirens and to the rumble of trucks headed downtown. At those times I would think about the twenty-four-hour Korean market almost directly across the street from my building. I would think about the white fluorescent light inside, so bright it was almost like a Kubler-Ross near-death experience, and how it spilled out onto the sidewalk between the displays that, in another hour, two young Korean men in white paper hats would begin to fill with fruit. I would think about the older man behind the counter, also Korean, also in a paper hat, and the formidable racks of cigarettes behind him, as big as the stone tablets Charlton Heston had brought down from Mount Sinai in *The Ten Commandments*. I would think about getting up, dressing, going over there, getting a pack of cigarettes (or maybe nine or ten of them), and sitting by the window, smoking one Marlboro after another as the sky lightened to the east and the sun came up. I never did, but on many early mornings I went to sleep counting cigarette brands instead of sheep: Winston . . . Winston 100s . . . Virginia Slims . . . Doral . . . Merit . . . Merit 100s . . . Camels . . . Camel Filters . . . Camel Lights.

Later—around the time I was starting to see the last three or four months of our marriage in a clearer light, as a matter of fact—I began to understand that my decision to quit smoking when I had was perhaps not so unconsidered as it at first seemed, and a very long way from ill-considered. I'm not a brilliant man, not a brave one, either, but that decision might have been both. It's certainly possible; sometimes we rise above ourselves. In any case, it gave my mind something concrete to pitch upon in the days after Diane left; it gave my misery a vocabulary it would not otherwise have had, if you see what I mean. Very likely you don't, but I can't think of any other way to put it.

Have I speculated that quitting when I did may have played a part in what happened at the Gotham Café that day? Of course I have . . . but I haven't lost any sleep over it. None of us can predict the final outcomes of our actions, after all, and few even try; most of us just do what we do to prolong a moment's pleasure or to stop the pain for a while. And even when we act for the noblest reasons, the last link of the chain all too often drips with someone's blood.

Humboldt called me again two weeks after the evening when I'd bombed West 83rd Street with my cigarettes, and this time he stuck with Mr. Davis as a form of address. He asked me how I was doing, and I told him I was doing fine. With that amenity out of the way, he told me that he had called on Diane's behalf. Diane, he said, wanted to sit down with me and discuss "certain aspects" of the marriage. I suspected that "certain aspects" meant the key to the safe deposit box—not to mention various other financial issues Diane might want to investigate before hauling her lawyer onstage—but what my head knew and what my body was doing were completely different things. I could feel my skin flush and my heart speed up; I could feel a pulse tapping away in the wrist of the hand holding the phone. You have to remember that I hadn't seen her since the morning of the day she'd left, and even then I hadn't really seen her; she'd been sleeping with her face buried in her pillow.

Still I retained enough sense to ask him just what aspects we were talking about here.

Humboldt chuckled fatly in my ear and said he would rather save that for our actual meeting.

"Are you sure this is a good idea?" I asked. As a question, it was nothing but a time-buyer. I *knew* it wasn't a good idea. I also knew I was going to do it. I wanted to see her again. Felt I had to see her again.

"Oh, yes, I think so." At once, no hesitation. Any question that Humboldt and Diane had worked this out very carefully between them (and yes, very likely with a lawyer's advice) evaporated. "It's always best to let some time pass before bringing the principals together, a little cooling-off period, but in my judgment a face-to-face meeting at this time would facilitate—"

"Let me get this straight," I said. "You're talking about—"

"Lunch," he said. "The day after tomorrow? Can you clear that on your schedule?" *Of course you can,* his voice said. *Just to see her again . . . to experience the slightest touch of her hand. Eh, Steve?*

"I don't have anything on for lunch Thursday anyhow, so that's not a problem. And I should bring my . . . my own therapist?"

The fat chuckle came again, shivering in my ear like something just turned out of a Jell-O mold. "Do you have one, Mr. Davis?"

"No, actually, I don't. Did you have a place in mind?" I wondered for a moment who would be paying for this lunch, and then had to smile at my own naïveté. I reached into my pocket for a cigarette and poked the tip of a toothpick under my thumbnail instead. I winced, brought the pick out, checked the tip for blood, saw none, and stuck it in my mouth.

Humboldt had said something, but I had missed it. The sight of the toothpick had reminded me all over again that I was floating cigaretteless on the waves of the world.

"Pardon me?"

"I asked if you know the Gotham Café on 53rd Street," he said, sounding a touch impatient now. "Between Madison and Park."

"No, but I'm sure I can find it."

"Noon?"

I thought of telling him to tell Diane to wear the green dress with the little black speckles and the deep slit up the side, then decided that would probably be counterproductive. "Noon will be fine," I said.

We said the things that you say when you're ending a conversation with someone you already don't like but have to deal with. When it was over, I settled back in front of my computer terminal and wondered how I was possibly going to be able to meet Diane again without at least one cigarette beforehand.

It wasn't fine with John Ring, none of it.

"He's setting you up," he said. "They both are. Under this arrangement, Diane's lawyer is there by remote control and I'm not in the picture at all. It stinks."

Maybe, but you never had her stick her tongue in your mouth when she feels you start to come, I thought. But since that wasn't the sort of thing you could say to a lawyer you'd just hired, I only told him I wanted to see her again, see if there was a chance to salvage things.

He sighed.

"Don't be a *putz*. You see him at this restaurant, you see *her*, you break bread, you drink a little wine, she crosses her legs, you look, you talk nice, she crosses her legs again, you look some more, maybe they talk you into a duplicate of the safe deposit key—"

"They won't."

"—and the next time you see them, you'll see them in court, and everything damaging you said while you were looking at her legs and thinking about how it was to have them wrapped around you will turn up on the record. And you're apt to say a lot of damaging stuff, because they'll come primed with all the right questions. I understand that you want to see her, I'm not insensitive to these things, *but this is not the way.* You're not Donald Trump and she's not Ivana, but this isn't a no-faulter we got here, either, buddy, and Humboldt knows it. Diane does, too."

"Nobody's been served with papers, and if she just wants to talk—"

"Don't be dense," he said. "Once you get to this stage of the party, no one wants to just talk. They either want to fuck or go home. *The divorce has already happened, Steven.* This meeting is a fishing expedition, pure and simple. You have nothing to gain and everything to lose. It's stupid."

"Just the same—"

"You've done very well for yourself, especially in the last five years—"

"I know, but—"

"—and, for thuh-*ree* of those years," Ring overrode me, now putting on his courtroom voice like an overcoat, "Diane Davis was not your wife, not your live-in companion, and not by any stretch of the imagination your helpmate. She was just Diane Coslaw from Pound Ridge, and she did not go before you tossing flower petals or blowing a cornet."

"No, but I want to see her." And what I was thinking would have driven him mad: I wanted to see if she was wearing the green dress with the black speckles, because she knew damned well it was my favorite.

He sighed again. "I can't have this discussion, or I'm going to end up drinking my lunch instead of eating it."

"Go and eat your lunch. Diet plate. Cottage cheese."

"Okay, but first I'm going to make one more effort to get through to you. A meeting like this is like a joust. They'll show up in full armor. You're going to be there dressed in nothing but a smile, without even a jock to hold up your balls. And that's exactly the region of your anatomy they're apt to go for first."

"I want to see her," I said. "I want to see how she is. I'm sorry."

He uttered a small, cynical laugh. "I'm not going to talk you out of it, am I?"

"No."

"All right, then I want you to follow certain instructions. If I find out you haven't, and that you've gummed up the works, I may decide it would be simpler to just resign the case. Are you hearing me?"

"I am."

"Good. Don't yell at her, Steven. They may set it up so you really feel like doing that, but *don't.* Okay?"

"Okay." I wasn't going to yell at her. If I could quit smoking two days after she had walked out—and stick to it—I thought I could get through a hundred minutes and three courses without calling her a bitch.

"Don't yell at *him,* that's number two."

"Okay."

"Don't just say okay. I know you don't like him, and he doesn't like you much, either."

"He's never even met me. He's a . . . a therapist. How can he have an opinion about me one way or another?"

"Don't be dense," he said. "He's being *paid* to have an opinion, that's how. If she tells him you flipped her over and raped her with a corncob, he doesn't say prove it, he says oh you poor thing and how many times. So say okay like you mean it."

"Okay like I mean it."

"Better." But *he* didn't say it like he really meant it; he said it like a man who wants to eat his lunch and forget the whole thing.

"Don't get into substantive matters," he said. "Don't discuss financial-settlement issues, not even on a 'What would you think if I suggested this' basis. Stick with all the touchy-feely stuff. If they get pissed off and ask why you kept the lunch date if you weren't going to discuss nuts and bolts, tell them just what you told me, that you wanted to see your wife again."

"Okay."

"And if they leave at that point, can you live with it?"

"Yes." I didn't know if I could or not, but I thought I could, and I strongly sensed that Ring wanted to be done with this conversation.

"As a lawyer—your lawyer—I'm telling you that this is a bullshit move, and that if it backfires in court, I'll call a recess just so I can pull you out into the hall and say I told you so. Now, have you got that?"

"Yes. Say hello to that diet plate for me."

"Fuck the diet plate," Ring said morosely. "If I can't have a double bourbon on the rocks at lunch anymore, I can at least have a double cheeseburger at Brew 'n Burger."

"*Rare*," I said.

"That's right, rare."

"Spoken like a true American."

"I hope she stands you up, Steven."

"I know you do."

He hung up and went out to get his alcohol substitute. When I saw him next, a few days later, there was something between us that didn't quite bear discussion, although I think we would have talked about it if we had known each other even a little bit better. I saw it in his eyes and I suppose he saw it in mine as well—the knowledge that if Humboldt had been a lawyer instead of a therapist, he, John Ring, would have been in on our luncheon meeting. And in that case he might have wound up as dead as William Humboldt.

I walked from my office to the Gotham Café, leaving at 11:15 and arriving across from the restaurant at 11:45. I got there early for my own peace of mind—to make sure the place was where Humboldt had said it was, in other words. That's the way I am, and pretty much the way I've always been. Diane used to call it "my obsessive streak" when we were first married, but I think that by the end she knew better. I don't trust the competence of others very easily, that's all. I realize it's a pain-in-the-ass characteristic, and I know it drove her crazy, but what she never seemed to realize was that I didn't exactly love it in myself, either. Some things take longer to change than others, though. And some things you can never change, no matter how hard you try.

The restaurant was right where Humboldt had said it would be, the location marked by a green awning with the words GOTHAM CAFÉ on it. A white city skyline was traced across the plate glass windows. It looked New York trendy. It also looked pretty ordinary, just one of the eight hundred or so pricey restaurants crammed together in Midtown.

With the meeting place located and my mind temporarily set at rest (about that, anyway; I was tense as hell about seeing Diane again and craving a cigarette like mad), I walked up to Madison and browsed in a luggage store for fifteen minutes. Mere window-shopping was no good; if Diane and Humboldt came from uptown, they might see me. Diane was liable to recognize me by the set of my shoulders and the hang of my topcoat even from behind, and I didn't want that. I didn't want them to know I'd arrived early. I thought it might look needy, even pitiable. So I went inside.

I bought an umbrella I didn't need and left the shop at straight-up noon by my watch, knowing I could step through the door of the Gotham Café at 12:05. My father's dictum: if you need to be there, show up five minutes early. If they need *you* to be there, show up five minutes late. I had reached a point where I didn't know who needed what or why or for how long, but my father's dictum seemed like the safest course. If it had been just Diane alone, I think I would have arrived dead on time.

No, that's probably a lie. I suppose if it had been just Diane, I would have gone in at 11:45, when I first arrived, and waited for her.

I stood under the awning for a moment, looking in. The place was bright, and I marked that down in its favor. I have an intense dislike for dark restaurants, where you can't see what you're eating or drinking. The walls were white and hung with vibrant impressionist paintings. You couldn't tell what they were, but that didn't matter; with their primary colors and broad, exuberant strokes, they hit your eyes like visual caffeine. I looked for Diane and saw a woman that might have been her, seated about halfway down the long room and by the wall. It was hard to say, because her back was turned and I don't have her knack of recognition under difficult circumstances. But the heavyset, balding man she was sitting with certainly looked like a Humboldt. I took a deep breath, opened the restaurant door, and went in.

There are two phases of withdrawal from tobacco, and I'm convinced that it's the second that causes most cases of recidivism. The physical withdrawal lasts ten days to two weeks, and then most of the symptoms—sweats, headaches, muscle twitches, pounding eyes, insomnia, irritability—disappear. What follows is a much longer period of mental withdrawal. These symptoms may include mild to moderate depression, mourning, some degree of anhedonia (emotional flatness, in other words), forgetfulness, even a species of transient dyslexia. I know all this stuff because I read up on it. Following what happened at the Gotham Café, it seemed very important that I do that. I suppose you'd have to say that my interest in the subject fell somewhere between the Land of Hobbies and the Kingdom of Obsession.

The most common symptom of phase-two withdrawal is a feeling of mild unreality. Nicotine improves synaptic transferral and improves concentration—widens the brain's information highway, in other words. It's not a big boost, and not really necessary to successful thinking (although most confirmed cigarette junkies believe differently), but when you take it away, you're left with a feeling—a pervasive feeling, in my case—that the world has taken on a decidedly dreamy cast. There were many times when it seemed to me that people and cars and the little sidewalk vignettes I observed were actually passing by me on a moving screen, a thing controlled by hidden stagehands turning enormous cranks and revolving enormous drums. It was also a little like being mildly stoned all the time, because the feeling was accompanied by a sense of helplessness and moral exhaustion, a feeling that things had to simply go on the way they were going, for good or for ill, because you (except of course it's me I'm talking about) were just too damned busy *not-smoking* to do much of anything else.

I'm not sure how much all this bears on what happened, but I know it has some bearing, because I was pretty sure something was wrong with the maître d' almost as soon as I saw him, and as soon as he spoke to me, I knew.

He was tall, maybe forty-five, slim (in his tux, at least; in ordinary clothes he would have been skinny), mustached. He had a leather-bound menu in one hand. He looked like battalions of maître d's in battalions of fancy New York restaurants, in other words. Except for his bow tie, which was askew, and something on his shirt, that is. A splotch just above the place where his jacket buttoned. It looked like either gravy or a glob of some dark jelly. Also, several strands of his hair stuck up defiantly in back, making me think of Alfalfa in the old *Little Rascals* one-reelers. That almost made me burst out laughing—I was very nervous, remember—and I had to bite my lips to keep it in.

"Yes, sir?" he asked as I approached the desk. It came out sounding like *Yais, sair?* All maître d's in New York City have accents, but it is never one you can positively identify. A girl I dated in the mideighties, one who did have a sense of humor (along with a fairly large drug habit, unfortunately), told me once that they all grew up on the same little island and hence all spoke the same language.

"What language is it?" I asked her.

"Snooti," she said, and I cracked up.

This thought came back to me as I looked past the desk to the woman I'd seen while outside—I was now almost positive it was Diane—and I had to bite the insides of my lips again. As a result, Humboldt's name came out of me sounding like a half-smothered sneeze.

The maître d's high, pale brow contracted in a frown. His eyes bored into mine. I had taken them for brown as I approached the desk, but now they looked black.

"Pardon, sir?" he asked. It came out sounding like *Pahdun, sair* and looking like *Fuck you, Jack*. His long fingers, as pale as his brow—concert pianist's fingers, they looked like—tapped nervously on the cover of the menu. The tassel sticking out of it like some sort of half-assed bookmark swung back and forth.

"Humboldt," I said. "Party of three." I found I couldn't take my eyes off his bow tie, so crooked that the left side of it was almost brushing the shelf under his chin, and that blob on his snowy white dress shirt. Now that I was closer, it didn't look like either gravy or jelly; it looked like partially dried blood.

He was looking down at his reservations book, the rogue tuft at the back of his head waving back and forth over the rest of his slicked-down hair. I could see his scalp through the grooves his comb had laid down, and a speckle of dandruff on the shoulders of his tux. It occurred to me that a good headwaiter might have fired an underling put together in such sloppy fashion.

"Ah, yes, *monsieur*." (*Ah yais, messoo*.) He had found the name. "Your party is—" He was starting to look up. He stopped abruptly, and his eyes sharpened even more, if that was possible, as he looked past me and down. "You cannot bring that dog in here," he said sharply. "How many times have I told you you can't bring that *dog* in here!"

He didn't quite shout, but spoke so loudly that several of the diners closest to his pulpitlike desk stopped eating and looked around curiously.

I looked around myself. He had been so emphatic I expected to see *somebody's* dog, but there was no one behind me and most certainly no dog. It occurred to me then, I don't know why, that he was talking about my umbrella, which I had forgotten to check. Perhaps on the Island of the Maître D's, *dog* was a slang term for umbrella, especially when carried by a patron on a day when rain did not look likely.

I looked back at the maître d' and saw that he had already started away from his desk, holding my menu in his hands. He must have sensed that I wasn't following, because he looked back over his shoulder, eyebrows slightly raised. There was nothing on his face now but polite inquiry—*Are you coming, messoo?*—and I came. I knew something was wrong with him, but I came. I could not take the time or effort to try to decide what might be wrong with the maître d' of a restaurant where I had never been before today and where I would probably never be again; I had Humboldt and Diane to deal with, I had to do it without smoking, and the maître d' of the Gotham Café would have to take care of his own problems, dog included.

Diane turned around and at first I saw nothing in her face and in her eyes but a kind of frozen politeness. Then, just below it, I saw anger . . . or thought I did. We'd done a lot of arguing during our last three or four months together, but I couldn't recall ever seeing the sort of concealed anger I sensed in her now, anger that was meant to be hidden by the makeup and the new dress (blue, no speckles, no slit up the side, deep or otherwise) and the new hairdo. The heavyset man she was with was saying something, and she reached out and touched his arm. As he turned toward me, beginning to get to his feet, I saw something else in her face. She was afraid of me as well as angry at me. And although she hadn't said a single word, I was already furious at her. The expression in her eyes was a dead negative; she might as well have been wearing a CLOSED UNTIL FURTHER NOTICE sign on her forehead between them. I thought I deserved better. Of course, that may just be a way of saying I'm human.

"Monsieur," the maître d' said, pulling out the chair to Diane's left. I barely heard him, and certainly any thought of his eccentric behavior and crooked bow tie had left my head. I think that even the subject of tobacco had briefly vacated my head for the first time since I'd quit smoking. I could only consider the careful composure of her face and marvel at how I could be angry at her and still want her so much it made me ache to look at her. Absence may or may not make the heart grow fonder, but it certainly freshens the eye.

I also found time to wonder if I had really seen all I'd surmised. Anger? Yes, that was possible, even likely. If she hadn't been angry with me to at least some degree, she never would have left in the first place, I supposed. But afraid? Why in God's name would Diane be afraid of me? I'd never laid a single finger on her. Yes, I suppose I had raised my voice during some of our arguments, but so had she.

"Enjoy your lunch, monsieur," the maître d' said from some other universe—the one where service people usually stay, only poking their heads into ours when we call them, either because we need something or to complain.

"Mr. Davis, I'm Bill Humboldt," Diane's companion said. He held out a large hand that looked reddish and chapped. I shook it briefly. The rest of him was as big as his hand, and his broad face wore the sort of flush habitual drinkers often get after the first one of the day. I put him in his midforties, about ten years away from the time when his sagging cheeks would turn into jowls.

"Pleasure," I said, not thinking about what I was saying any more than I was thinking about the maître d' with the blob on his shirt, only wanting to get the hand-shaking part over so I could turn back to the pretty blonde with the rose-and-cream complexion, the pale pink lips, and the trim, slim figure. The woman who had, not so long ago, liked to whisper "Do me do me do me" in my ear while she held onto my ass like a saddle with two pommels.

"We'll get you a drink," Humboldt said, looking around for a waiter like a man who did it a lot. Her therapist had all the bells and whistles of the incipient alcoholic. Wonderful.

"Perrier and lime is good."

"For what?" Humboldt inquired with a big smile. He picked up the half-finished martini in front of him on the table and drained it until the olive with the toothpick in it rested against his lips. He spat it back, then set the glass down and looked at me. "Well, perhaps we'd better get started."

I paid no attention. I already *had* gotten started; I'd done it the instant Diane looked up at me. "Hi, Diane," I said. It was marvelous, really, how she looked smarter and prettier than previous. More desirable than previous, too. As if she had learned things—yes, even after only two weeks of separation, and while living with Ernie and Dee Dee Coslaw in Pound Ridge—that I could never know.

"How are you, Steve?" she asked.

"Fine," I said. Then, "Not so fine, actually. I've missed you."

Only watchful silence from the lady greeted this. Those big blue-green eyes looking at me, no more. Certainly no return serve, no *I've missed you, too*.

"And I quit smoking. That's also played hell with my peace of mind."

"Did you, finally? Good for you."

I felt another flash of anger, this time a really ugly one, at her politely dismissive tone. As if I might not be telling the truth, but it didn't really matter if I was. She'd carped at me about the cigarettes every day for two years, it seemed—how they were going to give me cancer, how they were going to give *her* cancer, how she wouldn't even consider getting pregnant until I stopped, so I could just save any breath I might have been planning to waste on *that* subject—and now all at once it didn't matter anymore, because *I* didn't matter anymore.

"Steve—Mr. Davis," Humboldt said, "I thought we might begin by getting you to look at a list of grievances that Diane has worked out during our sessions—our exhaustive sessions, I might say—over the last couple of weeks. Certainly it can serve as a springboard to our main purpose for being here, which is how to order a period of separation that will allow growth on both of your parts."

There was a briefcase on the floor beside him. He picked it up with a grunt and set it on the table's one empty chair. Humboldt began unsnapping the clasps, but I quit paying attention at that point. I wasn't interested in springboards to separation, whatever that meant. I felt a combination of panic and anger that was, in some ways, the most peculiar emotion I have ever experienced.

I looked at Diane and said, "I want to try again. Can we reconcile? Is there any chance of that?"

The look of absolute horror on her face crashed hopes I hadn't even known I'd been holding onto. Horror was followed by anger. "Isn't that just like you!" she exclaimed.

"Diane—"

"Where's the safe-deposit box key, Steven? Where did you hide it?"

Humboldt looked alarmed. He reached out and touched her arm. "Diane . . . I thought we agreed—"

"What we agreed is that this son of a bitch will hide everything under the nearest rock and then plead poverty if we let him!"

"You searched the bedroom for it before you left, didn't you?" I asked quietly. "Tossed it like a burglar."

She flushed at that. I don't know if it was shame, anger, or both. "It's my box as well as yours! My *things* as well as yours!"

Humboldt was looking more alarmed than ever. Several diners had glanced around at us. Most of them looked amused, actually. People are surely God's most bizarre creatures. "Please . . . please, let's not—"

"Where did you hide it, Steven?"

"I didn't hide it. I never hid it. I left it up at the cabin by accident, that's all."

She smiled knowingly. "Oh, yes. By accident. Uh-huh." I said nothing, and the knowing smile slipped away. "I want it," she said, then amended hastily: "I want a *copy*."

People in hell want icewater, I thought. Out loud I said, "There's nothing to be done about it, is there?"

She hesitated, maybe hearing something in my voice she didn't actually want to hear, or to acknowledge. "No," she said. "The next time you see me, it will be with my lawyer. I'm divorcing you."

"Why?" What I heard in my voice now was a plaintive note like a sheep's bleat. I didn't like it, but there wasn't a goddamned thing I could do about it. "*Why?*"

"Oh, Jesus. Do you expect me to believe you're really that dense?"

"I just can't—"

Her cheeks were brighter than ever, the flush now rising almost to her temples. "Yes, probably you expect me to believe just that very thing. Isn't that *typical*." She picked up her water and spilled the top two inches on the tablecloth because her hand was trembling. I flashed back at once—I mean *kapow*—to the day she'd left, remembering how I'd knocked the glass of orange juice onto the floor and how I'd cautioned myself not to try picking up the broken pieces of glass until my hands had settled down, and how I'd gone ahead anyway and cut myself for my pains.

"Stop it, this is counterproductive," Humboldt said. He sounded like a playground monitor trying to stop a scuffle before it gets started, but he seemed to have forgotten all about Diane's shit-list; his eyes were sweeping the rear part of the room, looking for our waiter, or any waiter whose eye he could catch. He was a lot less interested in therapy, at that particular moment, than he was in obtaining what the British like to call the other half.

"I only want to know—" I began.

"What you want to *know* doesn't have anything to do with why we're *here*," Humboldt said, and for a moment he actually sounded alert.

"Yes, right, *finally*," Diane said. She spoke in a brittle, urgent voice. "Finally it's not about what you *want*, what you *need*."

"I don't know what that means, but I'm willing to listen," I said. "If you wanted to try joint counseling instead of . . . uh . . . therapy . . . whatever it is Humboldt does . . . I'm not against it if—"

She raised her hands to shoulder level, palms out. "Oh, God, Joe Camel goes New Age," she said, then dropped her hands back into her lap. "After all the days you rode off into the sunset, tall in the saddle. Say it ain't so, Joe."

"Stop it," Humboldt told her. He looked from his client to his client's soon-to-be ex-husband (it was going to happen, all right; even the slight unreality that comes with *not-smoking* couldn't conceal that self-evident truth from me by that point). "One more word from either of you and I'm going to declare this luncheon at an end." He gave us a small smile, one so obviously manufactured that I found it perversely endearing. "And we haven't even heard the specials yet."

That—the first mention of food since I'd joined them—was just before the bad things started to happen, and I remember smelling salmon from one of the nearby tables. In the two weeks since I'd quit smoking, my sense of smell had become incredibly sharp, but I do not count that as much of a blessing, especially when it comes to salmon. I used to like it, but now I can't abide the smell of it, let alone the taste. To me it smells of pain and fear and blood and death.

"He started it," Diane said sulkily.

You *started it*, you *were the one who tossed the joint and then walked out when you couldn't find what you wanted*, I thought, but I kept it to myself. Humboldt clearly meant what he said; he would take Diane by the hand and walk her out of the restaurant if we started that schoolyard *no-I-didn't*, *yes-you-did* shit. Not even the prospect of another drink would hold him here.

"Okay," I said mildly . . . and I had to work hard to achieve that mild tone, believe me. "I started it. What's next?" I knew, of course: the grievances. Diane's shit-list, in other words. And a lot more about the key to the lockbox. Probably the only satisfaction I was going to get out of this sorry situation was telling them that neither of them was going to see a copy of that key until an officer of the court presented me with a paper ordering me to turn one over. I hadn't touched the stuff in the box since Diane booked on out of my life, and I didn't intend to touch any of it in the immediate future . . . but she wasn't going to touch it, either. Let her chew crackers and try to whistle, as my grandmother used to say.

Humboldt took out a sheaf of papers. They were held together by one of those designer paper clips—the ones that come in different colors. It occurred to me that I had arrived abysmally unprepared for this meeting, and not just because my lawyer was jaw-deep in a cheeseburger somewhere, either. Diane had her new dress; Humboldt had his designer briefcase, plus Diane's shit-list held together by a color-coded designer paper clip; all I had was a new umbrella on a sunny day. I looked down at where it lay beside my chair and saw there was still a price tag dangling from the handle. All at once I felt like Minnie Pearl.

The room smelled wonderful, as most restaurants do since they banned smoking in them—of flowers and wine and fresh coffee and chocolate and pastry—but what I smelled most clearly was salmon. I remember thinking that it smelled very good, and that I would probably order some. I also remember thinking that if I could eat at a meeting like this, I could probably eat anywhere.

"The major problems your wife has articulated—so far, at least—are insensitivity on your part regarding her job, and an inability to trust in personal affairs," Humboldt said. "In regard to the second, I'd say your unwillingness to give Diane fair access to the safe-deposit box you maintain in common pretty well sums up the trust issue."

I opened my mouth to tell him I had a trust issue, too, that I didn't trust Diane not to take the whole works and then sit on it. Before I could say anything, however, I was interrupted by the maître d'. He was screaming as well as talking, and I've tried to indicate that, but a bunch of *e*'s strung together can't really convey the quality of that sound. It was as if he had a bellyful of steam and a teakettle whistle caught in his throat.

"*That dog . . . eeeeeeee! . . . I told you time and again about that dog. . . . Eeeeeee! . . . All that time I can't sleep. . . . Eeeeeee! . . . She says cut your face, that cunt. . . . Eeeeeee! . . . How you tease me! . . . Eeeeeee! . . . And now you bring that dog in here. . . . Eeeeeee!*"

The room fell silent at once, of course, diners looking up from their meals or their conversations as the thin, pale, black-clad figure came stalking across the room with its face outthrust and its long, storklike legs scissoring. No amusement on the surrounding faces now; only astonishment. The maître d's bow tie had turned a full ninety degrees from its normal position, so it now looked like the hands of a clock indicating the hour of six. His hands were clasped behind his back as he walked, and bent forward slightly from the waist as he was, he made me think of a drawing in my sixth-grade literature book, an illustration of Washington Irving's unfortunate schoolteacher, Ichabod Crane.

It was me he was looking at, me he was approaching. I stared at him, feeling almost hypnotized—it was like one of those dreams where you discover that you haven't studied for the bar exam you're supposed to take or that you're attending a White House dinner in your honor with no clothes on—and I might have stayed that way if Humboldt hadn't moved.

I heard his chair scrape back and glanced at him. He was standing up, his napkin held loosely in one hand. He looked surprised, but he also looked furious. I suddenly realized two things: that he was drunk, quite drunk, in fact, and that he saw this as a smirch on both his hospitality and his competence. He had chosen the restaurant, after all, and now look—the master of ceremonies had gone bonkers.

"*Eeeeee! . . . I teach you! For the last time I teach you . . .*"

"Oh, my God, he's wet his pants," a woman at a nearby table murmured. Her voice was low but perfectly audible in the silence as the maître d' drew in a fresh breath with which to scream, and I saw she was right. The crotch of the skinny man's dress pants was soaked.

"See here, you idiot," Humboldt said, turning to face him, and the maître d' brought his left hand out from behind his back. In it was the largest butcher knife I have ever seen. It had to have been two feet long, with the top part of its cutting edge slightly belled, like a cutlass in an old pirate movie.

"*Look out!*" I yelled at Humboldt, and at one of the tables against the wall, a skinny man in rimless spectacles screamed, ejecting a mouthful of chewed brown fragments of food onto the tablecloth in front of him.

Humboldt seemed to hear neither my yell nor the other man's scream. He was frowning thunderously at the maître d'. "You don't need to expect to see me in here again if this is the way—" Humboldt began.

"*Eeeeee! EEEEEEEEE!*" the maître d' screamed, and swung the butcher knife flat through the air. It made a kind of whickering sound, like a whispered sentence. The period was the sound of the blade burying itself in William Humboldt's right cheek. Blood exploded out of the wound in a furious spray of tiny droplets. They decorated the tablecloth in a fan-shaped stipplework, and I clearly saw (I will never forget it) one bright red drop fall into my water glass and then dive for the bottom with a pinkish filament like a tail stretching out behind it. It looked like a bloody tadpole.

Humboldt's cheek snapped open, revealing his teeth, and as he clapped his hand to the gouting wound, I saw something pinkish-white lying on the shoulder of his charcoal gray suitcoat. It wasn't until the whole thing was over that I realized it must have been his earlobe.

"*Tell this in your ears!*" the maître d' screamed furiously at Diane's bleeding therapist, who stood there with one hand clapped to his cheek. Except for the blood pouring over and between his fingers, Humboldt looked weirdly like Jack Benny doing one of his famous double-takes. "*Call this to your hateful tattle-tale friends of the street . . . you misery . . . eeeeee! . . . DOG LOVER!*"

Now other people were screaming, mostly at the sight of the blood, I think. Humboldt was a big man, and he was bleeding like a stuck pig. I could hear it pattering on the floor like water from a broken pipe, and the front of his white shirt was now red. His tie, which had been red to start with, was now black.

"Steve?" Diane said. "*Steven?*"

A man and a woman had been having lunch at the table behind her and slightly to her left. Now the man—about thirty and handsome in the way George Hamilton used to be—bolted to his feet and ran toward the front of the restaurant. "*Troy, don't go without me!*" his date screamed, but Troy never looked back. He'd forgotten all about a library book he was supposed to return, it seemed, or maybe about how he'd promised to wax the car.

If there had been a paralysis in the room—I can't actually say if there was or not, although I seem to have seen a great deal, and to remember it all—that broke it. There were more screams and other people got up. Several tables were overturned. Glasses and china shattered on the floor. I saw a man with his arm around the waist of his female companion hurry past behind the maître d'; her hand was clamped into his shoulder like a claw. For a moment her eyes met mine, and they were as empty as the eyes of a Greek bust. Her face was dead pale, haglike with horror.

All of this might have happened in ten seconds, or maybe twenty. I remember it like a series of photographs or filmstrips, but it has no timeline. Time ceased to exist for me at the moment Alfalfa the maître d' brought his left hand out from behind his back and I saw the butcher knife. During that time the man in the tuxedo continued to spew out a confusion of words in his special maître d's language, the one that old girlfriend of mine had called Snooti. Some of it really *was* in a foreign language, some of it was English but completely without sense, and some of it was striking . . . almost haunting. Have you ever read any of Dutch Schultz's long, confused deathbed statement? It was like that. Much of it I can't remember. What I can remember I suppose I'll never forget.

Humboldt staggered backward, still holding his lacerated cheek. The backs of his knees struck the seat of his chair, and he sat down heavily on it. *He looks like someone who's just been told he's got cancer,* I thought. He started to turn toward Diane and me, his eyes wide and shocked. I had time to see there were tears spilling out of them, and then the maître d' wrapped both hands around the handle of the butcher knife and buried it in the center of Humboldt's head. It made a sound like someone whacking a pile of towels with a cane.

"Boot!" Humboldt cried. I'm quite sure that's what his last word on planet earth was—"boot." Then his weeping eyes rolled up to whites and he slumped forward onto his plate, sweeping his own glassware off the table and onto the floor with one outflung hand. As this happened, the maître d'—all his hair was sticking up in back now, not just some of it—pried the long knife out of his head. Blood sprayed out of the head wound in a kind of vertical curtain, and splashed the front of Diane's dress. She raised her hands to her shoulders with the palms turned out once again, but this time it was in horror rather than exasperation. She shrieked, and then clapped her blood-spattered hands to her face, over her eyes. The maître d' paid no attention to her. Instead, he turned to me.

"That dog of yours," he said, speaking in an almost conversational tone. He registered absolutely no interest in or even knowledge of the screaming, terrified people stampeding behind him toward the doors. His eyes were very large, very dark. They looked brown to me again, but there seemed to be black circles around the irises. "That dog of yours is so much rage. All the radios of Coney Island don't make up to that dog, you motherfucker."

I had the umbrella in my hand, and the one thing I can't remember, no matter how hard I try, is when I grabbed it. I think it must have been while Humboldt was standing transfixed by the realization that his mouth had been expanded by eight inches or so, but I simply can't remember. I remember the man who looked like George Hamilton bolting for the door, and I know his name was Troy because that's what his companion called after him, but I can't remember picking up the umbrella I'd bought in the luggage store. It *was* in my hand, though, the price tag sticking out of the bottom of my fist, and when the maître d' bent forward as if bowing and ran the knife through the air at me—meaning, I think, to bury it in my throat—I raised it and brought it down on his wrist, like an old-time teacher whacking an unruly pupil with his hickory stick.

"Ud!" the maître d' grunted as his hand was driven sharply down, and the blade meant for my throat plowed through the soggy pinkish tablecloth instead. He held on, though, and pulled it back. If I'd tried to hit his knife hand again I'm sure I would have missed, but I didn't. I swung at his face, and fetched him an excellent lick—as excellent a lick as one can administer with an umbrella, anyway—up the side of his head. And as I did, the umbrella popped open like the visual punchline of a slapstick act.

I didn't think it was funny, though. The bloom of the umbrella hid him from me completely as he staggered backward with his free hand flying up to the place where I'd hit him, and I didn't like not being able to see him. Didn't like it? It terrified me. Not that I wasn't terrified already.

I grabbed Diane's wrist and yanked her to her feet. She came without a word, took a step toward me, then stumbled on her high heels and fell clumsily into my arms. I was aware of her breasts pushing against me, and the wet, warm clamminess over them.

"*Eeeee! You boinker!*" the maître d' screamed, or perhaps it was a "boinger" he called me. It probably doesn't matter, I know that, and yet it quite often seems to me that it does. Late at night, the little questions haunt me as much as the big ones. "*You boinking bastard! All these radios! Hush-do-baba! Fuck Cousin Brucie! Fuck YOU!*"

He started around the table toward us (the area behind him was completely empty now, and looked like the aftermath of a brawl in a Western movie saloon). My umbrella was still lying on the table with the opened top jutting off the far side, and the maître d' bumped it with his hip. It fell off in front of him, and while he kicked it aside, I set Diane back on her feet and pulled her toward the far side of the room. The front door was no good; it was probably too far away in any case, but even if we could get there, it was still jammed tight with frightened, screaming people. If he wanted me—or both of us—he would have no trouble catching us and carving us like a couple of turkeys.

"*Bugs! You bugs! . . . Eeeeee! . . . So much for your dog, eh? So much for your barking dog!*"

"Make him stop!" Diane screamed. "*Oh, Jesus, he's going to kill us both, make him stop!*"

"*I rot you, you abominations!*" Closer now. The umbrella hadn't held him up for long, that was for sure. "*I rot you all!*"

I saw three doors, two facing each other in a small alcove where there was also a pay telephone. Men's and women's rooms. No good. Even if they were single toilets with locks on the doors, they were no good. A nut like this would have no trouble bashing a bathroom lock off its screws, and we would have nowhere to run.

I dragged her toward the third door and shoved through it into a world of clean green tiles, strong fluorescent light, gleaming chrome, and steamy odors of food. The smell of salmon dominated. Humboldt had never gotten a chance to ask about the specials, but I thought I knew what at least one of them had been.

A waiter was standing there with a loaded tray balanced on the flat of one hand, his mouth agape and his eyes wide. He looked like Gimpel the Fool in that Isaac Singer story. "What—" he said, and then I shoved him aside. The tray went flying, with plates and glassware shattering against the wall.

"Ay!" a man yelled. He was huge, wearing a white smock and a white chef's hat like a cloud. There was a red bandanna around his neck, and in one hand he held a ladle that was dripping some sort of brown sauce. "Ay, you can't come in here likea dat!"

"We have to get out," I said. "He's crazy. He's—"

An idea struck me then, a way of explaining without explaining, and I put my hand over Diane's left breast for a moment, on the soaked cloth of her dress. It was the last time I ever touched her intimately, and I don't know if it felt good or not. I held my hand out to the chef, showing him a palm streaked with Humboldt's blood.

"Good Christ," he said. "Here. Inna da back."

At that instant the door we'd come through burst open again, and the maître d' rolled in, eyes wild, hair sticking out everywhere like fur on a hedgehog that's tucked itself into a ball. He looked around, saw the waiter, dismissed him, saw me, and rushed at me.

I bolted again, dragging Diane with me, shoving blindly at the soft-bellied bulk of the chef. We went past him, the front of Diane's dress leaving a smear of blood on the front of his tunic. I saw he wasn't coming with us, that he was turning toward the maître d' instead, and wanted to warn him, wanted to tell him that wouldn't work, that it was the worst idea in the world and likely to be the last idea he ever had, but there was no time.

"Ay!" the chef cried. "Ay, Guy, what's dis?" He said the maître d's name as the French do, so it rhymes with *free*, and then he didn't say anything at all. There was a heavy thud that made me think of the sound of the knife burying itself in Humboldt's skull, and then the cook screamed. It had a watery sound. It was followed by a thick, wet splat that haunts my dreams. I don't know what it was, and I don't want to know.

I yanked Diane down a narrow aisle between two stoves that baked a furious dull heat out at us. There was a door at the end, locked shut by two heavy steel bolts. I reached for the top one and then heard Guy, The Maître D' from Hell, coming after us, babbling.

I wanted to keep at the bolt, wanted to believe I could open the door and get us out before he could get within sticking distance, but part of me—the part that was determined to live—knew better. I pushed Diane against the door, stepped in front of her in a protective maneuver that must go all the way back to the Ice Age, and faced him.

He came running up the narrow aisle between the stoves with the knife gripped in his left hand and raised above his head. His mouth was open and pulled back from a set of dingy, eroded teeth. Any hope of help I might have had from Gimpel the Fool disappeared. He was cowering against the wall beside the door to the restaurant. His fingers were buried deep inside his mouth, and he looked more like the village idiot than ever.

"*Forgetful of me you shouldn't have been!*" Guy screamed, sounding like Yoda in the *Star Wars* movies. "*Your hateful dog! . . . Your loud music, so disharmonious! . . . Eeeee! . . . How you ever—*"

There was a large pot on one of the front burners of the left-hand stove. I reached out for it and slapped it at him. It was over an hour before I realized how badly I'd burned my hand doing that; I had a palmful of blisters like little buns, and more blisters on my three middle fingers. The pot skidded off its burner and tipped over in midair, dousing Guy from the waist down with what looked like corn, rice, and maybe two gallons of boiling water.

He screamed, staggered backward, and put the hand that wasn't holding the knife down on the other stove, almost directly into the blue-yellow gas flame underneath a skillet where mushrooms that had been sautéeing were now turning to charcoal.

He screamed again, this time in a register so high it hurt my ears, and held his hand up before his eyes, as if not able to believe it was connected to him.

I looked to my right and saw a little nestle of cleaning equipment beside the door—Glass-X and Clorox and Janitor In A Drum on a shelf, a broom with a dustpan stuck on top of the handle like a hat, and a mop in a steel bucket with a squeegee on the side.

As Guy came toward me again, holding the knife in the hand that wasn't red and swelling up like an inner tube, I grabbed the handle of the mop, used it to roll the bucket in front of me on its little casters, and then jabbed it out at him. Guy pulled back with his upper body but stood his ground. There was a peculiar, twitching little smile on his lips. He looked like a dog who has forgotten, temporarily, at least, how to snarl. He held the knife up in front of his face and made several mystic passes with it. The overhead fluorescents glimmered liquidly on the blade— where it wasn't caked with blood, that was. He didn't seem to feel any pain in his burned hand, or in his legs, although they had been doused with boiling water and his tuxedo pants were spackled with rice.

"Rotten bugger," Guy said, making his mystic passes. He was like a Crusader preparing to go into battle. If, that was, you could imagine a Crusader in a rice-caked tux. "Kill you like I did your nasty barking dog."

"I don't have a dog," I said. "I *can't* have a dog. It's in the lease."

I think it was the only thing I said to him during the whole nightmare, and I'm not entirely sure I *did* say it out loud. It might only have been a thought. Behind him, I could see the chef struggling to his feet. He had one hand wrapped around the handle of the kitchen's refrigerator and the other clapped to his bloodstained tunic, which was torn open across the swelling of his stomach in a big purple grin. He was doing his best to hold his plumbing in, but it was a battle he was losing. One loop of intestines, shiny and bruise-colored, already hung out, resting against his left side like some awful watch chain.

Guy feinted at me with his knife. I countered by shoving the mop bucket at him, and he drew back. I pulled it to me again and stood there with my hands wrapped around the wooden mop handle, ready to shove the bucket at him if he moved. My own hand was throbbing and I could feel sweat trickling down my cheeks like hot oil. Behind Guy, the cook had managed to get all the way up. Slowly, like an invalid in early recovery from a serious operation, he started working his way down the aisle toward Gimpel the Fool. I wished him well.

"Undo those bolts," I said to Diane.

"What?"

"The bolts on the *door.* Undo them."

"I can't move," she said. She was crying so hard I could barely understand her. "You're *crushing* me."

I moved forward a little to give her room. Guy bared his teeth at me. Mock-jabbed with the knife, then pulled it back, grinning his nervous, snarly little grin as I rolled the bucket at him again, on its squeaky casters.

"Bug-infested stinkpot," he said. He sounded like a man discussing the Mets' chances in the forthcoming season. "Let's see you play your radio this loud now, stinkpot. It gives you a change in your thinking, doesn't it? *Boink!*"

He jabbed. I rolled. But this time he didn't pull back as far, and I realized he was nerving himself up. He meant to go for it, and soon. I could feel Diane's breasts brush against my back as she gasped for breath. I'd given her room, but she hadn't turned around to work the bolts. She was just standing there.

"Open the door," I told her, speaking out of the side of my mouth like a prison con. "Pull the goddamn bolts, Diane."

"I can't," she sobbed. "I can't, I don't have any strength in my hands. Make him stop, Steven, don't stand there *talking* with him, make him *stop*."

She was driving me insane. I really thought she was. "You turn around and pull those bolts, Diane, or I'll just stand aside and let—"

"EEEEEEEEE!" he screamed, and charged, waving and stabbing with the knife.

I slammed the mop bucket forward with all the force I could muster, and swept his legs out from under him. He howled and brought the knife down in a long, desperate stroke. Any closer and it would have torn off the tip of my nose. Then he landed, spraddled awkwardly on wide-spread knees, with his face just above the mop-squeezing gadget hung on the side of the bucket. Perfect! I drove the mop head into the nape of his neck. The strings draggled down over the shoulders of his black jacket like a witch wig. His face slammed into the squeegee. I bent, grabbed the handle with my free hand, and clamped it shut. Guy shrieked with pain, the sound muffled by the mop.

"PULL THOSE BOLTS!" I screamed at Diane. "PULL THOSE BOLTS, YOU USELESS BITCH! PULL—"

Thud! Something hard and pointed slammed into my left buttock. I staggered forward with a yell—more surprise than pain, I think, although it *did* hurt. I went to one knee and lost my hold on the squeegee handle. Guy pulled back, slipping out from under the stringy head of the mop at the same time, breathing so loudly he sounded almost as if he were barking. It hadn't slowed him down much, though; he lashed out at me with the knife as soon as he was clear of the bucket. I pulled back, feeling the breeze as the blade cut the air beside my cheek.

It was only as I scrambled up that I realized what had happened, what she had done. I snatched a quick glance over my shoulder at her. She stared back defiantly, her back pressed against the door. A crazy thought came to me: she *wanted* me to get killed. Had perhaps even planned it, the whole thing. Found herself a crazy maître d' and—

Her eyes widened. *"Look out!"*

I turned back just in time to see him lunging at me. The sides of his face were bright red, except for the big white spots made by the drain holes in the squeegee. I rammed the mop head at him, aiming for the throat and getting his chest instead. I stopped his charge and actually knocked him backward a step. What happened then was only luck. He slipped in water from the overturned bucket and went down hard, slamming his head on the tiles. Not thinking and just vaguely aware that I was screaming, I snatched up the skillet of mushrooms from the stove and brought it down on his upturned face as hard as I could. There was a muffled thump, followed by a horrible (but mercifully brief) hissing sound as the skin of his cheeks and forehead boiled.

I turned, shoved Diane aside, and drew the bolts holding the door shut. I opened the door and sunlight hit me like a hammer. And the smell of the air. I can't remember air ever smelling better, not even when I was a kid and it was the first day of summer vacation.

I grabbed Diane's arm and pulled her out into a narrow alley lined with padlocked trash bins. At the far end of this narrow stone slit, like a vision of heaven, was 53rd Street with traffic going heedlessly back and forth. I looked over my shoulder and through the open kitchen door. Guy lay on his back with carbonized mushrooms circling his head like an existential diadem. The skillet had slid off to one side, revealing a face that was red and swelling with blisters. One of his eyes was open, but it looked unseeingly up at the fluorescent lights. Behind him, the kitchen was empty. There was a pool of blood on the floor and bloody handprints on the white enamel front of the walk-in fridge, but both the chef and Gimpel the Fool were gone.

I slammed the door shut and pointed down the alley. "Go on."

She didn't move, only looked at me.

I shoved her lightly on her left shoulder. "Go!"

She raised a hand like a traffic cop, shook her head, then pointed a finger at me. "Don't you touch me."

"What'll you do? Sic your therapist on me? I think he's dead, sweetheart."

"Don't you patronize me like that. Don't you *dare*. And don't touch me, Steven, I'm warning you."

The kitchen door burst open. Moving, not thinking but just moving, I slammed it shut again. I heard a muffled cry—whether anger or pain I didn't know and didn't care—just before it clicked shut. I leaned my back against it and braced my feet. "Do you want to stand here and discuss it?" I asked her. "He's still pretty lively, by the sound." He hit the door again. I rocked with it, then slammed it shut. I waited for him to try again, but he didn't.

Diane gave me a long look, glarey and uncertain, and then started walking up the alleyway with her head down and her hair hanging at the sides of her neck. I stood with my back against the door until she got about three-quarters of the way to the street, then stood away from it, watching it warily. No one came out, but I decided that wasn't going to guarantee any peace of mind. I dragged one of the trash bins in front of the door, then set off after Diane, jogging.

When I got to the mouth of the alley, she wasn't there anymore. I looked right, toward Madison, and didn't see her. I looked left and there she was, wandering slowly across 53rd on a diagonal, her head still down and her hair still hanging like curtains at the sides of her face. No one paid any attention to her; the people in front of the Gotham Café were gawking through the plate glass windows like people in front of the Boston Seaquarium shark tank at feeding time. Sirens were approaching, a lot of them.

I went across the street, reached for her shoulder, thought better of it. I settled for calling her name instead.

She turned around, her eyes dulled with horror and shock. The front of her dress had turned into a grisly purple bib. She stank of blood and spent adrenaline.

"Leave me alone," she said. "I never want to see you again."

"You kicked my ass in there, you bitch," I said. "You kicked my ass and almost got me killed. Both of us. I can't believe you."

"I've wanted to kick your ass for the last fourteen months," she said. "When it comes to fulfilling our dreams, we can't always pick our times, can w—"

I slapped her across the face. I didn't think about it, I just hauled off and did it, and few things in my adult life have given me so much pleasure. I'm ashamed of that, but I've come too far in this story to tell a lie, even one of omission.

Her head rocked back. Her eyes widened in shock and pain, losing that dull, traumatized look.

"You bastard!" she cried, her hand going to her cheek. Now tears were brimming in her eyes. "Oh, you *bastard!*"

"I saved your life," I said. "Don't you realize that? Doesn't that get through? *I saved your fucking life.*"

"You son of a bitch," she whispered. "You controlling, judgmental, small-minded, conceited, complacent son of a bitch. I hate you."

"Fuck that jerk-off crap. If it wasn't for the conceited, small-minded son of a bitch, you'd be dead now."

"If it wasn't for you, I wouldn't have been there in the first place," she said as the first three police cars came screaming down 53rd Street and pulled up in front of the Gotham Café. Cops poured out of them like clowns in a circus act. "If you ever touch me again, I'll scratch your eyes out, Steve," she said. "Stay away from me."

I had to put my hands in my armpits. They wanted to kill her, to reach out and wrap themselves around her neck and just kill her.

She walked seven or eight steps, then turned back to me. She was smiling. It was a terrible smile, more awful than any expression I had seen on the face of Guy the Demon Waiter. "I had lovers," she said, smiling her terrible smile. She was lying. The lie was all over her face, but that didn't make the lie hurt any less. She *wished* it was true; that was all over her face, too. "Three of them over the last year or so. You weren't any good at it, so I found men who were."

She turned and walked down the street, like a woman who was sixty-five instead of twenty-seven. I stood and watched her. Just before she reached the corner I shouted it again. It was the one thing I couldn't get past; it was stuck in my throat like a chicken bone. "I saved your *life!* Your goddamn *life!*"

She paused at the corner and turned back to me. The terrible smile was still on her face. "No," she said. "You didn't."

Then she went on around the corner. I haven't seen her since, although I suppose I will. I'll see her in court, as the saying goes.

I found a market on the next block and bought a package of Marlboros. When I got back to the corner of Madison and 53rd, 53rd had been blocked off with those blue sawhorses the cops use to protect crime scenes and parade routes. I could see the restaurant, though. I could see it just fine. I sat down on the curb, lit a cigarette, and observed developments. Half a dozen rescue vehicles arrived—a scream of ambulances, I guess you could say. The chef went into the first one, unconscious but apparently still alive. His brief appearance before his fans on 53rd Street was followed by a body bag on a stretcher—Humboldt. Next came Guy, strapped tightly to a stretcher and staring wildly around as he was loaded into the back of an ambulance. I thought that for just a moment his eyes met mine, but that was probably just my imagination.

As Guy's ambulance pulled away, rolling through a hole in the sawhorse barricade provided by two uniformed cops, I tossed the cigarette I'd been smoking in the gutter. I hadn't gone through this day just to start killing myself with tobacco again, I decided.

I looked after the departing ambulance and tried to imagine the man inside it living wherever maître d's live—Queens or Brooklyn or maybe even Rye or Mamaroneck. I tried to imagine what his dining room might look like, what pictures might be on the walls. I couldn't do that, but I found I could imagine his bedroom with relative ease, although not whether he shared it with a woman. I could see him lying awake but perfectly still, looking up at the ceiling in the small hours while the moon hung in the black firmament like the half-lidded eye of a corpse; I could imagine him lying there and listening to the neighbor's dog bark steadily and monotonously, going on and on until the sound was like a silver nail driving into his brain. I imagined him lying not far from a closet filled with tuxedos in plastic dry-cleaning bags. I could see them hanging there in the dark like executed felons. I wondered if he did have a wife. If so, had he killed her before coming to work? I thought of the blob on his shirt and decided it was a possibility. I also wondered about the neighbor's dog, the one that wouldn't shut up. And the neighbor's family.

But mostly it was Guy I thought about, lying sleepless through all the same nights I had lain sleepless, listening to the dog next door or down the street as I had listened to sirens and the rumble of trucks heading downtown. I thought of him lying there and looking up at the shadows the moon had tacked to the ceiling. Thought of that cry—*Eeeeeee!*—building up in his head like gas in a closed room.

"Eeeee," I said . . . just to see how it sounded. I dropped the package of Marlboros into the gutter and began stamping it methodically as I sat there on the curb. "Eeeee. Eeeee. Eeeeee."

One of the cops standing by the sawhorses looked over at me. "Hey, buddy, want to stop being a pain in the butt?" he called over. "We got us a situation here."

Of course you do, I thought. Don't we all.

I didn't say anything, though. I stopped stamping—the cigarette pack was pretty well flattened by then, anyway—and stopped making the noise. I could still hear it in my head, though, and why not? It makes as much sense as anything else.

Eeeeeee.

Eeeeeee.

Eeeeeee.

QUEEN OF KNIVES
Neil Gaiman

Neil Gaiman is a transplanted Briton who now lives in the American Midwest with his wife and children. He has worked as a journalist for a number of U.K. periodicals and newspapers. His graphic novels include *Violent Cases, Black Orchid,* and the *Sandman* series (one installment of which won the World Fantasy Award for Best Short Story in 1991). He is coauthor (with Terry Pratchett) of the novel *Good Omens*. His short fiction has been collected in *Angels and Visitations*. One of his most recent projects was the marvelous collaboration with artist Dave McKean on *Mr. Punch*. He is currently working on a fantasy TV series for the BBC, *Neverwhere*. This is his fourth consecutive appearance in *The Year's Best Fantasy & Horror*.

Gaiman often uses backgrounds, incidents, and flashes of memory from his own childhood, which may be why his occasional writings from a child's point of view are so effective (eg. *Violent Cases, Mr. Punch*). While I don't think the events in the poem "Queen of Knives" are actually from his childhood, the Gaiman flair for sucking the reader into his world is quite evident. The poem originally was published in *Tombs*, edited by Edward E. Kramer and Peter Crowther.

—E. D.

The re-appearance of the lady is a matter of individual taste.
—Will Goldston,
Tricks and Illusions

When I was a boy, from time to time,
I stayed with my grandparents
(old people: I knew they were old—
chocolates in their house
remained uneaten until I came to stay,
this, then, was aging).
My grandfather always made breakfast at sun-up:
A pot of tea, for her and him and me,
some toast and marmalade

(the Silver Shred and the Gold). Lunch and dinner,
those were my grandmother's to make, the kitchen
was again her domain, all the pans and spoons,
the mincer, all the whisks and knives, her loyal subjects.
She would prepare the food with them, singing her little songs:
Daisy Daisy give me your answer do,
or sometimes,
You made me love you, I didn't want to do it,
I didn't want to do it.
She had no voice, not one to speak of.

Business was very slow.
My grandfather spent his days at the top of the house,
in his tiny darkroom where I was not permitted to go,
bringing out paper faces from the darkness,
the cheerless smiles of other people's holidays.
My grandmother would take me for gray walks along the promenade.
Mostly I would explore
the small wet grassy space behind the house,
the blackberry brambles and the garden shed.

It was a hard week for my grandparents
forced to entertain a wide-eyed boy-child, so
one night they took me to the King's Theatre. The King's . . .

Variety!
The lights went down, red curtains rose.
A popular comedian of the day,
came on, stammered out his name (his catchphrase),
pulled out a sheet of glass, and stood half-behind it,
raising the arm and leg that we could see;
reflected
he seemed to fly—it was his trademark,
so we all laughed and cheered. He told a joke or two,
quite badly. His haplessness, his awkwardness,
these were what we had come to see.
Bemused and balding and bespectacled,
he reminded me a little of my grandfather.
And then the comedian was done.
Some ladies danced all legs across the stage.
A singer sang a song I didn't know.

The audience were old people,
like my grandparents, tired and retired,
all of them laughing and applauding.

In the interval my grandfather
queued for a choc-ice and a couple of tubs.

We ate our ices as the lights went down.
The "SAFETY CURTAIN" rose, and then the real curtain.

The ladies danced across the stage again,
and then the thunder rolled, the smoke went puff,
a conjurer appeared and bowed. We clapped.

The lady walked on, smiling from the wings:
glittered. Shimmered. Smiled.
We looked at her, and in that moment flowers grew,
and silks and pennants tumbled from his fingertips.

The flags of all nations, said my grandfather, nudging me.
They were up his sleeve.
Since he was a young man,
(I could not imagine him as a child)
my grandfather had been, by his own admission,
one of the people who knew how things worked.
He had built his own television,
my grandmother told me, when they were first married,
it was enormous, though the screen was small.
This was in the days before television programs;
they watched it, though,
unsure whether it was people or ghosts they were seeing.
He had a patent, too, for something he invented,
but it was never manufactured.
Stood for the local council, but he came in third.
He could repair a shaver or a wireless,
develop your film, or build a house for dolls.
(The dolls' house was my mother's. We still had it at my house,
shabby and old it sat out in the grass, all rained-on and forgot.)

The glitter lady wheeled on a box.
The box was tall: grown-up-person–sized, and black.
She opened up the front.
They turned it round and banged upon the back.
The lady stepped inside, still smiling,
The magician closed the door on her.
When it was opened she had gone.
He bowed.

Mirrors, explained my grandfather. *She's really still inside.*
At a gesture, the box collapsed to matchwood.
A trapdoor, assured my grandfather;
Grandma hissed him silent.

The magician smiled, his teeth were small and crowded;
he walked, slowly, out into the audience.

He pointed to my grandmother, he bowed,
a Middle-European bow,
and invited her to join him on the stage.
The other people clapped and cheered.
My grandmother demurred. I was so close
to the magician that I could smell his aftershave,
and whispered, "Me, oh, me. . . ." But still,
he reached his long fingers for my grandmother.

Pearl, go on up, said my grandfather. *Go with the man.*

My grandmother must have been, what? Sixty, then?
She had just stopped smoking,
was trying to lose some weight. She was proudest
of her teeth, which, though tobacco-stained, were all her own.
My grandfather had lost his, as a youth,
riding his bicycle; he had the bright idea
to hold on to a bus to pick up speed.
The bus had turned,
and Grandpa kissed the road.
She chewed hard liquorice, watching TV at night,
or sucked hard caramels, perhaps to make him wrong.

She stood up, then, a little slowly.
Put down the paper tub half full of ice cream,
the little wooden spoon—
went down the aisle, and up the steps.
And on the stage.

The conjurer applauded her once more—
A good sport. That was what she was. A sport.
Another glittering woman came from the wings,
bringing another box—
this one was red.

That's her, nodded my grandfather, *the one
who vanished off before. You see? That's her.*
Perhaps it was. All I could see
was a woman who sparkled, standing next to my grandmother,
(who fiddled with her pearls, and looked embarrassed).
The lady smiled and faced us, then she froze,
a statue, or a window mannequin,
The magician pulled the box,
with ease,
down to the front of stage, where my grandmother waited.
A moment or so of chitchat:
where she was from, her name, that kind of thing.
They'd never met before? She shook her head.

The magician opened the door,
my grandmother stepped in.

Perhaps it's not the same one, admitted my grandfather,
on reflection,
I think she had darker hair, the other girl.
I didn't know.
I was proud of my grandmother, but also embarrassed,
hoping she'd do nothing to make me squirm,
that she wouldn't sing one of her songs.

She walked into the box. They shut the door.
He opened a compartment at the top, a little door. We saw
my grandmother's face. *Pearl? Are you all right, Pearl?*
My grandmother smiled and nodded.
The magician closed the door.

The lady gave him a long thin case,
so he opened it. Took out a sword
and rammed it through the box.
And then another, and another
And my grandfather chuckled and explained
The blade slides in the hilt, and then a fake
slides out the other side.

Then he produced a sheet of metal, which
he slid into the box half the way up.
It cut the thing in half. The two of them,
the woman and the man, lifted the top
half of the box up and off, and put it on the stage,
with half my grandma in.

The top half.

He opened up the little door again, for a moment,
My grandmother's face beamed at us, trustingly.
When he closed the door before,
she went down a trapdoor,
And now she's standing halfway up,
my grandfather confided.
She'll tell us how it's done, when it's all over.
I wanted him to stop talking: I needed the magic.

Two knives now, through the half-a-box,
at neck-height.
Are you there, Pearl? asked the magician. *Let us know*
—do you know any songs?

My grandmother sang *Daisy Daisy*.
He picked up the part of the box,
with the little door in it—the head part—
and he walked about, and she sang
Daisy Daisy first at one side of the stage,
and at the other.

That's him, said my grandfather, *and he's throwing his voice.*
It sounds like Grandma, I said.
Of course it does, he said. *Of course it does.*
He's good, he said. *He's good. He's very good.*
The conjurer opened up the box again,
now hatbox-sized. My grandmother had finished *Daisy Daisy*,
and was on a song which went
My my here we go the driver's drunk and the horse won't go
now we're going back now we're going back
back back back to London Town.

She had been born in London. Told me ominous tales
from time to time to time
of her childhood. Of the children who ran into her father's shop
shouting *shonky shonky sheeny*, running away;
she would not let me wear a black shirt because,
she said, she remembered the marches through the East End.
Moseley's black-shirts. Her sister got an eye blackened.

The conjurer took a kitchen knife,
pushed it slowly through the red hatbox.
And then the singing stopped.

He put the boxes back together,
pulled out the knives and swords, one by one by one.
He opened the compartment in the top: my grandmother smiled,
embarrassed, at us, displaying her own old teeth.
He closed the compartment, hiding her from view.
Pulled out the last knife.
Opened the main door again,
and she was gone.
A gesture, and the red box vanished too.
It's up his sleeve, my grandfather explained, but seemed unsure.

The conjurer made two doves fly from a burning plate.
A puff of smoke, and he was gone as well.

She'll be under the stage now, or backstage,
said my grandfather,
having a cup of tea. She'll come back to us with flowers,
or with chocolates. I hoped for chocolates.

The comedian, for the last time.
And all of them came on together at the end.
The grand finale, said my grandfather. *Look sharp,
perhaps she'll be back on now.*

But no. They sang
*when you're riding along
on the crest of the wave
and the sun is in the sky.*

The curtain went down, and we shuffled out into the lobby.
We loitered for a while.
Then we went down to the stage door,
and waited for my grandmother to come out.
The conjurer came out in the street clothes;
the glitter woman looked so different in a mac.

My grandfather went to speak to him. He shrugged,
told us he spoke no English and produced
a half-a-crown from behind my ear,
and vanished off into the dark and rain.

I never saw my grandmother again.

We went back to their house, and carried on.
My grandfather now had to cook for us.
And so for breakfast, dinner, lunch, and tea
we had golden toast, and silver marmalade
and cups of tea.
Till I went home.

He got so old after that night
as if the years took him all in a rush.
Daisy Daisy, he'd sing, *give me your answer do.
If you were the only girl in the world and I were the only boy.
My old man said follow the van.*
My grandfather had the voice in the family,
they said he could have been a cantor,
but there were snapshots to develop,
radios and razors to repair . . .
his brothers were a singing duo: the Nightingales,
had been on television in the early days.

He bore it well. Although, quite late one night,
I woke, remembering the liquorice sticks in the pantry,
I walked downstairs:
my grandfather stood there in his bare feet.

And, in the kitchen, all alone,
I saw him stab a knife into a box.
You made me love you.
I didn't want to do it.

DRAGON-RAIN
Eileen Kernaghan

Canadian writer Eileen Kernaghan is the author of three lyrical fantasy novels: *Journey to Aprilioth* (winner of the "Porgy Award" from *The West Coast Review of Books*), *Songs from the Drowned Lands* (winner of the Canadian SF & Fantasy Award), and *The Sarsen Witch*. She has also published nonfiction, children's fiction, and stories for numerous magazines and anthologies. Kernaghan lives in British Columbia.

"Dragon-Rain" is a well-crafted work of Swords-and-Sorcery, a form of fantasy all too often written with a tin ear and a purple pen. Kernaghan shows the form at its best in this dry and delicious tale of a dragon and a reluctant sorceress. It is reprinted from an unusual source: *Magic*, a small-press anthology conceived, edited, and published by twelve-year-old Morgan Kopaska-Merkel, with the help of her father, David C. Kopaska-Merkel, in Tuscaloosa, Alabama.

—T.W.

The sorceress Jatsang stopped at a bend in the trail to scratch a fleabite. Gazing southward, she grunted in dismay. The valley below—once as lush as a length of emerald silk—was now the color of yak-dung. Where were the barley fields and pastures she remembered, the lapis lazuli pools and winding silver streams? By the time she reached level ground her mouth was so parched she could scarcely spit. Nearby were the ruins of a well. In a mood of profound pessimism she peered into its depths. Something skittered along the bottom, rasping its wings in a way that set her teeth on edge. There was no sign of water.

"May you be happy."

Jatsang swung round to see who was behind her. An elderly monk was watching her with mournful, red-rimmed eyes. "May you be peaceful," he added. "May you be free from care."

"I'd be a good deal happier," observed Jatsang, "if I had something to drink." She waved a vague arm towards the arid fields. "What has happened here? The place has gone to rack and ruin."

"Serpents," said the monk.

"Serpents?"

"Serpent-dragons, to be precise. A nest of nagas. At the bottom of our well."

"*This* well?"

"The very same. First they drank up all the water in the well, then they crawled out into the fields and emptied the ponds and streams. And as you see, we've had no rain at all this year. You'll find the begging poor, my lady. Since the drought came, we have had no food for our children, let alone anything to spare for pilgrims."

Jatsang reached into her travel-pack and pulled out her five-pointed sorcerer's hat. She put it on her head.

"I beg your pardon," said the monk. He looked confused. "You are a sorcerer, a *ngagspa*? Of what persuasion?"

"Bon-po," said Jatsang. "Black Bon," she added ominously.

"I saw a Black Bon sorcerer once," said the monk. "He wore a black cloak, a skull on his head, and an apron made of human bones. He was riding on a great black horse." He glanced dubiously at Jatsang's drooping white skirt and grubby waistcoat, the jagged rip in the sleeve of her shirt, the greasy black rope of hair that hung to her heels.

Jatsang asked impatiently, "Do you think we tramp around the mountains in our ceremonial dress?"

"Then Reverend Lady, if you are indeed a sorceress, you are the answer to our prayers."

"How so?"

"This drought has been caused by magic. We need a powerful magician to lift it."

Jatsang drew herself up to her full height. "I don't do magic for hire," she said. "Where's your village shaman?"

"Eaten," said the monk.

"*Eaten?*"

Dolefully, the monk explained. "He summoned a powerful demon to drive the nagas out of the well. But he got the last part of the spell wrong, and the demon ate him instead."

"How unfortunate," remarked Jatsang, without much sympathy. She had no patience with fools. "And what has this to do with me?"

"Reverend Lady, will you help us? Out of compassion. Think of the children. Many of them have fallen sick. Some have already perished. . . ."

Jatsang felt herself wavering. In the back of her mind, like lines of elegant black script, rose the words of the Precious Guru:

Mahayana, Secret Mantra, means to benefit others. It is essential for all tantric practitioners to cultivate great compassion in their being.

As though sensing her indecision, the monk leaned closer. His breath stank of hunger. "Reverend Lady, at least will you come with me to the monastery? Will you speak to our abbot?"

"Will you give me some water?"

"If need be, our last drop."

Jatsang shrugged, and followed him to a cluster of whitewashed buildings clinging haphazardly to the mountainside. Like all else in this stricken land, the monastery's aspect was ruinous. The monks looked tired and undernourished; the bottoms of their robes and their bare feet were gray with dust. The hum of prayer was dispirited, subdued; even the prayer wheels seemed to spin lethargically.

The abbot came out in person to greet Jatsang. When they had exchanged white scarves and he had settled her in a comfortable chair in his private sanctum, with a large jug of water close to hand, he said, "I'm told you are an adept of the Short Path, and a *ngagspa* of considerable attainment."

"It is not my habit," said Jatsang, "to speak publicly of such matters. Even within these walls, demons may be listening. Let me say this, merely: that as mistress of *tumo*, I've crouched naked on a mountain peak in the middle of a blizzard, warming my flesh with my own internal fires. As a *lung-gom-pa*, I have crossed three valleys and three mountains in a single day. Moreover, I have created fire-demons—no less than thirty at a time—not to mention tulpa knights and various other phantoms of the mind—"

"And how," interrupted the abbot, "does one so skilled in the mystic arts set about expelling demons?"

"One performs *chod*," replied Jatsang. She spoke without enthusiasm. She had performed *chod* only last month, because she felt the need to keep in practice. It had not been a happy experience. "Again, it would be a mistake to divulge too much. Suffice to say, when one celebrates *chod*, one tends to stir up any malign forces that may be present in the vicinity."

"And once you have drawn these demons out of their hiding place?"

"Then I will challenge them to destroy me, and by surviving, I will show them to be illusion. If you cease to believe in the power of demons, they will cease to harm you."

A flicker of disappointment—perhaps even of dismay—marred the perfect serenity of the abbot's face. "Is it not within your powers to destroy them on the spot?"

"You forget," said Jatsang, "that the very essence of *chod* is love and compassion for all things. Even demons. A Bon sorceress does not destroy malign spirits. Rather, she persuades herself of their nonexistence."

"I understand," said the abbot, looking unconvinced. "Before you begin *chod*, is there anything you require?"

"Several things. A sacred thunderbolt. A bell. A *damaru* drum. A thighbone trumpet. A moonless night. And silence."

"In two nights the moon is new. The rest is easily supplied."

"Very well," said Jatsang. "Then I will spend the intervening hours in meditation. To celebrate *chod* is to court madness and death. One does not embark upon it unprepared."

First she gave some thought to the location. Ideally, *chod* should be performed in a place where corpses had been chopped to bits and fed to the wolves and vultures. But the important thing was that the site should be wild, and haunted by malignant spirits. The patch of ground beside the naga-infested well, she decided, would adequately serve her purpose.

All that night she prepared herself, praying to the old Bon gods: to Father Khenpa, Master of the Heavens, riding on the White Dog of the Sky; and to Khon-ma, Mother of the Nine Earths, astride her ram. On the next night, an hour after midnight, under a dark and thunderous sky, Jatsang pitched her ritual tent. It was ornamented, in the prescribed manner, with the syllables "Aum," "A," and "Hum"; and flags in the Five Mystic Colors fluttered from its roof. It was time to begin the ceremony.

Sounding the thighbone trumpet, she visualized herself as the Goddess of All-Fulfilling Wisdom. Then she began the dances of the Five Directions, the Five

Obscuring Passions, and the Five Wisdoms. After that came the Spearing of the Elements of Self with the spears of the Five Orders of Celestial Spirits; and the offering up of the self in ritual sacrifice. Again she blew the sacred trumpet, spreading before the hungry demons a banquet of her own flesh, blood, and bones:

> This day I, the fearless yogin,
> am offering in sacrifice this fearless body of mine . . .
> Ye Eight Orders of Spirits, ye elementals and non-human beings,
> And ye mischievous and malignant hosts of flesh-eating sprites . . .
> Heaped up flesh, blood, and bones have been laid out as a sacrificial offering. . . .
> If you be in haste, bolt it down uncooked.
> If you have leisure, cook and eat it, piece by piece.
> And leave not a bit the size of an atom behind. . . .

There were noises at the bottom of the well. Slithering, hissing, seething noises. And all at once there boiled out of the mouth of the well a tangled, writhing mass of scales and talons, snapping jaws, and venomous yellow fangs.

The serpent-dragons seethed round Jatsang's ankles. She felt their supple, slime-covered coils tightening like steel bands around her knees and thighs. There was a smell like something long-dead dredged up from a stagnant pond. Scales scraped against scales.

They twined round her waist and her shoulders, hissed and spat in her ears, tangled their claws in the long rope of her hair. Jatsang's jaws clenched; her stomach knotted and twisted with disgust. There was a terrible crushing weight on her chest, so that she could not breathe. She felt as though her flesh was pierced with hundreds of dagger-points.

The intensity of the pain grew; she howled, writhed, convulsed with agony and terror. She had offered herself up as a banquet, as a Red Meal, and there was no turning back. This was how it felt to be eaten alive.

And all the while, she clung to the knowledge that these serpent-dragons were illusion, that they existed only in her fevered mind. As long as she did not believe in them, she could not be destroyed by them. If she died, it would be through her own all-devouring fear.

At last, when the pain was beyond endurance, beyond imagining, the crushing pressure eased, the coils slackened and fell away. Jatsang felt her blood gushing out of her terrible wounds, pooling thickly at her feet. Thirstily, the serpent-dragons lapped it up. "I give my flesh to the hungry, my blood to the thirsty, my bones as fuel to those who suffer from the cold. . . ." She was growing weaker. The rasping of the serpent's tongues grew faint, and faded away.

Now, after the Red Meal, came the Black Meal. She imagined herself as a small heap of charred bone, sinking slowly into a sea of black mud. She was nothing. The body she had willingly offered up to be devoured was nothing. All was illusion. At that instant she knew herself to be neither mad, nor dead. This much she had accomplished: she had survived.

She heard the wind flapping in the folds of her tent. She heard the whispering and shuffling of the villagers as they gathered round the well.

And then, to her sick dismay, she heard from the bottom of the well an ominous rustling and slithering, a dry susurrus of scales—and she knew that all her agony had been for nothing.

With despairing eyes the villagers stared at her. Angrily, she faced them down.

"Clearly, your belief was not strong enough," she told them. "I can do nothing to help you if you have no faith."

"Reverend Lady," said the old monk. "What will you do now?"

"What I should have done in the first place," snapped Jatsang. "I will continue my journey."

"But Reverend Lady," said the monk. His voice was imploring. "Think of the children...."

Against her better judgment, Jatsang glanced at the wan-faced children clinging to their mother's skirts. The last time she had traveled through this valley they had been plump and mischievous as puppies—giggling at her from doorways, trotting noisily at her heels, tumbling and shrieking and scuffling in the dirt. Now they gazed at her in reproachful silence, their eyes huge in their gray, pinched faces.

Jatsang looked, and remembered, and was lost. I am going to regret this, she thought, as she leaned over the well and shouted into its reeking depths: "Be warned, you spirits of ill will and unrighteousness, this is the sorceress Jatsang who addresses you. You who are the creatures of illusion, the inventions of my own mind. You have done your worst to destroy me, and I am unharmed. You are unworthy to inhabit my imagination. Now I am going to seek the aid of the Dragon King to drive you from this land.

"Fetch me a dragon-drum," she told the old monk; and when the villagers, in their ignorance, crowded round to see what she would do next, she howled and cursed and shook her fists to frighten them away. Settling down in the parched dust beside the well, she folded herself into the lotus position. For a day and a night she beat the dragon-drum and droned a mantra. Then she commenced the slow deep breathing and the mental exercises that would lead her into trance. For two days and two nights she meditated, gathering spiritual strength. She visualized herself as a storm-beaten flame on an ocean of fire; as a wrathful goddess wearing a necklace of human heads; as a radiant white skeleton huge as the universe itself. Then with the immense bounding strides of the *lung-gom-pa*, the far-traveler, she swooped over the gray fields and leafless woods; arriving at last at the mouth of a cave high on a sun-scorched mountainside.

Jatsang stepped out of the fierce white sunlight into a dark echoing hollow space that smelled of dank stone and moldering dust. Somewhere nearby she could hear the slow drip of water. Something hard and brittle—dry twigs, or bones—crunched under her feet.

She walked on slowly. The walls of the cavern narrowed, drew in upon her. The ground grew slick and treacherous. Soon water crept up over her feet, her ankles, her knees. As she went on, the beating of her heart stilled, the blood slowed in her veins, her throat closed, her lungs shrank in upon themselves. Black waters, warm and viscid as blood, closed over her; she drifted towards the jeweled, prismatic light that glittered in their farthest depths.

* * *

The gates of the Dragon-King's palace were emerald-encrusted, turquoise-studded, inlaid with jasper and lapis lazuli. They opened on a sudden blaze of lamplight, reflected from golden walls and fragile crystal columns. Beyond were corridors, courtyards, passageways, anterooms, reception chambers. There were rooms fashioned entirely of amethyst and rose-quartz; rooms paneled with peacock-colored silk, or mother-of-pearl, or the plumage of exotic birds; rooms symphonious with thousands of tiny crystal chimes; rooms filled with flowers. Jatsang strode purposefully on, through groves of ruby-fruited trees, down long aisles of onyx pillars. She could hear a sweet, faint music of flutes and bells; smelled frankincense and jasmine. Over everything lay a gentle subterranean light, diffuse and milky.

Seawater dripped from Jatsang's hair and garments. Her boots squelched, leaving a trail of muddy footprints on the silken rugs.

There slithered towards her, presently, three large cobras draped in the garnet robes of monks. "How may we help you?" one inquired; the others gazed with dismay at the spreading circle of damp where Jatsang stood.

"I seek an audience with the Dragon King."

"And you are?"

"The sorceress Jatsang."

"And is the king expecting you?"

"Probably not," replied Jatsang.

"Then we will convey your request to the king's secretary. Please tell us where you may be reached. You can expect a reply within the month."

"A little sooner than that, I hope," said Jatsang. Annoyed, she transformed her outward image into a Black Vulture-Headed All-Devouring Goddess, armed with a serpent-noose and an enormous club. Hissing with fright, the cobras scattered.

A useful trick, thought Jatsang. I must remember it. And Goddess-shaped, she shrieked and bellowed and bullied her way down several miles of silk-carpeted, jewel-encrusted corridors, arriving unheralded at the throne room of the Dragon King.

She found the Ruler Over All the Waters of the World recumbent on a bed of crimson brocade and silver latticework. On this occasion—reflecting, it was to be hoped, an accessible frame of mind—he had chosen to manifest himself in quasi-human form. His head might have belonged to any elegant, well-favored youth. His skin was smooth and ivory-hued, his features harmonious. Gleaming plaits of ebon hair framed large, half-hooded, cinnamon-colored eyes. His expression was mild if at this moment a trifle petulant.

From neck to tail he remained entirely dragonlike. His coils, enameled with brilliant, intricately patterned scales, were as muscular and thick as a boa constrictor's. His tail from time to time emitted tongues of flame. From his toes protruded the clutching, rending claws of a carrion bird.

"Sit down, sit down." The Dragon King's smile was expansive. With one of his forefeet he waved her towards a cushioned chair; with the other he proffered a bowl of honeyed orchids. Resuming her normal shape, Jatsang sank damply into the chair and stuffed a handful of orchids into her mouth. After several days of fasting, meditation, and cross-country travel, she was ravenous.

"So," said the Dragon King in an amicable tone. "What brings you to my palace?"

"A petition," Jatsang told him. She wiped her sticky fingers surreptitiously on the chair cushion.

The king groaned faintly, and settled his coils more comfortably on the bed. "Go on," he said, not very encouragingly. Jatsang observed that his mouth, though well shaped, was a trifle dissipated; and that his voice had a tendency to become shrill.

"Your subjects have . . ." she was about to say "infested" but thought better of it—"your subjects have invaded the Valley of Seven Streams. And they've sucked it dry."

"Yes, well, they are inclined to do that," said the King.

"But the valley is drought-stricken. The people are starving."

"We all have our problems," said the Dragon King. He sounded bored.

"Some of us more than others," Jatsang retorted.

"Oh, yes," said the king. "I know what you're going to say. That living as I do, I cannot understand what it is to suffer. Well, Madam, let me tell you something. The more exalted one's position in the universe, the greater the burdens one is expected to bear. Imagine this, if you can: that every morsel of food, every bamboo shoot or sugared banana-bud, every smallest spoonful of shark's-fin soup, turns to squirming toads in your mouth. Imagine moreover, that every woman you embrace is transformed into a serpent at the instant of your greatest pleasure. Are you imagining that?"

"I am," admitted Jatsang, feeling queasy.

"Then imagine, moreover, that all the scales on your back grow in contrary-wise direction—so that every smallest particle of sand, every tiny pebble that enters, causes shafts of exquisite pain that pierce your heart. And therefore do not think to envy me!"

"I would not dream of it," said Jatsang.

"Very well, then," said the Dragon King, looking somewhat mollified. "What is it you want of me?"

"A small thing, Your Highness. Order your subjects out of the well in the Valley of Seven Streams, and bring back the rain. A trivial task, for one who has power over the world's weather."

"Trivial perhaps—but also tedious. There will be a price."

Jatsang waited. She was thinking how pleasant it would be to slice that complacent, grinning head from its loathsome neck.

Do not examine the shortcomings of others, but examine your own, she reminded herself sternly.

The king said, "Food, as you can imagine, is no pleasure at all; making love serves only to enrage me. Music, art, the beauty of my gardens—all these have ceased to charm me. In a word, I am unendurably bored."

"And your price?"

"Is to be entertained."

"I am a Black Bon shaman of the Seventh Degree," said Jatsang stiffly. "I am not some village charlatan who swallows knives and vomits fire."

"My point exactly. Are not Black Bon-pos trained in the most arcane and exacting arts of magic?"

"True," agreed Jatsang.

"And when a king is asked to grant a favor, is he not entitled to demand of the supplicant three tests, or challenges?"

"Such a tradition exists, I'm given to understand."

"So then. I propose three tests of your shamanist skills."

"Such as?"

"Could you, for example, make stars out of yak-dung?"

"If I saw any purpose in it," said Jatsang.

"I might find it amusing," said the king. "Surely that is purpose enough?"

Jatsang glanced around the elaborately appointed room, with its glowing tapestries and carpets, its lacquered furnishings and golden chandeliers.

"And where," she inquired sardonically, "do you keep the yak-dung?"

Gleefully the Dragon King slapped his tail against the bedhead, setting a-chime a cluster of crystal bells. Moments later a servant—this one in human form—appeared as though by prearrangement, bearing a reeking mound of manure on a silver tray.

Jatsang eyed the yak-dung dubiously. "Stars, you said?"

"Stars," said the Dragon King. His tail spat fire in pleasurable anticipation.

Jatsang had brought with her none of the paraphernalia of her calling: neither drum nor cymbals, nor ram's head, nor magic mirror, nor sash of human bones. Still, for a sorceress who had once fended off wolves by creating thirty phantom fire-demons, this promised to be a simple task. She took out her ritual knife, adjusted her five-pointed wizard's hat, spoke some necessary incantations, and breathed her way into a deep trance.

Focusing her intense concentration on that steaming mass of dung, she caused it to separate gradually into lumps, then curds. The curds hardened, contracted, shriveled, like sun-dried apricots; turning eventually into black shiny lumps, like anthracite. She squeezed the lumps, compressed them with the power of her will, made them hard as diamonds. She imagined them translucent, colorless, then transparent: glittering, prismatic shards of purest crystal. Then she gathered them up in both hands, tossed them aloft like jewels from a broken necklace. They hung suspended just beneath the ornate ceiling, catching the lamplight and shattering it into a myriad points of fire.

Jatsang tipped back her head to admire her handiwork. She was pleased with the effect.

"Quite impressive," said the Dragon King. "Mere legerdemain, of course—a conjurer's trick—but somewhat amusing. Now as for the next test . . ."

Jatsang, who had been propelling the stars in intricate patterns around the ceiling, glanced down at the king.

"I want to see you raise a corpse," he said.

Jatsang's self-congratulatory mood changed abruptly to revulsion. "I don't do that," she said.

"But," persisted the king, "I have heard that it is a not uncommon practice of Black Bon sorcerers."

"That may be true. I've never done it. Nor do I plan to."

"Why not?" The king's eyes, now more coppery than cinnamon, had taken on a reptilian glitter.

"Because," said Jatsang, "the idea disgusts me."

"Ah, but consider the children," said the Dragon King. His voice was smooth as lotus petals, seductive as a *dramnyen* song. "Think of their parched throats and crusted eyes, their hunger-swollen bellies. Of what importance are your own selfish feelings, in the face of such suffering? And besides, is not all experience mere illusion?"

His logic was impeccable. Jatsang breathed a small prayer that the corpse would prove as fresh as the yak-dung.

Jatsang's gorge rose when she saw the task that confronted her. They had brought her the bloated corpse of a drowned man. Salt water streamed from his garments, dank strings of hair clung like seaweed to his grotesquely swollen, fish-white face. Behind her she heard a rasping and slithering as the king uncoiled himself, craning his neck for a better view.

Jatsang was all too familiar with the ritual for *rolang*, corpse-raising; she had seen it performed by other *ngagspas*, less fastidious than herself.

"The room must be dark," she informed the king; and she went round his bedchamber blowing out the candelabra, leaving only a single butter-lamp burning in a corner. Then, taking a deep breath, she lay down full length upon the corpse. It sloshed and gurgled horribly under her weight; noxious gases exploded from every orifice. She wrapped her arms around its flaccid middle, feeling through the sleeves of her shirt the dreadful seeping dankness of its flesh. Then, as the ancient ritual prescribed, she put her mouth to the corpse's mouth, and clearing all other thoughts from her head, she repeated, mentally, certain arcane and complex formulae.

She lost all sense of time. It might have been hours, or days, before she felt the first faint shuddering of the chill flesh beneath her, heard the first breath wheeze from the sodden lungs. The cadaver's limbs jerked spasmodically, its chest heaved. Jatsang turned her face aside just in time to avoid a gout of foul matter that erupted from its mouth; then once again applied herself to her loathsome task.

The drowned man's movements grew more vigorous; he struggled fiercely to sit up, then, pulling Jatsang with him, he hoisted himself to his feet. Jatsang clung to the corpse with desperate strength as he staggered drunkenly around the room. She knew that if this monstrous thing escaped her control, it would surely destroy her.

But now the cadaver, imbued with a sudden feverish energy, began to leap and bound around the bedchamber, scattering lamps and pillows and bric-a-brac in all directions. Still Jatsang clasped him in that frantic and macabre embrace.

Finally, there came the moment that, as often as she had witnessed it, still made her throat tighten and her belly twist with nausea. The dead man's tongue, black and swollen as a chunk of flyblown meat, protruded suddenly from between his gaping lips. Now, at once, unflinchingly and inescapably, Jatsang must perform the ritual's final act. She seized the ghastly tongue between her teeth and bit it off.

Jatsang spat out a mouthful of something indescribably vile. Then she bent over an ornate silver urn and retched until her guts seemed lodged in her throat. When at last she looked up she saw that the drowned man had collapsed like a punctured bladder. She stepped over the corpse, and fixing the Dragon King with a baleful eye, she snarled,

"What next?"

"You have accomplished the unusually difficult," the Dragon-King observed.

"You have performed the inexpressibly disgusting. Are you ready now to undertake the incalculably dangerous?"

"Get to the point," snapped Jatsang. The encounter with the corpse had left her with a headache and a queasy stomach. Her mood was less than amiable.

"If you want rain for your valley," said the Dragon-King, scratching absently behind his ear, "then you must seek out the Divine Naga, the Thunder-Dragon, who sleeps in a cave nine layers deep beneath the sea. He is the most powerful of my servants, for he holds beneath his chin the Pearl of All Desires. Who possesses the pearl has power over the thunder, rain, and lightning, over the phases of the moon, the ebb and flow of the tide, over all the processes of nature, and the course of life and death itself."

"And when I find this creature?"

"You must startle him out of his sleep, so that he flies up into the air and drops the pearl. Then you must snatch up the pearl and bring it to me. Only then will the drought end, and rain fall upon your valley. I trust you will find it an amusing challenge."

"We have different ideas," remarked Jatsang, "of what is amusing." But in fact this task seemed somewhat more congenial than the last. Though fierce and rough of nature, dragons on the whole were beneficent beasts, well intentioned toward humankind. To creep up on a dragon and surprise him in his sleep demanded no great cleverness or courage, no arcane magical arts—only a degree of stealth, and perhaps persistence, if the dragon should prove difficult to rouse.

Jatsang rummaged through the crowded shelves and storerooms of her memory, seeking what she knew of Weather-Dragons.

This much she remembered: they were fond of roasted swallows. They were afraid of centipedes, iron, and five-colored strands of silk.

Jatsang said, "I will need some items of equipment."

"Ask for whatever you require," replied the king. "Within reason, of course."

In less than an hour Jatsang was ready to set out. Thrust through her belt was a slender rod of polished iron. In her pouch was coiled a five-stranded length of silken thread, in colors of hyacinth, rose-madder, primrose, aubergine, and heliotrope. The basket on her back contained a brace of swallows marinated in wine and stuffed with sturgeon's eggs, and a jar of centipedes.

The king had provided detailed directions to the Weather-Dragon's lair. From the luxurious rooms of the upper palace she descended down ramps and staircases, through back hallways and postern doors, to shabbier nether regions. Here she found kitchens, storerooms, servants' quarters, then, at still deeper levels, a warren of cramped stone cells and narrow passageways glistening with damp. Her torchlight fell on rotten brick and mud-plaster eaten away by fungal growths. The air was stale and heavy, reeking of decay. From somewhere within the walls she could hear a slow dripping of water, and furtive scuttling sounds.

She turned at last into a downward sloping tunnel, so narrow that her shoulders brushed the walls on either side, so low that she was forced to stoop. It turned and twisted, looped back upon itself, plunged steeply, and becoming ever more constricted, looped again. As she penetrated ever deeper into its shadowy recesses Jatsang felt a growing sense of unease. She could cross a windswept gorge on a swaying bamboo bridge, could follow a goat-track along a chasm's edge with perfect equanimity. But caverns, tunnels, confined spaces—these made her throat tighten, her heart hammer in her chest.

At the farthest end of the tunnel she came to a vertical shaft sunk into the floor. Holding up her torch, she peered unhappily into its depths.

Though there was no sign of a rope or ladder, some rusty spikes had been driven at intervals into the sides of the shaft. Jatsang tied up the flapping ends of her skirt between her legs; cinched her belt; checked the fastenings on her pack. Then, hand over hand, she began the descent into the oubliette.

The walls of the shaft were slick with weed and slime. Green phosphorescence cast an eldritch light. This, thought Jatsang, must be how the dead feel, descending through the Eight Cold Hells. A chill crept up under her garments, like the clammy fingers of ghosts. I may soon be a ghost myself, she thought morosely, as her foot slipped on a spike and she caught herself just in time.

At the bottom of the well was yet another tunnel, which opened, some distance further on, into an enormous hollow space.

Hollow, but not empty. From wall to wall, from floor to ceiling, the cavern was filled with a vast recumbent shape.

It was like watching a mountain asleep, if mountains had hearts that reverberated in their depths like the monotonous thudding of a great skin drum; if the flanks of mountains rose and fell in time with their slow and ponderous breath; if mountains were coiled like serpents, with glittering carplike scales, and whiskers as thick as the trunks of trees hanging down on either side of their gaping jaws.

Jatsang knew too well the terrible power of mountains. She had seen what happened when the earth shuddered, when cliffs were wrenched asunder, when rivers of ice roared down from the heights like angry gods. She had seen villages vanish forever beneath the crushing weight of earth and stone. Jatsang feared neither man nor beast, knowing that what she could not outrun she could easily outwit. Neither did she fear ghosts, demigods, or demons, understanding them to be the inventions of her own mind. But the ponderous, mindless, implacable power of mountains—from such power, neither fleetness of foot nor quickness of mind could save her. From childhood a secret terror had haunted her dreams. She feared that one day the mountains would fall, and bury her alive.

No faintest ray of light penetrated these submarine depths, yet the cavern was dimly illuminated by a russet glow, the color of flames burning behind a curtain of mist. These, Jatsang realized after a moment, were the emanations of fire and smoke that issued, with each slumbering breath, from the dragon's maw. Her own throat was burning, her lungs afire, with the acrid stench that permeated that crowded space.

Her eyes were adjusting to the dim red light. Tilting back her head and peering through the smoke, she discovered the treasure she had been sent to steal. Tucked securely under the dragon's chin and half concealed in the rank herbage of his beard was a huge red pearl. Jagged flashes of light sparked out of it. From the bottom of it there erupted a kind of undulating sprout, like the first tender shoot from a bean.

Jatsang stood at the mouth of the cavern, pondering her next move. To rouse a sleeping dragon—it had seemed, on the face of it, a simple enough task. But she had not taken into account the sly and malevolent humor of the Dragon King. Asleep, his monstrous coils tightly wound, his great head sunk upon his neck, the dragon filled his sleeping chamber wall to wall and almost roof to floor, like some monstrous infant in the womb. What chance of escape for Jatsang, once she had prodded him into wakefulness? With one swipe of his foot he could crush her into the slime of the cavern floor. With one twitch of that glittering tail, he could smash her to jelly against the wall. To be crushed to death by a serpent-headed mountain—that, she recalled, was the fate reserved in hell for monks who had profaned the scriptures, for priests who had taken money for rituals not performed. If she were to be punished for pride, or stubbornness, or bad temper—well, there might be a certain justice in that. But her honesty had never been called into question.

So then. How to rouse this sleeping monster, and snatch away his treasure, and live to tell the tale? The sensible course of action would be a strategic retreat. She had done it before, when the cliff was too steep, the blizzard too fierce, the enemy too well armed. In the harsh, unforgiving land of Jatsang's birth, foolhardy courage was not counted a virtue. But then she thought of the piteous faces of the children; and worse still, she imagined the smirking triumph of the Dragon King, when she returned empty-handed, in defeat. . . .

Clearly, this time there was to be no turning back.

In the event, the weather-dragon proved to be a heavy sleeper. To begin with she tried a conservative approach, removing the lid from the basket of roasted swallows and—standing well out of range—letting their delicious odors waft through the cavern mouth. As the scent reached him, she saw the dragon's nostrils twitch. Two threads of saliva dripped from his jaws, and under his eyelids there appeared a thin line of red. Then his eyes drooped closed, and he slipped back into profound sleep.

Perhaps, thought Jatsang, this dragon has already dined too well.

She took a cautious step forward. Her feet, well rehearsed in stealth, made no sound on the cavern floor.

She drew the iron rod from her belt, and leaning forward, prodded the dragon in the space between two glistening coils. A kind of undulating ripple ran all down his length, from head to tail, like the light on shaken silk. Otherwise he took no more notice of the iron rod than if it had been the sting of a gnat. Growing bolder as she grew more impatient, Jatsang crept closer, and rapped the dragon sharply on one eagle-taloned foot. This time he made a rumbling sound deep in his throat, and the end of his tail flicked.

Jatsang reached into her pouch and took out the five-colored length of silk. After a moment's thought she wound the strands securely around a rock. Hurled with deadly accuracy and considerable strength, it hit the dragon squarely on the nose.

The dragon's head jerked and his eyes shot open. His tail lashed against the far wall, bringing a shower of mud and small stones raining down from the roof. His baleful red gaze fell on the silk-wrapped stone, which had come to rest near his left forefoot. With an air of petulance, five gargantuan claws scraped a concealing mound of dirt over the offending rock. Then the dragon yawned and went back to sleep. The Pearl of All Desires was tucked as securely as ever beneath his chin.

What now? thought Jatsang. Which of her hard-won sorcerer's arts could she most usefully employ? To make fire in her own flesh—she guessed that the dragon could teach her a trick or two at that game. To cover vast tracts of ground at a single stride—hardly helpful, she decided, when there was scarcely room in this place to scratch your behind. To far-speak—what use to reach out with her mind when there was no one within a ten-day's journey who might come to her aid?

She stared up at the dragon, observing the immense feet with their rending eagle's claws, the glowering, demonic head rearing high above the body's coiled serpentine mass. He was snake and four-footed beast and bird all at once, this creature—a marvelous synthesis of earth and air. And hard on the heels of that thought came another.

Earth. Air. To break the chains that bound her to the earth, to become as air, as wind . . . it would not be an easy feat. Not like far-striding, which through long practice had become a simple, half-unconscious act. Jatsang knew that her natural affinity was with earth, not air. Still, she had yet to test her skills to their full limit.

She sat down lotus-fashion on the cavern floor, and slowly, deeply, deliberately, drew breath in, let it out, drew it in again. She felt her head, her chest, her belly, her loins fill. Then, legs folded, she leaped as high as she could. On the first attempt she managed to rise only a foot or so, and fell back onto the cave floor with a thump that jarred the length of her spine.

Once again she began her breathing exercises. The second leap carried her a little higher; the third one higher still. And then, on the fourth jump, she felt the chains that held her to the earth loosening, stretching. She was a cloud, a scarf of mountain mist, a petal on a breath of wind. The sky was her element. She was filled with light. She drew one more breath, infinitely slow and infinitely sustained; and floating upwards, saw coil upon coil of the dragon's body winding away below her, until she was level with his eyes.

I'm not out of tricks yet, she thought; and reaching into her pack, she pulled out the jar of centipedes. Drifting in as close as she dared she snatched off the lid, and thrust the jar into the dragon's cavernous left nostril.

The dragon sneezed, once, twice, three times. The sound reverberated off the cave walls. Several boulders, suddenly dislodged, crashed past Jatsang's head. The dragon shook his head from side to side, pawing at his nose with his fore-claws; and then, tormented beyond endurance, he threw back his head and bellowed out his fury and dismay.

In that instant, the Pearl of All Desires slipped out from beneath his chin; and in that same instant Jatsang was there to catch it.

She had expected it to be perfectly hard and smooth, like marble, and yet to the touch it seemed strangely soft and yielding, with a velvety texture and a kind of living warmth to it. And at the same time it seemed marvelously fragile, hollow and weightless as an egg. As she clutched it against her chest it seemed to nestle there, nudging itself up into the hollow of her shoulder, pressing itself against her jaw. Holding it firmly she rose with it, until she was floating in the narrow space between the roof and the dragon's head; then she settled herself behind his ears as though she were Old Father Khen-pa himself, astride the White Dog of the Sky.

The dragon's ears twitched. He shook his head like a wet hound, trying to toss her off. The razor-sharp edges of his scales cut into her hands, but she took scant notice of the pain.

Writhing, undulating, the dragon tried to scrape her against the roof. His claws scored deep grooves in the floor of the cave, his breath scorched the walls. Then suddenly he was crashing his way through the cavern mouth, with Jatsang, still clutching the pearl, crouched low over his neck.

"So, Worm," shrieked Jatsang. Laughing, she held up the pearl, balanced lightly in one hand. She felt the vast bulk writhe in baffled rage beneath her. "Now I am mistress of the Pearl of All Desires, and you have no choice but to obey me. Take me to your master the Dragon King, or I will smash your precious Pearl to bits."

With that the dragon gave a kind of defeated sigh, and went down on his belly like a whipped dog.

"Up, up," said Jatsang severely. "You've slept long enough."

She clung to his head one-handed as he slithered through a maze of tunnels winding their tortuous way upward, like giant worm-holes, through the nine levels of the undersea. When they emerged at last into the upper world, they were standing in the palace of the Dragon King.

Jatsang had dirt in her hair and grit in her eyes. Small sharp stones had worked their way under her garments. Her wolfskin cape had a huge rent in it, and the dragon's scales had lacerated her tender flesh.

She thumped the dragon behind his ears with the rod of iron to remind him of his purpose; and together they trampled their way through the gorgeous rooms of silk and pearl and lapis and peacock feathers. Jatsang watched with grim enjoyment as the dragon's five-clawed feet scored ugly gouges in the polished floors; as his lashing tail ripped velvet cushions, silken carpets, and embroidered tapestries to shreds.

Thus they made their way from one end of the palace to the other, leaving devastation in their wake. At last they arrived at the bedroom of the Dragon King.

Cradling the Pearl of All Desires, Jatsang floated gently floorward. She discovered the Dragon King crouched wretchedly in the farthest corner, a velvet comforter pulled over his head. Behind her, there was an ominous splintering of wood.

"My Lord," said Jatsang gently, "it seems you are indisposed."

The Dragon King gazed up at her with anguished eyes.

"Your task," he complained, "was to steal from the dragon the Pearl of All Desires. I did not for one moment suggest that you steal the dragon."

Jatsang said, with asperity, "I did exactly as you asked. I have brought you your pearl. The dragon came along of his own free will."

Behind them, the dragon flicked his tail, shattering a crystal mirror and demolishing a priceless inlaid table. "He'll make an interesting pet," said Jatsang, cheerfully surveying the damage—"if you can ever manage to house-break him."

"You have gone too far," the Dragon King shrieked. "I wished to be entertained. I do not find this at all amusing."

"Nor I," agreed Jatsang. "I've been made to embrace a corpse, and climb down a well, and risk being drowned or set on fire or trodden upon. You've had your entertainment, and I've come to present your bill."

"I promised nothing," said the king. His voice was sullen.

Jatsang reminded herself of the words of the Precious Guru, Padmasambhva: "You must extinguish the scorching flames of anger with the water of loving-kindness. . . ." Accordingly, she swallowed her rage. "Perhaps not," she agreed, in a coldly reasonably voice. "But remember, I still have the Pearl of All Desires. And at this moment my greatest desire is to shake the sea-bed loose from its roots, and reduce your palace and everything in it to a heap of rubble."

As she spoke she lifted the pearl. A faint trembling could be felt beneath their feet. The shuddering grew stronger; there was a kind of wrenching jolt, and a grating noise like boulders being ground together. The chandelier swung back and forth, gathering speed as it went, all its glittering balls and pendants clashing. The Dragon-King's skin had gone the color of ash. He stared down in horror at the floor, which by now was lurching like a bamboo bridge in a winter gale. "Give back the pearl," he gasped out. "You shall have your rain."

"Very kind of you, I'm sure," said Jatsang, and she walked out, stepping carefully round the dragon, with the Pearl of All Desires tucked under her arm.

As she strode through the Valley of Seven Streams, where the sweet gray rain was falling, Jatsang was filled with a content that was perilously close to self-congratulation. In the end it is all illusion, she thought—and no illusion lasts forever. She grinned to herself as she shouldered her pack and started up the hill-path. She was thinking of that swarm of stars that surely by now would have ceased to circle above the Dragon-King's head.

LLANTOS DE LA LLORONA: WARNINGS FROM THE WAILER

Pat Mora

Pat Mora is a Chicana poet who hails from El Paso, Texas. She is the author of *Communion, Borders, Chants,* and *Nepantla: Essays from the Land in the Middle,* as well as a number of children's books. She has received an NEA Fellowship, a Kellogg National Fellowship, and three Southwest Book Awards.

This poem is based on the legend of La Llorona, a frightening, wailing creature who haunts dry riverbeds in the desert. According to folklore, she is the ghost of a woman who was abandoned by her high-born lover and then killed her own children in grief and rage. To encounter La Llorana is generally deemed to be fatal. . . .

The poem is one of four in the "Cuarteto Mexicano" section of Mora's excellent collection: *Agua Santa/Holy Water.* (The other three poems are recommended too, particularly "Coatlicue's Rules: Advice from an Aztec Goddess.")

—T.W.

    Every family has one.
        Even as a child, I'd hide
    and cry, *ay, ay, ay,*
        when people sneered
    at my parents as if they were
        below them in some hole
    of quivering vermin.

    Oye: Agua santa can come from our eyes.

    Early the whispers begin,
        persistent as the buzz
    of litanies. Flicking tongues
        say my mother X-*tabai*
    and I, *ay, ay, ay,*
        though beautiful as flaming
    sunsets, are dangerous.
        We start fires
    in the heart,
        and below the heart.
    Nights we wander near

Llantos de La Llorona: Warnings from the Wailer

    sighing rivers and streams,
our hair and voices rising.

Oye: Sing to confuse the gossips.

We hide, they say, in
    evening's thickshadows,
convert ourselves into trees,
    ceibas perhaps, disguise
our voices to sound like
    wives, *ay, ay, ay,*
alter ourselves to lure innocence,
    our hair and limbs tangling
round and round, like snakes
    hugging men to death.

Oye: Know your own strength.

After the Spaniard comes,
    rumor says I begin
having babies, *ay, ay, ay,*
    conceptions, remember?
I nestle them here
    when they finish nursing.
My mother *X-tabai*
    strokes their round heads,
soft as a ball of feathers.
    We whisper cuentos,
sing *rru-rru* lullabies.

Oye: Children are not bastards
    though sometimes their fathers are.

They say I drown the babies,
    bend down with them
heavy in my arms, *rru-rru*
    release them and their gur-
glings into night water,
    or do I, *ay, ay, ay,*
begin to like the feel
    of a dagger, long and thin,
one day plunge the tongue
    into those corazoncitos
to spare them
    other piquetitos,
Maybe I grow the dagger
    gleaming like my nails in moonlight.

Oye: Be resourceful. Grow what you need.

Perhaps I want to hurt the father
    who in his story
finds a woman who makes his parents smile,
    fair like every princess,
probably thinner and *ay, ay, ay,*
    silent too, and in those days,
I'm sure a virgin,
    immaculate.

Oye: Encourage any man looking for a virgin
    vessel to bear his own child.

The story is a watery
    or bloody mess and says
I wander wailing
    ay, ay, ay, near water,
por las orillas del río,
    for the souls I've lost,
"Hijas mías" I call
    like Malinche, mad women,
madbad ghostwomen
    roaming the dark.

Oye: Sometimes raising the voice does get attention.

Not all stabbings at the truth
    are fatal, as women
will attest, you daughters of a long line
    of celestial and earthly
women, knowers of serpent
    rumors, altars, silence,
suppressed sighs.

Don't think I wail every night.
    I'm a mother, not a martyr.
But try it. I wear a gown, white,
    flowing for effect
and walk by water. Desert women
    know about survival.

Join me sometime
    for there's much to bewail,
everywhere frail, lost souls.
    We'll cry, *ay, ay, ay.*

Oye: Never underestimate the power of the voice.

TOO SHORT A DEATH
Peter Crowther

Peter Crowther lives in Harrogate in Yorkshire, England, with his wife and two sons. He has had more than fifty stories published in such magazines and anthologies as *Fear*, *Interzone*, and *Dark Voices 4*. He is the editor of the anthology trilogy on superstitions: *Narrow Houses*, *Touch Wood*, and *Blue Motel*. He is also the coeditor of *Heaven Sent* (with Martin H. Greenberg), *Tombs*, and *Dante's Disciples* (both with Edward E. Kramer). His collaborative novel, *Escardy Gap*, written with James Lovegrove, will be published in September, and he has sold a script based on one of his stories to British television. In addition, he writes a semiregular review column for *Interzone*. A chapbook of his story "Forest Plains" is scheduled to be published by Silver Salamander Press in 1996 and a collection of his horror/fantasy stories, *The Longest Single Note and Other Strange Compositions*, will be published by White Wolf in 1997.

"Too Short a Death" is a bittersweet story about poetry, love, and death. One of the poets in the story did in fact exist. The story was originally published in *Celebrity Vampires*, edited by Martin H. Greenberg.

—E.D.

"Hey . . . *hey!*" The man on the stage was trying to make himself heard, laughing while he was doing it and waving his hands conspiratorially, as though he were Billy Crystal in the *Mr. Saturday Night* movie. But the sound that he was trying to drown out was not the sound of people enjoying *him* but rather of them enjoying each other or their food or their drinks.

"Yeah, Hillary Clinton." The man frowned and shook his hand as though he had picked up something that was too hot to hold. "You heard . . . you heard Bill wants six more secret service agents assigned to her, yeah? Well," he reasoned with a shrug, "after all, if anything happened to *her*, he'd have to become president."

In humor terms, it was one step—a small one—up from *Take my wife . . . please!* but somebody let out a loud guffaw and David MacDonald turned around on his seat to see who it had been. At one of the tables over by the coatracks two men were laughing, but it was clearly not at Jack Rilla.

"Thanks, Don," Jack Rilla shouted into his microphone. "My brother Don," he added for the audience's benefit. "Nice boy."

The man at the table—who was clearly no relation to the comedian—turned to face the stage and gave Jack Rilla the bird, receiving a warm burst of applause.

MacDonald had never enjoyed seeing somebody die on stage, so he turned back to his food.

He was enjoying the anonymity. All the effete photographers and the snot-nosed journos had gone, taken up their cameras and their tape recorders and walked. Gone back to the city.

He was no longer news. "The most innovative poet of his generation," *The New York Times* had trilled, mentioning—in the eighteen-paragraph, front-page lead devoted to his quest—the names of early pioneers such as William Carlos Williams, Edwin Arlington Robinson, and Ezra Pound; Kenneth Fearing, to whom they attached the appellation "The Ring Lardner of American verse"; the so-called war poets, including Richard Eberhart, Randall Jarrell, and Karl Shapiro—the Pulitzer winner whose "Auto Wreck" had been widely (and wrongly!) cited as the inspiration behind MacDonald's own "The Downer"; and even some of the Black Mountain College graduates, in particular Robert Creely and the college's head honcho, Charles Olson. This latter "revelation" enabled the hack responsible for the piece to tie it all back again to Williams and Pound, who, with their respective paeons "Paterson" and "Cantos," were commonly regarded as being among the North Carolina college's—and particularly Olson's—chief inspirations.

A neat job, but, in the main, entirely wrong.

MacDonald loved e. e. cummings, born a generation after Williams but infinitely more eloquent in his embrace of nature and naturalness and, to the end, delightfully whimsical. Similarly, he preferred Carl Sandburg—whose "Limited" he had used in its entirety (all six lines!) as the frontispiece to *Walton Flats*, a surreal and fabulous (in the true sense of the word) novel-length tale of godhood and redemption which he had written in collaboration with Jimmy Lovegrove—to the Runyonesque Kenneth Fearing. And as for the "war poets," MacDonald rated Randall Jarrell above all others—Shapiro and his "V-Letter" included—even to the point of learning Jarrell's "The Death of the Ball Turret Gunner" when he was only twelve years old.

When it came to open verse, MacDonald settled for the Beats—Ginsberg and Ferlinghetti in particular—over the inferior Black Mountain scribes, a fact which seemingly never ceased to amaze the self-styled poetry pundits. But it was *their* amazement that so astonished MacDonald, just as it astonished him how nobody seemed to give credit to the Harlem Renaissance and the fine work produced in the field of poetry by the likes of Etheridge Knight (of course), plus forerunners of the stature of Langston Hughes and Countee Cullen, and contempories such as Nikki Giovanni and Sonia Sanchez. As much as anyone—if not more than, in many cases—these writers, in MacDonald's opinion, were fundamental in recording the consciousness of a country at odds with itself, as he had gone to great pains to explain to a surprised David Letterman on live television a little over three years ago. Quoting the final few lines from Giovanni's "Nikki-Rosa"—in which the poet comments on the patronizing attitude of the whites—MacDonald took great relish in Letterman's damp forehead.

Sitting at the bar, MacDonald recalled the piece.

> ... I really hope that no white person ever has cause to write about me because they never understand Black love is Black wealth and they'll probably talk about my hard childhood and never understand that all the while I was quite happy.

But the attention he had received in the press the following day was nothing to the coverage afforded his bold announcement that he was to forgo the novel on which he was working and, instead, go in search of Weldon Kees.

That was almost a year ago now.

The newspapers and the magazines had all followed: followed him to dry Californian towns, tracked him into the wastes of New Mexico, dogged his footsteps into the inhospitable Texas plains, and now, back in the sleepy Nebraskan township of Beatrice, they had grown bored. After all, a fanatic is only of interest so long as he either looks like succeeding or looks like dying. Simple failure just isn't news.

Now no flashbulbs flashed as he walked still another dust-blown, night-time Main Street in some godforsaken town, in its own way just one more boil on the fat backside of indulgence, a lazy, going-nowhere/seen-nothing grouping of weatherworn buildings and choked-up autos clustered around an obligatory general store and wooden-floored bar . . . with maybe a railroad track where no trains stopped anymore thrown in for good measure.

Now no microphones were jammed between his mouth and some under- or overcooked indigenous delicacy as he continued his quest even through physical replenishment. Sometimes the questions had been more rewarding than the food. But the answers he gave were always the same, and the novelty had plain worn off.

Beatrice, Nebraska. A small, slow, company town lacerated by railroad tracks and gripped for eleven months of the year by permafrost or heat wave.

This was where he had started and, now, this was where it all ended. It was the latest—and, MacDonald now believed, the last—stop on this particular tour. Eleven months in the wilderness was enough for any man: even Moses only spent forty days, for Crissakes.

Whitman's America had come to a dead end on the shores of the Pacific and, like the land itself, rolling lazily down to the waterline seeking only oblivion, MacDonald was tired. Tired of honky-tonk bars where he would search through a maze of good ol' boys and raunchy women, rubbing against tattoos and beer bellies, straining to see and hear through cigarette smoke and jukebox rhythms, carrying home with him the secondhand, hybrid musk of sweat and cheap perfume; tired of the revivalist espresso houses in the Village, where he would search through intense poets and poetesses, all wearing only dark colors and frowns, the *de rigueur* uniform. They, like him, searching, always searching.

He pushed the plate forward on the table, the meal unfinished. It had been a bean-bedecked and fat-congealed mush that maybe could have passed for gumbo if he'd been about fifteen hundred miles to the southwest. He wiped his mouth across a napkin from a pile on the corner of the bar, their edges yellowed with age, and noted the faded photograph of a town square with picket fences that wouldn't have been out of place in an *Archie* comic book or a Rockwell painting. He'd walked through that town square—in reality, little more than a pause for breath between developments in what was merely a typical Nebraskan suburb—to get to the bar in which he was now sitting. There had been no sign of the picket fence.

Just like Rockwell himself, it was long gone. But he had seen from the swinging racks in the drugstore that Archie was still around, though his hair was longer now. Nothing stays the same forever. Maybe this town had been Rockwell once, but now it was Hopper, filled up with aimless people like Jack Rilla, the unfunny comedian, all living aimless lives, staring unsmiling out of seedy rooming house windows at the telegraph poles and their promise of distance.

Weldon Kees, where are you? he said to himself.

The bartender slouched over to him and lifted up the plate quizzically. "No good?" he said, his jowls shaking to the movement of his mouth.

MacDonald frowned and shook his head, rubbing his stomach with both hands. "*Au contraire,*" he said, effecting an English accent, "merely that you are too generous with your portions."

The bartender narrowed his eyes. "Aw *what?*"

"He said you gave him too much."

MacDonald turned in the direction of the voice to see a man in his early forties chasing an olive around a highball glass with a tiny yellow, plastic sword. The man looked like a movie star from the late fifties/early sixties, like maybe Tony Curtis or someone like that. He wore a plaid sportscoat, oxford button-down with a red-and-green striped necktie, and black pants rucked up at the knees to preserve two of the sharpest creases MacDonald had ever seen. Covering his feet, which rested lazily on the rail of his stool, were a pair of heavily polished Scotch grain shoes and, within them, a pair of gaudy argyle socks. MacDonald's eyes took it all in and then drifted back to the glass. There was no liquid it. He hadn't noticed the man before, but then he wouldn't have. The bar was crowded to capacity, a good turnout for the amateur talent night promised on a rash of handbills pasted around the town.

The bartender nodded and, with another puzzled glance at MacDonald, he turned around and slid the plate across the serving hatch. "Empties!" he shouted.

MacDonald swizzled the plastic palm tree in his club soda, twisted around on his seat and smiled. "Thanks. You want that freshened?"

The man turned to him and gave him a long, studied look, taking in MacDonald's plain gray jacket and pants, green, soft-collared sport shirt buttoned all the way to the neck, and nodded. "Yeah, why not, thanks. Vodka martini. On the rocks. Thanks again."

MacDonald raised his hand a few inches off the bar, and the bartender acknowledged with a short nod that looked more like a physical affliction.

"You here for the competition?"

MacDonald took a long drink and put his own glass back onto the bar. "That's right. You?"

"In a way," he said. "But really only to enjoy the efforts of others. I'm not actually a performer myself." The strange and self-knowing smile suggested hidden complexities in the statement.

MacDonald nodded and glanced at the stage, ignoring the opportunity to probe. At this stage of the journey he had had it with barroom confessions. Jack Rilla was telling a story about three men from different countries being sentenced to die . . . but being given a choice of the method of their execution. It was horrible.

"How about you?" the man said. "Are you a performer?"

"There's some that might say so," MacDonald replied, grateful to be able to turn away from what Jack Rilla was doing to stand-up comedy.

"What do you do?"

"I write poetry."

"That so?" The interest seemed genuine.

MacDonald nodded again and drained his glass as a crackly fanfare of trumpets sounded across the PA system to signal the end of the comedian. Nobody seemed to be clapping.

Turning around so they could watch the small stage at the end of the adjoining room, they saw a fat man with a Stetson starting to announce the next act. By his side were two younger men holding guitars and shuffling nervously from one foot to the other. The fat man led the halfhearted applause and backed away to the edge of the stage. The duo took a minute or so to tune their instruments and then lurched uneasily into a nasal rendition of "Blowing in the Wind."

MacDonald shook his head and held up the empty glass to the bartender, who had apparently forgotten them and had now taken to slouching against the back counter. "Refills over here," he shouted. The bartender lumbered over and refilled the glasses, all the while mouthing the words to the song. MacDonald took a sip of the soda.

"Not too good, huh?" the stranger said.

"The service or the entertainment?"

The man jerked his head at the stage.

"I've heard better," MacDonald said. "It's probably safe to say that Dylan'll sleep easy."

The man smiled and nodded. "I knew a poet once," he said.

"Yeah?"

"Uh-huh." He lifted the glass and drained it in one perfectly fluid motion. MacDonald recognized the art of serious drinking . . . drinking purely to forget or to remember. He had watched somebody he used to know quite well doing just the same thing over a couple of years . . . watched him in a thousand bar mirrors. He called those his wilderness years. The man set the glass down again and cleared his throat. "What kind of poetry you write?"

"Kind? It's just poetry."

"The rhyming kind?"

MacDonald gave a half-nod. "Sometimes," he said. "Depends on how I feel."

The pair of troubadours finished up their first song, receiving a smattering of applause, and launched immediately into another. This one was their own. It showed.

MacDonald reached into his pocket and pulled out the plastic button. The number on it was 23. He looked at the board at the side of the stage: beneath the number 22 was a piece of wipe-off card bearing the legend *Willis and Dobbs*.

While Willis and Dobbs crooned about some truck driver whose wife had left him for another woman—modern times!—a small group of four men and two women chatted animatedly at the table right down in front of the stage. A tall spindle of metal stood proud in the table center and boasted the word JUDGES. They didn't seem to be talking about Willis and Dobbs. Maybe it was just they didn't like country music.

Willis and Dobbs finished their song almost in unison and bowed while the audience applauded and whistled in relief. As the duo shuffled off the stage, the fat man with the Stetson shuffled on the other side, also applauding. As the fat man reached the microphone, MacDonald took another swig of the club soda and slid off his stool. "Wish me luck," he said to the stranger.

The man looked around. "You on now? Hey, break a leg," he said, slapping MacDonald on the arm as he walked past him.

The usual nervousness was there. It was always there. He made his way through the people standing up in the bar section and then walked down the two steps to the adjoining room where he threaded his way among the tables to the stage. All the time he walked he was memorizing the lines, though he knew them by heart. He reached the stage as the fat man told the audience to give a big hand to Davis MacDonald. The timing was impeccable.

He walked over to the microphone and nodded to the room, raising his hand in greeting. "Hi there," he said.

A smattering of nods and waves and mumbled returns acknowledged him. The man at the bar had turned full around on his stool to watch him. He raised his glass—which MacDonald saw had been replenished—and nodded. MacDonald nodded back. Then he faced the audience and lifted one finger to his mouth.

As always, the silence was almost immediate. It flowed over and around the people sitting at the tables, flowed through and into them, touching their insides and calming their heads. The only way you could recite poetry and feel it—whether reading it yourself or listening to it being read by others—was to do it in silence. After all, who ever heard of a painter painting onto a canvas that already had something on it?

There were a few nervous shuffles as MacDonald paced from one side of the stage to the other, his hands thrust deep into his pants pockets. At last, satisfied that this was as good as it was going to get, he removed the microphone, pointed over the heads of the onlookers to some impossible distance, and began.

> *She's down!*
> *Like a wounded mammoth, her body sags*
> *and, across the sidewalk,*
> *in a shower of fabled jewels,*
> *she spills the contents of her bags.*
>
> *The empty street becomes alive*
> *with do-gooders, tourists, and passersby,*
> *all holding breath.*
> *Transfixed, and with mouths agape,*
> *they see her features lighten under death*
> *while, alongside,*
> *the treasures once so richly cherished—*
> *a loaf, some toothpaste, matches, relish—*
> *lie discarded on the paving slabs.*
>
> *And ooohs and aaahs, the silence stab.*

> *It takes some time but, action done,*
> *the audience turns away its eye and,*
> *with a thought as though of one,*
> *thinks there one day goes I.*

On the final line, MacDonald turned his back on the audience, walked slowly back to the microphone stand, and replaced the microphone. A smattering of applause broke out around the tables. MacDonald nodded and raised his hand, mouthing the words *thank you, thank you.* He caught sight of the man at the bar. He looked as though he had seen a ghost.

After "The Downer," MacDonald recited his "Ode to the City."

> *Beneath the legends of the stars*
> *the drunks cry out in a thousand bars*
> *while pushers prowl in speeding cars . . .*
> *civilization is never far in the city.*
>
> *Bronchitic winos cough up more phlegm*
> *to mouth the glassy teat again,*
> *and venereal ladies stalk the concrete glens . . .*
> *though love has long since left the city.*
>
> *The neons wink cold, thoughtless lies,*
> *to flood the dark and strain the eyes,*
> *while the flasher opens wide his flies . . .*
> *because nothing hides inside the city.*

MacDonald lifted the microphone from the stand again and walked across to the left of the stage.

> *Smoke-bred cancers maim the flesh,*
> *the addict chokes his vein to strike the next*
> *while the abortionist clears away the mess . . .*
> *as all life dies within the city.*
>
> *The dropouts pass around the joint*
> *and the rapist hammers home his point,*
> *but the suicide doth himself anoint*
> *in the fetid, stagnant waters of the city.*
>
> *The kidnapper pastes together a note*
> *and then binds his charge with silken rope*
> *while frantic parents give up hope . . .*
> *which died long ago in the city.*

And now, as ever, the audience was his.

"In Mendaala When It Rains" came next, followed by "Dear Diary" and "Conversation." Then MacDonald paused and, unfastening the top button of his sport shirt, sat down on the front edge of the stage. "I want to finish up now with a couple of poems written by a man I never met," he said, the words coming softly, "but who I feel I've known all of my life.

"This man stole from us. He stole something which we possessed without even realizing . . . something which we could never replace. The thing he took from us . . . was himself." He shrugged out of his jacket and dropped it in a pile at his side. "On July twentieth, nineteen fifty-five, Harry Weldon Kees, one of *your*—" he pointed, sweeping his outstretched arm across the audience, "—your town's . . . most famous sons—disappeared from the north end of the Golden Gate Bridge.

"He left . . . he left many things behind him—not least a fifty-five Plymouth with the keys still in the ignition—but the worst things that he left were holes."

The faces in the audience looked puzzled.

"Those holes, ladies and gentlemen," MacDonald went on, "were the spaces that he would have filled with his poetry. Yes, he was a poet, Weldon Kees, and I'm here . . . here tonight, in Beatrice, Nebraska . . . his hometown . . . at the tail end of what has been almost a year-long search for him. Because, back in nineteen fifty-five, Weldon's body was never found. And because there have been some stories that he is still alive . . . somewhere out there. And if that's true, then I felt I had to find him." He stood up, shrugged, and said, "Well, I tried.

"Weldon . . . wherever you are . . . these are for you."

Reciting from heart, as he did with all of his "readings," Davis MacDonald recounted Kees's "Aspects Of Robinson" and, to finish, "Late Evening Song."

> *For a while*
> *Let it be enough:*
> *The responsive smile,*
> *Though effort goes into it.*
> *Across the warm room*
> *Shared in candlelight,*
> *This look beyond shame,*
> *Possible now, at night,*
> *Goes out to yours.*
> *Hidden by day*
> *And shaped by fires*
> *Grown dead, gone gray,*
> *That burned in other rooms I knew*
> *Too long ago to mark,*
> *It forms again. I look at you*
> *Across those fires and the dark.*

"Thank you, ladies and gentlemen . . . thank you for listening to me." MacDonald replaced the microphone and ran from the stage, leaving tumultuous applause behind and around him.

When he got back to the bar and slumped onto his stool, he saw that the man next to him was nursing his drink in his hands and, his head tilted back, staring into the long but narrow-angled mirror above the bar. MacDonald followed his stare and saw it all then: the bar, the back of the bartender's head as he moved by, the man's highball glass, and himself staring. But there was no reflection of the man himself.

He turned around quickly, mouth open, to stare right into the man's face and saw immediately that he had been crying.

"I'm Robinson," he said. "A friend of Weldon Kees."

MacDonald looked back at the mirror and shook his head. Then he looked back at the man and said, "How do you *do* that?"

"You tell a good story in your poems," he said. "I have a story, also, though I'm no weaver of words like you and Harry."

MacDonald slumped his elbows on the bar. "I think I need a drink."

The man stood up and straightened his jacket. "Come on, you can have one back at my place."

"Is . . . is Weldon Kees still alive?"

"No."

"Did he die that night? *Did* he jump off the bridge?"

The man shook his head. "Let's go. I'll explain on the way."

When they left the bar, the sidewalks were wet and shiny, reflecting shimmering neon signs and window displays. As he walked, MacDonald could also see his own malformed shape in the puddles but not that of the man who walked beside him. "I think I'm going mad," he said.

The man gave out a short, sharp laugh. "No, you're not."

MacDonald turned to him and grabbed hold of the arm in the plaid jacket—

> *Robinson in Glen plaid jacket, Scotch grain shoes,*
> *Black four-in-hand and oxford button-down*

The words of the poem he had just recited hit him suddenly and he pulled his hand back as though he had been burned. "How *can* you be Robinson? Robinson would have to be—" He thought for a moment. "He'd have to be around eighty or ninety years old."

"I'm actually much older even than that," the man said.

MacDonald looked down at the sidewalk, saw his reflection . . . alone. He pointed at the puddle. "And what about that?"

"The mirror from Mexico, stuck to the wall,

Reflects nothing at all. The glass is black."

He smiled and shrugged.

"Robinson alone provides the image Robinsonian."

"What are you?" MacDonald asked.

The man stared into MacDonald's eyes for what seemed to be an eternity, so long

> *His own head turned with mine*
> *And fixed me with dilated, terrifying eyes*
> *That stopped my blood. His voice*
> *Came at me like an echo in the dark.*

that MacDonald thought he was not ever going to answer his question. The worst part of that was that, while he stared, he simply did not care. "I think you can guess," he said, suddenly, releasing MacDonald from his gaze.

"Oh, come on!" MacDonald laughed. "A vampire? You're telling me you're a vampire?"

The man started to walk again. Over his shoulder, he said, "My kind go by many names. And, yes, vampire is one of them." MacDonald started after him, his mind ablaze with stanzas from Weldon Kees's poetry.

> *The dog stops barking after Robinson has gone.*
> *His act is over.*

And

> *These are the rooms of Robinson.*
> *Bleached, wan, and colorless this light, as though*
> *All the blurred daybreaks of the spring*
> *Found an asylum here, perhaps for Robinson alone.*

And even

> *This sleep is from exhaustion, but his old desire*
> *To die like this has known a lessening.*
> *Now there is only this coldness that he has to wear.*
> *But not in sleep.—Observant scholar, traveler,*
> *Or uncouth bearded figure squatting in a cave,*
> *A keen-eyed sniper on the barricades,*
> *A heretic in catacombs, a famed roue,*
> *A beggar on the streets, the confidant of Popes—*
> *All these are Robinsons in sleep, who mumbles as he*
>   *turns,*
> *"There is something in this madhouse that I*
>   *symbolize—*
> *This city-nightmare-black—"*
>   *He wakes in sweat*
> *To the terrible moonlight and what might be*
> *Silence. It drones like wires far beyond the roofs,*
> *And the long curtains blow into the room.*

MacDonald suddenly realized that he was running . . . running to catch up with the man. But, while the man was only walking, MacDonald was getting no nearer to him. *Good God,* he thought, *it's true. All of it.*

The man turned up some steps and stopped at the door of a house. As MacDonald reached the man, he stepped inside and waved for MacDonald to enter.

Inside, the house smelled of age and dirt. A narrow hallway gave onto some stairs and continued past two doors to a third door which was partly open. "I'll get you that drink," the man said and he walked along the hall to the end door. MacDonald followed without saying a word.

The room was a kitchen. Dirty dishes that looked as though they had been that way for weeks were piled up in and beside the sink. In the center of the room, a wooden table with a worn Formica top was strewn with packets and opened cans. MacDonald saw several cockroaches scurrying in the spilled food.

The man opened a cupboard and pulled out a bottle of Jim Beam and two glasses. He poured bourbon into the glasses and handed one to MacDonald. "I first met Harry back in 1943. He was writing for *Time* magazine and *The Nation* where he did an arts column." He pointed to a chair littered with newspapers. "Sit down." MacDonald sat and sipped his drink. The man continued with the story.

"He was also doing some newsreel scripts for Paramount—he'd just done the one about the first atomic bomb tests—and he had recently taken up painting. He was as good at that as he was at anything, exhibiting with Willem de Kooning, Rothko—" He paused and shook his head. "I'm sorry . . . are you acquainted with these names at all?"

MacDonald nodded.

"Ah, good. Yes, with Rothko and Pollock—and he was holding a few one-man shows. So, I guess it's fair to say that life for him was good.

"I met him one night in Washington Square. I say one night when, actually, it was well into the early hours of the morning." He paused and took a drink. "I was hunting."

"Hunting?"

"Yes. I was out looking for food."

"Are we back to the vampire shtick now?"

The man ignored the tone and continued. "I usually arise in the early evening. If it's too light outside, I stay indoors until the sun is about to set. Contrary to fable, we can exist in the sunlight although it hurts our eyes and causes headaches like your migraines. So we don't do it. Not usually.

"This particular evening, I had already fed upon a young woman down near Port Authority. She had just arrived in town from Cedar Rapids, Iowa, and she offered me herself for twenty dollars. That was a steep price for a prostitute back in 1943, I can tell you. But she was an attractive girl and she knew it. How could I refuse.

"I killed her in an alley, and drank my fill." He drained his glass and waved it at MacDonald. "More?"

"Huh? Oh, no. No more, thanks. I'm fine with this."

The man turned around and poured himself another three fingers. "Always the truth is simpler than the fiction, don't you find?" he said as he turned back to face MacDonald. "The truth is that we do not have to hunt every night. A complete feed will sustain us for many days—sometimes a couple of weeks—before we start to grow hungry again. Vampires, as you call us, are not naturally aggressive . . . anymore than humans, we hunt and kill merely to feed.

"Anyway . . . where was I? Ah, yes. When I met Harry—he was calling himself Harry back then, and I guess I just never lost the habit—when I met Harry, he was working on notes for his second book. He was walking through the Square where I was sitting. I was completely sated at this time, having—" He waved his hand—"the girl and so on."

MacDonald nodded and took a drink, eyeing the open door at his side.

"Anyway, he sat down beside me and we started to talk. We talked about the city and the night—both of which I know well—and then he mentioned that he was a writer. I think that's what Harry regarded himself as more than anything else: a writer.

"And he asked me if I enjoyed reading. I told him not very much at all. Then he mentioned his poetry: did I like poetry? I told him I really wasn't qualified to comment on it. I did have some books, I told him, but, I said, frankly they might as well be filled with blank pages for all the good they are to me.

"Some time later, of course," he said, leaning forward from his place against the kitchen counter, "he wrote—in the first of what I came to regard as my poems—

> *The pages in the books are blank.*
> *The books that Robinson has read.*"

MacDonald took another drink and hiccuped. "Did he know . . . did he know that you were a, you know . . . ?"

"Not immediately. But, eventually, of course, yes." He took a drink and rubbed his hand against the glass. "We were . . . we were alike, you know. Alike in so many ways."

"Alike? How?"

"Well, alienated. I suppose you could say that we were both outcasts from society. In those days I lived in New York.

"I have, of course, lived in many places—I won't bore you with the details: Harry covered some of them in his 'Robinson At Home' . . . uncouth bearded figure; keen-eyed sniper; a beggar on the streets; confidant of popes—but when I lived in New York, it grew too hot for me in the summertime. I used to go up to Maine, to a little coastal village called Wells. Do you know it?"

MacDonald shook his head. Holding out his empty glass, he said, "I think I *will* have that refill now."

The man took the glass. "Of course." He filled it to the brim and handed it back. "Harry didn't like me going off in the summer. He said it made him feel lonely."

"Lonely? Were you both . . . were you living together at that time?"

"Oh, gracious no. Harry was married—Ann was her name: nice girl, but entirely unable to cope with living with someone like Harry. And, of course, as he became more and more taken with my . . . shall we say, *company*, he became even less livable with." He sniggered. "Is there such a phrase as 'livable with?' "

MacDonald shrugged *why not?* and took another drink. The man smiled in agreement. "So, Ann took more and more to drinking. In 1954 she went into the hospital and—oh, of course, by this time we were in San Francisco. Did I mention that? We moved across to the West Coast in 1950. Harry took up with some new friends—Phyllis Diller, the comedienne? And Kenneth Rexroth?"

MacDonald nodded to both names.

"Wonderful poet, Ken Rexroth. Wonderful." He took a drink.

"We moved out west because, as I say, Harry hated the summers in New York when I was away. You remember 'Relating To Robinson?'

> *(But Robinson,*
> *I knew, was out of town: he summers at a place in Maine,*

*Sometimes on Fire Island, sometimes on the Cape,
Leaves town in June and comes back after Labor Day.)"*

He laughed suddenly. "I tell you, I never—*never*—went to Fire Island. Or the Cape. That was Harry. He was just so pissed off with me for leaving him." He shook his head and stared down into the swirling brown liquid in his glass. "So pissed off," he said again, but quieter.

"So—San Francisco. It was fine for a while, but Ann grew more and more restless. Harry had taken up playing jazz. He was good, too. Incredible man. So versatile. But our relationship—and the constraints placed upon it by his being married—was starting to take its toll. You see, Harry was growing older . . . and I was not.

"In 1953, he wrote 'The lacerating effects of middle age are dreadful, God knows . . . what the routes along this particular terrain are, I wish I knew. The trick of repeating *It can't get any worse* is certainly no good, when all the evidence points to quite the opposite.' " He shuffled around and lifted the bottle of Jim Beam. "You see," he said, flicking off the screw cap with his thumb, "I wanted Harry to let me taint him."

"Taint him? How do you mean?" MacDonald watched the cap roll to a stop on the dirty floor. Its sides were flattened.

"I mean . . . to make him like me."

"A vampire?"

"A vampire. He would have had eternal life, you see. It doesn't happen every time. Not every time we feed. That's another thing the legends have got wrong. We only taint our victims if we allow our own saliva to enter the wound. Most times, we do not.

"But, no, Harry wouldn't hear of it. He said that life was too precious—which was a paradox of a thing for him to say—and he couldn't face the prospect of hunting for his food. I told him that I would do all of that for him . . . but it was no use."

MacDonald took a deep breath and asked the question he had wanted to ask for several minutes. "Were you lovers?"

The man's eyes narrowed as he considered the question, and then he said, "Of a sort, yes. But not in the physical sense. We were soul mates, he and I. I had the information and the experiences of the millennia and Harry . . . Harry had the means to put them into words. Such beautiful words." He fell silent and, lifting the bottle to his mouth, took a long drink.

"By the time 1955 was upon us, we both knew that we couldn't carry on this way. In his poem 'January,' Harry wrote:

> *This wakening, this breath*
> *No longer real, this deep*
> *Darkness where we toss,*
> *Cover a life at the last."*

And MacDonald added: *"Sleep is too short a death."*

"You know it?" the man said, clearly amazed and apparently quite delighted.

"I know them all."

"Of course, you would.

"Well, that year, we decided that Harry would have to disappear. I suppose we had known it for some time. Harry had often toyed with the idea of his suicide—even before he met me. He kept a scrapbook of cuttings and notes, and a chronological list of writers who had killed themselves or simply disappeared. One of his favorites, you know, was Hart Crane. He threw himself off a ship."

"Yes, I know. His poem 'Voyages' is one of my own favorites."

"Harry's, too," said the man. He sighed and continued. "And so we decided that he would jump—or appear to jump—from the Golden Gate Bridge. The day he did it was one year to the day since his official separation from Ann."

"Where did you go?"

"Mexico. Mexico City. He lived in Mexico—*we* lived in Mexico, I should say—very happily. We led as close to a normal life as we could . . . which was very close indeed.

"Harry wrote poetry and short stories—many of them published under *noms de plume*—and we spent the nights together, talking. I would tell him of all the things that I had seen and experienced and Harry would put them into poems and stories.

"Then, in 1987, a journalist for the *San Francisco Examiner* wrote that he had met Harry in a bar in Mexico City back in 1957."

"That was true, then, that story?"

The man nodded enthusiastically. "Every word. Absolutely true. The journalist was Peter Hamill.

"Harry was pretty zilched-out that night, I remember," the man said wistfully. "He'd been drinking Jack Daniel's and then, because it was my night to hunt, he went off by himself—something he did very rarely—and polished off several bowls of marinated shrimp and most of a bottle of mescal. We thought nothing more about it until, like three decades later, for chrissakes, the story appeared in the *Examiner*. Needless to say, we left Mexico City within a few days."

"Where did you go then?"

"Oh, different places. Central America at first, but then Harry got to hankering for the States so we moved up to Texas." He took another drink from the bottle. "Then, when Harry's health got really bad, we moved back to Beatrice."

"What was it? What was wrong with him?"

"Cancer. He was riddled in the end. He died three weeks ago. I don't think I'm ever going to be able to cope."

MacDonald didn't know what to say.

"Even in the final days, I begged him to reconsider. If he'd let me taint him, he could have conquered the cancer. Then we could have lived forever. But he wouldn't." The man dropped the bottle and slid down the side of the counter to the floor. MacDonald jumped unsteadily from his chair and went to help him. He found a cloth by the side of the sink and ran cold water over it, flicking pieces of food and a couple of dead bugs into the sink. Then he rubbed the cloth over the man's face.

"I want . . . I want you to see him," he said. His voice was shaky and slurred.

"*See* him? I thought you said he was dead?"

The man nodded. "He is."

"He's dead and he's still here? Here in the house?"

Another nod.

"Where?"

"Upstairs. In his room."

MacDonald turned around and glanced back down the corridor towards the front door. Suddenly the smell of decay which permeated the house made sense. Kees had died three weeks ago. The weather was warm.

The man shuffled himself back up to a crouched position. "I . . . I want you to see him *now*."

MacDonald took his arm and helped him up. "Okay, okay."

"C'mon, then, let's go." The liquor was clearly having an effect. On MacDonald, it seemed to be having no effect at all. He felt as though he had never had a drink of alcohol in his entire life.

They staggered down the dark corridor to the foot of the stairs. "You sure you want to do this?" MacDonald asked.

"Sh—" he belched loudly and hiccuped. "Sure. Harry'd want to meet you."

They started up the stairs, swaying from side to side, MacDonald against the handrail and the man called Robinson buffeting against the wall.

At the top of the stairs, the smell was deeper and thicker. It was now pure decay.

"Thish way," Robinson said, and he took off by himself along the narrow corridor toward the end room. He reached it with a thud and took two steps backward, stretching his right hand out toward the handle.

MacDonald ran forward. "Here, let me," he said, against his better judgment. Robinson stepped aside.

MacDonald took hold of the handle and turned it. His first impression was that the air that escaped from the ancient pyramids must have smelled like this, only milder. It stank. He lifted his hand to his mouth and swallowed the bile that was even then shooting up his throat. He pushed the door open and stepped into the room.

It was almost pitch-black. The curtains were drawn across the narrow window, but a small night-light glowed beside a wide bed that ran from the side wall into the room. In front of the bed and along to the side beneath the window, stretched a long desk strewn with huge piles of manuscripts and sheets of paper. On the table was a typewriter, a confusion of pens and pencils and erasers, a half-full—or half-empty—bottle of Jack Daniel's, and an array of empty glasses, some upright and some on their sides.

On the bed itself was a body, though its resemblance to anything that might once have lived was tenuous. It was dark and wizened, and seemed to move and writhe where it lay. MacDonald realized that Harry Weldon Kees now provided a home for a multitude of insects and larvae.

The door clicked shut behind him.

MacDonald spun around and faced Robinson. "You . . . you're not drunk," he said.

The man smiled. "Sorry. I've had what you might say was a lot of practice in holding my liquor." Then he opened a cupboard by his side. "I have a job for you."

"A . . . a job? What kind of job?"

"I want you to kill me."

MacDonald laughed and made a move toward the door. "What the hell is this . . . ? I'm getting out—"

Robinson pushed him back and MacDonald stumbled against the bed, throwing his arm out to steady himself. MacDonald's hand sank into something which seemed damp and clammy. He felt things pop under its weight. "Oh, Jesus!" He jumped away from the bed and looked at his hand. It was covered in what looked like leafmold. He shook it frantically. "Oh, God," he said. "Oh, Jesus . . ."

"Here." Robinson reached into the open cupboard. He pulled out a flat-headed wooden hammer and handed it to MacDonald.

MacDonald took it and said, "Oh, Jesus!"

Then Robinson reached in again and pulled out a wooden pole, its end sharpened to a fine point.

MacDonald started to whimper.

"Here. You'll need this, too."

"No, I won't."

"You—"

"I'm not doing it. I'm not doing anything else. I'm getting out of this—"

Robinson took hold of MacDonald's jacket, crumpled it in his fist, and pulled the man toward him. "You'll do what I say you'll do . . . if you *do* want to get out of here."

MacDonald started shaking and stepped back away from Robinson. The man had spoken right into his face, breathed right over him . . . but the smell had not been of Jim Beam's, it had been of blood. Heavy and metallic. "Why? Why do you want me to do this? Why *me?*"

"Because I want to sleep the long sleep. Because . . . because I'm lonely. And because you are here."

"Is . . . is there no other way?"

Robinson shook his head. "At least one of the legends is true. A stake through the heart. It's the only way."

MacDonald looked at Robinson and fought off looking around at the thing on the bed. "What if I don't?"

"I'll kill you."

It didn't take long for them to get things organized. Robinson stretched out on the bed next to Weldon Kees and held the stake's point above his chest with his left hand. With his right hand, he held the hand of the body by his side.

While he thought about trying to make a break for it, MacDonald heard Robinson sigh a long, deep sigh. "It feels funny," he said. "Funny to be lying here at last, lying here waiting to die.

"I've come close a couple of times—well, more than a couple, I'd guess—but I've always managed to turn things to my advantage." He turned his head to Weldon Kees and smiled. "Old friend," he said softly. "You and me, forever now." He looked up at MacDonald, smiled at the man's shaking hands around the shaft of the hammer. "You've no idea, have you?" he said.

"About what?" MacDonald lowered the hammer, grateful for the pause.

"Loneliness. The ache of ages spent completely alone. I thought that loneliness was all behind me. I thought that Harry would eventually relent and let me taint him. But it was not to be. He even begged me not to bite him if he should slip into some kind of coma before the end. He said if I did, then he would never speak to me again." He shook his head. "I couldn't live without Harry's words. I *cannot* live without his words. Death can only be a release." He closed his eyes and shook the stake gently. "Do it. Do it now."

MacDonald lifted the hammer high. As he started to bring it down, Robinson's eyes opened and fixed upon him. "Burn us when you're through."

The hammer hit the stake squarely, as though MacDonald's hand had been guided right to the very end. The pole went into the body hard and lodged in the mattress beneath it. Robinson's body arched once, high in the air, and then slipped back.

MacDonald watched in fascination as the skin shriveled and pulled back, exposing teeth that looked nothing like what he expected a vampire's teeth to look like. The eyeballs jellied in their sockets and sank back out of sight. The flesh and muscle atrophied, the bones powdered, and within seconds Robinson's clothes sank back onto the dust. There was no blood.

As if in a daze, MacDonald put down the hammer and walked across to the desk. He lifted a pile of papers and scattered them about the desktop. He could not help himself. As he threw the sheets around, he tried to read some of the lines . . . some of the title pages. He started to cry.

He threw sheets onto the floor . . . high into the air, and watched them flutter onto the lone body on the bed. "Please . . . please, God, let me take just one sheet. . . ."

In his head, amidst the confusion, he heard a voice he did not recognize. It was an old voice, but it sounded gentle and wise. It said, *Take one sheet, then . . . but only one.*

MacDonald grabbed a sheet and jammed it into his sportscoat pocket. Then he picked up a book of matches, struck one, and ignited the whole book. He tossed it onto the scattered sheets, turned calmly around, and left the room.

The fire took longer to get going than he expected.

In the movies, the conflagration is always immediate. But here in reality, it took almost an hour. MacDonald watched it from across the street, watched the first flames reach up to the waiting curtains, watched the first glow in one of the downstairs rooms, smelled the first smoke-filled breeze blowing across the sidewalk.

Then it was done. And only then did MacDonald feel released from the power of Robinson's eyes.

As he started back to the heart of Beatrice, a gentle rain began to fall. MacDonald pulled the crumpled sheet from his pocket and, in the occasional glow of the streetlights, started to read. It was a poem. A complete work captured on a single sheet of paper. It was called "Robinson At Rest." It began:

> *Robinson watching a movie, safe*
> *In the darkness. The world outside spills by*
> *Along sidewalks freshened by rain.*
> *He says to the man by his side, "Is that clock correct?"*
> *"No," the answer comes. "It's stopped*
> *At last."*

And seventeen lines later it ended:

Weldon Kees (1914–1993)

THE JAMES DEAN GARAGE BAND
Rick Moody

Rick Moody is the author of *The Ice Storm*, a well-received collection of novellas, and one novel, *Garden State*. He lives in Brooklyn, New York.

"The James Dean Garage Band" is a rich and quirky fantasia about life in a small California town. And about what happened to James Dean *after* that infamous car wreck—which, as it turns out, wasn't actually a fatal crash after all. . . . This story was first published in the July issue of *Esquire* magazine, and also appeared in *The Ring of Brightest Angels Around Heaven: A Novella and Stories*.

—T.W.

He walked away from the accident, of course. He left the insurance adjusters and the film agents and lawyers to sift through the wreckage for his remains, and he walked away. Ahead, an old Ford sedan making a left turn. On Route 466. Dean had been driving all day. Speeding like a motherfucker. Rolf Wutherich riding shotgun. Wutherich had tuned up the car that morning. It was performing. This much is well known. Dean said, *That guy has to see us. He'll stop.* But the Ford didn't stop. And then Dean seemed to be steering straight for the Ford. *Wait,* said Wutherich. He had a wife and kids. Wutherich panicked. Grabbed for the wheel. Dean held him off. The Ford telescoped. The Porsche did a couple of jetés and came to rest top down in some scrub. Engine already in flames. A stillness. Again: the sound of the skid and of the chassis being reconfigured, sculpted by chance, the explosion, and the quiet. Dean told me later. Quiet. You could pass from one life to the next without a sound.

Besides the tweed jacket, he was wearing khaki pants, a white cotton tee, and Jack Purcells. He got out of the car and dusted off his jacket. He kicked the upside-down door of the Porsche. He hustled Wutherich from the passenger side and got him several yards away. Dean had to extinguish Rolf's hair, too. It was on fire. He worked desperately, shamefully. Wutherich also had a deep head wound. He was losing a lot of blood. But once Dean was satisfied that his friend was out of danger— the guy in the Ford was completely uninjured; he was standing nervously by Dean's side—once the practicalities were settled, the *opportunity* in this calamity became apparent. It was like an opening between cloud banks. It was like the interstices between fact and fiction. This opportunity was about motion. Leaving behind

Wutherich and lawsuits and countersuits and the paperwork and the medical bills and the studios and the tabloids. Leaving the scene of the accident. Dean started walking out into the desert. He was crying. The sun was on its way down. He had no water. But he felt impervious to scorpions or snakes or magic crows or thirst or anything else. He just started walking. And though he was no athlete, soon he was running. Running as fast as his skinny cinematic legs could carry him. Into the desert.

Three or four hours later. The only earthly light from a filling station a mile distant. Above, the stars bloomed like the lights on a marquee. With no good idea about the ramifications of his escape, except that it was going to have a sort of rugged individualism as part of it, James Dean was heading up into the hills. And that was how he arrived in *my town*. Lost Hills, that's the name of it, in Kern County. Fifty miles northwest of Bakersfield. Population, eleven hundred. No industry of any kind. Principal activity: drinking.

We were rehearsing that night.

Garage bands are always in the family. My brother and I were rehearsing, as we did a couple of nights a week, with a guy from up the street. We were in a rut, musically speaking. I can admit that now. We knew only a few songs. We had a couple of originals. We had been thinking about getting some horns, a saxophone player. In those days, you had to have a sax; they squawked sycophantically at all the dances.

We'd been rehearsing in the shed for two years. For my kit, I made do with a snare, a couple of toms, and a cymbal. My brother, Wallace, played stand-up bass. The third guy, Rocket, could do a passable imitation, on an electric guitar, of the kind of swamp blues that faith-healed, produced spontaneous tears, and conjured devils. Rocket could sort of play, actually. Which is more than I can say of Wallace and myself. I couldn't drum, and I still can't.

There was a knock outside, a knock we didn't hear really, a knock that registered only subliminally in us, and the garage door slid up. I remember thinking that the crickets seemed too loud that night. And the light of the moon was grand. There was this guy in a tweed jacket and khakis. Standing there.

My brother, Wallace, has said in a televised interview that Dean was wearing a tattered shirt and that his face and hands were dotted with blood. Wallace has said that Dean asked for first aid. What a lot of horseshit. Dean looked like any other guy from Lost Hills—he had that beleaguered, small-town, jobless look. There was nothing more to it. *You guys could peel paint with that shit*, he said. He meant the way we played. Then he stood there awkwardly, hands deep in his pockets. We didn't say anything. I wasn't terribly interested in making him comfortable. Rocket was fiddling with the knobs on his amplifier. I started adjusting the height of my stool. It happened, though, that there was an extra guitar, a Telecaster, standing against the wall, next to a rusty hoe. You know how coincidences work, these humdrum celestial interventions. It was a '51 Telecaster. First year they made the model, and I had saved up for months to buy it. Drove down to Bakersfield on a pilgrimage. With the garage door open that night, there was a portentous moonlight reflecting off the lacquer of the Telecaster. Really. That's how it was. Dean seemed to be looking at it. We were all looking at it. The guitar, the moonlight, and James Dean.

Can you play that? I asked.

James Dean said, *Can't really play shit, but I can teach you boys a trick or two. You gotta strum that thing like you're using it to harrow graves.*

Sure, you think I knew who he was. You think I read the papers back then, that I kept up with what was playing at the drive-in or on Main Street. But the papers didn't mean anything to me. I was an ugly kid. I wore glasses and was unnaturally thin, like a sickly version of Buddy Holly. Few girls had kissed me, not even my mom that I could remember, and I spent most of my time at the library. And I'll tell you what I *wasn't* reading. I wasn't reading *Drums Made Easy* or *Guitar for Beginners*. No, I was trying to read Kierkegaard and Nietzsche and the translations of the gnostic gospels (the Jung Codex)—on interlibrary loan from L.A.—and I didn't give a damn about the movies. Wallace was getting ready to do a mortuary-sciences degree. None of us went to the movies. Weren't interested. I was twenty-one and Wallace was a couple of years younger. Rocket could have been anywhere from twenty to forty-nine, *and he huffed glue.* Some kind of aeronautical solvent his dad brought back from the assembly line at McDonnell Douglas.

And it wasn't a garage, actually, where we were playing. Over the years people have asked if it was a real garage. It wasn't. It was a shed *with a garage door on it*. In fact, it was a fallout shelter. My parents, forward-thinking survivors of World War II, built the shelter after Eisenhower's "Atoms for Peace" initiative, about the same time that Fender introduced the Telecaster. The shelter was on an empty patch of desert. A couple of miles from my parents' house, on the outskirts of town. There was room there, on this empty stretch, for Lost Hills to get interested in civil defense. There were a half dozen shelters, like postindustrial burrows, on the land out there. The desert wasn't well irrigated yet. There were a few windmills fluttering around us, though. I loved windmills. I loved electricity.

When we saw that he wasn't going to leave right away, we set aside our equipment and took those old canvas folding chairs from the shed and set them out back. Weather balloons in the evening sky. Experimental aircraft. It was like there were fireworks out there; it was like the goddamned Fourth of July. And it was no coincidence, either, that we were sitting in that spot, no coincidence at all. That was where we always sat when we were dreaming big.

Dean told us he was James Dean and explained how he'd made a pretty good movie called *Rebel Without a Cause*, and that he was looking for some peace and quiet, and, well, *if you wanted to know the truth*, he was dodging this reputation, man, he was fighting off the calculation and spiritual impoverishment of fame, yep, and he had gotten into this accident and hurt a guy he cared about, and he was running from it and thinking he wanted to be a small-town bank teller and to manage his kid's Little League team and to be able to cry at Memorial Day parades and cheat on his taxes and get fat if he wanted and leave a bloated and pasty corpse and carry a pistol and sleep with his best friend's wife without a phalanx of photographers and reporters around, because, he said, *fame and remorse, boys, are one and the same thing.*

I thought he was just a handsome guy. Could have been a pansy maybe. Dean wasn't exactly charismatic when you get right down to it. Wallace, for example, was worried that he didn't *drink* enough. We'd been raised not to trust men who didn't drink. I'd read that in Mongolian culture to refuse an offered drink was dangerous—you could be killed for it—and the desert of central California was in those days a lot like Mongolia. In Mongolia, the shepherds and their great herds of yak and mutton just ambled this way and that, wherever the best grazing took them. And that was what we were doing, as adulthood overtook us. We were southwestern tumbleweeds, going end over end, according to the government of the winds.

I didn't know what Dean was talking about where fame was concerned. Sounded like a lot of complaining to me. Wallace knew, though. He could see the writing on the wall; he could *visualize* the quadrilateral shape of the James Dean Garage Band. He could see how Dean needed us, how he'd been brought here to experience the authenticity of our dim, narrow lives. And Wallace could see how we needed Dean. Pretty insightful for a guy whose job it is now to fill dead bodies with formaldehyde. After a few beers, my brother looked Dean right in the eye and put it to him: *Are you going to give us a hand with the combo?* Because we hadn't gotten out of the fallout shelter yet. We hadn't even played a church social or at the VFW or even for our parents. Our great expectations were locked deep in us. *Hey, why not*, Dean said, without conviction, *until you find someone else. Sure. But I can't sing at all.*

We nodded *yes*. Emphatically. The shooting stars burst in multiples over the sere part of the West.

We did it because we knew, even then, that a three-piece lineup wasn't enough, wasn't going to get to the sound we were hearing in our heads. We did it because we had some models, some music we liked, stuff like Edgard Varése and Robert Johnson and John Cage, who had just been doing the pentatonic scales, stuff like the kind of music La Monte Young would soon be making. We wanted to make these pieces that sounded like the wind blowing through a barn or like a neglected teakettle or like the little cry of pain that escapes your lips when you are really lonely. At least these were the sounds in my head, and I was trying to teach Wallace and Rocket about them, but I didn't really have the terminology yet. The thing we had in common then, as a band—and it was the thing that Dean helped us articulate later by applying Stanislavsky to the garage band format—was that we had been *forsaken by earthly affection*. That was the only lyric we needed. Everything else was just a restatement. Everything we played was just a simple sentence about our loneliness, about loneliness and the tan from aboveground tests, loneliness and jobs at filling stations, loneliness and homeliness and grade school humiliations, loneliness that we were only now digesting into song. Maybe we thought Dean could help us in this way. And maybe in the calculating lobes of our American skulls, we figured that having a movie-star guitarist would help us play the dance halls in Bakersfield. So we could quit our day jobs.

See, Wallace and I had bought a trailer out on the edge of Lost Hills with some money we had inherited from our grandmother. That was where we were living. I didn't know where we were going to put Dean, where in the trailer, but the way I saw it, an actor fleeing the studio system didn't need luxury accommodations. He could just sleep on the floor, as Wallace used to do on his way to blacking out. And that was what happened. That night, James Dean slept on the floor of our trailer, with dirty T-shirts as his pillow, with empties scattered around him. He woke with a stiff neck.

Next day, we went back to the fallout shelter, the four of us. We drove out in a dusty, hand-me-down DeSoto that my parents had given me when I turned sixteen. Dean probably never figured that he'd have to spend his time in a working-class vehicle like that. He probably thought he'd left that way of life back with the Hoosiers. We drove at cruising speed, just above the minimum. Windows down. Desert breezes in our crew cuts. We were eminences from a marginal culture.

The garage door creaked mournfully as it slid up. The shelter smelled like a crypt. I made Rocket use his own guitar at that first rehearsal, even though he was always bugging me to play the Telecaster. Instead, Dean strapped it on. We had a single-tube amp that looked like it was going to short out all the time. You could have fried an egg on that thing. No microphones. Tentatively, at first, we decided on one of the faster numbers, a thing by Rocket with lyrics he made up on the spot: "Rocket from the Tombs." I counted it off. And the engine of our success roared to life. Right away, the tempos were sped up. Right away. Because of Dean. As though the automotive ghost of his Porsche were urging us on, into the dusty attic of our small-town memories. In a couple of takes, the song started to sound pretty swell. That wasn't all, though. I want to let you know the enormity of what happened, the real miracle of the first rehearsal. We got Rocket's song—the lyrics seemed to concern dead people driving convertibles—up to, oh, about 150 beats per minute. That's what they'd say now: BPMs. And suddenly, instantly, effortlessly, Rocket landed on this certain riff, as though his fingers had been rehearsing it for months. It sounded appropriated, it was so right. *It was the Chuck Berry riff.* Before Chuck ever committed it to vinyl. Rocket's fingers did it. Dean pushed him into it. The song slotted into that groove. We were tilting at history.

Dean grew a beard. He wouldn't leave the shed after the rehearsal. So we let him stay there. Until his beard grew in. I wondered how, over the long haul, he was going to live in that tiny, airless space. He was used to Beverly Hills or Santa Monica bungalows with their artificial landscaping, air conditioners, toy dogs, ocean views. But as the days passed, we found him cooking canned beef stew over the olive flames of Sterno, sitting on the reinforced concrete, reading and rereading the opening of *The Diamond Sutra*. He looked, if not happy, at least relieved.

He started to grow his hair out, too, like a beatnik. Or that's what I supposed, though Wallace and Rocket and I didn't exactly know what beatniks looked like. I'd read Ginsberg and I liked the sound of his catalogs, but I was more interested in Continental thinking—Camus and Sartre. We hadn't actually seen any beatniks in Lost Hills, so we made up what we thought they were. They were figures of myth, like film actors. According to our imaginations, the beatniks had borrowed from every pertinent strain of Western thinking—strains both ascetic and decadent—and had thrown off anything they didn't like, anything that constrained the articulation of desire. Something like that. And these ambitions turned out to be Dean's ambitions. He taught them to us. He used sense memory. *He used the Method.*

When Dean finally had the beard, he agreed to go out in public. He had put on a little weight, too. He was getting himself one of those country midsections that spill over a turquoise belt buckle. He'd started to drink. No one ever gave him a look in town, though. They just didn't care. And even if they had known this was the guy from *Giant*, even if they'd known he was here among us to slip the noose of Hollywood, well, the people of Lost Hills weren't going to get in his way. No one ever walked up to him and said, *Hey, didn't you die in a car wreck a couple of months ago?* It would have been rude.

It was about this time when we got the gig at the jazz club, Wally's. In the weeks before, Dean led us through a crash course in free jazz. He'd blindfold us or make us play our instruments backward. He said we had to stop adhering so strictly to the downbeats. It was Wallace who had the first breakthrough in this area. And this breakthrough was truly emblematic of our sound, of what we did later. In fact, Wallace's jazz work is really important to any real critical exegesis of the James Dean Garage Band. If you were going to do a psychoanalytic reading of our dynamics, say, you would have to point to Wallace's relationship with my dad—always stormy and punctuated by long periods of parental neglect—and to his resultant need for a father figure, or at least an older-brother figure, who could make him feel secure enough to provide the bedrock structure—or in this case the *freedom from structure*—that we needed in the lower end of our sound. This need was fulfilled by the appearance of Dean. Through Dean, Wallace suddenly understood the way his bass could wander from the rigors of the blues as they were traditionally played. He ate better after that, too.

Having secured this first convert, Dean started holding me after rehearsals. *He had jammed on bongos with Monk and Coltrane,* he said, *and the thing they knew was how to let go of the time signature, just let go of it,* he said, *and see where the kit takes you after that, plug into the rigors of your feelings, man, and let go of the beat, not worry about it,* he said, *just play what you feel, just play anything, let it happen, feel your breathing, feel your pulse, the way it's faint and insistent, the way it comes and goes, the way it protests and whimpers and then sings, cries out its hortatory cries, just let it go, man, remember, remember.*

Of course, we couldn't play jazz fast—Wallace couldn't do those long, convoluted bass solos, I couldn't make the brushes work right—but Rocket was doing something wild. His guitar came to some terrible conclusions during our jazz period. He arrived at a system of accidentals and bad fingerings that sounded like infantile bereavement and rage trying, working, and ultimately *failing* to enunciate themselves. Just the way Strasberg talked about it. Later, of course, Hendrix was aiming for the same thing. It sounded as if Rocket were going to overcome the mechanism of his own breathing, as if the whole history of governmental oppression and religious intolerance were being digested and boiled down in his solos, and also the legacy of his uncomfortable childhood. He played melodies with the bittersweet pathos of silences.

Wally's was empty. There were maybe three or four guys on the premises the night we played, guys with really long hair, the kind of hair that Dean was growing, and they were all sitting at the bar. Bikers. I'd never seen any of them in Lost Hills. They'd never seen me, either. The tables by the stage were completely empty, little red candles flickering weakly on them. Dean looked like James Dean, you know, as we stepped onto the proscenium—he had shaved his beard by now—and we were playing in public—we were entertainers—but these guys at the bar, they looked right through us.

Here was Dean's bind: if he pretended he was nobody, he was condescending, and if he pretended he *was* somebody, he was putting on airs, he was arrogant. As a result, at the inaugural gig of the James Dean Garage Band, *Dean played with his back to the audience.* A couple of times, he stepped up to the extra mike, when we were singing backing vocals on a rave-up chorus, but mostly he was turned away. He was shaking so bad that his playing sounded great—the Telecaster was buzzing and warbling with tremolo. The guys in Wally's didn't give a shit. They never noticed a thing.

As a professional, you have so many preconceptions about playing out. You think because you're onstage that somehow you deserve or command respect. But once we got up there, we forgot everything we had learned in six months of rehearsals. We just plunged ahead. I remember looking at a set list—it was crayoned on a lobster bib and masking-taped to my drum case—and feeling like I was going to be sick. We were playing all those songs? One ended and another began, though, without nuance or detail, and we didn't have time to worry. Wallace broke a blister and by the end of the night his strings were covered in red cells and pus. And Rocket's throat closed up. Too much whiskey and epoxy. But it was okay. Rocket sounded like one of those eighty-year-old back-porch Delta blues guys whose lives have been a sequence of tragedies. Dean, in the meantime—in one of his forays into the recesses of the stage where no one could see what he was doing—had retuned his guitar. It was in some ornery sitar tuning. Sounded really lousy. He was trying to get the rhythm guitar to do some drone stuff. He was getting hip, he said, to Armenian düdük music.

At the same time, I was trying to hold down regular time. I was slipping between four-four and six-eight with these little bursts of sevens and fives. I didn't know what I was doing. As the set wore on, the desert rats at the bar got up and left. We cleaned the place out. We emptied it. Wally himself was shaking his head, mopping the floor as we finished the last few songs. The stench of spilled beer. The sound of the swabbing of Wally's mop. The ringing in my ears. Then: the skein of stars out in the desert. The sputtering of the DeSoto. The rasping sleepers beside me. As I made my way, at thirty-five miles per hour, through the desert.

Back to the garage. More rehearsal. Only way you bounce back from those off nights. Rocket was the next one to develop the avant-garde ambitions that were so crucial to our success. He was starting to learn the rudiments of *feedback* on his guitar. It happened like this. The old amp blew out, our single-tube amp. None of us really had the money to get another. Except Dean. Dean still had some residuals that he had secreted away someplace. In some foreign account. In a Swiss bank, or an offshore trust. With these funds, we made a trip to Bakersfield. We got two Fender amplifiers. One for Dean. One for Rocket.

We had the usual band fights about paying for this equipment. Rocket had to borrow money from Dean to kick in his fourth of any group purchase, and then he always tried to rig the repayments so that they favored his fiscal recklessness. I felt sorry for Rocket, so I intervened to arrange a quarterly repayment plan, which Dean, using negotiating experience from Hollywood, insisted would have to include interest. So I was paying Rocket's interest, quarterly, to Dean, while Rocket was borrowing money from Wallace to pay me back monthly, and also borrowing to repay the principal, which monies I would then, acting as middleman, pass on to

Dean to hold in escrow until the interest was paid off, when the actual, final payments on the principal would kick in.

It created some real friction among us.

In the meantime, Rocket started playing with the amps. This was 1957, or thereabouts. Fender had finally developed an amplifier that was loud enough for feedback, for that revolutionary noise. One day, Dean was mumbling, as he did, about money, and about songwriting credits in the band. (It should have been 80/20 Dean/band, he argued, as opposed to 50/50, like we'd already negotiated it. After all, it was *his name*.) Rocket had simply had enough. Rocket threw down his guitar in front of the amp—already cranked to capacity—and stormed out of the shed. Into the rain, if I remember correctly. A sudden and vehement desert rain. And the feedback from the pickups in the amplifier, in conjunction with the primitive electronics of the amp, commenced to gloriously *wail*. As if the guitar, the circuitry, the tubes, the pickups, as if all of this equipment were falling into lamentation, as if they were doing call and response with the lightning, over the plains, over the hills. It was a lovely, fuzzy overtone, almost aboriginal in its way. Rocket walked around in circles out in the rain, trying to get straight in his head whether or not to punch out Dean, and then I suppose he heard us laughing, heard Wallace and Dean and me laughing at the racket the amp was making. So he came back. Drenched. And he heard it, too. *Listen to that*, he said, grinning wildly, *damn. That is sweet.*

Right away, Rocket perched himself directly in front of the amplifier, sitting on the floor, with the guitar balanced on his knee, and worked with those ringing, bell-shaped electrical tones. He lived in that howl. Just lived in it. He was finally understanding that his body had borders, that he cast a shadow, that he was capable of acting and being acted upon. Rocket had ambitions now. He wanted to be famous. He wanted to be in love.

Feedback changed everything. For our sound, for the band, for the members of the band. It was ritualistic somehow. Feedback foreshortened the great distances between things and cleared up the mirages in the desert. It made all of the American West seem like a goddamned global village. It was the legend that wired up our thatched huts out in Lost Hills. For example, Wallace and I started stealing. It was a belated conversion to vice. We were catching up on the rock 'n' roll *lifestyle*. We were out stealing cars from the parking lots of repossession operations. Joyriding in the hills, drinking and driving. Driving into the desert, through endless stretches of sage and yucca and Mormon tea. Setting the cars on fire after, leaving them by the side of the road. We'd stay drunk all day. I had even begun propositioning girls. Groupies, you know? I'd see a girl at a diner and I'd say, *Hey, I'm the drummer in the James Dean Garage Band, and I think I need to put an arm around you.* No refusal was possible. The mere name of our band was persuasive. The neighbors started asking questions about us. The local constabulary forces began stopping us on the road.

And my business was going bankrupt. I'd been running a scrap-metal operation part-time since high school—it was mostly car parts and space junk or bomb casements. Stuff I found in the desert. At one time I was a canny and ambitious young man. At one time people were glad to make me part of their *scrap-metal needs*. Now the business was belly flopping from inattention. I was broke. We were broke. Just as we were making innovations in popular music that are still being felt today, we were all getting ready to go on public assistance. Dean bailed us out for a while, paid our expenses, but then even he began to get tight. According to his accountants, he was dead.

This all came to an end in '59, I think, when I actually robbed a drive-through hamburger joint over in Devils Den. The next town. They all knew me over there—they'd seen us in the DeSoto. I entered the Jiffy Burger franchise with a German service revolver. I demanded the contents of the register. I was never afraid, not even for a moment. They just *gave* me the money. The manager asked politely if I would pay it back later. It was the most forlorn holdup. I did it because we were playing *loud*, because noise was an unstable element, because we were waking up the dormant ghosts of the desert, and there was no way of knowing the effect this sound would have upon us. My dad had to come and give me a good talking to. He slapped me around once and told me if I didn't shape up, if I didn't look after my appearance, if I didn't let go of this childishness and assume my adult responsibilities, I was no son of his. There was no way I'd ever inherit the hardware store.

The real point here is that Dean didn't invent feedback, as the executors of his estate have claimed. The thing you have to remember is that the James Dean Garage Band was a *band*. Four distinct personalities, each with his own contributions and responsibilities. Our advances and experiments took place in a group context. There was a free exchange of ideas. No one person had any more say than anyone else. It was the unique meshing of our personalities, the interlocking of tastes and influences, that led us to excellence.

And Dean was going through a personal crisis. A desert initiation. As I've told you, he cooked his meals out back of the shed. He began using a regular campfire circle, with hot coals—as though he were some kind of Pueblo Indian. He let these coals smolder for days. One afternoon when I turned up to meet him, Dean had taken off his old beat-up Jack Purcells and was trying to walk barefoot over the coals. There was a strait through the middle of the bed where there were fewer hunks of this brimstone. To my amazement, he managed to scoot across with minimal damage. Two or three blisters, nothing more. I didn't believe it, so I asked him to do it again. Maybe he had access to some period hallucinogen. Whatever it was, he seemed to have no pain, and he was yammering the whole time, yammering about a priest from his childhood who had given him a copy of Jung's *Psychology and Alchemy* and told him, man, *that the search was the thing, and not the destination, that you had a path and it narrowed and it asked sacrifices of you, man, and you were bound to tread upon it, wherever it led.*

Mere spiritual investigation was fine, of course, it was part of the desert palette, except that Dean didn't seem to be able to withstand it. He was crying a lot. Sobbing like a girl. And complaining. And he didn't bathe and his teeth were going bad. A couple of days later, at rehearsal, he had a really horrible toothache. He told me he was going to wait through the three or four days of pain until the tooth died. Then it would just fall out of his head. Which it did.

After a few years of living in Lost Hills, the guy looked like shit. He couldn't have secured a part in the monster movies of the period. But he was embarked on some odyssey of personal discovery that didn't require citizenship in this world, an odyssey that probably was activated by and transcended the four formative psychic touchstones of his life: *his mother's death, his father's abandonment of him, the Quakerism of his youth, and the James Dean Garage Band.* It wasn't my place to be his spiritual adviser, but I tried. I tried to let him do whatever he wanted, as long as he showed up for rehearsal.

He had some pretty strange ideas for lyrics, too. Here, for example, is something he scrawled on a brown paper bag. He intended one day to use it for a song: *It's been two years since I touched a woman / It's been two years / Even back in New York when I was a hustler / I never went this long missing that chemistry / I'm missing brand-new refrigerators and lawns / The rich smell of freshly cut lawns / I just want to be held, you know / I don't need a studio contract.*

Nervous collapse was just around the next bend. I don't know what the term would be now. Anxiety-depression disorder. Borderline personality. Loss sensitivity. These days they would put him on a serotonin enhancer. He would bounce back and repudiate the melancholy of his early performances and become a producer of industrial films. But look at the situation for a moment from our point of view. Was Dean's erratic behavior affecting his personal or business life? *He had no personal life, really.* Was his eccentricity affecting the band? It was not. We could follow Dean and Rocket wherever their impulsive, shifting, whimsical, malevolent improvisations took us. Dean would teach us a couple of chords one day and the next day the same song would be totally different. He would challenge us to call up the worst incidents from our bumpkin childhoods and to dwell upon them—the accidental deaths of playmates, the sexual explorations of neighborhood girls—and then he would leave us there in the practice room and go down the steps into the shelter to drink by himself. He was erratic like the thunderheads that rolled across the desert were erratic, erratic like the rattlesnakes and the scorpions in the parched crevices of desert, the windmills, the UFOs.

Wallace started doing Sufi spins in the middle of the rehearsal space. He would put down the bass and stretch out his arms and begin dervishing to the riffs around him. The band seemed to be free-falling toward some disorder. There were days we had cases of beer on the floor and we would play "Rocket from the Tombs" twenty-five times, for hours and hours, *actually attempting to summon the American dead from their hellish convertibles.* We played until the rehearsals spilled out onto the empty acreage around the fallout shelter, and we would go sprinting—east and west, north and south—into the night, in search of angels who were never coming for us. In search of the agency that would lift us up and transport us from the lower middle class and from the small town where we'd been raised. Yes, the band had changed us. Dean's fame had contaminated us, and our obscurity had contaminated him. We weren't close, the four of us; we weren't heartfelt *discussers*, men's-movement guys, but we gathered out in the sage on these nights and made the campfires of desert mythology and we waited for signs.

It was the last of these nights that Dean gave us the news.

Fellas, he said to us, *I have to tell you something serious. I am sure sorry to bring it up, but I don't see any way around it, and there's no easy way to break the news, so I'm just going to have to tell you . . . I have to go home. Guys. I'm sorry. I'm really sorry. . . . I gotta go home, to L.A., because I'm . . . well, I think I'm falling apart. I don't know what's up or down, fellas. I'm all confused. I just can't stay here any longer. I want to. It's something I want to do, but I can't. Look, this has been coming to me in the last few weeks. You know, the energy's sort of getting strange out here, I'm feeling like the past is catching up with me. I'm losing it. I gotta admit I don't know why I'm out here . . . I don't know why I came out here. Because once you're the snack food for this thing, this system, boys, this celebrity, you're snack food for good. You might as well lie back and enjoy it, that's what I'm thinking. So what I'm saying is I don't see any choice, don't see any way around leaving. I hate to do it to you, because you've been like brothers to me. You guys took me in, gave me a place to sleep. But that's just the way it is. . . . It's . . . it's hurting me out here. Hey, listen, fellas, I know, I know, I'm gonna make it up to you. I'm gonna repay this debt I have here. I got a promise for you. I've done a little homework. I've made a few calls. I've booked us into the Café Vertigo. We're gonna play L.A. We're gonna play to the stars.*

It was great news, right? It was the end of our naïve ambitions and the beginning of our *total hegemony*. The hegemony of the James Dean Garage Band. It was the kind of good news that makes it hard to sit still. Your body gets a carbonated jumpiness. You can't sleep. You become a compulsive talker. Your posture changes. Your hair inexplicably parts the right way. It was great news! So, to say that Dean's offer *contained the destruction of everything we stood for, to say that going to L.A. to make it big was our biggest mistake*—that would be stupid, would be ungrateful, would be insolent. Well, but listen. There's evidence.

We started having artistic differences.

For example, I was feeling the constraints of the major chords, the major triads. I heard that D-A-G progression in rehearsal and I just about broke out in shingles. I didn't want to play any chords at all. Chords were like the demonic music of radio game shows and political rallies. And they were everywhere. Dean would count off and dive into that rut every time. It was a new thing for him—being conservative. That same old Chuck Berry shit. I would be tempted to throw my sticks; I would be tempted to walk out of the shed; I would be tempted to chuck it all and run. If I could have covered my ears and drummed at the same time, I would have. I was trying to get Rocket to tune all six strings to C. I wanted to invent punk rock. I wanted to play unrecognizable chords and shout the most lacerating words. I wanted to bury the popular song in sand, up to its neck. And Wallace was off on his own trip, too. He was still into jazz. He wanted to play hard bop. Theme/solo/solo/theme, that kind of stuff. Rocket was doing industrial/thrash/metal crossover noise. It was cacophony.

Dean also decided he should be the drummer. He tried to go behind my back with it, to the other guys. *Behind my back.* Can you believe this? He came over in rehearsal one day and just stuck out his hand for the sticks, with that smug, passionless expression of his. *If you can't play the darned things, someone else can do it for you, pal,* he said. *I've talked to the boys and they agree. We all agree. This isn't marching band hour. If I have to do it, I will.* I got up off the stool and threw it at him. The stool! And when it missed, I rushed at him with my balled fists. Because it wasn't about the band anymore. It was about a way of life! I had become a scrapper—Dean, with his invocations, had converted me himself—and I would stop at nothing now. With a trash-can lid, I began to beat him over the head. Until he was yelling for help. The little Hollywood fucker curled up like a ball. Protecting his million-dollar cheekbones from the absolutes of drumming, from the unavoidable in this desert life, the unavoidable that he had thought *would not apply to him* when he came to Lost Hills to hide.

Dean was trying to organize us—he was raising his hysterical mumble above the din—as if organizing us was going to be his next great creative comeback. He had become an explainer. *No, listen, guys, listen, we gotta rely on the sound that's going to work for these people in Los Angeles. We have to find a niche and occupy it. Just this once. C'mon guys, don't fuck it up. We have to play to the people this time. You know? That way we'll get more work. You guys want to work, right?* It was a debut for him, he kept saying, it was a debut. And the rest of us were supposed to be happy for the break, happy to accompany him. We were supposed to be happy about any old brush with *fame*. He tried to make us grateful for a break. But we'd seen now where fame led, we'd seen that no one gave a shit about talent lost or squandered or careers that fireballed to a close, that no one gave a shit about the famous at the moment they put the barrels of automatic weapons into their mouths and their lips tightened around that lavender steel, the famous leaping from highway overpasses or turning blue with needles in their arms, the famous in the state psychiatric hospitals shuffling the lengths of corridors on antipsychotic medications, the famous running from fame, the famous with night sweats trying to remember why they did what they did, no one gave a shit about them, then or now, except insofar as they could talk about it in public and brighten a conversation with friends who got to be anonymous at the end of the day. Dean was just trying to parlay what Rocket and Wallace and I had been building for four years into another film contract and some paid vacation at a fat farm where he could also have his dead teeth fixed, where he could have some light cosmetic surgery and get some new clothes and *that would be the end of us*. Right? What about me and Wallace and Rocket? What about the lost souls of Lost Hills? Did *the industry* think it could just pluck us out of the heartland and send us back? What kind of options were left to us?

In fact, there were some options. Maybe we could keep going when Dean left, when Dean sold out. Maybe we could get another rhythm guitarist. We could get one of those really great songwriters, like the guys who wrote "Heartbreak Hotel," one of those Memphis or Nashville guys, one of Elvis's team, and record a cynical and calculating tearjerker that would rocket up the charts. We could put away a little money—after we bought the Cadillacs with the fuzzy dice and souped-up engines. We could invest in pension plans or mutual funds so our children and children's children would attend first-rate private schools and come out at debutante balls and retire wealthy and always have health insurance and full-time nannies.

We went along with Dean. To L.A. We went along.

On January 1, 1960, we played our first date there, at the Café Vertigo. In a swirling sandstorm, we drove the DeSoto in from Lost Hills. We were tense with excitement. Because we were going to bring these jaded salesmen and women a little of what we knew, which was that life and love were just regret in three dimensions, and that the uplifting ballad, the spirited rocker, the heart-wrenching jazz torch song, these could all be *tools of the mass market*. We could have it all. We could move the hearts of Middle America *and* represent the delirium of guitars turned way up, out of tune, played badly.

I would like to tell you, as Wallace has claimed on the television talk-show circuit, that the Café Vertigo was packed, that there was a line around the block for this outfit called the James Dean Garage Band. I would like to tell you that, unlike our first gig at Wally's, our second was standing room only. But as we waited in the front of the café for the audience to trickle in, as we sat at a table, sipping drinks, the reality of the situation began to dawn on us. There was no audience. There would be no audience. It was like this: *James Dean was really dead,* as you and I know. His warm body, across the table from us, was an impertinence. No one wanted to know, no one wanted to hear about it. Even Rolf Wutherich, whose life Dean had saved back on the soft shoulder of Route 466, didn't show up that night. He was doing the NASCAR circuit, yanking those tires off in some pit stop. And Clift, Brando, Newman, Martin Landau, those guys? Dean's acquaintances from Strasberg's classes? Forget it. *They had the story of James Dean and that was enough.* Dean had even cut his hair for the occasion. He'd bought a new pair of jeans. He looked like a movie star, relatively speaking. He had a Mona Lisa smile. We were all four squeaky-clean pop singers from small-town America. We were going to seduce the daughters of Californians. But this wasn't how it turned out. Instead, we were facing the same disenchanted crowd we had faced at Wally's. Alcoholics. Guys with red eyes. Hell's Angels. Guys from flophouses.

In a state of geometrically increasing anxiety, we waited at a table in the back. Dean mumbled about betrayals and favors unreturned, swiveling desperately each time the door of the joint swung in. Long stretches of morbid silence. Some lovelorn country singer warbled on the jukebox. We drank. Then Dean asked me to write up the set lists. A preperformance ritual. We had planned on a program that relied on our most sanitized, our cheerfullest, our most reverential pop songs. I took the four moistened cocktail napkins from beneath our drinks. I produced a golf pencil I had brought for this purpose. I licked the tip of it. And then I made *four different set lists.* A different set for each of us. I took my own initiative. On Rocket's list, I wrote one song only. "Rocket from the Tombs." On Wallace's list, I wrote all the jazz songs. On my own, I listed only some items I needed from the grocery when I got home. And on Dean's napkin, I listed all of our pop songs—with their perfect pop-song structure and their sunny truths about love. *I did it because I didn't care, or because I did, or because I couldn't shake the town where I was born, like James Dean couldn't shake Indiana. I did it because I had to; because it was the last thing left to do.* When the bartender strode to the mike to announce us, I handed out these lists. In the commotion of our decline and fall, the three of them didn't even bother to look.

We climbed the three steps to the stage. Dean didn't greet the audience and he didn't introduce the song, and this is how I managed to effect my prank. Dean, with his back turned to the bar, just began to count off. *At a breakneck pace,* because the first song on Dean's list—in stark contrast to the lilting, Caribbean samba Wallace was about to tackle—was one of our faster numbers. However, the count didn't seem fast. It seemed interminable. The band knew there was trouble before it even happened. Wallace looked dumbfounded. He rushed over, again, to the spot where his set list was taped to the floor of the stage. Rocket turned entirely away from us and readied a completely ugly minor chord on the upper neck of his guitar. I used a mallet on the Chinese gong behind me. Dean arrived at the middle of the count. Another endlessly sustained gong crash. The feedback in Rocket's amplifier. The buzz of household wattage. The sound of glasses being set upon the bar. A siren outside. Rocket clearing his throat in the mike. And Wallace's simpering, melodious bass tiptoeing into the arrangement.

Dean reached *four*.

It started like a car crash. We fell upon this racket as if we had reason to suppose that popular music was trustworthy, that the cardiological regularity of four-four time and verse/chorus/verse/chorus/bridge/verse/chorus structure could in some way forestall our uncertainties. That's what we thought at first. But certainty itself became a delusion in the trajectory of our squall. Nothing was certain. The famous dead didn't even stay dead. The dead walked the street in new jeans exacting their prices, making big Hollywood deals. The living barely registered a pulse. Fame was a sham; the GNP, the GOP, the national census, the national debt—it was all the stuff of spooks, the living dead, the body-snatched. We were outside all that. Sensible things seemed ridiculous. We were lumbering through the most awful dissonance. We were playing in different keys. It wasn't going well. But you know what? We didn't stop. We never got to a second song. I kept going. I wouldn't stop. And Rocket was following me. And then Wallace's bass was suddenly strolling along with us. We had become some collective medium, some dictionary of signs and symbols that was wholly unconscious and full of the pitch and shit that no one wanted to think about; we had access to the store of all bad rock 'n' roll riffs past and future and to the encyclopedia of learning that stretched back through the Dark Ages to the gnostics and beyond to the earliest cave graffiti, and suddenly I realized that Dean was leading us again; he was our front man, his face screwed up like a kid whose lollipop has been taken from him, jigsawing these harsh chops on the Telecaster, and we were powerless to stop now and we were doing it because *we just were* and nothing could bring us to a stop. For forty-five minutes, the same two nasty dissonant chords over and over again, and then Rocket and Dean had stripped it down to one note they were trading off in call and response, messing with the knobs and the switches on their guitars so that this one droning note with its microtonal variations bent and faltered in the cavelike emptiness of the Café Vertigo, and I was riding on the toms now, staying off the snare so that the kit had some prehistoric tribal stuff coming out of it and I hallucinated Pleistocene dancers and hunter-gatherers on the stage on backing vocals and the legion of vision questers renouncing the world doing stage dances among us and then I saw a Southwest covered with radioactive glass and computer geeks dancing barefoot in it all night to synthesizer trances. When I woke from this dream, Wallace had let go of the bass and he was in the center of the stage, spinning.

The applause was diffident. There was almost no one there. It didn't matter. We had the giddy sense of a failure so complete that it seemed close, as an ideal, to sweetest success. We caught our breath in the men's room. I had my ass in a sink—there were no chairs—and I was smoking a reefer that Dean had passed to me. *Holy shit*, he said. *What was all that?* The joint was laced with some poisonous Middle Eastern hashish or something. Wallace was quietly overtone singing, as if he were a Tibetan monk. Rocket was passed out in a stall. And Dean was smiling his winningest Hollywood smile. He never was going to make it in this town again.

We were happy. Happy from the splendid coincidence of noise and space and exhaustion that marks a heartfelt night onstage, irrespective of its reception. We had no illusions about the two inches of press that the *L.A. Times* would devote to us in its rag the next morning. We waited at a motel, we waited for the calls, for the managers, for the booking agents, for the calls that never came. We waited. I remember pushing Wallace into the pool behind the motor lodge. Then Dean pushed me in. Lots of laughs. And then all of us drying out on the new plastic deck furniture they had by that chlorinated puddle. All of us knowing that the phone was never going to ring. Finally, after a couple of days, the money started to get short. In a week, we had exhausted all the cash we had. None of us, not even James Dean, the actor, had the money to live in L.A.

Wednesday morning I went to rouse Dean from his coma for the usual half dozen cups of black coffee. The door was open. His stuff was gone. Of course. The motel room had an antiseptic sadness. The motel room was just a motel room. The motel room was made up as artlessly as if he'd never been there, as though he had never graced our lives in those years after the wreck. In those thin towels and bleached sheets, there was no drama of rebirth or regeneration. There was no drama at all. The light drifting in through the draperies was anemic. My life was a desert highway stretching out in front of me. My life felt irredeemable. My ears were still ringing.

Here's the note he left crumpled on the bed: *Gone to Cleveland. Keep your mouth shut. Use the name if you want. Dean.*

And it was in Cleveland, of course, that he had his second crash.

Anyway, that's how we came by the name. The James Dean Garage Band. And that's how we came to record, in 1963, our one LP with its one hit, "Death Valley Dream Baby." That's the story, all right, and if you have a few more nights to spare, I've got a thousand more just like it, because I'm a desperate guy, and like all the anonymous, I have the urge to talk. You name it. I've got all kinds of stories, stories based on real stories, stories of the most rigorous truth, stories of legendary couples, stories of their partings, stories of the little guys who live in small towns tucked in back of air-force test sites. Who's to say? I have time. More than you, probably. This is how I see it: you have your luck as a kid and sooner or later that luck runs out. After that, what you have is memories. I run a Hallmark store in Cholame now. Get it? I'm fifty-seven years old. I sold my '51 Telecaster to make car payments. When I was twenty-eight, four or five years after I quit playing music, I married a postmistress. Because she was pretty. Because she was sweet and she loved me. So that we could have two sons who could both be drummers like their dad. For those reasons. But also so that I wouldn't have to wait for my mail. Because there's a letter coming, a letter from the actor James Dean. And here's what it will say: if the life you lead is not the one you dreamed about, *then flee.*

BECAUSE OF DUST
Christopher Kenworthy

Christopher Kenworthy was born in Preston, England, and has lived in many places around Britain, including London and Bath. He now lives in a country cottage near Garstang. He began writing fiction in 1986 and since then has contributed more than one hundred pieces of nonfiction to *Writers' Monthly*, *Prediction*, and *Encounters*. He says he "writes full time but dabbles in computer art, sacred geometry, photography, and is an infamous crop circle maker." In the early nineties he was editor and publisher of the acclaimed Barrington Press, publishing three noteworthy anthologies: *The Sun Rises Red*, *Sugar Sleep*, and *The Science of Sadness* and Nicholas Royle's first novel, *Counterparts*. Kenworthy's own short fiction has appeared in *Peeping Tom*, *Substance*, *Grotesque*, the *Northern Lights* anthology, and *The Third Alternative* (from which "Because of Dust" is reprinted).

"Because of Dust" is a simple yet haunting story about a young man who needs to keep something of the people he has known. Two other excellent stories by Kenworthy were published in *Peeping Tom* during 1995: "The Pig's Nose" and "Landing in the Grass."

—E.D.

When I think about Rachel I remember being locked out of my car with her on the Derwent Water car park. It was warmer than you'd think possible for October, the sunset dissipating while we waited for the A.A. recovery van to arrive. I kept apologizing, but she said it didn't matter. I'd only known her for one full day, but she wrapped her arms around me, making me acutely aware of her thin breasts pressing against my chest. As the air grew colder, the contact warmed our skin.

I'd met her a week previously at the Corner House cinema in Manchester. They were launching a new fiction magazine the same night, upstairs, so the theatre itself was virtually empty.

The film was Spanish, so I needed the subtitles. Reading them isn't normally a problem for me, but they were lower than usual on the screen, and every time I read a line my attention fixed on the back of somebody's head. She had blond hair, which was an obvious distraction. There was no movement from her until the credits ran, and then she wiped one hand around the back of her head, lifting her hair so that I caught a glimpse of neck.

I don't normally go into the bar on my own, but when I saw that she ventured in alone, I followed. She sat at a large table, which gave me an excuse to share it with her, because the smaller ones were crowding up.

"Did you enjoy that?" she asked.

I looked up from the program sheet, which I was pretending to read. "Oh yes. The bit where the boy walked up behind the woman hitcher, so slowly. Wonderful."

She nodded, then smiled. I wanted to ask her if she came here often, quite simply because I was curious to know why I'd never seen her before, but it was such a cliché that I didn't speak.

I read my program again, drinking frequently, trying to think of something less predictable to ask, but a few minutes later she rescued me by saying, "I've got to catch my train now," as she sidled out from behind the table.

Without thinking or hesitating I asked if she'd like to go out some time. I knew my expression was going to change from one of blank abandon to a pathetic sort of nervous query, but she said yes quickly, which was a relief.

It turned out that we were both free the following Sunday. I'd been planning to go to the Lakes, not for any serious walking, just a wander, and she said she'd love to go. Hadn't been up there since she was seven.

"Where do you live?" I asked.

"Hebden Bridge. It's in the middle of nowhere, but there are plenty of trains. I can meet you at your local station, early on."

We swapped phone numbers and she left. I drank slowly in case she missed her train and came back, but soon the bar lights were switched off, making me realize the time. Outside it had started to rain, a thin summery type of rain, not at all cold, and I smiled all the way back to my car.

On the way back from the Lakes we stopped at the Tebay service station, and over two treacly coffees, Rachel gave me a sugar cube; in fact it was a packet of two cubes, held together in a rectangle of white wrapping with a red T logo.

"It's a present," she said.

"I'll treasure it."

I'm sure she knew the intimacy of her gesture, because she looked into my eyes for a long time, but I don't know if she realized how tightly I'd hold onto her gift.

There is a shelf in my house where I store the few important objects that have been given to me. They are all soaked with memories, and when I put them in my hands I relive the moments when people offered slithers of themselves.

On the left is Mark's feather, held down with a blob of blue-tac. We were staying in north London at the time, during a relentless summer. The streets had a fine coating of sand, as though the dry air had sapped so much water from the town it had started to crumble. He picked a feather up as we headed for the Seven Sisters tube. It was mostly black, with a smear of orange and green along one edge. We debated whether it was real or dyed. Despite a lack of free-flying tropical birds in the city, we decided it was genuine, and he gave it to me.

"Look after that," he said.

When I hold the feather now I can smell the sweaty diesel scent of the tube, and I remember sitting next to Mark, looking at each other in reflection on the other side of the carriage as we talked. We laughed so much that we missed our stop and had to walk from Tottenham Court Road to Foley Street, making us late for the party.

Next to the feather are stones that Nick and Decko gave to me. I'd never been on a beach with so many different types of stone. For half an hour we picked out flat rocks and skimmed them on the lulling green waves which shattered around us, making us run back to preserve our feet. When the air softened with rain we exchanged stones. Nick gave me a dull pebble the colour of brick. Decko's stone looked like melted porcelain, with a vein of rouge.

If I hold those stones now, one in each hand, I can remember details I wasn't even aware of at the time: the seagulls' key-shifting song, the stink of marshland behind us, and the murmur of an ice cream van's engine, parked close by, its beige and red paint seeming to grow brighter as the ashen clouds turned black.

Rachel's sugar cube is on the right of the shelf, and when I touch it, my memories are bewildered; my eyes grow wet before I know what to think.

I only knew Rachel for one full day, so it's difficult to understand why she had such an effect on me. Within an hour of her climbing into the car, within ten minutes even, we relaxed. Instead of talking about who we were and what we did, we talked about what we'd seen on the news last night, the things we could see out the windows. We talked about small details. Normally it takes weeks for a relationship to settle into this sort of familiarity, but by the time we passed Forton Services, with its magic roundabout tower, I felt certain we weren't going to stumble.

With anybody else I would have felt a need to do specific things, to plan a series of events to prevent awkward silences. With some people in the past I'd even memorized lists of subjects to talk about, so that we wouldn't struggle. It's a shabby technique. How many times have I asked people what records they like, only to be worryingly disappointed? If somebody tells you that they like Barry Manilow on a first date, it's going to make you back off before you have any idea about your feelings for them. When you love somebody, such things are endearing.

I couldn't face another conversation asking what films somebody liked, whether they played a musical instrument, where they went to university, how they got on with their parents. I never asked Rachel any of these questions, and she didn't ask me. At the end of the day I knew very few facts about her, but I saw the way she ran her hands through the grass as we sat by Derwent Water, and knew more than if she had given me a history of preferences.

We drove up to Keswick along the astounding curves of the A66, where the west coast mountains are jagged silhouettes with a frosting of mist over them.

"I can't believe this weather," I said.

It was warm enough to wear T-shirts, and there were no clouds until late afternoon, though something about it being autumn made the air feel clean.

We found a quiet place to sit, south of Friar's Crag. The ground was dry and we sat there for hours, leaning against a tree, picking at the grass, fiddling with stones, listening to brittle leaves peeling from the trees and landing on the water. The lake itself was still, mercifully free of boats. The sun went behind Cat Bells cooling the valley with shadow.

Walking back to the car the air became so still that I stopped to watch the lake. Its surface was without ripples, one sheet of unmoving white.

A grassed area lead down to the water. Rachel followed me and stood to the side as I knelt close to the edge, putting my hands through the surface. Its fragile skin gave way and I put my arms in, almost to the elbow. Rings of dark circled outwards from me.

I drew my hands out when they were too cold, and droplets fell away. A few strips of transparent jelly remained on my skin like blisters of glass. I realized they were leeches and wiped them off on the turf.

My arms were dry by the time we reached the car, but after standing outside for twenty minutes waiting for the A.A., we were both frozen, apart from the places where our bodies pressed.

It was fully dark as we drove down the M6, and Rachel insisted that I drop her at Preston railway station. I kept offering to run her all the way.

"You'll be up all night. Trust me, there's a late train. I'll be OK. My house is one bus ride from the station, so I'll be quite safe."

She had countered all my planned arguments, so I could only say, "But I'd like to run you back."

"I don't like the thought of you driving home so late," she said, and her concern made me want to grin.

At the station she wouldn't even let me see her onto the platform.

"I'll wait a few minutes, in case you've missed it," I said.

"I'll be fine."

She was standing outside the car, leaning in to talk, which made it impossible for us to kiss. I smiled as she slammed the door and gave a wave. I looked round to see her one last time, but she'd already gone through.

I was absolutely certain that Rachel said she'd phone me, but when a week had passed I almost gave up on her.

Each night I promised to do something useful, even to go out, but I stayed in with the TV on, dying for the phone to ring. People did ring, proving that the line was working, but Rachel never called.

I was determined to wait for her, not out of stubbornness, but because I didn't want to look pushy.

It had happened to me once before, with Anna. I'd known Anna for about two years, vaguely, because she worked in my local newsagent. I always felt there was something movingly significant about the fact that my first words to her had been, "*Guardian* please." I was sure this meant we were fated to have a relationship. She agreed to go out with me for a drink when I finally asked, but we found each other unbearable dull. We both toyed with beermats in the Anchor while she told me that she played the organ, and that she liked Barry Manilow. At first I made polite comments about this, to fill the gaps in the conversation, but once I'd had a couple of drinks I asked her what the appeal was, made references to his nose. She said I was being a bit predictable.

For some reason we both tried to keep the momentum going, and went back to my place. Our conversation was even more nervous, and when I finally got round to kissing her, my arm over her back felt uncomfortable. It was the same sense of unease I feel when holding other people's children: a total lack of familiarity. Her lips, although soft, were narrow and didn't move much.

I rang Decko the next day and told him that she kissed like a frog. This was rude, but it indicated to me that I shouldn't let it go any further. Strangely, after I got off the phone to him I went to the bathroom and found a frog perched on the side of the toilet bowl. This unnerved me.

A week after having declared that she kissed like a frog, and determining not to see her again, I was desperate for her to ring. I finally decided that I would call, just in case she had lost my number, but before I had worked out how to word it my brother rang me up. He'd seen Anna in town with another man.

"It could be her brother," he said, "but they were holding hands."

Since then I've bought my newspapers elsewhere.

I decided that despite the risk of repeating history, I would call Rachel, just to see if she still had my number. After all, she could be sitting there hoping I'd get in touch, wondering what she did with that slip of paper. I might even give in and say that I couldn't wait for her to ring.

I barely knew her, but was quite obsessed. With Anna I'd been keen to see her again, even though we didn't get on, because of her sudden unavailability, her refusal to reconnect. With Rachel, my enthusiasm was for the way she made me feel. I liked the simplicity of this.

The voice that answered had a slight accent, similar to Rachel's, but sounded older.

"Is Rachel there please?"

There was a sound of swallowing.

"Hello?" I tried, but only heard the same sound, and then the phone was put down.

I tried the number again, quite annoyed, but at the same time worried.

It rang six times before it was picked up, and I could hear sobbing at the other end.

"Are you a friend?" the voice said, her breath catching.

"Yes."

"I'm so sorry," she said. "Rachel died last Monday. She was buried today."

I felt that I ought to keep talking, to be polite, but a silence followed where I could hear our breathing mingle in the phone.

More than anything I was astounded that it had happened on Monday, the day after we parted. I was frightened by the thought that I'd been picturing her alive, doing things, when she'd been in a morgue.

"What did she die of?" I asked.

"Her headaches, finally," the voice said, breaking up. I caught the word *hemorrhage* which was enough to clarify her meaning.

"I'm her mother," she said, and I couldn't help but notice that she was using the wrong tense.

When I managed to get off the phone I was aware that my whole body was waxy with sweat, and that my stomach had glued with something heavy. I'd never known anybody die, not even my parents. Having known Rachel such a short time didn't make it seem any better. I felt more cheated than if I'd been treated to a few years with her.

I experienced curiously selfish and sexual thoughts, such as annoyance at the fact that I would never know what her nipples looked like. I would never know how she kissed or what she smelled like after sex. I wanted to be able to put my hands on her belly while she breathed in sleep. I'd never even see her washing her hair.

It was difficult to picture her without imagining her being in the coffin. It would take a while for her body to rot fully, but I knew the initial sourness would have set in. They say that the softer parts give way first. The eyes moisten and slush, anus and vagina widen into mouldy clefts.

Already, decay would have made her hideous.

In my bedroom I clutched the sugar cube with my eyes closed, and smelled water, petrol, and something like warm wood, which I remembered was her hair.

Heading east on the train, the countryside lost its color. Autumn leafed trees gave way to barren trunks. There was old snow, dirtied and patchy, chimneys grizzling smoke into the sunless layering of clouds.

Hebden Bridge confused me because there weren't enough signs to find my way around. The roads surrounding the canal were all being worked on, so that amongst the pollution-stained buildings, were endless bright rags of safety ribbons and tangles of orange plastic fencing. The JCBs and earth movers were abandoned, their joints looking frozen.

The bus ride up to Heptonstall was unnerving, because the back wheels skidded and whined over the cobbles, and we drove up roads that I felt were too steep even to walk on. The bus driver indicated the stop I had asked for. "There you are, love," he said. I'd only been to Yorkshire once, and it took me a while to get used to men calling other men "love," but when he said it, I appreciated the kindness in his voice.

I'd talked to Rachel's mother again on the phone, and she was horrified that I had missed the funeral.

"I tried to call her friends," she said, her jerky breath crackling down the line, "but there weren't many I could track down. She didn't keep an address book. She memorized numbers and names."

"Were there many people at the funeral?"

"No. Not many."

She insisted that I go over and stop with her. I agreed, saying that I wanted to see the grave.

She said: "There's more for you to see than that."

The house was set back from the road down a stone path. Where there had once been a lawn, the ground was completely dug over, ploughed ridges cradling granular snow.

Rachel's mother opened the door and a hot rush of cooking wafted out. She was as tall as me but quite wide. She squinted permanently, and the wrinkles worsened when she tried to smile.

"I'm so glad you came."

I felt disoriented, again reminding myself how brief my relationship with Rachel had been, but knowing that I wanted more. I couldn't bear to let it end at that. I wanted to recover something of her.

By the time Mrs. Clarke had fed me scones and cake, along with several cups of dandelion tea, I knew it was too late to venture out to the grave. It was only just past six o'clock, but it had been dark since three.

She told me all sorts of stories about Rachel and her father. I smiled, nodded, added words of encouragement, but really I wanted to get some sleep.

"How did you know her?" she finally asked.

"It's difficult to say. Did she ever mention me?"

"Not by name."

I realized how ridiculous this was, because she wouldn't have had time to tell her mother anything about me.

"We both shared an interest in films," I said, worried that the formality of the phrase would reveal its lack of sincerity.

The woman nodded slowly.

"Did you love her?" she asked.

The question shocked me less than I would have thought. That she asked it wasn't much of a surprise, but the fact that I had to think before I could answer startled me.

"I don't really know," I said, my throat becoming hard. "I didn't really have time."

I took the plates into the kitchen and washed them. Trying to look out of the window into blackness I found it difficult to see anything. There were cobwebs and flies stuck to the other side of the glass, and a couple of moths flickered against the surface. I saw myself in the reflection then, noticing that my posture had lowered and my face was thin.

Leaning round the door to the front room, I said, "I think I'd better get some sleep, before tomorrow."

"I'll put you in the spare room," she said. "It's next to Rachel's. I haven't been in there since she died. It's still a mess. I can't face cleaning it up."

"I'll clear up in there if you like."

Her face sagged first, and even as she smiled at my request, her eyes were shiny with tears.

"You're welcome to look through her things," she said.

It was a peculiar thing to say, so I kept quiet for a few moments, until she led me to the spare room. I didn't expect to sleep at all because the room was freezing, but as soon as I had curled up under the itchy blankets, I fell into it dreamless.

I woke at half past six and the curtains were full of amber light. Outside there was a black and white valley, a new covering of snow over the coal colored ground, making the trees look sharp. A pool of mist had settled in the valley and the rising sun sent warmth through it. Sunrises have more clarity than sunsets, more like a concentrated shine instead of a wash. The sun turned red as it rose, then became a colorless circle as I watched the sky becoming blue, dampening with cloud.

My skin felt warm, but the room was still cold enough for my breath to form clouds.

I dressed without washing, because I was trying to be quiet, then went to Rachel's room. It was smaller than the one I'd slept in, but much warmer. There was a wardrobe, a cupboard with mirrors, and a bed. There were no posters on the walls. I examined the bottles of deodorant, perfume and moisturizer by the mirror, disappointed that this was so familiar and ordinary a bedroom.

I chose a jar of Vitamin E Facial Cream and unscrewed the cap. Inside the sticky stuff was swirled where her fingers had been. It smelled sweet, and as I looked closer I could see the tiny lines that had been left by the passing of her fingerprint.

I wanted to look at her clothes, to imagine her wearing them. When I opened the top drawer I found piles of folded white underwear. The bras were on one side, panties on the other. I lifted a pair out, their softness giving me an erection which made me frown with guilt. As I put the knickers back I noticed a slight yellowing along the gusset and closed the drawer quickly.

Until then I hadn't noticed anything wrong with the bed, and it took me a few moments of staring to work out what was bothering me. The bed hadn't been made since Rachel was lifted from it, and there was still an impression of her in the duvet. On the pillow there was a wide stain, which I thought must be blood.

The material was cold when I touched it, in contrast to the heat of the room, and I knew then that the room couldn't give me what I needed, so went downstairs.

From the front room I could see the church and the edge of the graveyard, about a minute's walk away. I would need hot water, so I went back into the kitchen. It was clear now why I hadn't been able to see anything out there at night; the kitchen window looked into an old conservatory. Each window was mottled with something that looked like birdlime. The windowsills were lined with potplants, all long dead, the soil dried so deeply that you could see their white roots, like grubs. Between the plants were hundreds of dead flies, scattered like raisins. I noticed the sound of those that were still alive, which until then I had presumed to be the hiss of the fridge. Some were spinning on their backs, legs jiggling.

Flies and moths circled wildly, a concentration of them in the far left-hand corner, crawling over the wood. I couldn't work out what they could be eating in there, or why there were so many.

The prospect of going in there to clear the place out was obviously too much for Mrs. Clarke. It must have been too much for Rachel as well, because they seemed to have been gathering for months. I thought that I would make an attempt to sweep the worst of them away, before going home. Depending on what happened at the grave.

I found a plastic bucket in a cupboard, took the mop out of it, then filled it with hot water. I squirted some Ecover into it and left the house without spilling any. The snow was difficult to walk on, especially as it had settled on ice, but as this meant I had more chance of being alone, I didn't mind. The bucket steamed like a nitrogen experiment on *Tomorrow's World*. I remember they used to put soft things, like fruit, into the liquid, and then shattered them with a hammer, for effect.

The church building wasn't impressive, but the old graveyard was unique. Where grass would usually be, the ground was plated with fallen headstones, more piled on top of them, leaning around and against each other. They reminded me of Stonehenge, and I remembered something Rachel had told me. She said that because worms create holes in the ground, depositing dust on the surface, they are slowly burying everything we have built. Stonehenge, she told me, was sinking at the rate of six inches per century.

"Just because of dust?" I asked.

"Yes. They bring minerals up from below for the plants, and all the stones go deeper. That's why old lawns and meadows are always free of stones, if you dig into them."

Round the back of the church I found the new field, only half scarred with graves. The last one was Rachel's, the soil mound having sagged into itself. I'd imagined more flowers, but there were only two roses, one bright yellow, the other a damaged brown. Both were rotten with frost, welded to the soil with ice. I chiselled some of the ice away with my fingertips, and pulled the brown one free. The outer crusting fell away, revealing petals as red as flesh.

There was nobody around, so I lifted the bucket and poured its content along the length of the soil. I didn't know whether it would be better to concentrate on one area, or spread it over her whole length. In the end I put more water in the place where I thought her head would be. The bucket had been heavy and difficult to carry, but once empty I was concerned that there wasn't nearly enough liquid to achieve the desired effect.

I needn't have worried, because the first worm heads appeared within moments.

Earthworms don't really have heads, but because there is a fold of nerves in the end which burrows, it's fair enough to think of it as a head. They don't have eyes either, which is probably why we think of them as being without true life or personality. When I was a teenager I charmed worms from the soil, then pulled them apart. Sometimes I'd cut them into several pieces, to see which squirmed the most. Invariably the gristle colored part, which controlled circulation, was the piece which moved the least.

The other segments coiled and wriggled until they dried out.

Although they are pink, it's difficult to think of worms as containing blood. Their blood is similar to ours; it even shares our hemoglobin. As they nosed onto the surface, I hoped these worms would share much more.

I guessed they had already cast a layer of Rachel's dust over the surface, in the days before I had arrived.

Although she wouldn't have rotted much, part of her would probably have melted through the base of the coffin, so that some of her essence was available to the soil. By bringing the worms out from there, I could gain access to her, put the moments of her into my hand.

The worms were slippery but covered with crumbs of dirt. They reminded me of something intestinal, a mass of peristalsis. Rolling on the mud they looked drugged. I gathered them up, watching their bodies fatten and shrink as they oozed around my fingers.

I remembered the sound of Rachel's voice and her small laugh, the smell of her T-shirt, perfumed by skin as we hugged in the darkening trees. I remembered the orange flashing lights of the A.A. van on her smiling face, and the tightening of her hug before she let go. She held my hand, for a second. I saw her face clearly, and knew that her eyes weren't watching me; they were looking into mine.

The sky was clear, blue as twilight, and despite the snow and ice I was aware of how grassy this field was. The worms shrank, turning white. In my hands they felt tiny and sharp nosed, like maggots. As the sun warmed onto my back the church bell began to chime.

I put the bucket away before Rachel's mother came through. We stood in the kitchen while she slotted bread into the toaster. I told her that I'd already been to the grave, and that I would be going soon.

"But you'll stay for breakfast."

"Yes, and then I'll go."

She lowered the bread with a metallic springing sound, and I could swear I heard the fibers of it drying out.

In the conservatory moths and flies rattled against the glass, and I tried to look away from them.

Sunlight came into the kitchen, showing up dust in the air. Somebody once told me that ninety percent of dust is skin. I often wonder what the other ten percent is. The way those particles sparkled, I thought they could have been gold.

LOOP
Douglas E. Winter

Douglas E. Winter was born in 1950 in St. Louis, Missouri, and has since gone on to become a partner in the international law firm of Bryan Cave. He is the author or editor of ten books, including *Stephen King: The Art of Darkness, Faces of Fear, Prime Evil,* and the upcoming anthology *Millennium.* He has published more than two hundred articles and short stories in such diverse markets as *The Washington Post, The Cleveland Plain Dealer, Book of the Dead, Cemetery Dance, Twilight Zone Magazine, Saturday Review, Gallery,* and *Video Watchdog.* He has won the World Fantasy Award for his criticism and has been nominated for the Hugo Award and the Horror Writers' Association's Bram Stoker Award. He's a member of the National Book Critics Circle, and his forthcoming projects include a critical biography of Clive Barker. Winter lives in a suburb of Washington, D.C., with his wife Lynne and their differently abled pekingeses.

Unfortunately, Winter writes far too few short stories. Each one is a disturbing, memorable gem. "Loop," like "Splatter," which appeared in the first annual of this series, strikes at the heart of current societal concerns. How far is too far in violence ("Splatter") and in sex? Winter seems a literary expert on the convergence of the two. "Loop" just may be the ultimate striptease. It is reprinted from *Dark Love* edited by Nancy A. Collins, Edward E. Kramer, and Martin H. Greenberg.

—E.D.

> *You'd better hope and pray*
> *That you'll wake one day*
> *In your own world . . .*
> —Shakespear's Sister

You know this dream. It takes you by the hand and leads you out of the wilderness of your office, away from the paper-patterned desk and ever-ringing telephone and into the first of the many hallways. Your secretary is smiling, not at you, but at the air somewhere to the left of you; her telephone receiver is balanced between shoulder and ear, and you hear her talk of dates and times and places. The weekend, always planning for the weekend: a dental appointment, a son's soccer practice, a tryst in a darkened motel room. You wish for a new lie to tell her, but your wrist pokes the Rolex President from beneath the embroidered initials of your starched white cuff and you give the timepiece that practiced impatient stare. The bank, actually a savings and loan, will close at four, and you tell your secretary what you usually tell her. She nods without losing her smile and talks on.

You know these hallways, too. A flurry of birds swoops from the canvas at the first corner. The open doors, although there are few of them, offer glimpses of the other offices, identical furniture and file cabinets, the same gilt-framed trophies on display: subdued photographs of wives or husbands, diplomas from the finer law schools, certificates of admission to the proper courts. This hallway leads to another, and then another, and at last you are wandering the lobby, nodding back to the receptionist before ducking into the men's room.

You relieve yourself of the afternoon's cups of coffee, knowing that more will be needed if you are to finish writing the brief that even now, with luck, the word processing department is retyping. But you are thinking far ahead—never a good sign.

You must not forget the Kleenex. You pull five, six sheets from the dispenser, fold them neatly into a square, and tuck them into the inner pocket of your Paul Stuart suit coat.

Now you are ready. You take a last look into the mirror, squaring the knot of your tie and drawing in a stomach-tightening breath. The man who looks back at you seems tired but knowing, in control of his own destiny and that of his clients.

You wonder why it is that mirrors always lie.

The clock is running, and Delacorte, if anything, is punctual. He has thirty minutes for his errand and enough paper waiting on his desk to keep him busy half the night. He drags a comb through his hair, carefully buttons his double-breasted jacket. He decides to wash his hands again, and tosses the wad of paper towel the length of the washroom, a swish, before he exits. The receptionist waves a farewell to his call of "Back in twenty," and then he is riding the elevator to the pavement.

The streets of the capital have no names. In this quadrant, letters run in alphabetical order, absent the J, from south to north, while numbers count ever higher east to west. Some mad Frenchman is responsible.

Delacorte needs no grid systems, no tourist maps, no directions. He has made this pilgrimage nearly every week for the past year, and his eyes may as well blink closed. It is no longer a walk but a migration. He prefers the east side of 13th Street, crossing at I Street to enter Franklin Park, where he endures the usual gauntlet of broken men: gristled faces, shriveled bodies, brown-bagged bottles. An elderly black woman wearing a mottled DuRag maneuvers her shopping cart in an endless circle, stopping on occasion to rearrange the newspapers inside. At a bench near the fountain sits a man Delacorte knows only as Ernie, for this is the name sewn above the pocket of the gray-purple Texaco jumpsuit that is apparently his only clothing. Ernie smiles at the sight of him and asks for bus fare—the same question, the same words, he offers each time Delacorte has passed. Delacorte slips a dollar from his wallet and presses it into Ernie's trembling hand: "Go home," he tells Ernie, the same advice he has always offered. Ernie nods and sits back down on his bench.

On the far side of the park is 14th Street, across which waits a brownstone enigma, the liquor store and its angled alley, the last remnants of the invasion of mirrored glass and marble facade known as urban renewal. To the south was once a block of bars and burlesque clubs, bookstores and model studios, a shadowland tended mostly by women, frequented mostly by men. Now it is a furrow of bright concrete dwarfed by multistory monoliths. Inside these buildings are law firms and lobbyists, bankers and businessmen, the endlessly expanding hive of frantic worker bees. Delacorte looks both ways before crossing.

The windows of the liquor store offer the wet dreams of beer and bikini teams, but Delacorte isn't buying. There is time for three dollars, no more, no less. He thinks himself invisible and veers into the alleyway, takes the ten or so footsteps that lead to the decrepit portico lurking at its north side. Into the doorway, into the dark.

The smell, as always, astounds him, a stew of stale breath and sweaty armpits, Lysol cleanser and spent semen. He calms his surging stomach and looks down the waiting avenue of booths; one day, he is certain, he will meet someone here whom he knows. Though he does know the bull-necked Jamaican who minds the cash register; he knows him rather well, in the same way that he knows the man whose jumpsuit name tag reads Ernie. Most every weekday he hands each of them dollars.

Today Delacorte deals three portraits of George Washington onto the countertop and takes three stacks of quarters in return. He drops eleven of the quarters into his jacket pocket; the twelfth he holds between thumb and forefinger as he nods a wordless thank-you to the man at the cash register. A woman known as Taylor Wayne hovers at the man's shoulder, twisted in some impossibly alluring contortion across a glossy poster, nearly life-size, fully nude. Last week it was a woman known as PJ Sparxx, and the week before that, a woman known as Aja: the ever blond, ever naked, ever willing. They mean nothing to him.

His favorite booth is 7: truly a lucky number, for it was there that he met her. It happened years ago, before the video monitors were installed, when the backs of the doors of each booth were laminated with tiny white-speckled screens onto which robot projectors tickered their five- and ten-minute film loops. There was no sound, not yet. It must have been 1978, 1979—that long ago. He had come to this place only once or twice before, for reasons that he could not even begin to explain: an impulse, a vague need, idle curiosity. He thought of the visits as a kind of vulgar release, the kind of sex, like that with the occasional secretary, that could be appreciated and despised—quick and easy and forgettable.

But he could not forget her. One look, and he belonged to her, just as she, in time, would belong to him. There was no title on the tattered remnant of a film box that had been taped to the door of booth 7. She was nowhere to be seen in the lurid photographs on its splayed front and back. She was not even a featured player; those roles were reserved for the long forgotten and now, perhaps, long dead. The centerpiece of this loop was a threesome, a man and two women so blond and tanned and athletic as to be almost indistinguishable as they coiled in urgent pantomime on a spotlit, silk-skinned dais. Around them in huddled, humping shadows lurked the minor players in this filmic orgy, quaffing imaginary wine from empty bottles and biting at plastic grapes. She was but one of them, a shadow within shadows—set dressing, nothing more than fleshy backdrop, until the closing seconds of that short reel, when the featured trio, momentarily spent, untangled their knot, the women kissing each other gently as the Adonis stood, reaching up into the darkness for a bottle. A portly gray-haired celebrant rises from his decorous deed, flaccid pencil of a penis flapping beneath a furred belly, and through a trick of the light she is exposed, alone, no longer something but someone: a person. She is young, no doubt underage—fifteen, sixteen years old, corn-bred in some Midwest nowhere, Nebraska or Iowa, run away from the usual things: alcoholic mother, abusive stepfather, boring high school. She is too thin, her hips sharp and pointed, her breasts flat and tiny. her hair is blue black and Dachau short. But her pose, the vague and vulnerable gesture: the pose has it own purity, its own perfection. She reclines into the shadows, helpless, waiting, wanting, wishing . . . for you. You must stand in the tiny booth, the sudden erection cramped and painful.

The film spools from end back to beginning, and you push more quarters into the mouth of the meter and wait patiently through the minutes, the images blurring into a kind of meaningless newsreel until she appears again, and again, and again, and here, in this dark confessional, you visit her each day, feed quarter after quarter into the coin box bolted to the plywood wall, the clank of the metal a kind of overture, an expectant signal that brings your mind and body awake with total intensity, watching but not watching this ten-minute loop of grainy film until you know its every nuance, and hers: those timeless twenty seconds from shadow to light to shadow again. The sagging carcass of her partner, tilting forward, bottle in hand, and in his gray wake the silver of alabaster skin that widens into the pair of adolescent breasts and then into the upper torso of a woman, head turned aside, looking not at the camera but to some vision that just escapes your sight off-frame, and then the first breath, almost a sigh, that raises her nipples and her shoulders, her left arm moving back, her hand, invisible, seeking some purchase on the pillows beneath her, lips parting, a look both pliant and puzzled and then, with a second breath, her leg angling up and then the pose, the sublime pose, and darkness.

You watch her and you watch her and you watch her and then, one day, she is gone. Taped to the door of booth 7 is a shiny new cardboard box, and inside, when you sit, disbelieving, hoping, praying, and offer a shiny quarter to the coin box, the projector whirs out a new film, a different film, something called *Hardcore Hookers*. You watch with dutiful resignation, but of course she is not there. You ask the man at the cash register—at the time, a scowling Filipino troll whose throaty laugh collapsed into a cough. "Gone," he said. You even offered him money, but he knew nothing about the film, nothing but "Gone, gone." His hand waved to the door, as if the reel itself had arisen from the wet darkness of the booth and slouched out into the alley.

Years later, scrounging the racks of dusty boxes in a place called Top-Flite Video, just off Times Square in the ragtag reach of the Port Authority Terminal, you found and bought that first Super 8 film, even though you owned no projector. Just touching the plastic reel was enough to bring back the vision, and with it that feeling, the one like no other, the one that took you out of this world and into hers. The loop, you learned, was called *Roman Hands*, and though the foxed yellow carton listed the names of its stars, none of them was hers. But by then you didn't need to know her name. She was famous.

The years had passed with increasing intensity. These were the 1980s—your thirties—and you measured them with money. You lived the law, slept the law, worked the partnership track until there was no doubt that you would be among the tenured few. The visits to Peepland slowed, and as the weeks multiplied into months, and the months into years, you finally brought an end to what you saw as a boyish fling, the last gasp of adolescence. It was like visiting your mother's grave, a desire that in time became an obligation and at last lost all vestiges of sentiment. Once you dated a woman who reminded you vaguely of her, but in bed, her body folded beneath you, she did not transform. Her kisses were dry, her breath stale. As you slid into her, there were gasps, not silence. Sooner or later you had to call her by name: Jane it was, or Jean. Janine. In the morning, when you woke up next to her, you wanted to cry. You bought her breakfast instead, and never called her again.

In a few months you met Melinda, our lady of investment banking; Melinda of the business suits and wire-rimmed glasses, forever clinking glasses of chardonnay and daring you to unfurl that braid of ash blonde at the nape of her neck. Her voice filled your silence and, for a time, even touched that silence inside, the place in your mind and heart and gut where only the picture people walked and talked and made love in silent shadows.

Melinda, who stole into your life on a rainy afternoon, late in April or early in May, and who left, not at all quietly, almost four years later. Melinda of the Georgetown condominium; Melinda of the Nordic Trac; Melinda of the unwanted pregnancy; Melinda of the career that mattered most.

Melinda, whose photograph you need to bring back memories of her face.

Your first wife, Melinda.

Nothing has changed inside booth 7: four walls and a roof of painted plywood, the plastic bench bolted to the wall opposite the coin box, a closet of monastic simplicity bathed in the cool blue light of the television monitor. The television and her first video, *Fourplay*, were waiting there, waiting for Delacorte's return. It was the summer of 1983, and after a three-martini lunch that sealed the settlement of another lawsuit, Delacorte found himself wandering north along 14th Street, watching the next of its ancient buildings fall prey to the swinging metal ram of the demolition crane. Three stories of red brick and dirty windows, haven of strip shows and massage parlors, were broken in half, blasted into dust. An adult bookstore would follow, the final domino, and the block would be cleansed, made ready for secretarial pools and stock options.

Whether his footsteps were impulsive or merely inevitable, he found the alleyway and escaped the August sun in the dank solace of Peepland. The old ways came back to him too easily. The crumpled dollars from his pants pocket were transmuted into quarters, and he made his way to booth 7 with nervous certainty: that she would be waiting, that she would be gone, and disappointment settled into his gut as the video played out its plotless episodes, the random collision of anonymous bodies in anonymous rooms. The male star, a mustachioed Ron Jeremy, plied his smirking sex play on a series of listless bodies until one dollar, two dollar, three dollar, four brought on the final scene, the gigolo and his latest conquest, a slutty Amber Lynn, tangling the sheets of a soundstage bed. Through an angle of light, a French maid enters, black fishnets and white ruffles, and feigns surprise with a silent surge of her lips. A latticed door is the shield through which she peers at the writhing couple, whose contortions urge her own fingers to touch her breasts, her stomach, and at last between her legs. There is no doubt that it is her. The hair is brunette, a shag cut, like Fonda in *Klute*, and she is no longer thin but lean, her stance effortless and athletic and all so knowing as she works open the buttons of the insipid uniform, unveils a budding body, still so young, so pale, so fragile and yet so willing: her mouth and at last her taut darkness taking in her fingers with such singleminded joy.

This time she did not escape him. Delacorte insisted on buying the video, haggling with the clerk until, after a phone call, the man accepted a hundred dollars, cash. As Delacorte returned to the sunbaked street, tape tucked beneath his arm, he blinked at the relentless light and knew with a sudden certainty where the visions would go, coiled in black cases, unleashed from the rundown storefronts, the back alley theaters, the bygone houses of the holy and sent into the living rooms, the bedrooms, the dens of suburbia, where video decks in the thousands, the millions, would loop out her secret life and, in time, make it public.

Her name is Charli Prince. It is a new name, taken for her headline role in the Vivid Video production known as *Air Force Brat*. Or perhaps the name was always hers, but only now, in her newfound fame, is it worthy of revelation. For her very first film credit, a seven-minute Swedish Erotica loop in which she gave a dreamy blowjob to a dusky construction worker, she was known simply as Cherie. The loop ran in booth 12 of Peepland for five weeks in the winter of 1980: hostages held in Iran, Reagan's election, the space shuttle taking flight. Then came a series of loops for Pleasure Principle Productions in which she took third or fourth billing as Cheri Redd. Her hair was long and wicked, thickets of crimson fire that she flung furiously from side to side as men in ones and twos were taken into her mouth and then her vagina before spilling necklaces of pearly white across her throat and chest.

When he first heard her voice—that throttled cry of "Yeah, yeah . . . *yes*" cut short by gasps so pained that she may as well have been knifed—she was known as Lotte Love. He was huddled in what he hoped was a clean seat at the Olympic Theatre at 15th Street, just below H Street; a bank building now towers over its grave. He was watching her first feature film, directed by Radley Metzger and called *Carnal Souls*. Though Metzger's films have found a skewed legitimacy, this one seems to have disappeared, with rare and usually oblique references in the filmographies. For years Delacorte had to settle for two weatherbeaten publicity stills, found in a pricy collector's catalog; in 1989, after his biotech clients consumed their leading competitor, he bought a 16mm print. His memories of the movie, except for those of her scene, were muddled by the years, but the story was one he could not forget. A church organist, played with coy perfection by Kelly Nichols, fellates the hunky parish priest and then leaves a small midwestern farm town in shame, reckless with remorse, only to die when her car plunges from a bridge. Awakening in purgatory, she expiates her sins through a series of triple-X encounters with other lost souls. One of the dear departed—none other than Lotte Love—laments having never made love to a woman, and Kelly has no choice but to comply.

It is one of his favorite scenes. She takes Kelly to the floor like a famished lion, not so much kissing as tasting her, from mouth to breasts to cunt and then back again. Her lips are fuller now, pouty and stung by bees. Her complexion is clear, burnished carefully by sun or sunlamp, and those blue eyes shine with a singleminded desire. The red of her hair is brighter, slashed with black. She owns the scene; she controls each gesture, each movement, even when she lies supine, Kelly's fingers inside her.

He remembered one other thing about *Carnal Souls*. It was that night, early in the eighties, that he entered the bookstore next to the Olympic and began to buy the magazines. Not many of them, not at first, just one or two each month: *Adam Film Quarterly, Triple X World*, and the rest, devoted to the burgeoning adult movie trade. Searching, ever searching, for photos of her, and rewarded again and again as she flashed and fondled and fucked her way out of obscurity and into his eager heart. In *Gent* she straddled a jockstrapped football player, teasing his erection with her cheerleader's pompons; in *Knave* she sucked the spike heel of a Nazi-uniformed prison matron. Her wrists were circled with rope in *Bondage Life*; she knelt, her buttocks striped with welts, in *Submission*; she glistened, in red and in black, in *Latex Lovers Guide*.

In the January 1986 issue of *Gallery*, she shed the skin of Lotte Love to pose as the "Girl Next Door" from Missouri, Sherry Ellen Locke: birthdate 6/11/64, passions for cowboy films, white chocolate, the Indy 500. He might not have noticed but for the pose on page 103: the tilt of her shoulders as she leaned over the hood of a vintage Ford Mustang, the careless but knowing thrust of her chin and breasts and hips. It took only a second look, and by then it was obviously her.

Her hair was straight and silky, insufferably blond, the kind of blond that mingles silver and white; her breasts had inflated to ripe and impossibly firm grapefruits. A deep tan, cooked under California sun, was slit with the blue stripe of a T-back bikini bottom. On the following pages she is beyond glorious, bending and twisting in white garter belt and stockings, draping a poolside lounge chair in nothing but high heels and suntan oil, spreading her legs wide for all to see.

With each new magazine, each new video, each new vista, she opens herself to you, shows you some wisdom in a world of skin and muscle, nylon and silk, latex and rubber, leather and chain, where the unknowable is expressed by the down of blond peach fuzz, a taut stomach, tensed thigh. She is immaculate and she is invincible, a wingless angel, unreachable perfection—and she is insatiable. She is now called Sherilyn, as you learn when paging through an issue of *Video Xcitement*, your fingertips bruised with cheap newsprint. You order her solo video from Southern Shore and watch her undress and dance to the distant sound of rock 'n' roll while the picture fades into sunsets and at last a silver dildo.

She is Cher Lucke when going wall-to-wall with Jamie Gillis in Hollywood Video's *Ultrafoxes*. She is Cheri in *Naughty Night* and *Creampuffs 2*. In a video from B&D Pleasures, she is title material: *Sherri Bound*. Her costars are Kiri Kelly, a docile, bleach-maned submissive, and a whipmaster by the name of Jay Dee, a potbellied graybeard with a taste for riding boots and those bygone clichés of the S/M underworld. When he calls her "slave" you nearly laugh, for there is no doubt just who is master here; she owns the camera, and everything that it sees.

It is your local video store that announces her to you as Charli Prince. There, in rental offerings hidden between the covers of a three-ring binder, awaits the erotic elite, and in *Air Force Brat* she took her rightful place among them. The next night you selected her tryst with Tracy Adams and Tyffany Minx in *Flirtysomething*, a video by Insatiable Gold. You watched her mouth, her eyes, for a clue, some knowing smile, a nod and a wink that would tell you she is acting, that she knows you are watching, wishing, wanting as her voice called to you in her trademark "Yeah, yeah . . . *yes*" and she pulled herself, and you, to orgasm.

With each new tape, some of them purchased, others rented and copied, but all of them made part of your collection, there is a revelation: the seductive debut on Active Video with the bombshell blond known, like so many of her sisters, by a single name, in this case, Savannah; the intensity of her interracial licking at the lips of Heather Hunter; and the desperation of her cries in the closing moments of *Deep into Charli*, in what *Adult Video News* describes as "her first anal encounter."

You find yourself thinking about her at the least likely moments, and this, of course, means that you are in love. You are taking the deposition of a grim-faced young mother, her child the slobbering, brain-dead victim of a pharmaceutical cartel's multimillion-dollar mistake, and just as you ask again about this woman's history of venereal disease, you flash on the notorious set piece from *Ultimate*, the video that gave your secret love her first fifteen minutes of fame, that took her from the furtive shadows and into the public eye, and the look of absolute abandon that shone from her face as the five thick-muscled, over-endowed men closed in on her, forming the points of a star. Two of them penetrate her, front and back. A third dips his cock into her wide and waiting mouth. Her hands grasp the risen gristle of the fourth and fifth, pulling at them in a frantic rhythm that seems, like her body, to pulse, to move slowly from pattern to passion to pageantry as she brings them simultaneously to climax.

It is this scene, impossible to imagine, that replays again on the night that you bedded Alice, the sister of your tennis buddy's assistant at the Ex-Im Bank, and during the following nine months of life together you found no moment as fulfilling. Later you wondered why it took that long to find Alice's flaw, to understand that subtle imperfection. Perhaps you were distracted. There was so much work to be done as the mergers and acquisitions tumbled into bankruptcies and dissolutions—and there was so much yet to be seen.

For here in booth 7, she is yours, and you are hers. She looks out at you from the pulsing screen, licks her willing lips, and smiles her never ending smile. "Yeah, yeah . . . *yes*." Smiling on the bed, the sofa, the divan, the lounge chair, the carpet, the hardwood tile, the pool table, the kitchen table, the lawn, the leaves, the desert, even the blacktop of an outdoor basketball court. In the car, front seat and back. In the flatbed of a pickup truck; in the cab of an eighteen-wheeler; in the trough of a concrete mixer. In the swimming pool, in the Jacuzzi, the tub, the current, the tide. Under a shower of water and, yes, once, of urine. "Yeah, yeah . . . *yes*." Smiling as the deeds are done by her and to her, smiling as the nipples and the pussies and the cocks are pushed into her mouth, taken by her hand; smiling as the handcuffs are secured, the cloth gag thrust between her lips, the lashes laid across her buttocks and her back; smiling as the kisses descend, ascend, linger, the wet tongues lick and lap; as the come shots are replayed in slow motion, the favorite target her face, though of course her breasts and so many times her stomach are bathed in the essence of her worshipers.

Smiling. Always smiling.

"Yeah, yeah . . . *yes*."

Delacorte slips another quarter from his pocket. The television monitor, inches from his face, hums with white noise that dampens the sound from the booth next door, a riot of muted moans and then a tinny voice that declares, "I'm coming . . . I'm coming" as the screen blinks its message, red on blue, summoning Delacorte to insert another coin. Once, wondering just what his quarters might buy, he timed the tape loop, the gift of twenty-five cents. It was a meaningless gesture. Inside the booths there is no inflationary spiral; his coins buy ecstasy just as cheaply now as then. It is the ecstasy itself that has spiraled, crossing over from the darkness, out of the grainy loops of film, out of the thing called pornography into something new and different, something called adult entertainment. From this journey came a new ecstasy, a strangely cleansed and sanitized ecstasy, bright and shining moments of orgasmic glory in videotapes of startling clarity made by cameras that peered and probed from every angle. A world where lovers, should he say fuckers, practiced safe sex and portrayed no violence. A world where friends, lovers, even husband and wife, might watch. A world where a vision might rise from the shadows and walk into the light.

In the year before the accident, the name, the face, and, of course, the perfect body of Charli Prince sped across the pages of the magazines, the covers of videos, the screens of televisions. Suddenly she was everywhere: not a week went by without another sight of Charli Prince. Aerosmith's new music video. The cover of *Penthouse*. Lingerie modeling for *Elle*, swimsuits for *Inside Sports*. A brief feature in *Entertainment Weekly*. A cameo on Letterman. Brian De Palma was quoted in *Daily Variety*: he would cast Charli Prince in his next movie.

She was no longer seen but shown. She was being covered with clothes. Her lips and tongue were open, but forming words—words and sentences.

Whether she fled or was forced from the light of this nude dawn, Charli Prince stole quickly back into the darkness, making of all things some tawdry horror film, an erotic thriller for the mad Italian Gualtiere. Why she should have settled for this role is as mysterious as her fate. In the footnote focus of *Hard Copy* and *Inside Edition*, there was only the somber suggestion that making an R-rated film could somehow give her a new life, something that was lacking in an X-rated world. The smirking irony, the undertone of vicious glee, burned at your heart. De Palma never had his chance to work with Charli Prince, to stalk her with his Steadicam, to make her his victim. Giacomo Gualtiere, for whatever reason—an agent's instinct, the Tallis script, a favor owed—was there first and last and forever.

In an instant, she was a goddess.

In another instant, she was dead.

But love never dies. Love fills the little closet, the one with the lock, in the guest bedroom of your riverfront Victorian in McLean; and this is no ordinary love, not the love of gestures, of flowers and sentimental greeting cards. This is a love that is hard fact, love that can be sorted and counted: fifty-four videos, seventy reels of film, magazines in the hundreds. Two calendars, a sheaf of promotional stills, the cover of that Pearl Jam CD. A poster of her, the famous wet bikini in the boardroom that inflamed feminists and, no doubt, the passions of ten thousand college boys, looks down upon this testament of your love.

Everything is here, from that first loop of film to the final performance. Delacorte found that video at his local Blockbuster, not hidden behind a ring binder, but displayed openly on the shelf for all to rent and see: *Death American Style*. The laconic narrator, who once sang beach boy ballads and starred in an NBC made-for-TV movie, offers homilies about gun control and capital punishment to a cavalcade of atrocities, many of them real, some of them staged. There, following George Holliday's amateur video of the beating of Rodney King—fifty-six times in eighty-one seconds—is the in-store camera recording of a Korean convenience store owner as she shoots a fifteen-year-old girl in the back of the head. Hotel balconies collapse amidst New Year revelry; religious communes are set afire by the FBI. United Airlines Flight 232 cartwheels into flames in a crash landing at Sioux City, Iowa. Pennsylvania State Treasurer R. Budd Dwyer, facing a prison sentence for bribery, calls a press conference, thrusts a .357 Magnum into his mouth, and blows out the back of his head. On the set of *Twilight Zone: The Movie*, Vic Morrow is decapitated by a crashing helicopter, the two refugee children torn from him, and from us, forever. Suffering and pain, fire and blood, images without context, killings without cause or effect, killings without meaning but for their moment, the moment that they are recorded, the moment that they are seen.

Then, saving the best for last, is the outtake from *Bloody Roses*, as a clapboard introduces scene and take, and in an instant Charli Prince is there, she is alive and she is moving in high-heeled wonder toward the camera, toward you, on a soundstage somewhere in Salt Lake City, and it is the final week of shooting, you know that from your file of news clippings and obituaries, and Giuseppe Tinelli is at the camera and he frames her in medium close-up, struggling from the arms of a tall brutish Italian whose stage name is George Eastman, and from somewhere off camera the culprit comes, igniting from the cartridge of the rigged stage pistol, as her left hand circles Eastman's forearm, then pushes away, spinning her back toward the camera, toward the superheated discharge that erupts in the darkness, even as she takes a single step, moving into the overloaded blank that rockets from the barrel of the gun and spits its dull fragments of metal into her suddenly heaving chest, that tunnels through her too quickly for even the unblinking eye of the lens to record, that sprays the air with blood and flesh, that spins her around and sends her falling down even as the cameraman moves miraculously to close-up and that is when her lips move, and although there is only silence, there is no sound, you can hear her voice, you can hear her calling "Yeah, yeah . . . *yes*" before her mouth fills with blood, before all is red, hemorrhaging from her nostrils in a flood as she sprawls, kicking, onto the floor, and the camera holds the shot, never letting it go as her lungs seek air and her chest heaves once, then again, and then and then and then is still.

Delacorte could not help himself; he stood, pants tenting as his hard-on rose in triumph. Then he took the remote control, stabbed at its buttons, rewound the scene to its beginning.

He unzipped his pants and pressed the slow-motion.

You knew then that your love could never die. You kept the rental tape until the copy you ordered arrived, and you paid the late fee with a gold card and a smile. You asked after a laserdisc of *Death American Style* and the clerk expressed doubt, though he had heard about the possibility of a CD-ROM. He would check and let you know.

For weeks you watched the tape, fast-forwarding through the mayhem until you reached the ninety-minute mark, and you studied this fifty-five-second smear of colors, you ran it back and forth, you ran it in slow motion, frame by frame, at double speed, in reverse, until you knew its every brilliance and blemish, the odd streak of light that flares into the upper left-hand corner of the frame at the seventeen-second mark; the black spot of the entry wound that appears at twenty-four seconds, preceding her first jerking response by almost two heartbeats; each frame has its own story to tell, and you sit and you watch until there is nothing left to know.

Then you put the tape into your closet and you wait and you wait but you know too well what has happened, and you need no sullen peepshow counterman to tell you: "gone." It is the end, it is over, and at night, as you fight for sleep, you imagine how the next night will end, and the night after that, how a parade of taut-bodied, long-legged goddesses will serve your every need and be gone when you awaken, ready for another day of work. But the next night is spent with Sally, and in the morning, eyeshadow smeared and body smelling of sweat, she talks with Delacorte about commitment, and the night after that he spends alone.

After Sally there is Kate, who likes to play Harry Connick CDs and wants you to wear a condom; and after Kate there is the new paralegal, Alyson, and after Alyson is a brief meeting with your managing partner, who reviews the firm policy on sexual harassment. You are thinking about Alyson, about the clipped fingernails, the mole on her left shoulder, why she never wore lipstick, when you hear about the videotape. It is idle conversation, overheard in a bar, a half whisper at your shoulder, a laugh, somewhere in the shallow background of pennies for thoughts and pickup lines, but you sat in a circle of suits, talking about tax codes, unable to turn and ask, unable to say even a word. Later you doubted what you had heard. You tried not to think about it, but the thoughts were unrelenting, the thoughts would not stop promising that it was real. It was not long afterward that you saw the words, or something very much like them, in print. The city's underground newspaper spoke them, loud and clear, in a derisive rant on the missing links of Americana: aliens in Hangar 18, Dillinger's penis, JFK's brain, mimed moonlandings, dead, drug-addled crooners, and yes, of course, a certain video.

True lies, all of them, the stuff of tabloids and talk shows and too many cocktails. Still: you had money, and you had time. You rented the post office box and you placed the classified ads here and there and you waited and you waited, but you didn't have to wait long.

The letter was postmarked ROCHESTER NY, but the telephone number was from a suburb of Pittsburgh. You did not believe, you knew it was a hoax, a con, but you made the call, and the call made you wonder, and the wonder brought on the hunger, and the hunger was for love. It wasn't long before you said yes.

It was the most expensive video you have ever seen: $200 for the viewing and then the plane fare to Chicago, nearly two thousand quarters. What it bought you was a darkened motel room near O'Hare, a half circle of seats facing into a television screen, and a squat Hitachi videodeck whose clock blinked out 12:00; it was the first time you had watched her when you were not alone. You paid your money to a shadow and you sat down in the closest of the chairs. An older man, someone's grandfather, arrived five minutes late and nervous; he coughed, too loudly, and shrugged inside his frayed corduroy jacket. The other two men were friends, acquaintances, huddling like conspirators in the corner to your right; they looked pretty much like you, and would not meet your eyes.

"Gentlemen," said the voice of the shadow. "Please be seated." And seated you were, with an uneasy atmosphere of embarrassed expectancy that divided you from the others more convincingly than the wooden walls of booth 7 could have done. You leaned toward the television and its veil of gray haze as the shadow reached the cassette into the videodeck. Then there was nothing left for you to do but what you do best: watch.

On the videotape there is no sound, though from somewhere in the room comes a sharp intake of breath, whether of shock or sudden desire you do not know, as the picture rolls, steadies, blurs, then steadies again and finds focus. It is grainy, fourth- or perhaps even fifth-generation, like the signal of some distant television station, transmissions from the end of the world, and it is a view in black and white, from a fixed position, high above, no doubt mounted on the ceiling, peering down from an angle slightly to her left.

For she is there. She lies before you, eyes closed, palms upward, legs spread ever so invitingly—and nude. You squint but cannot quite make out her expression, though you are certain that it is a smile. The video jumps, its only edit, and you now look upon a close-up of a single sheet of paper, an official-looking document, a form marked in ink with circles and checks, the outline of a human form, and handwriting and a signature. You ignore its codes and comments, searching for the box with her name: Charlotte Pressman. A cold and anonymous name, as cold and anonymous as her corpse.

You let the words find your lips as the picture jumps again and the fixed camera angle returns, and now you know her, every inch of her, you know her gray and mottled skin, her deflated breasts, her matted tangle of hair, as the deputy medical examiner closes in, scalpel in hand, to dance this last dance.

The striptease of flesh begins. From the left shoulder cutting downward, then the right, and then a single stroke of the blade along her stomach, a ragged letter Y. The folds of skin are taken in his hands, and the layers of her outer flesh are peeled back, revealing the glories within: strips of muscle, yellow pouches of fat, wet bone. In a frozen forever, man and metal probe the shattered breastbone, forceps dip and pull at her broken heart. A silvery rotary saw descends and, when its work is done, the glistening organs are pulled out one by one, examined and weighed and cataloged as you hear the voice, the voice that has been speaking for minutes but only now is heard: pancreas, unremarkable; adrenals, unremarkable; spleen, unremarkable. The flat voice, the drone of a dial tone—unremarkable, unremarkable—as he reaches deep inside her, to the places that tongues and pricks could not venture, and with each touch takes more and more until at last she is a gutted husk. But there is, of course, more: the swift pass of the scalpel from ear to jaw to ear, and her face is peeled back, flimsy and forgotten, before the saw spins again and shears the top of her head. The gray mass is lifted, weighed—unremarkable, unremarkable—and the drama is done. At last you have seen all of her.

You stand and you walk away, out of the room, out of the hotel, out of Chicago, and you hear the voice of one of the men behind you, wondering aloud about the price of a second showing. But there is no price, not one that you can afford; you have only your quarters, and you will always have her:

She is faceless; she is nameless; she is meat.

Each week you returned to Peepland; each week for the first month, once or twice or three times a week and now it is every day, every afternoon, that you leave your desk and you walk the few short blocks to this tiny outpost, the last of its kind in this city, and you trade your dollar bills for quarters and you find your way to a booth, more often than not this booth, lucky 7, and you sit in the darkness and you look through the window of the video screen and you see the naked, the women and the men, you see them rage and rut, and you see nothing there for you, nothing at all, nothing but the lean face of Delacorte reflected in the glass, looking back at you.

In time, the loop will run out, and Delacorte will raise himself up off the bench, and he will return to the office, squaring the knot of his tie, ready to sit behind his desk and take his telephone calls and revise his brief well into the night. But you: you are alone, and although you are waiting and you are watching, there is nothing left to be seen.

When what your last quarter bought you winds down to blue, then nothing, you lean your forehead against the monitor, feel its light and warmth fade into black. Your eyes, trapped in the vanished picture, look into the darkness and offer their plea. But there is no escape.

You sit in booth 7 and you watch the black screen, waiting for the shadow to move, the shadow to shift from darkness into light and then never find the darkness again. You realize then how very much you want to cry, to find the way that tears are made, but of course, as always, your cock has wept for you.

You take the fold of Kleenex from your pocket, wipe the red and swollen tip of your penis and then your hands. In the moment before you stand, ready to open the door and step back into the world, you let the Kleenex fall to the floor, where the life that was inside you trickles down a crack in the cold concrete.

For David J. Schow

LA LOMA, LA LUNA
Sue Kepros Hartman

Sue Kepros Hartman has been a reporter and features writer in and around Colorado for a number of years. Her fiction has been published in various small literary magazines.

"La Loma, La Luna" is contemporary fantasy set in the Rocky Mountains. The author evokes a strong sense of place, creates memorable characters, and infuses the everyday world with magic in this story of people who are drawn to the wild. It comes from *High Fantastic*, a collection of stories from Colorado edited by Steve Rasnic Tem.

—T.W.

At gloaming, when the amber sunset dissolves into the pewter shadows of twilight, the hour of dusk when hoodoos and haints, saints and spirits yawningly arise for this night's mischief, Niko drifts ahead, darting behind a bush, his one warning a throaty growl as he launches over our heads and we see only the sleek fur of his underbelly, a spume of silver snow.

Sawyer laughs, an unusual behavior for her when she's walking her wolves. "Don't be afraid, Cara. That's wolf mischief. Hide and seek."

Luna, the white wolf and Niko's mate, darts up from behind and slams into the back of my knees. I keel over.

"You can't show fear, but when one challenges you, don't ever stare directly into their eyes."

From flat on my stomach in the snow, there is little danger of me doing that. As I struggle to my feet, Luna stands on her hind legs and braces her paws on my shoulders; she's a full head taller and her paw prints look larger than my not-so-dainty size eights.

"Most excellent, Cara." Sawyer's still laughing. "You've been adopted. Remember, though, to let them know who's dominant. I bite them on the nose; it works!"

Later in the evening, in the better light of the inn, I see a thin and ancient scar running from the bridge of Sawyer's nose down her left nostril into her upper lip, causing it to curl up slightly on that side.

High in the Colorado Rockies there is, and there no longer is a ramshackle and historic inn near the shores of Twin Lakes on Highway 82, which links the old mining town of Leadville to the high-end sizzle of stars and bars that is Aspen, over Independence Pass, in the shadow of Mount Elbert, the state's steepest and most frigid peak at 14,433 feet.

In the 1880s, the inn was the stagecoach stop and layover. Moreover, it hosted the only House of Ill Repute for twenty miles in any direction in the mountains and that is a long horseback ride, colder than frost in your beard in February. Even with clapboard additions to the main split-log building, what with the stage travelers and respectable guests, there could never be more than three to four girls working the house, and they were often banished to the unheated shack across the roadway in order to accommodate more socially acceptable guests in the inn proper. With being cast into the cold to entertain on straw pallets instead of the inn's famous feather beds, and given the fact that there was no shortage of bachelor miners in the region, the Parlor Girls didn't stay in the employ of Miss Lorette for any duration. After the murders in Rooms 5 and 7 and Immaculate Jane's overdose in Room 6 from laudanum, Miss Lorette's business took a definite decline and only the two most loyal of her employees stayed on, those for a very brief period.

The second resurrection occurred in the 1920s, when the old bordello was patched up to house The Young Gentlemen's Hunt Club, to which the elite membership would retreat to the male-only pursuit of game—deer, elk, bear, five-card stud, illegal hootch, and occasionally, young women of dubious character. True to form, this incarnation invited its own tragic scandal and the eight-year run of The Young Gentlemen's Hunt Club ended abruptly, with the death of a spirited Manitou Springs matron, whose body was found in the snow amidst the budding red lilies, elks lip, and lupine, beside Lake Creek, wearing an ivory silk camisa, limbs frozen blue stiff, curled in on herself, with her husband's two favorite elk-hounds huddled against her, their coats frosty with ice. Dead as their mistress. Such exquisite loyalty.

"I bought it in 1980," Sawyer informs a guest. "I remodeled it myself, with the help of my two cousins, Durrina and Gaydell, but once the carpentry was complete, they hightailed it back to Sealbone—Twin Lakes was too fast-paced to suit them, even though there are only eighteen residents in the village. Imagine that." Sometimes she tells people that Durrina and Gaydell were homesick for their mother, her great aunt Florella; that's why they left. Different days, different stories. Two other women were involved in the reconstruction of the inn—tales of townsfolk verify that—but who they really were and why they left depends on who you talk to.

Sawyer is a woman with a mission—no nonsense, chainsmoking, hard-muscled, under five foot, with a crew cut—not a spike, mind you, but a man's three-dollar buzz—whose male clothes, haircut, and style could never disguise her being a woman. Men flock to Sawyer, but like me, she's avoided them for years, sexually dormant, celibate as a priestess in her mountain lodge, hosting travelers too tired to drive on, providing food and warmth and the original soft-to-the-point-of-decadence feather beds with down comforters for her guests, entertaining them with historic and hair-raising stories, whichever their pleasure, and nurturing her pack of black Arctic tundra wolves and wolf-dog hybrids, which are the region's greatest draw: Casa de la Luna, Twin Lakes, Colorado.

To be accurate, I must tell you that even the black wolves are not purebreds—it being against the law to harbor a wild wolf. They are all—as far as Sawyer will admit—seven-eighths wolf, one-eighth husky, malamute, shepherd, something. Ironically, the more wolf-bred the animal is, the safer it becomes for human companionship; it is dog blood that turns them erratic and aggressive.

In the first years of operation, at dusk, after the first supper rush and once the overnight guests are safely ensconced in their tiny, dim-lit rooms, Sawyer takes Niko, the black alpha male, for a run around the lakes. It is often my privilege to accompany them on their walks where Niko lopes ahead in the darkening night until he can barely be seen, the flash of his moonstone-white eyes all that shows in the camouflage silver-tipped black fur. A beauty, born leader, Niko becomes the black wolf of a lifetime of dreams, in this place of faraway travelers. And did I tell you that Sawyer whistles the way that men used to, tuneful and serene—and that whistling is a beacon to Niko, keeping him within the boundaries of her will?

"He's amazing," I say, picking up the albino pup by the scruff as he squirms in my grasp. "Fur as white as new-dawn snow, pale blue eyes like icicles."

"Stunningly special," Sawyer concurs, more than slightly sarcastic. To her, wolves are beyond description, language is a reductive medium. I wish she would try to be a little tactful.

"Welcome to my family, Raggs the Digger II. Thank you, Alex."

She nods to Alex, whose creased forehead displays his sacrifice in adopting out the orphan, whose wolf mother and husky/wolf father were poisoned by neighbors in Leadville. There have always been those who hate and fear wolves.

"Raggs the First was the infamous Cathedral Bluffs albino renegade of the 1870s." For the attention they pay to me, I might as well have stayed back at the inn and painted, do what I'm here to do.

"I'll help pay for his keep, Sawyer." Alex is sad to the point of weeping. I wonder if Alex, a fellow member of Colorado Wolf Rescue, may come to regret his marriage to the native Leadvillite which corralled his wandering nature, and cost him his lupine companions, but he doesn't say so. One of his marriage vows is loyalty, and like the wolf, he mates for life.

"My hell, Alex. Don't look so hang-dog. It's only sixteen miles to my place. You can come visit Raggs anytime, night or day."

Lord, that Sawyer is a surprise with men. When Alex grins back at her, I know for sure that he, like most men she encounters, is smitten, and will always be enchanted by her no matter what else lures him, and, even so, this man will never come on a personal visit.

"I'd want to kill someone who harmed one of my wolves. There's nothing worse than poison. It's a coward's way."

"The way I pieced it together is that Raggs's mother sensed the rat poison in the rabbit, and dropped scat on it, even in its final twitching, but the redtail who tore off parts of the carcass got snatched up by Raggs's father, who dragged it to the den. I was bottle-feeding this runt, so Raggs is my only survivor."

"Albinos are supposed to be the smartest. I read that the first Raggs raided ranches wherever and whenever he wanted to, and evaded his hunters for twenty years." That's all I know about the subject; I hope it's enough.

"Strychnine, Alex?" Sawyer is still excluding me. "If I caught someone trying that, I'd kill him."

We believe her.

Sawyer snatches Raggs and he yips, nipping at her forearm. "As for contributing to his keep, that won't be necessary as long as hunters keep donating their elk and deer scraps. The way the pack's growing, though, we'll see. If I need help, I'll ask."

In the wild, a wolf can eat up to twenty pounds of meat at one sitting, a domesticated one who eats regularly somewhat less, but even so, it's quite costly to feed a wolf pack; the hunters' donations are a godsend.

To kill any parasites in the wild game scraps, Sawyer boils it before feeding it to the wolves, simmering it in the same iron cauldron she uses to make chili. During lean months, I sometimes wonder what she's dicing into the chili pot, but unfortunately, I am too ravenous and not daring enough to ask.

I've never been sure if I like that white wolf, Raggs, so much as I admire his physical prowess, respect his damnable will. Especially since he challenged and displaced Niko as alpha. I've never wanted to rough Ragg's coat or probe for muscle and sinew as I do Niko and Luna, playing growling, wrestling, dodging a clumsy paw, clamping their muzzles, discovering, remembering my way, memorizing to my fingerbones how to render them into clay, into bronze, into memory.

I do not know what Sawyer and I are to each other—perhaps mere allies, if not friends, but I do know that even during late September, during her peak period, the week of the Great Tomato Wars, Sawyer holds Room 6 for me on the weekends, in case I feel like driving three hours from my home in East Denver, even though there are at least fifty Texans camped outside, willing to pay triple rates to sleep there. Lord knows why—these aren't deluxe accommodations: the forty-watt electric lanterns blink off and on at their convenience; the wood floors sag to the point of worry (and squeak after midnight); cooking smoke wafts upstairs and under the doorjambs; if the tenant next door snores, you know it; and don't forget to mention the ghost of Immaculate Jane who occasionally appears at the edge of the oval mirror. And the bathroom with the clawfoot tub is down the hall. At least it's not down the path—as Eric would say.

Perhaps Sawyer's loyalty to me displays a latent respect for art or perhaps it's a misplaced sense of guilt, because she's recently initiated a relationship with my best artist friend and long-past lover, Eric, who's moved to Twin Lakes as Casa de la Luna's cook. As I've told you, she never reveals her secrets to me, nor I to her, for that matter, so what we've agreed to hold in common is an admiration of Twin Lakes, wolves, and Eric Corcoran. Since some in Leadville territory don't have much to occupy them—especially in the deep cold winters—at least the romance between Eric and Sawyer ends certain speculations. I've finally concluded that it doesn't matter whether strangers think my visits to Casa de la Luna are for other purposes than healing my heart and honing my art. People will think what they will, no matter how many pains you go to in correcting them.

From the luggage storage under the stairway, Sawyer retrieves a daguerreotype of Miss Lorette. The only facts generally agreed upon by local historians are that Casa de la Luna was the stage stop; and it was a whorehouse whose madame's portrait was once painted on the wooden floor of a Leadville saloon—and it was not a pretty sight. Miss Lorette was long of nose, small of eyes and exceedingly square-jawed. The daguerreotype confirms this description and it, along with a perfectly preserved Basque jacket of apple-green taffeta, tiny waisted with maroon velvet lapels, adorned with brass and floral velvet perfume buttons—wherein perfume was dabbed into the velvet insets in order not to stain the jacket fabric, and gave off an odor of Ashes of Roses Toilet Water well into the twentieth century—are all that remains of the legendary Lorette. There is, however, a ghostly presence of stiff comportment that staff and lodgers see lurking in the hallway, outside the girls' rooms, particularly during full moons of the quieter winter months, following the autumn rush during the era of the Great Tomato Wars.

The Tomato Wars turned deadly serious in the third year, when native Coloradans felt threatened by the influx of Texas oil shale workers while the local molybdenum market crashed, causing further layoffs at the mines. Leadville men had time on their hands and those who before had avoided the rotten-tomato pitching contest began taking interest in slaughtering the Texas Tomatillos. Everyone hurled tomatoes at everyone else; it was a melee and if you got hit, you were out. The team with the last man standing was the winner and for three luckless seasons, Colorado lost.

Some townspeople resented Sawyer for attracting even more Texans into the Leadville/Twin Lakes region with the wars, and it was about that time that the rumors about Sawyer went wild.

I am playing pool at Alex's club, the Drubbing, with a local named Brant Lockhardt and his underage brother, Ramsey, who is so drunk that he drawls a lewd proposition at me in spite of the twelve-year difference. He drools too, hardly seductive; I tell him to kiss off, so he heads for the men's room, passing out with his head in the urinal, which is not an unusual occurrence, according to Alex. The sheriff overlooks the violation of liquor laws only in certain circumstances, and I suppose that being the son of upstanding citizen and alpaca entrepreneur Garland Lockhardt allows some special privileges in Leadville. Unlike his baby brother, Brant is a world-class guzzler, and now that Ramsey's out of commission for a while, Brant starts in on me.

"I saw your friend yesterday morning when I was shooting ducks. All her beasts were there too, and they were dancing and howling by the lakes. It was barely getting light, so I got my binoculars to focus better, and you know what?"

I should know better than to ask, but I can't resist a dangler. "What, Brant?"

"She was naked." He whistles.

I drove up from Denver last night so I can't say for sure what happened, but neither can I let this pass. "I doubt it. She only lets them out three at a time at most, and always at sundown. Besides, who'd be crazy enough to be outside nude when it's this cold?"

Brant smiles. "My point exactly."

"I'll lay you twenty it never happened. Prove it, or shut up."

Brant raises one eyebrow. Men love a challenge. He refills my beer glass.

I ought to leave this be, but . . . "Did you take pictures, Brant? Let's see them."

He winks at me. I drop the eight, followed by the cue ball into the corner pocket. I didn't want to play in the first place.

Alex stops polishing the immaculate counter. Why doesn't he say something, can't he defend her? She took on that albino orphan of his.

Jason, the postman poet, looks up from his usual volume of Robert—it is always either Frost or Bly, and at this point, it doesn't matter which.

"Maybe you ought to say something to her, Cara," Jason states. Even him? He ought to go back to Robert, and stay out of my battles.

Brant is warming up. "Folks say that she's loco, call her the wild wolf woman."

"They aren't the least wild." I lie. I'm getting sucked into something, I'm sure, but I can't back off now. "I play with the wolves. I bottle-fed the white alpha male myself—so did Alex. Ask him. He gave Raggs to Sawyer in the first place."

Alex shoots me a glare; it might pass for a warning.

"You mean the freaky white one with the weird eyes?"

"Raggs is the most loyal and protective of all. Until he grew so huge that he could challenge the old alpha, Raggs used to sleep on the foot of her bed."

Brant grins like a fool and winks again.

"Something wrong with your eye, Lockhardt?"

Jason clears his throat, a sure sign that he's about to butt in.

Brant looks sheepish; he knows when he pushes too far. "Hey, you want to play a game?" He waves his cue at Jason.

"Wouldn't mind." Jason chalks up. "I can shed some light on this wolf thing. One might say that I had a transpersonal experience concerning them."

Normally quiet to the point of invisibility, when Jason sees that he's caught someone's interest, he's like a dry gulch after a thunderstorm, no holding back.

"It was late last spring as I recall, because I was wearing my shorts. I finished my route early, so I pulled over by the lodge near the lakes. I strolled awhile, stopping to peel an orange and peruse some Ginsberg,"

At least it wasn't Robert.

"I must have fallen asleep in the sun and when I awoke, it was quite cool and close to dark; I'd be in trouble for not checking out at the P.O. Somehow I got turned around and found myself on the other side of Twin Lakes from the spot where I parked the jeep.

"I hear crashing leaves, growls, and yelps. I unclip my mace from my belt hook and run toward the nearest stand of trees. The entire wolf pack is loose and snapping at my heels as I hoist myself above their slobbering teeth just in time but I snag and tear the sleeve of my new sweater—which I pay for myself, by the way—on a branch of the pine that I am climbing. The black wolves wait below."

Brant's mouth is actually hanging open; he reminds me of a catfish snapping at a yellowjacket. "What did you do?"

"What could I do? I stayed there, hollering, hoping that someone would hear my cries for help, but no one did. I sat up in that pine tree, getting hungry, hoarse, and cold until it was nearly dawn and a flock of crows—or was it ravens—which has the curved beak? Never mind, the ravens, let's say, landed in the nearest tree, cawing themselves silly, as if they were laughing at my ridiculous predicament. It was humiliating, although the dawn, as I recall, was a coral-shell color, lovely, as was the haunting melody of a whistler, who I never truly saw, which drew the wolves away, toward the wetland."

Alex shakes his head and draws Jason a fresh one on the house. A story of that proportion never goes unrewarded.

"That's not the worst part," Jason continues. "My boss's supervisor called in the one postal inspector in the whole region to search for the lost mail and its carrier so when I got in to work and told Adele what happened, she docked me instead of approving overtime, and she wrote me up for keeping the vehicle overnight and she's been riding my ass ever since."

"That's bad, man," Brant sympathizes, and turns to grin at me. He thinks that he's won.

"That's still not the worst," Jason claims. "The worst part is that I don't get it. I don't understand. What is the metaphor, being treed by wolves in the latter days of the twentieth century?" He heads toward the men's room where I hope that he has to haul Ramsey out of the way to use the urinal. This is not my most generous moment.

"He said that they were all black wolves," I complain to Alex. "Raggs is alpha now and there's no mistaking that he's white as that marble countertop. We both know that the pack wouldn't be out without him. Hell, the pack wouldn't go anywhere without Sawyer!"

Alex shrugs. "Lighten up, Cara. Hell, it's a good tale. Jason's a mailman. They've always got a vicious dog story; everybody knows that."

"So you both think that was the boy-who-cried-wolf stuff?" Brant looks the way certain back-country men look after a hard day's drinking, eyes slitted and blind like a prairie rattler's, skin drawn tight across the cheekbones, slack of mouth, and full of lies. "I'll tell you what I think: I think that Sawyer is some kind of Indian witch, just like they say, and I've got a mind to borrow some wolfhounds from my buddy in Wheatridge and see what's roaming around Twin Lakes at night with that lady timber nigger."

I'm not going to stick around to listen to that kind of idiocy, but I stay long enough to take a parting shot at Jason—Brant's too far gone to bother with. "Well, Jason," I say, "there's a pack of mangy coyotes that sneaks into Twin Lakes at night—to steal the bones and scraps around the wolf pens. That's what's running wild at night—besides people's imaginations. I wouldn't admit it if I got treed by coyotes either."

Jason looks hurt and turns to Brant. "What plugged her in?"

I spot three coyotes on my way back from a chilly run, my first trip since Eric and Sawyer got married three weeks ago. From across the lake, I watch my friends walking two of the beta female wolves. I am not lonely, but solitary; I am actually relieved that Eric has found someone else. I always feel responsible for the unhappiness of my former lovers, all the while knowing that I am not. When the coyotes wail, several wolves yip and yell back. It is so cold that the snowcrust snaps beneath my feet as I scurry back to the lodge, drawn by the drifting pine smoke, the promise of a popping fire. Now there is silence, the wintery gloom silhouetting the taller, pony-tailed male and the smaller female with the square cut, her two silvery wolves at her side.

The pine boards are cold on my soles; I drop my winter nightgown over my head and scoot across the room to the overstuffed feather bed. I confess that the first time I slept here I was nervous about fleas, bedbugs, mites, some unlikely survivor of the four-poster's history—the bedding of a bordello—but the flannel sheets are warm, the down so deep and accommodating, I learn to ignore former and current apprehensions, drifting into dreams much quieter and more peaceful than ever has been my waking life.

The rising full moon awakens me, round, blue white, and icy. As the corolla shines above the lodgepoles, Raggs the Digger, sensing me in the window above him, turns and lifts his head. He paces up and down his run, wolf eyes meeting mine, pleading, breaking away, darting back, piercing the soul. He throws back his head and howls.

The hackles on my neck rise. Shivers snake up my spine. This is it—sublime terror, congenital fear.

The pack answers Raggs, one voice at a time, an eerie harmonic chorus, primal beyond understanding, basic as primordial fear. Delicious.

I know what he wants. What right has Sawyer to pen a wolf? To keep him safe, she'd say. But to chain and stun collar and housebreak him? Where could he go, once domesticated? Still, to confine an animal like Raggs, keeping him chained under an Owl Moon?

I tug on my jogging shoes, don't bother with socks, slip on my down vest. I know better than to mess with the wolves, but I am haunted by Raggs's howling. It's earsplitting in the empty valley.

Raggs licks my hand as I fumble with the latch on his run. He tears out, me dashing behind, tramping the snow, crashing through the brittle crust as he bounds along the surface. We cross the road, across the frozen path between Twin Lakes.

Leap of a hare, casting snow crystal. Air too cold to feel cold. Dry tears. He is gone. What if I can't find him; what if he never comes back? And look at the moon, the heart-breaking moon man. Even as a child, I couldn't believe that he was benign. Something's amiss. Light that pure and full is female. That grinning man-in-the-moon must have hidden her away, stuffed her light into his bag of tricks, thinking that he could get away with it.

Aha! He's back! Raggs jumps into my path, darting past and returning. He brings to me a snowshoe hare, his white muzzle stained with blood the color of cherry compote, dropping it at my feet like a well-trained retriever, then tears it to pieces before my eyes, fur flying in chunks like a downy pillow fight at a party where there will be no slumber.

Across Twin Lakes, we spy two shadows, the woman from the moon, slender with her shaggy wolf. But it is only Sawyer, sending Niko ahead, to call us back, to make us answer for our misbehavior.

She looks us up and down, my hair in total disarray, roaming about in winter in a nightgown, bringing back her precious Raggs, her white wolf bloodied. I can tell her that I am sorry, that I've been overcome by moonlight. I can say that. If she gives me the chance.

"It's only rabbit blood, Sawyer."

She shoves before she speaks. I slide and fall.

Raggs intervenes, flattening his ears, showing his teeth. He snarls.

Which brings in Niko. He steps between Raggs and Sawyer. I am sorry that I started all this with my half-assed romantic notions, but it is too late.

Growling, Niko bares his teeth in a tight smile, seeing his chance to reestablish supremacy as alpha male. He assumes a crouch and inches closer to where I lie on the snow with the bloody-faced dog/wolf looming over me, his shaggy head eclipsing the triumphant moon man's grin.

I am scared out of my wits, and I can see by Sawyer's eggshell pallor and tightened lips that she is likewise frightened. That surprises me; I believed that nothing could scare Sawyer.

She grapples for the radio remote in her parka pocket, and pushes the stun button.

Raggs yelps, leaps straight up in the air, furiously twisting to bite at his electronic collar.

Niko stands full height, sensing his opponent's weakness. Niko is ready to spring.

"No, Niko, *no!*" Sawyer yells.

He stops, confused. He turns his head and cocks it to one side. I hear it. A solitary whistler. Dvorak's "New World," I think.

Niko slinks back, withdrawing from the contest.

Eric overtakes us on the path, where he's come to search out Sawyer. Some late and boisterous guests have pulled in, wanting breakfast now and bed later, and demanding to hear the legendary ghost stories that Sawyer tells of Miss Lorette and her Parlor Girls.

Sawyer apologizes for the state of disarray that the inn is in, the tufts of down in the air. She would have vacuumed had she known . . .

"If cleanliness is next to godliness," she laughs—too loudly, angrily—"I guess you know where I stand. But you wouldn't have driven this far—especially this time of night—if an immaculate room is what you wanted, and you've obviously ignored what the Leadvillites call my wolves. The Devil's Dogs, my ass! They ought to listen to the Cheyenne instead of the Brothers Grimm. The Cheyenne say that wolves are spirit messengers; that they talk to the departed at night."

I decline to stay up and join the revelry but wait until Eric's back from penning Niko and Raggs.

"Thanks," I whisper, "for whistling Niko off. You saved my butt, all our butts."

"I never learned how to whistle, or how to blow bubbles with gum. Deprived childhood, I guess," he whispers back, hugging me goodnight. I look up to see Sawyer watching us as she launches into a Lorette legend.

I hear Sawyer still laughing late in the night as I will myself to sleep. It takes more than this night's events to spook me off. I dream about a square-jawed Woman-in-the-Moon who uses a buggy whip to keep her girls in line and I half awaken several times to hear clicking taps of tiny heels pacing outside my doorway. I have to pee so I force myself up, cautiously open the door, and of course, no one is there. The hall is empty. The bathroom is cold. The clock downstairs chimes three.

A giant of an infant with an egg-shaped head pulls his pale body out of the crater and stretches to reach the man whose back is turned. He wants to stuff the man into his mouth. "The hungry heart is on the loose, it would devour the moon." Quite articulate for a baby. No, I tell him, *no!* I scream but my words are silent. The screams are real. I struggle with the comforter, tugging me down. The alarm clock reads 4:30. Yelping. The howl of a wolf. I pull myself up and out of sleep and run toward the ungodly ruckus.

Eric needs one hundred stitches to close the wounds to his right arm, his painting arm. There's quite a lot of blood splattered across their room, sheets soaked, but he refuses to be transferred to a hospital.

"It looks like a crazy quilt," he tells me, "but I'll be fine. I'll need your help, though, to pack my gear. Who needs a one-armed cook?"

Eric is agitated; it must be the painkiller Dr. Kincaid gave him that makes Eric more talkative than I've ever seen him, while Sawyer, usually the garrulous one, is completely silent.

There is no trace of hostility that I can see in their relationship. Eric claims that it is just a branch in the road where they will take separate routes. It is I who will likely weep over this, although not in their sight.

When I get Eric's gear loaded into my car and while he finishes up inside, Sawyer comes out and offers her hand. "I'll be seeing you, at least, at the Tomato Wars, won't I?" It is a challenge and I accept. She and Eric might be finished, but we aren't.

Even though the air is frigid, Eric rolls his window down to hear the calling wolves, as the pale light of Casa de la Luna becomes a pinprick of a beacon gradually vanishing in my rearview mirror. As the clicking windshield wipers sweep away the sleet from the glass, dragging arcs of ice across the glass, Eric tells his story:

"I told her it was a bad idea to bring Raggs back in the bedroom but Sawyer was afraid someone would let him out again."

"I wouldn't have, Eric. I'm not stupid."

"I know, honey, that's what I said, but Sawyer was still riled up about earlier, and she was worried about that carload of drunks, too. Booze and wolves."

"I'm sorry, Eric. It's my fault."

"No. Nobody's fault. I was too tired to fight her about Raggs sleeping inside, and she was so tired she forgot to put the stun control on the bedside table. Raggs didn't want to lie on the hearth and she kept kicking him off the foot of the bed. Everybody was cranky, Cara, and exhausted. When we started making love he must have thought I was hurting her and just like any alpha male, he'd defend a female in his pack. It was instinct, that's all. No villains, no blame. Okay?"

"But you're leaving her."

"For now. Later on, we'll see."

"She hates me."

"Nope. Next to me, you're her best friend."

"Oh, sure. That's why she's so warm and huggy."

"She's scared of people, can't you tell? The wolves are her family. Hell, they're everything. If I don't stick around, there's no evidence. And if I won't file a complaint, nobody can do anything to Raggs, although I believe she shouldn't keep him around people. Well, around men, anyway. The way he came at me . . ."

Eric shakes his head. "I finally decide to remarry and look what happens. I choose another stubborn woman, only this one's a hermit who harbors wolves."

"That's why I respect her. I wish I was more like her—able to stand the cold and isolation to do what I want. I don't know anybody else who could handle a pack of wolves. That's why I wanted to be her friend."

"You still can be."

"She did ask me to come for the Tomato Wars."

"See? She doesn't hate you, Cara. If you want to, you should go. No hard feelings. Okay?"

"It didn't sound like she'll be expecting you." I already know that Eric won't come; he never liked the Tomato Wars.

"I wish she wouldn't call them wars," Eric says. "What you call something matters. Calling a drunken vegetable fight a war is as far off as calling a wolf a dog."

His head jerks forward and his breathing is slower. Except for an occasional moan from Eric, the scrape of the wipers, and the droning engine, I find the quiet I need to bawl on the two-hour drive to his sister's home.

We are the only women enlisted in the fifth and what is to be the final Holy Tomato War. Sawyer takes to the Texas team, the Tomatillos, because she knows that I'd never betray my home state, Colorado. I've been working out to stay fit. I hope that she's taken up smoking again.

Some of the Texas veteran warriors don't want a middle-aged woman on their team, but as the numbers of participants on both teams have dropped the last two years, and since it is Sawyer's lodge and her two truckloads of rotten tomatoes, she is adopted by the Tomatillos. My team isn't as hungover as the twenty members of hers, but thirteen of the Colorado Beefsteaks look like college leftovers from the sixties, stringy hair, red eyes, goofy grins. Hemp experts, if you will. Except for Jason, the postal carrier, and Brant Lockhardt with his brother Ramsey—who aren't yet drunk—I'll be on my own defending Colorado.

We are down to two members on each team. Sawyer was eliminated early, splattered by Jason, who seems to think that he's protecting me. I'm in it for stubbornness now and because I feel Sawyer watching, perched on the flatbed by the kegs, several converts to her charm gathered around her.

I pick the two fattest, squishiest tomatoes from the bushel basket nearest me and stand up from behind the hay bale barricade. I hurl them at one Texan, a big guy, who simultaneously takes one from Jason as each of my tomatoes hits with a satisfying splat. Jason is immediately eliminated by the last Tomatillo who seems to be in kamikaze mode. I pelt him with a succession of five fat ones.

I turn to see Sawyer's reaction, but she is gone and though I've won the day for Colorado, I don't give a damn. While some of the boys from my team are using up the leftover tomatoes in a slingshot, shooting them willy-nilly across the road, I hose off my arms, hands, and feet before returning to my room. When I pass the wolf pens, a tomato smashes into the chicken wire over my head.

"Knock it off! The war's over!"

A tomato flies over the top of the pen and splatters on Raggs's head and muzzle. He yelps.

"Damn it! Stop!" I turn and see the Lockhardt brothers guzzling something other than beer from a fifth. If they're going to start again, and if Sawyer isn't even a good sport enough to congratulate me, then maybe I'll just stay somewhere else tonight.

I hear about the ugly finale to the Tomato Wars the next morning from the owner of the elegant bed and breakfast where I stay in Leadville. It's Victorian and regal even when it's not compared to Casa de la Luna—glossy antique furniture, crisp linens, a firm mattress, no one and nothing prowling the premises at night. In the early morning the aroma of baking bread, warm sugar, cinnamon, and coffee wakens me. The shingles outside my window shine with moisture and there's a fine dusting of autumn's first snow glistening on the grass until the late morning sun can dissolve the chill.

As the Guatemalan proprietress sets a crystal glass of mango-papaya juice with a lime wedge in front of me, she says, "Those tomato boys are very bad. I am glad you left there, señorita."

Her English is heavily accented so at first I do not understand.

"A nice father, Garland, such bad boys," she repeats, bustling about the table with baskets of pastries and a platter of scrambled eggs with chorizo for me, her only guest.

The china platter is garnished with sprigs of cilantro. At Sawyer's, a garnish is something you do to a wayward cook's wages.

"Those boys get to shooting off their mouths and before you can know it, it's their guns shooting, too."

I feel the world slide sideways and for a moment I see a girl in her nightgown near the bay window.

"Señorita, they shot them, you know? The pens were on fire and even before the wolves got out, they started shooting, So terrible to shoot an animal in a pen—there's nowhere for him to hide."

No. Not that.

"My husband. He is the veterinarian. She called him in the middle of the night to come see what he could do."

"How bad?" I have to know.

"One dead, the female mate of the big black wolf. He, too, shot, but will live. He's in back, in our clinic. The white one, though, instead of running away, turned and jumped the younger boy, the one who set the fire."

"How is he?"

"Face and shoulders mauled and bitten." Then she sees my face. "You mean the wolf. He escaped, but left a trail of blood in the snow. That's where my husband is now, with the young woman, tracking her wolf before the other Lockhardt and the posse find it. An injured wolf can't be left to roam."

Niko shot. Luna dead. Raggs, wounded and loose, hunted.

"They say so many things about that woman, but no, she is kind. She stayed and held the head of the dying wolf while they put her down, even though the blood spurted terribly, she was gut-shot, and that's bad to see, even for a doctor, like my husband."

I eat my rolls, the eggs, and chorizo with salsa as she speaks; she is such a caring hostess and I mustn't seem ungrateful. Besides, what is to be done?

"Maybe they got away with this carnage. The sheriff goes out there this morning, he asks questions, tells the boys not to leave town, but I think that they will not be punished. They will go free because of what people say about her. It is shameful what they say about her and the animals."

The woman looks at me, and decides to trust.

"They say she and the white wolf are lovers, the woman and the beast, they say it is the reason the young man almost lost his arm before and now this with Garland's boy. Imagine such a vicious lie told in these times, in your country."

Unfortunately, I can well imagine.

* * *

I am stroking Niko's fur. His left rear leg is bandaged, but other than a slight limp, he seems physically the same. But there's something in his eyes; he's missing Luna and will always miss her. He will not mate again.

Can you love another species more than you'll ever love a fellow human? I'll ask Sawyer, she'll know.

I never get the chance. I do not know where Sawyer went after the shootings. Within a week, she disappeared, along with the remaining members of her pack. I'd like to believe that she recovered Raggs from the mountains and that Niko grieved for Luna, and regained his rightful status as alpha male. I suspect that he died of mourning.

No one else knows where Sawyer went either, or where she came from in the first place, except maybe Eric, who's also moved on. None of us even know for sure if Sawyer is her first name or her last name or even a real name. The sheriff seemed more interested in the disappearance of Brant Lockhardt than he was in the fate of Sawyer, except the coincidence of both disappearing at the same time.

Now I don't give a damn what happened to Brant, but I do have my suspicions. It's Sawyer's fate, or to be accurate, the wolf pack's destiny, that concerns me. I'd like to know how they moved so quickly out of our lives, leaving no trace. Alex hopes that members of Wolf Rescue came in and hauled the wolves out, a caravan of pickups roaring over Independence Pass in the middle of a moonless night. But if that were so, someone would know.

Jason delivered a message after the slaughter—Sawyer told him to thank me for letting the wolves out when the fire started, but I wasn't even there. No one's figured out who the woman was who rescued most of the pack and that's still part of the puzzle.

A drunk told Alex that Sawyer had relocated, pack and parcel, in some small town whose name started with a "p," but Jason claims that even the post office has no forwarding address, so her mail's been collecting dust in her personal dead letter office in his basement for almost ten years.

Several autumns ago, I heard about the Palisade Peach Crusades, so I drove there searching for Sawyer, but it was just a sad rip-off of the glorious Tomato Wars. Since then, I've checked out Paonia, and both Parachute and Paradox while I was on the Western Slope, but no luck.

Nobody's been able to make a go of Casa de la Luna since Sawyer left, either, with six different owners and as many new names in the duration. The courtyard that once housed the wolf pens is restored to a summer veranda with smoking barbecue pits by the newest owners, a pleasant retired Dallas couple. When the aroma of sizzling pork ribs drifts across the lakes, above the pine trees, and into the tumbling clouds, locals often claim that they hear the howling of wolves and that it makes their skin crawl. It's unmistakable: you know the howl of a wolf from a coyote or a feral dog, once you've heard it. There are other strange goings on: flickering lights at night in the log house across the road that once served as the bordello, pacing footsteps in the deserted upstairs hallways, a pale woman in a sheer dress dashing along the shores of Twin Lakes—stretching stride-for-stride with her two huge dogs, soon to fade in the predawn mists. I am tempted to tell them that these things all went on before things got bad for Sawyer, but decide against speaking. Those legends will fade, too, just as the daguerreotype of Miss Lorette blurs with time on the wall of the landing of the curving staircase above the silver-framed print of The Lone Wolf, in the dark and smoke-stained entry of Casa de la Luna, near the shores of Twin Lakes, near Independence Pass, high in the Colorado Rockies.

WOMEN'S STORIES and SWAN/PRINCESS
Jane Yolen

Poet, novelist, and children's book writer Jane Yolen has published over one hundred and fifty books to date. She is also a folklorist, lecturer, teacher, and the editor of the Jane Yolen Books imprint at Harcourt Brace. As a poet, her works have been published in a wide variety of magazines and collections. "Women's Stories" comes from the *Sisters in Fantasy* anthology edited by Susan Shwartz and Martin H. Greenberg; "Swan/Princess" comes from Yolen's own anthology, *Xanadu 3*. Yolen and her husband divide their time between homes in western Massachusetts and St. Andrews, Scotland.

—T.W.

Women's Stories

*There are two fathers I do not understand:
the one at the bridge,
devil's bargain still warm on his mouth,
kissing his daughter first, saying:
"Do I have a husband for you";
and Abraham, with his traitor's hand,
leading Isaac up the hill to God.*

*These are not women's stories.
Even before I birthed my three,
and the one bled out before its time,
and the one encysted in the tube,
even before that I would have thrust the knife
in my own breast, before God;
I would have swallowed the kiss,
gone back to the beast myself.*

Job's wife has her own story.
Lot's pillar of salt cried tears
indistinguishable from her eyes.
Who invented a glass slipper
never had to dance.

Do not try to climb my hair.
Do not circle me with a hedge of thorns.
My stories are not your stories.
We women go out into the desert together,
or not at all.

Swan / Princess

1

When the change came
she was sitting in the garden
embroidering an altar cloth,
thin gold thread working the crown of Christ.
First her neck
arching like cathedral vaultings.
Dress ripping at the shoulders accommodated wings:
white-vaned, white-feathered like Oriental smocking.
Hands and feet tangling into orange legs,
inelegant, powerful as camshafts.
When her head went, she cried,
not for pain but for the loss
of her soft, thin lips
so recently kissed by the prince.
Not even the sweet air,
not even earth unfolding beneath her
recompensed for those lost kisses
or the comfort of his human arms.

2

When the change came
she was floating in the millpond,
foam like white lace tracing her wake.
First her neck shrinking,
candle to candleholder,
the color of old, used wax.
Wings collapsing like fans;
one feather left,
floating memory on the churning water.
Powerful legs devolving;
powerful beak dissolving.
She would have cried for the pain of it
had not remembrance of sky sustained her.
A startled look on the miller's face
as she rose, naked and dripping,
recalled her to laughter,
the only thing she had really missed as a swan.

SWITCH
Lucy Taylor

Lucy Taylor is a former resident of Florida who now lives in the hills outside Boulder, Colorado, with her six cats. She is a full-time writer whose short fiction has appeared in such venues as *Little Deaths, Hotter Blood, Cemetery Dance, Pulphouse, The Mammoth Book of Erotic Horror, Northern Frights,* and *Women of Darkness.* Her collections include *Close to the Bone, The Flesh Artist,* and *Unnatural Acts and other Stories.* Her first novel, *The Safety of Unknown Cities,* was published in 1995 by Darkside Press. In the past few years Taylor has achieved recognition as an exceptional writer of erotic horror.

However, "Switch"—an unnerving little story from *David Copperfield's Tales of the Impossible,* edited by David Copperfield and Janet Berliner—is a complete change of pace for Taylor, with echoes of a horrific Oz.

—E.D.

In her sleep, twelve-year-old Erika heard the wind scream like a woman being slashed. She wanted to wake up, but she couldn't. She was trapped in the dream.

"Pick a card, any card," cooed the magician. His voice was oily and wheedling. He wore a crimson beret and white gloves that were frayed at the fingertips. His face looked as yellow as old mayonnaise. His breath smelled fruity and bitter at the same time, like marmalade. He leaned down toward Erika, offering the cards spread out in a fan shape in his gloved hand.

"Which one?" she said nervously, fearing a trick.

"Any one!" He grinned back fiercely, showing so many teeth that she thought he was going to bite out a chunk of her flesh.

She reached out toward the cards. Which one to pick?

"Gotcha!" cried the magician before she could choose. He flung the cards high into the air. All the colors of the rainbow, all the designs her imagination could conceive, tumbling helter-skelter, hither and yon, all swirling around like gaudy leaves cast to the wind. She saw places and names hurtle past and faces—some that she didn't recognize and some that were schoolmates and neighbors and family.

Like seeing the world through a kaleidoscope designed by a lunatic.

All out of sequence, in wild disarray.

With a cry of dismay, Erika fell to her knees, tried to gather the cards and put them back in their proper order. They were slippery and fell through her fingers.

She started to pray.

The magician laughed till he screamed.

She awoke from the nightmare to the shriek of a furious chinook, the fierce dry wind that blew down onto the plains of Colorado from the eastern slope of the Rockies in the winter and spring. Like a hundred freight trains thundering past, it rocked and pummeled the house.

Living out on the plains of eastern Colorado, Erika had heard the chinooks before, the wild winds that blew off loose shingles and rattled the windowpanes in their frames. They terrified her, the way they rushed past the house like something savage and out of control, diabolical in their frenzy.

Tonight, though, the wind was worse than she'd ever heard it, brutal and angry and purposeful, like a madman pounding the roof with a ball-peen hammer while he tittered and hissed. Like a giant pugilist throwing combination punches at the walls.

Erika clutched the covers over her head and chewed on the tip of one braid, a habit she'd picked up when she was small and her brother Brock teased her for sucking her thumb. She hated herself for acting like a little kid—*I'm almost grown-up*, she reminded herself—but the chinook was shaking and battering the house now, violently seeking entry. The bed, the floor, began vibrating, creaking. Erika stopped trying not to be scared and screamed for her parents.

No one came.

She yelled for her brother Brock, whose room was right next to hers. He didn't answer.

Maybe they can't hear me for the wind.

She got up and ran first to Brock's room and then to her parents'. Their beds looked slept in, but they were empty.

Fear felt like a hand wriggling down Erika's throat all the way to her belly. The wind was tearing things loose from the house, shaking the house like a salt shaker and, if it didn't stop, Erika was afraid she and her family would fall out the broken windows and doors like so many grains of white salt.

Her vision blurred. Smeary colors dripped from the ceiling and streamed down the walls. Her flesh seemed to be liquefying into long, goopy strands. Her bones felt as flimsy as Styrofoam, as though she was about to be tossed away like one of the cards she'd seen in her dream, pitched high in the air to land where the winds of chance blew it.

She knew only one way to protect herself. She shut her eyes and tried to duplicate the trick she'd used years ago, when Uncle Dub came visiting from Garden City and put his hand down her panties when he took her out to the Dairy Queen: she pretended her head was a TV set and she clicked it off and unplugged it.

Then she was safe. Or had seemed to be.

She'd watched what Uncle Dub was doing to her and tried to convince herself it wasn't real, it was only an illusion. *Real* was up here in her head, not down there, where Uncle Dub's hand groped in her panties.

She escaped that way now, her consciousness sliding out of the spot between her eyebrows and drifting up through the shifting colors and shimmery walls into the overpowering screech of the chinook.

Out the window she could see shingles and trash can tops, children's toys sailing high in the air, spinning in the moonlight. They looked like light bright shiny cards.

Her sleep was like a gauzy twilight, where dreams flickered instead of stars. She was in the school gym doing push-ups. A squinty-eyed woman with sparse lips and no chin was yelling at her to do the exercise faster. "I can't, dammit, leave me alone!" Erika yelled. The woman with no chin grabbed Erika by her braids and yanked her head back. She had a witch's sharp nose and nailfile-on-glass voice. "Go to the principal's office!" she shouted. "Now!"

Then Erika was as wide awake as if someone had snapped their fingers inside her head. She sat up. The wind had died down. She was afraid the clock might have stopped during the eyeblink-brief night, but it said a little after seven o'clock and the digital display changed as she watched it.

But the house itself—the *aliveness* of the house seemed to have come to a halt in some mysterious way. There was no sound, no clatter of breakfast dishes, no doors being slammed or newspapers folded. The silence expanded and deepened, like the vibrations of a great bell tolling in a deaf ear.

She remembered the night before—the empty beds in her parents' and brother's rooms. Wherever they'd gone last night, surely they were back now.

She lay there listening intently, listening for all the things she should have heard but didn't. The house, the street outside, were draped in silence thick as a fog, a solid, pregnant quiet dense with its own profundity.

When she was very young, Erika's older cousin Penny had teased her with a terrifying threat: if she were bad, one day when she was asleep or in the bathtub or watching TV, Ma and Pa and Brock would slip quietly out of the house, get into the car, and drive away, leaving her behind. She knew now that Penny was just being mean, but now the awful words came back to her. What if Penny had known something she didn't? What if her parents and brother had really left her?

"Ma?" Erika whispered.

No one answered.

"Ma! Pa! Where is everybody!"

The silence rang in her head like a taunt.

Trembling, Erika got out of bed. She found her parents' and Brock's bedrooms were still empty. So was the kitchen, where this time of day Ma would be cleaning up the breakfast dishes, maybe nibbling a waffle or piece of toast that somebody'd left on their plate.

Today there was only that unbearably rich, fertile silence, silence like turned earth roiling with creepy-crawlers and worms. Silence like the inside of a coffin.

Erika put on her jacket and buckled her fanny pack around her waist. In it were her allowance money and hairbrush, a tube of Tooty-Fruity Lipgloss, half a dozen POGs, and some photos she'd taken of her family's recent trip to Yellowstone, which she was planning to show Denny Capshaw, a seventh grade boy she was starting to like.

She walked next door to the neighbors' and banged on the door, shouting hello. No one came. Not even a dog yapped. So it was with all the houses on the block, no amount of tearful screaming and pleading and shouting brought the slightest response from any of the locked, mausoleumlike houses.

Erika started to run. She ran through the deserted streets to Buford Junior High School, but she already knew . . . she *knew* . . . the school was still locked from the day before. The playground was barren, the classrooms, when Erika peered in the windows, were empty as well.

For an instant, standing on the glass shards of a broken bottle as she looked through a window into the empty gymnasium, Erika remembered the dream in which she was lying on her belly, sweaty and exhausted, struggling to do push-ups while a witch in blue shorts and white tennis shoes yelled at her. Now she remembered more: scribbling a nasty poem about the witch on the wall of the girl's restroom and then trudging to the principal's office, where a frowning secretary with bubblegum pink lips phoned her parents to come get her.

Had she dreamed that part, too?

Erika gazed at the deserted school, the empty streets, and neighborhood. She picked up a sharp-edged piece of glass off the ground, closed her eyes, and thrust the jagged fragment into the heel of her hand. Pain jolted her. Blood bloomed in her palm like a rose plucked from the air by a magician.

She didn't wake up.

They've really all gone. The whole world's disappeared. I'm all alone.

She could not imagine enduring such awesome aloneness for long. Never to see her parents again, her brother, her friends. Never to hear a human voice except her own. She looked at the piece of glass she was holding and thought about what she must eventually do—it was a sin, but God would have to understand.

She sat down on the bench by the bus stop and sobbed until her throat felt like she'd swallowed a mouthful of kitty litter.

The cold wrapped itself around her like a shawl. The wind, that strange yowling chinook from the night before, was beginning to clamor again. It swirled trash through the air and blew grit off the playground into Erika's face. Her eyes stung with tears and the school and the houses around it grew blurry and bendable, the way they had on the previous night, like soft toys made of rubber. Everything seemed to be losing its substance, turning to shadow and smoke.

The chinook kicked gravel at Erika as she fled to the nearest house and huddled under the porch, shielding her face with her jacket. She considered running right out into the wind, letting it sweep her away, but she couldn't make herself do such a foolhardy thing. She was afraid to find out where the wind might take her.

The wind shrieked like a witch with a toothache. It filled every cranny and space of the vast, thrumming silence. It poured into her ears, into her head like shards of blood red, glassy sand.

Please don't take me away, too, she thought, and that was the last thing she knew.

Pick a card, any card, said the magician in his sly, singsongy voice. His grin was like Uncle Dub's. Erika wasn't so sure she was dreaming this time. The magician offered her the same wide fan of cards. The cards gleamed like polished tiles, like bright, miniature stained-glass windows. Each one gem-perfect and brilliant.

Pick a card.

Erika reached out her hand.

That's it now, pick a card. It won't bite you.

The magician's leering face, his phony-sweet whisper were just the way Uncle Dub's had been. Suddenly Erika knew—it was another trick. She would pick the wrong card. She knew it! The trick was set up so she had to pick the wrong card, because the Erika card wasn't there in the deck at all. She'd somehow held onto her card during the terrible wind when all the other cards had blown away and everyone disappeared. And now . . .

The magician hopped up and down like a maddened toad.

He hurled the cards down and they fell end to end in a line, like a road paved with jewels snaking off into the distance.

Pick a card! Pick a card! Pick a card!

Erika woke up beneath the porch of the strange house, hugging her knees to her chest. Her hand throbbed where she had deliberately cut herself. The wound was covered with a crust of dried blood.

She listened. And her heart leaped with hope because she could tell that the world had returned. Cars were rolling by in the street. Children played ball. Somewhere a radio was playing and a couple of women were chatting about whether or not to henna their hair.

Everything sounded like it was supposed to, the way it had sounded *before*.

Why, then, was she still so afraid?

Erika stretched her stiff, tired muscles and started for home.

Or to where home used to be.

She turned east on Demeres Road and walked north for four blocks on Prestwick Drive till she got to her house. There was a strange Buick in the drive, but she figured her parents had guests, maybe someone left homeless when their roof had blown off. Marching up the steps, she rang the bell, which responded, not with its usual raspy buzz, but an unfamiliar, bell-like trill.

A woman Erika had never seen before opened the door. She was big-boned and blond with deep smile lines etching her eyes and a missing side tooth. Her nails were long and fake and polished the color of cinnamon buns. She stared at Erika.

"Lizbeth," she said. "What are you doing home from school this time of day?" Her bluesy voice had a soft, West Texas drawl. "You sick or somethin'?"

Erika blinked hard, said nothing.

"Well, come on in the kitchen. I just took a tray of brownies out of the oven. You can tell me what's going on while we eat."

Erika bit her lip to keep from crying. She followed the strange woman into the kitchen.

Did she have the wrong house? Could the woman possibly be so nearsighted that she mistook Erika for her daughter Lizbeth?

But it wasn't the wrong house, it was *her* house, Erika realized, right down to the hat tree in the hall and the dark, star-shaped stain on the rug in the dining room where Brock had once spilled a mug of hot cocoa. Except the furniture . . . the furniture was all wrong. It was flowery stuff with bright patterns and ruffled lamps, whereas theirs had been pale blue and white French Provincial. And in the kitchen was a big butcher-block table and a cage with two parakeets in it instead of the TV that Ma liked to watch while she cooked.

"I . . . I think I must have the wrong house," Erika said in a small, skittish voice.

The blond woman looked up from slicing the brownies. "Oh, come on, it hasn't been *that* long since I baked brownies."

"No, I mean really . . . who lives here?"

"Lizbeth, that's not funny no more. I don't care for sarcasm, okay?"

"Hey, Lizzie, what are you doin' home?"

A man opened the back door and strode in. He was tall and broad as a Kodiak bear and almost as hairy, with a full reddish beard sprouting out of his fleshy jowls and chin. "You been sent home for sassin' your phys. ed. teacher again?"

"She's in a mood," said the woman. "Bein' smart-assed."

The big man, who reminded Erika of a picture she'd seen in a storybook of Paul Bunyan, scowled. "Now you know what I told you would happen if you got sent home from school again. I don't care if you do hate phys. ed., you gotta take it to graduate. Did you get punished with push-ups again?"

Erika felt the fear inching up her spine like a cockroach parade. Her tongue felt blistered and dry. She drew herself up and tried to speak in the clear, strong voice of the trial attorney she hoped to be when she grew up. "I don't know who you are or what you're talking about. My name's Erika Spence, and this is my home, and I want to know what have you done with my parents, Sarah and Jim Spence and my older brother, Brock Spence? Where are they? Who are you? What have you done with them?"

The man and the woman stared at her. The woman spoke first, timidly, "Lizbeth, honey, what—" but the man cut her off. "What are you talkin' about? What the hell is this, some kinda game? Who the hell are these Spence people?"

Erika reached in her fanny pack and pulled out a photo of Ma and Pa and Brock at Yellowstone the month before. She'd taken it with her favorite Christmas present, an instant Polaroid camera.

"These are my parents and my brother," she said. "They're supposed to be living here. What have you done with them?"

The blond woman had set down the knife and come around the table. She looked at the photo for a long time and frowned, showed it to the man. They exchanged puzzled looks.

Then the man shrugged and started unbuckling his belt with hairy, thick-knuckled hands.

"You got one more chance to explain yourself, Lizzie, to cut out this foolishness or I swear, you ain't too old to take upstairs, you ain't too old to . . ."

"Hank, please," said the woman.

"Now, Prudy, just stop, let me handle this, okay? I don't know what damn-fool game she's playin' or where she got that picture, but—"

"Hank, I don't think it's a game. I think . . . Lizzie, just talk to me. Tell me what's going on."

She reached out to Erika.

"Don't touch me!" Erika smacked the strange woman in the mouth. The woman yelped as blood streamed from her lip. The man bellowed. Erika dashed for the door.

She plunged into the street, dodging a furniture van that swerved and squealed its tires to avoid her, then darted between two houses and hid under some box-bushes in the backyard while the man named Hank and the woman named Prudy searched for her. Her heart was double its size, slamdancing her throat. She bit her tongue to keep from crying.

Afternoon shadows crawled over Erika's hiding place. It had been over an hour since she heard the man and the woman calling for her. She crawled out from under the bushes.

A white Scottish terrier wearing a green collar and tags approached Erika. She recognized the dog at once: the Barrys' Scotty, Felix the Lion-Hearted, who could catch a mean Frisbee despite his short legs and stout body. Erika fed him and walked him whenever the Barrys went out of town.

She dropped to her knees.

"Felix, come here. Are you lost, too?"

Felix flattened his ears. His snarl looked like a smaller version of a pit bull ready for battle. Erika stood up and jumped backward as Felix sprang. His pint-sized killer-dog teeth pierced her socks and punched through the skin of her ankle.

Erika screamed and kicked Felix away. He came at her again. She ran to a parked car and climbed onto the trunk. She waited there until Felix lost interest and wandered away, then her tears flowed. Felix the Lion-Hearted had been like her own dog.

She climbed down from the car hood. Her shoe felt squishy and weird. She looked down and saw it was filling with blood.

Up ahead, she saw a mailman turn the corner and start up the block. It was a skinny, olive-skinned man, not the regular mailman, Mr. Simms, but she ran up to him anyway.

"Do you know where . . . ?"

The olive-skinned man stuffed a handful of letters into a mailbox and tugged on the fat lobe of an ear that stuck out from the side of his head like a miniature satellite dish. "Lizbeth Buchanon, I just passed your folks a few blocks from here and they're lookin' for you. Your dad, he looked madder'n a wet hen. I'd head on home if—Lizbeth, Lizbeth wait, where you goin'? Didn't you hear what I said? Your parents are lookin' for you! Hey, what happened to your foot?"

Erika darted across the street and ran through several backyards until she could no longer hear him yelling. Her heart was pounding the way it did the summer before when she had to go off the high diving board at the public pool and then just stood there, toes wrapped over the edge, looking down into the terrible bottomless blue.

She was hungry and thirsty. There were four dollars and change in her jeans pocket, but she didn't dare walk to the convenience store up the street for fear the strange people who thought they were her parents would be there.

Assuming, of course, the convenience store was still where she remembered it to be. Maybe that had changed, too. And maybe her mind was altered, too, making her have memories about being punished in gym class that really belonged to some girl named Lizbeth Buchanon.

That was the scariest notion of all.

She was entering an unfamiliar neighborhood, one of tall, close-spaced apartment buildings with tiny, sparse yards. A group of girls shot basketball on a litter-strewn court. They had sleek, coltish muscles and scolded each other in some language that Erika did not understand. The street signs now were written in a language other than English.

Erika paused at the corner to look in the window of a small grocery store. The bins on display were full of items she didn't recognize: fat, bulbous yellow fruit and long tuberous things that might have been gigantic string beans or maybe monstrous, deformed melons. The signs identifying these objects were written in fanciful red letters that looked like small houses pierced with a variety of slashes and strokes. They ran up and down, not left and right.

Erika peered in and squinted.

Erika's Grandma Bertie hobbled to the door of the shop and stared out. Part of her face hung lopsided, like she was made of Play-Doh that somebody'd stretched out to make a funny-ugly face. That was the result of Grandma Bertie's stroke the year before. Erika flung her arms about the old woman.

"Grandma Bertie? Grandma Bertie, it's me! It's Erika."

The old lady acted like Erika'd puked on her. She jabbed the knob of her cane into Erika's chest, hissing spittle and strange words at Erika. The words made no sense and seemed to be grouped into one long period-less paragraph. The syllables sounded stretched out and melted together like Grandma Bertie's face.

"Grandma, why are you talkin' like that. Speak so's I can understand you, Grandma, please!"

The old woman chattered and glowered and banged Erika on the shin with her cane. Erika squealed.

A man with round owlish eyes and a mouth like a slit in a piggy bank ran up and dragged the Grandma Bertie person away from the door.

"Did you hit that girl? Did you? Good Christ, May, you senile old bag, do you want to get us sued again?"

The old woman began to gibber her birdcall-like words.

"Are you all right, miss?" the slit-mouthed man asked. "She didn't hurt you, did she? No problem here, right? Okay?"

Erika shook her head, backing away.

"Come here and let me take a look at your leg."

He wiggled slim, spidery fingers. *Come here.*

Erika ran.

The strange part of town with the people who spoke funny words began to peter out, but the roads here were no less unfamiliar, narrow and two-laned. Some were dirt roads leading out toward a horizon as flat and dark as the edge of a ruler. Erika tried not to wonder what had become of Denver, whose downtown buildings could normally be seen silhouetted against the sky like some far-off magical kingdom.

A familiar-looking, brown convertible bore down on Erika. She recognized it at once—she could never forget it. It belonged to Uncle Dub. Last time she'd sat in it had been when his thick, cold fingers—chilled from holding the cup of vanilla/chocolate swirl—had wiggled and waggled in the niche between her legs.

But to Erika's relief and amazement Uncle Dub wasn't driving the car—which he had proclaimed loudly and often could not be driven by anyone but himself. Behind the wheel sat redhaired Darlene Markson, Erika's math teacher. Darlene was a plump, pan-faced lady whose hobby was jigsaw puzzles. Her husband Bruce, who coached Little League, collected Civil War relics. Erika liked the Marksons and their sons, Wayne and Jeff. She'd spent two weeks with them once when Ma and Pa had some difficulties and split up temporarily and Ma said she needed time to herself "to think." During that time, Darlene Markson had taught Erika how to make pies from scratch and how to play chess. The Marksons all liked to quote Scripture; they prayed before every meal and read the bible together at night. So when Darlene Markson pulled the car to a stop alongside her, Erika was so happy to see her that she got in without saying a word.

"Is it . . . is it really Erika Spence . . . or are you some other girl now?" said Mrs. Markson hesitantly.

Erika jumped at the sound of her own name as though it were something foreign to her.

"Yes, yes! It's Erika! I can't find my parents or my brother. I don't even know where I am any more, and I'm hungry, and my foot's hurt and everything's changed. Can you help me?"

Mrs. Markson stared at Erika so hard it was like she was trying to see through her skin.

"Yes, of course, Erika. I'll help you. Come home with me first, I'll get you something to eat." She added in a small, strained voice, "Bruce and the boys, I haven't seen them since last night."

It was a different house from the one that Erika had visited before, a big gawky frame house with a huge oak tree in the front yard, but Erika didn't remark on this. Inside, she noted that Mrs. Markson had several jigsaw puzzles going at once, just like she always did whenever Erika had visited her at the old house, wherever that was now. Darlene Markson washed Erika's foot and gave her a pair of her own satin bedroom slippers to wear. Then she put out a big plate of cold fried chicken and coleslaw and potato chips and they sat at the dining room table. Erika ate ravenously.

"Do your parents know where you are?" asked Mrs. Markson.

Her real parents, Erika wondered, or those strangers Prudy and Hank? In either case, the answer was no. She shook her head.

"So you just took off on your own?" said Mrs. Markson, forking pink, stringy coleslaw into her mouth.

"There was a wind," Erika said softly. "It blew real hard and either it blew me to a new place or it blew everybody else far away. Things got all confused and mixed up. Nobody has the right name now. Nobody lives where they're s'posed to. The magician did it, I think. He sent the wind. Did you hear it?"

Darlene Markson sank small white teeth into a lip that look swollen and bitten. "You know, then."

Know what, Erika wanted to ask. She chewed her food and stayed silent.

"Yes, I heard the wind," Mrs. Markson continued. She gave a choked laugh. "Matter of fact, it blew so hard, I think it blew Jeff and Wayne and Bruce clear away. Some other man tried to get in here, said he was my husband, but I wouldn't let him in. . . ."

"The people, they all got switched around," said Erika quietly. "What happened? Where did they go?"

"I don't know," murmured Mrs. Markson. "I don't understand this. Bruce and me, we were expectin' the Rapture, when God takes His own up to Heaven, but not this. Not everyone all stirred up and put back wrong." She got up and walked over to a completed jigsaw puzzle on the card table next to the TV. "Like God got bored and He went and did—*this*." She gave the card table a terrible smack with both fists. The puzzle bounced and broke apart. Pieces fell to the floor, rolled this way and that. "And the worst part is, we don't know if this is the first time or if . . . if it's been happening all along . . . things getting switched around . . . and nobody ever remembered it had been any different."

Erika cringed from the ferocity behind Darlene Markson's blow. "So why didn't it happen to you, too?" she asked finally. "How come you're still you?"

Darlene Markson put her bleeding fist to her mouth. "I'm not sure. I was real tired and blue the night the wind started up and I took a whole handful of my pills . . . Bruce doesn't know I take pills, he'd say it was unChristian, but I need them, I need my pills to relax and . . . I dreamed God came down all painted up and evil and he mixed everyone up. But he couldn't touch me, 'cause the pills had washed over my mind like an ocean and he . . . couldn't get to it." She stared at Erika as if suddenly realizing something. "What about you? Did you hide your mind, too?"

"Kind of," said Erika, wishing for the first time that maybe she hadn't used the power she'd learned from her experience with Uncle Dub, wishing she'd just let the wind take her, blow her someplace new, into some other girl, maybe that girl named Lizbeth who hated phys. ed. and had a mama named Prudy and a daddy who looked like Paul Bunyan.

"What should we do?" asked Erika.

"I don't know," said Mrs. Markson. "I've got enough sleeping pills left . . . if things get real bad . . . if I never find Bruce and the boys again . . . maybe I could . . ." she trailed off.

"I've thought of that, too," Erika said, "but I don't want to die. I want my family back. I want *everything* back the way it was before."

"I don't think it can go back," said Mrs. Markson. She put a hand under Erika's chin, lifted it up. "And we can't tell people everything's different now, because they won't believe us. They'll think we're crazy. But we can stick together—we've got to. There may be other people like us—people who didn't get switched around for some reason, who remember the way it was. Right now I think we should pray. We'll pray for courage to get us through—"

The doorbell rang.

Mrs. Markson jumped up. "Maybe it's Bruce and the boys."

Erika stayed at the table nibbling chips, but she could hear Mrs. Markson opening the front door and saying hello. By the tone of her voice, Erika knew it wasn't her husband or sons at the door.

She heard a man talking, then a woman. She heard her own name! She jumped up, recognizing the voices. It was Ma and Pa, asking to see her.

Erika burst into the hallway, ignoring the two police officers who stood straight as tin soldiers on either side of the door. She threw her arms about her mother, sobbing. Her mother bent down, comforting. "There, there, hon, there, there."

Erika suddenly stopped crying and whirled around. One of the policemen was clicking handcuffs onto Mrs. Markson, the other reading her something like the cops on TV—"My Randy" rights, Brock called them sarcastically.

"What are you *doing*?"

"They're just going to question her, honey," said Erika's mother. "About the kidnapping and all . . . a bulletin was put out that you'd run away and then the policeman saw you go by in Mrs. Gordon's car. . . ."

"Mrs. *Markson*," screamed Erika, "her name's Mrs. Markson!"

". . . like I was saying, in Mrs. Gordon's convertible, so then Hank and Prudy called us and . . ."

"She didn't kidnap me. She was taking care of me. Don't hurt her, please."

They took Mrs. Markson away, still calling her by the wrong name. She was begging and babbling about needing to go back for her pills.

"I'm glad we found you," said Erika's mother. "So glad . . ."

Ma took Erika's hand on one side, Pa took the other. They walked out the front door—

—into the arms of Paul Bunyan and Prudy, who looked sour and scared, but broke out in nervous, relieved laughter when they saw Erika emerge from the Markson house.

"It *was* her! You found her!" boomed Paul Bunyon.

"Thank God," said Prudy. "And thank you so much, both of you, for helping us out. I don't know what's happened, if she's on drugs or what, but she stood right in our kitchen and swore up and down that Sarah and Jim Spence were her parents and then she showed us your picture. Don't know where she got it from, but we recognized you, of course, the Hollys from the PTA and the bridge club. But she'd got your names wrong, said your name was Spence. Then when the police called to say they'd seen her go into the house with Mrs. Gordon . . . I thought maybe it would calm her down if you should be the ones to approach her and pretend to be these people she thinks are her folks."

Erika's father looked at the photo Prudy showed him. "That's one of the pictures got lost after our trip to Yellowstone last year. Our boy Peter took it."

Erika's mother shook her head. "At least now you can get help for the poor confused child. God bless you."

"I know the name of a top-notch psychiatrist," said Erika's dad. "He specializes in delusional psychosis. I could give you his number."

"We'd appreciate that," said Prudy, squeezing Erika's hand. "I can't imagine what's happened to her—maybe Mrs. Gordon's been giving her pills—it sounds to me like the woman has a drug problem."

"Lizbeth's gonna need plenty of treatment to straighten her out," growled Paul Bunyan.

"Let me pick a card! Let me pick a card!" pleaded Erika.

The magician held the deck up high out of her reach. "It isn't time yet," he singsonged. "It isn't time yet to reshuffle the deck."

Still, Erika leaped for the cards in his hand. Leaped like her life depended on it.

The magician made a tsk-tsk sound with his pursed, purple lips. He closed the cards up into a neat deck and turned away.

Erika awoke in her bed in the place that smelled like cough drops and pee, the place where everything was bolted down—the chairs, the bed, the TV set. They were so afraid you were going to hurt yourself with something, pick something up and hit somebody with it that they had everything fastened down.

And the people, they were fastened down, too. With straps across their wrists and locks on their doors, with pills the doctors said would keep their minds from bolting away like so many spooked horses, but really just made them sit there like scared-looking dolls.

Please make it all go away, Erika thought.
Put everything back like it was.
Put it back.

Erika turned her face to the strange wall in the strange room in the strange world. She prayed for the wind to come back.

SCARING THE TRAIN
Terry Dowling

Terry Dowling lives in Sydney, Australia, and is one of that country's most respected writers of speculative fiction. His short fiction has appeared in Australian magazines such as *Aphelion*, *Eidolon*, and *Australian Short Stories*, in the U.S. magazines *Strange Plasma* and *The Magazine of Fantasy & Science Fiction*, and in the anthologies *Urban Fantasies*, *Matilda at the Speed of Light*, *Terror Australis*, *Intimate Armageddons*, and *The Year's Best Fantasy & Horror*. His novels included *Rynosseros* and *Blue Tyson*. His science fiction collection, *Wormwood*, won the Readercon Small Press Award for Best Collection in 1991. His horror stories have been collected in *An Intimate Knowledge of the Night* from which "Scaring the Train" has been taken.

I've never encountered the game the characters play in "Scaring the Train" but at least one person I know is familiar with the idea behind it. It's dangerous enough for the participants and victims without supernatural elements joining in the fun.

—E.D.

Because for us, something might appear in the heart of the day that would not be the day, something in an atmosphere of light and limpidity that would represent the shiver of fear out of which the day came?
—Maurice Blanchot,
The Infinite Conversation

1

Portobello 1962

Every summer during our childhood holidays at Portobello, Maximillian and I would spend an hour every third day scaring the train. Every third day meant twenty-one days before we'd duplicate a day, which seemed clever at the time, neither of us realizing that it made its own pattern.

It never took more than a few exhilarating moments, of course, the scaring itself, but the hour gave preparation time, let us prepare our chosen section of track, the particular sheltered stretch or cutting, never using the same one twice in a week unless that became part of the strategy.

It gave us time to avoid the local constabulary (and, naturally, the frightened drivers, firemen, and concerned locals did get the police onto us, though never with any luck). When constables Pike and Harlow came on their bicycles, or now and then with Sergeant Jeffers in the district's single squad car, we were crouching behind the long grass, peering through greenery, never seen, or were miles away with relatives and friends, secure in our alibis.

The scaring itself? It was anything from running to a spot on the track moments before the locomotive reached it, to doing an oh-shock-horror!, freeze-frame, hands up, wide-eyed terror reaction or a classy matador flourish before leaping aside. Twice Max did his damsel-in-distress routine, lying across the line; we even did up a chicken wire and papier mâché boulder, though by then the engineers knew to call our bluff. With a scream of the steam whistle, the great engine plunged upon it, making us wish the boulder had been real.

We countered with the old dressed-up store dummy, its arm severed and painted with "blood." The engineers barely flinched. They had our measure right enough, had made their private decisions and adjustments. They would have driven through a massacre on that stretch of track after what we'd given them over four golden summers.

The whole thing entered a new phase when Sergeant Jeffers, rather belatedly, put two and two together and realized—at probably the same time we did—that since these "reckless and dangerous pranks" (as he had the *Portobello Weekly Mail* put it in one front-page write-up) happened only in the summer, it might well be the kids of families visiting from out of town.

Max and I weren't to be outdone. We made sure of our alibis, both with adults and the kids we hung out with, and took to using disguises more and more often—jumpers and caps, even wigs bought in hometown thrift shops and theatrical supply stores, taking pains to throw suspicion on local kids we didn't especially like.

Planning and timing became perfect; each scaring was a precisely calculated masterpiece and more exciting than ever. Of necessity, we had grown to be masters of those rare things in thirteen-year-old boys, restraint and patience. One evening, while I was conspicuously at a local party with my folks, Max put the first empty four-gallon drum on the left side of Hank's Creek cutting. It took him twenty-six minutes, there and back, riding without a light. Two nights later, I added the one on the right and linked them with multiple strands of heavy-gauge fishing-line souvenired from fifteen-year-old, ace-bully Rusty Cramer's fishing basket (an exploit in itself!).

Max and I didn't need to be there for the outcome but snatched thirty minutes from a Sunday family picnic to pedal furiously to Manton's Hill, there used our borrowed binoculars (birdwatching, right?) to observe the 10:58 from Madrigal plunging over the Hank's Creek bridge, the drums crashing down, bouncing off to the side—kaboom! kaboom!—clear as the bells of doom in the morning quiet (so we imagined; the train's own sound swallowed it all, perhaps even for the engineers, though they would have seen the drums plunging down; possibly did hear them pounding against the sides of the cab).

Max turned to me when it was over, eyes flashing. "We could've derailed that train if we'd wanted to, y'know, Paul."

"Reckon. Or blown up the bridge. Stolen dynamite."

"I'm serious."

He was, but on that hot quiet morning the talk went no further, for Max had his binoculars turned on the cutting.

"Hey, look!"

I raised Dad's glasses, swept my gaze in two big coins of dislocation suddenly made one across trees, fences, and sunny fields till I found the place, saw the solitary figure standing by the tracks at this end of the cutting. Almost a mile away, no clear features, but someone in a thoughtful stance it seemed, not Jeffers or Pike or Harlow, no one I knew, just some stranger drawn by Maximillian Sefti and Paul Danner's double booms of fate. He seemed to be looking down at the tracks, perhaps at the crumpled, dented drums and their trailing, incriminating lengths of line.

"Who is it?" I asked.

"No idea," Max said. But then, though it was a mile or more, though there were trees and fields and we were down on our bellies out of sight in the tree-shadow, our bikes back in the long grass so nothing glinted, nothing, the man looked directly out at us, directly at us. We couldn't see the smile or the nod though we imagined them well enough, but we both gasped when he raised an arm and waved, acknowledging us, someone, anyone who might be watching across all that bright sunny air.

We lowered our binoculars long enough, instinctively enough, to give each other a reassuring glance—we were both there, both seeing it—then looked back.

He was gone, of course, which completed the fright perfectly, had us scanning the intervening fields, noticing the pockets of shade like our own, patches of tree-shadow, the gloom in wind-dancing, sun-dappled copses, sockets of darkness where other watchers might now be watching us.

"Jeffers, I betcha!" Max cried as we scrambled down to our bikes, though we both knew it wasn't. "He's set us up."

But there was no one else about and no interception as we pedalled back to the picnic grounds. All I could think of—and Max, too, I knew—was all that vast sunny space, the airy distances, the man waving, the sudden holes of black you just never noticed till you looked for them, then saw so suddenly, so nakedly.

Curiosity got the better of fear, of course. By the time we were cycling home at the end of the day, following the billowing dust of our parents' cars, we were no longer spooked. The mysterious stranger was no Bogeyman, just someone who had heard the racket and come down to investigate, who then seemed to be looking out at us, had seen a companion, an acquaintance, someone he knew, and simply waved in greeting. Nothing to do with Jeffers, nothing to do with vigilant local farmers setting a trap.

But enough of the fear remained, the mood of that morning hour, to power our curiosity. We were determined to stage another scaring on the Tuesday, breaking our third-day ruling but needing to do something, needing to be sure.

By the time we reached Hayvenhurst Avenue we had our plan. The four rolls of three-inch gray masking tape from Bidder's barn were perfect and, as we weren't the only kids to take regular shortcuts across the Bidders property to get from Hayvenhurst to the creek, we judged the risk well worth it.

In thick woodland three miles out of town, close to the Manton cutting, we laid out seventeen-by-seventeen eight-foot strips of tape in a grid, carefully backed so we finally had a steel-gray portcullis, what looked like an iron grate to be fixed over the track on more of Rusty Cramer's fishing line.

We threaded line at the corners and sides, rolled up our grid, then did a few partial run-throughs, got the thing to the edge of the cutting and unrolled in less than four minutes. The hard part, scrambling down to get the end of the line hiked up and tethered to a tree on the other side, then weighting down the bottom lines with stones to get the tension needed, we figured would take another four to six, allowing for fumbles. We tossed a coin for the privilege and Max won.

We stored the grid in some bushes, rode back to town by a leisurely roundabout route, even stopped at the library to borrow a book on local bird life, establishing our alibis there and justifying borrowing our folks' binoculars again.

On the Tuesday we were out at the Manton cutting twenty-four minutes ahead of the 12:10 freight. It was hot and very still in the cutting. Cicadas droned in the trees; only the slightest breeze stirred the dry grass stalks along the tracks. The rails gleamed like streaks of chrome in the noon heat.

In moments we had the grid unrolled, tethered, and tossed down. Max scrambled after it, soon appeared on the other side, hauled the grid taut, and fastened it, then weighted the trailing tethers with rocks. That done, he scrambled back and lay panting beside me, admiring our handiwork.

It was as if it had always been that way—a gated track, the lines like poured quicksilver coming and going, running off into the day, nothing else but insect song, dried grass stirring in the thermals off the rails, the barest flutter of breeze in the treetops.

"Let's go!" Max said, and we were up and on our way, cycling out to Byle's Lookout, using the long sweep of Salter's Hill to put us up the other side in a record six minutes. We were on our stomachs, panting, binoculars up and focused before our front wheels had finished turning.

We were a lot closer than at Hank's Creek and could make out the whole scene—the cutting exposed from this angle just before the tracks curved away towards Madrigal, everything as we'd left it, the scene deserted but for the grasses stirring and the improbable iron gate athwart the track. We could already hear the train approaching, a low sliding roar, building and building.

It was over in moments. The 12:10 was suddenly there, plunging at the grid like a demon. There was a scream of the steam whistle, oddly attenuated, it seemed, as if dampened by the cutting or the trees, then—*thwap!* (imagined not heard)—the grid was hit, carried away, and the eighteen bogies were clack-clacking their way off towards Madrigal.

But neither Max nor I jumped up to leave. Without having agreed on it, even mentioned it, we stayed where we lay, watching the tracks through our glasses.

And the man was there, just stepped into view from behind the embankment, seemed to be studying the rails where our gate had been.

Prickles of fear ran down my spine.

"Christ!" Max said. "Who is that guy?"

"Let's go, Max!" I spoke in a harsh whisper, not wanting to see him look out and wave, not again. I remembered all the dark places in the trees, saw them again right there.

"Wait, will ya!" Max said, feeling a need to wait, and I probably couldn't have left anyway. I needed it too somehow, this part of what we'd started.

And sure enough, the figure looked up, much closer than before, much closer, a man in his early fifties or thereabouts, in dark work shirt and drab workman's pants, wisps of gray hair stirring on his mostly bald head, deepset eyes peering out. And he smiled as if in understanding, possibly a grim smile, and nodded, yes, yes, I know, and not waving this time, just turned and stepped out of sight behind the embankment.

"Who is that guy?" Max asked again, but more to himself than to me.

Death, for my money, I wanted to shout. *Pavor diurnus.* Day terror. The Bogeyman.

"Has to be planted," Max continued. "They've been watching for us is what. Keeping an eye out. Listen, Paul." He turned on his side to face me. "That may not be the guy from the other day. They've got help. Guys from the railway maybe. Planted them at likely places. Maybe they're onto us, maybe not. So they wind us up by acting like they've seen us. He didn't see us just now, just knew we'd be watchin'. They're goosin' us, Paul. Rattlin' us."

It made sense. Blessed good sense.

"What do we do?" My voice was still broken by fear, embarrassingly querulous.

"We've got a week left. We can plan good stuff for next year. Real good stuff!"

"Lay low now, you reckon?"

"Not on your life. We get 'em a good one. One last scare."

"They could be watchin'. What do we do?"

"A night scare, Paul."

"They're not as good."

"No, so we do it where we never have before. Where they'd never expect."

"Like where?"

"In town."

"Town!"

"At night. Late at night. We rig up something at the end of the platform."

"But at night, Max. They just don't see enough."

"Yeah, so we rig something that uses that. We use the engine's head-lamp. Okay?"

"You got a plan?"

"Believe it, my man."

For the last scare of the last week of what was to be our final summer at Portobello; though we didn't know it then, we picked the Thursday, the 11:40 freight out of Madrigal, nonstop through Portobello at 12:16.

A monograph from the library—*Night Birds* by George Lowry—furnished us with our alibi, while a coin toss gave me the privilege of the scare itself. Not something I actually wanted, but I wouldn't let Max know that for the world.

We sneaked out at 11:45, pedaled into town, hid our bikes, and slid down to the station. It was deserted on this late-summer night, the air already cooling towards autumn, with crickets sounding and an occasional fragment of a night bird's song to justify our visit if anyone found us.

The lights from Main Street and Hayvenhurst barely reached the platform; only the lights in the waiting room and the twin lampposts at either end showed where Portobello Station existed in the night.

We had minimal equipment just in case: a twenty-foot length of sturdy rope.

Max's plan was simple. The rope would be tied round my waist and fixed to the lamppost at the southern end. I would lean out at a bizarre forty-five degrees from the platform's edge, giving the engineers enough time to see me before Max hauled me back.

It would be a dreadful sight for the engineers, a frantically waving figure leaning out—an impossible image to take with them as they plunged on through the darkness. So simple. So effective. Our bravura piece before we went our separate ways for another year, so we thought.

We rigged it up, did a few rehearsals so I could be sure of my footing and Max could get used to my weight. We agreed I would pull back myself if I wanted to— all we needed was for me to be glimpsed for a few seconds after all, and the approach was long enough. But leaving it to the last moment would make it the *pièce de résistance* of scarings.

At 12:05 we checked the knots, and Max took his place behind the post. I leaned out over the track, satisfied myself that there was ample visibility, and waited the few minutes, counting bits of the darkness like the worry beads Max's Mum used at mass, noticing it all: the dim lines made by fences, trees, cast-iron fittings, the soft lights of Main Street reaching out, striking into my eyes—look here! look here!—the red and green signal lights, the double tracks themselves, made into sliding sweeps of silver by a moon we couldn't see. There were just the crickets, the warble of a bird sounding far off, a few barks from a dog even further away.

"Get ready," Max said, needlessly.

I hung there, leaning out, sharp with anticipation and too much darkness, noticing it all, listening, straining for the slow sliding roar that would grow, edge up, come as both a wave of sound and a shiver underfoot, watched for the single eye, the shouts of steam. I strained for that unmistakable train rhythm—

locomotive locomotive locomotive

There it was! Yes!

And there were words on that rush of sound as well.

"What do you two think you're doing?"

We froze in disbelief, Max gripping the rope, me leaning out.

And there was Rusty Cramer, fifteen, burly (fat), vindictive (blamed, implicated by the fishing line), and angry (dangerous).

"I said what do you two think you're doing?" He came towards us like a big block of night, something dislodged from the ordinary world and sent careening, spinning out wildly into all this calm.

"Wait and see!" Max cried, not wanting to lose our chance, not now.

"Yeah, well I knew I'd catch up with you assholes sooner or later."

He was close and threatening, still improbable, but Max tried to keep him talking. "It's a joke we're pulling, see. Watch what happens now."

"You're both for it, you dumb shits! I'm gonna bust ya!"

"Watch the train first, okay. Here! Wow, look at that!"

"What?" Rusty Cramer said, and turned, saw the freight thundering on its run through the town, looked back, tried to figure exactly what it was we meant to do, turned again just as the light hit me and the whistle screamed in warning, terrifying me and keeping Rusty distracted. "What the hell!"

I remembered to wave my arms frantically, judged my own jumpback only to have Max haul me back first.

Actually I fell back, and the locomotive was there, past, gone, leaving the steady thunder of bogies howling after it. And Max ran at Rusty, pushed him hard, sent him slamming into the iron sides of a bogey, where he sprang away again, slammed into the lamppost, thud after sickening thud.

I was on my feet in seconds, staring, horrified, dangerously close to the track myself, saw Rusty Cramer pinball from bogey to post to the gravel, saw him flat, torn, and dead. Saw Max wide-eyed, determined to have his alibi, his scapegoat, never for a moment saw the guard's van rushing up, dim and forgotten, or the bar or strap or trailing line, whatever it was that struck my skull and sent me flying, falling, and thinking as I fell: "I'm dead too!"

I didn't die. I spent three months in hospital with a fractured skull and got used to having a metal plate over the weak spot as a constant reminder of how lucky I was. Mum didn't say much about what happened, mostly: "There, there, Pauly, you just rest." But Dad gave me most of it.

"That damn fool Cramer kid!" he said on my second day out of a seventy-day coma. "What do you remember, son?"

I played dumb, frowned a lot, asked him to tell me more.

"Rusty Cramer's dead, you know, Paul?"

"What about Max?"

"Max. He phoned it in. Said you were after night birds, stumbled on the Cramer kid doing one of those pranks on the station."

"Right. That sounds right. Don't remember too much though."

"Course you don't. You startled him and he got hit, then something brained you good. You're very lucky, Paul."

"Seem to remember that. Where's Max?"

"Where do you think, son? School's been back nearly ten weeks. He said he'd write or call, keep in touch."

"Right. So Rusty Cramer did all those things."

"That's what the cops said. Blaming it on outatowners. Thug of a kid. I guess it's just as well he blew it."

"Why's that, Dad?"

"You remember he had a rope fixed to a post and was leaning out—how Max said you found him? Well, he scared the train drivers good this time. One had a heart attack from it, they reckon; died right there at the throttle. The other guy says Rusty must've scared him to death hanging out waving like that. You probably stopped other deaths happening, son. I'd try and look at it that way."

"I will, Dad. I will. I guess it's the only way."

Max and I did get to speak about it after a fashion, but on the phone, long distance, three weeks later. I didn't ask him the most important question: *how* he could have done it, *how*, actually avoided it, convincing myself that it had been spur of the moment (though it hadn't been, of course, definitely hadn't been!), just something implicit in all our earlier games of death and mayhem, one more unreality, cartoonlike almost, not to be dwelt upon too much. And while we made our peace, alluded to his quick-thinking, run-to-the-phone-for-an-ambulance call, spoke of

Rusty's death (murder!) guardedly, and that of the engineer (manslaughter), even mentioned the newspaper clipping from the *Mail* Dad had kept about how the autopsies on Rusty Cramer and the driver were botched, we had to postpone the full weight of our discussion and debriefing, the reality of it, till our next meeting— other important things like the mysterious man at the cuttings, the botched autopsies, all the stuff that mattered all of a sudden.

"I'll write to you," Max said, far off across the country. "And we can talk about it in the summer."

Which didn't happen, of course. After the accident, Max's parents didn't choose Portobello that year, and with my sister dating, we didn't get there either. Two years after that, Dad's job took us down to Australia; I finished high school in Sydney, and in 1967 went on to do an arts degree at Sydney University, and Max Sefti and my scaring the train became one more unresolved part of that ineffably dear, long, slow, blink-and-it's-gone, quickly stolen thing called childhood.

2

Sydney University 1967

Imagine what it was like then towards the end of first term, sitting with nine other first-year students in our English tutorial, when the door opened and in came a student forced by part-time employment commitments to change tutorial groups, who turned out to be none other than Max Sefti—*here* in Australia, in Sydney, at *this* university, walking into *this* room.

It shattered the smooth consensual reality in a moment, was wonderful and utterly bizarre, even vaguely alarming. We had shared lectures in Wallace and Carslaw but hadn't spotted one another. There were no words to capture it, absolutely none. The tutor's remarks, the *Innocence and Experience* poetry of William Blake, stood no chance except as vivid counterpoint, but afterwards, over coffee in the Refectory, I found out about those missing parts of my life.

It wasn't an optimum spiel because Janice and Becky, two girls from our tutorial group, tagged along with a friend of theirs, an intense-looking, dark-haired young guy named Lucian. Consequently what might have been an incredible yet surprisingly natural bridging of days became the kind of narrative back-tracking I'm giving here. It was certainly interesting in itself since I was able to hear Max tell his version of it at last, filled with his forthright young adult confidence and my own self-conscious, artless lapses into cliché, an understandable refrain of: "My God, but you here!"

The facts came out all the same, though as part of some incredible freak accident, certainly not as premeditated (however briefly) murder: Rusty lying dead, the unseen guard's van, my being struck hard enough to fracture my skull, send me into coma, and require a long convalescence. That helped win back Janice and Becky's attention; they asked about the plate in my skull, exactly where it was, could they touch it, things like that. Dark-haired Lucian frowned and seemed clearly fascinated.

I heard how Max had given the police—the very ones we'd caused such trouble— an account of finding Rusty on the station, startling him in midscare, causing him to stumble and fall so he was hit and flung back into the lamppost. He told how an unfastened strap or buckle flailing about had struck me on the side of the head, and how ready the authorities were to believe, actually believe, because Rusty had been such a swine of a kid all his young life and we did have our birdwatching book and all.

I learned, too, how Max had had the presence of mind to retie the rope from my waist around Rusty's, had got that done minutes before the police and the ambulance arrived so everyone believed, so no one even for a moment thought to suggest we might have been in collusion with him, a local kid working with two outatowners.

That was the version he gave anyway: Rusty catching us at it, tripping during a scuffle, being hit; our arranging things so he was implicated, but all an accident. Just a terrible accident.

Max added a detail then that sent a chill through me in that sunny corner of the Refectory.

"Paul, something happened while I was retying the rope round Rusty's waist...."

"You saw the guy!" I blurted it out. The bits of fear had all connected up. The far-off reality was real again, finally, not pushed aside, not hidden away.

"No. No, I didn't." His tone gave me the "but" before he said it. "But I looked for him, you know? I'd knelt on something sharp and just looked up. Expected to see the guy—like in that Charles Dickens story."

"But nothing?"

"Nothing. Just a feeling, you know. It was a really bad moment. I was fumbling with the rope, trying to get it under Rusty's body and tied before the cops arrived. I was breathless from running from the phone, my knee was hurting from whatever I'd knelt on, you were lying there covered in blood. I had Rusty's blood all over me. It was pretty awful."

I made myself ask it. "So what about the autopsy reports, Max? They were messed up you said."

"I did? Oh yes. Right. On the phone that night. The *Mail* had a bit on it. The train driver died of a heart attack, but the autopsy for cause of death said the blood had changed."

"Changed? What do you mean, changed?"

"Just that. Changed. Altered somehow. It didn't say. But the Cramer kid had the same thing. His blood had gone funny."

"But what does that mean?"

People at other tables were giving us looks.

"Paul, it didn't say. Just that the lab people had stuffed up."

I calmed myself. "But you sensed the guy?"

"Something. I went back to the station the next day. You were over in Madrigal, still on the critical list, still in a coma. They had already operated to relieve pressure on your brain, to get out the bone fragments too smashed up to leave there, they told us."

It was frustrating. He was talking for the others.

"See anything?"

"Just where it all happened. The post was actually bent where Rusty hit it. They hadn't sanded over the bloodstains properly yet. I saw the nail I'd knelt on before getting the feeling. It was just—eerie, you know?"

"But no sign of the guy?"

"Uh uh. But it was like he was there, you know? I kept looking up expecting to see him."

Lucian spoke then, the first words I'd heard him say that morning but for monosyllables.

"It's convergent energy. How you think of a thing makes a thing. How you name a thing defines a thing."

Thanks, Lucian, if that's your real name. I'd only known him by sight before that morning, but it was the kind of patter you expected, looking at him, all Plato and Socrates, Sufis and Sophistry, Castanada and *Sergeant Pepper's*.

Max looked from him to me and back. "Say again."

"You probably haunted yourself," Lucian said. "We all do it. Set up expectations. Rope the unconscious into it—all that energy."

"Uh uh," Max said. "I meant the other bit."

"Power of names. Naming gives shape. Summons. Bestows power. All part of primitive people's singing up the land, renaming things, remaking things. The Navajo—"

"Yeah, right." Max had heard enough.

But Lucian continued, and just as well. "It's like these scarings. At what point did they become rituals?"

"Rituals?" I showed *my* annoyance now.

But Max was intrigued. "*Did* become?"

"All right. Do become, though I suspect they already have. And, yeah, rituals because we always do more than we know. Simple acts become metaphor, symbolic, representational as well as just themselves. We're left to find what they really mean."

Who's your friend? Max said in a look, but was interested in spite of himself.

Lucian probably read that look. "You have to admit it, Max. You were both pretty fixated. The blood and death and all. That man you saw. Lots of fertile stuff there. Of course there are going to be ramifications. All that emotion and psychic force; both of you looking for answers."

"Maybe." Max was yielding, plainly needed something of the reassurance dark assured Lucian seemed to be providing. "What do you suggest?"

"Suggest?" Lucian managed to look both surprised and confident all at once. "Why, restage the event—with us along as unbiased controls." He already had that good scientific word. "See what you get."

"A scaring? Here?"

Becky liked the idea. "Why not? It'd be fun."

"We've got trains," Janice said. "Lots of stations."

Now I was the one with the doubts. "Too crowded. Doesn't feel right."

"Okay," Lucian said. "I should be able to borrow a holiday house at Glenbrook. That's in the Blue Mountains if you don't know, about two hours away. Term vacation's, what, in two weeks? We could go up for a few days. Lots of little stations. Springwood. Blackheath. Medlow Bath. Hazelbrook. Wentworth Falls. Just pick one."

Max turned to me. "Paul? What do you think?"

"Yes," I said, connecting up the years, feeling relieved, reprieved somehow, giving all that had occurred its due place in my life, its correct perspective and proportion, getting another chance at—just something important. "Yes, I want to."

My certainty surprised me.

"What do you say?" Lucian asked Max diplomatically.

Max, so suddenly here, so dramatically in my life again just by being here, frowned, murmured: "Hmm," then said: "Yeah. Okay. Why not?"

I believe he thought he was doing it for me: allowing a psychotherapy, completing an equation, but deep down I knew he needed something out of this too: perhaps as elusive as redemption, expiation for harm done, control lost, perhaps as simple as nostalgia for what had been.

Our only days.

3

Glenbrook 1967

Late Monday afternoon was it. The five of us set out from the small wooden house in Glenbrook and drove through the Blue Mountains towns in Lucian's Holden. We had a rather tense and silent afternoon tea at the Paragon in Katoomba, then continued out to Mount Victoria, only to retrace our route, stopping and looking, stopping and looking, till we finally found a suitable station sufficiently hidden away from the road.

All things considered, we should have known better than to go ahead with it that particular evening; everything about the last hour of the day felt wrong. Rain was due and there was that low mean sideways light coming at us below an overcast, and a cool breeze hugging the land, moving the trees and grasses but leaving low clouds locked in place, wrinkled and bellying down.

Strange weather, the light sliding in from the edge of the world like that, giving us a disturbing overlit quality so we glowed like tricked-up idealizations of ourselves, figures in some garish symbolist painting.

Even as we went down the steps into the shadow of the platform, something of that quality remained—a silvering, gilding, flaring in the sunset edges of the trees and waving grasses, each leaf and blade picked out, detailed, each whorl and valance of the locked and threatening sky.

"This is weird," Janice said, perfect bathos, typical Janice, and the rest of us laughed; it was so beyond words.

"Elemental, dear Janice," said Lucian, which she didn't get, but it was probably the right word: we were elemental on that lowering, fading, fateful evening, in one of those moments of incidental framing reality where every commonplace surprises you.

I know, I'm overdoing this, but that's how it was for me, and the others too, I felt. Some days, some evenings, night just happens as a background to other things, but here it was, being made, perceptibly forming out of cracks and corners, the blackness of the short tunnel pushing out, flowing up, as if prying itself loose, all of it heightened by the dramatic closing light we had just now left behind, shed from ourselves in return for discrete shadows, the self-same drab as the clouds overhead.

There were people, just a few, waiting for the next commuter train up from

Sydney to take them on to nearby Mountains stops and beyond, or the express to take them down to the Emu Plains and out to the coast.

We stayed just long enough to work out the details, which side to use (left-hand facing west—the train would plunge straight into the quick darkness of the tunnel—blink, blink—did we imagine that?), how to make an easy getaway through the shallow tunnel itself. We stayed until the 5:50 from Sydney had dropped off its passengers and moved on, waited till they had vanished into the night and the lone ticket collector had gone back in out of the wind, then made our way to the car, headed back to Katoomba.

"I'm not sure about this," Max said as we were driving along.

Lucian must have expected it; he was clearly our motivating force now and still the perfect diplomat. "I know what you mean, Max. It's been a weird afternoon. What about you, Paul?"

Again I surprised myself. "Might as well go ahead with it now." Something about the quality of the light back at the station had fascinated me, given me a sense of imminence, something. But I didn't speak it, and must have even sounded a bit indifferent.

Lucian pulled over, turned to face us in the back seat. "Listen, you two," he said, but carefully, caringly. "Five years ago you got close to something really important for you. It affected you in all sorts of ways, I can tell. We don't have to do this. We can call it off. But it needs a bit of enthusiasm, okay? If we go ahead."

Janice grinned at him. "I'm enthusiastic."

"Right," Max said, to Janice or Lucian, you couldn't tell. "It was just so"—dramatic? frightening? vivid? I wondered what he'd say—"incomplete."

"So we're doing this now. Completing it." Lucian spoke as if he understood it all, and maybe he did. "Next question. If we do it, your call, who leans out?"

I spoke first. "Me!"

"I will!" Max said.

"Toss for it!"

"My turn!"

Lucian, captain of the car, the whole night, decided. "Maybe it should be Paul, Max. He needs to do this. Okay?"

Max nodded. "You up to it, Paul?"

"I'm fine."

So we drove on, took in a movie in Katoomba, got back to our chosen spot at 11:02, in plenty of time for the 11:40 freight. Since we figured the train would probably sound its whistle when the scaring took place, we left the car half a mile from the station and walked there, not wanting disturbed locals to see us driving away afterwards. Our plan was to walk along the tracks and cut up to the highway.

The night had closed in, chill and windy, and though the overcast stole the starlight, the rain had held off. As we moved down to the platform, the wind soughed in the power lines, whistled round the stanchions, gusted in the trees. Grass bent low on the embankments. The dark hole of the tunnel seemed thicker, deeper, seemed to pull at us, pull then push in distinct night rhythms. I wasn't the only one to imagine it; the others made comments too, seemed to find it eerie, but then we were all oversensitive to such things.

The platform itself was deserted as we expected, with just a few lights showing in either direction, the four double lampposts, the two sets of signal lights showing their comforting red and green. The waiting room was lit too and cozily warm. A fire had been left in the generous hearth, with wood to one side. The honour system prevailed and, despite our mission, we fed it for anyone who might arrive during the long night that would follow.

It took moments to fasten the rope first to the westernmost lamppost just before the tunnel, then to my waist, less than a minute or two to let me reprise my long-ago act of leaning out over the left-hand line, feet on the lip, Lucian and Max hauling me back a few times on Max's call. All straightforward, an anticlimax if anything after the build-up of our boyhood scarings, something almost pointless and foolish, stripped of context.

But Lucian was clearly excited and Max was becoming so. We were all on edge; any lingering sense of anticlimax was kept at bay by the night itself, so vivid and powerful, the constant, unsettling keening of the wind, the shuddering grasses above the cutting, the tossing trees, so many inexplicable sudden sounds. The darkness of the tunnel seemed even deeper—pushed, pulled, waiting.

This wasn't Portobello in the warm summer night of 1962. This was a small Australian mountain station racked by a chill, late-autumn sou'easter. This was a consummation somehow, a fitting resolve. Some kind of redemption.

Max knew it; dark-eyed Lucian did. Becky no doubt. Janice said she was cold and became in a moment *persona non grata* forevermore in all our minds.

The time drew near. The girls hid; I leant out; Lucian and Max took their places, gripped the lifeline double-handed.

No one came. No hint of the stranger. No Rusty Cramer this time (though, paradox, I did wish it could be so, generous in my need). The wind blew and blew; the rails shone by any light they could steal—found firelight, lamplight, stole light from our eyes to keep the silver there in that heaving autumn dark.

Train came impressed on that fragile darkness, a roar below, behind, above the wind, suddenly there in smouldering running lights, in the headlight beating out, a great diesel bearing down.

I stretched out my arms, waved, waved frantically, pinned in the hideous, devouring glare. The whistle screamed, screamed where it never had before, at an hour when it never should.

I waved in the terror-rushing-darkness. How many heart attacks this time? How many? All fall down! Everyone!

Was hauled back, ricocheted as the raw and angry train ran by and was swallowed by the frame of the tunnel, swallowed whole, gulped in carriage by rachetting, sliding, angrily snapping bogey, vertebra by vertebra as its dark spine was sucked in, gone.

Max and Lucian had both caught me. There was a moment of exhilaration, of sheer delight at what we'd done, all our earlier fear turned into that. Becky was smiling, Janice too, though she still looked scared. Would we be caught? Would we?

But we didn't wait for some curious local to call in a complaint, or a lone patrol car wandering through these towns to investigate why a through freight would shatter sleep around midnight this way.

Max untied the rope and coiled it ready for throwing aside later, then we helped one another down onto the tracks and began our retreat, following the double lines to the shallow tunnel.

Max couldn't restrain his delight. "It worked, Paul! It worked!"

"Smooth as clockwork," Lucian said, sounding pleased too, then added: "We need to listen though. For vibrations in the rails."

"Could a train come?" Janice asked, first time of four or five.

Perversely I said, "Sure could." Scaring the Janice. Hating her insensitivity to this, her finding only the Bogeyman when it was so much more.

The tunnel was only twenty or so paces long, and a train-wind pushed at us all the way, though it was just the sou'easter finding a way through. But when we came out the other side we noticed the changes at once. The trees still blew above us on the embankments, the grasses still leaned in waves; the wind was sounding, hitting at us, but it was as if stillness had been imposed on all that—those things drawn off, suspended somehow, changed.

And more. It was as if one of those heavily shadowed, cliff-locked, deep-tunneled coastal stations south of Sydney—Otford, Stanwell Tops, Helensburg, I wasn't sure of the names—had been superimposed on this one. The tunnel had been too deep; now the sides of the cutting seemed way too high. Details were wrong, out of place.

Perhaps it was adrenalin rush, nerves firing with the excitement, all that noise and light replaced by the compressed dark of the tunnel and the windy silence, but we all noticed it, showed it by the looks we gave, though nothing was said, not even when we saw that there was fog in the cutting ahead.

Fog on a windy overcast night! It snatched the streetlight too, gave some to the tracks so they ran as quicksilver glint, drawn off and lost in the silvery pall.

But *fog*.

The next surprise: the line branched ahead. Branched! We were not even fifty meters from the tunnel and the left-hand westbound track we were following had a line running silver and fogbound into a cutting, steep-sided and not on any of the maps Lucian said he had studied.

This wasn't the stranger of summers gone, not Rusty Cramer bouncing pinball ricochet off the midnight freight to Madrigal. This was the world gone wrong.

"We go back now," Lucian said, and echoed that key word. "This is wrong."

"Something's there!" Janice cried.

locomotive!

We all heard it. A shuffle, snuffle, muttered, stolen back.

"Run!" Max said, and we did, not up the sides, it was too steep, not ahead to cross that branch-line, but back.

locomotive! locomotive!

Unmistakable. Something waited in the old, new, different cutting. Something.

We ran on and on, entered the tunnel again, found it long, long, far longer, deeper than it had been moments ago, ran on, panting, breathing hard, Janice giving off a wail that never quite made it to a scream.

locomotive! locomotive! locomotive!

Pursued by the night, we fled, felt the train-wind at our backs, were pinned in headlight, light made from darkness, rail silver, stolen streetlamps, window-shine, and eye glitter, dazzling, numbing, chilling light.

"Against the wall!" someone cried, Max, Lucian, I couldn't tell. "On the other side! On the other side!" And I ran with the others, trusting that someone had indeed calculated which track would carry the—*locomotive! locomotive!*—presently at the tunnel's mouth. *Train*. As if that covered it.

We rushed, clattered, and stumbled to the tunnel wall, that wrong, south-coast tunnel wall, flattened ourselves against the slick, damp bricks, cold, so cold, too cold, tried to push into the hard wet surface, air coursing over us, smelling of train friction, metal on metal, ozone, dried blood, night-bitter, blood-bitter, *locomotive! locomotive!*

It ran past, whatever it was, going the wrong way on the wrong line at the wrong hour, in a tunnel that was wrong, wrong, with all of night and hell and angry disregard in its rush.

And we pulled back, peeled away, only when there was no sound (and no fog and no cutting, I was certain), no train wind or hint of its returning, no sign at all of that ultimate Night Train.

Janice was dead when we found her. All that carefully packed life bludgeoned— no—drawn out thin and gone, cut free, snatched away. No wound that we could tell in the meagre light, just wiped of life and light and fear, all in a moment, there in that space—a mere twenty or so paces deep. Normal again, hah! Never normal. Never again.

And when the police finally came and took us back to Katoomba and asked their hours of questions, it was left as heart attack and stupid uni students walking the tracks (apparently the engineers had not bothered to report the scaring). Sure, Lucian phoned around and word got back to us later that there was a glitch in the autopsy forensics; all the iron had been leached from her blood.

So that couldn't be the end of it for us.

We went back, three of us did, some months after the court hearing. Becky and Lucian were living together by this stage, but she decided not to go along. So Lucian, Max, and I drove up one Saturday night, arriving late with our torches and memorial bunch of flowers (our excuse if anyone found us at it), and after entering the tunnel from the western end to make sure there was no extra line, no branch cutting beyond, we finally agreed on the spot where Janice had died.

There were no bloodstains, of course, nothing on the hard round stones before that slick wall but moss, old cigarette packets, a candy bar wrapping, leaves and dried grass stalks, two bottle tops, and a rusty nail.

Not quite knowing why I did so, I took the nail, put it in my pocket; it was something that was real, after all, part of it, part of the place and the time and the death. Of poor, brief, stupid Janice.

We left the flowers and drove away.

4

Town Hall Station 1972–1994

There were four openings for this account I'm doing here, one for each version I've tried putting down, depending on which starting point I chose. One line you already have: "Every summer during our childhood holidays at Portobello, Maximillian and I would spend an hour every third day scaring the train." But I could just as easily have started *in media res*, as in an earlier attempt, with: "The train winds are the best in Sceptre City"—a good line: short, gripping, promising mysterious things—then worked back through it as Dr. Day suggested I do.

Stealing a bit, really, because Sydney didn't get its third real skyline landmark—

Bridge, Opera House, finally the Sydney Tower: God's Microphone, the Sceptre—until 1981, but as you discover as you get older in the eternal. Now, you reach a point when it never seems otherwise, and you have to concentrate to remember how it really was then.

The line is as true for 1967 as today—tonight—and writing this down again, I do remember that name as part of that time.

Glancing back over what I've written, it seems that Lucian promised to be some sinister reincarnation of that stranger Max and I saw years ago. Sinister he was with his dark good looks and strange notions, but while Max and I remained in one another's lives after we graduated in 1970, we lost touch with Lucian and Becky who, last we heard, got married and mortgaged and snatched aside from the flow of life (or into it, depending on your view of such things).

Max got married too, to a young high-school teacher named Pauline. Me, why I'm Mr. Popular, with relationships pretty well constantly, but have stayed single, communicating something unresolved in myself (I was told by one girlfriend who went away, vanished from my life, never answered the phone again), something tense and gripped too tightly. And I screamed during nightmares I never remembered. So, sure, I had ladies, partners, companions, in one-night, six-week, two-month lots, but never futures.

But Max stayed in touch and stayed interested (there was too much unresolved between us as well) and he was the one who phoned in May 1972 and asked me to meet him at Giovanni's Pizzeria at Town Hall Station to discuss train winds.

What he said. Train winds.

We'd tried Sydney's train winds before, back in '68 and '69, standing on Town Hall, Wynyard, St. James, and Museum, feeling the plunging piston push of air before trains arrived, the unmistakable slipstream, warm, redolent of oil, ozone, raw metal, and dark places. It could delight you, thrill you, or scare you silly, and we kept at it because we almost understood something every time, recognized or remembered something, though never quite what.

So began a decades-long series of infrequent, almost ritualistic meetings that usually started with a meal and ended with us going down onto the platforms and just experiencing the elusive telling-us-something quality of the train winds.

All routine until a week ago.

This time his voice on the phone had been troubled, urgent. Would I meet him? Yes. The usual place (now Alexander's Cafe). Sure.

I found him drinking coffee right there before the breathing stairwells of the Town Hall underground. He didn't say much, not then, but we bought City Circle tickets and went to the final level where there was the weight of the city and the lives, and the familiar twin tracks laid taut, silver, and humming between their double gulps of darkness. Tunnels are like seashells; you hear impossible seas when you listen close.

We stood, toes to the edge, peering off into one of those snatching gaps and then, then, we could talk, eyes on the dark in darkness, then we could.

"You know what Janice said that night, Paul?"

Janice? Janice? Years, moments, lives rammed together in an instant.

That Janice.

"What? When?"

"Before she died. Before we went up to Glenbrook that weekend."

"No. I didn't. No, I don't, Max. What did she say?"

Toes to the edge, we peered off into gloom, minds attuned to the faintest breath, listening, listening for the tiniest ghost-rush and whisper.

"She'd had dreams, she said. The same dream. Ever since we decided to do the scaring. She dreamt she'd die there."

I resisted the hard knot of guilt, fought shame and denial, emotion locking my gut. Bloody Janice! Bloody, changed-blood Janice!

"So?" Calm. Hard. Keeping it hard.

"Something sharp would take her. Something sharp."

Thanks a lot, Max. Bringing me this. "A train?"

There, I had named it, said it, peering into gloom. The Night Train.

locomotive!

And listened, watched the veins in the earth, those warm taut lines, worm lines, snail-slide of silver, watched the blocked black, ocean-shell darkness. For train. *Train.*

"Something sharp. I asked that too—a train?—before we set out that day."

"And? Come on, Max! And?"

"She asked if trains were sharp."

Ohmigod! Poor dizzy Janice. So brave, so driven. So changed.

"You never told me."

"Told no one, mate. You didn't want to hear. You wouldn't have then, would you? Another death?"

"No." Small word. No. Remembering Janice. Years. Summers.

"I kept it from everyone."

"Lucian?"

"No way. He'd have gone off on one of his theories. We put it aside. Just like with Rusty Cramer."

"So why tell me now?" Though I knew what he'd say.

"I've had the dreams too, mate. Four of them. Something sharp. About trains."

We felt the faintest kiss of air, a hint, a flutter. It was. Oceans falling on midnight shores.

"So we don't do this anymore. We put it aside again, Max. It's just memory serving up old stuff. We've carried it with us too long."

We step back right now, Max, I wanted to say. We step back. No more scaring either way.

Feathers of air stroked our faces.

"I just had to tell you. Had to let you know."

"Down here?" What I didn't say was: Did the dreams scare Pauline away?

"Needed that too. Just did, you know? It's been too long."

The rush, the unmistakable smell of the pushing air, the smell. Metal on metal. Ozone. Electric fire in the underworld. Sharp fire deep down.

"It has." Step back now, Max. I took his arm; he let me draw him back with me, one step, two, another. "We should include Lucian. Let him know too. Talk it out."

"Already have."

"What? When?"

"He suggested this. Said I needed this."

The train was there, shattering, battering, squealing down to just a silver, ribbed 10:08 to Hornsby, modern and safe, harmless again.

We waited as people came and went, waited till the doors slid shut and it had pulled off into the undernight. I imagined it drawing the air from our lungs after it, pulling it into sighs, drawing it thin. Earth, fire, water, and air.

Max did sigh. "I'm scared, Paul. Really scared, you know."

"So we keep away from places like this."

"Does no good. I see lines."

"You what?"

"I see train lines everywhere. Just look down a street or an alley. There they are, clear and bright as anything."

Like the dark holes under trees. Black spaces in sunshine.

"You mean it?"

"Look again and they're gone. But it's not corner of the eye stuff, Paul. They're right there. I hear a noise at night, look out the window and see them going down the street. See them in the drive, going across backyards, running right through fences. I go out to the fridge. There are lines in the living room, Paul, just right there, you know."

I still had his arm, was gripping it hard. I made him listen to me, told him about my own visits to Dr. Day, got him to quiz me on why I'd do such a thing. No, I wasn't having dreams or seeing lines. But I had anxieties, I said, problems relating, connecting. I had to write it out, I told him, which did seem to help. I said he hadn't done that was all, hadn't sorted the coincidence of the deaths, hadn't worked through it. Been debriefed. Talked down. That's all.

We agreed: no more scarings. We'd meet with Lucian, patch up the ragged bits, talk it through, the three of us. Stay in touch this time. He was easier as we left the station; I was easier, having focused my own fear and edges through Max's own. He gave me Lucian's address, then we phoned, arranged to meet on the Friday night. Then I put Max in a cab and never saw him again.

5

7:13 P.M.

Last night I found Lucian's nail.

Third opening of the four. This is the one I had before I decided to do it via Internet, get it out as far and as fast as I could. It can't be everywhere at once. It can't look everywhere. There have to be gaps, ways through, yes, openings.

But time for this line anyway, bringing it nearly to the moment. One to go.

Last night I found Lucian's nail. Two inches long, flat round head, round body, the sort of short, dark, rusty nail you find by the dozens, hundreds, in the recycle bins of older hardware stores and in old paling fences.

But his. His.

Found it on the night of the very day Lucian's package arrived with its ninety-minute TDK audio tape and the little cardboard box and the note—the package brought in by Tilly and used to weigh down her own goodbye note on the afternoon she too had had enough of remoteness, screams in the night, failure to commit, whatever she decoded it as.

Her note didn't surprise me. She'd tried; I'd tried, believed I had, believed I believed I had. I tried to wish her well.

But Lucian's note chilled me where I stood in the hall, the words scrawled in pencil, more disturbing somehow than if they had been in blood or purple ink.

> *Max's nail. Hide it. Tell no one.*
> *Look for mine. Hide them both. Stop it here.*

I resented the melodrama, the emotional grab on top of losing Tilly (with all the cumulative guilt of losing Louise and Jill, it just went on and on, back, back), but I was deeply and singly terrified too.

Max's nail. I opened the tiny box and saw it—just like Janice's, like Lucian's too I bet!—and knew Max was dead. Knew somehow, somewhere, he would be found with his blood changed, the iron gone to make this.

Nail.

I started to understand it then, you see. Standing in the hall, holding the small white box, with Tilly gone and the tape to play and the stupid note.

But not Lucian. Not Lucian dead too!

Two thoughts. Three. You've left me alone with this. Betrayed me. And: the Train was getting nearer.

Then the phone rang.

Standing there in front of it, compressed with loss, terror, and disbelief, with too much unraveling of the ordinary world, I cried out and swore and would've shouted down the line except I thought: Tilly. Please, God, yes.

"Paul? It's Becky. Sorry to bother you but have you seen Lucian?"

"No. No, I haven't, Beck. What's happened?"

It went from there. Could I come over? Of course I would, left the tape waiting, unplayed, went to her place, heard how Lucian had gone with no word, no explanation. She'd waited the drunk-binge, affair-guilt, drug-down twenty-four hours (apparently he'd been hitting it hard in every sense of the word, goosed by ideas that wouldn't go away), made the appropriate calls to friends (well, closer friends), hospitals, the police, answered their questions: no, no sign of foul play, had finally, finally, two days on, phoned me on the off chance.

Off chance! *On*, more like it: the very day his package arrived.

The last time she'd seen him was as she'd left for work, sitting at the kitchen table, the morning after being out with Max till all hours. With Max.

I asked about that, heard they'd been seeing a lot of one another (without including me? So much for our meeting up again), allowed that the tape would tell me all about that.

I looked in the kitchen as surreptitiously as possible, looked there again while brewing Becky and me coffee, found it just sitting there on the bench top as if pushed to one side, that exact size and shape, would never have noticed it without looking for it.

His. It was.

"What's this?" I actually asked her when she came in to help.

She shrugged. "Don't know. Found it on the floor."

No real curiosity about such an ordinary thing. It's true when they say there is nothing more sinister than what we never suspect: teapots, cracks in sidewalks, the flutter of a curtain, the bang of a screen door, lawn sprinklers.

Where's the body then? I wondered. Thinking of Janice, the nail in the tunnel where she had died, the sharp thing Max had knelt on tying the rope around dead, changed Rusty. (I *was* putting it all together, you see.)

We ended up sitting at the kitchen table and I pocketed the nail when I went to pour us refills, then spent the next hour considering anything and everything, me trying to be calm and caring but frantic with the need to find Lucian's body, wanting more than anything to get out of there so I could play the tape. No police, no telling anyone till I'd played that.

But Becky's question brought me up short. Not the expected theories: the prospect of a clean break, running away with someone, not the improbabilities of an amnesia-inducing accident or even a thrill-kill, but words about our first days.

"It's all to do with Portobello, isn't it? That convergent energy thing."

How you think of a thing makes a thing. How you name a thing defines a thing.

I might have said No, gone on about how wrong it was to make Lucian's ideas the only handle on this. But Becky had had twenty-seven more years of such talk. No doubt it did follow on, did connect up. She kept at it.

"That's when it all started, didn't it?"

I might have told her then, mentioned the nail—the nails—the tape, the scrawled note, but needed perspective, desperately needed detachment if I could get it.

"Let me think this over, Beck. Let me go through my old diaries, just think it through, you know, see what I come up with. I'll call you tomorrow."

Fortunately I'd been there long enough, sitting through the silences with her, that it didn't seem like I was abandoning her. We'd exhausted possibilities, gone from plausible to improbable, from rational to irrational. At last I could leave.

"There's nothing else, Paul. There's just nothing else," she said as we went to the front door.

I hated her certainty, feared it. "I'll call, I promise. The moment I have anything."

Then I drove home thinking, wondering, bringing it all back.

I could have started the account like that, you see, with finding the nail, then gone back to Portobello and 1962. But I needed to pace through it for myself, just to get it out, and I'm nearly done.

I went home and put Lucian's nail in the box with Max's, then slipped the tape into my sound system, pressed play.

There was nothing. Nothing. Just the running noise of the capstans turning, a no-sound, like the vacuum of space against an open mike, a constant waiting changelessness.

Now that I've had words fade on the page in front of me, I know what to expect, but even then I wasn't the least surprised. Once you granted the nails, the changed blood, of course you allowed for tapes that erased. Allowed them all as parts of a system—something just being recognized.

I drank more scotch than I should have and slept, thank God, slept right through.

Not because I was brave, more that I missed Tilly and was lonely, I went out walking that cold windy Saturday morning (this morning), just went across to the park, loving the autumn chill, how the leaves blew in waves, scurried and rustled on the paths.

I had the nails in my pocket and had half a mind to drive up into the Blue Mountains, go to the tunnel where Janice had died, or easier, closer, go down onto Town Hall's lowest level and just sit there, wait out the day—in case Lucian might come to me from some impossible cutting or out of some narrow squeezed-back, folded-in part of the undernight.

I was halfway across the deserted park when the hallucinations began: the hint and glint of rails among the scattering leaves, the sense of a train wind: ozone, steel on steel, feather-flutter in the midst of the cold southwesterly, like a warm breath into chilled hands.

I kept waiting for attendant sounds, imagined—*locomotive!*—yes, in the bending, shuddering trees.

And I knew. Just knew.

How Max had died. Rusty's death. Janice's.

Leaning out. Tethered. Lucian hauling, misjudging, some error. Max dead, a nail left from his changed blood, wrested out. Every adult human carried at least a two-inch nail's worth of iron in the blood. Carrying oxygen to the brain or something. What a death! Train pummeling through, laved in train wind, a kiss, a stroke, out goes the iron. The mind, the body, knowing what it lacked, stultified with the knowledge of the clean sweep. Something sharp. Bitter iron taste like blood in the mouth.

I kicked at the leaves, hands in pockets, walking, walking, catching hints of silver lines in the windy day, coming at me from under the trees, glinting in bushes, raw quicksilver, pared chrome, drawing off and off and away, treacherous as razors.

The lines. All the lines.

Somewhere, somewhere, I knew, as I turned out into Buckingham Street, passed sealed, windlocked houses, leaves scattering, blowing out of beleaguered trees, Max's body lay changed and dead, perhaps in a forgotten tunnel, overlooked in a culvert, someplace where Lucian had done—or not done—his deed.

But Lucian, where?

I turned from Buckingham into Wentworth, circled the park, crossed it again, expecting Lucian at any moment, sitting on a bench, standing under a tree, dead eyes looking straight out, face white, leached, starved. But no, nothing, and the hints of lines faded in the bleak afternoon, vanished altogether.

Yet had told me something. Accelerating affect. The lines leading out.

I phoned Becky from a payphone on the corner, meaning to be brutally direct ("Where did you leave the body, Beck?"), but there was no answer.

I caught a cab to her house, entered by the unlocked back door, and found her dead on the kitchen floor, plundered, changed, eyes wide, her own nail by her right hand, held but dropped in death.

I added it to the others in my pocket, wiped the door handle, and left, went back into the windy afternoon and took a bus into the city, went down onto the lowest level of Town Hall Station. No tether for me, just a quick moment of agony, a small tragic ritual in this dead afternoon hour, only a few people about.

If you've gotten this far, get to see this much at all, then you know I didn't do it, of course.

As I waited, peering into darkness, I saw someone looking back at me. Standing on the track, barest hint of shadow in shadow, of eyeshine and pale, pale skin, someone.

Lucian, was my first thought, first certainty. Lucian, you bastard, my second. Not your nail in the kitchen. Some other poor bugger's to mislead us.

No one else was watching. No one else saw me jump down onto the line, stride into the warm, pulsing throat of the tunnel. No one called after me. I went up to the figure standing in the middle of the track, was about to grab him by the front of his jacket, demand: What have you done? What have you done, bastard? Had the words right there, but stopped short.

It was Lucian all right. I saw that in the glow of platform light over my shoulder, in the white of skin and the glitter of sightless, staring eyes. He was staring into light.

It's hard to say now what he looked like, what the loss of iron had done. What skin I could see was like marble, tight and cold. He just stood, dead, changed, scarecrow upright, arms dangling, but worse, worst of all, his mouth hung open, and through it, from it, came a wind, that wind, and the whisper—*locomotive!*—of barest noise-in-a-seashell words.

"Not yet, Paul." Named. Naming me. *It* did. The Night Train did. This Bogey-man. Bogie-man. "Not yet, little Paul."

I fled then, turned and ran out of the tunnel, clambered up onto the platform even as the sliding thunder came and—an unforgettable meat-slammed-on-a-table sound—dead Lucian was impaled, carried, dumped, and rolled by the silver severed thread of a train—my sweet, unknowing, latest, alibi train.

I took out the box, opened it, saw that the nails were gone.

And knew.

6

7:38 P.M.

So, you've guessed. Well, I took longer than you, but I worked it out then, refined it tonight, writing this.

The plate in my skull: not plastic or stainless steel, no, not for me. If you looked, you'd find dead black iron. Intimate iron. I'm sure of it. A mirror curved onto thought, raw but never doing harm. Not to me.

How many lives, I wonder, for that piece of metal, just so this demon, this devil, can have its psychopomp, one who goes before? One of many, who knows? Successors, perhaps, to our man at Portobello so long ago.

How many of us, driven to silence? Needing to speak, drawn to tell, what do I do? Go on seeing the glint of rails across parks, in rainy avenues, flashing in the moonlight when there is no moon, twin lines of there/not there quicksilver, feeling the train wind in the tiniest breath and pulse, in the play of dust devils in an empty street?

Go on drawing others to me, those whose blood will be changed in the sharpened dark?

I don't expect you to believe any of this, if ever it does get out there. Just don't be surprised. That Becky died. That Dr. Day didn't answer his phone tonight, will probably never answer it again. That I'm still alive.

We all like trains. We do. But how many of us did it take to build this train and its endless thundering bogies? (Bogies, oh yes!) And tracks that go on and on and spill into the ordinary world worn thin? How many nails? How many?

My final opening line? Easy now. Perfect ending.

Let me write it. Let me write it before the words fade again. You would have liked it.

Now I know what Death is.

There.

And here. The knock at the door. Someone—Sue or Carmen, maybe Tilly back again. Or maybe that new guy from the office. Gerry. He said he might drop by. Any old iron.

Even as I close this off, press send one more time, there are rails, hints of lines off down the hall, running into night, but not for me. Not for the Bogie-man.

There's the far-off sound, a warm familiar pressure in my skull, and the wind is already blowing.

BLOOD KNOT
Steve Rasnic Tem

Steve Rasnic Tem grew up in the Appalachian mountains of Virginia and now lives in Colorado with his wife, writer Melanie Tem, and their children. His novel *Excavations*, was published in 1987 but he is better known for his short stories and poetry. He won the British Fantasy Award in 1988 for his story "Leaks." His work has been widely published in such magazines and anthologies as *Hardboiled, Bloodsongs, All Hallows, Pirate Writings, The Mammoth Book of Vampires, Metahorror, Borderlands, Love in Vein, Snow White, Blood Red, It Came From the Drive-In, Xanadu, The Year's Best Fantasy & Horror*, and *Best New Horror*. He edited the Colorado anthology *High Fantastic* (Ocean View Press) and has a collection of poetry, *Dream Machines*, coming from Unnameable Press.

"Blood Knot" is about fathers and daughters and the difficulty one particular father has in accepting the incipient womanhood in his little girls. It is reprinted from *Forbidden Acts* edited by Nancy A. Collins and Edward E. Kramer.

—E.D.

"Just a damn knot. You can't untie it; you can't burn it off. Older you get, the tighter it gets. Might as well accept it, 'cause that's the way it is. What else you going to do? Kill everybody in the family? Jesus Christ, it's a goddamned blood knot."

I heard my daddy say this when I was thirteen, fourteen, something like that. We were at our last family reunion: Daddy, me, and sis, and Daddy's fourth wife, June. "June bug," he called her—I guess because she was so much younger than he. Flash-forward ten years later and there Daddy is in a hospital bed coughing his lungs out. He pulls me closer—I was in my Army fatigues—and with breath that smelled like shit he tells me, "I married my June bug 'cause she was so young I knew the rest of the family wouldn't approve and they'd have nothing to do with her. Had me a ready-made excuse to stay away from the rest of them, give myself some breathin' room. With your family, well, you're who you are, but then you're not who you are, you know what I mean? Because you can't move. You can't change. Too bad she was so damn dumb."

I thought he was a fool. He had everything I'd ever wanted: kids, and a house, and more than one wife who'd loved him more than he'd deserved, surely more than was good for her. By then I'd found out that I had no talent for girlfriends, not even bad ones. They never lasted long enough to get bad. They never lasted long enough to be a pleasant memory after they were over. I was too reckless, or I wasn't reckless enough. I was too kind, or I wasn't kind enough. Something. Whatever it was that brought out the skittishness, the scared-dog look, in those women, I had. In plentiful supply. I asked, even begged sometimes, for answers, and it was always something like, "Maybe it's the way you talk," or, "Maybe it's all that stuff you think about." And that was if I *really* made them give me an answer. But they didn't know. I didn't know, and they didn't know. Hell, I thought being a little weird *attracted* some women. But not in my case.

"Some things are fated. Maybe you've got bad fate, or something, Harold." That was Linda, the night before she left me. She held me, and she let me cry in her bed, and she listened while I spilled my guts about needing a family of my own, someone I could love like I was supposed to, and she was good, so good she brushed away my embarrassment when she brushed away my tears, and the next day she left me. Fate, I guess.

Well, fuck her. She was good to me that night, but fuck her.

I'm not sure, but I think Daddy killed June one night, shortly after I'd turned eighteen. I don't know—we just never saw her around again. There'd been a lot of noise, a lot of drinking. I'm sorry to say that at the time I felt a big load had been taken off, because of the way she looked at me, the funny way she made me feel. Daddy always said she never really was part of the family. She kept herself apart and, after all, she wasn't blood. And she was young, too young to understand him, or us, or much of anything about living, I guess. Maybe that was why I could feel about her the way I did—my own stepmother after all. She wasn't blood, and like he'd always told me himself, blood is everything.

I don't know what Daddy would have made of my three daughters. I don't want to know. If he had lived I wouldn't have let him anywhere near them—even if somebody'd pulled off his arms and snipped off his balls. I had that dream once, where somebody cut him up like that. He didn't even scream. In fact, he thanked the man, the man in the shadows holding the razor. He smiled and said, "Thank you very much—I sure needed that," even as the blood spurted from his crotch like some kind of orgasm that had been going on too long. I don't know if it was a nightmare or not.

"It don't matter if you like your family or not. You're tied to 'em; might as well accept that. It's in the blood."

So, yeah, it finally happened. I met my own June, only her name was Julie, and she was quite a bit younger, and not very smart. I oughtta be embarrassed saying that, I guess. But I'm not. I did love her; still do, I'm sure. A person doesn't have to be smart, or the right age, for you to love them.

I'm never going to know, I guess, if she really loved me, or if it was just because she was younger, and not knowing what love is really, and then the girls came along; and so, like any good mother—and I'll always swear that she was a good mother—she stuck with the father of those children—however strange his thinking—and said that she loved him with all her heart. And maybe she did. Maybe she did. I've never really understood women. Not my wife. And not my daughters.

But oh, I've loved my daughters. All three of them, precious as tears. Only a couple of years apart—Julie for some crazy reason thought I wanted a son, so she insisted we keep trying, but I was overjoyed, I felt blessed, to have daughters—but my oldest, Marcie, was small for her age, and my youngest, Ann, was taller than average, and my middle daughter, Billie, was just like the middle bear, *just* right, so the three of them together were taken all the time for triplets. We were always told how adorable they were, how beautiful. People were just naturally attracted to them. And the boys? Boys are always just naturally drawn to something a little different. I know.

Things were pretty much okay until the girls got to be teenagers. Don't tell me about that being a hard time of life. I know that's a hard time of life, but knowing that still doesn't help a father much. The girls started wanting dates and it was okay with their mother, because Julie just didn't know no better, I guess. They were too damned young and I said so, but of course they went and done it anyway, and after a while I just got tired of watching them and chasing after them and let them just go right ahead and date too young and ruin their lives—what was I supposed to do?

Oh, I still loved them, you can count on that, but I have to say I was mad at them most of the time.

But my girls sure looked beautiful in those date dresses of theirs—so beautiful I couldn't stand to look at them when they were all dolled up.

They tell you on *Oprah* and *Donahue* and every other damn program what to do with your kids, but they don't tell you a damn thing that helps. They act like kids and their families are separate people that have to *negotiate* every damn thing. They just don't understand that a family's got to be all tied up in knots you can't get loose of no matter how hard you try. Cut those knots apart and somebody's bound to wind up bleeding to death on the floor.

I don't know if my girls knew I still loved them. I couldn't be sure, 'cause I stopped telling them I loved them once the oldest got to be thirteen. That might not have been the right thing to do, but I just didn't feel right, telling a young, fresh-faced beauty of thirteen that I loved her. Perverts do that, not a good family man. Not a father.

Besides, they shoulda known. They shoulda always known. We were blood, weren't we, all tied together?

The girls started their periods early. Hell, the youngest—my baby Ann—was nine, and you know that can't be right. My wife handled that stuff, of course, but she still talked to me about it—I don't know why women like to talk about such things. She told me the baby *was* young to be having her period, but that was becoming more and more common these days; but as far as I was concerned, that was hardly any kind of recommendation. Not much right about these days, what with baby girls having periods and watching actual live sex acts on the TV when their daddies ain't around. And their mothers making it a secret, too. Mothers and daughters, they always have these secrets that no man alive can understand.

What was I supposed to do about any of it? What could I do?

People expect the man to change the world, but the world is a damned hard thing to change—it just rolls on pretty much the way it wants to until it runs right over you.

Sometimes all the females in the house had their periods at the same time and the blood stank up everything and I'd wake up in the middle of the night and sometimes Julie wouldn't be in the bed and then she'd come back and say *why* she'd just been down the hall in the bathroom, but the bathroom was near where the girls slept and I'd think every time, I'd sit there in the dark and think, *What if Julie and my girls are down the hall drinking some man's blood?*

Now, I know that ain't true and it's a pretty crazy way to think, but I wasn't always sure at the time. My girls' breasts were getting bigger every day and it seemed to me they weren't eating enough at meals to be puttin' on that kind of weight.

Then one day I thought I had it figured out—they were bleeding out and they were getting breasts and hair in return, breasts and hair so they could fuck as many guys as they could before they got too old to enjoy it.

And, of course, what they were bleeding out was the family blood, dumping it like it was something dirty and all used up and something they didn't need anymore.

They were fools, of course. Like you could untie the knot by disrespecting it that way. What right did they have anyway? I was tied to them so hard I wasn't ever going to get loose, so why should *they* get their freedom? What had they ever done to earn it? Here I was, having done everything for Julie and the girls, and I was going to be tied to it forever. I wasn't ever going to be rid of the taste of their blood, their dirt, their skin. I was going to die choking on it.

I can't even say I didn't like the taste of that knot. That salty, ocean taste, like it was everything we'd ever come from for thousands of years. I can't say I didn't like it—maybe if you have something shoved in your face long enough, you hate it for a while, but maybe there comes a point—years maybe—when it's been shoved there so often you just start liking it again. You feed on it and after a while maybe that's all you live for, practically.

That was me and my wife and my girls. Our blood knot. I loved them and I hated them and then I loved them so much I couldn't be without them, couldn't let them out of my sight. It was like I had the taste of them in my mouth all the time and I was liking that taste more and more, and I just couldn't live without it, no way.

If they'd stayed home more often, things probably would've turned out okay. Maybe I would get tired of them, tired of the taste and smell of them, and I'd get tired of it all like I did when they first wanted to date, and then I'd just let them do what they damn well pleased. Julie could have made them stay home if she'd had the mind, but I married her too young and she was just too damned dumb. A good mother in every other way, but too dumb for my girls, I'm sorry to say.

I loved my girls; I loved them dear. I started trying to tell them that so maybe they'd stay at home, but it didn't work. My youngest, my baby Ann, she even laughed at me, and what's a man supposed to do with that? I would've hit her real hard right then and there, but at that point I still couldn't hit my baby girl. The other two, but not her.

I should've had boys, should've made Julie give me boys, but I never could've loved boys that way. I don't know if that's a good thing or a bad thing.

Let me explain something: I know I wasn't always the best father and husband. If I had been, I wouldn't have let things get so far. A good father and husband keeps a lid on things, keeps things from going so far. Keeping things from going so far—with his kids, his wife, the neighbors—that's the main thing a father's supposed to be doing. And I know I failed at that one.

Things collect, and they don't go away. Things get together, you get too many of them, and then things go too far.

Knots get untied. Blood gets spilled on the old, dry wooden floor, and the floor soaks it up so fast you can't believe it, lots faster than you can clean it up, and pretty soon the whole floor is stained red and everything you look at looks red.

I think they all four must have been having their period. They weren't complaining about it, but the whole house smelled like it and I tasted it in every meal for two days and I breathed that blood in every time I opened my mouth and all my clothes smelled like it and even the newspaper, and two nights running my dreams were so red I couldn't make out a thing in them.

Marcie had come back from one of her "dates." Fuck fests, more like it, but a father can't say that in front of his daughters and still be a good father. I just smiled at her and asked, "Have a nice time?" And she just stared at me, looking scared. There was no point in that—I loved her—didn't she know that?

Then I saw that my baby Ann was with her.

"What the fuck!" I yelled and immediately felt bad, saying the F word in front of my girls, but it was already out there and I couldn't get it back inside.

"Had me my first date, Daddy!" Ann piped up with her little dolly's voice. "Mom said it was okay with her. Me and Marcie, we *doubled*."

I couldn't say a damn thing, just stared at the two of them all made up like models, or whores. They'd put me down in a box, and I couldn't see how to climb my way out. I turned around and went into the bedroom and closed the door, sat down to think. Once you got a family, you don't get too much time to think.

I felt all loose with myself. I felt *untied*. The women in a family, they have a way of doing that to their men.

Being in a family is like being in a dream. You don't know if it's a good dream or a bad dream. You don't know if you're up or down. Everything moves sideways, until, before you know it, you're back where you started again, like you hadn't moved anywhere at all. That's where I was, moving sideways so fast but not going nowhere.

My girls, they started the untying. It wasn't me that did that part. My beautiful, beautiful girls. I just finished what they started.

But when you start untying that blood knot, it's more blood than anyone can imagine. It goes back forever, that blood. You taste it and you breathe it and it stains the floor and it stains the walls and it stains the skin, until you're some kind of cartoon running around stabbing and chopping and tasting.

My babies' breasts . . . aaah . . . like apples, like sweet onions, like tomatoes.

Once they were all in the blood, it was like they were being born again, crying out, "I love you, Daddy," and I could kiss them and there was not a damn thing wrong with any of it, 'cause daddies are supposed to love their babies.

Because they're your blood, you see. And you're tied to them forever.

THE GIRL WHO MARRIED THE REINDEER
Eiléan Ní Chuilleanáin

Eiléan Ní Chuilleanáin's most recent book of poetry was published by the Wake Forest University Press, and is titled *The Brazen Serpent*. She is Senior Lecturer at the School of English at Trinity College, which is part of the University of Dublin.

THE OTTER WOMAN
Mary O'Malley

Mary O'Malley is the author of two poetry collections, *Where the Rocks Float* (Salmon, 1993) and *Consideration of Silk* (Salmon, 1990). She lives in Ireland.

Both of these poets use imagery from the magical "shape-shifter" animal legends to be found across their native Ireland and throughout Europe. The poems are reprinted from *The Southern Review*, Autumn 1995 issue.

—T.W.

The Girl Who Married the Reindeer

I

When she came to the finger-post
She turned right and walked as far as the mountains.
Patches of snow lay under the thorny bush
That was blue with sloes. She filled her pockets.
The sloes piled into the hollow of her skirt.
The sunset wind blew cold against her belly
And light shrank between the branches
While her hands raked in the hard fruit.

The reindeer halted before her
And claimed her as his wife.
She rode home on his back without speaking,
Holding her rolled-up skirt,

Her free hand grasping the wide antlers
To keep her steady on the long ride.

II

How could they let her go back to stay
In that cold house with that strange beast?
So the old queen said, whose son her sister had married.

Thirteen months after she left home
She'd travelled hunched on the deck of a trader
Southwards to her sister's wedding.

Her eyes reflected acres of snow,
Her breasts were large from suckling,
There was salt in her hair.

They met her staggering on the quay;
They put her in a scented bath,
Found a silk dress, combed her hair out.
They slipped a powder in her drink
So she forgot her child, her friend,
The snow, and the sloe gin.

III

The reindeer died when his child was ten years old.
Naked in death his body was a man's.
Young, with an old man's face and scored with grief.

When the old woman felt his curse she sickened,
She lay in her tower bedroom and could not speak.
The young woman who had nursed her grandchildren nursed her.

The old witch could not undo her spell
Or the spells of time, though she groaned for power.
The nurse went downstairs to sit in the sun.

IV

The boy from the north stood in the archway
That looked into the courtyard where water fell,
His arm around the neck of his companion—
A wild reindeer staggered by sunlight.
His hair was bleached, his skin blistered.
He saw the woman in wide silk trousers
Come out of the door at the foot of the stair,

Sit on a cushion, and stretch her right hand for a hammer.
She hammered the dried, broad beans one by one,
While the swallows timed her, swinging side to side:
The hard skin fell away, and the left hand
Tossed the bean into the big brass pot.
It would surely take her all day to do them all.
She saw the child watching, her face did not change.

A light wind fled over them
As the witch died in the high tower.
She knew her child in that moment:
His body poured into her vision
Like a snake pouring over the ground,
Like a double-mouthed fountain of two nymphs,
The light groove scored on his chest
Like the meeting of two tidal roads, two oceans.

The Otter Woman

Against the wisdom of shorewomen
She stood on the forbidden line too long
And crossed the confluence of sea and river.
One shake of her body on O'Brien's Bridge
And the sea was off her.
A glorious swing from haunch to shoulder
Sent water arcing in the sunlight.
A fan of small diamonds flicked open,
Held, fell. Her smooth pelt rose into fur.

He stood and watched her from the shadows
And moved to steal her tears scattered on the riverbank.
Now he could take his time. He smoked.

She was all warm animal following the river,
Trying her new skin like a glove.
He trailed her, magnetised by the power to transform
The occasional bliss on her face, her awakened body.
Once or twice she saw him.
Her instincts were trusting on land.
They smiled. This took the whole summer.

He took her by a lake in autumn,
A sliced half moon and every star out.
The plough ready to bite the earth.

She left him on a street corner
With no choice and no glance back,
Spring and a bomber's moon.
In between their loosed demons
Played havoc in the town.

2

He pinned her to the ground, his element.
This was not what she came for
But what she got.
Soon the nap of her skin rose only for him.
It was too late to turn back.
She grew heavy out of water.

Indifferent to all but the old glory
He never asked why she always walked
By the shore, what she craved,
Why she never cried when every wave
Crescendoed like an orchestra of bones.

She stood again on the low bridge
The night of the full moon.
One sweet, deep breath and she slipped in
Where the river fills the sea.
She saw him clearly in the street light—his puzzlement.
Rid of him she let out
One low, strange cry for her human sacrifice,
For the death of love,
For the treacherous undertow of the tribe,
And dived, less marvelous forever in her element.

RESOLVE AND RESISTANCE
S. N. Dyer

"Resolve and Resistance" is a strange and splendid *homage* to the works of Jane Austen, which seems particularly appropriate in a year chock full of Austen adaptations for the screen. The story that follows, however, is unlike anything produced by the BBC . . . although it *is* a costume drama of sorts. And it does have an all-star cast.

S. N. Dyer is the pseudonym of a full-time physician in private practice. Dyer's fiction has been nominated for the Hugo, Nebula, and World Fantasy awards. "Resolve and Resistance" comes from the April issue of *Omni* magazine.

—T.W.

The beggar was in the ruins of London, leaning against the stump of a tree in the blighted field which had once been Hyde Park, watching the foreign conquerors parade arm in arm with trollops, and with girls who would not have been trollops had their fathers and sweethearts not perished in house-to-house fighting. And perhaps some of the girls were not trollops; the invasion was a year past, and the young have short memories.

The beggar shifted slightly, suppressing a moan. His absent arm and his blind eye had long since ceased to ache, but the loss of his leg was still fresh. Perhaps because he had lost it in defeat, it continued to trouble him. It was if the foot were present, each missing toe throbbing continually in phantom agony.

Sensing him move, the ginger tomcat on his shoulder began to purr, and his parrot looked over from its perch on his empty cap. "Do your duty, do your duty," it said.

He saw some officers approaching in their savage finery, led by a servile Englishman. Soon he could hear the man's voice, and recognized the broad nasal accents of his own native Norfolk. The beggar ducked his head and tried to appear asleep, leaning his face so that the cat obscured it.

"You there. Do your pets do tricks?"

He sighed. Norfolk was a large county; he could only hope that the man would not recognize him. He preferred to think that none who had ever known him could become collaborators.

"Aye, me lords," he said. "Now Nappy, where's Farmer George?" He shrugged so that the cat jumped down.

The parrot began to strut, shouting "Hooray for Boneyparte! Hooray for Boneyparte!" Then it leapt upon the cat's back and rode about contentedly.

The French officers laughed happily, and each tossed a coin into the cap. The Norfolkman bent down. "I knew a bird like that once—smaller, it was, belonged to a boatswain's mate when I was a lad."

The collaborator stared at the beggar, his gaze dissecting away the tangled shock of white hair, the disgusting beard, the missing teeth, and focusing instead upon the long thin nose, the huge black eyes. He drew in a quick breath, his own eyes widening.

"I'm done for," thought the beggar. The thought was nowhere near so unpleasant as he had expected. After losing the last battle and his leg, his hope had been of vengeance and salvation. But this year of wandering had buried any hope, even that of escape.

The Norfolkman said, "No, the parrot I knew had some yellow to him," and whispered before he drew away, "Darcy. Pemberley."

That night some roughs came and took his coins, dealt him a few blows for no good reason, and tossed his crutch away for the sheer pleasure of watching him crawl after it. Nappy and Farmer George had taken refuge together in one of the few standing trees, and watched their master's new humiliation with impassive eyes.

The beggar did not care. He raised himself upon his crutch and hobbled back, whistling for his pets. He had a destination now, though he had no idea where Pemberley might be, or what manner of man Darcy. But for the first time in a year he had more to his life than pain and the shadow of inchoate yearnings.

And so, smiling, a green Indies parrot upon his left shoulder, a flearidden orange cat curled in his lap, Horatio Lord Nelson, Viscount Bronte, Knight of the Bath, Commander in Chief of the Channel Fleet, fell asleep and dreamed of battles that would never be and of others that would never end.

Two months later he arrived at Pemberley. The nights had turned cold, and he knew that if he did not find refuge here, he would not survive the winter.

The village was surprisingly prosperous, as if bypassed by the war and the blockade. He saw French soldiers laughing outside a pub, ruffling the hair of a child, and he felt unreasoning hatred for these simple country folk. In Norfolk, in Yorkshire, even in Scotland and Wales, those wild lands with the least claim of loyalty to their Hanoverian king—there guerrillas fought a war that was vicious and unrelenting. In the ports and harbours of England, old men and boys halfheartedly rebuilt burned-out shipyards and raised scuttled vessels, all that had been left by the navy and merchant ships which even now set forth from colonial ports under the guidance of the exiled Prince of Wales. England still ruled the waves, she just did not rule herself. But here, now, it was if the war had never occurred, and the Frenchmen were the invited guests of Mad George.

He stopped by the pump, drank his fill, then cupped his hands for his comrades. The parrot stood upon the cat's back to drink, and they soon had a small audience for their small performance.

A pair of French officers emerged from a shop and watched Nelson.

"*Très amusant,*" said one.

"He must come with us," said the other. "The fair Elisabeth appreciates oddities."

They mounted their horses, nervous Thoroughbreds who were obvious booty from the stables of some Englishman of taste. "You there," an officer called.

Nelson looked blank until the fellow spoke to him again in English. "You there, beggar, come with us. Madame will give you dinner and a place to sleep."

Nelson nodded and tugged on his hat in a crippled imitation of servility. He whistled. Farmer George's sole trick was to leap up to his shoulder. As ever the cat managed to make it seem he had done it of his own accord as well as a great favor to his master.

The Frenchmen rode slowly, admiring the fine hedgerows and fertile fields where they soon intended to hunt, while Nelson stumped along behind. They were entirely unaware that he understood them, and probably would not have cared had they known.

"You will like Elisabeth, Jean-Paul, but remember—she will not award you her favors. I believe she is holding out for the emperor himself."

"Perhaps he'll let me search her."

Nelson gritted his teeth and gripped his crutch more firmly, longing to dash out the man's brain. The casual joke encompassed a tragedy which had struck him as severely as the fall of his country, and even now made his one good eye see through a crimson fog. Emma. His beautiful Emma. She had gone to Bonaparte in the guise of a lover and the role of an assassin, and had met her fate at the guillotine that had replaced the gallows at Tyburn field. While she died in futile bravery, he skulked anonymously about the country, senselessly preserving his life. Emma had died in a vainglorious gesture for her country—and now she was reduced to a sniggering policy of caution.

"Elisabeth may set her sights high," the Frenchman continued. "She is quite the original. Your average Englishwoman, of course, will sleep with anyone for a dram of gin, and not be worth the price."

Once more, Nelson's fingers tightened about his crutch. What beneficent God would reduce him so, and now force him to smile as the women of his country were denigrated? Nappy chanted again, "Do your duty, do your duty."

"The sisters, tell me again of the sisters."

"Ah. *Les belles filles Bennetts*. Jane is the most beautiful, but she is faithful to her boring husband Bingley. Mary is a bluestocking; any man who tries to seduce her will die of boredom. Lydia, though—ah Lydia." It was clear from his lascivious tones exactly how friendly Lydia might be.

"She is a widow, and you know how they are. Kitty, now, she is malleable and will do what she sees others are doing."

"I see," said Jean-Paul. "But in this fine household of Madame Darcy, I have one question. . . ."

At the name Darcy, Nelson's heart began to beat faster, and not merely from the exertion.

"Where might be Monsieur Darcy?"

"You must ask Elisabeth, she says it so amusingly. How foolish he acted, she will say. Did he not know how interesting and entertaining we soldiers of the Empire would be? It certainly served her husband right, to refuse us hospitality and to be shot instantly dead."

One may toss a bucket overboard, a bucket of slop, of blood, of fine wine. It does not matter. It will strike the water, spread forth, and in seconds dissolve entirely, no trace of it remaining in the grand, cruel ocean. So it was, then, with Nelson's last hope.

Sometimes, in the grip of extreme hunger or fatigue, he felt his mind slip into a delirium the equal of those which had tormented him during his various tropical fevers. Now, hurrying after the horsemen, he felt the waking dreams come upon him once more. He was in charge again of the fleet, but this time the invasion force did not slip past him in the fog, as had previous French fleets at Alexandria and Toulon. This time he did not sate his fury upon empty vessels, nor send Hardy and the ships to Brighton to rescue whom they might while he and his marines hopelessly pursued the vast army on land. . . .

This time he came instead upon the fleet a mile off Portsmouth, and set his own ships amongst it, pell-mell, without regard to the line. Cannons exploded, ships burned, and he gave no quarter, listening to the screams of drowning men and horses, while in reality he walked a sunlit path, smelling late autumn roses and hearing the song of the mockingbird.

In his mind he had fought not only this battle but others, his tactical sense and his rage so heightened that, did he only think he might go to some harbor without being recognized and captured, might find some vessel to smuggle him away to the colonies, might meet up with his men again and command a fleet—then he should be the invincible arm of terror and destruction. Then no Continental ship should ever leave its port, no ship at all touch shore upon his besieged island home. . . .

And to what avail, even in his dreams? He who was thought dead and was as good as such; no hero in hiding, to save his nation. Only a crippled and sun-touched old sailor, masquerading as a buffoon for so long that it no longer seemed a masque.

His reverie ended at the finely wrought gates of Pemberley. The great home, like its village, seemed untouched by conflict. Perhaps more horses had once graced its stables, perhaps famous pictures and crystal chandeliers no longer decorated its halls. No matter, it seemed whole and inviolate.

The only curiosity was a building beside the stable, its equal in size but with walls of canvas. Odd sounds emanated from the massive shed.

"Philippe, what is that?" asked the younger officer, echoing Nelson's silent question.

"Did I not tell you that Elisabeth loves oddities? She has given refuge to a genuine ancient eccentric, who is building . . ." Here he paused to laugh, and could barely continue, ". . . building a balloon that will travel to the moon."

"But that is absurd. It could not fly high enough. . . ."

"Ah yes, but he uses chemicals rather than hot air, and . . ." Again he interrupted himself, this time with a fit of ungentlemanly giggling ". . . and he will harness birds to it, and they will pull it to the moon!"

"Oh dear," said Jean-Paul. "And so if the lovely ladies take us hunting, as you said they would, then we will be slaying the steeds of this noble effort!" He, too, succumbed to merriment.

And so, reflected Nelson, I seek refuge with a woman whose sense of cruelty delights in allowing madmen to make fools of themselves. I should be most welcome.

* * *

Farmer George and Nappy performed their act at the doorstep for Madame Darcy and her sisters. The women were indeed beauty incarnate, wearing fashionable gowns of simple, sheer silk that were testimony to their collusion with the enemy. They watched with vague ennui, never gracing Nelson with more than the briefest of superior glances.

The lady of the house then ordered her butler to take the beggar below and bathe him—"Twice," she added imperiously—and bring him to dinner. He protested, but her odd whims seemed to be law.

This, Nelson reflected, might be a danger equal to any he had faced since being wounded and finding refuge in the hidden cellar of a smuggler—a man who had made his living circumventing the law and profiting from the enemy, but who in the throes of invasion proved himself a better friend to his country than so many who had adhered to the conventional path, and ultimately dying a more virtuous death than many.

Nelson submitted to the bath and allowed himself to be dressed in coat and breeches which must have belonged to the late and apparently unlamented Mr. Darcy, but he refused to be shaved. Examining his now trimmed coif and beard in a small mirror, even he could barely recognize his famous features, sunburned and lined with illness and fatigue. Still he took pains to rearrange his hair so that it stood at odd angles, and to put the neckerchief in disarray.

Dinner was a bizarre yet festive occasion, so great a feast that one would not suspect the nation to be under the yoke of a dictator, the people starving from the thievery of the conquerors and from the half-successful blockade of the remnants of their own navy.

Madame Darcy had placed the French colonel at the head of the table and flirted with him shamelessly and relentlessly, though with an undercurrent of coldness that signified a resolution to maintain her virtue. Her sister Jane and husband Bingley were bluff English gentry, polite, hearty, and entirely ignorant of the fact that they were engaged in giving comfort to the enemy. Lydia Wickham, evidently the widow of an army captain who had died in service, was even more the strumpet than the Frenchman had implied, and her sister, Kitty Bennett, seemed to possess that lack of discrimination which was common to the animal for which she had been named.

The final sister, Mary Bennett, was actually engaged in reading at table. Beside her sat an ancient wearing an ornate, outmoded long wig and a dressing gown, who babbled on to himself about something called chymical economy. Occasionally Mary would look up from her book and address a question to this Lord Henry, and then their conversation would become so abstruse as to seem to be conducted in a foreign tongue. Madame Darcy's father, Mr. Bennett, finished the party, an oblivious gentleman who did not seem perturbed by his daughters' scandalous behavior.

No one at this table of ignorance, licentiousness, and madness spoke a word to Nelson. He thought back to his meals with his sailors, and tried to behave in the uncouth nature of the untutored, eating with his fingers or a knife, downing his watered wine in a single gulp. And indeed, after a year of living upon the rude charity of the road, he did not have to entirely feign the manners of a starveling.

He ate in fear of committing some error which might call attention to the reality of himself. His identity itself must be safe, for he was presumed dead. His boatswain, after entrusting the care of his parrot to the wounded admiral—or perhaps it had been the opposite—had taken Nelson's bloodstained coat and attempted to sell its wealth of medals. Eager French officials had known it immediately to be a relic of the missing Nelson; the boatswain had then bragged of stripping the coat from a corpse hastily tossed into some mire, and held to this brave contention even to his death.

But while no one would suspect this pitiful beggar of being the late commander in chief, surely they could recognize him as a fugitive gentleman. Investigation would then identify him—and he would be disposed of swiftly by firing squad, or slowly and visibly with farcical trial. Or most likely, and most detestable, he would be pardoned in a humiliating show of magnanimity to the fallen nation, to be kept as a crippled caricature of his former dignity. Kept as a house pet, fed and groomed and brought out at state dinners to shout "Hooray for Boneyparte."

"Has your cat lost as many lives as you?"

Nelson started back to the moment. Miss Mary Bennett was speaking to him. "Whatever d'ye mean, milady?"

"It is said that a cat has nine lives. You have obviously had a number of misadventures, losing your leg and your arm. Your right eye would also seem to be weak. . . ."

He cursed it silently. It did not appear scarred or shrunken as did so many sightless eyes, but the damned thing had lately taken to wandering.

". . . and that scar you attempt to hide with your hair is most impressive. In fact, the mere fact that your hair is entirely gray and your age not so very advanced—fifty, I should judge—bespeaks a life of action. . . ."

"Sister," yawned Elisabeth Darcy, cutting short the disquisition, "you are wont to experiment thoroughly with boring subjects, and as such have quite lost the ability to be entertaining. Philippe here has been telling us that the emperor will soon come to residence in the city, and you would rather hear the sanguine life story of an accident-prone drunkard."

And so the table was instead regaled with news of the imminent resumption of the social scene. Madame Darcy ended dinner with the announcement that she would, indeed, winter in London, and enjoy the opportunities of which the metropolis provided. Next the gentlemen called for brandy and the women briefly retired, and Nelson was escorted to a windowless room with a cot, where his pets awaited. He was instructed to remain there, no matter what he might hear.

He woke after midnight to the sound of an opening door, and groped for the feeble defense of his crutch. Farmer George, foolish beast, began to purr as he always did upon half-wakening, and Nappy, now off his best behaviour, squawked, "Do your duty, men. Do your duty."

A figure stood in the doorway—Madame Darcy, with her hair down now, and clad in a simple muslin gown which gleamed ghastly in the light of a candle.

Marvels abound, thought Nelson. Did her interest in oddities thus include their amatory prowess? He had been celibate for a long time, at first with a sailor's tired stoicism. Then his mistress had been executed and his wife Fanny, determined not to be outshone even in death by her rival, had succumbed in some equally foolish show of resistance. In this act of sublime stupid bravery she had been joined by his stepson Josiah, who had saved his life at Tenerife. . . . And with the deaths of those women he had loved had died also any carnal longings.

Nor did he think his ill and battered body, whose suffering was equal to that of his spirit, willing to acquiesce to any erotic adventure. But Madame Darcy was lovely and spirited, if devious and cruel. And if such a woman was of a mind to seduce this wretched bit of humanity, he doubted not that she would possess the means to bring him to the mark.

She slipped into the room, closing the door, and waved the candle at his eyes. "As I thought," she said. "The right does react less swiftly. You are blind in that eye, are you not?"

"Ey, mum, this ain't done now. . . ." he whined.

"Enough." She spoke as one used to command. "I observed you at table. Your ill manners were most well done, but I sensed the inner battle against proper behavior. You are a gentleman, are you not? And a man blind in his right eye, absent his right arm, with evidence of a serious head wound . . ."

He had an uncomfortable presentiment where this trail might end. "Missing me left peg, too, mum."

She waved dismissively. "One cannot expect things to remain static. Sir, I must know—are you Admiral Nelson?"

He sighed. It was over. "That I am, madame. At your service." He waved his left arm in a parody of a flourish, unable to bow as the scene demanded.

To his surprise, she fell to her knees, clasped his hand in hers, and raised it to a face now glistening with tears. "Oh milord, how I have prayed for such a happenstance as this!"

She led him through a house strangely active, then outside. It seemed that half the yeomen of the district were present. "Will you not wake the Frenchmen?"

She laughed. "They think themselves exhausted by Lydia and Kitty, but in truth it is Mary's botanicals."

The studious sister, leading out the ancient eccentric, said, "A simple dissolution of laudanum and extraction of . . ."

"Later, sister," sighed Elisabeth Darcy. They passed men practicing with rifles. When one is constantly entertaining hunters, the lady explained, it was only natural that some weapons and charge might disappear, and be put to better use.

They came to the huge shed. The canvas had been drawn up. A strange vessel rested there, a framework of light wood above an open boat. Four similar craft sat behind it.

"What then, do you need my knowledge to invade the moon?"

"No," replied Madame Darcy, "to invade London."

She turned and curtsied. "Lord Nelson, your fleet awaits."

In reality, his fleet was nowhere near ready. The moonboats were not, as Nelson had feared, mere balloons harnessed together. Rather than hot air, they relied upon a heretofore unknown substance which Lord Henry Cavendish referred to as dephlogisticated air, which he formed of water and electricity.

"Lord Henry, you must know," Miss Mary Bennett took pains to inform Nelson, "is the man who weighed the earth."

"A boon to humanity, I am sure," he replied. But he was pleasantly surprised the first time he took his flagship up. It veritably sprang into the air, angered at restraint, and reaccepted the ground only grudgingly as the odd gas was returned into storage vats.

"Did I mention," asked Lord Henry casually as he flew with Nelson one night above the trees, "that dephlogisticated air is remarkably inflammable and will explode upon any contact with fire or lightning?"

"Musket fire as well?"

"A direct hit to a gasbag would prove fatal," the desiccated old man replied. "I trust that I have placed the bags high enough, and sealed them adequately, to prevent the sparks of our own flints from igniting them. But one must lack certainty without the opportunity of direct observation."

Ah well. Nelson had seen first rates explode when fire reached their magazines, had risked it himself. No one who had ever witnessed such a conflagration—the awful roar, the instant extinction of hundreds of men—no one could forget such a sight. Yet one still sailed into battle.

There was much to do. Before teaching the crews, Nelson had first to devise methods of flying. It was a bit like sailing, in that one was at the mercy of wind and weather, but it differed in the addition of the vertical.

Long sails might be extended laterally from a ship, to aid in steering. These might even be manned as oars, if the ship were to become becalmed.

The crew, when aloft, wore ropes about their waists in case of turbulence. Nelson had a set of leather belts with which he strapped himself to a forward strut, whence he might survey both the ship and the path ahead. From this odd perch, jutting out somewhat like a figurehead, he could see sepulchral wisps of cloud, and the dark fields below, divided by fence and hedge and sparkling ribbons of water. At times it seemed almost inviting, calling to him to step away, to fly freely. . . . And then he was glad of his bonds, like Odysseus tied to his mast, listening to the song of the siren maidens.

There were signals to devise, and marksmen to train. His sergeants in this were a pair of poachers known as the Wheat brothers, Dick and Rees, unruly men who could hide in a tree and shoot a rabbit through the eye. This seemed a valuable talent, and soon Nelson was sending all his new marines into treetops, both to impart to them the skill of shooting accurately downward, and to steel them to heights. His men were armed with rifles, which gave them some small advantage— they might accurately shoot three times the distance of a French musket. But those French muskets, of course, outnumbered them by the thousands.

There was no lack of volunteers. Madame Darcy's collection of oddities, it seemed, contained several former soldiers and a surveyor, all pretending to be farmhands. Nelson's own lamentable cover identity was Mad Tom the human scarecrow: on pleasant days he stood in the housegarden and waved his crutch at birds. It was a humiliating performance that he found himself entering with no qualms, to the extent that he sometimes abased himself further, to earn a coin from an amused French visitor.

He began each night as a beggar, rag-clad, red-eyed. Yet as he entered the shed and passed amongst the shadows of the moonboats he became a different man, standing straighter, pain ignored, voice deep and resolute. Those who laughed at him by day took his orders by night, and wondered to themselves who their new admiral might be.

And so he would find himself in the helm of a moonboat, snapping commands to the boys as they ran aloft in the riggings—for other than the few old soldiers designated for boarding, and the indispensable Wheat brothers, it seemed best to have lightweight crewmen. This allowed the boat to go higher, and gave them the luxury of lining the underside of the balloon casings with a padding of burlap—sufficient, it was to be hoped, to prevent musket fire from piercing the bags and igniting the dephlogisticated air.

One cloudy night he determined to take his men up all together, to practice some vague concept of formation flying. The surveyor was complaining bitterly—he had just finished painting figureheads upon the boat, carved wood seeming an excessive weight, and the paint was not yet dry on Nelson's flagship, the *Electra*. The name amused him, as he remembered his triumphs in the *Agamemnon*.

He had thought himself immune to surprise, but as he donned an extra coat—for it was cold aloft, and cloaks tended to become entangled in the rigging—he saw the five Bennett sisters approach him, scandalously attired in breeches and jackets.

"Ladies!" he said. "We do not embark upon a pleasure voyage."

He did not share the superstition that women were bad luck aboard a ship, and in any event, they had yet to invent new superstitions suitable to the airships.

"This is not a cruise," agreed Elisabeth Darcy. "We have always intended to captain these ships ourselves. We are smaller even than your village lads, we are familiar with London and its troop dispositions due to our recent journey of reconnaissance. And if we are ignorant of seamanship—why, so are the men of this county, and all humanity is equally ignorant of airmanship. To further my qualifications I am also, as you are no doubt aware, the general as it were of the Free Patriot Army of this part of England."

He actually had not been aware, but it did explain some of the surreptitious visitors and odd meetings he had noticed. It also explained his old shipmate's message to him. "But . . ."

"And besides . . ." said Lydia, a dueling pistol appearing suddenly in her hand. She aimed at a rat which was skulking in shadow toward the stables. There was a brief thunderclap, the smell of powder, and the rodent fell twitching. Lydia smiled, her small teeth gleaming ferally in the moonlight. . . . "And besides, our solicitous French friends have turned us all into crack shots. And we are, I do not blush to say, utterly ruthless."

He had some question regarding that—he had seen Jane cry over a wounded sparrow, and thought Mary might be quite distracted from combat by the sight of an interesting toadstool, but he did admit that Elisabeth and Lydia had the makings of diligent and stern warriors, and that Kitty might be relied on to do whatever the others did, only more vigorously.

"Very well," he said. "But be warned that, as admiral of this fleet, I shall not temper my language or orders out of regard for your sex."

"Be certain you do not," snapped Elisabeth, and she and her sisters each betook themselves to the helm of a moonboat.

Mr. Bennett tended to be somewhat overwhelmed by the activities of his daughters, though he was often heard to say, "If Lizzy believes it correct, I shall abide by her decision." He spent most of his days in the nursery, supervising the education of the various tiny Bingleys, Darcys, and Wickhams who were trotted out intermittently after meals or on sunny afternoons, and were otherwise kept in seclusion.

One day Bennett came to Nelson's small room. One of Nelson's periodic fevers had recurred, and he lay drenched in sweat, sipping bitter quinine and hoping that he would recover in time for their proposed action upon Boxing Day, or weather not permitting, upon the New Year's Day. It seemed wise to attack when the better part of their foes, complacent with garrison duty, would be obtunded from holiday celebrations.

As always when his master had a fever, Farmer George hovered closely, delighting in the heat and adding his own feline warmth to Nelson's discomfort.

"Brought you something, Mad Tom," said Bennett, with a slight cough of disparagement. He, as all the men, held clueless suspicions regarding Nelson's identity.

"Thought you might like it," he continued, and held up an antique scarlet uniform coat. "My great uncle's. Can't have you going into battle dressed as a beggar now, can we? Meaning no offense, of course," as he recalled that the man was a beggar.

Nelson thanked him. It did suit his purpose. His crew were to wear no signs of identification, to aid in their escape should such be necessary. He, however, lacking various limbs as he did, had no chance of escape, and would prefer to die in the uniform of his nation. Even a uniform some fifty years outdated.

They held their final conference on Christmas morning. The Yule log roared in the fire, and Cavendish rattled on a bit about the hazards of the explosive grenades he had concocted, the need to watch the temperature of the air in relation to the balloon's ascension, and various other facts with which Nelson was already depressingly familiar.

"And now," said the aged scholar, "I believe I have finished my role in this comedy of patriotism. I have noticed certain properties in stationary bodies of water which make me believe it will be possible to weigh the moon, and I have delayed my investigations into this matter long enough." He left the room, and only Elisabeth's peremptory command kept her sister Mary from hurrying off to discuss this interesting mathematical question with the old gentleman.

"Very well," said Elisabeth. They went over the plans again. The Free Patriot Army—a motley selection of allied individual groups which tended to the occasional act of terror or thievery—was to be alerted but only when the fleet was already above London, to keep any from suspecting trouble and rousing the troops. Their own men were to begin the day's action, however, by silently capturing the semaphore stations which allowed messages to be transmitted across country at a shocking speed. They would send their own message, but only when the moonboats had begun their action.

Mr. Bennett entered the room as they were ending their conference. "I had thought we ought to ask the vicar to dine tonight, and hold services for the holy day," he said.

"It will not be convenient, Father. We have planned otherwise," replied Elisabeth. "Tonight we leave to invade and conquer London."

"If you think it advisable, Lizzy," her father returned.

Then they went to prepare for the night's action. Nelson allowed himself to be shaved, and his hair to be tied back with a riband. His cat, meanwhile, bathed in equal self-satisfaction, and the parrot groomed its feathers.

"We are," he remarked, "the Spartan army, bathing and oiling that they might look well as they die." It felt good to be back in uniform, even this foolish antiquated one, and to speak again in his own voice.

The troops seemed taken aback by Mad Tom's transformation. He leaned against the railing of the *Electra*, uniformed, his gaze hard and steady, as the crews gathered in the twilight by the moonboats. The craft had taken on a full load of dephlogisticated air, and they strained against their bonds like cavalry horses eager for battle. He called for their attention.

"England expects every man—and woman—to do his—or her—duty."

Elisabeth Bennett stepped forward. "My friends"—only a woman would exhort warriors so—"tonight, with the Almighty's help, we will liberate our captive nation, and free ourselves from the onerous and odious foreigners. And lest you doubt that God has already given us every sign of his favor, let me remind you that in our hour of need he sent us this man to lead us into battle. Sent us Horatio Nelson, hero of the Nile, Commander in Chief of the British Navy."

Her troops exchanged astonished glances, then began to cheer. It was only with a loud shout and his much enhanced reputation that Nelson was able to restore order.

Then suddenly the damned parrot had flown onto his shoulder and was shouting, "Do your duty, do your duty."

He was never sure what fool had set them loose, but the cat was there as well, scrabbling up into the rigging, and the parrot had flown amongst the gasbags. It would take too long to catch them; they would simply have to come along. And when he stopped to consider it, they were in fact the only veterans of naval combat at his command.

"Set sail," he ordered. High above, Nappy called, "Hooray for Boneyparte! Do your duty!"

The most astonishing thing about air travel was its utter silence. Floating now above the clouds, guided only by compass and the surveyor's dead reckoning, linked by dark lanterns flashing code, they were alone in a world of black sky and white clouds. There were, to be sure, various creaks and aching sounds from the rigging, the soft ripples of the billowing sail, and the occasional odd beat of the mechanical wings as they corrected course, but in all the impression was of silence. They traveled within the clouds themselves, cleaving through the ghastly, fluffy field of white. The cold haze of the clouds was nothing like the salt spray of the ocean. But Nelson felt strangely at home.

The ships seemed to fly as if possessed, and the crews as well. Nelson found himself under constant scrutiny, village lads looking at him with what could only be termed worship. When the *Meryton* came alongside, he even surprised Mr. Bingley (acting as second in command to his wife) with a similar expression. The jaded, familiar voices of the Bennett women, immune to hero worship, were a relief.

"You should not have told them, Captain Darcy," he said to Elisabeth. She was perched high in the prow beside him, telescope at the ready. "They now feel themselves invincible."

She merely smiled.

Travel without regard to roads and waterways was remarkably quick. They were over London within hours; odd how one disregarded the stench of the place when one approached slowly by land or sea, but how it struck one almost physically as one floated down gently from above.

Until now, if seen at all, they must have been considered part of the clouds. As they began to draw lower they would be apparent to those below. Nelson suspected, however, that most who noticed them at this hour would be drunk, and the rest (he hoped) disbelieving or awestruck.

Their good luck was, indeed, unbelievable unless (as Mistress Darcy would have it, and Nelson might once have been inclined to accept) God was for them. They hovered far above the Tower of London.

"If Bonaparte is not there, we are done for," said Nelson.

Elisabeth, peering below with her telescope, made an impatient sound. "Remember the cowardice of the man. He could not sleep in a captive nation but inside a fortress. Besides, I have had intelligence from within."

One could hardly argue with that. Nelson nodded. Perhaps he should give some new, bold signal to his fleet—but he had not the heart.

Instead, he signaled for commencement of their plan. The *Electra* and *Boadicea* were to land, whilst aboard the *Boyle*, Mary Bennett would discover whether the grenades were truly effective by dropping them upon the guardhouses. Nelson hoped that there were not many Englishmen amongst the French, then shook his head quickly. If so, they were collaborators, and deserved what fate might overtake them.

The *Beryton* and the *Canada* contained the bulk of their sharpshooters, and were to stay above, offering covering fire.

Nelson sighed, slipping free of his restraints and wrapping his arm about the post. He was about to land in the enemy stronghold, he was beplumed and dressed in an absurd outfit of bright red, he could not run—one might think him nothing but a target to draw fire. Yet had not he always stayed upon the quarterdeck during melees, dressed in his every medal, seeming to dare the sharpshooters to take him? Best to do battle in the same manner he always had before.

They were halfway down—landing was always a bit unsettling, the ground rushing up beneath you, your stomach lagging a good ten paces behind, and the hope that the illiterate blacksmith's apprentice piloting the ship had judged the descent properly, lest all come to resemble a pudding dropped from a bell tower—when a guardsman looked up and began to scream.

Nelson heard a sharp retort, and saw the guard fall. "Never has so much been owed to a handful of poachers," he thought. Around him, rifles began to fire. His men had the advantage. He saw the Wheat brothers calmly take aim and fire, lads behind them reloading, while the terrified French soldiers could not even reach the ships with their musket fire, which then tended to return to them. . . . But then they had fallen within musket range.

"Do your duty!" screamed his bird.

"Get above, you idiot," Nelson cursed, and immediately swore again, as he felt sharp claws dig into his shoulder. The terrorized Farmer George was moving on to his accustomed refuge.

The surprise unbalanced him entirely and he pitched backward, but not before hearing a musket ball pass far too close. It singed his scalp and tore the unfortunate cat off his shoulder and into eternity. Another had died for his sake—and if the cat had not surprised him, it would instead be he who had been sent to greet his forebears.

Elisabeth skidded down beside him. "Admiral? Are you . . ."

"Damnation! Help me up," he said. He was bleeding, but this time it mercifully poured over his blind eye, leaving his vision unencumbered. "Then see to that lad."

That lad was beyond help—a belly wound. But deferring his own medical help in favor of the sailors had always won Nelson their hearts, and this time was no different.

There was an explosion, and great gouts of flame leapt up beyond the wall. Evidently Cavendish's inventions had succeeded again.

The *Electra* thumped to her rest upon the ground, Nelson barely retaining footing. The crew was half off already, screaming and drawing weapons for close fighting—a few swords and cutlasses, more pitchforks and scythes. "For England! For Nelson! For George!" they shouted and their admiral, a bit concussed by the bullet, wondered if that final cheer were for his cat.

Then he was out of the moonboat, hobbling furiously for cover. Soldiers were approaching from the opposite side of the ship. Elisabeth turned, smiling with narrowed lips and eyes, and shot directly into the central airbag. The dephlogisticated air exploded, destroying the *Electra* and taking out the majority of the pursuers. Still though, she had been a noble ship and he regretted her loss.

They could hear shouts and firing inside the Tower. As Elisabeth had expected—she was so much the optimist—the English servants had fallen upon their foreign masters.

They met up with the crew of the *Boadicea*. Nelson watched as Lydia, a knife in her teeth and her blouse open to the waist in a remarkable display, put a bullet through a guardsman's chest and a second bullet through another's throat, then paused calmly amidst the carnage to reload her pistols.

They entered the Tower. He found himself lagging far behind, stumbling now and then over the body of a foe or friend. Once he rounded a corner only to find himself staring directly into the muzzle of a French officer's pistol. Only then the man's mistress smashed a chamberpot down upon his head.

"Thank you, madame," said Nelson. Leaning against the wall, he was able to doff his absurd feathered hat. Of course, the parrot upon his shoulder made the gesture a bit less courtly.

"My pleasure, sir," she replied, taking up the loaded gun and departing, in search of new game, he presumed.

Then he was in a large ornate bedchamber with his men (and women) holding guns outstretched on one side, and on the other Napoleon Bonaparte himself, clad in an astonishing saffron nightgown and surrounded by loyal guards.

"You cannot escape," said Elisabeth. Outside a building exploded. Damn! Had they not expressly asked Mary to spare the magazine, of which they might have future need?

"What will it be?" Elisabeth continued. "Die now, and let your men fight on to keep the country? Little good that will do you!"

The emperor's pudgy face contorted as he thought. What to choose, safety and surrender, or glorious death? It was certain that, while he would ordinarily not hesitate to opt for the former, he was having unexpected difficulty with the choice. The man was not entirely without honor.

"I cannot surrender—not to rabble, not to women," he cried.

"Then surrender to me," said Nelson, limping forward. He bent down and shook off his hat, then looked directly at Bonaparte. Would his famous profile, his well-known haunted eyes, reveal his identity despite the comic but blood-soaked costume and the parrot?

Napoleon's eyes widened and his jaw dropped in the moment of recognition. Then he smirked. "If I have been defeated, it has been at the hands of a dead hero."

"My death, perhaps, was reported prematurely, sir," replied Nelson. "May I have your sword?"

Bonaparte gestured to his men to put down their guns, then proffered his sword, hilt outward.

Nelson smiled, and waved his hand dismissively. "I fear I cannot oblige you without help. Captain Darcy?"

And to the emperor's eternal scandal, the woman went forward to accept the token of surrender.

At that moment Nappy began to squawk. "Hooray for Boneyparte," he said. "Hooray!"

The admiral of the airfleet and savior of England sighed. He was obviously going to have to work on his pet's repertoire.

It is a truth universally acknowledged that a single woman in possession of the gratitude of her nation must be in want of a husband.

Nelson, newly bandaged, having set guards about the castle and having supervised the incarceration of the prisoners and the sending of messages regarding the victory, as well as briefly paying his respects to his oblivious mad monarch, had been pleased to discover his own medals in the possession of the emperor. Their familiar weight gave solidity to the scarlet coat. All this exertion, far from tiring him, had exhilarated him. He found, also, that for the first time in a year his missing left leg no longer ached.

He located the Bennett sisters in a drawing room, finely painted though its decorations and the bulk of its furnishings had been removed as booty long ago. They sat demurely, pistols beside them, as the staff served tea. Jane was silent; Mr. Bingley had been amongst the casualties. However Kitty, one arm in a sling, was remarkably ebullient.

"It is settled then, Elisabeth," she was saying. "You shall accept no less than the Prince of Wales."

He sat, and allowed the captain of his late flagship to pour him a cup of tea. Nelson admitted that it did seem a good match. One felt that this year of fugitive adversity must have matured George, honing him from a dissipated selfish fop into a stern, dedicated patriot. Or so one, at least, hoped.

"And for Jane?" That sister wiped away a tear. It was clear she would maintain deep mourning for at least a year. "Another royal duke?"

"I think not," said Elisabeth thoughtfully. "We shall need the royal dukes single, to induce treaties. So many sovereigns have marriageable daughters."

"Allow me to recommend my executive officer and dear friend Captain Hardy," said Nelson, entering into the spirit of the thing. "A capable man, and I'm sure he has been promoted to admiral in my absence."

Jane allowed that she might take it under advisement.

"Well, I want a duke," said Kitty, and began to pout. "Foreign would do, just not from too far east."

"And you, Mary?"

The studious sister glanced up from a book of philosophy she had discovered in Napoleon's bedchamber. "I suppose I shall have to marry Lord Henry. I do, after all, bear his child."

This comment had the insalubrious effect of ending all conversation for the space of several minutes.

Then Nelson wished the ladies happy, and rose. He imagined he had more to do that evening, to ensure their safety until the navy returned and the army was reconstituted.

"Does no one intend to ask my future?" asked Lydia suddenly.

Nelson paused. "I had presumed, Captain Wickham, that you would wish to remain with your ship, and make a career, as it were, of flight." The new air navy would need experienced officers.

"Not enough," she said, and rose to walk over to where he stood leaning upon his crutch. She took his lapels in her hands, and came very close. "Not enough to be a captain. I wish an admiral."

Nelson felt a sudden odd weakness before her predatory gaze, and realized something else. For so long his life had been circumscribed by pain and want. And now, in his time of triumph, pain had retreated—and he felt the first stirring of that other long dormant phantom, of pleasure.

"It may yet be arranged," he replied.

LA DAME
Tanith Lee

Tanith Lee lives with her husband John Kaiine by the sea in Great Britain and is a highly esteemed and prolific writer of fantasy, science fiction, and horror. Her most recent books include *Darkness, I; Vivia; Eva Fairdeath; Reigning Cats and Dogs; Gold Unicorn; Elephantasm;* and *Nightshades: a novella and stories.* Her dark fairy tales have been collected in *Red as Blood, or Tales From the Sister Grimmer,* and other stories have been collected in *Forests of the Night, Women as Demons,* and *Dreams of Dark and Light.* Lee has won the World Fantasy Award for her short fiction and has had stories reprinted in previous volumes of *The Year's Best Fantasy & Horror.*

"La Dame" is a lush tale about a unique seductress from *Sisters of the Night,* edited by Barbara Hambly and Martin H. Greenberg.

—E.D.

> "The game is done! I've won! I've won!"
> Quoth she, and whistles thrice.
> —Coleridge, *The Ancient Mariner*

Of the land, and what the land gave you—war, pestilence, hunger, pain—he had had enough. It was the sea he wanted. The sea he went looking for. His grandfather had been a fisherman, and he had been taken on the ships in his boyhood. He remembered enough. He had never been afraid. Not of water, still or stormy. It was the ground he had done with, full of graves and mud.

His name was Jeluc, and he had been a soldier fourteen of his twenty-eight years. He looked a soldier as he walked into the village above the sea.

Some ragged children playing with sticks called out foul names after him. And one ran up and said, "Give us a coin." "Go to hell," he answered, and the child let him alone. It was not a rich village.

The houses huddled one against another. But at the end of the struggling, straggling street, a long stone pier went out and over the beach, out into the water. On the beach there were boats lying in the slick sand, but at the end of the pier was a ship, tied fast, dipping slightly like a swan.

She was pale as ashes, and graceful, pointed, and slender, with a single mast, the yard across it with a sail the color of turned milk bound up. She would take a crew of three, but one man could handle her. She had a little cabin with a hollow window and door.

Birds flew scavenging round and round the beach; they sat on the house roofs between, or on the boats. But none alighted on the ship.

Jeluc knocked on the first door. No one came. He tried the second and third doors, and at the fourth a woman appeared, sour and scrawny.

"What is it?" She eyed him like the devil. He was a stranger.

"Who owns the pale ship?"

"The ship? Is Fatty's ship."

"And where would I find Fatty?"

"From the wars, are you?" she asked. He said nothing. "I have a boy to the wars. He never came back."

Jeluc thought, Poor bitch. Your son's making flowers in the muck. But then, the thought, What would he have done here?

He said again, "Where will I find Fatty?"

"Up at the drinking-house," she said, and pointed.

He thanked her and she stared. Probably she was not often thanked.

The drinking-house was out of the village and up the hill, where sometimes you found the church. There seemed to be no church here.

It was a building of wood and bits of stone, with a sloping roof, and inside there was the smell of staleness and ale.

They all looked up, the ten or so fellows in the house, from their benches.

He stood just inside the door and said, "Who owns the pale ship?"

"I do," said the one the woman had called Fatty. He was gaunt as a rope. He said, "What's it to you?"

"You don't use her much."

"Nor I do. How do you know?"

"She has no proper smell of fish, or the birds would be at her."

"There you're wrong," said Fatty. He slurped some ale. He did have a fat mouth, perhaps that was the reason for his name. "She's respected, my lady. Even the birds respect her."

"I'll buy your ship," said Jeluc. "How much?"

All the men murmured.

Fatty said, "Not for sale."

Jeluc had expected that. He said, "I've been paid off from my regiment. I've got money here, look." And he took out some pieces of silver.

The men came round like beasts to be fed, and Jeluc wondered if they would set on him, and got ready to knock them down. But they knew him for a soldier. He was dangerous beside them, poor drunken sods.

"I'll give you this," said Jeluc to Fatty.

Fatty pulled at his big lips.

"She's worth more, my lady."

"Is that her name?" said Jeluc. "That's what men call the sea. *La Dame*. She's not worth so much, but I won't worry about that."

Fatty was sullen. He did not know what to do.

Then one of the other men said to him. "You could take that to the town. You could spend two whole nights with a whore, and drink the place dry."

"Or," said another, "you could buy the makings to mend your old house."

Fatty said, "I don't know. Is my ship. Was my dad's."

"Let her go," said another man. "She's not lucky for you. Nor for him."

Jeluc said, "Not lucky, eh? Shall I lower my price?"

"Some daft tale," said Fatty. "She's all right. I've kept her trim."

"He has," the others agreed.

"I could see," said Jeluc. He put the money on a table. "There it is."

Fatty gave him a long, bended look. "Take her then. She's the lady."

"I'll want provisions," he said. "I mean to sail over to the islands."

A gray little man bobbed forward. "You got more silver? My wife'll see to you. Come with me."

The gray man's wife left the sack of meal, and the dried pork and apples, and the cask of water, at the village end of the pier, and Jeluc carried them out to the ship.

Her beauty impressed him as he walked towards her. To another maybe she would only have been a vessel. But he saw her lines. She was shapely. And the mast was slender and strong.

He stored the food and water, and the extra things, the ale and rope and blankets, the pan for hot coals, in the cabin. It was bare, but for its cupboard and the wooden bunk. He lay here a moment, trying it. It felt familiar as his own skin.

The deck was clean and scrubbed, and above the tied sail was bundled on the creaking yard, whiter than the sky. He checked her over. Nothing amiss.

The feel of her, dipping and bobbing as the tide turned, gave him a wonderful sensation of escape.

He would cast off before sunset, get out on to the sea, in case the oafs of the village had any amusing plans. They were superstitious of the ship, would not use her but possibly did not like to see her go. She was their one elegant thing, like a madonna in the church, if they had had one.

Her name was on her side, written dark.

The wind rose as the leaden sun began to sink.

He let down her sail, and it spread like a swan's wing. It was after all discolored, of course, yet from a distance it would look very white. Like a woman's arm that had freckles when you saw it close.

The darkness came, and by then the land was out of sight. All the stars swarmed up, brilliant, as the clouds melted away. A glow was on the tips of the waves, such as he remembered. Tomorrow he would set lines for fish, baiting them with scraps of pork.

He cooked his supper of meal cakes on the coals, then lit a pipe of tobacco. He watched the smoke go up against the stars, and listened to the sail, turning a little to the wind.

The sea made noises, rushes, and stirrings, and sometimes far away would come some sound, a soft booming or a slender cry, such as were never heard on land. He did not know what made these voices, if it were wind or water, or some creature. Perhaps he had known in his boyhood, for it seemed he recalled them.

When he went to the cabin, leaving the ship on her course, with the rope from the tiller tied to his waist, he knew that he would sleep as he had not slept on the beds of the earth.

The sea too was full of the dead, but they were a long way down. Theirs was a clean finish among the mouths of fishes.

He thought of mermaids swimming alongside, revealing their breasts, and laughing at him that he did not get up and look at them.

He slept.

Jeluc dreamed he was walking down the stone pier out of the village. It was starlight, night, and the pale ship was tied there at the pier's end as she had been. But between him and the ship stood a tall gaunt figure. It was not Fatty or the gray man, for as Jeluc came near, he saw it wore a black robe like a priest's, and a hood concealed all its skull face but for a broad white forehead.

As he got closer, Jeluc tried to see the being's face, but could not. Instead a white thin hand came up and plucked from him a silver coin.

It was Charon, the Ferryman of the Dead, taking his fee.

Jeluc opened his eyes.

He was in the cabin of the ship called *La Dame*, and all was still, only the music of the water and the wind, and through the window he saw the stars sprinkle by.

The rope at his waist gave its little tug, now this way, now that, as it should. All was well.

Jeluc shut his eyes.

He imagined his lids weighted by silver coins.

He heard a soft voice singing, a woman's voice. It was very high and sweet, not kind, no lullaby.

In the morning he was tired, although his sleep had gone very deep. But it had been a long walk he had had to the village.

He saw to the lines, baiting them carefully, and went over the ship, but she was as she should be. He cooked some more cakes, and ate a little of the greasy pork. The ale was flat and bitter, but he had tasted far worse.

He stood all morning by the tiller.

The weather was brisk but calm enough, and at this rate he would sight the first of the islands by the day after tomorrow. He might be sorry at that, but then he need not linger longer. He could be off again.

In the afternoon he drowsed. And when he woke, the sun was over to the west like a bullet in a dull dark rent in the sky.

Jeluc glimpsed something. He turned, and saw three thin men with ragged dripping hair, who stood on the far side of the cabin on the afterdeck. They were quite still, colorless, and dumb. Then they were gone.

Perhaps it had been some formation of the clouds, some shadow cast for a moment by the sail. Or his eyes, playing tricks.

But he said aloud to the ship, "Are you haunted, my dear? Is that your secret?"

When he checked his lines, he had caught nothing, but there was no law which said he must.

The wind dropped low and, as yesterday, the clouds dissolved when the darkness fell, and he saw the stars blaze out like diamonds, but no moon.

It seemed to him he should have seen her, the moon, but maybe some little overcast had remained, or he had made a mistake.

He concocted a stew with the pork and some garlic and apple, ate, smoked his pipe, listened to the noises of the sea.

He might be anywhere. A hundred miles from any land. He had seen no birds all day.

Jeluc went to the cabin, tied the rope, and lay down. He slept at once. He was on the ship, and at his side sat one of his old comrades, a man who had died from a cannon shot two years before. He kept his hat over the wound shyly, and said to Jeluc, "Where are you bound? The islands? Do you think you'll get there?"

"This lady'll take me there," said Jeluc.

"Oh, she'll take you somewhere."

Then the old soldier showed him the compass, and the needle had gone mad, reared up and poked down, right down, as if indicating hell.

Jeluc opened his eyes and the rope twitched at his waist, this way, that.

He got up, and walked out on to the deck.

The stars were bright as white flames, and the shadow of the mast fell hard as iron on the deck. But it was all wrong.

Jeluc looked up, and on the mast of the ship hung a wiry man, with his long gray hair all tangled round the yard and trailing down the sail, crawling on it, like the limbs of a spider.

This man Jeluc did not know, but the man grinned, and he began to pull off silver rings from his fingers and cast them at Jeluc. They fell with loud, cold notes. A huge, round moon, white as snow, rose behind the apparition. Its hand tugged and tugged, and Jeluc heard it curse. The finger had come off with the ring, and fell on his boot.

"What do you want with me?" said Jeluc, but the man on the mast faded, and the severed finger was only a drop of spray.

Opening his eyes again, Jeluc lay on the bunk, and he smelled a soft warm perfume. It was like flowers on a summer day. It was the aroma of a woman.

"Am I awake now?"

Jeluc got up, and stood on the bobbing floor, then he went outside. There was no moon, and only the sail moved on the yard.

One of the lines was jerking, and he went to it slowly. But when he tested it, nothing was there.

The smell of heat and plants was still faintly about him, and now he took it for the foretaste of the islands, blown out to him.

He returned to the cabin and lay wakeful, until near dawn he slept and dreamed a mermaid had come over the ship's rail. She was pale as pale, with ash blond hair, and he wondered if it would be feasible to make love to her, for she had a fish's tail, and no woman's parts at all that he could see.

Dawn was so pale it seemed the ship had grown darker. She had a sort of flush, her sides and deck, her smooth mast, her outspread sail.

He could not scent the islands anymore.

Rain fell, and he went into the cabin, and there examined his possessions, as once or twice he had done before a battle. His knife, his neckscarf of silk, which a girl had given him years before, a lucky coin he had kept without believing in it, a bullet that had missed him and gone into a tree. His money, his boots, his pipe. Not much.

Then he thought that the ship was now his possession, too, *his* lady.
He went and stood in the rain and looked at her.
There was nothing on the lines.
He ate pork for supper.
The rain eased, and in the cabin he slept.

The woman stood at the tiller.
She rested her hand on it, quietly.
She was very pale, her hair long and blond, and her old-fashioned dress the shade of good paper.
He stood and watched her for some time, but she did not respond, although he knew she was aware of him, and that he watched.
Finally he walked up to her, and she turned her head.
She was very thin, her face all bones, and she had great glowing pale gleaming eyes, and these stared now right through him.
She took her hand off the tiller and put it on his shoulder, and he felt her touch go through him like her look, straight down his body, through his heart, belly, and loins, and out at his feet.
He thought, She'll want to go into the cabin with me.
So he gave her his arm.
They walked, along the deck, and he let her pass into the cabin first.
She turned about, as she had turned her head, slowly, looking at everything, the food and the pan of coals, which did not burn now, the blankets on the bunk.
Then she moved to the bunk and lay down, on her back, calm as any woman who had done such a thing a thousand times.
Jeluc went to her at once, but he did not wait to undo his clothing. He found, surprising himself, that he lay down on top of her, straight down, letting her frail body have all his weight, his chest on her bosom, his loins on her loins, but separated by their garments, legs on her legs. And last of all, his face on her face, his lips against hers.
Rather than lust it was the sensuality of a dream he felt, for of course it was a dream. His whole body sweetly ached, and the center of joy seemed at his lips rather than anywhere else, his lips that touched her lips, quite closed, not even moist nor very warm.
Light delicious spasms passed through him, one after another, ebbing, flowing, resonant, and ceaseless.
He did not want to change it, did not want it to end. And it did not end.
But eventually, he seemed to drift away from it, back into sleep. And this was so comfortable that, although he regretted the sensation's loss, he did not mind so much.

When he woke, he heard them laughing at him. Many men, laughing, low voices and higher ones, coarse and rough as if torn from tin throats and voice boxes of rust. "He's going the same way." "So he is too."
Going the way that they had gone. The three he had seen on the deck, the one above the sail.
It was the ship. The ship had him.

He got up slowly, for he was giddy and chilled. Wrapping one of the blankets about him, he stepped out into the daylight.

The sky was white with hammerheads of black. The sea had a dull yet oily glitter.

He checked his lines. They were empty. No fish had come to the bait, as no birds had come to the mast.

He gazed back over the ship.

She was no longer pale. No, she was rosy now. She had a dainty blush to her, as if of pleasure. Even the sail was like the petal of a rose.

An old man stood on the afterdeck and shook his head and vanished.

Jeluc thought of lying on the bunk, facedown, and his vital juices or their essence draining into the wood. He could not avoid it. Everywhere here he must touch her. He could not lie to sleep in the sea.

He raised his head. No smell of land.

By now, surely, the islands should be in view, up against those clouds there— But there was nothing. Only the water on all sides and below, and the cold sky above, and over that, the void.

During the afternoon, as he watched by the tiller for the land, Jeluc slept.

He found that he lay with his head on her lap, and she was lovely now, prettier than any woman he had ever known. Her hair was honey, and her dress like a rose. Her white skin flushed with health and in her cheeks and lips three flames. Her eyes were dark now, very fine. They shone on him.

She leaned down, and covered his mouth with hers.

Such bliss—

He woke.

He was lying on his back, he had rolled, and the sail tilted over his face.

He got up, staggering, and trimmed the sail.

Jeluc attended to the ship.

The sunset came and a ghost slipped round the cabin, hiding its sneering mouth with its hand.

Jeluc tried to cook a meal, but he was clumsy and scorched his fingers. As he sucked them, he thought of her kisses. If kisses were what they were.

No land.

The sun set. It was a dull grim sky, with a hole of whiteness that turned gray, yet the ship flared up.

She was red now, *La Dame*, her cabin like a live coal, her sides like wine, her sail like blood.

Of course, he could keep awake through the night. He had done so before. And tomorrow he would sight the land.

He paced the deck, and the stars came out, white as ice or knives. There was no moon.

He marked the compass, saw to the sail, set fresh meat on the lines that he knew no fish would touch.

Jeluc sang old songs of his campaigns, but hours after he heard himself sing, over and over:

"*She the ship*
"*She the sea*
"*She the she.*"

His grandfather had told him stories of the ocean, of how it was a woman, a female thing, and that the ships that went out upon it were female also, for it would not stand any human male to go about on it unless something were between him and—her. But the sea was jealous too. She did not like women, true human women, to travel on ships. She must be reverenced, and now and then demanded sacrifice.

His grandfather had told him how, once, they had had to throw a man overboard because he spat into the sea. It seemed he had spat a certain way, or at the wrong season. He had had, too, the temerity to learn to swim, which few sailors were fool enough to do. It had taken a long while for him to go down. They had told the widow the water washed him overboard.

Later, Jeluc believed that the ship had eyes painted on her prow, and these saw her way, but now they closed. She did not care where she went. And then too he thought she had a figurehead, like a great vessel of her kind, and this was a woman who clawed at the ship's sides, howling.

But he woke up, in time.

He kept awake all night.

In the morning the sun rose, lax and pallid as an ember, while the ship burned red as fire.

Jeluc looked over and saw her red reflection in the dark water.

There was no land on any side.

He made a breakfast of undercooked meal cakes, and ate a little. He felt her tingling through the soles of his boots.

He tested the sail and the lines, her tiller, and her compass. There was something odd with its needle.

No fish gave evidence of themselves in the water, and no birds flew overhead.

The sea rolled in vast glaucous swells.

He could not help himself. He slept.

There were birds!

He heard them calling, and looked up.

The sky, pale gray, a cinder, was full of them, against a sea of stars that were too faint for night.

And the birds, so black, were gulls. And yet, they were gulls of bone. Their beaks were shut like needles. They wheeled and soared, never alighting on the mast or yard or rails of the ship.

I'm dreaming, God help me. God wake me—

The gulls swooped over and on, and now, against the distant diluted dark, he saw the tower of a lighthouse rising. It was the land, at last, and he was saved.

But oh, the lighthouse sent out its ray, and from the opposing side there came another, the lamp flashing out. And then another, and another. They were before him and behind him, and all round. The lit points of them crossed each other on the blank somber sparkle of the sea. A hundred lighthouses, sending their signals to hell.

Jeluc stared around him. And then he heard the deep roaring in the ocean bed, a million miles below.

And one by one, the houses of the light sank, they went into the water, their long necks like Leviathan's, and vanished in a cream of foam.

All light was gone. The birds were gone.

She came, then.

She was beautiful now. He had never, maybe, seen a beautiful woman.

Her skin was white, but her lips were red. And her hair was the red of gold. Her gown was the red of winter berries. She walked with a little gliding step.

"Lady," he said, "you don't want me."

But she smiled.

Then he looked beyond the ship, for it felt not right to him, and the sea was all lying down. It was like the tide going from the shore, or, perhaps, water from a basin. It ran away, and the ship dropped after it.

And then they were still in a pale nothingness, a sort of beach of sand that stretched in all directions. Utterly becalmed.

"But I don't want the land."

He remembered what the land had given him. Old hurts, drear pains. Comrades dead. Wars lost. Youth gone.

"Not the land," he said.

But she smiled.

And over the waste of it, that sea of salt, came a shrill high whistling, once and twice and three times. Some sound of the ocean he had never heard.

Then she had reached him. Jeluc felt her smooth hands on his neck. He said, "Woman, let me go into the water, at least." But it was no use. Her lips were soft as roses on his throat.

He saw the sun rise, and it was red as red could be. But then, like the ship in his dream, he closed his eyes. He thought, But there was no land.

There never is.

The ship stood fiery crimson on the rising sun that lit her like a bonfire. Her sides, her deck, her cabin, her mast and sail, like fresh, pure blood.

Presently the sea, which moved under her in dark silk, began to lip this blood away.

At first, it was only a reflection in the water, but next it was a stain, like heavy dye.

The sea drank from the color of the ship, for the sea too was feminine and a devourer of men.

The sea drained *La Dame* of every drop, so gradually she turned back paler and paler into a vessel like ashes.

And when the sea had sucked everything out of her, it let her go, the ship, white as a bone, to drift away down the morning.

CIRCE'S POWER
Louise Glück

Louise Glück, who hails from New York City, has won many awards for her poetry over a long, distinguished career, in addition to a Guggenheim fellowship. Her poetry collections include *House on the Marshlands, The Descending Figure,* and *Firstborn.*

  "Circe's Power" meditates on a figure who is given rather short shrift in Homer's *Odyssey.* . . . It is reprinted from the April 10 issue of *The New Yorker.*

—T.W.

> I never turned anyone into a pig.
> Some people are pigs; I make them
> look like pigs.
>
> I'm sick of your world
> that lets the outside disguise the inside.
>
> Your men weren't bad men;
> undisciplined life
> did that to them. As pigs,
>
> under the care of
> me and my ladies, they
> sweetened right up.
>
> Then I reversed the spell,
> showing you my goodness
> as well as my power. I saw

we could be happy here,
as men and women are
when their needs are simple. In the same breath,

I foresaw your departure,
your men with my help braving
the crying and pounding sea. You think

a few tears upset me? My friend,
every sorceress is
a pragmatist at heart; nobody
sees essence who can't
face limitation. If I wanted only to hold you

I could hold you prisoner.

DRAGON'S FIN SOUP
S. P. Somtow

S. P. Somtow is a dazzling writer—his output is prodigous, yet each story seems to be as distinctive, and as entertaining, as the tale that follows. His novels include *The Darkling Wind*, *The Wizard's Apprentice*, *Vampire Junction*, and (for children) *The Fallen Country*. He was a composer and performer before turning to writing; he is also a screenwriter and film director. He was born in Bangkok, Thailand, raised in Europe, educated at Eton and Cambridge, and currently resides in the U.S.

"Dragon's Fin Soup" is a wild contemporary fantasy set in a small Bangkok restaurant. It was published in *The Ultimate Dragon*, edited by Byron Preiss, John Betancourt, and Keith R. A. DeCandido.

—T.W.

At the heart of Bangkok's Chinatown, in the district known as Yaowaraj, there is a restaurant called the Rainbow Café which, every Wednesday, features a blue plate special they call dragon's fin soup. Though little known through most of its hundred-year existence, the café enjoyed a brief flirtation with fame during the early 1990s because of an article in the Bangkok *Post* extolling the virtues of the *specialité de la maison*. The article was written by the enigmatic Ueng-Ang Thalay, whose true identity few had ever guessed. It was only I and a few close friends who knew that Ueng-Ang was actually a Chestertonian American named Bob Halliday, ex–concert pianist and Washington *Post* book critic, who had fled the mundane madness of the western world for the more fantastical, cutting-edge madness of the Orient. It was only in Bangkok, the bastard daughter of feudalism and futurism, that Bob had finally been able to be himself, though what *himself* was, he alone seemed to know.

But we were speaking of the dragon's fin soup.

Perhaps I should quote the relevant section of Ueng-Ang's article:

> Succulent! Aromatic! Subtle! Profound! Transcendental! These are but a few of the adjectives your skeptical food columnist has been hearing from the clients of the Rainbow Café in Yaowaraj as they rhapsodize about the mysterious dish known as dragon's fin soup, served only on Wednesdays. Last Wednesday your humble columnist was forced to try it out. The

restaurant is exceedingly hard to find, being on the third floor of the only building still extant from before the Chinatown riots of 1945. There is no sign, either in English or Thai, and as I cannot read Chinese, I cannot say whether there is one in that language either. On Wednesday afternoons, however, there are a large number of official-looking Mercedes and BMWs double-parked all the way down the narrow soi, and dozens of uniformed chauffeurs leaning warily against their cars; so, unable to figure out the restaurant's location from the hastily scrawled fax I had received from a friend of mine who works at the Ministry of Education, I decided to follow the luxury cars . . . and my nose . . . instead. The alley became narrower and shabbier. Then, all of a sudden, I turned a corner, and found myself joining a line of people, all dressed to the teeth, snaking single file up the rickety wooden steps into the small, unair-conditioned, and decidedly unassuming restaurant. It was a kind of time-travel. This was not the Bangkok we all know, the Bangkok of insane traffic jams, of smörgasbord sexuality, of iridescent skyscrapers and stagnant canals. The people in line all waited patiently; when I was finally ushered inside, I found the restaurant to be as quiet and as numinous as a Buddhist temple. Old men with floor-length beards played mah jongg; a woman in a cheongsam directed me to a table beneath the solitary ceiling fan; the menu contained not a word of Thai or English. Nevertheless, without my having to ask, a steaming bowl of the notorious soup was soon served to me, along with a cup of piping-hot chrysanthemum tea.

At first I was conscious only of the dish's bitterness, and I wondered whether its fame was a hoax or I, as the only pale-faced rube in the room, was actually being proffered a bowl full of microwaved Robitussin. Then, suddenly, it seemed to me that the bitterness of the soup was a kind of veil or filter through which its true taste, too overwhelming to be perceived directly, might be enjoyed . . . rather as the dark glasses one must wear in order to gaze directly at the sun. But as for the taste itself, it cannot truly be described at all. At first I thought it must be a variant of the familiar shark's fin, perhaps marinated in some geriatric wine. But it also seemed to partake somewhat of the subtle tang of bird's nest soup, which draws its flavor from the coagulated saliva of cave-dwelling swallows. I also felt a kind of coldness in my joints and extremities, the tingling sensation familiar to those who have tasted fugu, the elusive and expensive Japanese puffer fish, which, improperly prepared, causes paralysis and death within minutes. The dish tasted like all these things and none of them, and I found, for the first time in my life, my jaundiced tongue confounded and bewildered. I asked the beautiful longhaired waitress in the cheongsam whether she could answer a few questions about the dish; she said, "Certainly, as long as I don't have to divulge any of the ingredients, for they are an ancient family secret." She spoke an antique and grammatically quaint sort of Thai, as though she had never watched television, listened to pop songs, or hung out in the myriad coffee shops of the city. She saw my surprise and went on in English, "It's not my first language, you see; I'm a lot more comfortable in English."

"Berkeley?" I asked her, suspecting a hint of Northern California in her speech.

She smiled broadly then, and said, "Santa Cruz, actually. It's a relief to meet another American around here; they don't let me out much since I came home from college."

"American?"

"Well, I'm a dual national. But my great-grandparents were forty-niners. Gold rush chinks. My name's Janice Lim. Or Lam or Lin, take your pick."

"Tell me then," I inquired, "since you can't tell me what's in the soup . . . why is it that you only serve it on Wednesdays?"

"Wednesday, in Thai, is Wan Phutth . . . the day of Buddha. My father feels that dragon's flesh should only be served on that day of the week that is sacred to the Lord Buddha, when we can reflect on the transitory nature of our existence."

At this point it should be pointed out that I, your narrator, am the woman with the long hair and the *cheongsam*, and that Bob Halliday has, in his article, somewhat exaggerated my personal charms. I shall not exaggerate his. Bob is a large man; his girth has earned him the sobriquet of "Elephant" among his Thai friends. He is an intellectual; he speaks such languages as Hungarian and Cambodian as well as he does Thai, and he listens to *Lulu* and *Wozzeck* before breakfast. For relaxation, he curls up with Umberto Eco, and I don't mean Eco's novels, I mean his academic papers on semiotics. Bob is a rabid agoraphobe, and flees as soon as there are more than about ten people at a party. His friends speculate endlessly about his sex life, but in fact he seems to have none at all.

Because he was the only American to have found his way to the Rainbow Café since I returned to Thailand from California, and because he seemed to my father (my mother having passed away in childbirth) to be somehow unthreatening, I found myself spending a good deal of time with him when I wasn't working at the restaurant. My aunt Ling-ling, who doesn't speak a word of Thai or English, was the official chaperone; if we went for a quiet cup of coffee at the Regent, for example, she was to be found a couple of tables away, sipping a glass of chrysanthemum tea.

It was Bob who taught me what kind of a place Bangkok really was. You see, I had lived until the age of eighteen without ever setting foot outside our family compound. I had had a tutor to help me with my English. We had one hour of television a day, the news; that was how I had learned Thai. My father was obsessed with our family's purity; he never used our dearly bought, royally granted Thai surname of Suntharapornsunthornpanich, but insisted on signing all documents Sae Lim, as though the Great Integration of the Chinese had never occurred and our people were still a nation within a nation, still loyal to the vast and distant Middle Kingdom. My brave new world had been California, and it remained for Bob to show me that an even braver one had lain at my doorstep all my life.

Bangkoks within Bangkoks. Yes, that charmingly hackneyed metaphor of the Chinese boxes comes to mind. Quiet places with pavilions that overlooked reflecting ponds. Galleries hung with postmodern art. Japanese-style coffee houses with melon-flavored ice cream floats and individual shrimp pizzas. Grungy noodle stands beneath flimsy awnings over open sewers; stratospherically upscale French patisseries and Italian gelaterias. Bob knew where they all were, and he was willing to share all his secrets, even though Aunt Ling-ling was always along for the ride. After a time, it seemed to me that perhaps it was my turn to reveal some secret, and so one Sunday afternoon, in one of the coffee lounges overlooking the atrium of the Sogo shopping mall, I decided to tell him the biggest of all secrets. "Do you really want to know," I said, "why we only serve the dragon fin soup on Wednesday?"

"Yes," he said, "and I promise I won't print it."

"Well you see," I said, "it takes about a week for the tissue to regenerate."

That was about as much as I could safely say without spilling the whole can of soup. The dragon had been in our family since the late Ming Dynasty, when a multi-multi-great-uncle of mine, a eunuch who was the emperor's trade representative between Peking and the Siamese Kingdom of Ayuthaya, had tricked him into following his junk all the way down the Chao Phraya River, had imprisoned him beneath the canals of the little village that was later to become Bangkok, City of Angels, Dwelling Place of Vishnu, Residence of the Nine Jewels, and so on and so forth (read the *Guinness Book of Records* to obtain the full name of the city), known affectionately to its residents as City of Angels Etc. This was because the dragon had revealed to my multi-great-uncle that the seemingly invincible Kingdom of Ayuthaya would one day be sacked by the King of Pegu and that the capital of Siam would be moved down to this unpretentious village in the Chao Phraya delta. The dragon had told him this because, as everyone knows, a mortally wounded dragon, when properly constrained, is obliged to answer three questions truthfully. Multi-great-uncle wasted his other questions on trying to find out whether he would ever regain his manhood and be able to experience an orgasm; the dragon had merely laughed at this, and his laughter had caused a minor earthquake which destroyed the summer palace of Lord Kuykendaal, a Dutchman who had married into the lowest echelon of the Siamese aristocracy, which earthquake in turn precipitated the Opium War of 1677, which, as it is not in the history books, remains alive only in our family tradition.

Our family tradition also states that each member of the family may only tell one outsider about the dragon's existence. If he chooses the right outsider, he will have a happy life; if he chooses unwisely, and the outsider turns out to be untrustworthy, then misfortune will dog both the revealer and his confidant.

I wasn't completely sure about Bob yet, and I didn't want to blow my one opportunity. But that evening, as I supervised the ritual slicing of the dragon's fin, my father dropped a bombshell.

The dragon could not, of course, be seen all in one piece. There was, in the kitchen of the Rainbow Café, a hole in one wall, about nine feet in diameter. One coil of the dragon came through this wall and curved toward a similar opening in the ceiling. I did not know where the dragon ended or began. One assumed this was a tail section because it was so narrow. I had seen a dragon whole only in my dreams, or in pictures. Rumor had it that this dragon stretched all the way to Nonthaburi, his slender body twisting through ancient sewer pipes and under the foundations of century-old buildings. He was bound to my family by an ancient spell in a scroll that sat on the altar of the household gods, just above the cash register inside the restaurant proper. He was unimaginably old and unimaginably jaded, stunned rigid by three thousand years of human magic; his scales so lusterless that I had to buff them with furniture polish to give them some semblance of draconian majesty. He was, of course, still mortally wounded from the battle he had endured with multi-great-uncle; nevertheless, it takes them a long, long time to die, especially when held captive by a scroll such as the one we possessed.

You could tell the dragon was still alive, though. Once in a very long while, he breathed. Or rather, a kind of rippling welled up him, and you could hear a distant wheeze, like an old house settling on its foundations. And of course, he regenerated. If it wasn't for that, the restaurant would never have stayed in business all these years.

The fin we harvested was a ventral fin and hung down over the main charcoal stove of the restaurant kitchen. It took some slicing to get it off. We had a new chef, Ah Quoc, just up from Penang, and he was having a lot of trouble. "You'd better heat up the carving knife some more," I was telling him. "Make sure it's red hot."

He stuck the knife back in the embers. Today, the dragon was remarkably sluggish; I had not detected a breath in hours; and the flesh was hard as stone. I wondered whether the event our family dreaded most, the dragon's death, was finally going to come upon us.

"Muoi, muoi," he said, "the flesh just won't give."

"Don't call me *muoi*," I said. "I'm not your little sister, I'm the boss's daughter. In fact, don't speak Chiuchow at all. English is a lot simpler."

"Okey-doke, Miss Janice. But Chinese or English, meat just no slice, la."

He was hacking away at the fin. The flesh was stony, recalcitrant. I didn't want to use the spell of binding, but I had to. I ran into the restaurant—it was closed and there were only a few old men playing mah jongg—grabbed the scroll from the altar, stormed back into the kitchen, and tapped the scaly skin, whispering the word of power that only members of our family can speak. I felt a shudder deep within the dragon's bowels. I put my ear up to the clammy hide. I thought I could hear, from infinitely far away, the hollow clanging of the dragon's heart, the glacial oozing of his blood through kilometer after kilometer of leaden veins and arteries. "Run, blood, run," I shouted, and I started whipping him with the brittle paper.

Aunt Ling-ling came scurrying in at that moment, a tiny creature in a widow's dress, shouting, "You'll rip the scroll, don't hit so hard!"

But then, indeed, the blood began to roar. "Now you can slice him," I said to Ah Quoc. "Quickly. It has to soak in the marinade for at least twenty-four hours, and we're running late as it is."

"Okay! Knife hot enough now, la." Ah Quoc slashed through the whole fin in a single motion, like an imperial headsman. I could see now why my father had hired him to replace Ah Chen, who had become distracted, gone native—even gone so far as to march in the 1992 democracy riots—as if the politics of the Thais were any of our business.

Aunt Ling-ling had the vat of marinade all ready. Ah Quoc sliced quickly and methodically, tossing the pieces of dragon's fin into the bubbling liquid. With shark's fin, you have to soak it in water for a long time to soften it up for eating. Bob Halliday had speculated about the nature of the marinade. He was right about the garlic and the chilies, but it would perhaps have been unwise to tell him about the sulfuric acid.

It was at that point that my father came in. "The scroll, the scroll," he said distractedly. Then he saw it and snatched it from me.

"We're safe for another week," I said, following him out of the kitchen into the restaurant. Another of my aunts, the emaciated Jasmine, was counting a pile of money, doing calculations with an abacus, and making entries into a leatherbound ledger.

My father put the scroll back. Then he looked directly into my eyes—something he had done only once or twice in my adult life—and, scratching his beard, said, "I've found you a husband."

That was the bombshell.

I didn't feel it was my place to respond right away. In fact, I was so flustered by his announcement that I had absolutely nothing to say. In a way, I had been expecting it, of course, but for some reason . . . perhaps it was because of my time at Santa Cruz . . . it just hadn't occurred to me that my father would be so . . . so . . . old-fashioned about it. I mean, my God, it was like being stuck in an Amy Tan novel or something.

That's how I ended up in Bob Halliday's office at the Bangkok *Post*, sobbing my guts out without any regard for propriety or good manners. Bob, who is a natural empath, allowed me to yammer on and on; he sent a boy down to the market to fetch some steaming noodles wrapped in banana leaves and iced coffee in little PVC bags. I daresay I didn't make too much sense. "My father's living in the nineteenth century . . . or worse," I said. "He should never have let me set foot outside the house . . . outside the restaurant. I mean, Santa Cruz, for God's sake! Wait till I tell him I'm not even a virgin anymore. The price is going to plummet, he's going to take a bath on whatever deal it is he's drawn up. I'm so mad at him. And even though he did send me to America, he never let me so much as set foot in the Silom Complex, two miles from our house, without a chaperone. I've never had a life! Or rather, I've had two half-lives—half American coed, half Chinese dragon lady—I'm like two half-people that don't make a whole. And this is Thailand, it's not America and it's not China. It's the most alien landscape of them all."

Later, because I didn't want to go home to face the grisly details of my impending marriage contract, I rode back to Bob's apartment with him in a *tuk-tuk*. The motorized rickshaw darted skillfully through jammed streets and minuscule alleys and once again—as so often with Bob—I found myself in an area of Bangkok I had never seen before, a district overgrown with weeds and wild banana trees; the *soi* came to an abrupt end and there was a lone elephant, swaying back and forth, being hosed down by a country boy wearing nothing but a *phakhomah*. "You must be used to slumming by now," Bob said, "with all the places I've taken you."

In his apartment, a grizzled cook served up a screamingly piquant *kaeng khieu waan*, and I must confess that though I usually can't stand Thai food, the heat of this sweet green curry blew me away. We listened to Wagner. Bob has the most amazing collection of CDs known to man. He has twelve recordings of *The Magic Flute*, but only three of Wagner's *Ring* cycle—three more than most people I know. "Just listen to that!" he said. I'm not a big fan of opera, but the kind of singing that issued from Bob's stereo sounded hauntingly familiar . . . it had the hollow echo of a sound I'd heard that very afternoon, the low and distant pounding of the dragon's heart.

"What is it?" I said.

"Oh, it's the scene where Siegfried slays the dragon," Bob said. "You know, this is the Solti recording, where the dragon's voice is electronically enhanced. I'm not sure I like it."

It sent chills down my spine.

"Funny story," Bob said. "For the original production, you know, in the 1860s . . . they had a special dragon built . . . in England . . . in little segments. They were supposed to ship the sections to Bayreuth for the première, but the neck was accidentally sent to Beirut instead. That dragon never did have a neck. Imagine those people in Beirut when they opened that crate! What do you do with a disembodied segment of dragon anyway?"

"I could think of a few uses," I said.

"It sets me to thinking about dragon's fin soup."

"No can divulge, la," I said, laughing, in my best Singapore English.

The dragon gave out a roar and fell, mortally wounded, in a spectacular orchestral climax. He crashed to the floor of the primeval forest. I had seen this scene once in the Fritz Lang silent film *Siegfried*, which we'd watched in our History of Cinema class at Santa Cruz. After the crash there came more singing.

"This is the fun part, now," Bob told me. "If you approach a dying dragon, it *has* to answer your questions . . . three questions usually . . . and it has to answer them truthfully."

"Even if he's been dying for a thousand years?" I said.

"Never thought of that, Janice," said Bob. "You think the dragon's truthseeing abilities might become a little clouded?"

Despite my long and tearful outpouring in his office, Bob had not once mentioned the subject of my Damoclean doom. Perhaps he was about to raise it now; there was one of those long pregnant pauses that tend to portend portentousness. I wanted to put it off a little longer, so I asked him, "If you had access to a dragon . . . and the dragon were dying, and you came upon him in just the right circumstances . . . what *would* you ask him?"

Bob laughed. "So many questions . . . so much I want to know . . . so many arcane truths that the cosmos hangs on! I think I'd have a lot to ask. Why? You have a dragon for me?"

I didn't get back to Yaowaraj until very late that night. I had hoped that everyone would have gone to bed, but when I reached the restaurant (the family compound itself is reached through a back stairwell beyond the kitchen) I found my father still awake, sitting at the carving table, and Aunt Ling-ling and Aunt Jasmine stirring the vat of softening dragon's fin. The sulfuric acid had now been emptied and replaced with a pungent brew of vinegar, ginseng, garlic, soy sauce, and the ejaculate of a young boy, obtainable in Patpong for about one hundred baht. The whole place stank, but I knew that it would whittle down to the subtlest, sweetest, bitterest, most nostalgic of aromas.

My father said to me, "Perhaps you're upset with me, Janice; I know it was a little sudden."

"Sudden!" I said. "Give me a break, Papa, this was more than sudden. You're so old-fashioned suddenly . . . and you're not even that old. Marrying me off like you're cashing in your blue chip stocks or something."

"There's a worldwide recession, in case you haven't noticed. We need an infusion of cash. I don't know how much longer the dragon will hold out. Look, this contract . . ." He pushed it across the table. It was in Chinese, of course, and full of flowery and legalistic terms. "He's not the youngest I could have found, but his blood runs pure; he's from the village." The village being, of course, the village of my ancestors, on whose soil my family has not set foot in seven hundred years.

"What do you mean, not the youngest, Papa?"

"To be honest, he's somewhat elderly. But that's for the best, isn't it? I mean, he'll soon be past, as it were, the age of lovemaking . . ."

"Papa, I'm not a virgin."

"Oh, not to worry, dear; I had a feeling something like that might happen over there in Californ' . . . we'll send you to Tokyo for the operation. Their hymen implants are as good as new, I'm told."

My hymen was not the problem. This was probably not the time to tell my father that the deflowerer of my maidenhead had been a young, fast-talking, vigorous, muscular specimen of corn-fed Americana by the name of Linda Horovitz.

"You don't seem very excited, my dear."

"Well, what do you expect me to say?" I had never raised my voice to my father, and I really didn't quite know how to do it.

"Look, I've really worked very hard on this match, trying to find the least offensive person who could meet the minimum criteria for bailing us out of this financial mess—this one, he has a condominium in Vancouver, owns a computer franchise, would probably not demand of you, you know, too terribly degrading a sexual performance—"

Sullenly, I looked at the floor.

He stared at me for a long time. Then he said, "You're in love, aren't you?"

I didn't answer.

My father slammed his fists down on the table. "Those damned lascivious Thai men with their honeyed words and their backstabbing habits . . . it's one of them, isn't it? My only daughter . . . and my wife dead in her grave these twenty-two years . . . it kills me."

"And what if it *had* been a Thai man?" I said. "Don't we have Thai passports? Don't we have one of those fifteen-syllable Thai names which *your* grandfather purchased from the king? Aren't we living on Thai soil, stewing up our birthright for Thai citizens to eat, depositing our hard-earned Thai thousand-baht bills in a Thai bank?"

He slapped my face.

He had never done that before. I was more stunned than hurt. I was not to feel the hurt until much later.

"Let me tell you, for the four hundredth time, how your grandmother died," he said, so softly I could hardly hear him above the bubbling of the dragon's fin. "My father had come to Bangkok to fetch his new wife and bring her back to Californ'. It was his cousin, my uncle, who managed the Rainbow Café in those days. It was the 1920s and the city was cool and quiet and serenely beautiful. There were only a few motor-cars in the whole city; one of them, a Ford, belonged to

Uncle Shenghua. My father was in love with the City of Angels Etc. and he loved your grandmother even before he set eyes on her. And he never went back to Californ', but moved into this family compound, flouting the law that a woman should move into her husband's home. Oh, he was so much in love! And he believed that here, in a land where men did not look so different from himself, there would be no prejudice—no bars with signs that said *No Dogs or Chinamen*— no parts of town forbidden to him—no forced assimilation of an alien tongue. After all, hadn't King Chulalongkorn himself taken Chinese concubines to ensure the cultural diversity of the highest ranks of the aristocracy?"

My cheek still burned; I knew the story almost by heart; I hated my father for using his past to ruin my life. Angrily I looked at the floor, at the walls, at the taut curve of the dragon's body as it hung cold, glittering, and motionless.

"But then, you see, there was the revolution, the coming of what they called democracy. No more the many ancient cultures of Siam existing side by side. The closing of the Chinese-language schools. Laws restricting those of ethnic Chinese descent from certain occupations. . . . True, there were no concentration camps, but in some ways the Jews had it easier than we did . . . someone *noticed*. Now listen! You're not listening!"

"Yes, Papa," I said, but in fact my mind was racing, trying to find a way out of this intolerable situation. My Chinese self calling out to my American self, though she was stranded in another country, and perhaps near death, like the dragon whose flesh sustained my family's coffers.

"Nineteen forty-five," my father said. "The war was over, and Chiang Kai-Shek was demanding that Siam be ceded to China. There was singing and dancing in the streets of Yaowaraj! Our civil rights were finally going to be restored to us . . . and the Thais were going to get their comeuppance! We marched with joy in our hearts . . . and then the soldiers came . . . and then we too had rifles in our hands . . . as though by magic. Uncle Shenghua's car was smashed. They smeared the seats with shit and painted the windshield with the words 'Go home, you slanty-eyed scum.' Do you know why the restaurant wasn't torched? One of the soldiers was raping a woman against the doorway and his friends wanted to give him time to finish. The woman was your grandmother. It broke my father's heart."

I had never had the nerve to say it before, but today I was so enraged that I spat it out, threw it in his face. "You don't know that he *was* your father, Papa. Don't think I haven't done the math. You were born in 1946. So much for your obsession with racial purity."

He acted as though he hadn't heard me, just went on with his preset lecture: "And that's why I don't want you to consort with any of them. They're lazy, self-indulgent people who think only of sex. I just know that one of them's got his tentacles wrapped around your heart."

"Papa, you're consumed by this bullshit. You're a slave to this ancient curse . . . just like the damn dragon." Suddenly, dimly, I had begun to see a way out. "But it's not a Thai I'm in love with. It's an American."

"A *white* person!" he was screaming at the top of his lungs. My two aunts looked up from their stirring. "Is he at least rich?"

"No. He's a poor journalist."

"Some blond young thing batting his long eyelashes at you—"

"Oh, no, he's almost fifty. And he's fat." I was starting to enjoy this.

"I forbid you to see him! It's that man from the *Post*, isn't it? That bloated thing who tricked me with his talk of music and literature into thinking him harmless. Was it he who violated you? I'll have him killed, I swear."

"No, you won't," I said, as another piece of my plan fell into place. "I have the right to choose one human being on this earth to whom I shall reveal the secret of the family's dragon. My maidenhead is yours to give away, but not this. This right is the only thing I can truly call my own, and I'm going to give it to Bob Halliday."

It was because he could do nothing about my choice that my father agreed to the match between Bob Halliday and me; he knew that, once told of the secret, Bob's fate would necessarily be intertwined with the fate of the Clan of Lim no matter what, for a man who knew of the dragon could not be allowed to escape from the family's clutches. Unfortunately, I had taken Bob's name in vain. He was not the marrying kind. But perhaps, I reasoned, I could get him to go along with the charade for a while, until old Mr. Hong from the Old Country stopped pressing his suit. Especially if I gave him the option of questioning the dragon. After all, I had heard him wax poetic about all the questions he could ask . . . questions about the meaning of existence, of the creation and destruction of the universe, profound conundrums about love and death.

Thus it was that Bob Halliday came to the Rainbow Café one more time—it was Thursday—and dined on such mundane delicacies as beggar chicken, braised sea cucumbers stuffed with pork, cold jellyfish tentacles, and suckling pig. As a kind of *coup de grâce*, my father even trotted out a small dish of dragon's fin which he had managed to keep refrigerated from the day before (it won't keep past twenty-four hours) which Bob consumed with gusto. He also impressed my father no end by speaking a Mandarin of such consonant-grinding purity that my father, whose groveling deference to those of superior accent was millennially etched within his genes, could not help addressing him in terms of deepest and most cringing respect. He discoursed learnedly on the dragon lore of many cultures, from the salubrious, fertility-bestowing water dragons of China to the fire-breathing, maiden-ravishing monsters of the West; lectured on the theory that the racial memory of dinosaurs might have contributed to the draconian mythos, although he allowed as how humans never coexisted with dinosaurs, so the racial memory must go back as far as marmosets and shrews and such creatures; he lauded the soup in high astounding terms, using terminology so poetic and ancient that he was forced to draw the calligraphy in the air with a stubby finger before my father was able vaguely to grasp his metaphors; and finally—the clincher—alluded to a great-great-great-great-aunt of his in San Francisco who had once had a brief, illicit, and wildly romantic interlude with a Chinese opium smuggler who might *just possibly* have been one of the very Lims who had come from *that* village in Southern Yunnan, you know the village I'm talking about, that very village . . . at which point my father, whisking away all the *haute cuisine* dishes and replacing them with an enormous blueberry cheesecake flown in, he said, from Leo Lindy's of New York, said, "All right, all right, I'm sold. You have no money, but I daresay someone of your intellectual brilliance can conjure up some money somehow. My son, it is with great pleasure that I bestow upon you the hand of my wayward, worthless, and hideous daughter."

I hadn't forewarned Bob about this. Well, I had meant to, but words had failed me at the last moment. Papa had moved in for the kill a lot more quickly than I had thought he would. Before Bob could say anything at all, therefore, I decided to pop a revelation of my own. "I think, Papa," I said, "that it's time for me to show him the dragon."

We all trooped into the kitchen.

The dragon was even more inanimate than usual. Bob put his ear up to the scales; he knocked his knuckles raw. When I listened, I could hear nothing at all at first; the whisper of the sea was my own blood surging through my brain's capillaries, constricted as they were with worry. Bob said, "This is what I've been eating, Janice?"

I directed him over to where Ah Quoc was now seasoning the vat, chopping the herbs with one hand and sprinkling with the other, while my two aunts stirred, prodded, and gossiped like the witches from *Macbeth*. "Look, look," I said, and I pointed out the mass of still unpulped fin that protruded from the glop, "see how its texture matches that of the two dorsal fins."

"It hardly seems alive," Bob said, trying to pry a scale loose so he could peer at the quick.

"You'll need a red-hot paring knife to do that," I said. Then, when Papa wasn't listening, I whispered in his ear, "Please, just go along with all this. It really looks like 'fate worse than death' time for me if you don't. I know that marriage is the farthest thing from your mind right now, but I'll make it up to you somehow. You can get concubines. I'll even help pick them out. Papa won't mind that, it'll only make him think you're a stud."

Bob said, and it was the thing I'd hoped he'd say, "Well, there *are* certain questions that have always nagged at me . . . certain questions which, if only I knew the answers to them, well . . . let's just say I'd die happy."

My father positively beamed at this. "My son," he said, clapping Bob resoundingly on the back, "I *already* know that I shall die happy. At least my daughter won't be marrying a Thai. I just couldn't stand the thought of one of those loathsome creatures dirtying the blood of the House of Lim."

I looked at my father full in the face. Could he have already forgotten that only last night I had called him a bastard? Could he be that deeply in denial? "Bob," I said softly, "I'm going to take you to confront the dragon." Which was more than my father had ever done, or I myself.

Confronting the dragon was, indeed, a rather tall order, for no one had done so since the 1930s, and Bangkok had grown from a sleepy backwater town into a monster of a metropolis; we knew only that the dragon's coils reached deep into the city's foundations, crossed the river at several points, and, well, we weren't sure if he did extend all the way to Nonthaburi; luckily, there is a new expressway now, and once out of the crazy traffic of the old part of the city it did not take long, riding the sleek air-conditioned Nissan taxicab my father had chartered for us, to reach the outskirts of the city. On the way, I caught glimpses of many more Bangkoks that my father's blindness had denied me; I saw the *Blade Runner*esque towers threaded with mist and smog; saw the buildings shaped like giant robots and computer circuit boards designed by that eccentric genius, Dr. Sumet; saw the not-very-ancient and very-very-multicolored temples that dotted the cityscape like rhinestones in a cowboy's boot; saw the slums and the palaces, cheek by jowl, and the squamous rooftops that could perhaps have also been little segments of the dragon poking up from the miasmal collage; we zoomed down the road at breakneck speed to the strains of Natalie Cole, who, our driver opined, is "even better than Mai and Christina."

How to find the dragon? Simple. I had the scroll. Now and then, there was a faint vibration of the parchment. It was a kind of dousing.

"This off-ramp," I said, "then left, I think." And to Bob I said, "Don't worry about a thing. Once we reach the dragon, you'll ask him how to get out of this whole mess. He can tell you, *has* to tell you actually; once that's all done, you'll be free of me, I'll be free of my father's craziness, *he'll* be free of his obsession."

Bob said, "You really shouldn't put too much stock in what the dragon has to tell you."

I said, "But he *always* tells the truth!"

"Well yes, but as a certain wily Roman politician once said, 'What is truth?' Or was that Ronald Reagan?"

"Oh, Bob," I said, "if push really came to shove, if there's no solution to this whole crisis . . . could you actually bring yourself to marry me?"

"You're very beautiful," Bob said. He loves to be all things to all people. But I don't think there's enough of him to go round. I mean, basically, there are a couple of dozen Janice Lims waiting in line for the opportunity to sit at Bob's feet. But, you know, when you're alone with him, he has this ability to give you every scintilla of his attention, his concern, his love, even; it's just that there's this nagging concern that he'd feel the same way if he were alone with a Beethoven string quartet, say, or a plate of exquisitely spiced *naem sod*.

We were driving through young paddy fields now; the nascent rice has a neon-green color too garish to describe. The scroll was shaking continuously and I realized we must be rather close to our goal; I have to admit that I was scared out of my wits.

The driver took us through the gates of a Buddhist temple. The scroll vibrated even more energetically. Past the main chapel, there were more gates; they led to a Brahmin sanctuary; past the Indian temple there was yet another set of gates, over which, in rusty wrought iron, hung the character *Lim*, which is two trees standing next to one another. The taxi stopped. The scroll's shaking had quieted to an insistent purr. "It's around here *somewhere*," I said, getting out of the cab.

The courtyard we found ourselves in (the sun was setting at this point, and the shadows were long and gloomy, and the marble flagstones red as blood) was a mishmash of nineteenth-century *chinoiserie*. There were stone lions, statues of bearded men, twisted little trees peering up from crannies in the stone; and tall, obelisklike columns in front of a weathered stone building that resembled a ruined ziggurat. It took me a moment to realize that the building was, in fact, the dragon's head, so petrified by time and the slow process of dying that it had turned into an antique shrine. Someone still worshipped here at least. I could smell burning joss-sticks; in front of the pointed columns—which, I now could see, were actually the dragon's teeth—somebody had left a silver tray containing a glass of wine, a pig's head, and a garland of decaying jasmine.

"Yes, yes," said Bob, "I see it too; I feel it even."

"How do you mean?"

"It's the air or something. It tastes of the same bitterness that's in the dragon's fin soup. Only when you've taken a few breaths of it can you smell the underlying sensations . . . the joy, the love, the infinite regret."

"Yes, yes, all right," I said, "but don't forget to ask him for a way out of our dilemma."

"Why don't you ask him yourself?" Bob said.

I became all flustered at this. "Well, it's just that, I don't know, I'm too young, I don't want to use up all my questions, it's not the right time yet . . . you're a mature person, you don't . . ."

". . . have that much longer to live, I suppose," Bob said wryly.

"Oh, you know I didn't mean it in quite that way."

"Ah, but, sucking in the dragon's breath the way we are, we too are forced to blurt out the truth, aren't we?" he said.

I didn't like that.

"Don't want to let the genie out of the bottle, do you?" Bob said. "Want to clutch it to your breast, don't want to let go . . ."

"That's my father you're describing, not me."

Bob smiled. "How do you work this thing?"

"You take the scroll and you tap the dragon's lips."

"Lips?"

I pointed at the long stucco frieze that extended all the way around the row of teeth. "And don't forget to ask him," I said yet again.

"All right. I will."

Bob went up to the steps that led into the dragon's mouth. On the second floor were two flared windows that were his nostrils; above them, two slitty windows seemed to be his eyes; the light from them was dim, and seemed to come from candlelight. I followed him two steps behind—it was almost as though we were already married!—and I was ready when he put out his hand for the scroll. Gingerly, he tapped the dragon's lips.

This was how the dragon's voice sounded: it seemed at first to be the wind, or the tinkling of the temple bells, or the far-off lowing of the water buffalo that wallowed in the paddy, or the distant cawing of a raven, the cry of a newborn child, the creak of a teak house on its stilts, the hiss of a slithering snake. Only gradually did these sounds coalesce into words, and once spoken the words seemed to hang in the air, to jangle and clatter like a loaded dishwasher.

The dragon said, *We seldom have visitors anymore.*

I said, "Quick, Bob, ask."

"Okay, okay," said Bob. He got ready, I think, to ask the dragon what I wanted him to ask, but instead, he blurted out a completely different question. "How different," he said, "would the history of music be, if Mozart had managed to live another ten years?"

"Bob!" I said. "I thought you wanted to ask deep, cosmic questions about the nature of the universe—"

"Can't get much deeper than that," he said, and then the answer came, all at once, out of the twilight air. It was music of a kind. To me it sounded dissonant and disturbing; choirs singing out of tune, donkeys fiddling with their own tails. But you know, Bob stood there with his eyes closed, and his face was suffused with an ineffable serenity; and the music surged to a noisome clanging and a yowling and a caterwauling, and a slow smile broke out on his lips; and as it all began to die away he was whispering to himself, "Of course . . . apoggiaturas piled on appogiaturas, bound to lead to integral serialism in the midromantic period instead, then minimalism mating with impressionism running full tilt into the Wagnerian *gesamtkunstwerk* and colliding with the pointillism of late Webern. . . ."

At last he opened his eyes, and it was as though he had seen the face of God. But what about me and my miserable life? It came to me now. These *were* Bob's idea of what constituted the really important questions. I couldn't begrudge him a few answers. He'd probably save the main course for last; then we'd be out of there and could get on with our lives. I settled back to suffer through another arcane question, and it was, indeed, arcane.

Bob said, "You know, I've always been troubled by one of the hundred-letter words in *Finnegan's Wake*. You know the words I mean, the supposed 'thunder-claps' that divide Joyce's novel into its main sections . . . well, its the ninth one of those . . . I can't seem to get it to split into its component parts. Maybe it seems trivial, but it's worried me for the last twenty-nine years."

The sky grew very dark then. Dry lightning forked and unforked across gathering clouds. The dragon spoke once more, but this time it seemed to be a cacophony of broken words, disjointed phonemes, strings of frenetic fricatives and explosive plosives; once again it was mere noise to me, but to Bob Halliday it was the sweetest music. I saw that gazing-on-the-face-of-divinity expression steal across his features one more time as again he closed his eyes. The man was having an orgasm. No wonder he didn't need sex. I marveled at him. Ideas themselves were sensual things to him. But he didn't lust after knowledge, he wasn't greedy about it like Faust; too much knowledge could not damn Bob Halliday, it could only redeem him.

Once more, the madness died away. A monsoon shower had come and gone in the midst of the dragon's response, and we were drenched; but presently, in the hot breeze that sprang up, our clothes began to dry.

"You've had your fun now, Bob. Please, please," I said, "let's get to the business at hand."

Bob said, "All right." He tapped the dragon's lips again, and said, "Dragon, dragon, I want to know . . ."

The clouds parted and Bob was bathed in moonlight.

Bob said, "Is there a proof for Fermat's Last Theorem?"

Well, I had had it with him now. I could see my whole life swirling down the toilet bowl of lost opportunities. "Bob!" I screamed, and began pummeling his stomach with my fists . . . the flesh was not as soft as I'd imagined it would be. . . . I think I sprained my wrist.

"What did I do wrong?"

"Bob, you idiot, what about *us?*"

"I'm sorry, Janice. Guess I got a little carried away."

Yes, said the dragon. Presumably, since Bob had not actually asked him to prove Fermat's Last Theorem, all he had to do was say yes or no.

What a waste. I couldn't believe that Bob had done that to me. I was going to have to ask the dragon myself after all. I wrested the scroll from Bob's hands, and furiously marched up the steps toward that row of teeth, phosphorescent in the moonlight.

"Dragon," I screamed, "dragon, dragon, dragon, dragon, dragon."

So, Ah Muoi, you've come to me at last. So good of you. I am old; I have seen my beginning and my end; it is in your eyes. You've come to set me free.

Our family tradition states clearly that it is always good to give the dragon the impression that you are going to set him free. He's usually a lot more cooperative. Of course, you never do set him free. You would think that, being almost omniscient, the dragon would be wise to this, but mythical beasts always seem to have their fatal flaws. I was too angry for casuistic foreplay.

"You've got to tell me what I need to know." Furiously, I whipped the crumbling stone with the old scroll.

I'm dying, you are my mistress; what else is new?

"How can I free myself from all the baggage that my family has laid on me?"

The dragon said:

> *There is a sleek swift segment of my soul*
> *That whips against the waters of renewal;*
> *You too have such a portion of yourself;*
> *Divide it in a thousand pieces;*
> *Make soup;*
> *Then shall we all be free.*

"That doesn't make sense!" I said. The dragon must be trying to cheat me somehow. I slammed the scroll against the nearest tooth. The stucco loosened; I heard a distant rumbling. "Give me a straight answer, will you? How can I rid my father of the past that torments him and won't let him face who he is, who I am, what we're not?"

The dragon responded:

> *There is a sly secretion from my scales*
> *That drives a man through madness into joy;*
> *You too have such a portion of yourself;*
> *Divide it in a thousand pieces;*
> *Make soup;*
> *Then shall we all be free.*

This was making me really mad. I started kicking the tooth. I screamed, "Bob was right . . . you're too senile, your mind is too clouded to see anything that's important. . . . All you're good for is Bob's great big esoteric enigmas . . . but I'm just a human being here, and I'm in bondage, and I want out . . . what's it going to take to get a straight answer out of you?" Too late, I realized that I had phrased my last words in the form of a question. And the answer came on the jasmine-scented breeze even before I had finished asking:

> *There is a locked door deep inside my flesh*
> *A dam against bewilderment and fear;*
> *You too have such a portion of yourself;*
> *Divide it in a thousand pieces;*
> *Make soup;*
> *Then shall we all be free.*

But I wasn't even listening, so sure was I that all was lost. For all my life I had been defined by others—my father, now Bob, now the dragon, even, briefly, by Linda Horovitz. I was a series of half-women, never a whole. Frustrated beyond repair, I flagellated the dragon's lips with that scroll, shrieking like a premenstrual fishwife: "Why can't I have a life like other people?" I'd seen the American girls with their casual ways, their cars, speaking of men as though they were hunks of meat; and the Thai girls, arrogant, plotting lovers' trysts on their cellular phones as they breezed through the spanking-new shopping mall of their lives. Why was I the one who was trapped, chained up, enslaved? But I had used up the three questions.

I slammed the scroll so hard against the stucco that it began to tear.

"Watch out!" Bob cried. "You'll lose your power over him!"

"Don't speak to me of empowerment," I shouted bitterly, and the parchment ripped all at once, split into a million itty-bitty pieces that danced like shooting stars in the brilliant moonlight.

That was it, then. I had cut off the family's only source of income, too. I was going to have to marry Mr. Hong after all.

Then the dragon's eyes lit up, and his jaws began slowly to open, and his breath, heady, bitter, and pungent, poured into the humid night air.

"My God," Bob said, "there *is* some life to him after all."

My life, the dragon whispered, *is but a few brief bittersweet moments of imagined freedom; for is not life itself enslavement to the wheel of* sansara? *Yet you, man and woman, base clay though you are, have been the means of my deliverance. I thank you.*

The dragon's mouth gaped wide. Within, an abyss of thickest blackness; but when I stared long and hard at it, I could see flashes of oh, such wondrous things . . . far planets, twisted forests, chaotic cities . . . "Shall we go in?" said Bob.

"Do you want to?"

"Yes," Bob said, "but I can't, not without you; dying, he's still *your* dragon, no one else's; you know how it is; you kill your dragon, I kill mine."

"Okay," I said, realizing that now, finally, had come the moment for me to seize my personhood in my hands, "but come with me, for old times' sake; after all, you did give me a pretty thorough tour of *your* dying dragon. . . ."

"Ah, yes; the City of Angels Etc. But that's not dying for a few millennia yet."

I took Bob by the hand and ran up the steps into the dragon's mouth. He followed me. Inside the antechamber, the dragon's palate glistened with crystallized drool. Strings of baroque pearls hung from the ceiling, and the dragon's tongue was coated with clusters of calcite. Further down, the abyss of many colors yawned.

"Come on," I said.

"What do you think he meant," Bob said, "when he said you should slice off little pieces of yourself, make them into soup, and *that* would set us all free?"

"I think," I said, "that it's the centuries of being nibbled away by little parasites. . . ." But I was no longer that interested in the dragon's oracular pronouncements. I mean, for the first time in my life, since my long imprisonment in my family compound and the confines of the Rainbow Café's kitchen, since my three years of rollercoastering through the alien wharves of Santa Cruz, I was in territory that I instinctively recognized as my own. Past the bronze uvula that depended from the cavern ceiling like a soundless bell, we came to a mother-of-pearl staircase that led ever downward. "This must be the way to the esophagus," I said. "Yeah." There came a gurgling sound. A dull, foul water sloshed about our ankles. "Maybe there's a boat," I said. We turned and saw it moored to the banister, a golden barque with a silken sail blazoned with the ideograph *Lim*.

Bob laughed. "You're a sort of goddess in this kingdom, a creatrix, an earth-mother. But I'm the one with the waistline for earth-mothering."

"Perhaps we could somehow meld together and be one." After all, his mothering instinct was a lot stronger than mine.

"Cosmic!" he said, and laughed again.

"Like the character *Lim* itself," I told him, "two trees straining to be one."

"Erotic!"

And I too laughed as we set sail down the gullet of the dying dragon. The waters were sluggish at first. But they started to deepen. Soon we were having the flume ride of our lives, careening down the bronze-lined walls that boomed with the echo of our laughter . . . the bronze was dark for a long long time till it started to shine with a light that rose from the heat of our bodies, the first warmth to invade the dragon's innards in a thousand years . . . and then, in the mirror surface of the walls, we began to see visions. Yes! There was the dragon himself, youthful, pissing the monsoon as he soared above the South China Sea. Look, look, my multi-great-great-uncle bearing the urn of his severed genitals as he marched from the gates of the Forbidden City, setting sail for Siam! Look, look, now multi-great-great-uncle in the Chinese Quarter of the great metropolis of Ayuthaya, constraining the dragon as he breached the raging waters of the Chao Phraya! Look, look, another great-great-uncle panning for gold, his queue bobbing up and down in the California sun! Look, look, another uncle, marching alongside the great Chinese General Taksin, who wrested Siam back from the Burmese and was in turn put to an ignominious death! And look, look closer now, the soldier raping my grandmother in the doorway of the family compound . . . look, look, my grandfather standing by, his anger curbed by an intolerable terror . . . look, look, even that was there . . . and me . . . yielding to the stately Linda Horovitz in the back seat of a rusty Toyota . . . me, stirring the vat of dragon's fin soup . . . me, talking back to my father for the first time, getting slapped in the face, me, smashing the scroll of power into smithereens.

And Bob? Bob saw other things. He heard the music of the spheres. He saw the Sistine Chapel in its pristine beauty. He speed-read his way through Joyce and Proust and Tolstoy, unexpurgated and unedited. And you know, it was turning him on.

And me, too. I don't know quite when we started making love. Perhaps it was when we hit what felt like terminal velocity, and I could feel the friction and the body heat begin to ignite his shirt and my *cheongsam*. Blue flame embraced our bodies, fire that was water, heat that was cold. The flame was burning up my past, racing through the dirt roads of the ancestral village; the fire was engulfing Chinatown, the rollercoasters of Santa Cruz were blazing gold and ruddy against the setting sun, and even the Forbidden City was on fire, even the great portrait of Chairman Mao and the Great Wall and the Great Inextinguishable Middle Kingdom itself, all burning, burning, burning, all cold, all turned to stone, and all because I was discovering new continents of pleasure in the folds of Bob Halliday's flesh, so rich and convoluted that it was like making love to three hundred pounds of brain; and you know, he was considerate in ways I'd never dreamed; that mothering instinct, I supposed, that empathy; when I popped, he made me feel like the apple that received the arrowhead of William Tell and with it freedom from oppression; oh, God, I'm straining, aren't I, but you know, those things are so hard to describe; we're plummeting headlong through the mist and foam and flame and spray and surge and swell and brine and ice and hell and incandescence and then:

In the eye of the storm:

A deep gash opening and:

Naked, we're falling into the vat beneath the dragon's flanks as the ginsu-wielding Ah Quoc is hacking away at the disintegrating flesh and:

"No!" my father shouted. "Hold the sulfuric acid!"

We were bobbing up and down in a tub of bile and semen and lubricous fluids, and Aunt Ling-ling was frantically snatching away the flask of concentrated H_2SO_4 from the kvetching Jasmine.

"Mr. Elephant, la!" cried Ah Quoc. "What you do, Miss Janice? No can! No can!"

"You've gone and killed the dragon!" shrieked my father. "Now what are we going to do for a living?"

And he was right. Once harder than titanium carbide, the coil of flesh was dissipating into the kitchen's musty air; the scales were becoming circlets of rainbow light in the steam from the bamboo *cha shu bao* containers; as archetypes are wont to do, the dragon was returning to the realm of myth.

"Oh, Papa, don't make such a fuss," I said, and was surprised to see him back off right away. "We're still going to make soup today."

"Well, I'd like to know how. Do you know you were gone for three weeks? It's Wednesday again, and the line for dragon's fin soup is stretching all the way to Chicken Alley! There's some kind of weird rumor going around that the soup today is especially *heng*, and I'm not about to go back out there and tell them I'm going to be handing out rain checks."

"Speaking of rain—" said Aunt Ling-ling.

Rain indeed. We could hear it, cascading across the corrugated iron rooftops, sluicing down the awnings, splashing the dead-end canals, running in the streets.

"Papa," I said, "we *shall* make soup. It will be the last and finest soupmaking of the Clan of Lim."

And then—for Bob Halliday and I were still entwined in each other's arms, and his flesh was still throbbing inside my flesh, bursting with pleasure as the thunderclouds above—we rose up, he and I, he with his left arm stretched to one side, I with my right arm to the other, and together we spelled out the *two trees melding into one* in the calligraphy of carnal desire—and, basically, what happened next was that I released into the effervescing soup stock the *sleek swift segment of my soul, the sly secretion from my scales*, and, last but not least, the *locked door deep inside my flesh*; and these things (as the two trees broke apart) did indeed divide into a thousand pieces, and so we made our soup; not from a concrete dragon, time-frozen in its moment of dying, but from an insubstantial spirit-dragon that was woman, me, alive.

"Well, well," said Bob Halliday, "I'm not sure I'll be able to write this up for the *Post*."

* * *

Now this is what transpired next, in the heart of Bangkok's Chinatown, in the district known as Yaowaraj, in a restaurant called the Rainbow Café, on a Wednesday lunchtime in the midmonsoon season:

There wasn't very much soup, but the more we ladled out, the more there seemed to be left. We had thought to eke it out with black mushrooms and *bok choi* and a little sliced chicken, but even those extra ingredients multiplied miraculously. It wasn't quite the feeding of the five thousand, but, unlike the evangelist, we didn't find it necessary to count.

After a few moments, the effects were clearly visible. At one table, a group of politicians began removing their clothes. They leaped up onto the lazy Susan and began to spin around, chanting "Freedom! Freedom!" at the top of their lungs. At the next table, three transvestites from the drag show down the street began to make mad passionate love to a platter of duck. A young man in a pinstripe suit draped himself in the printout from his cellular fax and danced the hula with a shriveled crone. Children somersaulted from table to table like monkeys.

And Bob Halliday, my father, and I?

My father, drinking deeply, said, "I really don't give a shit who you marry."

And I said, "I guess it's about time I told you this, but there's a strapping Jewish tomboy from Milwaukee that I want you to meet. Oh, but maybe I *will* marry Mr. Hong—why not?—some men aren't as self-centered and domineering as you might think. If you'd stop sitting around trying to be Chinese all the time—"

"I guess it's about time I told you this," said my father, "but I stopped caring about this baggage from the past a long time ago. I was only keeping it up so you wouldn't think I was some kind of bloodless half-breed."

"I guess it's about time I told you this," I said, "but I *like* living in Thailand. It's wild, it's maddening, it's obscenely beautiful, and it's very, very, very un-American."

"I guess it's about time I told you this," my father said, "but I've bought me a one-way ticket to Californ', and I'm going to close up the restaurant and get a new wife and buy myself a little self-respect."

"I guess it's about time I told you this," I said, "I love you."

That stopped him cold. He whistled softly to himself, then sucked up the remaining dregs of soup with a slurp like a farting buffalo. Then he flung the bowl against the peeling wall and cried out, "And I love you too."

And that was the first and only time we were ever to exchange those words.

But you know, there were no such revelations from Bob Halliday. He drank deeply and reverently; he didn't slurp; he savored; of all the *dramatis personae* of this tale, it was he alone who seemed, for a moment, to have cut himself free from the wheel of *sansara* to gaze, however briefly, on nirvana.

As I have said, there was a limitless supply of soup. We gulped it down till our sides ached. We laughed so hard we were sitting ankle-deep in our tears.

But do you know what?

An hour later we were hungry again.

THE GRANDDAUGHTER
Vivian Vande Velde

Vivian Vande Velde is the author of A *Hidden Magic* and A *Well-Timed Enchantment*, charming fantasy novels for children. "The Granddaughter" comes from her new collection of stories, *Tales from the Brothers Grimm and the Sisters Weird*. This wicked little retelling of the "Little Red Riding Hood" story is reminiscent of those old, hilarious "Fractured Fairy Tale" cartoons. Here, the author casts the wolf in a sympathetic role, for once in the poor bugger's life. . . .

—T.W.

Once upon a time in a land and time when animals could speak and people could understand them, there lived an old woman whose best friend was a wolf. Because they were best friends, they told each other everything, and one of the things that Granny told the wolf was that she dreaded visits from her granddaughter, Lucinda.

"I'm afraid my son and his wife have spoiled her," Granny said to the wolf as they shared tea in the parlor of the little cottage Granny had in the woods.

"Children will be children," the wolf said graciously. He had no children of his own and could afford to be gracious. "I'm sure she can't be all that bad."

"You'll see," Granny told him. "You haven't seen Lucinda since she was a tiny baby who couldn't even talk, but now she's old enough that her mother has said she can come through the woods on her own to visit me."

"Lucky you," the wolf said with a smile.

"Lucky me," Granny said, but she didn't smile.

The wolf didn't visit Granny for nearly a week, being busy with wolf business in another section of the forest where he was advising three porcine brothers on home construction. After he came back, though, he was walking near the path leading from the meadow to Granny's house when he saw a little girl with a picnic basket. He recognized her right away from the picture Granny kept on her mantel.

"Hello," he said, loping up to the child. "You must be Lucinda."

"Don't call me that," the girl snapped. She stopped to glare at him. "I'm Little Red Riding Hood."

The wolf paused to consider. "A little red riding hood is what you're wearing," he said. "It's not a name."

"It's my stage name," the girl said. She swirled her red cape dramatically. "I'm going to be a famous actress one day, and I'm going to travel all around the world, and when I do, all my clothes will be red velvet. It'll be my trademark."

The wolf nodded and opened his mouth, but before he could get a word out, Little Red continued: "Madame Yvette—she's my acting instructor—Madame Yvette says every great actor or actress needs a trademark. Mine will be red velvet because Madame Yvette says I look stunning in red velvet. Not everybody can carry off such a dramatic color, you know, but I have the coloring and the flair for it."

The wolf nodded and opened his mouth, but before he could get a sound out, Little Red continued: "I played Mary in our church's Easter pageant, and my performance was so touching everyone in the congregation wept—they actually wept. Even the priest had tears in his eyes, and you've got to believe he's seen an Easter pageant or two in his time, so you *know* I must have been stunning, even though they told me Mary had to wear white linen and not red velvet."

The wolf nodded, but before he could get his mouth open, Little Red continued: "When I go on tour, I'm going to demand that all the theaters I perform in must have red velvet seats, and I'll travel in a coach with red velvet cushions, and kings and queens and emperors and popes will stand in lines by the roads, waiting for hours for a chance to catch a glimpse of me."

Little Red paused for a breath.

The wolf was pretty sure there was only one pope, and that—since there was only the one—he probably wasn't permitted to stand on roadsides, waiting for actresses to pass by. But he didn't want to waste his opportunity to speak and decided he'd better say something important. He said: "Well, probably I should introduce myself—"

"Oh, I know who you are," Little Red interrupted. "You're that wolf who's my grandmother's friend. Yes, I noticed the scratch marks your claws left on her hardwood floors. I told her, I said, 'I don't know how you put up with it. I mean, having a nonhuman friend is one thing,' I told her, 'but scratches and dings on the floors and furniture, which just make the whole house look shabby, is another. After all, I have an image to maintain for my fans.' "

Little Red leaned forward to lay her hand on the wolf's shoulder. She didn't seem to notice that his eyes were beginning to glaze over. She said, "I know I can speak frankly with you because you've been a friend of the family, so to speak, for ages, so you've got to know I'm only telling you this for your own good, but you really should consider meeting my grandmother outside in the garden. She could sit in a nice comfy lawn chair, and then you wouldn't have to worry about scratch marks or shedding or fleas or anything like that."

Fleas? the wolf thought. *Fleas?*

But Little Red continued on. " 'And meanwhile,' I told Granny, 'have you ever tried Professor Patterson's Wood-Replenishing Cream? Madame Yvette uses it to polish the stage. It's great for bringing out the natural shine of wood.' Granny had never heard of it—which, of course, I'd already guessed by the state her furniture was in—but I told her I was sure my mother would be willing to spare a jar of hers, since Granny's floors were in such obviously desperate need."

Little Red stopped for another breath, but by then the wolf's head was spinning. He was just opening his mouth to protest that he did not have fleas, but he wasn't fast enough. Little Red started telling him about other products that her mother used around the home, and once she started, he wasn't able to get a word in edgewise.

After a few minutes that felt like an hour or two, the wolf was thinking that he was in serious danger of being bored to death.

The next time Little Red paused to inhale, he pointed at the sun overhead and exclaimed, all in one rush so Little Red couldn't interrupt, "My goodness, look at the time, I had no idea it was so late, I'm late for an appointment, it was real nice meeting you, good-bye!"

He also had the sense to start moving as soon as he started talking.

Which was a good thing, because Little Red started telling him, even as he left, about the clock her father had bought, which had been made in Switzerland, and it had a dial to show the phases of the moon and you could set it to any one of three different kinds of chimes, and it was carved with something-or-other—but by then the wolf had speeded up and was out of earshot.

He felt ready to collapse with exhaustion. The only thing that kept him going was the thought of poor Granny, and the knowledge that she had to be warned.

Luckily, he knew a shortcut.

Racing ahead, he got to Granny's house and pounded on the door.

Though it was midmorning, Granny came to the door wearing her nightie and slippers, with a shawl wrapped around her shoulders.

Before she could get a word out, the wolf said: "I met her, I know what you mean, she's on her way—quick, get dressed, there's still time to escape out the back door."

Granny sneezed. Twice. Three times. The wolf thought Little Red would probably blame him for giving her grandmother allergies, but Granny said, "She gave me her cold, and now I'm too sick to leave. I hoped her mother wouldn't let her come again today. What am I going to do? I'm not up to one of her visits."

"Tell her she can't come in," the wolf suggested.

"You can't say that to family," Granny said. She blew her nose in her hankie. "I can't face her. She'll tell me it isn't a cold and that I'm sneezing because of all the dust in my house. Can you believe she told me my house is one huge dust trap and that her mother wouldn't stand for it?"

"Yes," the wolf said, "I believe it." Looking out the window, he added, "Here she comes up the walk."

"She's sure to have all sorts of remedies and advice," Granny said. "Well, I'm hiding in the closet. Call me when it's safe to come out again."

She stepped into the closet and pulled the door closed behind her.

Something has to be done about that little girl, the wolf thought, *or she'll never leave*. He grabbed a spare nightie and nightcap out of the chest at the foot of the bed and leapt into Granny's bed, pulling the covers up to his chin just as Little Red walked in without knocking or waiting for an invitation.

"I got the most beautiful azaleas out of our garden for you to cheer you up," Little Red said, reaching into her basket, "along with the regular cakes and bread and jams and other goodies my mother usually packs for you. I'll bet you thought it was too early in the year for azaleas, but we have the very first ones, because what we do is we force them by putting burlap bags on the ground to . . ."

Little Red stopped talking, and it was the first time the wolf had heard such a thing.

"What are you doing here?" she demanded.

"Why, dear," the wolf said, trying to sound like Granny, "I'm your grandmother. I live here."

"You're not Granny," Little Red said. "You're that rude wolf."

Rude! the wolf thought. "No, dear," he insisted in a high, shaky voice, "I'm Granny. I'm feeling much better today, but very contagious. Why don't you leave the basket of goodies on the night table and go back home?"

Little Red put the basket down on the floor, but she picked up a wooden spoon with which Granny had been eating a bowl of oatmeal, and she approached the bed. "If you're Granny," she said, and jabbed the wolf's front leg with the spoon, "why do you have such big, hairy arms?"

The wolf winced but ignored the oatmeal, which stuck to his fur. He forced himself to speak gently and lovingly. "The better to hug you with, my dear," he said.

"And if you're Granny, why do you have such big, hairy ears?" She poked him on the side of the head with the spoon, leaving behind another glob of oatmeal.

"Ouch! The better to hear you with, my dear." He forced himself to smile.

"And if you're Granny, why do you have such big, sharp teeth?" She smacked him on the muzzle with the spoon—which hurt a lot.

The wolf lost his temper. "The better to eat you with!" he yelled. He didn't mean it, of course. He was angry, but not angry enough to eat his best friend's granddaughter.

But as he jumped out of bed, intending only to frighten Little Red a bit, his back leg caught on the blankets and he half fell on her.

Landing heavily on the floor, she began to scream.

Loudly.

Very loudly.

Extremely loudly.

She scrambled backward, knocking Granny's chair over, and continued screaming, all the while whacking away at the wolf with the wooden spoon.

The wolf, still caught in the bed linens, flailed about, shredding the sheets with his claws, and began to howl.

Granny, hearing all the commotion, tried to open the closet door, but the tipped chair was in the way. She was sure an intruder had come into the house and was killing both her best friend and her granddaughter. "Help!" she began to scream, knowing that there were woodcutters working nearby. "Help!"

And one of the woodcutters, a neighbor man named Bob, heard her.

Bob shifted his ax to his left hand and swept up his hunting musket as he took off running across Granny's yard.

Throwing open the front door, he saw the snarling wolf dressed in Granny's clothes, and he saw Little Red, still on the floor, screaming. He assumed the worst and fired the musket . . .

. . . just as he stepped into Little Red's basket of goodies.

The bullet missed the wolf and shattered the bowl of oatmeal on the night table.

"What idiot's shooting guns off in my house?" Granny yelled, but nobody could hear her because of Little Red's screaming.

Bob dropped the musket, which was only good for one shot before it needed to be reloaded, and switched the ax back to his right hand, all the while trying to shake the basket off his foot at the same time he was approaching the bed. Dragging Little Red out of the way, he swung his ax at the wolf . . .

 . . . just as Granny heaved herself against the closet door, scraping the fallen chair across the floor.

The ax embedded itself in the edge of the door.

Granny looked from the ax head, three inches away from her nose, to Bob.

There was a moment of stunned silence. The wolf stopped struggling against the tangled bedsheets. Even Little Red stopped screaming.

"What in the world did you do that for?" Granny demanded.

"I thought the wolf ate you," Bob said. "I was trying to rescue your granddaughter."

Too shocked for words, the wolf shook his head to indicate he'd never eat Granny.

"Well!" Little Red said. "Some rescue! First you barge in here, tracking your muddy boots all over the floor"—Bob opened his mouth to apologize, but Little Red continued—"which I know wasn't in very good shape to begin with, Granny being the indifferent housekeeper she is—I know she doesn't mind my saying that because I only mention it for her own good, and believe me, when I'm a famous actress I'll hire a maid to give her a hand, because, heaven knows, she isn't getting any younger." The wolf saw that Bob's eyes were beginning to bulge as his hand slipped from the handle of his ax, but Little Red continued: "But even leaving Granny's messy habits out of it, you come in here trailing big globs of mud and grass, shoot a hole through the bowl, which *my family* bought Granny for Christmas last year, gouge a perfectly fine door with your ax, not to mention pulling my hair, and look at this—*look at this!*" Everybody looked. "You are stepping in the goodies my mother made and which I brought here for my sick granny, never mind that I had to walk for hours to get here and that I'm even now missing a class with Madame Yvette to be here, inhaling wolf dander, and catching a chill from sitting on this floor, which no doubt will ruin my stunning speaking voice. And you call this a rescue?"

Bob shook the basket off his foot.

The wolf saw that the azaleas were crunched, but the food was surprisingly undamaged. He straightened the nightcap, which had fallen to cover one eye. He, Granny, and Bob looked at one another. They looked at the basket of goodies. They looked at Little Red.

There was only one thing they could do.

They locked Little Red in the closet, then they went out in the backyard and had a picnic.

DAPHNE AND LAURA AND SO FORTH

Margaret Atwood

Canadian author Margaret Atwood has drawn upon themes from myth and folklore in previous works such as *The Robber Bride* (a novel), *Bluebeard's Egg* (short stories), and in her poetry. She is one of the finest writers working today, and these are highly recommended. Her latest collection of poems is *Morning in the Burned House*, a lovely volume which I also strongly recommend—although, I admit, it has only a few poems with mythic/folkloric/ magical imagery. The poem that follows is one.

—T.W.

He was the one who saw me
just before I changed,
before bark/fur/snow closed over
my mouth, before my eyes grew gray.

I should not have shown fear,
or so much leg.

His look of disbelief—
I didn't mean to!
Just, her neck was so much more
fragile than I thought.

The gods don't listen to reason,
they need what they need—
that suntan line at the bottom
of the spine, those teeth like mouthwash,
that drop of sweat pearling
the upper lip—
or that's what gets said in court.

Why talk when you can whisper?
Rustle, like dried leaves.
Under the bed.

It's ugly here, but safer.
I have eight fingers
and a shell, and live in corners.
I'm free to stay up all night.
I'm working on
these ideas of my own:
venom, a web, a hat,
some last resort.

He was running,
he was asking something,
he wanted something or other.

A LAMIA IN THE CÉVENNES
A. S. Byatt

British writer A. S. Byatt, winner of the 1990 Booker Prize, is also a distinguished literary critic and has taught at University College, London. Byatt has written several works of fiction, three of which are of particular note to fantasy readers: *The Djinn in the Nightingale's Eye*, a collection of five adult fairy stories; *Angels and Insects*, one novella which was recently made into a film with the same title; and *Possession*, an extraordinary novel which no lover of fantasy (or books, or Victoriana) should miss—a literary mystery with a fairytale at its heart.

"A Lamia in the Cévennes" is a sensual and thought-provoking tale, set in the countryside of France. It comes from the July issue of *The Atlantic Monthly*.

—T.W.

In the mid-1980s Bernard Lycett-Kean decided that Margaret Thatcher's Britain was uninhabitable, a land of dog eat dog, lung-corroding ozone, and floating money, of which there was at once far too much and far too little. He sold his West Hampstead flat and bought a small stone house on a Cévenol hillside. He had three rooms and a large barn, which he weatherproofed, using it as a studio in winter and as a storehouse in summer. He did not know how he would take to solitude, and laid in a large quantity of red wine, of which he drank a good deal at first, and much less afterward. He discovered that the effect of the air and the light and the extremes of heat and cold was enough—indeed, too much—without alcohol. He stood on the terrace in front of his house and battled with these things, with mistral and thunderbolts and howling clouds. The Cévennes is a place of extreme weather. There were days of white heat, and days of yellow heat, and days of burning blue heat. He produced some paintings of heat and light, with very little else in them, and some other paintings of the small river that ran along the foot of the steep, terraced hill on which his house stood; these were dark green and dotted with the bright blue of the kingfisher and the electric blue of the dragonflies.

These paintings he packed in his van and took to London and sold for largish sums of the despised money. He went to a private viewing of his own work and found that he had lost the habit of conversation. He stared and snorted. He was a big man, a burly man, whose stare seemed aggressive when it was largely baffled. His old friends were annoyed. He himself found London just as rushing and evil-smelling and unreal as he had been imagining it. He hurried back to the Cévennes. With his earnings he built himself a swimming pool where once there had been a patch of baked mud and a few bushes.

To say he built it is not quite right. It was built by the Jardinerie Emeraude, two enterprising young men, who dug and lined and carried mud and monstrous stones, and built a humming pump house full of taps and pipes and a swirling cauldron of filter sand. The pool was blue, a swimming-pool blue, lined with a glittering tile mosaic, and with a mosaic dolphin cavorting amiably in its depths— a dark-blue dolphin with a pale-blue eye. It was not a boring rectangular pool but an irregular, rounded triangle, hugging the contour of the terrace in which it lay. It had a white-stone rim, molded to the hand, delightful to touch when it was hot in the sun.

The two young men were surprised that Bernard wanted it blue. Blue was a little *moche*, they thought. People now were making pools steel gray or emerald green, or even dark wine red. But Bernard's mind was full of the blue dots that were visible across the southern mountains when one traveled from Paris to Montpellier by air. It was a recalcitrant blue, a blue that asked to be painted by David Hockney and only by David Hockney. He felt that something else could and must be done with that blue. It was a blue he needed to know and fight. His painting was combative painting. That blue, that amiable, non-natural aquamarine, was different in the uncompromising mountains from what it was in Hollywood. There were no naked male backsides by his pool, no umbrellas, no tennis courts. The river water was somber and weedy, full of little shoals of needlefish and their shadows, of curling water snakes and the triangular divisions of flow around pebbles and boulders. This mild blue, here, was to be seen in *that* terrain.

He swam more and more, trying to understand the blue, which was different when it was under the nose, ahead of the eyes, over and around the sweeping hands and the flickering toes and the groin and the armpits and the hairs of his chest, which held bubbles of air for a time. His shadow in the blue moved over a pale eggshell mosaic; it was a darker blue, with huge, paddle-shaped hands. The light changed, and with it, everything. The best days were under racing cloud, when the aquamarine took on a cool, gray tone, which was then chased back, or rolled away, by the flickering gold-in-blue of yellow light in liquid. In front of his prow, or chin, in the brightest lights moved a mesh of hexagonal threads, flashing rainbow colors, flashing liquid silver-gilt, with a hint of molten glass; on such days lines of liquid fire, rosy and yellow and clear, ran across the dolphin, who lent them a thread of intense blue. But the surface could be a reflective plane, with the trees hanging in it, with two white diagonals where the aluminum steps entered. The shadows of the sides were a deeper blue but not a deep blue, a blue not reflective and yet lying flatly *under* reflections. The pool was deep, for the Emeraude young men had envisaged much diving. The wind changed the surface, frilled and furred it, flecked it with diamond drops, shirred it and made a witless patchwork of its plane. His own motion changed the surface—the longer he swam, the faster he swam, the more the glassy hills and valleys chopped and changed and ran back on each other.

Swimming was *volupté*—he used the French word, because of Matisse. *Luxe, calme, et volupté*. Swimming was a strenuous battle with immense problems, of geometry, of chemistry, of apprehension, of style, of other colors. He put pots of petunias and geraniums near the pool. The bright hot pinks and purples were dangerous. They did something to that blue.

The stone was easy. Almost too blandly easy. He could paint chalky white and creamy sand and cool gray and paradoxical hot gray; he could understand the shadows in the high rough wall of enormous cobblestones that bounded his land.

The problem was the sky. Swimming in one direction, he was headed toward a great rounded green mountain, thick with the bright yellow-green of dense chestnut trees, making a slightly innocent, simple arc against the sky. Whereas the other way, he swam toward crags, toward a bowl of bald crags with a few pines and lines of dark shale. And against the green hump the blue sky was one blue, and against the bald stone another, even when for a brief few hours it was uniformly blue overhead, that rich blue, that cobalt deepwashed blue of the South, which fought all the blues of the pool, all the green-tinged, duck-egg-tinged blues of the shifting water. But the sky had also its greenish days, and its powdery-haze days, and its theatrical threatening days, and none of these blues and whites and golds and ultramarines and faded washes harmonized in any way with the pool blues, though they all went through their changes and splendors in the same world, in which he and his shadow swam, in which he and his shadow stood in the sun and struggled to record them.

He muttered to himself. Why bother? Why does this *matter* so much? *What difference does it make to anything if I solve this blue* and just start again? I could just sit down and drink wine. I could go and be useful in a cholera camp in Ethiopia. *Why bother to render the transparency in solid paint or air on a bit of board?* I could *just stop.*

He could not.

He tried oil paint and acrylic, watercolor and gouache, large designs and small plain planes and complicated juxtaposed planes. He tried trapping light on impasto and tried also glazing his surfaces flat and glossy, like seventeenth-century Dutch or Spanish paintings of silk. One of these almost pleased him—done at night, with the lights under the water and the dark round the stone, on an oval bit of board. But then he thought it was sentimental. He tried veils of watery blues on white in watercolor; he tried Matisse-like patches of blue and petunia (pool blue, sky blue, petunia); he tried Bonnard's mixtures of pastel and gouache.

His brain hurt, and his eyes stared, and he felt whipped by winds and dried by suns.

He was happy, in one of the ways human beings have found in which to be happy.

One day he got up as usual, and as usual flung himself naked into the water to watch the dawn in the sky and the blue come out of the black and gray in the water.

There was a hissing in his ears, and a stench in his nostrils—perhaps a sulfurous stench, he was not sure; his eyes were sharp, but his profession, with spirits and turpentine, had dulled his nostrils. As he moved through the sluggish surface, he stirred up bubbles, which broke, foamed, frothed, and crusted. He began to leave a trail of white, which reminded him of polluted rivers, of the waste pipes of tanneries, of deserted mines. He came out rapidly and showered. He sent a fax to the Jardinerie Emeraude. "What was Paradise is become the Infernal Pit. Where once I smelled lavender and salt, now I have a mephitic stench. What have you done to my water? Undo it, undo it. I cannot coexist with these exhalations." His French was more florid than his English. "I am polluted, my work is polluted, *I cannot go on.*" How could the two young men be brought to recognize the extent of the insult? He paced the terrace like an angry panther. The sickly smell crept like marsh gas over the flowerpots, through the lavender bushes. An emerald-green van drew up, with a painted swimming pool and a painted palm tree. Every time he saw the van, he was pleased and irritated that this commercial emerald-and-blue had found an exact balance for the difficult aquamarine without admitting any difficulty.

The young men ran along the edge of the pool, peering in, their muscular legs brown under their shorts, their plimsolls padding. The sun came up over the green hill and showed the plague-stricken water skin, ashy and suppurating. It is all okay, said the young man, this is a product we put in to fight algae, not because you *have* algae, M. Bernard, but in case algae might appear, as a precaution. It will all be exhaled in a week or two; the mousse will go; the water will clear.

"Empty the pool," Bernard said. "*Now.* Empty it now. I will not coexist for two weeks with this vapor. Give me back my clean salty water. *This water is my lifework.* Empty it *now.*"

"It will take days to fill," one young man said, with a French acceptance of Bernard's desperation. "Also there is the question of the allocation of water, of how much you are permitted to take."

"We could fetch it up from the river," the other said. In French this is, literally, we could draw it *in* the river, *puiser dans le ruisseau*, like fishing. "It will be cold, ice cold from the source, up the mountain," said the Emeraude young men.

"Do it," Bernard said. "Fill it from the river. I am an Englishman, I swim in the North Sea, I like cold water. Do it. *Now.*"

The young men ran up and down. They turned huge taps in the gray-plastic pipes that debouched from the side of the mountain. The swimming pool soughed and sighed and began, still sighing, to sink, while down below, on the hillside, a frothing flood spread and laughed and pranced and curled and divided and swept into the river. Bernard stalked behind the young men, admonishing them. "Look at the froth. We are polluting the river."

"It is only two liters. It is perfectly safe. Everyone has it in his pool, M. Bernard. It is tried and tested; it is a product for *purifying water.*" Only you, his pleasant voice implied, are pigheaded enough to insist on voiding it.

The pool became a pit. The mosaic sparkled a little in the sun, but it was a sad sight. It was a deep blue pit of an entirely unproblematic dull texture. Almost like a bathroom floor. The dolphin lost his movement and his fire and his curvetting ripples, and became a stolid fish in two dimensions. Bernard peered in from the deep end and from the shallow end, and looked over the terrace wall at the hillside, where froth was expiring on nettles and brambles. The pool took almost all day to empty and began to make sounds like a gigantic version of the bath-plug terrors of Bernard's infant dreams.

The two young men appeared carrying an immense boa constrictor of heavy black-plastic pipe and an implement that looked like a torpedo, or a diver's oxygen pack. The mountainside was steep, and the river ran green and chuckling at its foot. Bernard stood and watched. The coil of pipe was uncoiled, the electricity was connected in his humming pump house, and a strange sound began, a regular boom-boom, like the beat of a giant heart, echoing off the green mountain. Water began to gush from the mouth of the pipe lying in the sad, dry depths of his pool-pit. Where it trickled upward, the mosaic took on a little life again, like crystals glinting.

"It will take all night to fill," the young men said. "But do not be afraid: even if the pool overflows, water will not come in your house; the slope is too steep, and it will run away back to the river. And tomorrow we will come and regulate it and filter it and you may swim. But it will be very cold."

"*Tant pis,*" Bernard said.

All night the black tube on the hillside wailed like a monstrous bullfrog, boom-boom, boom-boom. All night the water rose, silent and powerful. Bernard could not sleep; he paced his terrace and watched the silver line creep up the sides of the pit, watched the greenish water sway. Finally he slept, and in the morning his world was awash with river water, and the heartbeat machine was still howling on the riverbank, boom-boom, boom-boom. He watched a small fish skid and slide across his terrace, flow over the edge, and slip in a stream of water down the hillside and back into the river. Everything smelled wet and lively, with no hint of sulfur and no clear smell of purified water. His friend Raymond Potter telephoned from London to say that he might come on a visit; Bernard, who could not cope with visitors, was noncommittal, and tried to describe his delicious flood as a minor disaster.

"You don't want river water," Raymond Potter said. "What about liver flukes and things, and bilharzia?"

"They don't have bilharzia in the Cévennes," Bernard said.

The Emeraude young men came and turned off the machine, which groaned, made a sipping sound, and relapsed into silence. The water in the pool had a grassy depth it hadn't had. It was a lovely color, a natural color, a color that harmonized with the hills, and it was not the problem Bernard was preoccupied with. It would clear, the young men assured him, once the filtration was working again.

Bernard went swimming in the green water. His body slipped into its usual movements. He looked down for his shadow and thought he saw out of the corner of his eye a swirling movement in the depths, a shadowy coiling. It would be strange, he said to himself, if a big snake were down there, moving around. The dolphin was blue in green gloom. Bernard spread his arms and legs and floated. He heard a rippling sound of movement, turned his head, and found he was swimming alongside a yellow-green frog, a frog with a salmon patch on its cheek and another on its butt, the color of the roe of scallops. It made vigorous thrusts with its hind legs and vanished into the skimmer, from the mouth of which it peered out at Bernard. The underside of its throat beat, beat, cream colored. When it emerged, Bernard cupped his hands under its cool wet body and lifted it over the edge: it clung to his fingers with its own tiny fingers, and then went away, in long hops. Bernard went on swimming. There was still a kind of movement in the depths that was not his own.

* * *

The odd stirrings persisted for some days, although the young men set the filter in motion, tipped in sacks of white salt, and did indeed restore the aquamarine transparency, as promised. Now and then he saw a shadow that was not his; now and then something moved behind him; he felt the water swirl and tug. This did not alarm him, because he both believed and disbelieved his senses. He liked to imagine a snake. Bernard liked snakes. He liked the darting river snakes and the long silver-brown grass snakes that traveled through the grasses beside the river.

Sometimes he swam at night, which is when he first definitely saw the snake, only for a few moments, after he had switched on the underwater lights, which made the water look like turquoise milk. There under the milk was something very large, something coiled in two intertwined figures of eight and like no snake he had ever seen—a velvety black, it seemed, with long bars of crimson and peacock-eyed spots, gold, green, blue, mixed with silver moon shapes, all of which appeared to dim and brighten and breathe under the deep water. Bernard did not try to touch; he sat down carefully and stared. He could see neither head nor tail; the form appeared to be a continuous coil, like a Möbius strip. And the colors changed as he watched them: the gold and silver lit up and went out, like lamps; the eyes expanded and contracted; the bars and stripes flamed with electric vermilion and crimson and then changed to purple, to blue, to green, moving through the rainbow. He tried professionally to commit the forms and the colors to memory. He looked up for a moment at the night sky. The Plough hung very low, and the stars in Orion's belt glittered white-gold on thick midnight velvet. When he looked back, the pearly water was vacant.

Many men might have run roaring in terror; the courageous might have prodded with a pool net; the extravagant might have reached for a shotgun. What Bernard saw was a solution to his professional problem—at least a nocturnal solution. Between the night sky and the breathing, dissolving eyes and moons in the depths, the color of the water was solved, dissolved; it became a medium to contain a darkness spangled with living colors. He went in and took notes in watercolor and gouache. He went out and stared, and the pool was empty.

For several days he neither saw nor felt the snake. He tried to remember it, and to trace its markings into his pool paintings, which became very tentative and watery. He swam even more than usual, invoking the creature from time to time. "Come back," he said to the pleasant blue depths, to the twisting, coiling lines of rainbow light. "Come back—I need you."

And then, one day, when a thunderstorm was gathering behind the crest of the mountains, when the sky darkened and the pool was unreflective, he felt the alien tug of the other current again and looked round quick, quick, to catch it. And there was a head, urging itself sinuously through the water beside his own, and there below his body coiled the miraculous black-velvet rope or tube, with its shimmering moons and stars, its peacock eyes, its crimson bands.

The head was a snake's head, diamond-shaped, half the size of his own head, swarthy and scaled, with a strange little crown of pale lights hanging above it like its own rainbow. He turned cautiously to look at it and saw that it had large eyes with fringed eyelashes—human eyes, very lustrous, very liquid, very black. He opened his mouth, swallowed water by accident, coughed. The creature watched him and then opened its mouth in turn, which was full of small, even, pearly human teeth. Between these protruded a flickering, dark forked tongue, entirely serpentine. Bernard felt a prick of recognition. The creature sighed. It spoke. It spoke in Cévenol French, very sibilant but comprehensible.

"I am so unhappy," it said.

"I am sorry," Bernard said stupidly, treading water. He felt the black coils slide against his naked legs, a tail tip across his private parts.

"You are a very beautiful man," the snake said in a languishing voice.

"You are a very beautiful snake," Bernard replied courteously, watching the absurd eyelashes dip and lift.

"I am not entirely a snake. I am an enchanted spirit, a lamia. If you will kiss my mouth, I will become a most beautiful woman; and if you will marry me, I will be eternally faithful and gain an immortal soul. I will also bring you power, and riches, and knowledge you never dreamed of. But you must have faith in me."

Bernard turned over on his side and floated, disentangling his brown legs from the twining colored coils. The snake sighed.

"You do not believe me. You find my present form too loathsome to touch. I love you. I have watched you for months, and I love and worship your every movement, your powerful body, your formidable brow, the movements of your hands when you paint. Never in all my thousands of years have I seen so perfect a male being. I will do *anything* for you—"

"Anything?"

"Oh, *anything*. Ask. Do not reject me."

"What I want," Bernard said, swimming toward the craggy end of the pool, with the snake stretched out behind him, "what I want is to be able to paint your portrait, *as you are*, for certain reasons of my own, and because I find you very beautiful. If you would consent to remain here for a little time, as a snake, with all these amazing colors and lights, if I could paint you *in my pool*, just for a little time . . ."

"And then you will kiss me, and we will be married, and I shall have an immortal soul."

"Nobody nowadays believes in immortal souls," Bernard said.

"It does not matter if you believe in them or not," the snake said. "You have one, and it will be horribly tormented if you break your pact with me."

Bernard did not point out that he had not made a pact, not having answered her request yes or no. He wanted quite desperately that she should remain in his pool, in her present form, until he had solved the colors, and was almost prepared for a Faustian damnation.

A few weeks of hectic activity followed. The lamia lingered agreeably in the pool disposing herself wherever she was asked, under or on the water, in the figure three or six or eight or zero, in spirals and tight coils. Bernard painted and swam and painted and swam. He swam less, because he found the lamia's wreathing flirtatiousness oppressive, though occasionally, to encourage her, he stroked her sleek sides, or wound her tail round his arm or his arm round her tail. He never painted her head, which he found hideous and repulsive. Bernard liked snakes but he did not like women. The lamia, with female intuition, began to sense his lack of enthusiasm for this aspect of her. "My teeth," she told him, "will be lovely in rosy lips, my eyes will be melting and mysterious in a human face. Kiss me, Bernard, and you will see."

"Not yet, not yet," Bernard said.

"I will not wait forever," the lamia said.

Bernard remembered where he had seen her before. He looked her up one evening in Keats, and there she was—teeth, eyelashes, frecklings, streaks and bars, sapphires, greens, amethyst, and rubious-argent. He had always found the teeth and eyelashes repulsive, and had supposed that Keats was, as usual, piling excess on excess. Now he decided that Keats must have seen one himself, or read someone who had, and must have felt the same mixture of aesthetic frenzy and repulsion. Mary Douglas, the anthropologist, says that *mixed* things—neither flesh nor fowl, so to speak—always excite repulsion and prohibition. The poor lamia was a mess, as far as her head went. Her beseeching eyes were horrible. He looked up from his reading and saw her snake face peering sadly in at the window, her halo shimmering, her teeth shining like pearls. He saw to his locks: he was not about to be unwittingly kissed in his sleep. They were each other's prisoners, he and she. He would paint his painting and think how to escape.

The painting was getting somewhere. The snake colors were a fourth term in the equation of pool and sky and mountains-trees. Their movement in the aquamarines linked and divided delectably, firing the neurons in Bernard's brain to greater and greater activity, and thus causing the lamia to become sulkier and eventually duller and less brilliant.

"I am *so sad*, Bernard. I want to be a woman."

"You've had thousands of years already. Give me a few more days."

"You see how kind I am, when I am in pain."

What would have happened if Raymond Potter had not kept his word will never be known. Bernard had quite forgotten the liver-fluke conversation and Raymond's promised, or threatened, visit. But one day he heard wheels on his track, and saw Potter's dark-red BMW creeping up the slope.

"Hide," he said to the lamia. "Keep still. It's a dreadful Englishman of the fe-fi-fo-fum sort; he has a shouting voice, he *makes jokes*, he smokes cigars, he's bad news, *hide*."

The lamia slipped underwater in a flurry of bubbles like the Milky Way.

Raymond Potter came out of the car smiling, and carried in a leg of wild boar, the ingredients for a ratatouille, a crate of red wine, and several bottles of eau de vie Poire Williams.

"Brought my own provisions. Show me the stove." He cooked. They ate on the terrace, in the evening. Bernard did not switch on the lights in the pool and did not suggest that Raymond might swim. Raymond in fact did not like swimming; he was too fat to wish to be seen, and preferred eating and smoking. Both men drank rather a lot of red wine and then rather a lot of eau de vie. The smell of the mountain was laced with the smells of pork crackling and cigar smoke. Raymond peered drunkenly at Bernard's current painting. He pronounced it rather sinister, very striking, a bit weird, not quite usual, funny-colored, a bit over the top?— looking at Bernard each time for a response and getting none, as Bernard, exhausted and a little drunk, was largely asleep. They went to bed, and Bernard woke once in the night to realize that he had not shut his bedroom window as he usually did; a shutter was banging. But he was unkissed and solitary; he slid back into unconsciousness.

The next morning Bernard was up first. He made coffee; he cycled to the village and bought croissants, bread, and peaches; he laid the table on the terrace and poured heated milk into a blue-and-white jug. The pool lay flat and still, quietly and incompatibly shining at the quiet sky.

Raymond made rather a noise coming downstairs. This was because his arm was round a young woman with a great deal of hennaed black hair, who wore a garment of that see-through cheesecloth from India which is sold in every southern French market. The garment was calf-length, clinging, with little shoulder straps, and dyed in a rather musty brownish black, spattered with little round green spots like peas. It could have been a sundress or a nightdress; it was only too easy to see that the woman wore nothing at all underneath it. The black triangle of her pubic hair swayed with her hips. Her breasts were large and thrusting—that was the word that sprang to Bernard's mind. The nipples stood out in the cheesecloth.

"This is Melanie," Raymond announced, pulling out a chair for her. She flung back her hair with an actressy gesture of her hands and sat down gracefully, pulling the cheesecloth round her knees and staring down at her ankles. She had long, pale, hairless legs with very pretty feet. Her toenails were varnished with a pearly pink varnish. She turned them this way and that, admiring them. She wore rather a lot of very pink lipstick and smiled in a satisfied way at her own toes.

"Do you want coffee?" Bernard said to Melanie.

"She doesn't speak English," Raymond said. He leaned over and made a guzzling, kissing noise in the hollow of her collarbone. "Do you, darling?"

He was obviously going to make no attempt to explain her presence. It was not even quite clear that he felt Bernard had a right to an explanation, or that he himself had any idea where Melanie had come from. He was simply obsessed. His fingers were pulled toward her hair like needles to a magnet: he kept standing up and kissing her breasts, her shoulders, her ears. With considerable distaste Bernard watched Raymond's fat tongue explore the coil of Melanie's ear.

"Will you have coffee?" he asked Melanie in French. He indicated the coffeepot. She bent her head toward it with a quick curving movement, sniffed it, and then hovered briefly over the milk jug.

"This," she said, indicating the hot milk. "I will drink this."

She looked at Bernard with huge black eyes under long lashes.

"I wish you joy," Bernard said in Cévenol French, "of your immortal soul."

"Hey," Raymond said. "Don't flirt with my girl in foreign languages."

"I don't flirt," Bernard said. "I paint."

"And we'll be off after breakfast and leave you to your painting," Raymond said. "Won't we, my sweet darling? Melanie wants . . . Melanie hasn't got . . . she didn't exactly bring . . . you understand—all her clothes and things. We're going to go to Cannes and buy some real clothes. Melanie wants to see the film festival and the stars. You won't mind, old friend; you didn't want me in the first place. I don't want to interrupt your *painting. Chacun à sa boue,* as we used to say in the army; I know that much French."

Melanie held out her pretty, plump hands and turned them over and over with considerable satisfaction. They were pinkly pale and also ornamented with pearly nail varnish. She did not look at Raymond but simply twisted her head about with what could have been pleasure at his little sallies of physical affection, or could have been irritation. She did not speak. She smiled a little over her milk, like a satisfied cat, displaying two rows of sweet little pearly teeth between her glossy pink lips.

Raymond's packing did not take long. Melanie turned out to have one piece of luggage—a large green leather bag containing rattling coins, by the sound. Raymond saw her into the car like a princess, and came back to say good-bye to his friend.

"Have a good time," Bernard said. "Beware of philosophers."

"Where would I find any philosophers?" asked Raymond, who had done theater design at art school with Bernard and now designed sets for a successful children's TV program called *The A-Mazing Maze of Monsters*. "Philosophers are extinct. I think your wits are turning, old friend, with stomping around on your own. You need a girlfriend."

"I don't," Bernard said. "Have a good holiday."

"We're going to be married," Raymond said, looking surprised, as though he himself had not known this until he said it. The face of Melanie swam at the car window, the pearly teeth visible inside the soft lips, the dark eyes staring. "I must go," Raymond said. "Melanie's waiting."

Left to himself, Bernard settled back into the bliss of solitude. He looked at his latest work and saw that it was good. Encouraged, he looked at his earlier work and saw that it, too, was good. All those blues, all those curious questions, all those almost answers. The only problem was where to go now. He walked up and down; he remembered the philosopher and laughed. He got out his Keats. He reread the dreadful moment in *Lamia* when the bride vanished away under the coldly malevolent eye of the philosopher.

>   do not all charms fly
> At the mere touch of cold philosophy?
> There was an awful rainbow once in heaven:
> We know her woof, her texture; she is given
> In the dull catalogue of common things.
> Philosophy will clip an Angel's wings,
> Conquer all mysteries by rule and line,
> Empty the haunted air and gnomed mine—
> Unweave a rainbow, as it erstwhile made
> The tender-personed Lamia melt into a shade.

Personally, Bernard said to himself, he had never gone along with Keats about all that stuff. By "philosophy" Keats seemed to mean natural science, and, personally, he, Bernard, would rather have the optical mysteries of waves and particles in the water and the light of the rainbow than any old gnome or fay. He had been at least as interested in the problems of reflection and refraction when he had had the lovely snake in his pool as he had been in its oddity—in its *otherness*—as snakes went. He hoped that no natural scientist would come along and find Melanie's blood group to be that of some sort of *Herpes*, or do an x-ray and see something odd in her spine. She made a very good blowsy sort of a woman, just right for Raymond. He wondered what sort of a woman she would have become for him, and dismissed the problem. He didn't want a woman. He wanted another visual idea. A mystery to be explained by rule and line. He looked around his breakfast table. A rather plain orange-brown butterfly was sipping the juice of the rejected peaches. It had a golden eye at the base of its wings and a lovely white streak, shaped like a tiny dragon's wing. It stood on the glistening, rich yellow peach flesh and maneuvered its body to sip the sugary juices, and suddenly it was not orange-brown at all; it was a rich, gleaming, intense purple. And then it was both at once, orange-gold and purple-veiled, and then it was purple again, and then it folded its wings and the undersides had a purple eye and a soft green streak, and tan, and white edged with charcoal. . . .

When he came back with his paint box, it was still turning and sipping. He mixed purple, he mixed orange, he made browns. It was done with a dusting of scales, with refractions of rays. The pigments were discovered and measured, the scales on the wings were noted and *seen*, everything was a mystery—serpents and water and light. He was off again. Exact study would not clip this creature's wings; it would dazzle his eyes with its brightness. Don't go, he begged it, watching and learning, don't go. Purple and orange is a terrible and violent fate. There are months of work in it. Bernard attacked it. He was happy, in one of the ways in which human beings are happy.

THE GUILTY PARTY
Susan Moody

Susan Moody is a British mystery novelist best known in the U.S. for her two detective series, the first featuring Penny Wanawake and the more recent featuring Cassie Swann. The former chairman of the British Crime Writers Association, she also writes romantic suspense. Her most recent novel, *Misselthwaith* (published in the U.K.), is the sequel to the much-beloved *The Secret Garden*.

Moody does a beautiful job conveying post–WWII England—the mothers distracted by grief or worry, the children merely bored as children can be during a long summer—and creates a brief yet tragic morality play. The story is reprinted from *No Alibi*, a British anthology edited by Maxim Jakubowski.

—E.D.

MAN FOUND HANGED, I read. REFUGEE TAKES OWN LIFE.

At first I wondered why my mother should have kept this cutting when, as her death approached, she had thrown so much else away. I thought she had long ago forgotten the events of that distant summer, though I had never done so; now it seemed she had not. Afterwards she had never explained, and I had never asked. In those days, children did not question. We did as we were told, we accepted.

But now, reading the piece of worn newsprint, the questions rose in me again like bile.

I was eleven, that July. It was one of those long hot summers soon after the war, the sort which linger on in the memory and stand as the paradigm of all the summers of our youth. Day after day the sun blazed from an empty sky, turning our gray Kentish sea to an almost Mediterranean turquoise. We spent every day on the beach, swimming or endlessly competing against each other to see who could throw a stone the furthest, who could hit a floating piece of driftwood first, who could chuck a pebble into the air and hit it with another.

Although I was a girl and the rest were boys, we competed on equal terms; sex had not yet sneaked into our consciousness. There was no television to make us precocious before our time, and although we were permitted to go to the cinema once a week, we groaned when the hero kissed the heroine, or looked away, embarrassed. We were not allowed to read Enid Blyton; sweets were still rationed; strawberries were only available in season; appearances mattered.

We wore shorts and Aertex shirts. On our feet were Clark's sandals or white tennis shoes which we Blanco'ed vigorously when they grew grubby, setting them out on a windowsill overnight to dry a stiff chalky white. We never wore black plimsolls: black ones were common. Fish and chips was also common, and so was eating in the street. So the pleasure and delight of buying three pennorth of chips and devouring them, hot and vinegary, straight from the newspaper wrapping, was made all the more delicious by the guilty fear that our mothers might see us.

It was always our mothers we worried about. Fathers were nonexistent or rare. We never asked about them, partly because, in those years following the war, they were not a species to which we were used, and partly because the answer might be too painful to give or to receive. My brother and I had a father, though we scarcely knew him; David and Nicholas and the brothers, Charles and Julian, did not. Ours was still in Germany, helping, so my mother said, to rebuild it: whenever I thought of him, which was seldom, I envisaged my scholarly father in his shirtsleeves, setting bricks into mortar.

This was a naval town and there had been many local casualties. Looking back, I imagine the mothers had nowhere else to go and so they stayed on, tucked inside their private griefs, bringing up their orphaned children, contriving to send them away to the kind of schools their officer husbands would have wanted, making do, drawing only a modicum of comfort from each other. Our accents were middle class, our poverty genteel.

Why my mother had chosen to come here while she waited for my father to return from rebuilding Germany I am not sure. We had no local connections and she hated the sea, the corrosive salt air, the lumps of tar we tracked in from the beach to ruin her worn carpets, the gales which prowled beneath the roof tiles and brought the prospect of unpayable bills.

We, on the other hand, loved it. It was an extravagant town to spend our holidays in. From the windows of our vast houses, which were separated from the beach only by a quiet road and a stretch of green, we had an extensive view, bounded at one side by a chalky headland covered in a cap of bright grass, on the other by a pier broken in two halves. As summer lengthened, the vista simplified itself into parallels of color: blue sky, turquoise sea, butterscotch shingle, the parrot-green grass, silver railings. Beyond the pier wallowed a rusting hulk, the victim of enemy action. On the horizon, the spars of wrecked ships stuck up like the arms of drowning men, and when the light was right, you could see across the Channel to France, maybe even Dunkirk. On the esplanade, a red-painted land mine solicited alms for shipwrecked sailors. Although it was never spoken of, the war was part of our lives.

In winter, the wind was so strong you could spread your arms and lean back on it. There was a lifeboat, too, and sometimes we would be wakened by the sound of the maroon going off to call in the lifeboatmen. At night, bugles from the barracks played the last post: every morning, we were woken by reveille.

But that summer, as we waited for adolescence, we were bored. There were still weeks to go before we returned to the routines of boarding school. Apart from the weekly visit to the cinema, nobody offered us entertainment; we made our own from such pinchbeck as was available. Our perpetually anxious mothers were not involved with us; although they fed us, saw that we washed our hair regularly, got us up in the morning, they did not talk to us. In those days, the adults in our lives ended at our eye level: I cannot remember ever seeing my parents' faces, only their clothes. My rarely glimpsed father, I remembered, had a penchant for Leander-pink ties; my mother wore crossover flowered dresses, but what their faces were like I can only reconstruct from looking at photographs.

My brother and I had a wind-up gramophone, and half a dozen records which we played endlessly that summer: the "Teddy Bears' Picnic," "In The Mood," and "Jealousy," and the drinking song from *The Student Prince*, over and over again until one dramatic afternoon my mother rushed in like a whirlwind and hurled whatever was on the turntable to the ground, where it smashed into several shiny black pieces. To our surprise, we saw she was crying. "For God's *sake!*" she shouted. Our homes were full of hidden tension.

Quite why my mother had decided I was to take piano lessons with Mr. Hartman, I don't know. Perhaps she had decided I was becoming too much of a tomboy. Perhaps she was worried that when I went away to my new school in the autumn, I would be found wanting. Perhaps it was because Mrs. Summerfield was sending her daughter Rosie to him.

Whatever the reason, I found myself one hot afternoon standing in the fusty front room of Mr. Hartman's flat, in the house four down from ours. A grand piano dominated most of the bay window. Through it, I could see the heads of the boys down on the beach, aimlessly chucking stones into the sea. Vaguely I understood that Mr. Hartman had come from Germany before the war. He had a foreign accent and wore a Fair Isle pullover with holes in the elbows. His teeth were the color of honey.

How old was he? Now, I can see that he was probably in his late thirties, but at the time he seemed immeasurably aged in his grubby uncollared shirt and round tortoiseshell spectacles. My brother had a similar pair: I knew that you could prise the tortoiseshell off, like a scab. I wondered if Mr. Hartman had discovered this.

That first afternoon he sat down at the piano stool and placed me between his knees. "We shall start with the scale of C," he announced, and proceeded to play it. He put a warm hand over mine and bent my fingers one after another up the keyboard and down again. "Up," he said. "And down again. Up—and down."

His cluttered room smelled of coffee and tobacco and aniseed. It was an alien smell, and curiously exciting, quite different from other houses I had visited. Bookcases overflowed with volumes in German; a sabre hung from the wall with a little blue velvet gold-tasselled cap tied to it. There were faded sepia pictures on the walls of naked girls gazing into streams or leaning pensively back against pillows. Records in tattered brown slip-covers lay piled on the floor; a rack of china-bowled pipes stood on the mantelpiece and beside it, a tin where Mr Hartman kept tobacco, with a girl painted on it, her long hair rippling over but not hiding her unformed body. A red glass decanter stood on the window-sill and, instead of lying on the floor, an oriental carpet was fixed to the wall.

A record player in a shiny wooden cabinet stood beside the fireplace: whenever I climbed the stairs to his flat, I would hear him playing Schubert's *Trout Quintet* and for me, now, that music is inextricably associated with guilt and Mr. Hartman.

On top of the record player stood a primitive radio, with antennae protruding from the top, and beside it lay a pair of headphones.

Twice a week that summer I walked out of our gate and down to Mr. Hartman's flat. I progressed from scales with one hand to scales with both, and then on to arpeggios and the ripple of chromatics. I could pick out "Twinkle-Twinkle Little Star" on the piano in my own house, and "Three Blind Mice." One afternoon, Mr. Hartman declared that I should learn a simple tune, which I would play first with one hand and then, when I had mastered it, with both. "*Müss i' den, müss i' den, zum stätle hinaus,*" he crooned into my ear. He gripped me between his knees as he put his hands inside my shirt and squeezed my waist. "You will like this, I think." His hands were warm and slightly rough; a finger moved slowly over my bare skin. "*Und du, mein schatz, bleibst hier.*"

The boys were waiting for me when my hour with Mr. Hartman was up. Why did they choose that afternoon to scoff at me and at him? They had never done so before. Jealousy, perhaps, or a recognition of the fact that I was changing?

"Silly old Hartman," jeered my brother, as loudly as he dared, glancing up at Hartman's window.

"Hartman, fartman," said Julian, older than the rest of us, and more knowing.

The boys found this deliciously comic. "Hartman, fartman," they said. "How can you *bear* it, stuck up in some stuffy old flat all afternoon with a horrible German?"

"A beastly Hun."

"A bloody," Julian said daringly, "Kraut."

And why did I choose that afternoon to say: "I think he's a spy"? Was it from boredom? Or a desire to establish that I was still one of them? Or was it from some deeper alarm? As soon as I had uttered the words, I wanted them unsaid, but it was too late.

The boys pounced. "A spy? What do you mean? How can he be? How do you know?"

My credibility was at stake. "He's got a radio," I said, "one of those ones that spies use, with bits sticking out of the top. And headphones."

"Headphones?" The boys stared at each other.

"There's still lots of spies about," Charles announced. "I heard about it at school. It's to do with the Cold War."

We could see that he did not know what the Cold War was, and politely refrained from asking him.

"Do you think national security could be at stake?" asked Nicholas, made knowledgeable by the *Rover* which he borrowed surreptitiously from a friend.

"I think we ought to investigate old Fartman," said my brother. "I mean, if he's a spy, and everything."

"How're you going to do that?" I asked scornfully. I wished I had never spoken. All I'd seen was the radio and some German books; all I had was a sense of something about Mr. Hartman which might be dangerous.

"We could keep a watch on him," said Julian, importantly.

And that's what we did. We hung about on the green, swinging on the silver railings, staring up at his window. We followed him when he walked past the lifeboat into town; we followed him home again. Julian produced a notebook and a pencil and we kept a record of his comings and goings. We noted the arrival of Rosie Summerfield, and her departures. Darkness fell late, and our mothers, preoccupied, knowing we would not, in any case, sleep, did not insist on early bedtimes. We were out there every evening, watching him.

Because his flat was on the first floor, we could not see into his room but occasionally he came to the window and stared down at us. And once, Julian, balancing on the railings, claimed he could see him, with his headphones on, tapping away at something.

Once, Mr. Hartman asked me what we were doing. "Come here," he said. He sat down in the armchair beside the cold fireplace and I sat on his lap. His warm rough hands held my thighs. I liked him; I wondered if my father would have this same male smell when he came home. "What are you children doing, playing outside my window all the time?"

"Nothing," I muttered. If I told him we believed he was a spy, he might stop my piano lessons, or move away. I would miss him. I realized then that I missed my father.

He seemed sadder than usual. "I don't like being watched," he said. "I have been watched too much."

Was this a threat? When I reported back to the boys, they grew excited. "He's obviously been under observation before," Julian, our ringleader declared. "We'll keep a watch at the back of the house as well as the front. We'd better be a bit more careful."

We skulked behind lampposts and gates; we stared up at Mr. Hartman's windows from behind hedges and garden walls. When he walked, we darted from doorway to doorway behind him, our breath coming faster when he paused or looked behind him.

He never challenged us. When I went for my lesson, he stood behind me at the piano, his hands on my shoulders or slowly stroking my bare arms. Sometimes his hands moved to cover my Aertex-shirted chest. He kept me longer, afterwards, leaning back in his armchair with me astride his thighs, his hands clasping my legs, a finger slowly climbing higher and then returning. Sometimes he bounced me up and down, and sighed.

"It's only a game," he said to me one afternoon. Outside, the sun whitened the yellow shingle; between the red velvet curtains a shaft of light was solid with dust.

"What is?"

His hands cradled my buttocks. "Life," he said. "You, my dear, and me. It's only a game. And sometimes I am tired of playing it, of moving on, of keeping to the rules."

I had no idea what he meant.

One day, Julian announced that he had sent Mr. Hartman an anonymous letter, had pushed it through the front door of the house the evening before, then ran like the wind before anyone saw him. He had cut the words out of a newspaper, just like they did in books.

"What did you say?" We gasped at the daring.

"I told him we were on to him," said Julian. "Told him we knew exactly what he was up to."

"He'll probably make a bolt for it now," said Charles.

"Where would he bolt to?" I said. I could hear in my head his sad voice, singing. *Und du, mein schatz, bleibst hier.*

"Back to his paymasters," said Nicholas.

"Who're they?" I demanded. I was frightened; Julian had gone too far. It was supposed to be a game, wasn't it? And now it had become serious.

"The Russkies, I should think."

"We ought to send a letter to the police," Julian said.

"Anonymous, do you mean?" asked my brother.

"Yes. That'd scare him, if the police came round, asking questions."

"We'd probably get a medal or something," Nicholas said.

"How can we, if the letter's anonymous?"

"Fingerprints," Nicholas said.

When I came home from my next lesson, my mother was waiting. "How're you getting on?" she said.

"All right."

"Why don't you play me something," she said.

I was embarrassed, unused to so much attention. I launched into "Three Blind Mice." If she was impressed, she didn't say so.

"How do you get on with Mr. Hartman?" she asked. There was something about her demeanor which made me uneasy.

"Very well," I muttered. "He's nice."

"Does he ever . . ."

"What?"

"Touch you?"

"Of *course* not." And, to put her off, I added: "The boys think he's a spy."

"Silly things. He's a refugee. Poor Mr. Hartman. Do you want to go on with the lessons?"

"Yes please," I said.

But I never went back to Mr. Hartman's flat.

He hanged himself that night, using a tie, in the big old wardrobe of his bedroom.

I cried. The boys were subdued. All of us blamed Julian for precipitating the suicide, but we knew ourselves to be equally guilty. We had driven him to it, watching him, dogging his footsteps, never leaving him alone. It was only a game; we knew perfectly well that he was not a spy, poor Mr. Hartman who had been forced to flee his country by the Nazi threat and find refuge and safety in England.

MAN FOUND HANGED.

I read the cutting again. Why had I never asked? And why had my mother never explained, never reassured? Was she afraid of what I would tell her? She knew I blamed myself for the suicide. She knew that. Now, for the first time, I read the evidence given at the inquest by Mrs. Mary Summerfield, the last person known to have seen Mr. Hartman alive. She stated that she had gone round to discuss a certain matter concerning her daughter, Rosemary Summerfield aged ten; that the discussion had grown heated, that she had threatened to inform the police if he did not in future keep his hands to himself.

My mother had known all this, so why did she not speak of it to me? And if she had, what difference would it have made? I thought I had killed him by accusing him of being a spy. I believed that between us, the boys and I had driven him to his death. And now, after all, I had discovered that if there was a guilty party in all this, it was not I.

If my mother had explained to me then, had put aside her own worries and looked at mine, would I have married, had children, lived the kind of life which might have been anticipated for me that summer when I was eleven?

Or would I always have feared that if I ever again let a man put his hand on my thigh, or touch my breasts, he would kill himself?

SHE'S NOT THERE
Pat Cadigan

Pat Cadigan was born in Schenectady, New York, and now lives in Overland Park, Kansas, with her son. She was coeditor of *Shayol*, perhaps the best of the semiprofessional magazines of the late 1970s; it was honored with a World Fantasy Award in 1981. Cadigan made her first professional sale in 1980, and has subsequently come to be regarded as one of the best science fiction writers of her generation. She is the author of three novels to date: *Mindplayers*, *Synners*, and *Fools*, the latter two of which each won the Arthur C. Clarke Award in England. She has recently published a series of novellas about future Japan that will be incorporated into a new novel, and she is also working on a novel called *Parasites*. In addition to being one of the original "cyberpunks," Cadigan has written an amazing array of sf, fantasy, and horror stories throughout her career, and has been published in such magazines and anthologies as *The Magazine of Fantasy & Science Fiction*, *Omni*, *Asimov's Science Fiction*, *Tropical Chills*, *Light Years and Dark*, *Little Deaths*, *Alien Sex*, and *Blood Is Not Enough*. She has published three collections of her short work: *Patterns*, *Home by the Sea*, and *Dirty Work*.

Cadigan is one of a handful of writers who seemingly can work within any genre. "She's Not There," originally published in Gardner Dozois's anthology *Killing Me Softly*, is a subtle and disturbing story that asks the question: Is there anything in this life for which you'd give up everything?

—E.D.

There was once such a thing as a single, as in music, as in rock 'n' roll, as in hear it on a radio with a speaker that made it sound like listening to music over the telephone. Didn't matter—if the speaker was small, the music was big. *Big*. What made it big could reach out through that fuzzy-muzzy speaker and change the world, change the universe. At least change your life.

Don't you remember how music changed your life? Of course not, why am I even asking? You *couldn't* remember, even though you were there.

How would you know, why would you care . . . ?

That's not how you remember the line, I know. But that's how it was originally sung. Not by a group of young guys who managed to chart one more near-miss before passing into nostalgia, but by a young woman who committed suicide the day after it hit number one, cementing her place in the pantheon of rock music deities for all time and sending a good part of the civilized world into a mourning that eclipsed the deaths of Buddy Holly, Elvis, and John Lennon combined.

You've never heard of her.

It was a dirty little town. I mean that literally. Grimy little industrial town, blot on the New England landscape. There are those who even now will tell you that it was and is a pretty town, but they probably lived up on the west side or out on Summer Street. I lived where the dirt settled.

Kathy didn't. The Beaver would have been at home in her neighborhood. In mine, we'd have mugged him for his lunch money, and then made him pay protection so we wouldn't do it again. And then we'd have done it again anyway, just to see the look on his face. *That's right, kid, there ain't no justice in* this *world*.

You think that's bad—punching out a harmless, mediocre little kid like the Beav? Well, it was. But the Beav got over it. He had a nice home to run to, June kissed his boo-boos, Ward taught him a few boxing moves, and he never walked through our turf again anyway.

And just for the record, *I* never laid a glove on him. I wasn't even there that day. I was in my room, studying. Because there were three things I knew better than anything:

1. There's no justice.
2. There's no Santa Claus.
3. I was getting *out*.

Kathy was the first one who ever believed me. Believed *in* me. We were little girls in Catholic school; navy-blue jumper dresses over white blouses and sky-blue bow ties, with kneesocks and saddle shoes, marching two by two into school in the morning. People would say, *Bet you hate it, all that Catholic school stuff, all that regimentation, all that praying, those uniforms.* Yeah, sure, all of it, except the uniforms. I secretly loved the uniforms even while I pretended to hate them. When you had a flock of kids in identical uniforms, you couldn't tell who was from Summer Street and who was from that patch of blight just two blocks down from the church. You couldn't tell unless you already knew. Kathy knew; she was from Summer Street. She didn't care.

She was always solemn, one of those skinny, paper-white girls you figure will grow up to be a professional neurotic. Because she was so brilliant. *Brilliant.* One of the Smart Kids in the class.

I was Smart, too, but they made me fight for it. So I fought like I was mugging the Beaver, taking everything he owned. Because it was supposed to be useless for me—my kind didn't go to college, dirt didn't get *out*. *They* said.

The music told me different. Listen, you think a fuzzy-muzzy transistor radio is a silly thing to hang on to? It was the music, really; when there was no radio, I played it in my head. Anything on that list of Things They Can't Take Away From You, what you know and what you hear in your head, that's what I hung on to. Maybe you've got something better. If you do, don't go walking through my old neighborhood with it.

Then I heard Kathy sing, and I knew what *she* was hanging on to.

* * *

I hit the eighth grade the year that Kennedy hit the White House. A Catholic makes president—that must mean there's a God, right? Well, there was something; maybe it was a pony. My face was breaking out; my *breasts* were breaking out, God help me. And Kathy was getting thinner.

She was the only one doing *that* that *I* could see. I keep thinking it got cold early in the fall of 1960, but nobody else remembers it that way. No one else remembers it being especially cold or hot or anything else. An unremarkable year except for the election of the first Catholic president in history, which was supposed to mean something good to all us women in uniform, good little Catholic girls and the nuns who taught us.

Every autumn, that's what I think of—those weeks leading up to the election and after, the air growing cold, the last of the leaves falling off the trees, and, in spite of everything, in spite of where I was, what I was, and how it was then, I feel that same happy-sad feeling that comes with remembering really good things you don't have anymore. But then, I guess that about sums it all up, doesn't it?

By the time we were all saying a rosary in class every day to thank Holy Mary for interceding with her Son to make Kennedy president, I had already heard Kathy sing. One afternoon over at her house, up in her room, she'd suddenly jumped up off the bed in the middle of some forgettable conversation, put a record on her record player, and then just stood in the middle of the room and *sang*. It was some folk song I'd never heard before, but if she'd been singing "Mary Had a Little Lamb" it would have been something I'd never heard before. She didn't just have a voice, she had a voice, a *voice*. *The Voice.* Two seconds and I'd forgotten what a strange thing it was for her to do, just get up and perform. I was just so glad she'd done it for me, that *I* could hear it. And after she finished, I'd been going to make some kind of weak joke about getting her to sing at my wedding to some movie star or other, except that when she was through, I couldn't say a word. I remember feeling like the sound of my voice would profane the quiet left after hers. I remember that it *was* quiet, too, very quiet, because there was no one else in the house that day.

That didn't happen often, that there would be no one home at Kathy's. Her mother was a licensed practical nurse who worked at a convalescent home mostly and sometimes filled in a Tri-County General Hospital, usually around the holidays when the combination of vacations and sick leave would leave them shorthanded. Her father was an electrician or something, and I figured he made his own hours, because there wasn't any pattern to when he was home and when he wasn't. Kathy's older sister, Sarah, was in high school, a place that was as mysterious to me as Timbuktu or Cleveland. The younger sister, Barbara, wasn't home either—good thing for her, because Kathy was always chasing her out, telling her to go find something to do and some friend to do it with. I didn't really understand that, because the kid never bothered her. She was okay, the kid; I'd have let her stay and even hang around us, but Kathy wouldn't hear of it. One time I asked her why.

"Because I can't miss her if she won't go away," she snapped. It should have been funny, but Kathy really wasn't much for humor. There's only one joke she ever told me, so long ago, two lifetimes ago, but I still remember it. Because it was not the sort of joke I'd have expected her to tell me and I didn't get it at the time. It went like this:

> Kathy: *Do you know how to use the word "pagoda" in a sentence?*
> Me: *There's a pagoda in Japan?*
> Kathy: *My father said, "Kathy, go to your room" and I said, "Pagoda hell."*

I'd get it now. A lot of people would. But in 1960, at the beginning of the first American Catholic administration, nobody got it.

"Does anybody else know you can sing?" It took me two days to get up the nerve to ask her that question because I had the feeling she was pretty sensitive about her singing. Now that I had, it sounded so damned vapid.

Kathy only twisted her shoulders in an awkward shrug. "Anyone like who? Sister Mary Aloysius? Mrs. What's-Her-Name, the choir director? Dick Clark? My father?"

She looked away. We were standing just inside the doors of the public library, protected from the raw pre-Christmas wind (though not the damp, which was creeping up my ankles from my toes), watching the bus stop for our respective buses home. I took the Putnam Park Via Water Street; Kathy rode the less frequent Lunenburg Via John Bell Hwy. It was getting dark fast, earlier every day. I'd always hated the darkening descent to the Christmas season. Even though the days started getting longer just before Christmas Day, it never felt that way to me. I found winter depressing; so did Kathy, as far as I could tell.

"Did you ever think of—you know, doing something with your, um, music?"

"You mean, singing in front of people?" She turned to look at me, and I thought she'd be irritated with me—she'd sounded irritated—but the expression on her face was more frightened than anything else. "How? Where? And for who?"

"The Glee Club? Or the choir?" Her eyes might have been boring two holes through me. "The Shangri-Las?"

That made her smile, but it was a small one, sad and fleeting. "I don't want them to know."

I waited for her to say something else, to say she thought that kind of thing was a big waste of time, that she didn't want to sing moldy old show tunes and hymns, but she just kept staring at me, chewing on the inside of her lower lip. Waiting, I realized, for reassurance from me.

"Well, for heaven's sake, Kath, who's going to tell them? Not me, you can bet the farm on that. I'm sick of how the Shangri-Las never take my advice anyway."

She started to smile again at that but she forced herself not to. "Okay. That's the way I want it."

"Well, okay," I said.

And then her bus came, for once ahead of mine, and I watched her bustle out and join the small group waiting in front of the bus door. She almost looked over her shoulder at me, except the scarf on her head was tucked into her coat collar and she couldn't quite manage it.

It wasn't actually my business—I mean, I was curious, and in those days, you tended to feel like you deserved a full explanation for any weirdness that might crop up in a friend. Usually, you'd get it. But I never did. I'd ask her from time to time, broaching the subject carefully. Most times, she just ignored any questions—everything was too personal. Or she wouldn't even hear me. Frustration? I'll tell the world.

I also wanted to tell the world about Kathy's voice. Well, I wanted to tell somebody. Someone important, someone who would count, who could do something, give her the reward she deserved for having such a talent. I wanted somebody to put a smile on her pale face; I wanted that so bad I could taste it.

Actually, I wanted it to be *me* so bad I could taste it. That's how it is when you want to rescue someone, rush into whatever bad shit is going on in their lives and be the big hero. Of course, you want to do that in your own way, because it's someone else you're rescuing but it's yourself that you're gratifying.

I thought about that one so much afterwards that I don't have to think about it anymore. It's in me the way oxygen's in the atmosphere.

Anyway, I discovered that there *was* someone who could put a smile on her face. He went to the boys' branch of the school, which was a block away from the girls' building. They kept us separated and penned up, so that by the time we went off to any of the coed high schools, the hormones were virtually audible.

Eddie Gibbs was the name on Kathy's smile. I could see why. He was cute but nice, too, not stuck-up like a lot of the more popular boys. We all got to see each other briefly during the daily lunch hour—our school let us out for lunch in those days—but for much longer and more substantially every Friday evening, when most of us would go to Miss Fran's School of Ballroom Dancing where, to our wicked, sinful delight, the girls and boys could even *touch* each other.

Miss Fran's was a rite of puberty. Not to enroll was tantamount to checking the yes box for *Have you ever been hospitalized for mental illness?* on an employment application; you were marked permanently as odd, and nobody wanted that. So everyone signed up and went fox-trotting and box-waltzing and cha-cha-ing on Friday nights, even the oddest kids, the class outcasts and misfits, future doctors and future ex-cons, even me. Everyone, except Kathy.

Now, somehow, all those years of hanging out with me hadn't done anything to diminish her stature among our classmates, or with our teachers. She was Kathy, after all, Kathy who lived on Summer Street, and I guess they all figured that someday she'd outgrow her silly attachment to me. Sometimes one of the popular girls would take it into her head that she should Talk To Kathy About Her Friend. I guessed they were afraid that someday they'd look out the front window of their sorority house and see me following Kathy up the walk to the pledge party. Kathy would tell me about it sometimes, and one girl actually did say she would be pledging her mother's sorority in college, and Kathy could, too, but I couldn't. Can't tell you how crushed I was.

Anyway, what her association with me couldn't do, her absence from Miss Fran's did. It was more than odd, it was shocking and unnatural, and it wasn't because of me. Suddenly, they were Talking To Me About Kathy.

I don't know what I would have told them if I'd known the truth. What I could say, in all honesty, was that I didn't know. I didn't know why she wasn't there, I really didn't. I asked her a couple of times, but she would just shake her head and look miserable. She was all pulled into herself, closed off; even her posture was like that, she was walking around with her chest all caved in. She looked thinner than ever, too. Everybody was talking, but to give them credit (something I don't do too easily), all the talk was still pretty kind. Maybe she was sick, maybe someone she knew was sick, maybe her parents were fighting. That last could have meant anything from chronic arguing to having the police at your house every Saturday night, telling your father to sober the hell up (and your mother to shut the hell up).

Kathy wouldn't say, but she stopped inviting me over, and she stopped coming over to my place. I thought maybe she was mad at me, maybe one of those future sorority sisters had told her I'd cut her up, trying to break up our friendship. All I finally got out of her was that she was being punished. I didn't ask her what for. Having to tell all in confession was humiliating enough; nobody wanted to have to tell anything sensitive to someone who *wasn't* bound by the secrecy of the confessional.

I'd have let it go even with Kathy getting sadder and thinner all the time, except that Eddie Gibbs came to me about her.

I didn't realize it was about her at first. I thought Eddie had a crush on *me*. It wasn't so impossible. Ron Robillard had had a crush on me for a while early in the school year, and he was the most popular boy. Of course, he hated having a crush on me, and I always had to be careful to stay out of his way at Miss Fran's because he'd stomp on my foot or pinch my arm or whisper something mean. It made me glad he wasn't in love with me for real.

Eddie was different, though. Eddie was kind, a real nice guy. Where Ron was your basic crew-cut blond all-American athlete and wife-beater-in-training, Eddie was slender and dark. My mother saw him once and said he was Mediterranean. He was a Smart Kid, too, and it only took a tiny little bit of extra attention from him to hook me, choosing me to dance with at Miss Fran's, even sitting in the same pew at church one Sunday. And as we walked out together after Mass was over, he asked me why Kathy didn't come to Miss Fran's.

I felt pretty dumb, but that lasted all of about a minute. Well, of *course*, Kathy. Why not Kathy? I couldn't even be jealous about it, not really. I didn't fit into that scheme, but Kathy did.

Still, I felt pretty good that Eddie Gibbs had come to me, rather than one of the accepted girls. To me, it meant that I had his respect if not his heart, and knowing that gave me a bigger charge than him having a crush on me ever could have. That was why I did what I did.

Actually, I didn't do so much in the beginning. I promised Eddie three things: one, I would find out why she didn't go to Miss Fran's (well, I would *try*); two, I would show him how to get to her house. And then three, I would talk to her about him, find out if she liked him, too. Then they could officially be *going out*. This didn't mean they were going anywhere together, just that they were boyfriend and girlfriend. Thirteen used to be too young to date.

The easiest thing was, of course, showing him where Kathy lived. The Summer Street address didn't even make him blink. He managed to contrive all kinds of excuses to pass by it. Sometimes he'd even ask me to go with him and I would. I thought maybe if Kathy's family saw me with Eddie, they'd think he was my boyfriend instead of hers, and she wouldn't get into trouble.

I'm not sure what put that thought in my head, that Kathy's family would object to her having a boyfriend. And hell, Eddie wasn't her boyfriend, not formally. I wasn't sure she even knew his name. Maybe it was just that they wouldn't let her go to Miss Fran's. Everybody knows a few kids with families like that, who overprotect them so much that they can't wait to go to college and go nuts. Except I was pretty sure that Kathy wouldn't, unless her folks stayed unreasonable after she got to high school.

But the summer before high school, her father caught us, and she almost didn't get there at all.

Saying her father caught us makes it sound a lot more than it was, and yet, that doesn't begin to tell it. A whole lot of people saw it; nobody saw it. All that showed on that sunny afternoon in early July was Eddie and I on the sidewalk in front of Kathy's house, and Kathy sitting on the porch. Kathy's father came out, looked at us, and then looked at her; she got up from her chair and went inside and we walked away.

But that's not what happened.

What happened was, Eddie had talked me into walking over the Fifth Street bridge and down Hayward to Summer so he could check out Kathy's, maybe see her outside and get a chance to talk to her. At that point, I couldn't tell if Eddie really had it that bad for her, or whether he was dying of curiosity as to how any girl could be so resistant to his good looks and hot status. *I* wasn't resisting him— even though he never made like he was interested in me in that way, even though I knew he wouldn't have bothered even making friends with me if I hadn't been a way to get next to Kathy, I went along with whatever he wanted. God knows, in this life the only reason anyone ever bothers with anyone else is for purposes of usefulness. In this life, or any other.

So there we were, Eddie and I, walking along like we really were good buddies, even talking about this and that. Eddie had this surprisingly high political awareness—he was the only kid I knew who could actually discuss HUAC and Senator Joseph McCarthy. Well, the only kid besides Kathy, of course. Kathy seemed to know about a lot of things.

The front of Kathy's house was visible from the corner of Summer and Hayward, and we could see her on the porch as soon as we crossed the intersection. Eddie started to walk faster, and some impulse made me tug on his shirt and tell him to slow down. "You don't want to stampede her, do you?" I said, only half joking.

He looked puzzled; why would any girl object to the sight of the great Eddie Gibbs coming toward her as fast as possible? Well, maybe that's not fair, but it's not totally unfair, either. In any case, Eddie slowed up, and we finally got to the middle of the block where Kathy's house was without him exploding with frustration or hormones.

I made Eddie stand there on the sidewalk until I could get Kathy's attention. I was thinking we had to do this fast, say hello, get her to come with us, and be gone before someone else in the family saw the three of us together.

Looking back on it, I think that she must have seen us all along and she was trying to ignore us into going away. But discouraging Eddie Gibbs wasn't that easy.

I felt envious; I couldn't imagine that any handsome guy was ever going to chase *me* so persistently, and I couldn't figure out why Kathy wasn't thrilled, or at least flattered.

She sat there for a long time paging through the Sears catalog, of all things, and not looking up. The neighbors on either side of her were out in their gardens and doing some lawn work and they'd noticed us. Not in any big way, they just waved at me and I waved back. Eddie went from baffled to annoyed. "Kathy?" he asked.

It wasn't that his voice was so loud as that it just carried well, through all those outdoor sounds to the porch. Kathy finally looked up, and my first thought on seeing her face was, *Who died?*

That moment became one of those mental snapshots you can never lose, no matter how much changes afterwards. I could see that the white posts were going to need painting before the summer was out, that some of the boards were a little bit warped, that someone had put out some geraniums to be planted. There was a transistor radio sitting on a small wicker table to Kathy's right. She was wearing what I thought of as a school blouse, with a softly rounded collar, a silver crucifix, and one of her good skirts. I wondered if she were going somewhere.

Then I realized it wasn't sadness on Kathy's face but rage. The last thing she could have wished for was to have someone like Eddie Gibbs standing in front of her house, looking at her. I thought I saw her make a move to get up, and I don't know whether she meant to come down the walk to us or go inside to get away from us, because before she could do anything at all, her father came out onto the porch.

He wasn't a big man, Kathy's father, neither exceptionally ugly nor handsome nor anything else. My impression was that I could stare at him all day and forget what he looked like as soon as I turned away. He gazed at me and Eddie as if he suspected we'd come to steal the silver. After some unmeasurable span of time, he turned to Kathy.

Pagoda hell. It might as well have been painted on her forehead. This was bad, I thought; this was really, really bad, whatever was going on between them. But even that wasn't so remarkable. Lots of people our age were at war with one or both parents; it was the way things went. I kept thinking that was all it was, one of those generation gap problems, as, in response to some cue I hadn't caught, Kathy got up without a word and went into the house.

Eddie and I looked at each other. An airplane droned overhead, and when I looked back to Kathy's house, the porch was empty. I turned back to Eddie and shrugged. "I don't know."

"Me, either," Eddie replied, and we went back the way we had come. I was sort of hoping that Eddie would ask me to be his girlfriend, since Kathy's rejection had been unmistakable, but Eddie seemed to be lost in thought. Probably needed some time, I decided as our paths diverged at the corner of Hayward and Fifth.

Two days later, I called Kathy, thinking I'd sound her out about Eddie—was she interested or not? His interest in her had lasted longer than the usual crush, and I wasn't sure whether to be worried by Eddie's attention span or just impressed.

The line was busy, and still busy when I tried again a half hour later. After three hours, I gave up. Maybe someone had knocked the phone off the hook.

The phone was still beeping busy the following morning, so I figured I'd just walk over and see what the problem was. Without Eddie, this time; considering the expression on Kathy's father's face, I didn't think I should bring anyone with me. No, scratch that—any *boy*. Some parents got overly nervous. I wouldn't have thought Kathy's would be, but there was no telling, really; I just didn't know them very well.

This time, Kathy's mother was sitting on the porch, with the newspaper and a big glass of pink lemonade. Not an uncommon sight in July, but there was something weird about it. Kathy's mother looked like she was posing for a picture. Or just posing—I kept thinking that the lemonade and the paper were props, but that didn't make any sense.

Maybe some of what I was feeling showed on my face; Kathy's mother got this defensive look, as if she expected me to challenge her right to do this, sit on her own porch with a cold drink. Or maybe she was just worried that I'd ask her for a sip, or even my own glass. Neither of Kathy's parents had ever been in danger of winning a medal for hospitality.

I was kind of annoyed, so I just walked right up onto the porch and said, "Hi, Kathy home?"

She stared straight ahead, newspaper in one hand, lemonade in the other. "No."

"Oh." I waited for a few moments. "Will she be back soon?"

Now the woman shrugged. Lemonade sloshed over the rim of the glass and spotted her white pants.

"Okay, then, when would be a good time for me to call her?"

She didn't say anything for the longest time. I'd been going to wait her out, and then decided I was tired of her game, whatever it was. No wonder Kathy was so strange, I thought as I stumped down the porch steps. Next to her parents, she was positively normal.

"Kathy's in the hospital."

I turned around to see Barbara standing just inside the screen door. Her mother gave her a really furious look, but Barbara ignored her, hugging herself. Barbara was built much more solidly, not thin like Kathy.

"She's in the hospital with blood poisoning," Barbara said. "She's going to be all right, but she can't have any visitors. Because of *germs*."

That was the last straw for her mother, I guess. She got up in a big hurry, and Barbara fled. Her mother yanked open the screen door with such force that it flew all the way back, banging against the front of the house. I waited, thinking I'd hear some yelling and find out what Kathy's mother was so upset about, but there wasn't a sound. Yelling would have been embarrassing, but the silence was downright weird. I went home and phoned Eddie. I figured he should know.

As it turned out, Eddie's older sister was a nurse in training at the hospital, so he could find out more than I could. I made him promise to tell me when he did, and he kept assuring me that he would, don't worry.

Guys lie. All guys, young and old, boyfriends, fathers, brothers, all of them. They lie and lie and lie. Either that or they don't pay any attention to what they're saying while they say it. He found out. He even sneaked in and saw her. And after that he wouldn't even speak to me.

Kathy had to be an invalid for the rest of the summer, or so her mother the nurse said. She got hold of a wheelchair—maybe borrowed it from the convalescent home. Kathy sat in it on the porch for the last part of July and all of August, listening to the radio. She couldn't go anywhere or spend much time with anyone.

I only went over when her house would be at its emptiest. And even so, she wouldn't say much. Not just about how she happened to end up in the hospital, but about anything. Trying to hold a conversation with her was impossible.

I was pretty mad at Kathy's mother, and also at Eddie Gibbs for being such a fair-weather boyfriend. I didn't know what his problem was, except he obviously wasn't interested in Kathy anymore. Maybe some cheerleader with big breasts had given him a tumble, I thought. Guys were a lot more trouble than they were worth.

Toward the end of August, Kathy seemed to be getting a lot better, but she was still in that damned wheelchair. "Why does your mother insist on keeping you in that thing?" I asked her finally. "You can walk, can't you?"

She shook her head.

"You can't walk?" I couldn't believe it.

"No, it's not my mother. My father makes me stay in the chair."

"Well, that's ridiculous," I said. "How are you supposed to stay healthy—"

"My father doesn't want me to put any excess strain on my heart before school starts." She turned up the radio, which was supposed to end the conversation.

"But that doesn't make any sense," I said, raising my voice to talk over Elvis. "Your mother's a nurse, she could tell him—"

"No, she can't," Kathy said. "She can't, and we can't. Nobody can tell him anything."

After that, she didn't want to talk about anything anymore, but I was getting tired of that and all her neurotic shit. Her and her mother and her weirdo father—by far, the only sensible one seemed to be Barbara, and I was starting to wonder about her.

"I think this year you ought to do something with *your* singing," I told her abruptly, reaching over to turn Elvis down. "Get involved with the Glee Club and the choir. They'll probably make you a soloist. Looks good on your transcript when you apply to college."

"Oh, I plan to do something with my singing," she said, giving me this sideways look.

"What?" I asked her.

"You'll see."

"Come on, Kathy, *what*."

"You'll *see*." Suddenly she smiled. "You will." She turned up the radio again and was happy for all of fifteen seconds. Her father materialized on the porch like a magic trick. He snapped off the radio, then picked it up, yanked the batteries out of the compartment in the bottom, and put them in his pocket.

"Trash," he said, glaring at Kathy. "You know what kind of people listen to that trash, don't you?" His gaze moved to me. "Don't you, Katherine? Answer me."

She ducked her head and I thought I heard her whisper, *"Yes, Daddy."*

"People like *her*." He jerked his thumb toward the sidewalk. "Hit the road, trash. I don't want you near my daughters, any of them. The next time one of those horny young apes you go around with gets a yen for some, you take him to the whores you live with. Do I make myself clear to you?"

It all came out in such a quiet, calm voice, I wasn't sure that I'd actually heard what I heard. And then Kathy whispered, *"Go. Please. Get out of here."*

I was so shocked, that was just what I did. Maybe her father had blown some kind of gasket in his brain, I thought. I'd have to ask Kathy when I saw her at school, even though she would probably be embarrassed to death over it. Because she lived on Summer Street; in my neighborhood, I'd have just figured him for yet another guy who got mean when he got drunk.

Actually, it was the last time I saw Kathy for years. The week before school started, she ran away. Without the wheelchair.

High school was hell anyway, but without Kathy, it was even more rotten. I was so mad at her for leaving me to face it alone, after we'd stuck together for so long. At the same time, I couldn't blame her. What wasn't boring was incomprehensible or embarrassing. I fell into my radio and stayed there.

Not the local stations, which were all easy listening or country-western or yak-yak-yak, but the ones from Boston and Worcester, where everything seemed to be faster, happier, better. I loved to sit alone and listen after school. In Worcester, the kids called in requests every afternoon, and it sounded like they all knew each other. I daydreamed about getting out, finding my way to some place like that. Maybe that was what Kathy had done, gone off to find some better place to be, where her parents couldn't keep her in a wheelchair, and as soon as she was sure it really was a better place, she'd let me know. Somehow, she'd send me a message to come join her without giving it away to her parents or anyone else.

I hung on to that for a while, even though I knew it was a complete fantasy. But as long as it *was* a complete fantasy, I pulled out all the stops and imagined that her message would come in the music. Like we were spies or secret agents in hostile country, trying to get home.

So fourteen and fifteen is a little old to be playing Spy. It was better than playing with Eddie Gibbs. He'd gone on to become high school aristocracy, and, as near as I could tell, he'd forgotten all about Kathy and me. I gave him a dirty look every time I saw him; he would stare right through me, like he didn't see me at all.

Yeah, well, like I should have expected more out of a fourteen-year-old guy.

I spent my junior year sleeping with Jasper Townshend. It was the next best thing to getting *out*.

Every night of the week, I could drift off to sleep at the sound of Jasper's low, velvety voice urging me to believe in the power of my own dreams. It didn't bother me that he said this to *everyone* who slept with him. I didn't expect a whole lot of Jasper; all I wanted to do was forget this world for seven or eight hours, and Jasper knew exactly how to help me do that.

Being so good at what he did, he became a very popular guy, number one in the overnight time slot. All the other radio stations might as well have been off the air. It wasn't just that he had the best voice in the business, or a lot of great things to say. It was that he really knew how to program the music, and when to shut up.

You could tell the music meant a lot to him. I think it meant as much to him as it did to me. With Kathy gone, it meant more to me than it ever had. Sometimes I'd even forget that my little fantasy wasn't real, and I'd listen for Kathy's voice, the song she would sing to let me know she'd found someplace safe.

I guess if you listen hard enough for something, you'll finally hear it.

* * *

The first time I heard it was in a dream, literally. I was back in Kathy's room and she was singing for me, but it wasn't the folk song I remembered but something slow called "In My Room." I seemed to remember some surfer-types singing it and it had sounded pretty lame. But Kathy had stolen it and made it into some kind of hymn to privacy. And why not a hymn? All us good little Catholic girls sang hymns best.

The song ended and I was captivated all over again. I didn't want anything to break the silence that fell after that last pure note, I wanted to listen to it echo in my mind, but Kathy's father suddenly barged in without knocking. I thought he was going to tell me I was trash and throw me out. Instead, he started singing, too.

Shock woke me up. But Kathy's father was still singing, and I realized I was hearing the radio. I could feel my emotions going up and down, like a flock of seagulls riding on waves. I mean, I was *really* glad Kathy's father wasn't singing *or* throwing me out, but I was really sorry the Kathy version of "In My Room" wasn't available.

Then I found out I was wrong, and I didn't know *how* I felt.

I wish you still knew what happened after that—it would make all of this so simple. But I've resigned myself to the fact that no one remembers The Voice except me.

That was what they called her—*Billboard, Variety, Hit Parade,* Dick-for-chrissakes-Clark. George Martin, too; he'd been trying to get some British group with funny haircuts to smooth out their sound, get respectable. When he heard The Voice, he dropped them and hopped a jet for America. He tracked her down in L.A. and spent three months wooing her with promises of all kinds.

I could have told him she'd have been a tough nut to crack. I giggled whenever I thought of some high-powered music promoter or manager or whatever they were coming to me for advice on how to reach The Voice. I'd have told them just not to bother. The Voice couldn't be bought, wasn't for sale.

I didn't really expect her to think of me, either. She'd run away from all of it years ago, me included. I didn't know *why* it included me; I didn't want to know, either. I was afraid I'd find out that her father had finally brainwashed her into believing I was the trash he said I was. Instead, I went on pretending that she was sending me messages in the music, messages of encouragement. I hung on to the music and hung on to her.

And what the hell—the miracle came to pass, and I got my ticket *out.* It was labeled *Full Scholarship, State University.* One way only, and that was all right with me.

That was the time that I was really tempted to try to get in touch with her, to show her that I'd done it after all, the way she had always believed I would. I thought maybe she really might want me to get in touch with her now. She may have been The Voice to the world, but I was the one who had heard The Voice first. Before she had sung for anyone else, she had sung for *me.*

I wish you all remembered her world tour. I was at the State University then, majoring in parties and becoming radicalized, when I found out she was going to play that blot on the New England escutcheon we had both escaped. I'd go see her in both places, I decided. I was still going back to see my mother once in a while; I could make an extra trip for Kathy.

Eddie Gibbs was long gone, as far as I knew. He'd joined the Army right after graduation and been shipped off to somewhere in southeast Asia. Too bad, I thought, he'd never get a chance to see what he'd missed.

So I went. She was as thin as ever, maybe even a little thinner. Her hair had grown out long, down past her shoulders. Sometimes, when she moved her head in a certain way, it reminded me of a nun's veil; I wondered how she was living and with who, if anyone.

I wondered through her rendition of "Tobacco Road," and then was startled to hear my name mentioned.

"This next song I also stole, from four good kids who could probably have a hit single with it, and maybe they will. But not till I'm done with it. This is for my friend who always said she was getting *out*. I hope she got out."

A wave of laughter swept through the audience—I swear, she could have stood up there and castigated everyone and they would all still have loved her. She waited a beat and then launched into "I'm Not There."

> No one told you about me
> The way I cried . . .
> Nobody told you about me
> How many people cried . . .
> . . . don't bother trying to find me
> I'm not there . . .

Very spooky song, and not in a good way. If there was such a thing as being allergic to a song, I was allergic to that one. I couldn't stand to listen to it, watching her move back and forth across the stage, looking carefully at all the upturned faces.

I knew she was searching for *me*, and, suddenly, I didn't want her to find me. During the break, I pushed through all the people milling around and got outside none too soon. My stomach had been turning over and over. Much to the disapproval of some of the well-muscled group in T-shirts that proclaimed Security front and back, I puked into a garbage can just outside the hall and then went back to my mother's. I figured that would be the end of it, but I was wrong. Again.

"It took a while to find you," she said on the telephone. Her speaking voice, as well as The Voice, sounded just the way I remembered, full and textured.

"What do you want?" I asked her. "I mean, you seem to have everything."

"I'd give it all up just to get some peace of mind." I thought that was a pretty weird thing to say. I couldn't think of how to respond her. "There aren't any easy answers," she added, as if she had read my mind. "I'm just letting you know how I feel."

I switched the receiver to my other ear." And how *do* you feel?"

"Did you stay long enough to hear 'I'm Not There?' " she asked suddenly. "That's the song I stole. That's what they call it when you take a song someone else wrote and change it to fit your own preference. Did you like it?"

"It was strange," I said.

"But did you *like* it?" There was such an urgent note in her voice, I felt I had to be completely honest.

"No."

She gave a short laugh. "No. You wouldn't. Because you *are* there, aren't you?"

"Yeah. I'm here." I paused. "You're the one who left."

"No," she said patiently, "I wasn't there to begin with. I was never there. Because no one told you about me."

"Don't," I said.

"Don't what—tell you?"

"You're not telling me anything, you're just spooking me. I was hanging on because you were supposed to be there to hang on with me. You believed—"

"No, *you* believed," she said snappishly.

"And *you* let me."

There was a long pause. "Yes," she said at last. "I suppose I did." She paused again. "Is there anything—has there ever been anything—that you'd give it all up for?"

I laughed. "What have *I* ever had to give up?"

"Everything."

I laughed some more. " 'Everything.' Jesus, Kathy, I think you're getting *your* 'everything' confused with *my* 'everything.' In case you hadn't noticed, you've got a hell of a lot more in your 'everything' than I do in mine."

"It wasn't always that way," she said gravely. I squirmed a little because I had just been thinking something along the same lines.

"No, but it sure is now, isn't it?" I sighed. "What did you call for, Kathy? And how did you know to call me here?"

"I was hoping I'd find you."

"You were hoping I'd still be living here?"

"No. That you'd come back here for the concert."

I was annoyed with myself for being so predictable. "Okay. So *why* did you call?"

"I wanted to ask you if you thought there was anything in this life that you'd give up everything for?"

I sighed. "Don't tell me—you're top of the charts and suddenly you think you have a calling to become a nun."

"No."

"Then what?"

"Answer the question."

"I can't," I said, annoyed. "It's *your* question, not mine. I don't know what you're talking about."

Another one of those pauses. I couldn't even hear her breathe. "You're right. I can't ask you a question I'm supposed to answer. So let me ask you this: Do you think you could ever forgive me?"

I hadn't expected that one at all. "For what? For leaving me to get it all figured out on my own? Build my own life?"

"Among . . . other things," she said, a bit hesitant.

"Yeah, sure. What the hell. Forgiveness is one of the cornerstones of the Church we grew up in. And you can take the girl out of the Church, but you can't take the Church out of the girl, right?"

Kathy didn't laugh. "Oh, you'd be surprised what you can do if you want to badly enough."

"I would?"

"You will." Dead line. It was the last thing she ever said to me. In *that* life.

"I'm Not There" took off like an epidemic. It was really like that. People got infected with it. I didn't understand it, it was the world's biggest downer, and yet it seemed like you couldn't put on a radio without hearing it five times an hour. The world tour kept adding shows and dates, and it looked like she planned to spend the rest of her life touring and singing "I'm Not There." Rock groups were fighting each other to open for her, and she couldn't walk down a street in any city or town without getting mobbed.

Still, the news about her was either very sparse or very controlled. What interviews she gave were enigmatic at best, and made her sound like a weirdo at worst. Which I guess she was, thanks to her parents.

I thought about them a lot, wondered if they were touched by Kathy's good fortune. The house always looked the same on my visits back to Blight City, and there was never anything about her parents or her hometown in the news about her. As if she had x-ed it all out of her life and reinvented herself. She wouldn't have been the first.

Ultimately, I couldn't blame her. Some impulse made me drop into the chapel on campus and light a candle for both Kathy and me. *Peace between us*, I thought. Or maybe prayed is a better word for it. I hoped that when she called again—if she ever did—we'd be friends.

My clock radio woke me the next morning with the news of her suicide.

There was the usual controversy, lots of editorials about how fame, success, and money couldn't buy happiness. Crowds holding vigils outside the concert hall where she was to have performed that night, prayer services, tributes by various of the rock aristocracy.

I spent that day in a state of shock. Without thinking about it, I threw some clothes and books in a bag, went down to the bus station, and bought a ticket home. I was too much of a zombie to cope with anything more demanding than a bus. I couldn't even register the passage of time—I got on the bus, then I got off the bus. Then I walked one step after another through a darkness until I saw the lights in the windows and I knew I was at the house.

Kathy's mother answered the door. She only looked at me and then turned away, disappearing into the kitchen. Barbara and Sarah were sitting on the couch in the living room. All these years and it was the same couch. Sarah looked as if someone had been threatening her with a beating; she was all but cowering while Barbara sat holding both her hands. Barbara was bigger than she'd been the last time I'd seen her, not fat, just husky, like an athlete.

Barbara and I gazed at each other for a long moment. Then she flicked a glance at the staircase leading to the second floor. I nodded and went up.

Her father was in her room, sitting on her bed with his hands on his knees. "What do *you* want?" he said.

The room was just as it had been back when she had sung for me, a thousand years ago in this empty house. I went over to her desk and put on her radio.

". . . vigil in London at the Odeon, as well as in cities across America," a disc jockey was saying solemnly. "At a candlelight service in Manhattan, protest singer Bob Dylan performed a new song he called 'Sad-Eyed Lady of the Lowlands,' which he says he wrote specifically for—"

Kathy's father was at the desk so quickly I flinched. He snapped the radio off. "*Lady*," he sneered. "She was no *lady*. She was just another teenaged whore with hot pants. Like *you*. She took off because what she was getting here wasn't enough for her, she had to have them by the dozens—"

I backed away from him, looking around for something to defend myself with, in case he got violent.

"I knew *you* would start bringing them around here for her. I know your kind, I *know*."

Even if there had been anything vaguely like a weapon handy, I don't think I'd have known how to use it. I felt as if I were shrinking in the face of his creature passing for human. I turned and ran for the door.

He caught the back of my collar just as I put my hand on the doorknob. The neck of my shirt pressed into my windpipe, choking me, but I managed to get the door open. He was trying to reel me in, but I clamped both hands on either side of the doorway, braced myself, and opened my mouth to scream.

Kathy was standing in the hallway, near the top of the stairs. The sight startled me so much, I froze. Fortunately, Kathy's father saw her too, and stopped struggling with me as well.

"*You!*" he growled at her, and shoved me aside. I fell to the floor and scrambled up again quickly, watching him advance on Kathy. She didn't yell or scream or try to run away—she just stood there and let him come at her.

For a few moments, his body hid her completely, and I screamed as hard and as loud as I could, as if I were trying to stun him with sound. "*Stop!*"

Kathy's father turned on me, letting her go. She sagged against the banister and I saw that it wasn't Kathy as I had last seen her, but Kathy at fourteen. "Lesbo!" he snarled at me. "Is that it, you're teaching her your dirty little girlie tricks, is that it, lesbo?"

Panic was like an electric shock. I couldn't make myself do anything except point at Kathy, fourteen-year-old Kathy on the stairs, watching her father and me with the strangest expression of calm detachment. Was she really there, was she—?

His hand went completely around my bicep, because suddenly I was only fourteen myself. He dragged me toward the stairs as if I weighed nothing. I tried to pull away and I thought my arm would tear out of the socket. He was cursing and ranting about dirty little girls and pulling me to the head of the stairs. I clung to the banister just next to where Kathy was standing and looked up at her. She seemed about to say something, but then I felt my feet become entangled with her father's legs. There wasn't even time to yell *Ouch*—we were on our way down the stairs together the quick way.

I was pretty sure we hit every step, separately and together. At each impact, I could hear a collection of different noises, some of it music, some of it just voices, and sometimes just *her* voice. *The* Voice.

No one told you about me
Though they all knew . . .

Sometime later, I had stopped falling down the stairs, but a big hole must have opened up in the floor because I was still falling, but through empty space, unimpeded even by the vision of Kathy leaning over me and explaining, ". . . *my eyes are clear and bright, but I'm not there."*

And she wasn't, and neither was I.

I woke up here, where you all believe I've been waking up every day for ten of the last thirty years. I'm not disoriented, I can remember what you remember of this world. But I also remember *that* world. I know there's no going back to the way things were.

The funny thing is, if she'd asked me, if Kathy had *just asked me*, I might have done it for her anyway. Except I'd have tried a lot harder to fix it so that we could both come out with something better for each of us.

If she had told me, back then, I would have helped her. I wouldn't have just looked the other way, I'd have believed her. After all, she believed in *me*.

But for some reason, she couldn't believe in herself, I guess. Which was why she needed me. She didn't believe she could get *out*, you see. She didn't believe there would ever be an escape for her, so she took *mine*. My escape, and my belief. And it worked.

It took some big sacrifices on her part, though. She couldn't just *take*, she had to give up something in return. That was the suicide after the day "I'm Not There" hit number one, the sacrifice she had to offer to get my faith for her own.

She gave up The Voice, too. Maybe someone else wouldn't have, but then, someone else didn't have to endure her father's weight on top of her in her own room, crushing her spirit. But she had to give up *all* of The Voice. That was the big price, the biggest price of all, really.

So it turned out that I was *there* that afternoon when we were both fourteen, and her father came home to find that she had disobeyed his rules about no visitors, and I went tumbling down the stairs with him. You see that sort of thing in the movies and it never occurs to you that it's the sort of thing you can break your back doing. Of course, it could have been worse—Kathy's father might have lived.

The parish was very good to me and my mother, but even a church collection plate isn't a bottomless well. My mother's insurance should keep me in this place for maybe another five years. After that—well, I don't know. Maybe I'll be getting *out*. You know? That's a joke, you can laugh.

I keep hoping that Kathy will suddenly reappear, come back from wherever she went—someone told me she became a nurse, but out of state somewhere. I keep hoping she'll come back and thank me. I keep hoping, and hoping, and hoping. I don't believe I'll ever be getting out of this chair, but I've been trying to make myself believe that Kathy's coming back.

I can *see* her, too. I can see just how she'll look, and suddenly I'll get this feeling that if I turn around real quick—

But of course, she's still not there.

THE WHITE ROAD
Neil Gaiman

Gaiman's poem "The White Road" is a variation on the traditional fairy tale "Mr. Fox." In the original, Mr. Fox gets his just desserts; in Gaiman's version, this may not be the case. The poem originally appeared in Terri Windling and my anthology *Ruby Slippers, Golden Tears*.

—E.D.

". . . I wish that you would visit me one day, in my house.
There are such sights I would show you."

My intended lowers her eyes, and, yes, she shivers.
Her father and his friends all hoot and cheer.

"*That's* never a story, Mister Fox," chides a pale woman
in the corner of the room, her hair corn-fair,
her eyes the gray of cloud, meat on her bones,
she curves, and smiles crooked and amused.

"Madam, I am no storyteller," and I bow, and ask,
"Perhaps, you have a story for us?" I raise an eyebrow.
Her smile remains.

She nods, then stands, her lips move:

"A girl from the town, a plain girl, was betrayed by her lover,
a scholar. So when her blood stopped flowing,
and her belly swole beyond disguising,
she went to him, and wept hot tears. He stroked her hair,
swore that they would marry, that they would run,
in the night,
together,
to his aunt. She believed him;
even though she had seen the glances in the hall

he gave to his master's daughter,
who was fair, and rich, she believed him.
Or she believed that she believed.

"There was something sly about his smile,
his eyes so black and sharp, his rufous hair. Something
that sent her early to their trysting place,
beneath the oak, beside the thornbush,
something that made her climb the tree and wait.
Climb a tree, and in her condition.
Her love arrived at dusk, skulking by owl-light,
carrying a bag,
from which he took a mattock, shovel, knife.
He worked with a will, beside the thornbush,
beneath the oaken tree,
he whistled gently, and he sang, as he dug her grave,
that old song . . .
shall I sing it for you, now, good folk?"

She pauses, and as a one we clap and we holloa
—or almost as a one:
My intended, her hair so dark, her cheeks so pink,
her lips so red,
seems distracted.

The fair girl (who is she? A guest of the inn, I hazard) sings:

"*A fox went out on a shiny night
And he begged for the moon to give him light
For he'd many miles to go that night
Before he'd reach his den-O!
Den-O! Den-O!
He'd many miles to go that night, before he'd reach his den-O.*"

Her voice is sweet and fine, but the voice of my intended is finer.

"And when her grave was dug—
A small hole it was, for she was a little thing,
even big with child she was a little thing—
he walked below her, back and a forth,
rehearsing her hearsing, thus:
—*Good evening, my pigsnie, my love,
my, but you look a treat in the moon's light,
mother of my child-to-be. Come, let me hold you.*
And he'd embrace the midnight air with one hand,
and with the other, holding his short but wicked knife,
he'd stab and stab the dark.

"She trembled in her oak above him. Breathed so softly,
but still she shook. And once he looked up, and said,
—*Owls, I'll wager*, and another time, *Fie! is that a cat
up there? Here puss* . . . but she was still,
bethought herself a branch, a leaf, a twig. At dawn
he took his mattock, spade, and knife, and left
all grumbling and gudgeoned of his prey.

"They found her later wandering, her wits
had left her. There were oak leaves in her hair,
and she sang,
*'The bough did bend
The bough did break
I saw the hole
The fox did make*

*'We swore to love
We swore to marry
I saw the blade
The fox did carry'*

"They say that her babe, when it was born,
had a fox's paw on her and not a hand.
Fear is the sculptress, midwives claim. The scholar fled."

And she sits down, to general applause.
The smile twitches, hides about her lips: I know it's there,
it waits in her gray eyes. She stares at me, amused.

"I read that in the Orient foxes follow priests and scholars,
in disguise as women, houses, mountains, gods, processions,
always discovered by their tails—" so I begin,
but my intended's father intercedes.
"Speaking of tales—my dear, you said you had a tale?"

My intended flushes. There are no rose petals,
save for her cheeks. She nods, and says:

"My story, father? My story is the story of a dream I dreamed."

Her voice is so quiet and soft, we hush ourselves to hear,
outside the inn just the night sounds: an owl hoots,
but, as the old folk say, I live too near the wood
to be frightened by an owl.

She looks at me.

"You, sir. In my dream you rode to me, and called,

—*Come to my house, my sweet, away down the white road.*
There are such sights I would show you.
I asked how I would find your house, down the white chalk road,
for it's a long road, and a dark one, under trees
that make the light all green and gold when the sun is high,
but shade the road at other times. At night
it's pitch-black; there is no moonlight on the white road . . .

"And you said, Mister Fox—and this is most curious, but dreams
are treacherous and curious and dark—
that you would cut the throat of a sow-pig,
and you would walk her home behind your fine black stallion.
You smiled,
smiled, Mister Fox, with your red lips and your green eyes,
eyes that could snare a maiden's soul, and your yellow teeth,
which could eat her heart—"

"God forbid," I smiled. All eyes were on me, then, not her,
though hers was the story. Eyes, such eyes.

"So, in my dream, it became my fancy to visit your great house,
as you had so often entreated me to do,
to walk its glades and paths, to see the pools,
the statues you had brought from Greece, the yews,
the poplar-walk, the grotto, and the bower.
And, as this was but a dream, I did not wish
to take a chaperone
—some withered, juiceless prune
who would not appreciate your house, Mister Fox; who
would not appreciate your pale skin,
nor your green eyes,
nor your engaging ways.

"So I rode the white chalk road, following the red blood path,
on Betsy, my filly. The trees above were green.
A dozen miles straight, and then the blood
led me off across meadows, over ditches, down a gravel path,
(but now I needed sharp eyes to catch the blood—
a drip, a drop: the pig must have been dead as anything)
and I reined my filly in in front of a house.
And such a house. A Palladian delight, immense,
a landscape of its own, windows, columns,
a white stone monument to verticality, expansive.

"There was a sculpture in the garden, before the house,
a Spartan child, stolen fox half concealed in its robe,
the fox biting the child's stomach, gnawing the vitals away,
the stoic child bravely saying nothing—

what could it say, cold marble that it was?
There was pain in its eyes, and it stood,
upon a plinth upon which were carved eight words.
I walked around it and I read:
Be bold,
Be bold,
but not too bold.

"I tethered little Betsy in the stables,
between a dozen night black stallions
each with blood and madness in his eyes.
I saw no one.
I walked to the front of the house, and up the great steps.
The huge doors were locked fast,
no servants came to greet me, when I knocked.
In my dream (for do not forget, Mister Fox, that this was my dream.
You look so pale) the house fascinated me, the kind of curiosity (you know this,
Mister Fox, I see it in your eyes) that kills cats.

"I found a door, a small door, off the latch,
and pushed my way inside.
Walked corridors, lined with oak, with shelves,
with busts, with trinkets,
I walked, my feet silent on the scarlet carpet,
until I reached the great hall.
It was there again, in red stones that glittered,
set into the white marble of the floor,
it said:
Be bold,
be bold,
but not too bold
Or else your life's blood
shall run cold.

"There were stairs, wide, carpeted in scarlet,
off the great hall,
and I walked up them, silently, silently.
Oak doors: and now
I was in the dining room, or so I am convinced,
for the remnants of a grisly supper
were abandoned, cold and fly-buzzed.
Here was a half-chewed hand, there, crisped and picked,
a face, a woman's face, who must in life, I fear,
have looked like me."

"Heavens defend us all from such dark dreams," her father cried.
"Can such things be?"

"It is not so," I assured him. The fair woman's smile
glittered behind her gray eyes. People
need assurances.

"Beyond the supper room was a room,
a huge room, this inn would fit in that room,
piled promiscuously with rings and bracelets,
necklaces, pearl drops, ball gowns, fur wraps,
lace petticoats, silks and satins. Ladies' boots,
and muffs, and bonnets: a treasure cave and dressing room—
diamonds and rubies underneath my feet.

"Beyond that room I knew myself in Hell.
In my dream . . .
I saw many heads. The heads of young women. I saw a wall
on which dismembered limbs were nailed.
A heap of breasts. The piles of guts, of livers, lights, the eyes,
  the . . .
No. I cannot say. And all around the flies were buzzing,
one low droning buzz.
—*Bëelzebubzebubzebub* they buzzed. I could not breathe,
I ran from there and sobbed against a wall."

"A fox's lair indeed," says the fair woman.
("It was not so," I mutter.)
"They are untidy creatures, so to litter,
about their dens the bones and skins and feathers
of their prey. The French call him *Renard*,
the Scottish, *Tod*."

"One cannot help one's name," says my intended's father.
He is almost panting now, they all are:
in the firelight, the fire's heat, lapping their ale.
The wall of the inn was hung with sporting prints.

She continues:
"From outside I heard a crash and a commotion.
I ran back the way I had come, along the red carpet,
down the wide staircase—too late!—the main door was opening!
I threw myself down the stairs—rolling, tumbling—
fetched up hopelessly beneath a table,
where I waited, shivered, prayed."

She points at me. "Yes, you, sir. You came in,
crashed open the door, staggered in, you sir,
dragging a young woman
by her red hair and by her throat.
Her hair was long and unconfined, she screamed and strove

to free herself. You laughed, deep in your throat,
were all a-sweat, and grinned from ear to ear."

She glares at me. The color's in her cheeks.
"You pulled a short old broadsword, Mister Fox, and as she
    screamed,
you slit her throat, again from ear to ear,
I listened to her bubbling, sighing, shriek
and closed my eyes and prayed until she stopped.
And after much, much, much too long, she stopped.
"And I looked out. You smiled, held up your sword,
your hands agore-blood—"

"In your dream," I tell her.

"In my dream.
She lay there on the marble, as you sliced
you hacked, you wrenched, you panted, and you stabbed.
You took her head from her shoulders,
thrust your tongue between her red wet lips.
You cut off her hands. Her pale white hands.
You sliced open her bodice, you removed each breast.
Then you began to sob and howl.
Of a sudden,
clutching her head, which you carried by the hair,
the flame red hair,
you ran up the stairs.

"As soon as you were out of sight,
I fled through the open door.
I rode my Betsy home, down the white road."

All eyes upon me now. I put down my ale,
on the old wood of the table.
"It is not so,"
I told her,
told all of them.
"It was not so, and
God forbid
it should be so. It was
an evil dream. I wish such dreams
on no one."

"Before I fled the charnel house,
before I rode poor Betsy into a lather,
before we fled down the White Road,
the blood still red
(and was it a pig whose throat you slit, Mister Fox?)

before I came to my father's inn,
before I fell before them speechless,
my father, brothers, friends—"

All honest farmers, fox-hunting men.
They are stamping their boots, their black boots.

"—before that, Mister Fox,
I seized, from the floor, from the bloody floor,
her hand, Mister Fox. The hand of the woman
you hacked apart before my eyes."

"It is not so—"

"It was no dream. You Landru. You Bluebeard."

"It was not so—"

"You Gilles de Rais. You monster."

"And God forbid it should be so!"

She smiles now, lacking mirth or warmth.
The brown hair curls around her face,
roses twining about a bower.
Two spots of red are burning on her cheeks.

"Behold, Mister Fox! Her hand! Her poor pale hand!"
She pulls it from her breasts (gently freckled,
I had dreamed of those breasts)
tosses it down upon the table.
It lies in front of me.
Her father, brothers, friends,
they stare at me hungrily,
and I pick up the small thing.

The hair was red indeed, and rank. The pads and claws
were rough. One end was bloody
but the blood had dried.

"This is no hand," I tell them. But the first
fist knocks the wind from out of me,
an oaken cudgel hits my shoulder,
as I stagger,
the first black boot kicks me down onto the floor.
And then a rain of blows beats down on me,
I curl and mewl and pray and grip the paw
so tightly.

Perhaps I weep.

I see her then,
the pale, fair girl, the smile has reached her lips,
her skirts so long as she slips, gray-eyed,
amused beyond all bearing, from the room.
She'd many a mile to go, that night.
And as she leaves,
from my vantage place upon the floor,
I see the brush, the tail between her legs;
I would have called,
but I could speak no more. Tonight she'll be running
four-footed, surefooted, down the White Road.

What if the hunters come?
What if they come?

Be bold, I whisper once, before I die. *But not too bold* . . .

And then my tale is done.

REFRIGERATOR HEAVEN
David J. Schow

David J. Schow lives in southern California with his wife, Christa Faust. He is known primarily in the horror field for his powerful, award-winning short fiction, and for editing *Silver Scream*. He has had two novels published, *The Kill Riff* and *The Shaft*. In 1989 he branched out into films and television, scripting "the unsavory activities of such social lions as Leatherface and Freddy Krueger." His most recent screenplay credit was for *The Crow*. His short fiction has been collected in *Seeing Red*, *Lost Angels*, and *Black Leather Required*.

It's good to have Schow back writing short fiction. "Refrigerator Heaven" shows him at the top his form with crisp language, deft characterization, and a dark theme. Originally published in the anthology *Dark Love* edited by Nancy A. Collins, Edward E. Kramer, and Martin H. Greenberg, Schow's story probably takes the theme of that anthology farthest.

—E.D.

The light is beatific. More than beautiful. Garrett sees the light and allows the awe to flow from him.

Garrett can't *not* see the light. His eyelids are slammed tightly shut; tears trickle from aching slits at both corners. The light seeks out the corners and penetrates them. It is so hotly white it obliterates Garrett's view of the thin veinwork on the obverse of his own inadequate eyelids.

He tries to measure time by the beat of his own heart; no good.

The light has always been with him, it seems. It is eternal, omnipotent. Garrett gasps, but not in pain, not *true* pain—no, for the light is a superior force, and he owes it his wonder. It is so much *more* than he is, so intense that he can *bear* it caress his flesh, seeking out his secret places, his organs, his thoughts, illuminating each fissure and furrow in his very brain.

Garrett slams his palms over closed eyes and marvels that the light does not care and offers no quarter. Garrett feels pathetic; the light, he feels, is unequivocal and pure.

Garrett has looked into the light and formulated a new definition of what God must be like. He feels honored that he, among mortals, has been permitted this glimpse of the divine. His mind interprets the light as hot, though he does not feel the anticipated baking of his flesh. So pure, so total . . .

He has never in his pathetic, mortal life borne witness to a spectacle like it.

Finally, the light is too much. Garrett must avert his gaze, but he cannot. No matter which way he turns his head, the light is there, cleansing away agendas and guilt and human foibles and the mistakes of the past, as well as mistaken notions of the future. The light, forever, there in Garrett's head.

He reaches to find words to offer up to the light, and he can only find limited human conceits, like love.

A woman is in bed with her husband. They are between bouts of lovemaking, and the woman's eyes are hooded and blue in the semidarkness, with that unique glow—a radiance that tells the man he is all she sees, or cares to see right now.

She tells him she loves him. Unnecessarily. The words in the dark do him spiritual good anyway.

She touches his nose with her fingertip and draws it slowly down. You. I love. He knows.

He is about to say something in response, if for no other reason than not to maroon her in their warm, postcoital quiet, stranding her alone with her words of love. He is trying to think of something sexy and witty and genuinely loving, to prove he cares.

He is on his back, and one of her legs, warm and moist on the softest part of the inner thigh, is draped over his. You are mine, the embrace says. You are what I want.

The man is still struggling with words that won't come. He misses his chance. If you miss the moment, other forces rush in to fill the dead air for you, and rarely does one have control or choice.

Later, the man thinks, if only he had spoken, none of the bad things would have happened.

There are some loud noises. The next thing the man knows, his wife is screaming and he is facedown, cheek bulled roughly against the carpet. His wife is screaming questions that will not be answered in this lifetime.

The man's hands are cuffed behind his back. He is lifted by the cuffs, naked, as lights click on in the bedroom.

He twists his head, tries to see. He is backhanded, very hard, by one of his captors. The image he snatches is of his wife, also naked, held by her throat against the bedroom wall, by a man in a tight business suit. With his free hand the suit is holding an automatic an inch from her nose and telling her in no uncertain verbiage to shut up if she knows what is good for her.

Like a bad gangster movie, thinks the man.

He sees all this in an eighth of a second. Then, *bang*. He hits the floor again, feeling the wetness of fresh blood oozing from a split eyebrow.

His ankles are ziplocked together—one of those vinyl slipknot cuffs used by police. Then he is hoisted bodily, penis dangling, and carried out of his own bedroom like a roast on a spit.

He fights to see his wife before his captors have him out the door. In this moment, seeing her one last time becomes the most important imperative ever to burn in his mind.

As he is hauled away, he says he loves her. He has no way of knowing whether she hears. He cannot see her as he speaks the words. In the end, the words come easily.

He never sees his wife again.

Donnelly regarded the box with a funny expression tilting his face to starboard. He took a long draw on his smoke, which made a quarter inch of ash, then shrugged the way a comedian does when he *knows* he's just delivered a knee-slapper . . . and the audience is too stupid to appreciate it.

"So what did this guy *do*?" he said with artificial levity.

"That's classified," said Cambreaux. "That's none of your beeswax. That, Chester, is a dumb question, and you oughta know better."

"Just testing," said Donnelly. "I'm supposed to jump-quiz smartasses like you to make sure there are no security leaks. So what did he do?"

"He's a reporter, from what I gather. He was in the wrong place at the right time with a camera and a tape recorder, neither of which we can find. They sent down orders to scoop him."

"Very funny."

"Scoop him up, I mean." Cambreaux popped four codeine-coated aspirin like M&Ms. "Do you have any more questions?"

"What did he see? What did he hear?"

"Let me ask *you* a question: Do you want to keep your job? Do you want me to lose *my* job?"

"That's two questions." Donnelly was having fun.

"You asked two questions first."

"Yeah, but your answers are cooler. You want a cigarette?"

"No." Cambreaux really wanted the smoke, but thought this was a habit over which he should exert more control. There was a definite lack of things to do with one's hands down in this little, secure room, and he was grateful for Donnelly's company, this shift. "They locked this guy in a cell for four days, your basic sweat-out. No phone calls. No go. So then Human Factors beats the crap out of him; still nothing. They used one of those canvas tubes filled with iron filings."

"Mm." Donnelly finished his cigarette and looked around for an ashtray. Finally he ground out the butt on the sole of his shoe. "No exterior marks, except for a bruise or two, and your organs get pureed."

"Yeah. They used a phone book, too."

"And he read the phone book and said, 'This has got a lot of great characters, but the plot sucks.' "

"Boy, you got a million of 'em. And they all stink."

"Thanks." Donnelly patted himself down for a fresh smoke. It was a habit he swore he needed to quit. The pat-down, not the smoking. "Then what?"

"Then what. They brought in Medical Assist. They tried sodium pentothal; no dice. Then psychedelics, then electroshock. Still zero. So here we be."

Donnelly looked twice. Yes, that *was* a kitchen timer on top of Cambreaux's console. Donnelly's wife had one just like it—round clock face, adjustable for sixty minutes. She used it to brew coffee precisely; she was fastidious about things like perfect coffee. Donnelly indicated the timer, then the big box. "You baking him in there?"

"Yeah. He's not done yet."

The box was about five feet square and resembled an industrial refrigerator. It was enameled white, steel-reinforced, and featureless except for a big screw-down hatch lock like the ones Donnelly had seen while touring an aircraft carrier. Thick 220-volt cables snaked from the box to Cambreaux's console.

"You got gypped," said Donnelly. "No ice-maker."

Cambreaux made the face he always made at Donnelly's jokes. Donnelly noticed—not for the first time—that Cambreaux's head seemed perfectly round, a moon head distinguished by a perfect crescent of hair at eyebrow level, punctuated by round mad-scientist specs with flecks of blue and gold in the rims.

"New glasses?"

"Yeah, the old ones were too tight on my head. Torture. Gave me the strokes, right here." Cambreaux indicated his temples. "Pure fucking torture. Man, you ever need any info out of me, just make me wear my old glasses and I'll kill my children for you."

Donnelly strolled around the box, one full circuit. "What do we call this?"

"The refrigerator. What else?"

"A *reporter*? Funny. Most journalists don't have the spine or the sperm for this sort of marathon."

"If he'd talked, he wouldn't be here."

"Point. Agreed."

"What are you *staring* at, Chester?"

"I love to watch a man who enjoys his work."

Cambreaux gave him the finger. "You going to stand around admiring me all afternoon, or can I talk you into setting up a fresh pot on the machine?"

Cambreaux's timer went *ding*.

"I was waiting to see what happens when our reporter is done basting," said Donnelly.

"What happens is this." Cambreaux lifted the timer and cranked it back to sixty minutes.

Donnelly squinted at him. "Jesus. How long have you been here today?"

"Six hours. New regs call for eight hours up."

"Oh. Cream and sugar?"

"Just a spot of each. Just enough cream to discolor the coffee."

"You're starting to sound like my wife."

"Grope me and I'll shoot you in the balls."

"This is probably a stupid question—"

"Guaranteed, from you," Cambreaux overrode.

"—but can I get anything for our pal the reporter?"

Cambreaux pushed back from the console, the racketing of his chair casters loud and hollow in the room, like the too harsh ticking of the appliance timer. He winnowed his fingers beneath his glasses and rubbed his eyes until they were pink.

"Did I say this guy is a reporter? Scratch that. He *was* a reporter. When he comes out of the fridge, he won't need anything except maybe a padded cell. Or a casket."

Donnelly kept staring at the box. It was just weird enough, the sort of anomaly you can't take your eye from.

"How about I just bring him a shot of good ole government-issue cyanide?"

"Not just yet," said Cambreaux, touching his timer as if for inspiration, then jotting a note on a gray legal pad. "Not just yet, my friend."

Elapsed time has ceased to have meaning, and this is good for Garrett.

A relief. He has been released from what were once boundaries, and the mundane of the day-to-day. There is no day here, no night, no time. He has been liberated. Elemental input, and the limitations of his physical form, have become his sole realities. He had once read that the next step in human evolution might be to a formless intellect, eternal, almost cosmic, undying, immortal, transcendent.

If the light had been God, then the cold is Sleep. New rules, new deities.

He is curled into a fetal ball like a beaten animal, shuddering uncontrollably while his lit-up mind wrestles with the problems of how to properly pay obeisance to this latest god.

His *bones* feel cold; his hands and feet, distant and insensate. Respiration is a knife of ice, boring in to pierce his lungs in tandem. He shallows his breath and prays that his rawed esophagus might lend the air a mote of metabolic heat before it plunges mercilessly into his lung tissue.

He is still merely tissue.

He knows the cold will not steal more than a few critical degrees of his core heat. The cold will not murder him; it is testing him, inviting him to discover his own extremes. To kill Garrett would be too easy, and pointless. He would not have survived the light only to perish by the cold. The cold cares about him, as the light had, as an uncaring god is said to care for the flock that is crippled, tormented, and killed . . . only to profess renewed faith.

The cold is intimate in a way that surpasses his mere flesh.

His fingers and toes are now remote tributaries of forgotten feeling. Garrett curls on his right side, then his left, to spell each of his lungs in turn, to stave off the workload of chilly pain by reducing it to processable fragments.

He allows the sub-zero ambience to flow *through*, not batter against, the inadequate walls of his skin. He thinks of the felled tree in the forest. He is here so the cold will have a purpose. He is the proof of sound in the silent, snowbound woodland; the freezing air needed him as much as he needed it to verify his own existence.

Huddled, then, and shivering, still naked, his blood retarded to a thick crawl in unthawed veins, Garret permits the cold to have him. He welcomes its forward nature, its brashness.

Garrett closes his eyes. Feels bliss. Smiling, with clenched teeth, he sleeps.

On the dirty coffee table in front of Alvarado there were several items of interest: A bottle of Laphroaig scotch, a big camera, a snubnosed gun, and an unopened letter.

The camera was an autofocusing rig with flashless 1600 ASA color film and a blimped speedwinder, for silent work. Twenty-one exposures had been recorded in scant seconds. The Laphroaig was very mellow and half gone. The gun was a Charter Arms .44 Bulldog, no shots used yet.

Whenever the building made a slight nighttime noise around him, Alvarado tensed, his heart thudding briskly with anticipation. Moment to moment, he was safe . . . though the next moment might bring last call.

He had driven all the way into the San Fernando Valley to mail his preaddressed packets, copies of his precious tapes and photos. Now his backstop was secure, his evidence was damning, and the only reason he could think of for still hanging around his apartment was because he, too, felt damned. Soiled somehow.

New evidence waited inside his camera. Rawer, more toxic, dangerously good stuff to reinforce his already strong case.

Alvarado lifted the envelope and read the address for the thousandth time. It was a cable TV bill for Garrett, his next-door neighbor. Once upon a time, the gods running computerized mailing lists had hiccuped, fouled their numbers. Rather than rectify the irritant with fruitless phone calls, Alvarado and Garrett had been trading mail for nearly a year now, sliding it beneath each other's respective doors when they were out. They both traveled a lot. The mail thing had become an after-hours joke between them.

Garrett was an ad agent for a publishing company. He toured his turf with a folio of new releases and pitched store to store. Alvarado had been staff at the *Los Angeles Times* until he was let go in a seasonal pruning, followed by a hiring freeze blamed on the latest recession. He made do as a freelancer until his time rolled around again; he had made his living professionally long enough to believe in karmic work rhythms. Freelancing had propelled him into some very odd new places. Alternative papers. Tabloids. Pop magazines.

Investigative journalism, self-motivated.

Now, if his backstop allies made proper use of the duplicate tapes and photos now safely in postal transit, Alvarado would be back on the map, big time. The waiting was not the worst part, though it *had* made his life pretty suspenseful during the past few hellish days.

Sometimes reporters got assassinated for their reportage. It happened, though the public rarely heard about it. Thus, Alvarado had emplaced his elaborate backstop network.

Sometimes reporters got *worse* than killed. Thus the gun, yes, loaded, and this quiet vigil in a dark room.

It had happened four or five days ago. Say a week. Alvarado's schedule and sleeptime had become totally bollixed, of combat necessity.

A week ago, he had heard a noisy commotion in the night. His damning photos and tapes had not yet been copied or mailed. He was awake from his snooze on the sofa in a silent instant, fully alert. At first he thought the disturbance was a simple domestic—Garrett and his wife or girlfriend having some temporary and loud disagreement in the middle of the night, as lovers sometimes do.

Alvarado's mind decoded the noises he heard. This was no argument.

He remembered grabbing his camera and moving to the balcony. After a second of hesitation he had stepped around to Garrett's adjoining balcony, and recognized immediately that very bad shit was going on inside.

He witnessed most of it through his viewfinder, focusing on the slit of light permitted by the curtains on Garrett's sliding door. He saw Garrett naked, trussed and manhandled by an efficiently fast goon squad in the very best JCPenney's Secret Service wash-and-wear. Garrett's wife or girlfriend, also naked, was being abused and threatened on the far side of the bedroom. The men moved like they had a purpose.

Twenty-one rapid-fire exposures later, Garrett was out, abducted, gone . . . and

Alvarado was off to the mailbox with older, no less scary business. He had his own future to protect.

Now, tonight, Alvarado sat staring at the cable bill addressed to Garrett. He had received it. And Garrett had received a late-night visit intended for his neighbor.

Intended for *me*, Alvarado knew.

It was a coincidence almost divine, winning Alvarado the time to get his material to safety. Garrett had picked up the check, and perhaps that was why Alvarado was still hanging around.

Just like that, his life had become bad film noir. Here he was, drinking, fondling his gun, and fantasizing about the inevitable confrontation. Blam, blam, and in a blaze of glory *everybody* gets to be in the papers.

Post-mortem.

Provided the bad guys got the address right this time.

If the light was God, and the cold Sleep, then the sound was Love.

Garrett decides he is being tempered and refined for some very special purpose, duty, or chosen destiny. He feels proud and fulfilled. He cannot be the recipient of so many revelations for some nothing purpose . . . and so he pays very close attention to the lessons the sound brings him.

He is quite the attentive little godling in training.

The extremes he withstands are the signposts of his own evolution. He began as a normal man. He is becoming more.

It is exhilarating.

He eagerly awaits Heat, and Silence, and Darkness, and whatever he needs beyond them.

"You want to hear a funny?" said Cambreaux.

Donnelly felt he was not going to walk away amused. "I do the jokes in this toilet."

"Not as boffo as this: Our reporter? Janitorial collected him at three o'clock this morning. We've had the wrong guy in the refrigerator for a week."

Donnelly did not laugh. He never laughed when he could feel his stomach dropping away like a clipped elevator, skimming his balls enroute to Hell. "You mean this guy is *innocent?*"

Cambreaux's style did not admit of sheepishness, or comeback. "I wouldn't say that."

"Everybody's guilty of something, is that it?"

"No. I wouldn't say that our friend in the box is innocent. Not anymore."

They both stared at the refrigerator. Locked inside was a man who had been subjected to stresses and extremes known to fracture the toughest operatives going. His brain had to be string cheese by now. And he hadn't *done* anything . . . except be innocent.

"Fucking Janitorial," Donnelly snorted. "They're always screwing up the work orders."

"Bunch of gung-ho bullet boys," Cambreaux agreed. Better to fault another department, always.

"So . . . you going to let him out?"

"Not my call." Both he and Donnelly knew that the man in the box had to be released, but neither of them would budge until the right documents dropped down the correct chute.

"What's he on now?"

"High-frequency sound. Metered for—oh, *shit!*"

Donnelly saw Cambreaux rocket from his chair to grab the kitchen timer and hurl it across the chamber. It disintegrated into frags. Then Cambreaux was frantically snapping off switches, cranking dials down.

"Goddamn timer froze! It stopped!"

Donnelly immediately looked at the fridge.

"It was on too high for too long, Chet! Goddamn timer!"

Both of them wondered what they would see when the lid was finally opened.

Garrett feels at last that he is being pushed too far, that he must extract too high a price from himself.

He endures, because he must. He hovers on the brink of a human millennium. He is the first. He must experience the change with his eyes open.

The sound removed everything from Garrett's world.

Not too late at last, Garrett says *I love you.*

He has to scream it. Not too late.

Then his eardrums burst.

Cambreaux was drinking coffee in the lounge, shoulders sagging, elbows planted on knees, penitent.

"Ever hear the one about the self-protecting fuse?" said Donnelly. "The one that protects itself by blowing up your whole stereo?" No reaction. "I saw the fridge open. When did they take our boy?"

"This morning. I was on the console when the orders finally came down."

"Hey—your hands are shaking."

"Chet, I feel like I have to cry, almost. I saw that guy come out of the fridge. I've never seen anything like it."

Donnelly sat down beside Cambreaux. "Bad?"

"Bad." A poisonous laugh escaped him. It was more like a cough, or a bark. "We opened the box. And that guy looked at us like we'd just stolen his soul. He had blood all over him, mostly from his ears. He started hollering. Chet, he didn't want us to take him out."

This didn't sound good, spilling from a professional like Cambreaux. Donnelly let out a measured breath, leavening his own racing metabolism.

"But you took him out."

"Yes sir, we did. Orders. And when we got him out, he broke, and clawed his own eyes out, and choked to death on his tongue."

"Jesus Christ . . ."

"Janitorial took him."

"Disposal's the one thing those bozos are good at."

"You got a cigarette?"

Donnelly handed it over and lit it for him. He lit himself one.

"Chet, did you ever read 'The Pit and the Pendulum?' "

"I saw the movie."

"The story is basically about a guy who gets tortured for days by the Inquisition.

Right before he makes his final fall into the pit, he gets rescued by the French army."

"Fiction."

"Yeah, happy endings and all. We did the same thing. Except the guy didn't want to leave. He *found* something in there, Chet. Something you or I don't ever have a chance at. And we took him out, away from the thing he discovered. . . ."

"And he died."

"Yeah."

They were silent together for a few minutes. Neither of them was very spiritual; they were men who were paid for their ability to do their jobs. Yet neither could resist the idea of what Garrett might have seen in the box.

Neither of them would ever climb into the box to find out. Too many reasons not to. Thousands.

"I got you a present," Donnelly said.

He handed over a factory-fresh appliance timer. This one came with a warranty and guarantee. That made Cambreaux smile. A bit.

"Take it slow, old buddy. Duty calls. We'll have a drink later."

Cambreaux nodded and accepted Donnelly's fraternal pat on the shoulder. He had just done his job. No sin in that.

Donnelly walked along the fluorescent-lit corridor, very consciously avoiding the route that would take him past the room where the refrigerator was. He did not want to see it hanging open just now.

He made a mental note to look up the Poe story. He loved a good read.

AFTER THE ELEPHANT BALLET
Gary A. Braunbeck

Gary A. Braunbeck was born in 1960 and now lives in Columbus, Ohio, with his wife Leslie and two cats. He held jobs as a carny "stick," crisis center counselor, newspaper reporter, short-order cook, bartender, and dog groomer before he began writing full time in 1991. He has sold stories to magazines and anthologies such as *Not One of Us*, *Cemetery Dance*, *Borderlands 4*, *Tombs*, *Masques III*, *Frankenstein: The Monster Wakes*, *Werewolves*, *The Earth Strikes Back*, *Murder Most Delicious*, *Fantastic Alice*, and *The Year's Best Fantasy & Horror*. His first collection, *Things Left Behind*, will be out this year from Cemetery Dance Publications.

"After the Elephant Ballet," which has ghosts, guardian angels, and several elephants, is ultimately about forgiving our parents and getting on with our lives. It was originally published in *Heaven Sent* edited by Peter Crowther and Martin H. Greenberg.

—E.D.

> *Our acts our angels are, or good or ill,*
> *Our fatal shadows that walk by us still.*
> —John Fletcher (1579–1625),
> *An Honest Man's Fortune*, Epilogue

The little girl might have been pretty once, but flames had taken care of that: burned skin hung about her neck in brownish wattles; one yellowed eye was almost completely hidden underneath the drooping scar tissue of her forehead; her mouth twisted downward on both sides with pockets of dead, greasy-looking flesh at the corners; and her cheeks resembled the globs of congealed wax that form at the base of a candle.

I couldn't stop staring at her or cursing myself for doing it. She passed by the table where I was sitting, giving me a glimpse of her only normal-looking feature: her left eye was a startling bright green, a jade gemstone. Buried as it was in that ruined face, its vibrance seemed a cruel joke.

She took a seat in the back.

Way in the back.

"Mr. Dysart?"

A woman in her midthirties held out a copy of my latest storybook. I smiled as I took it, chancing one last glance at the disfigured little girl in the back, then autographed the title page.

I have been writing and illustrating children's books for the last six years, and though I'm far from a household name I do have a Newbery Award proudly displayed on a shelf in my office. One critic, evidently after a few too many Grand Marniers, once wrote: "Dysart's books are a treasure chest of wonders for children and adults alike. He is part Maurice Sendak, part Hans Christian Andersen, and part Madeline L'Engle." (I always thought of my books as being a cross between Buster Keaton and the Brothers Grimm—what does *that* tell you about creative objectivity?)

I handed the book back to the woman as Gina Foster, director of the Cedar Hill Public Library, came up to the table. We had been dating for about two weeks; romance had yet to rear its ugly head, but I was hopeful.

"Well, are we ready?" she asked.

" 'We' want to step outside for a cigarette."

"I thought you were trying to quit."

"And failing miserably." I made my way to the special "judge's chair." "How many entries are there?"

"Twenty-five. But don't worry, they can show you only one illustration and the story can't be longer than four minutes. We still on for coffee and dessert afterward?"

"Unless some eight-year-old Casanova steals your heart away."

"Hey, you pays your money, you takes your chances."

"You're an evil woman."

"Famous for it."

"Tell me again: How did you rope me into being the judge for this?"

"When I mentioned that this was National Literacy Month, you assaulted me with a speech about the importance of promoting a love for creativity among children."

"I must've been drunk." I don't drink—that's my mother's department.

Gina looked at her watch, took a deep breath as she gave me a "here-we-go" look, then turned to face the room. "Good evening," she said in a sparkling voice that always reminded me of bells. "Welcome to the library's first annual storybook contest." Everyone applauded. I tried slinking my way into the woodwork. Crowds make me nervous. Actually, most things make me nervous.

"I'll just wish all our contestants good luck and introduce our judge, award-winning local children's book author Andrew Dysart." She began the applause this time, then mouthed *You're on your own* before gliding to an empty chair.

"Thank you," I said, the words crawling out of my throat as if they were afraid of the light. "I . . . uh, I'm sure that all of you have been working very hard, and I want you to know that we're going to make copies of all your storybooks, bind them, and put them on the shelves here in the library right next to my own." Unable to add any more dazzle to that stunning speech, I took my seat, consulted the list, and called the first contestant forward.

A chubby boy with round glasses shuffled up as if he were being led in front of a firing squad. He faced the room, gave a terrified grin, then wiped some sweat from his forehead as he held up a pretty good sketch of a cow riding a tractor.

"My name is Jimmy Campbell and my story is called 'The Day The Cows Took Over.' " He held the picture higher. "See there? The cow is riding the tractor and the farmer is out grazing in the field."

"What's the farmer's name?" I asked.

He looked at me and said, "Uh . . . h-how about Old MacDonald?" He shrugged his shoulders. "I'd give him a better name, but I don't know no farmers."

I laughed along with the rest of the room, forgetting all about the odd, damaged little girl who had caught my attention earlier.

Jimmy did very well—I had to fight to keep my laughter from getting too loud. I didn't want him to think I was making fun of him, but the kid was *genuinely* funny; his story had an off-kilter sense of humor that reminded me of Ernie Kovacs. I decided to give him the maximum fifty points. I'm a pushover for kids. So sue me.

The next forty minutes went by with nary a tear or panic attack, but after eight stories I could see that several of the children were getting fidgety, so I signaled to Gina that we'd take a break after the next contestant.

I read: "Lucy Simpkins."

There was the soft rustling of movement in the back as the burned girl came forward.

Everyone stared at her. The cumulative anxiety in the room was squatting on her shoulders like a stone gargoyle—

—yet she wore an unwavering smile.

I returned the smile and gestured for her to begin.

She held up a watercolor painting.

I think my mouth may have dropped open.

The painting was excellent: a deftly rendered portrait of several people—some very tall, others quite short, still others who were deformed—standing in a semicircle around a statue which marked a grave. All wore the brightly colored costumes of circus performers. Each face had an expression of profound sadness; the nuances were breathtaking. But the thing that really impressed me was the cloud in the sky; it was shaped like an elephant, but not in any obvious way. It reminded you of summer afternoons when you still had enough imagination and wonder to lie on a hillside and dream that you saw giant shapes in the pillowy white above.

"My name is Lucy Simpkins," she said in a clear, almost musical voice, "and my story is called 'Old Bet's Gone Away.'"

"One night in Africa, in the secret elephant graveyard, the angels of all the elephants got together to tell stories. Tonight it was Martin's, the Bull Elephant's, turn. He wandered around until he found his old bones, then he sat on top of them like they were a throne and said, 'I want to tell you the story of Old Bet, the one who never found her way back to us.'

"And he said:

" 'In 1824 a man in Somers, New York, bought an elephant named Old Bet from a traveling circus. He gave her the best hay and always fed her peanuts on the weekends. Children would pet her trunk and take rides on her back in a special saddle that the man made.

" 'Then one day the reverend brought his daughter to ride on Old Bet. Old Bet was really tired, but she thought the reverend's little girl looked nice so she gave her a ride and even sang the elephant song, which went like this:

> " 'I go along, thud-thud,
> I go along.
> And I sing my elephant song.
> I stomp in the grass, and I roll in the mud,
> And when I go a-walking, I go along THUD!
> It's a happy sound, and this is my happy song.
> Won't you sing it with me? It doesn't take long.
> I go along, thud-thud,
> I go along.

" 'Old Bet accidentally tripped over a log and fell, and the reverend's daughter broke both of her legs and had to go to the hospital.

" 'Old Bet was really sorry, but the reverend yelled at her and smacked her with a horsewhip and got her so scared that she ran away into the deep woods.

" 'The next day the reverend got all the people of the town together and told them that Old Bet was the Devil in disguise and should be killed before she could hurt other children. So the menfolk took their shotguns and went into the woods. They found Bet by the river. She was looking at her reflection in the water and singing:

> " 'I ran away, uh-oh,
> I ran away.
> And I hurt my little friend.
> I didn't mean to fall, but I'm clumsy and old
> I'm big and ugly and the circus didn't want me anymore.
> I wish they hadn't sold me.
> I want to go home.

" 'The reverend wanted to shoot her, but the man who'd bought her from the circus said, "Best I be the one who does the deed. After all, she's mine." But the man wasn't too young either and his aim was a bit off and when he fired the bullet it hit Old Bet in the rear and it hurt and it scared her *so much!* She tried to run away, run back to the circus.

" 'She didn't mean to kill anyone, but two men got under her and she crushed them and her heart broke because of that. By now the judge had come around to see what all the trouble was, and he saw the two dead men and decreed right there on the spot that Old Bet was guilty of murder and sentenced her to hang by the neck until she was dead.

" 'They took her to the rail yard and strung her up on a railroad crane, but she broke it down because she was so heavy. They got a stronger crane and hanged her from that. After three hours, Old Bet finally died while five thousand people watched. She was buried there in Somers and the man who bought her had a statue raised above the grave. Ever since, it has been a shrine for circus people. They travel to her grave and stop to pay their respects and remember that, as long as people laugh at you and smile, they won't kill you. And they say that if you look in the sky on a bright summer's day, you can see Old Bet up there in the clouds, smiling down at everyone and singing the elephant song as she tries to find her way back to Africa and the secret elephant graveyard.'

"Then it was morning, and the sun came up, and the elephants made their way back to a place even more secret than the elephant graveyard. They all dreamed about Old Bet, and wished her well.

"My name is Lucy Simpkins and my story was called 'Old Bet's Gone Away.' Thank you."

The others applauded her, softly at first, as if they were afraid it was the wrong thing to do, but it wasn't long before their clapping grew louder and more ardent. Gina sat forward, applauding to beat the band. She looked at the audience, gave a shrug that was more an inward decision than an outward action, and stood.

Lucy Simpkins managed something like a smile, then handed me her watercolor. "You should have this," she said, and made her way out of the room toward the refreshment table.

As everyone was dispersing, I took Gina's hand and pulled her aside. "My God, did you hear that?"

"I thought it was incredibly moving."

"*Moving*? Maybe in the same way the last thirty minutes of *The Wild Bunch* or *Straw Dogs* is moving, yes, but if you're talking warm and fuzzy and *It's A Wonderful Life*, you're way the hell off-base!"

Her eyes clouded over. "Jesus, Andy. You're shaking."

"Damn straight I'm shaking. Do you have any idea what that girl has to have been through? Can you imagine the kind of life which would cause a child to tell a story like that?" I took a deep breath, clenching my teeth. "Christ! I don't know which I want more: to wrap her up and take her home with me, or find her parents and break a baseball bat over their skulls!"

"That's a bit . . . strong, isn't it?"

"No. An imagination that can invent something like that story is not the result of a healthy, loving household."

"Don't be so arrogant. You aren't all-knowing about these things. You don't have any idea what her family life is really like."

"I suppose, Mother Goose, that you're more experienced in this area?" I don't know why I said something like that. Sometimes I'm not a nice person. In fact, sometimes I stink on ice.

Her face melted into a placid mask, except for a small twitch in the upper left corner of her mouth that threatened to become a sneer.

"My sister had epilepsy. All her life the doctors kept changing her medication as she got older; a stronger dose of what she was already taking, or some new drug altogether. Those periods were murder because her seizures always got worse while her system adjusted. Her seizures were violent as hell, but she refused to wear any kind of protective gear. 'I don't wanna look like a goon,' she'd say. So she'd walk around with facial scrapes and cuts and ugly bruises; she sprained her arm a couple of times and once dislocated her shoulder. People in the neighborhood started noticing, but no one said anything to us. Someone finally called the police and Child Welfare. They came down on us like a curse from heaven. They were, of course, embarrassed when they found out about Lorraine's condition—she'd always insisted that we keep it a secret—but nothing changed the fact that people who were supposedly our friends assumed that her injuries were the result of child abuse. Lorraine had never been so humiliated, and from that day on she saw herself as being handicapped. I think that, as much as the epilepsy, helped to kill her. So don't go jumping to any conclusions about that girl's parents or the life she's had because you *can't know.* And anything you might say or do out of anger could plant an idea in her head that has no business being there."

"What do you suggest?"

"I suggest that you go out there and tell her how much you enjoyed her story. I suggest we try to make her feel special and admired because she deserves to feel that way, if only for tonight."

I squeezed her hand. "It couldn't have been a picnic for you, either, Lorraine's epilepsy."

"She should have lived to be a hundred. And just so you know—this has a tendency to slip out of my mouth from time to time—Lorraine committed suicide. She couldn't live with the knowledge that she was 'a cripple.' I cried for a year."

"I'm sorry for acting like a jerk."

She smiled, then looked at her watch. "Break's almost over. If you want to step outside and smoke six minutes off your life, you'd better do it now. I'll snag some punch and cookies for you."

I couldn't find Lucy; one parent told me she'd gone into the restroom, so I stepped out for my smoke. The rest of the evening went quickly and enjoyably. At the end of the night, I found myself with a tie: Lucy Simpkins (how could I not?) and my junior-league Ernie Kovaks who didn't know no farmers.

Ernie was ecstatic.

Lucy was gone.

I have only the vaguest memories of my father. When I was four, he was killed in an accident at the steel mill where he worked. He left only a handful of impressions: the smell of machine grease, the rough texture of a callused hand touching my cheek, the smell of Old Spice. What I know of him I learned from my mother.

His death shattered her. She grew sad and overweight and began drinking. Over the years there have been times of laughter and dieting, but the drinking remained constant, evidenced by the flush of her cheeks and the reddened bulbous nose that I used to think cute when I was a child because it made her look like W. C. Fields; now it only disgusts me.

After my father's death, nothing I did was ever good enough; I fought like hell for her approval and affection but often settled for indifference and courtesy.

Don't misunderstand—I loved her when she was sober.

When she was drunk, I thought her the most repulsive human being on the face of the earth.

I bring this up to help you make sense of everything that happened later, starting with the surprise I found waiting on my doorstep when, after coffee and cheesecake, Gina drove me back to my house.

Someone on the street was having a party so we had to park half a block away and walk. That was fine by me; it gave us time to hold hands and enjoy the night and each other's company. The world was new again, at least for this evening—

—which went right into the toilet when something lurched out of the shadows on my porch.

". . . been waitin' here . . . long time. . . ." Her voice was thick and slurred and the stench of too much gin was enough to make me gag.

"Mom? Jesus, what are you—" I cast an embarrassed glance at Gina "—doing here?"

She pointed unsteadily to her watch and gave a soft, wet belch. ". . . s' after midnight . . . s' my birthday now . . ."

She wobbled back and forth for a moment before slipping on the rubber welcome mat and falling toward me.

I caught her. "Oh, for chrissakes!" I turned toward Gina. "God . . . I don't know what . . . I'm sorry about . . ."

"Is there anything I can do?"

Mom slipped a little more and mumbled something. I hooked my arms around her torso and said, "My . . . dammit . . . my keys are in my left jacket pocket. Would you—"

Gina took them out, unlocked the front door, and turned on the inside lights. I spun Mom around and shook her until she regained some composure, then led her to the kitchen where I poured her into a chair and started a pot of coffee. Gina remained in the front room, turning on the television and adjusting the volume, her way of letting me know she wouldn't listen to anything that might be said.

The coffee finished brewing, and I poured a large cup for Mom. "How the hell did you get here?"

The shock of having someone other than myself see her in this state forced her to pull herself together; when she spoke again, her voice wasn't as slurred. "I walked. It's a nice . . . nice night." She took a sip of the coffee, then sat watching the steam curl over the rim of the cup. Her lower lip started to quiver. "I'm . . . I'm sorry, Andy . . . didn't know you were gonna have company." She sighed, then fished a cigarette from the pocket of her blouse and lit it with an unsteady hand.

"Why are you here?"

"I just got to . . . you know, thinking about your dad and was feeling blue . . . 'sides, I wanted to remind you that you're taking me out for my birthday."

My right hand balled into a fist. "Have I *ever* forgotten your birthday?"

". . . no . . ."

"Then why would I start now?"

She leaned back in the chair and fixed me with an icy stare, smoke crawling from her nostrils like flames from a dragon's snout. "Maybe you think you've gotten too good for me. Maybe you think because I wasn't a story writer or artist like you, you don't have to bother with me any more."

Time to go.

"Sit here and drink your coffee. I'm going to walk my friend to her car and then I'll come back and take you home."

". . . didn't get it from me, that's for damn sure . . . does you no good anyway . . . drop dead at forty-five and no one'll care about your silly books. . . ."

I threw up my hands and started out of the kitchen.

". . . what's this?" she said, pulling Lucy's watercolor from my pocket. "Oh, a picture. They used to let us draw pictures when I was in the children's home . . . did I ever tell you about—"

She was making me sick.

I stormed out of the kitchen and into the front room in time to see Jimmy Stewart grab Donna Reed and say, "I don't want to get married, understand?"

"Don't worry," said Gina. "They get together in the end." She put her arms around me. I felt like Jason being wrapped in the Golden Fleece.

"I'm so sorry about this," I said. "She's never done this before—"

"Never?"

I looked into her eyes and couldn't make any excuses. "I mean . . . she's never come *here* drunk before."

"How long has she been this way?"

"I can't ever remember a week from my life when she didn't get drunk at least once."

"Have you ever tried to get her some help?"

"Of course I have. She tries it for a while, but she always . . . always—"

"—I understand. It's okay. Don't be embarrassed."

That's easy to say, I thought. What I said was: "I appreciate this, Gina. I really do." I wished that she would just leave, so I could get the rest of this over with.

She seemed to sense this and stepped back, saying, "I guess I should, uh, go—"

A loud crash from the kitchen startled both of us.

I ran in and saw Mom on the floor; she'd been trying to pour herself another cup of coffee and had collapsed, taking the coffee pot with her. Shattered sections of sharp glass covered the floor and she had split open one of her shins. Scurrying on her hands and knees, she looked up and saw me standing there, saw Gina behind me, and pointed at the table.

"W-where did you . . . did you get that?"

"Get *what?*"

". . . that goddamn . . . picture!"

I moved toward her. She doubled over and began vomiting.

I grabbed her, trying to pull her up to the sink—making it to the bathroom was out of the question—but I slipped and lost my grip—

—Mom gave a wet gurgling sound and puked on my chest—

—Gina came in, grabbed a towel, and helped me get her over the sink—

—and Mom gripped the edge, emptying her stomach down the drain.

The stench was incredible.

Feeling the heat of humiliation cover my face, I looked at Gina and fumbled for something to say, but what *could* I say? We were holding a drunk who was spewing all over—

—what could you say?

Gina returned my gaze. "So, how 'bout them Mets, huh? Fuckin-A!"

That's what you could say.

I didn't feel so dirty.

Gina surprised me the next morning by showing up on my doorstep at eight-thirty with hot coffee and croissants. When I explained to her that I had to take Mom's birthday cake over to her house, Gina said, "I'd like to come along, if you don't mind."

I did and told her so.

"Come on," she said, taking my hand and giving me a little kiss on the cheek. "Think about it; if she's hung over and sees that I'm with you, she might behave herself. If she doesn't behave, then you can use me as an excuse not to stick around."

I argued with her some more; she won. I don't think I've ever won an argument with a woman; they're far too sharp.

Besides an ersatz apology ("I feel so *silly!*") and a bandage around the gash on her shin, Mom showed no signs that last night had ever happened. Her hair was freshly cleaned, she wore a new dress, and her makeup was, for a change, subtly applied; she looked like your typical healthy matriarch.

We stayed for breakfast. Gina surprised me a second time that morning by reaching into her purse and pulling out a large birthday card that she handed to Mom.

Well, that just made Mom's day. She must have thanked Gina half a dozen times and even went so far as to give her a hug, saying, "I'm glad to see he finally found a good one."

"Blind shithouse luck," replied Gina. She and Mom got a tremendous guffaw out of that. I gritted my teeth and smiled at them. Hardy-har-har.

"So," Mom said to Gina. "Will you be coming with us?"

"I don't know," Gina replied, turning to me with a Pollyanna-pitiful look in her eyes. "Am I?"

"You stink at coy," was my answer.

"Good!" said Mom. "The three of us. It'll be a lot of fun."

"Have you decided where you want to go?"

"Yeee-eeessss, I have."

Oh, good; another surprise.

"Where?"

She winked at me and squeezed Gina's hand. "It's a secret. I'll tell you when we're on our way." This was a little game she loved to play—"I Know Something You Don't Know"—and it usually got on my nerves.

But not that morning. Somehow Gina's presence made it seem as if everything was going to work out just fine.

Our first stop was the mall, where Gina insisted on buying Mom a copy of the new Stephen King opus and paying for lunch. After we'd eaten, Mom looked at her watch and informed us it was time to go.

"Where are we going?" I asked as we got on the highway.

Mom leaned forward from the backseat. "Riverfront Coliseum."

"*Cincinnati?* You want to drive three hours to—"

"It's my birthday."

"But—"

Gina squeezed my leg. "It's her birthday."

I acquiesced. I should have remembered that no good deed goes unpunished.

"A *circus!*" shouted Gina as we approached the coliseum entrance.

I slowed my step, genuinely surprised. I have been to many circuses in my life, but never with my mother. I always thought she'd have no interest in this sort of thing.

"Surprised?" said Mom, taking my arm.

"Well, yes, but . . . why?"

Her eyes filled with a curious kind of desperation. "All our lives we've never done anything *fun* together. I've been a real shit to you sometimes and I'll never be able to apologize enough, let alone make up for it. I've never told you how proud I am of you—I've read all your books. Bet you didn't know that, did you?" Her eyes began tearing. "Oh, hon, I ain't been much of a mother to you, what with the . . . drinking and such, but, if you'll be patient with me, I'd like to . . . to give it a try, us being friends. If you don't mind."

This part was familiar. I bit down on my tongue, hoping that she wasn't going to launch into a heartfelt promise to get back into A.A. and stop hitting the bottle and turn her life around, blah-blah-blah.

She didn't.

"Well," she whispered. "We'd best go get our tickets."

"Do we get cotton candy?" asked Gina.

"Of course you do. And hot dogs—"

"—and cherry colas—"

"—and peanuts—"

"—and an ulcer," I said. They both stared at me.

"You never were any fun," said Mom, smiling. I couldn't tell if she was joking or not.

"I never claimed to be."

Gina smacked me on the ass. "Then it's about time you started."

It was a blast. Acrobats and lion tamers and trained seals and a big brass band and a sword-swallower, not to mention the fire-eating bear (that was a real trip) and the bald guy who wrestled a crocodile that was roughly the size of your average Mexican chihuahua (A DEATH-DEFYING BATTLE BETWEEN MAN AND BEAST, proclaimed the program. "Compared to what?" asked Gina. "Changing a diaper?"). All of it was an absolute joy, right up to the elephants and clowns.

Not that anything happened with the elephants; they did a marvelously funny kickline to a Scott Joplin tune, but the sight of them triggered memories of Lucy Simpkins's story. I looked at Gina and saw that she was thinking about it as well.

Mom thought the elephants were the most precious things she'd ever seen—and since she used to say the same about my baby pictures, I wondered if my paranoia about my nose being too large was unjustified after all.

At the end of the show, when every performer and animal came marching out for the Grand Finale Parade, the clowns broke away and ran into the audience. After tossing out confetti and lollipops and balloons, one clown ran over to Mom and handed her a small stuffed animal; then, with a last burst of confetti from the large flower in the center of his costume, he honked his horn and dashed back into the parade.

I looked at Mom and saw, just for a moment, the ghost of the vibrant, lovely woman who populated several pages of the family photo albums; in that light, with all the laughter and music swirling around us, I saw her smile and could almost believe that she was going to really change this time. I suspected that it might just be wishful thinking on my part, but sometimes a delusion is the best thing in the world—especially if you *know* it's a delusion.

So, for that moment, Mom was a changed woman who might find some measure of peace and happiness in the remainder of her life, and I was a son who harbored no anger or disgust for her, la-dee-da.

It was kind of nice.

* * *

We made our way through the crowd and toward the exit. I don't like crowds, as I've said, and soon felt the first heavy rivulets of sweat rolling down my face.

Gina sensed what was happening and led us to a section near a concession stand where the crowd was much thinner.

As I stood there catching my breath, Gina nudged Mom and asked about the stuffed animal. Mom looked at it then for the first time.

"Oh, my. Isn't that . . . something?" She was smiling, yet she cringed as she touched the tiny fired-clay tusks of the small stuffed elephant in a ballerina pose, wearing a ridiculous pink tutu. Cottony angel's wings jutted from its back.

"That's *adorable*," laughed Gina.

"Yes . . . yes, it is," whispered Mom. Her smile faltered for just a moment. I have seen my mother worried before, but this went beyond that; something in her was genuinely *afraid* of that stuffed toy.

"Janet Walters!" shouted a voice that sounded like old nails being wrenched from rotted wood.

Mom looked up at me. "Walters" was her maiden name.

"What the—?"

The nun came toward us.

That in itself wasn't all that unusual; it was easy to assume that the nun was here with some church group. What *was* unusual was the way this nun was dressed; pick your favorite singing sister from *The Sound of Music* and you'll have some idea. Nuns don't have to dress this way anymore, but this one did. The whole outfit was at least fifty years out of date. Her stockings were four times too heavy for the weather and her shoes would have looked right at home in a Frankenstein movie.

Sister Frankenstein barreled right up to Mom and grabbed her arm. "Would you like to hear a story?"

Mom's face drained of all color.

I didn't give a good goddamn if this woman was a nun.

"Excuse me, Sister, but I think you're hurting—"

Sister Frankenstein fixed me with a glare that could have frozen fire, then said to Mom: "He was led across the railroad yards to his private car. It was late at night. No train was scheduled, but an express came through. A baby elephant had strayed from the rest of the pack and stood on the tracks in front of the oncoming train, so scared it couldn't move. Jumbo saw it and ran over, shoved the baby aside, and met the locomotive head-on. He was killed instantly and the train was derailed."

My mother began moaning soft and low, gripping the stuffed toy like a life preserver.

Sister Frankenstein let fly with a series of loud, racking, painful-sounding coughs and began to stomp away (*I go along, thud-thud*), then turned back and said, "Only good little girls ever see Africa!"

A crowd of teenagers ran through and the nun vanished behind them.

I was reeling; it had happened so *fast*.

Mom marched over to the only concession stand still open—

—which sold beer.

She took the large plastic cup in her hands and said, "P-please don't start with me, Andy. Just a beer, okay? It's just a beer. I need to . . . to steady . . . my—"

"Who the hell *was* that?"

"Not now." She tipped the cup back and finished the brew in five deep gulps.

Gina took my hand and whispered, "Don't push it."

Right. Psycho Nun On The Rampage and I'm supposed to let it drop.

Gina raised an eyebrow at me.

"Fine," I whispered.

Mom fell asleep the minute we got in the car and didn't wake up until we hit Columbus.

Mom took her mail from the box, then insisted we come in for a slice of cake.

As I was pouring the coffee, Mom opened a large manila envelope that was among the mail.

Her gasp sounded like the strangled cry of a suicide when the rope snaps tight. I turned. "What is it?"

Gina was leaning over her shoulder, looking at the large piece of heavy white paper that Mom had pulled from the envelope.

"Andy," said Gina in a low, cautious voice. "I think you'd better take a look at this."

It was a watercolor painting of the center ring of a circus where a dozen elephants all wore the same kind of absurd pink tutu as the stuffed toy, all had angel's wings unfurling from their shoulders, and all were dancing through a wall of flames. The stands were empty except for one little girl whose face was the saddest I'd ever seen.

There was no doubt in my mind—or Gina's, as I later found out—about who had painted it.

There was no return address on the envelope, nor was there a postmark.

After a tense silence, Mom lit a cigarette and said, "Would you two mind . . . mind sitting with me for a while? I got something I need to tell you about."

"When I was six years old, the county took me and my three brothers away from our parents and put us in the Catholic Childrens' Home. . . ."

I faded away for a minute or two. I'd heard this countless times before and was embarrassed that Gina would have to listen to it now.

Most of what Mom said early on was directed more toward Gina than me. The Same Old Prologue.

In a nutshell:

Mom's parents were dirt poor and heavy drinkers both. Too many complaints from the school and neighbors resulted in a visit by the authorities. My mother and her brothers remained under the care of the Catholics and the county until they were fifteen; then they were each given five dollars, a new set of clothes, and pushed out the door.

"There wasn't really much to enjoy, except our Friday art classes with Sister Elizabeth. If we worked hard, she'd make popcorn in the evening and tell us stories before we went to bed, stories that she made up. There was one that was our favorite, all about these dancing elephants and their adventures with the circus. I don't know why I was so surprised to see Sister Elizabeth tonight; she always loved circuses.

"She'd start each story the same way, describing the circus tent and giving the names of all the elephants, then she'd make up a story about one elephant in particular. Each Friday it was a new story about a different elephant. The stories were real funny, and we always got a good laugh from them.

"Then she got sick. Turned out to be cancer. She kept getting sadder and angrier all the time, so we started to draw pictures of the elephants for her, but it didn't lift her spirits any.

"The stories started getting so . . . bitter. There was one about an elephant that got hanged that gave some of the girls bad dreams for a week. Then Sister quit telling us stories. We heard that she was gonna go in the hospital, so we bought her flowers and asked her to tell us one last story about the elephants.

"God, she looked so thin. She'd been going to Columbus for cobalt treatments. Her scalp was all moist looking and had only a few strands of wiry hair and her color was awful . . . but her eyes were the worst. She couldn't hide how scared she was.

"She told us one more story. But this one didn't start with the circus tent. It started in Africa."

I leaned forward. This was new to me.

"I never forgot it," said Mom. "It went like this: The elder of the pack gathered together all of the elephants and told them that he had spoken with God, and God had said the elder elephant was going to die, but first he was to pass on a message.

"God had said there were men on their way to Africa, sailing in great ships, coming to take the elephants away so people could see them. And people would think that the elephants were strange and wonderful and funny. God felt bad about that 'funny' part, and He asked the elder to apologize to the others and tell them that as long as they stayed good of heart and true to themselves they would never be funny in His eyes.

"The elder named Martin the Bull Elephant as the new leader, then lumbered away to the secret elephant graveyard and died.

"The men came in their ships and rounded up the elephants and put them in chains and stuffed them into the ships and took them away. They were sold to the circus where they were made to do tricks and dances for people to laugh at. Then they were trained to dance ballet for one big special show. The elephants worked real hard because they wanted to do well.

"The night of the big show came, and the elephants did their best. They really did. They got all the steps and twirls and dips exactly right and felt very proud. But the people laughed and laughed at them because they were so big and clumsy and looked so silly in the pink tutus they wore. Even though they did their best, they felt ashamed because everyone laughed at them.

"Later that night, after the circus was quiet and the laughing people went home, the elephants were alone. One of them told Martin that all of their hearts were broken. Martin gave a sad nod of his head and said, 'Yes, it's time for us to go back home.' So he reached out with his trunk through the bars of the cage and picked up a dying cigar butt and dropped it in the hay and started a big fire.

"The elephants died in that fire, but when the circus people and firemen looked above the flames they saw smoke clouds dancing across the sky. They were shaped like elephants and they drifted across the continents until they reached the secret elephant graveyard in Africa. And when they touched down the elder was waiting for them, and he smiled as an angel came down and said to all of them, 'Come, the blessed children of my Father, and receive the world prepared for you. . . .' "

She cleared her throat, lit another cigarette, and stared at us.

"That's *horrible*," said Gina.

"I know," whispered Mom. "Sister Elizabeth didn't say anything after she finished the story, she just got up and left. It really bothered all of us, but the sisters had taught us that we had to comfort each other whenever something happened that upset one or all of us. They even assigned each of us another girl that we could go to if something was wrong and there wasn't any sisters around. Sister Elizabeth used to say that we were all guardian angels of each other's spirits. It was kinda nice.

"The girl I had, her name was Lucy Simpkins. She'd been really close to Sister, and I think it all made her a little crazy. On the night Sister Elizabeth died, Lucy got to crying and crying until I thought she'd waste away. She kept asking everyone how she could go to Africa and be with Sister Elizabeth and the elephants.

"Everyone just sort of looked at her and didn't say anything because we knew she was upset. She was a strange girl, always singing to herself and drawing. . . .

"She never said anything to me. Not even when I went to her and asked. At least, that's how I remember it.

"You see, sometime during the night she got out of bed and snuck down to the janitor's closet, found some kerosene, and set herself on fire. She was dead before anyone could get the flames out."

Mom rose from the table, crossed to the counter, and looked at her birthday cake. "I never told anyone that before."

She took a knife from the cutlery drawer and cut three slices of cake. We ate in silence.

She went to bed a little while later, and Gina came over to my place to spend the night.

At one point she nudged me, and said, "Have you ever read any Ray Bradbury?"

"Of course."

"Don't you envy him? There's so much joy and wonder in his stories. They jump out at you like happy puppies. They make you believe that you can hang on to that joy forever." She kissed me, then snuggled against my chest. "Wouldn't it be nice to pinpoint the exact moment in your childhood when you lost that joy and wonder, then go back and warn yourself as a child? Tell yourself that you mustn't ever let go of that joy and hope. Then you wouldn't have to worry about any . . . regrets coming back."

"I think it's a little late to go back and warn Mom."

"I know," she whispered. "You really love her, don't you? In spite of everything."

"Yes, I do. Sometimes I've wished that I didn't, it would have made things easier." I tried to imagine what my mother must have been like as a child but couldn't: to me, she was always old.

"I can't do this to myself, Gina. I can't start feeling responsible for the way her life has turned out. I've done everything I'm capable of, but it seems as if . . . she doesn't *want* to be happy. Dad's being alive filled some kind of void in her, and when he died, something else crawled into his spot and began sucking the life out of her.

"I remember once reading about something called 'The Bridge of the Separator.' In Zoroastrianism it's believed that when you die you meet your conscience on a bridge. I can't help but wonder if . . ."

"If what?"

"I used to look at Mom and think that here was a woman who had died a long time ago but just forgot to drop dead. And maybe that's not so far from the truth. Maybe the really *alive* part of her, the Bradbury part of joy and wonder and hope, died with my father—or maybe it died with Lucy and that nun.

"Whatever the reason, it's dead and there's no bringing it back, so is it so hard to believe that her conscience has gotten tired of waiting at the bridge and has decided to come and get her?"

I awoke a little after five A.M. and climbed quietly out of bed so as not to wake Gina. I stood in the darkness of the bedroom, inhaling deeply. Something smelled.

I puzzled over it—

—sawdust and hay, the aroma of cigarettes and beer and warm cotton candy and popcorn and countless exotic manures—

—I was smelling the circus.

The curtains over the bedroom window fluttered.

The circus smell grew almost overpowering.

I put on my robe and crossed to the window—

—pulled back the curtains—

—looked out into the field behind my house—

—where Lucy Simpkins stood, her sad, damaged hands petting the trunk of an old elephant whose skin was mottled, gray, and wrinkled. Its tusks were cracked and yellowed with age. When Lucy fed it peanuts, its tail slapped happily against its back legs.

A bit of moonlight bounced off Lucy's green eye and touched my gaze. The old elephant looked at me through eyes that were caked with age and dirt and filled with the errant ghosts of many secrets.

My first impulse was to wake Gina, but something in Lucy's smile told me that they had come to see only me. I went downstairs and out the back door.

I became aware of the damp hay and sawdust under my feet. If I had thought this was a dream, a small splinter gouging into my heel put that notion to rest. I cried out, more from surprise than pain, and shook my head as I saw blood trickle from the wound. Leave it to me to go out in the middle of the night without putting on my slippers.

Lucy smiled and ran to me, throwing her arms around my waist, pressing her face into my chest. I returned her embrace.

She led me to the elephant.

"I thought you might like to meet Old Bet—well, that's what I call her. To Sister Elizabeth, this is Martin."

"And to my mother?"

"This would be Jumbo. Everyone has a different name for it."

The elephant wound the end of its trunk around my wrist: How'ya doin'? Pleased to meet you.

I fed it some peanuts and marveled at its cumbersome grandeur. "Is this my mother's conscience?"

Lucy gave a little-girl shrug. "You could call it that, I guess. Sister Elizabeth calls it 'the carrier of weary souls.' She says that when we grow too old and tired after a lifetime of work, then it will lift us onto its back and carry us over the bridge."

It will remind us of all we've forgotten. It knows the history of the whole world, everyone who's lived before us, and everyone who will come after us. It's very wise."

I stroked its trunk. "Have you come to take my mother?"

Lucy shook her head. "No. We're not allowed to take anyone—they have to come to us. We're only here now to remind."

She tapped the elephant; it unwound its trunk from my wrist so she could take both of my hands in hers. I was shocked by their touch; though they looked burned and fused and twisted, they felt healthy and normal—two soft, small, five-fingered hands.

Her voice was the sound of a lullaby sung over a baby's cradle: "There's a place not too far from here, a secret place, where all the greatest moments of our lives are kept. You see, everyone has really good moments their whole life long, but somewhere along the line there is one moment, one great, golden moment, when a person does something so splendid that nothing before or after will ever come close. And they remember these moments. They tuck them away like a precious gem for safekeeping. Because it's from that one grand moment that each guardian angel is born. As the rest of life goes on and a person grows old and starts to regret things, something—" she gave a smile "—*reminds* them of that golden moment.

"But sometimes there are people who become so beaten-down they forget they ever had such a moment. And they need to be reminded." She turned toward the elephant. "They need to know that when the time comes and Old Bet carries them across the bridge, that moment will be waiting, that it will be given back to them in all its original splendor and make everything all right. Again. Forever."

". . . and Mom has forgotten about her . . . moment?"

"So have you. You were there. You remember it. You don't think you do, but. . . ."

"I don't—"

"Shh. Watch closely."

The elephant reared back on its hind legs and trumpeted. When it slammed back down, its face was only inches from mine. Its trunk wrapped around my waist and lifted me off the ground until my eyes were level with one of its own—

—which was the same startling jade-green as Lucy's.

I saw myself as clearly in its gaze as any mirror, and I watched my reflection begin to shimmer and change: me at thirty, at twenty-one, then at fourteen and, at last, the six-year-old boy my father never lived to see.

He was sitting in his room—a large pad of drawing paper on his lap, a charcoal pencil clutched in his hand—drawing furiously. His face was tight with concentration.

His mother came into the room. Even then she looked beaten down and used up and sadder than any human being should ever be.

She leaned over the boy's shoulder and examined his work.

"Remember now?" whispered Lucy.

". . . yes. I'd kept my drawing a secret. After Dad died, Mom didn't spend much time with me because . . . because she said I looked too much like him. This was the first time in ages that she'd come into my room. It was the first time in ages I'd seen her sober."

The woman put a hand on the little boy's shoulder and said something to him.

My chest hitched.

I didn't want to remember this; it was easier to just stay angry with her.

"What happened?"

"She looked through all the drawings and . . . she started to cry. I was still mad as hell at her because of the way she'd been treating me, the way she never hugged me or kissed me or said that she loved me, the way she spent all her time drinking . . . but she sat there with my drawings, shaking her head and crying, and I felt so embarrassed. I finally asked her what the big deal was and she looked up at me and said . . ."

"—said that you had a great talent and were going to be famous for it someday. She knew this from looking at those drawings. She knew you were going to grow up to be what you are today. She told you that she was very proud of you and that she wanted you to keep on drawing, and maybe you could even start making up stories to go with the pictures—"

"—because she used to know someone who did that when she was a little girl," I said. "She said that would be nice because . . . oh, Christ! . . . it would be nice if I'd do that because it would make her feel like someone else besides her was remembering her childhood."

Old Bet gently lowered me to the ground. My legs gave out and I slammed ass-first into the dirt, shaking. "I remember how much that surprised me, and I just sat there staring at her. She looked so proud. Her smile was one of the greatest things I'd ever seen and I think . . . no, no, wait . . . I *know* I smiled back at her."

"And that was it," said Lucy. "That was her moment. Do you have any idea how much it all meant to her? The drawings and your smile? When you smiled at her, she knew for certain that you were going to be just what you are. And for that moment, she felt as though it was all because of her. The world was new again." She brushed some hair out of my eyes. "Do you remember what happened next?"

"I went over to give her a hug because it felt like I'd just gotten my mother back, then I smelled the liquor on her breath and got angry and yelled at her and made her leave my room."

"But that doesn't matter, don't you see? What matters is the moment before. That's what's waiting for her. That's what she's forgotten."

". . . Jesus . . ."

"You have to remember one thing, Andy. It wasn't your fault. None of it. You were only a child. Promise me that you'll remember that?"

"I'll try."

She smiled. "Good. Everything's all right, then."

I rose and embraced her, then patted Old Bet. The elephant reached out and lifted Lucy onto its back.

"Are you going back without Mom?" I asked.

She *tsk*-ed at me and put her hands on her hips, an annoyed little girl. "Dummy! I told you once. We aren't allowed to take people. Only remind them. Except this time, we had to ask you to help us."

"Are . . . are you her guardian angel?"

She didn't hear me as Old Bet turned around and the two of them lumbered off, eventually vanishing into the layers of mist that rose from the distant edge of the field.

The chill latched onto my bones and sent me jogging back inside for hot coffee.

Gina was already brewing some as I entered the kitchen. She was wearing my extra bathrobe. Her hair was mussed and her cheeks were flushed and I'd never seen such a beautiful sight. She looked at me, saw something in my face, and smiled. "Look at you. Hm. I must be better than I thought."

I laughed and took her hand, pulling her close, feeling the warmth of her body, the electricity of her touch. The world was new again. At least until the phone rang.

A man identifying himself as Chief Something-or-Other from the Cedar Hill Fire Department asked me if I was the same Andrew Dysart whose mother lived at—

—something in the back of my head whispered *Africa*.

Good little girls. Going home.

My new book, *After The Elephant Ballet*, was published five weeks ago. The dedication reads: "To my mother and her own private Africa; receive the world prepared for you." Gina has started a scrapbook for the reviews, which have been the best I've ever received.

The other day when Gina and I were cleaning the house ("A new wife has to make sure her husband hasn't got any little black books stashed around," she'd said) I came across an old sketch pad: MY DrAWiNG TaLlAnt, bY ANdY DySArT, age 6. It's filled with pictures of rockets and clowns and baseball players and scary monsters and every last one of them is terrible.

There are no drawings of angels.

ANdY DySArT, age 6, didn't believe in them because he'd never seen proof of their existence.

In the back there's a drawing of a woman wearing an apron and washing dishes. She's got a big smile on her face and underneath are the words My mOM, thE nICE lAdy.

The arson investigators told me it was an accident. She had probably been drinking and had fallen asleep in bed with a cigarette still burning. One of them asked if Mom had kept any stuffed animals on her bed. When I asked why, he handed me a pair of small, curved, fired-clay tusks.

On the way to Montreal for our honeymoon, Gina took a long detour. "I have a surprise for you."

We went to Somers, New York.

An elephant named Old Bet actually existed. There really is a shrine there. Circus performers make pilgrimages to visit her grave. We had a picnic at the base of the gorgeous green hill where the grave lies. Afterward, I lay back and stared at the clouds and thought about guardian angels and a smiling woman and her smiling little boy who's holding a drawing pad, and I wondered what Bradbury would do with that image.

Then decided it didn't matter.

The moment waits. Still.

I go along, thud-thud.

For my mother

HENRY V, PART 2
Marcia Guthridge

"Henry V, Part 2," is one of the most hilarious midlife crisis stories I've ever encountered. It comes from the Fall issue of the *The Paris Review*.

Marcia Guthridge has had other short fiction published in *The Paris Review*, and has a collection of short fiction in the works. She lives in Chicago.

—T.W.

She was choosing cucumbers at the grocery store and wondering what sorts of genitalia cicadas had when someone touched her on the shoulder. She prepared her public face and turned, expecting to see her friend the produce man. There was no one behind her. The automatic sprinkler over the vegetables switched on and soaked the sleeve of her new suede jacket. She wanted someone to be behind her. She turned all the way round and there, at the far end of her cart in a wet mist which rose faintly pink from a heap of red cabbages, stood Henry V of England.

"He's awfully young," she said aloud, or nearly aloud. There was no one else around. She hastily chose a cucumber and a red cabbage, though her sons hated red cabbage, wheeled her cart in a half-circle and went fast away from the boy-king past the oranges and the garlic, to the checkout counter. He strode behind her. She did not look back, but she could hear his sword hitting his boot at every step. He helped her unload her groceries for the cashier, who asked her if she was in a hurry. Maureen didn't answer. Henry V followed her out the door to the parking lot, carrying both bags of groceries. She told the bag boy she didn't need his help. The king walked to the rear of her car and waited, grinning, while she fetched the keys to open the trunk. After setting the bags inside he tossed his mop of blond hair, which was cut as if with a bowl and stood out like eaves over his longish ears and away from his forehead, with a twist of his neck. Then he stood straight and grinned some more. He made Maureen think of a golden retriever puppy her parents had bought her as a child, which had dug under the fence and disappeared after two weeks.

"Where did this guy come from?" she asked herself. The after-work rush was beginning. Several people passed by her car without staring. Could they possibly be so anxious to get their shopping done that they don't notice a boy wearing studded gloves, a tooled scabbard, and a tunic emblazoned with the Lancaster lions straddling two parking places behind a Honda Accord? Henry V, for his part, didn't seem to notice any of the hurrying shoppers or the line of cars building up behind Maureen's, waiting for her to vacate her parking place. He only had eyes for Maureen. "I must have made him up," she decided. "This is very sick. This is terrible."

She decided to kill him quickly. After all, he'd been dead already for hundreds of years. Who would arrest her? She jerked open the car door. It stuck a bit because of the dent from a couple of weeks ago. She scrambled into the driver's seat and it hit her that she didn't have the keys. He had opened the trunk and held onto the keys. How could she run over him when he had her car keys? Suddenly his large head appeared at her window. She started. He tapped on the glass, still grinning. He was so close she could see that his teeth were very bad: brown nubs, medieval teeth, disgusting. She rolled down the window to accept the keys he dangled between their faces, and she smelled wood smoke and manure. When she had taken the keys and started the car he walked back behind it again and stood waiting for her to mow him down, grinning into the rearview mirror. Her fingers tapped the emergency brake but didn't release it. She had always suspected that her puppy had been run over by a car and that her parents had never told her. One of the cars behind her ground its gears irritably and screeched away, and the next car in line honked loudly. She closed her eyes and let her head sink back against the headrest. Henry V bounded along the side of the car and appeared in the seat next to her. "I definitely dreamed him up. But I had no idea he was going to arrive; I am not prepared," she said to herself, and to him: "Fasten your seat belt. I'm a conservative person." He obeyed immediately.

She had a good deal of trouble getting used to him. That first night and several afterward he spent in the garage. When she got into the car to drive to work the next day he was in his seat waiting for her, his seat belt snugly buckled. He stayed in the car while she answered phones at the radio station where she worked. He followed her into the house that afternoon and sat at the kitchen table while she fixed supper. Once or twice he rose to look out the window, but mostly he stared at her. She stared back. She asked herself questions: how long would he stay, could he speak? When one of her sons came thundering up the basement stairs to report that someone had spilt something black and oily on the beige carpet downstairs, she jumped so high she broke a plate. She gazed blankly at her son, cleaned up the broken china, and went to the pantry for baking soda. She gave it to him and told him to pour it on the carpet and to leave her alone, she was busy. She realized as he thundered back down that she had given him the wrong stuff; she turned dizzily to call him back and ran into Henry V who had followed her into the pantry. She tripped on his armor-toed boot, and he caught her by the hand to stop her falling. She thought once more of the golden retriever pup, who had been always underfoot, whose nose had been soft and damp like Henry's glove; and who had slept in the garage.

She pulled her hand away from his and raised it to him as a warning, against what she wasn't sure. She felt it was time for her to say something. Her thoughts were disorganized. She had never been good at initiating conversation. She didn't even know if he would understand her sort of English. But she began anyway.

"I'm having some difficulty," she said. "I seem to have a transition to make here, and I'm afraid it's too much. You know I remember when my sons were babies both of them were fussy babies. It's funny, I don't know anymore which one did what cute thing or bad thing, which one's first word was *mine* and which one's *mama*. They run together. My sister-in-law was always giving me scrapbooks with those plastic quilted covers, you know the ones—no, of course you don't—and telling me I'd be sorry if I didn't write things down, my babies would be gone forever. Well anyway, they were both fussy, that I remember, and I'm not too sorry that's gone forever either, it wasn't colic or anything, they were just always fussing. And the pediatrician asked me if they cried when I picked them up or when I put them down or when I changed their diapers or when I started feeding them or when I was finished, and I said, 'Yes, yes, yes, all of those,' and she wrote DIT in her file. That's for 'Difficulty in Transition.' That's what I'm having. Can you talk?" Henry V stared at her, his gloved hand still outstretched where it had held hers. "Please sit down again," she said.

She sat down with him at the kitchen table and looked him over carefully. He had a couple of days' growth of beard (a soft, flimsy teenage beard like the whiskers her sons were beginning to sprout) with a pink Celtic skin underneath, a deep round scar on his lower left cheek—smallpox, an arrow? But his face was essentially unclear to her; even when she gazed at it point-blank it seemed curiously as if she were looking through welling tears. The setting sun blazed in through the window behind his head and cast him still further into shadow.

She sighed. "So maybe the deal is, since I made you up I can do anything I want to do with you, if I want to do anything. If I do anything, the first thing I'll do is send you to the dentist."

She balled her hands into fists and closed her eyes. She willed Henry V's teeth capped, opened her eyes, and took a breath. He was gone. She didn't know whether to be relieved or disappointed. There was no trace of him left. His pungent smell had disappeared. The glove he had removed in order to scratch himself was no longer on the table. Then she heard a clatter behind her, by the sink. She turned and saw him rummaging in the dish drainer, then raising a colander toward the window into a shaft of sunlight. The light gently freckled his face through the holes in the colander. She breathed again.

"Grin at me," she said. He did. His teeth were beautiful. They glinted in the sun shaft like a movie star's. She blinked her eyes and yellowed them a bit. She didn't want him to be a movie star. The teeth were now perfect; nevertheless, she could not avoid thinking that she might as well have a lemur hunkering at her sink, so primitive a primate was this man, so attenuated was their connection on the evolutionary time line. He gave her the shivers.

He, on the other hand, appeared to be comfortably settled in her kitchen. Having found a knife in the dish drainer, with one foot propped on the table, he was scraping mud from his boot, his mouth folded inward in concentration. But how could she manage to squeeze herself into his unfathomable life? Did Maureen come before Queen Katharine or after? Was Falstaff dead? Had the boy-king known sorrow? Boredom? Impotence? How could she fit him into her life?

This would be more difficult than the teeth. She dragged a broom over and began sweeping clods of dirt from under the table: he had finished cleaning his boots. He picked something from his wild hair—she worried he might give fleas to her sons' pet white mice—squashed it on his thumbnail, turned his face up to her and obligingly showed his new teeth. She was proud of her dentistry, and hoped it hadn't caused him any pain. So this was how she would proceed: she would ignore Falstaff and Katharine and make him fit her, if she had the power.

She got to work right after supper that night. She dug out both *Henry IVs* and *Henry V*, and the encyclopedia. She looked him up in the indexes of her college Western Civilization textbooks. There was not much to be found out that she didn't know already: two paragraphs in each text and one in the encyclopedia. The *Henry IVs* she ended by skimming: she did not enjoy seeing this boy as a jackanapes. It wasn't constructive. She decided to go to the video store the next day and rent Olivier's *Henry V*, though only in the spirit of scholarly thoroughness. She knew already Olivier would be too elegant for her. So it seemed her ministrations would have to be delicate. In all her imaginings she still couldn't imagine why it was such a man she had come up with. "God knows there have been plenty of things I wanted to change about nearly every man I've known," she confided to Henry as he helped her empty the dishwasher. "And I couldn't fix them either."

Getting ready for bed that night she wondered if it would work to make him the actor from the new *Henry V* movie she had seen recently. She didn't think so, but she decided to give it some consideration. At least the actor, whose name she couldn't remember, could be dressed in a shirt and jeans. Maureen was put off by those studded gloves. So she ran down the stairs with her toothbrush in her mouth, passing her husband on his way up (Kirk didn't seem to see her), swallowing toothpaste. She rummaged through old newspapers until she found an ad for the movie. To her surprise, the actor in the picture bore little resemblance to her Henry V; the blurry newsprint picture was as inscrutable as her Henry's fuzzy face. A fantasy life with an actor wouldn't work anyway, she said to herself as she refolded the paper and stacked it on the recycling pile. Most of them are gay, she had surmised from meeting them when they came to read at the radio station where she worked, also self-centered. And if he weren't gay, who could tell when she might pick up *People* magazine and find pictures of this guy with his gorgeous wife and his cottage in the country and his two unctuous Siamese cats. No, the idea of an actor was too unruly. Though as a medieval warlord he might prove stubborn, Henry, being dead, could at least be pinned down.

Then there was the question of age. His youth was embarrassing to Maureen. But he had died young—it had happened—and here he was now, with her. The encyclopedia didn't say how he had died, and she simply decided she couldn't worry about that for now, nor his studded gloves, nor even his age. She spent a sleepless night and a long day at her office phone, in her car and on her kitchen stool fooling with Henry's clothes, his adolescent grin, his wispy budding beard; and she couldn't do anything about them. Apparently she had to live with him a while before she was sure what she wanted and how much she could do. At least she'd taken care of those teeth. Fuzzy as he looked, he had a hard center and she would have to leave that alone for now. And, need she worry about his age? Why should *she* be embarrassed? Who would see them and laugh? And after all, princes matured early, didn't they? They had to. This boy had whored with Falstaff, fathered a king, decimated the French army. She spent days trying to figure things out. She kept tripping over Henry in the kitchen and locking him in the garage every night. "Fuck it," one day she said to the whistling kettle, where she was boiling water for tea. She had switched from coffee to tea because it was British. She told Kirk she hadn't been sleeping well and was cutting down on caffeine; when she offered him some tea he made a nauseated face. "Fuck it and 'od's bodkins. It's my fantasy, isn't it? I'll imagine that nothing matters. Maybe I'll change a few things gradually, and then I won't have so much trouble with transitions. Meanwhile this is the king I'm stuck with."

She decided to work on her seduction. She sat on her stool at the kitchen counter with a pot of steamed beets in front of her needing to be peeled and sliced and closed her eyes to begin an outline. She wondered about his underwear. Did he wear any? She thought not, dispatching hastily from behind her closed eyes a picture of him in a chainmail jock strap. She could not think of any appropriate words, so there would be none. They could come later. Leave the wordy wooing to Shakespeare.

First she tried squeezing herself into the nightdress of the newlywed Queen Katharine. Demure and virginal she could muster, but no, in her fantasy she didn't want to be anyone's wife—not even the wife of a boy barbarian. She would have to be Maureen, keeping Kirk, stretch marks, and all.

She got down to details. She tried out a soap-opera type kiss—necks twisting, mouths wide open. It wasn't right for his big canine head, too modern; she felt sodden from it. She tried a continental kiss on the hand. That was wrong too, not Gaelic enough. She kept her eyes closed tightly through an interruption from her son Justin, who reported that indeed his white mice had gotten fleas. She snapped: "Don't be ridiculous, mice don't get fleas. And even if they did, where would they have gotten fleas?" Justin asked why her eyes were closed, she ignored him and after a while he clomped clumsily back down the stairs.

Then she remembered a scene from the movie, and she knew she had her scenario. After the Battle of Agincourt, Henry and his men had carried their dead a long distance across the bloody battlefield, tripping over dead horses, to heap the bodies onto a cart, while singing a requiem. She sketched her scene briefly. She didn't want to prepare too much. She wanted it to happen. She thought at first she would keep her eyes closed, that it would be easier that way. But by the time he had moved across the kitchen and reached for her, she didn't know whether her eyes were open or closed. Her arms flailed and upset the beets. Red steamy juice spilled over the counter and trickled onto the floor. Henry heaved her over his shoulder so that her head and one arm dangled down his back and bounced as he walked. He carried her up the stairs, huffing through his mouth. She couldn't see anything: her hair was in her face. When they entered the bedroom he kicked the door closed and stooped to set her on her feet. She staggered. His cheeks were red, and he breathed heavily into her face. She smelled leeks and vinegar and sank stiffly backward onto the bed.

He towered over her like a hero, his feet planted widely apart. One of the lions on his tunic was almost completely obscured by gray dirt. The others heaved with his breathing. His eyelids fluttered, as if he were about to sink into a trance. Maureen thought for a moment he might faint or disappear, but instead he fumbled under his tunic with his left hand and drew his sword with his right; she was pleased to see he had shed somewhere his studded gauntlets. Maureen clutched a handful of skin on her stomach—loose skin from pregnancies—and wondered if he could kill her.

He brandished the sword three times over his head. She turned her face to the side in fear, saw the orange daisies on the bedspread, heard the swish of the sword in the air. Then he cried, "Once more unto the breech!", threw the sword clanging against the wall and leapt on top of her. She gasped, felt him between her legs. He thrust at her once: "For England!" he yelled painfully into her ear. Twice: "For Harry!" Again: "And for St. George!"

She felt him quiver and go limp. He must be densely built, more muscular than he looked, from jumping onto moving horses. He was absurdly heavy. Her lungs and belly were squashed. Her eyes felt like they would pop soon. She struggled for a breath. He was motionless. She managed to wriggle one of her arms out from under him. She pushed frantically at his shoulder—dead weight. Finally she got hold of the thick shock of hair at his forehead and jerked his head back from her chest. Something cracked in his neck, but she was able to inhale. His face was as limp as the rest of him. His jaw fell open and he drooled a little. "Poor thing. I'm not a horse," she sighed. "We're going back to the drawing board."

So in the weeks that followed Maureen made subtle adjustments. She still wanted to be careful, not do too much; for essentially she was satisfied. Orgasms were simply a matter of mechanics. For all his puppy-dog gracelessness, and despite the deceptive ease she had fixing his teeth, she came to appreciate this man's royal recalcitrance. She had some power. He was hers. But she could not remove the dusty lions from his chest, nor, unless he took them off of his own accord, his spiky gloves. Clearly there was something important—a clumsy, importunate, entitled, colossal swagger—which she could not, would not, must not mar. She needed this about him. She needed as well his bumptious vigor, the susceptibility of his youth. She needed his utter strangeness. She was not at all sure where his intransigence left off and her needs began.

And sex was not the main thing here, after all. She knew Henry needed some modernizing. But, she feared that as the lover of a modern man she wasn't married to, she would have to be "good in bed," and she had almost no notion of what that meant. She knew from novels that some women dressed in bizarre outfits and did stripteases for men to excite them. Of course that wasn't in bed, exactly. Anyway, if she could keep Henry in the Middle Ages, she wouldn't have to worry about being good in bed. She wanted a little more romance than he'd supplied that first time (she didn't want to be just a receptacle), but not too much awareness. She didn't want his expectations moving into the twentieth century.

First she circumcised him ("This won't hurt much more than the teeth," she promised him with a wavering smile) because that was what she was used to. Then after a nasty outbreak of acne around his mouth made it difficult for her to look at him she firmly aged him a touch. He began to speak in a language she could never have spoken herself, but which she understood perfectly, effortlessly. His words were vague like music, like the sound an ocean makes, simple but arcane, archaic but neither Shakespearean nor Chaucerian, spiritual and earthy. He read poetry to her while she cooked.

They liked the same poems. He read Tennyson's "Morte D'Arthur" over and over to her one night while she stirred a white sauce which refused to thicken. Each time Bedivere whipped Excalibur in the air, trying to let it go, she saw Henry and his sword and the orange daisies on her bedspread. She trembled, and her whisk sprinkled floury milk all over the stove; when the mysterious arm rose from the water, "clothed in white samite, mystic, wonderful," and caught the sword, she wept again and again.

He was particularly fond of Marvell's "To His Coy Mistress." While he read it, his beautiful metaphysical voice filled her up, and she stared at the red stain from the beet juice they had spilled that first time. She was hypnotized into an ethereal passion. From Marvell he flipped back a few pages in her anthology of the metaphysical poets and found the Donne poems her English teachers had skipped. She left a roast beef blackening in the oven the day he found this:

> *And yet no greater, but more eminent,*
> *Love by the spring is growne;*
> *As, in the firmament,*
> *Starres by the Sunne are not inlarg'd, but showne.*
> *Gentle love deeds, as blossomes on a bough,*
> *From loves awakened root do bud out now.*

She did not count the centuries by which Henry antedated Donne (they had world enough and time). She was only astonished at how long she had yearned for some gentle love deeds. They understood each other perfectly, effortlessly.

She went from day to day flushed and flustered, half aware of the material world. Her friends asked if she had changed her makeup. Her husband wanted to know if she was having hot flashes. Her skin felt tight; she was full as an egg. She saw beautiful people—beautiful men, rather—everywhere. At the coffee shop downstairs from the radio station she sat at the counter between two men so lovely she moved to a table so she could see them better. Henry wasn't with her. The one on the left had a sumptuous beard and burly hands. The other had sad downslanting eyes and a wide mouth like Rudolf Nureyev's. She forgot to drink her tea. She still didn't care much for tea anyway. She kept trying to drink it because Henry liked it. She felt sexy. She felt that, perhaps, if the beautiful men were to turn around, they might look at her too. She had a revelation. She had always assumed that sexy women attracted men. Now it occurred to her that it might be the other way round: that the ones who have plenty of sex look sexy. And she was, after a fashion, experiencing such plenty. She may even have become, without knowing it, "good in bed." Very likely there wasn't as much to it as she had used to think. And sure enough, she fancied, as she stood at the cash register paying her bill, that bearded man was staring at her. She was afraid to look up; as she walked up the five flights of stairs back to the station (she had decided to try to lose a few pounds), she was sure she did look different, having reacted to Henry's lustful gaze like a plant to the sun.

She felt sexy even around her husband. She wore sweaters she'd kept since before the boys were born (they fit tightly now) and lipstick. When Henry was not around, she sat beside Kirk on the couch during the TV news and let her shoulder graze his. She laid her hand on his thigh; once she kissed him good night with her mouth wet and open, then (abandoning memory) shoved her face behind his ear and breathed: "What could I do to turn you on?" He neither moved nor spoke. She drew back to look at his face. He was frankly considering.

"Leave me alone maybe," he said at length, not unkindly. "You're scaring me."

After that, she left him alone, and he seemed to want to pick a fight with her. He complained that she wasn't paying attention to anything. When she served him and the boys a supper of peas, broccoli, coleslaw, and warm milk, Kirk gagged and beat his fists on the table. He went in his underwear to the dryer to get his sweatpants and reported angrily to Maureen that he had found the dryer running hot but empty. His sweatpants were still wet in the washer. They went to watch their sons play basketball at the high school one evening, and he squirmed through a conversation Maureen began with the coach's wife about the beauty of the young boys' bodies, and how she preferred basketball to football because the uniforms showed them off so much better.

"You don't make sense anymore. The lights are on but nobody's home," Kirk said to her in the car on the way home.

She smiled and languidly apologized.

"The elevator doesn't go to the top floor."

She was driving. She had come recently to the conclusion that she liked to drive. Henry found the certainty with which she moved the stick shift arousing.

"You don't have all the little dots on your dice. Where did you get that watch?"

"What watch?"

"What watch?" he yelled back at her. "This watch." He snatched her right arm from the steering wheel and waved it in the air between them. Maureen's hand flopped loosely from the wrist. "This expensive-looking watch here with all the shiny jewels on it."

She turned into their street, using one arm. He held onto the other one. "I bought it for myself. I've always wanted a nice watch." She glanced at him. His nose was moving up and down as if it itched, but he didn't scratch it. He let her arm go so she could downshift to enter the driveway. "You can check the Visa bill," she added.

She called the boy-king Hal now. He still wore his gloves and his high leather boots with the steel-armored toes, but the noisy sword and scabbard had disappeared, his tunic was cleaner, and his face was changing. It occurred to Maureen that the scantly shrinking ears and lengthening jaw were suggestive of a boy she had had a crush on in high school, but she couldn't remember what that boy had looked like. She wasn't too sure what anyone looked like anymore, except Henry, and even he could be capriciously unstable and, at times, still fuzzy around the edges.

He sat silently in the shadowy kitchen one evening while Maureen and Iris Millikin stuffed invitations for the PTA auction into envelopes. Cicadas had begun that week to appear. One had chased Maureen to the car that morning, flying upside down. Iris and she worked in the dining room. Maureen couldn't see Hal, but she could feel him there in the next room, breathing, listening to her talk about her job and her car and her teenagers, waiting for her. Iris asked about the new watch.

"I hadn't realized it was so conspicuous," said Maureen. "Several people have asked me about it."

"My God, Maureen, it's the flashiest watch I've ever seen. It's dripping with stones. Are they real?"

Maureen nodded, blushing. "My lover gave it to me." Iris looked slowly up from the invitation she was folding. Maureen giggled. She hadn't told anyone else. She didn't know Iris well enough for large confidences, but now she'd begun. Hal stirred in the next room; his steel toe clanged against a chair. Maureen hoped she hadn't disturbed him by telling.

Iris gaped. Maureen continued talking, deciding as she talked that talking was good: a verification.

"It's the best thing that's ever happened to me. We understand each other perfectly, effortlessly. We read poetry together. He talks to me while I cook. When he reads Tennyson the room shakes, he has such a voice. And I read aloud too, and when I'm with him my voice isn't a bit nasal."

"Shhhh!" urged Iris, tipping her head toward the living room. "Kirk is right in there."

"The TV is too loud. He can't hear anything."

Iris's face shed some shock and turned eager. "Is it anyone I know?"

"I don't think so. You may have heard of him, but I'm not going to say his name. Look." Maureen unclasped her watch and handed it to Iris.

"You mean he's famous?" Iris took the watch and reverently inspected it. "It's perfectly gorgeous. Do you wear it all the time? Hasn't Kirk seen it?"

"I told him I bought it for myself. Look at the inscription."

Lightly etched in florid italic behind the face was "Had we but world enough and time . . ."

"Oh my God," Iris groaned, as if with pain or longing. She returned the watch to Maureen. They were quiet while they finished the envelopes, except that every few minutes Iris looked at Maureen, shook her head and sighed.

Iris left by the back door. She had pulled her car into the driveway. Maureen went outside with her to help her load the boxes of envelopes into the trunk. Several cicadas clacked in the hawthorn tree by the garage. Lifting the top box off Iris's stack, Maureen whispered, "His skin is fiery to the touch." Iris let the remaining two boxes slide, and stuffed envelopes splattered onto the driveway.

He never, after that first time, carried her up the stairs. Rather, he waited for her to go up ahead of him. She knew, though she didn't look back, that he liked to watch her haunches shift and flex beneath her clothes, lifting her weight deftly. She stopped wearing underwear, and she rolled up the stairs on the balls of her feet, her torso listing easily forward. She had never felt so lithe. She could see, though she didn't look back, his face as he watched her, interested merely at first, then lit by joy and a certain youthful astonishment. She heard his naive, grateful breathing at the foot of the stairs.

Soon he would follow her. She would wait for him in bed with a book open, her husband sleeping beside her. He would enter the room naked. He was covered with down: hair light and soft as corn silk, invisible in the daytime. But in the light from the bedside lamp it shimmered around him. His face and forearms glowed. "You look like an angel," she would whisper, and she would move quietly and lift the comforter to let him into bed beside her. "An archangel."

Late one night she sat in the kitchen with the lights off, and there came the familiar thunking clamor up the basement stairs. Her eyes popped open so suddenly she almost fell off her stool; and she braced herself for a niggling barrage from one of the boys: a shirt needed ironing, a book needed buying, a failed summer-school test needed signing. She turned an irritated face toward the head of the stairway, and Kirk emerged. He had been working on the monthly bills downstairs at the family-room desk. He carried a creased piece of paper, which he slammed onto the counter in front of her, covering the beet stain. It was the Visa bill.

"I've had it." He swung his arm at the light switch, missed, aimed again, swung furiously as if he were trying to kill a bat. Fluorescence flickered, flashed, then illuminated the room. Maureen blinked. Hal stood up from his chair by the table and vanished.

Kirk's voice became quiet, and his face came close to Maureen's. His lips moved with a frightening elasticity. "You sit in the dark and talk nonsense." His mouth stretched toward his ears. Maureen flinched. "You, I used to know, I can't talk to you. You spend two thousand dollars on a watch when you already have a watch." He turned away from her. He sobbed once. His shirt was damp between the shoulder blades. "I wish someone else had bought it for you." He spoke normally now, as if after one sob he felt better. "I think you should see a doctor."

"Never," she said with equanimity. She guessed she would have something interesting to talk about to one now, but a doctor would surely kill Hal, expertly and without remorse.

She slid the Visa bill aside so she could see the red stain on the wood counter. It had soaked into the grain and gone brown. It could have been anything now: grape juice, mildew, a scorch from a hot saucepan, blood.

"I think you'd better get your brain in gear. Shape up. The next time you wreck the car the kids are likely to be with you. Really. Straighten up and fly right."

"Kirk, I wouldn't exactly call it a wreck."

"What would you call it?"

"A ding. Somebody sideswiped me in the grocery store lot. I wasn't even there. It wasn't my fault. I was parked just fine."

"I don't even know what you're talking about. So what else is new?" He flung his arms over his head hopelessly. "I'm talking about running into the light pole!"

"Oh, that." Maureen had forgotten. At work she had backed out of her parking place the week before . . . into a pole, crunching in the trunk of the car. Hal had been with her. He had laughed at the dismayed look on her face and at the way the damaged car looked—like a big blue duck, he said, with its turned-up tail.

Kirk got quiet again. "What's wrong with you?" he asked.

She saw the familiar mole on his forehead and a wet dab on his mustache—a tear? Something thick rose in her throat. "I want you to laugh when I bang in the car. I want you to understand me; and when you don't, I don't want to be told I'm crazy. I want to be told I'm mysterious."

Kirk pushed out his lower lip and blew a long breath upward, as if he were trying to dry the tear from his mustache. "Well, don't look at me," he said, leaving the room. "I'm telling you you're a pain in the ass."

She was sorry to have made Kirk angry; she didn't like to fight with him. But it gave her satisfaction to have expressed her simple desires in a straightforward manner. If they made him angry, she couldn't help it.

Meanwhile, her days with Hal went happily along. Some days Hal came to work with her. It was early summer, and together they took long walks through the neighborhood to see the trees sprouting new leaves. It had been a dryish spring—no storms to rattle the foliage—so the flowering shrubbery kept blooming through June. They had to push heavy lilac boughs from their faces as they walked the sidewalks. Hal kept pace beside her in his ambling, arm-swinging way. He walked unlike other men she knew, like someone who had never carried a briefcase. His own favorite was a pair of ornamental crab apples in a yard a few blocks from Maureen's house. Maureen did not know who lived there, but Hal admired the little pink trees so much that one evening they sat down under them and watched the dusk and listened to the neighborhood dogs start barking at each other until Maureen glanced at the house and saw one of the front room curtains jerk open and someone look out. They got up and moved lazily down the street, the length of their forearms touching.

At home, she heard his steel toes lightly clicking on the floors even when he was not visible. The sound reminded her of a time years before when one of her sons had decided to be a tap dancer. She had signed him up for lessons, bought him tap shoes; and for the next two months, until his interest waned, instead of walking he had inelegantly tapped everywhere, especially favoring the tiled bathroom floor. The clattering, the silvery marks throughout the house, and the danger of broken tiles had annoyed Kirk to no end; but Maureen was sure she remembered enjoying those noisy days, even before Hal's echoings highlighted their preciousness.

Hal usually came to the grocery store with her these days, and her mind was more on him than on food. They were playful and happy there. It was a hallowed place for them, because they had met there. Weekly they bought pounds of leeks. Maureen giggled and blushed whenever they came to the cucumbers, and made the same joke each time: "One still has to buy cucumbers, doesn't one?" And each time Hal laughed. She danced to the jazz on the piped-in radio. She dropped things: they seemed to turn slimy and slip through her fingers. Often she came home with bruised apples and melons preposterously squashed. Her boys insisted she should switch grocery stores: the fruit was no good anymore at this one. Once, during a discussion of warhorses and their saddles, she dropped a stack of five chicken potpies on the way from the freezer to her cart; and the grocer helped her pick them up and gave her five new ones, because the pastry might be broken. Rather oversolicitously, Maureen thought, he helped her unload at the register. "I think he thinks I'm palsied or dim-witted," she confided later to Hal.

The produce man showed a similar solicitude, which she couldn't quite analyze. It may have stemmed from the fact that she looked like a woman with sex on her mind, or it may have been that she simply looked odd, goonily tittering over cucumbers. He managed to let her know he was separated from his wife. She couldn't quite reconstruct the conversation in which he had said this, but somehow she had found it out. One day he appeared away from his department, at the meat counter, where Maureen stood comparing cuts of pork for price. She held a tray of pork chops in one hand and a shoulder roast in the other. The produce man told her he'd show her some time how to cook turnip greens. He thought they'd be better with a roast, contrary to popular wisdom, and would make a less fatty meal. He had put his hand on her waist and was boasting that he didn't need to use any bacon grease in his greens—he spiced them with chopped carrots and onions. Maureen was embarrassed, unable to decide how or whether to continue a flirtatious conversation about vegetables. Finally, with a squeeze of his fingers against her ribs and a wink, he said: "Take a shoulder." Suddenly Hal's voice sounded in her other ear: "Take a king," he whispered. She dropped the roast. Its plastic tray cracked and pink juice seeped out onto the floor. The produce man went to find a bag boy with a mop. Maureen called after him: "Would you see if you have any leeks in the back? I couldn't find them where they usually are."

He turned and walked backward, smiling at her. "I sure do have some leeks," he said. "We were running short so I took you a nice bunch and put them aside. I know you always buy leeks." She and Hal followed him toward the produce department.

"Is something wrong?" she asked Hal while the produce man was gone. Hal shook his head and looked down at his steel toes. He stood with his arms folded and his lips pulled back from his perfect teeth in a stiff grimace. The sharp points on his gauntlets glinted in the harsh commercial light. He jiggled his legs. The scar on his cheek had turned red. "You look as if something were the matter," she said.

He looked up at her from under one eyebrow, his head still tilted down, and spoke urgently. "I am inside you always, you know, not only in the act of love. I came to life inside you and there I will remain: moving, moving you, changing you, growing, stretching you."

"I know," said Maureen. They understood each other perfectly, effortlessly. She took the leeks from the produce man without thanking him, and after they loaded the groceries into the backseat (the trunk wouldn't open any more), they made love in the car without removing their clothes.

Maureen was as unprepared for Hal's death as she had been for his arrival. The encyclopedia didn't say how it happened, nor did Shakespeare, who left him gaily wooing in one play and took up the next at his funeral. Kirk was out of town at the time, at a convention of public-works executives. The last cicada had attacked that day. It had veered at her drunkenly from behind the back door as she was returning from dropping the boys at baseball practice. She had ducked and closed her eyes so she wouldn't see its fierce, red-eyed foolish face; and when she made it panting into the house, she went straight upstairs to get a sweater. She was cold, whether from a chill in the air, fear of the cicada, or from a premonition of sorrow she didn't know. She entered the bedroom and headed for the dresser, but stopped short at the sight of a figure sitting on her bed. She thought at first it was Hal, but only for a second. It was a squat, menacing man, she saw, when he rose noisily to stand, fully armored. Its arms splayed out far from its sides because of the bulk of metal in its armpits; it could not bring its legs very close together either, so it teetered as it rose, then stood by Maureen's bed as if astride a short, invisible horse. It was Hal's uncle, the Earl of Exeter. She recognized him from the movie. He looked a little like an actor she had seen once or twice on Masterpiece Theatre. She had wondered, watching the movie, why, since this fellow was apparently the only Briton who could afford a proper suit of armor, he hadn't at least bought one for his nephew the king, who went to battle in that flimsy padded tunic covered with dirty lions. Immediately, before he even spoke, she felt resentment toward her visitor. She decided she would take up with him the questions of armor, stinginess, and the value of the king's body once they had introduced themselves. But after a creaky bow and before she had a chance to open her mouth, Exeter launched into a speech:

> *We mourn in black: why mourn we not in blood?*
> *Henry is dead, and never shall revive:*
> *Upon a wooden coffin we attend;*

> And Death's dishonourable victory
> We with our stately presence glorify,
> Like captives bound to a triumphant car.
> What! shall we curse the planets of mishap
> That plotted thus our glory's overthrow?
> Or shall we think the subtle-witted French
> Conjurers and sorcerers, that, afraid of him
> By magic verses have contriv'd his end?

Without a pause he clanged out of the bedroom and was gone.

It took Maureen some while to digest his meaning. When she understood that Hal was dead, she lay down on her bed like an effigy, with her hands folded across her belly. She had cramps. She knew the French had nothing to do with her king's death: it was the planets of mishap. She knew she had to construct a proper death. It would be good for her, something to occupy her mind. Illness was inappropriate— too undramatic. He had to die in battle or be hit by a bus. She settled upon battle. She rose, in pain, to do her little research, then lay back down, grateful after all for the insubstantialities of Exeter's and the encyclopedia's accounts. How nice that she would be allowed to give Hal the sort of glorious passage to Valhalla he would enjoy. She devised a wound, but not too bloody a one, and nothing that would mark his ruddy young face. She'd given birth to him without pain, and she wanted to give him as little as possible in return when she killed him. An arrow in the shoulder would be good, like cowboys used to get in the movies, but more serious. As he expired in the arms of a weeping foot soldier, he spoke of her, and gave the soldier one of his muddy studded gloves to take to her. Somehow it got lost later. Hordes of haggard warriors massed round him, heads bowed, and hummed a requiem as he expired. Ravens the size of large cats tipped the branches of a nearby oak. His horse stood over him until the last breath (sweet pungent breath), then whinnied, reared, whirled, and galloped away into the hills.

Maybe she had known since the parking lot, when she had decided not to run him over with her car, that eventually she would have to kill him. There was no avoiding the treacherous ambiguities of their affair. (It had occurred to her, before he had spoken, that Exeter had come to accuse her of incest and haul her to the Tower, where she would melt into a retroactive footnote.) She planned to choke back the feeling that she was guilty of murder: some more or less scandalous end had been inevitable.

After she had arranged the death, Maureen turned to her grief. She cried every night for two weeks in the kitchen. Two of her sons' white mice died the day after Hal did, electrocuted by a naked wire behind the basement refrigerator where they had fled when Maureen left the cage door ajar after feeding them. The boys assumed, when she served them supper sobbing, that she was wracked with guilt because of her absentmindedness. Kirk stayed out of town for a week and a half and when he returned he tried not to see her mourning. Perhaps he accepted, by default, the mouse explanation from the boys. He talked to her a little about his convention, about people he had run into that she knew. "It's nice of you to talk to me," she warbled, licking tears from her upper lip.

When she finally stopped crying, she still had her memories. She remembered

Hal's untameable hair. She recreated his renderings of Keats, rifling through her messy library till she found the lines from *Endymion*—

> *Why, I have been a butterfly, a lord*
> *Of flowers, garlands, love-knots, silly posies,*
> *Groves, meadows, melodies, and arbour roses*

—and she remembered, without exactly locating it, ". . . the spirit is beside thee whom thou seekest . . ." Keats had been one of their joint favorites; *Endymion* took on new proportions for her now—the story of a boy dreaming of loving the moon—though she could not make the poetry sound like Hal had. She remembered his lathery laughing mouth when she had taught him how to brush his gleaming new teeth. She remembered his acne, his habit of fiddling with his right earlobe, and the way he liked to chomp his leeks raw and unclean.

Her grief achieved now a certain calm, but these scattered recollections were not quite satisfying; so she stayed home from work one day and relived everything from beginning to end—from cucumbers to Exeter, through beet juice to the blood of the roast beef, which she saw now as allied omens of startings and finishings. She stayed awake that night and was done by the next afternoon. She moved fast, but never got tired. It was recreation. The wild hair on his large head was not as real as it could be. This murder turned out to be the best thing she had made. Memory was memory, after all: who could doubt it? Not even Kirk, nor Iris. She was now a bona fide widow, as deserving of her sadness as any woman who had lost a lover or husband, because what she had now was as real as what any of them had. She was queen of England and France, and still alive to boot, unlike the poor widow Katharine, who hadn't even any brain scraps left to play among.

Several weeks later, when the next generation of cicadas had dug deep into the ground and all their parents were dead, Maureen lay in the bed of the produce man thinking of the dirge from *Cymbeline*, but not sadly. She was moved to make a speech, a thing that did not happen to her often. But emotion was bubbling in her like yeast, bloating her.

"I guess you know how much this—what shall I call it? I don't like 'affair'—our recreation means to me," she said. His head turned toward her. Because she was beginning to know the things he would do before he did them, she thought he must have smiled, but she couldn't see his face. He was a matte black shadow. They had pulled the shades against the afternoon sun. "I want you to know," she continued, "that you are very big to me, very very big." He guffawed. "I'm not talking about anything physical, so don't laugh, or I guess you can laugh if you want to. I guess I'm not sure whether I'm talking about anything physical or not. I guess I'm not too sure any more what's physical and what isn't. I don't know where your body stops and my mind starts." He took her hand in his.

"Your body is like a dream of magic, like an ancient legendary artifact kept secret through the centuries by the alchemists, searched for by Nostradamus, Zoroaster and the Masonic Brotherhood, finally revealed to me. To me." He hiked one leg up under the sheet and scratched his knee.

"You fill me, complete me, probe and touch something deeply buried and uncivilized in me. I lose my balance, I fly upside down, I become savage, and finally I surpass completion and become not-me. I die, in the Donneian sense. I feel we die together." He let go her hand, rose with a little hop from the bed and went to the window. He pulled the shade toward him to look out onto the street. In the light she could see his broad black back shiny with sweat, and also that he had stopped understanding her. She knew he favored conversations about asparagus. But she continued: "You are downy, iridescent. Royal."

MRS. GREASY
Robert Reed

Robert Reed lives in Lincoln, Nebraska, and is best known for his science fiction contributions to *The Magazine of Fantasy & Science Fiction, Asimov's Science Fiction, New Destinies, Universe, Tomorrow,* and *Synergy.* His novels include *The Lee Shore, The Hormone Jungle, Black Milk, The Remarkables, Down the Bright Way, Beyond the Veil of Stars,* and *An Exaltation of Larks.* His stories have appeared in several volumes of Gardner Dozois's *The Year's Best Science Fiction* series.

Familiar as I am with Reed's science fiction, I was caught completely off guard by the exceedingly creepy "Mrs. Greasy," which appeared in *Tomorrow* magazine, edited by A.J. Budrys.

—E.D.

Dad found the island advertised in a sportsman's magazine. Fishing and hunting at reasonable rates; summer cabins with kitchens, flush toilets, and a scenic lodge on the Minnesota-Ontario border. It wasn't yet Christmas, but he knew Mom and guessed what kind of campaign was required. He sent off for pamphlets, then put one in each of their red stockings—stiff yellowed pamphlets showing rustic cabins and tall pine trees, various smiling vacationers holding walleye and northern pike up to the cameras.

It looked like paradise to his son, Jimmy. Teasing his little sisters, Jimmy pretended to be a hungry pike rising through a lake of torn wrapping paper.

Dad gave him a warning glare before starting in with Mom, telling her how it was never too early. At these prices, he argued, they'd need to get their reservations in soon. Before spring, certainly. And Mom did listen—no small accomplishment—as she silently studied her pamphlet with her usual suspicious expression.

"Well," Dad concluded, "what do you think?"

Mom shrugged and looked at the ceiling. "But we're not outdoor people," was her retort, the voice calm and responsible. "Remember the last time you took us camping?"

"Oh," Dad growled, "that was a fluke." He made a show of opening and closing his left hand. "See? All healed."

Mom said nothing.

"Besides," Dad added, "this isn't camping. We'll be in a cabin. There's a gas stove and a refrigerator—"

"—And the usual maid, too. Me."

Jimmy's father was an optimist, and it was blinding optimism that led him into traps. He had a big useless smile and boyish sensibilities, and fifteen years of marriage had taught him little. "I didn't mean that," he pleaded. Then the smile brightened, and he added, "You don't even have to wear your maid's uniform."

If they had been beside a lake then, it would have frozen solid. Ice to the horizon, blue and eternal.

Dad sensed his error, swallowing and his smile wobbling. "Oh, I'm kidding. I'll help you. With the cooking and the girls, and everything. . . ."

Mom stared at him, unamused and thoroughly unimpressed.

"And so will Jimmy," Dad added.

She turned to watch her son snapping his teeth, pike-fashion. "What do you think, Jimmy?"

He was eleven, almost twelve, and the idea of his own island on a wilderness lake sounded perfect. It was the answer to a wish he'd never consciously wished, and he gave a little smile, trying to avoid her traps. Don't offer her anything she could dismiss, he knew. That's why he skipped to a mournful expression, asking, "Why not?"

Mom's gaze seemed to flicker, for just an instant.

"I don't want to drive around the world again." Last summer's vacation still weighed on their collective memories. "I didn't like that."

What could she say?

"I want to go," Jimmy added, scrupulously honest. "I want Dad to teach me how to fish."

Mom was trapped. She loved complaining that Dad and Jimmy didn't do enough shared projects, that their male-bonding was inadequate. What was more male than hunting giant predatory fish?

Dad smelled victory. "It's cheap," he interjected. "We could afford to stay two weeks, if we wanted."

"Please, please," said Jimmy. "Can we go?"

The twins joined in, out of habit. "Can we go see the island, Mommy? Can we, please, can we?"

And she looked at the old pamphlet once again, trying to find some loophole. By nature, Mom was rational and pessimistic; but there was no rational reason to say no. The best she could manage was to sniff the pamphlet, telling everyone, "It smells musty." Then she gave a sigh and a vague shrug, adding, "We can consider it, I guess. Maybe."

Seven months later, they were standing on a stony beach, watching loons fish the clear glacial waters. This was the Great North, nothing in front of them but green wilderness stretching towards a white one. Their Volvo station wagon—a tank with tires—stood at the end of a logging road, emptied and locked tight. Beside them was a small mountain of suitcases, boxes, and coolers. They had provisions for two weeks, which sounded like forever. They'd been waiting for two hours, one hour past the appointed rendezvous time; when they heard the big inboard motor there was a collective sigh, faces turning, watching a good-sized boat coming off the open water.

The loons sang out and tried to fly, wings pumping and their feet running across the water until they were out of sight.

The boat throttled down, turning in against a little moss-carpeted dock. The pilot was an oldish man wearing stained jeans and a filthy white T-shirt. He climbed onto the dock and tied up, giving wet grunts when he bent and when he stood again. "You the Hansons?" said an old wet voice.

Dad stepped forwards, by himself.

"Bert Gressy." It sounded as if he'd said *Bent Greasy*, which was a fair description of the man. Mr. Gressy was large but stood hunched forwards, a vigorous full gut straining against the T-shirt. He must have been young once, but Jimmy couldn't tell when. His head seemed three sizes too large. His features were ugly. One of his ears had been whittled down to a fleshy nub, and his teeth—what teeth remained—were badly stained and clinging to rotting gums. "Looks like I'm late," he announced, amused.

"Not very," Dad replied, shaking the man's hand.

"Had to go to town. For parts." The old man had sour breath; Jimmy smelled it from a distance. "If I'm late, that's why."

"Parts?" said Mom.

"For the generator, yeah."

Mom said, "Generator?"

Mr. Gressy was looking at Dad, red eyes narrowing and the wet voice saying, "Yeah, there's no juice in the cabins. For now."

"No electricity?" Mom persisted.

"Happens." Then a big shrug, as if to say, "It's only a little important."

"But you'll fix it," Dad interjected. "You did get the part—"

"Today. Tomorrow, at the latest." The big head nodded, and he wiped his sickly mouth with a hand. "Or the day after, for sure."

Mom said nothing, which was remarkable. Their coolers were full of defrosting meats, and she had to be concerned. Dad thought to ask if there was ice on the island. Mr. Gressy shook his head, saying, "Fact is, the camp's been dark all week."

And still Mom said nothing. Maybe she was worn out by the traveling, or maybe she thought no purpose would be served by making noise. Or maybe, most likely, she was laying a careful trap to catch Dad, this vacation always sounding too good to be true and an important lesson about to be learned. Without one cross word, she helped Dad and Jimmy load the boat, Mr. Gressy saying nothing, doing nothing but sitting on his swiveling chair. The family ended up scrunching together at the stern, the motor roaring and the wind roaring and Dad leaning, speaking into Mom's ear. "It'll be fine," he promised. "Just wait."

She never said a word.

Jimmy recognized the island from the pamphlets. It was bigger than he had imagined, the A-frame lodge on high ground and half a dozen cabins on a broad peninsula. They entered a little cove, sliding in alongside a floating dock. "The skiff's yours," said their host. He gestured at a small aluminum boat. "She's gassed and ready. When you need more gas, look in the lodge. In the big red cans."

"Which cabin is ours?" asked Mom.

"You pick," said Mr. Gressy. "Any one you want."

There was a moment of silence, then Dad attempted a smile. "Where are the other people?" he asked.

"Aren't any." Mr. Gressy gave a disinterested shrug. "You've got the run of the place."

They could have asked to leave, to be taken back to the security of their Volvo. But why? The old man watched them unload their gear, sometimes shaking his head as if amused. Were they that inadequate? Jimmy wondered. As vacationers went, did they measure up that badly?

Their last cooler was set against the hull. Jimmy grabbed it and gave a jerk, then saw the butt of the rifle tucked into a special-made slot, almost invisible. An instant later, Mr. Gressy said, "Shot a bear, just last week," and gave a scornful little laugh.

Nobody else noticed the rifle or the words.

Jimmy hurriedly dragged the cooler to Dad, both of them lifting it up and over. Then the old man was saying, "Rules, folks. I've got one big important rule."

Even the twins paused, standing there with their dolls clenched to their chests.

He told them, "I live on the other side of the island, alone, and I like my privacy. If you need me, blow the boat horn up at the lodge. Blast till I show." He stared at Dad, his expression dismissive. "'Less of course I'm gone, which puts you on your own."

Mom grasped Dad's hand and squeezed.

Dad coughed and said, "Climb on over, son."

Jimmy joined them. The dock rode low in the water, weighed down by their luggage.

"Enjoy yourselves," said Mr. Gressy, laughing for no clear reason. Then he untied himself and raced out of the cove, probably going home. The dock moved over his wake, then everything turned hot and still, almost silent. Finally Mom dropped Dad's hand and said, "Well, I guess we pick our cabin." But nobody seemed eager to step onto solid land, some tiny precognitive voice warning them against that simple act.

There wasn't time to fish that first day, what with unpacking and the need to clean out their cabin. Whoever was there last had left the floor muddy and the trash cans filled. Mom cooked the meat that had defrosted, burying the rest in the last of the truckstop ice. Dinner was hamburgers fried on the filthy little stove. Showers were mandatory, the hot water gone before Jimmy had his turn. Nightfall arrived, but not the lights. Everyone went to bed early, Jimmy relegated to an army cot in the kitchen, and he lay awake most of the night, the air muggy and herds of mice running wild through the cabinets and beneath the floor.

But the next day started better. He and Dad went fishing, armed with nautical maps and state-of-the-art tackle, taking the little skiff deeper into Canada and ending up in a weedy bay that Dad claimed was ideal for pike. Years of reading sportsman's magazines made him expert. They used fierce bright lures with grappling hooks and steel leaders and strong monofilament line, bluer than the sky. They stayed the day, eating soggy sandwiches between casts, arms tiring and necks burning and about eighty pounds of green weeds caught by late afternoon. Nothing else.

They started back for dinner, leaving the fishless bay to discover that the wind had come up, blowing straight for them. Whitecaps stretched ahead for a treacherous mile. At one point, hunkering down on the bow, Jimmy looked back and saw his father holding the throttle with both hands, a puffy, frightened expression on his face. Every wave had to be climbed, cold white spray making them shiver. Jimmy thought they would die. He saw himself sinking into the bottomless water, past the reach of sunlight, a thousand burly pike ready to gnaw him to the bone.

But they made their island, their cove, the wind abating and Mom watching from the dock, hands on hips. One storm had been left for another. "How is it?" she asked, her voice giving fair warning.

"Oh," Dad sputtered, "they weren't biting."

"I mean the wind." She was pale from anger. "You could have waited for the wind to drop."

Neither of them spoke.

Then she changed topics, saying, "By the way, we've moved. We're in the next cabin up."

Dad attempted a smile. "Are we?"

"Our toilet quit." She watched them shakily climb out of the little skiff. "I used the boat horn, as ordered, but Mr. Greasy must not have heard me. I haven't seen him today."

Had she called him *Mr. Greasy?*

Dad didn't seem to notice anything, telling her, "I'm sure the new cabin is fine."

"The girls and I found the generator too," she grumbled.

Nobody wanted to ask the obvious question.

She answered anyway. "It's in the lodge, and it's halfway dismantled. Which is good, I guess. Someone's been working on it, I guess."

Jimmy looked at the open water, amazed by the fierce waves and feeling thankful to have survived. Life felt precious now. He promised himself never to take anything for granted. Never, never again.

Mom shook her head, admitting to them, "I'm beginning to wonder about our Mr. Greasy."

There. She'd said *Greasy.*

And Dad said, "Honey," with a disapproving tone.

"But hey," Mom concluded, "everything is reasonably priced. And isn't that what counts?"

The weather changed overnight, turning cold with a hard driving rain. They spent the next day and a half inside their new cabin, playing cards and reading, sometimes using the stove's burners for heat. Every meal had some cut of beef or chicken. Jimmy and his sisters quarreled over small things. Mom and Dad conspicuously avoided fighting over anything. The storm let up that second afternoon, a chill drizzle falling, and Dad decided to fish that same distant bay. Was Jimmy interested? Not really, he admitted. Dad went alone, looking miserably cold before he was out of sight. Jimmy put on his poncho and went for a delightful solitary walk.

The A-frame lodge was dark and dirty. There was a pool table where balls rolled to the low end, and a Ping-Pong table with a tattered net and bandaged paddles. The main entertainment, he decided, was an old wall with a thousand names and dates carved into it. Using his pocket knife, he put *Jimmy Hanson* between Ferris Murlock and Henry Waggle. The oldest date was '56, which seemed impressive, and he found himself wondering about these vanished people, fingertips trying to pull the past from the deeply etched wood.

The generator was in the back room, its pieces scattered on the sloping floor. No Mr. Greasy. Jimmy wandered back outside, finding a modest trail that led off across the island. He followed until he came upon a hand-painted skull-and-crossbones sign, its message reading:

TRESPASSERS SHOT
AND GUTTED ON SIGHT!!!

Shot *and* gutted? He shivered and retreated to the warm cabin, never mentioning the generator or the sign. Eventually Dad returned, no luck with the wary pike, and the family ate like cougars, consuming most of a roast meant to last for several days. Afterwards Jimmy studied Dad's nautical maps, trying to picture the forbidden places. Their island was an irregular quarter-sized rock surrounded by glacial blood. The nearest town wasn't even on the map. Tiny square and rectangular dots marked the cabins and lodge, and a lone square was on the opposite side. Mr. Greasy's home. Judging by the squiggly lines, there was a ridge in the water offshore. Didn't fish like ridges? he asked. "Sometimes," Dad conceded, nodding and looking at the map for himself. He didn't mention Mr. Greasy, but he gave Jimmy a sly little smile, telling everyone, "We'll have walleye for dinner tomorrow night. How's that sound?"

Despite the drizzle, Jimmy accompanied him that next day. They worked the island's shoreline, drifting and trolling, their destination never mentioned. By noon they could see a dock and the familiar speedboat, Dad observing, "Our friend must be home." Yet there wasn't any other trace of Mr. Greasy. A low granite cliff was topped with towering pines. They waited for the man to appear, trolling back and forth over the next couple hours, not a single walleye bothering their lures. Finally Dad said, "He won't mind," and turned towards shore. And as if they needed more reasons, he added, "Your mother's about to explode over this electricity business."

They tied up and climbed out. Rickety wooden stairs led up the cliff face. Dad led the way, again saying, "I'm sure he won't mind." Another skull-and-crossbones sign read:

TRESPASSERS
BUTCHERED ALIVE!!!

That brought a pause, a deep sigh, then Dad remarked, "Yes, but we're not really trespassing. And he promised us power by now. Am I right?"

They continued through the trees, entering a large clearing. Jimmy saw the satellite dish, then the rows of polished black panels, everything pointing skyward. Those were solar panels, he realized. They made electricity. And the dish meant Mr. Greasy had a TV with a thousand channels, which seemed like the strangest, most astonishing wonder he could have seen. The wide trail went between the rows, and they walked slowly, neither of them speaking. Straight ahead was a house, square and simple, built from old squared-off logs. Around the house was a high chain-link fence with barbed wire on top. Jimmy thought of a prison's fence, except wasn't the wire hanging the wrong way? It stuck out over the outside, odd as it seemed. And just then Dad whispered the word, "Survivalist."

Whatever that meant, thought Jimmy.

They retreated, almost hurrying, back to their boat and out onto the water and Dad eventually leaning towards Jimmy, whispering for no reason. "Don't mention this to Mom," he said. "It would just make things worse."

Worse how? Because Mr. Greasy had electricity? Because he had TV? Because there was a prison fence around his house? Or because the old man was nuts, and who knew what he might do?

"Promise me, Jimmy."

He promised.

"Good, then."

Jimmy shut his eyes, imagining the log house and the barbed wire meant to ward off intruders; and he discovered that he could feel something, some clear *presence* that he could pinpoint to the nearest inch. The presence was inside the log house, moving a few steps and stopping, then moving again. Was it Mr. Greasy? But he knew it couldn't be. He just knew. It was something else, stranger than any satellite dish, and now the something stepped closer to him, whispering Hello with a voice no one else could hear. *Hello there, you. Hello.*

They never caught any walleye. Dinner was tunafish, and Dad joked about how he'd hooked the tuna and wasn't it delicious? Nobody laughed, including him. Then in the morning he left for a new bay, vowing to bring back something edible; and the drizzle began again, nothing visible but their island and the endless gray water.

Jimmy decided to walk, no destination planned. No plans whatsoever. Curiosity moved him towards the island's center. He kept off the trail, thinking he could claim ignorance if the old man found him. Eventually he had no clear idea where he was or how to get home. The ground was low and wet, blacker than coal and covered with brush. He couldn't see far, but three times he found deer skulls with polished antlers still attached. Then came a glade and a trash heap—old furniture half burned; rotting food making Jimmy squeamish—and he pressed forwards, spotting the lake at long last. The ground turned to rock carpeted with pine needles. When he came onto an open ledge, Mr. Greasy's dock below on his right and his boat missing, the mortal danger suddenly lifted.

He stepped without looking, too cocky for his own good.

His left foot slid on wet needles, the right foot following its lead, and suddenly Jimmy was airborne, falling fast, some calm secure part of him thinking that at least there was water under him and everything would be fine. Which it would have been, except for the rock. Sticking up from the water was a tough survivor of the glaciers, its sharp crest cutting through his jeans and into his shin. He didn't feel the injury until he had swum ashore, soaked and aching and thoroughly embarrassed. He climbed up the brief rock face and started to limp, then paused and saw the torn denim and blood, and the last of his adrenaline fell away.

He had to get home as soon as possible.

Jimmy broke into a limping trot, crossing the trail between the fancy solar panels. He planned to run around Mr. Greasy's house. He barely looked at it as he moved, glad that the owner was gone and that his guts could remain happy inside him for the time being—

"Hello? Hello? Who are you, hello?"

It was a woman's voice. Jimmy halted out of shock; talking pines wouldn't have been a bigger surprise.

"Darling?" said the voice. "Oh, you're hurt."

He managed to turn, spotting a woman standing in the doorway. They were forty feet apart and the light wasn't perfect, but she certainly looked younger than Mr. Greasy. She had to be his daughter, he thought; except she was beautiful, pale like china and smiling at him with big eyes, her smooth platinum hair falling over her shoulders. She was wearing an old-fashioned housecoat over a lacy nightgown. She was Mom's age, Jimmy decided. Then he squinted and thought, no, she was younger.

"Did you fall in the lake, darling?"

He gave a weak nod.

"Your poor little leg . . . how does it feel, love?" She had a caring voice, not loud but perfectly audible despite the distance between them. It was just one of many oddities that he sensed and accepted and then dismissed. Another oddity was her knowledge of his wound, which she couldn't see. "Show me," she insisted; and Jimmy had lifted his poncho to show it. "You must have struck a stone when you fell," she told him. "That nasty stone."

Suddenly Jimmy was glad to be bleeding. He made a show of limping, managing a few strides towards the front of the house and the tall locked gate. The woman stayed in the doorway, bare feet showing. They were almost forty feet apart, yet he could see every toe, how each of the perfect nails was painted red and how the toes curled over the splintery wood. He loved those feet. He could nearly taste them against his open mouth. Lifting his gaze, he saw hints of her legs and knees and her breasts, tasting salt and a rich musk inside his closed mouth. Then he stared hard at her face, and began to shiver from being wet and nervous. With the softest possible voice, he asked, "Who are you?"

She heard him. Smiling, she said, "Mrs. Greasy," and she broke into an amused laugh.

Had he heard her correctly? No, she must have said Gressy—

"I have bandages in here," she continued. "I have medicines."

The padlock on the gate was larger than two fists.

"Sometimes he leaves a spare key under one of those pink stones."

Jimmy turned over every stone, pink or not. No key to be found. Mrs. Greasy promised, "It's warm in here," and he actually shook the locked gate, making the padlock jump. Frustration mounted, then it fell away again. Suddenly he was outside himself, aware of how strange he looked . . . a boy wrestling with chain-link, trying to reach an old man's wife. He was feverish. He had to be insane. And when she saw hesitation, she asked, "What is your name?"

"Jimmy—"

"Jimmy," she repeated, almost before he had said it. "Are you staying in one of the cabins, Jimmy?"

He nodded, leaning against the gate.

"He didn't mention guests. He almost never does anymore." She licked her lips, showing him a pouting expression. It was lovely pouting, and he felt too weak to stand by himself.

"You're chilled, Jimmy."

"Yes," he muttered.

"Did you come here to visit me, Jimmy?"

He said, "Yes," before he realized it was impossible and crazy. How could he have known she was here?

"Break the lock, Jimmy. Take a stone and hit it hard." She smiled while she spoke, telling him, "My husband won't mind. You are his guest, and you're cold and wet. And hurt." A long pause, then she added, "I can feed you. Do you like soup?"

He was famished, yes.

"With oyster crackers?"

He could beat on the padlock with a chunk of granite, yes. Or maybe he could dig beneath the fence somewhere, his gaze trying to find a likely place. Except the ground was rock and Mr. Greasy had poured concrete in every little gap.

"Do you like my house, Jimmy?"

He looked at it with care and a growing astonishment. The log walls seemed ancient, carved with hammers and wedges and axes, and the foundation was made of native stones cemented together with care. It occurred to Jimmy that the house had been here longer than Mr. Greasy had been alive, and what made it all the more bizarre was how the woman crouched, letting him see inside. The single room was lit up with lights and a big-screen television, the television turned to one of the shopping channels. He could see part of a stove and the end of a brass bed, and there wasn't a lot of room left over.

"He went to town." She meant Mr. Greasy. "He doesn't like leaving me, but one of his panels is sick. We need some fancy part. I don't understand what it is. Do you know about fancy machines, Jimmy?" Then she said, "I bet you do understand them."

He said nothing.

"Whenever he goes there," she said, "he brings back a nice little gift. I like gifts. If you were my husband, would you bring me gifts?"

He managed a step backwards.

"You're such a lovely boy, I think." She was much younger than Mom; he noticed it all at once. "Is anyone else staying in the cabins, Jimmy?"

"No," he muttered.

"Oh, you're here by yourself, are you?"

"My folks, and my sisters—"

"Is your father lovely like you? Is he?"

Jimmy was frightened, a great black dread forcing him to step back again. He watched the woman pull one of her lovely hands up and down the doorjamb, unbothered by splinters. She seemed to be caressing her home, still crouching, some kind of phony diamond being sold on the television behind her and her other hand in her lap, fingers curling, the housecoat and gown inching higher. The pale legs were smooth and the impossibly red toes wiggled and the quiet voice was telling him, "I feel so lonely, darling. Will you take pity on me, please?"

He saw between her legs, for an instant. Then came panic, and he was running before he made a conscious decision to run, rounding the fence and finding the trail again. He was oblivious to pain until he was past the skull-and-crossbones sign. Then he slowed, feeling cowardly, his wet clothes making him shiver and the limp returning, his entire leg sore. He could scarcely walk by the time he reached the cabin.

Mom asked, "What happened?" with an angry, caring voice.

He felt safe again. He wasn't sure how he was at risk before, but here he was safe.

"Let me look," she said. And he was a boy again, stripping and putting on sweatclothes, one pants leg pulled up over his knee. His sisters teased him, saying, "Jimmy's in trouble now." He didn't care. Mom washed the wound, then bandaged it and told him twenty times not to get it wet. Then again she asked, "What happened?"

He told about his fall, making it sound as if it happened nearby.

"Stay away from the lake," she advised. "We're a long ways from any hospital. Please don't be stupid."

Jimmy said he would be careful—now he had a promise with each parent—and he shut his eyes, pulling a scratchy blanket around himself. His sisters quit teasing, sensing that it did no good. He was left alone. On the sly he touched himself, finding an astonishing rigidity that took him by surprise; and he imagined Mrs. Greasy sitting on her brass bed, doctoring his leg, dipping her pretty face, and kissing the wound, blood like lipstick on her smiling mouth and her telling him, "And now we are married, my love."

The next astonishing event happened the next day, the sun breaking from the clouds and baking the island dry. That was followed by Mr. Greasy's appearance at the cabin door. He was smiling with his gruesome teeth, except it wasn't exactly a smile. He had a gift, a peace offering, handing Mom a heavy, hard package of white butcher paper. "Venison," he said. "I feel bad about not getting the power running. I thought maybe you'd like some venison steaks."

Mom muttered something like, "Oh, we've managed."

Dad was back from another fishless morning. "This is lovely," he sang. "Isn't it lovely, dear?"

Mom had to say, "It's nice, yes."

Mr. Greasy was watching Dad, that non-smile blending into something harder, red eyes smoldering. It took Jimmy a few moments to comprehend. The old man came home yesterday and found the rocks overturned at his gate, and who had seen his wife? He suspected Dad. He stared and gave an angry little snort, wiping at his mouth. Then he was saying, "I know what. Why don't I take you out tomorrow, show you some spots? I know where the big old pike hide."

Dad said, "Would you?"

"Like I say, I feel bad about things."

Jimmy felt cold, and he stepped backwards.

"A real guide," Dad was singing. "This is perfect."

The old man wiped at his mouth again, then noticed Jimmy. Jimmy was wearing shorts, his bandaged shin obvious. "Get winged, did you?"

With a certain pride, Dad said, "Oh, he went exploring. Had some little adventure, I guess."

Mr. Greasy read Jimmy's face, his thoughts. It took him an instant to comprehend everything, knowing that it wasn't Dad he wanted, and a real smile starting to show. This was just a kid, a nobody, and he dismissed Jimmy with a growling laugh.

Mom said, "Thank you for the meat."

Mr. Greasy turned to her and said, "Know where I got it?"

Nobody spoke.

"Every fall," he said, "there's always a few bucks who swim over here from the mainland. Always."

"Why?" asked Dad

A shrug of the shoulders. "They're in rut," he explained. "Bucks in rut do all kinds of crazy shit."

Dad said, "I see."

The ugly old man winked at Jimmy, saying, "They're nuisances, and know what I do with nuisances?" He bent his finger as if pulling on a trigger, firing twice.

Nobody spoke.

He turned back to Dad, saying, "See you at dawn. And hey, bring the boy. If he's up to some hard fishing, that is."

"Oh, he is. We both are."

Jimmy felt himself starting to melt.

Mr. Greasy walked out the door, saying, "Yeah, we'll have ourselves an adventure tomorrow."

"See?" Dad said. "Everything's looking up."

Mom watched Mr. Greasy vanish into the trees, heading home. Shaking her head, she said, "He feels bad, but he somehow doesn't get the electricity working again. Notice?" She lifted the steaks and remarked, "Frozen solid. Or didn't you notice?"

Nobody made a sound.

Jimmy became ill. It was one of those carefully structured flu bugs that kids master. He couldn't sleep, what with his worries, and he made a point of sitting in the bathroom for a big chunk of the night. Mom came to the door and knocked, asking if he was all right. He said, "I'm fine," but without conviction. Then he picked at his predawn breakfast, the oatmeal cooling and Mom asking again how he felt. "Fine," he replied. "I'm all right."

It was nearly nine o'clock when Mr. Greasy finally arrived. Jimmy heard the boat approaching, and he made a small sickly noise, rising and starting for the bathroom again.

"You aren't all right," said Mom.

Dad was picking up his tackle. "Come on, Jim. We've got to get out there."

Mom snagged Jimmy as he passed, putting a hand on his forehead. "Your son doesn't feel well."

It was news to Dad. "Since when?"

"I'm okay," Jimmy whimpered.

"What's the matter?" asked Dad.

He was sick from fear, if anyone cared.

Boots clomped on the porch. "Hello? Hello?"

"Is it the runs?" asked Mom.

"Yeah," Jimmy lied.

Mr. Greasy was looking in through the screen door. He was wearing a life jacket over the usual T-shirt, and he asked, "What's running?"

"It looks like it's just you and me," Dad reported. "And the pike."

"Yeah?"

"The boy's got a touch of something." Dad opened the door while holding all of his tackle, giving Jimmy a teasing wink. "Too bad you can't come with us. It'll be fun."

Mr. Greasy was glaring in at him. "He doesn't look that sick."

"I am," Jimmy protested, scarcely above a whisper.

"It's the water," Mom offered. "It'll pass."

"That it does," Mr. Greasy agreed. He sounded certain, telling Jimmy, "If you want to get well, son, stay close to home. Stay in bed, if you know what's good for you."

Dad was off the porch, tackle box in one hand and two poles in the other. "Is it too late to get the big ones?"

Mr. Greasy shook his head.

Mom got up to get the thermometer.

"A twenty-pound pike," said Dad. "That's what I want."

Once again, Mr. Greasy pulled the imaginary trigger, killing another rut-crazed deer.

Jimmy went to bed, as instructed by Mr. Greasy and Mom, and he managed to sleep hard for a couple hours, exhaustion combined with relief at having escaped. He dreamed and woke, touching himself afterwards and feeling that astonishing stiffness again. What did he dream? He couldn't recall anything more than a vague warmth and someone crying out. In pain? He couldn't decide. Sitting up on his cot, he blinked and wiped at his eyes, realizing the cabin was empty. Mom had taken his sisters somewhere, probably to let him sleep.

The day was bright and warm. Jimmy found himself outside, walking fast, passing the skull-and-crossbones sign and then starting to run. There was a pile of deer skulls and antlers off in the brush; he hadn't noticed them before. The farther he went, the louder birds sang. Behind the log home was a shed where a bear hide had been hung up to dry, the pelt black and glossy. And fresh. Jimmy kept running, around to the front, to the gate, starting to turn the rocks over in a crazy panic. Where was the key—?

"Jimmy?" said Mrs. Greasy. "Oh, I was hoping you would come see me. And here you are!"

The boy felt faint, rising and turning, grasping the chain-link and his eyes having trouble with the simple task of focusing. Mrs. Greasy was standing in the doorway, just like the other day. She was wearing a new nightgown but no housecoat, those same red toes curling over the doorjamb.

But her face wasn't the same—

"He knows about you, Jimmy. I didn't tell him, but he knows."

—and he realized how her face had changed. She looked younger, and not just a little bit. Mrs. Greasy looked sixteen, at the oldest. Her gown was sheer and the sunshine reached to her skin. He could see her breasts and ribs and how her waist narrowed, how her long legs were a little apart and how there wasn't any hair between them. There was still forty feet between them, yet he could see minuscule details whenever he looked at her. Pink flesh glowed with its own inner light. The rest of the world was out of focus, inconsequential.

She was saying, "He doesn't like visitors coming to see me," and she laughed, sounding like a teenage girl pleased with being popular. "But I doubt if he fears you very much. Not much."

He shook the gate once, then again.

"Would you like some soup, Jimmy?"

"Come open this," he whispered.

"I cannot," she replied. "You know that."

"Why not?"

"You know why."

And she was right. More than beautiful, she had an enormous simplicity. One long look could teach any man or boy everything he would ever need to know about her. "How is your leg, Jimmy?"

He blinked and said, "Better."

"Come show me, Jimmy."

He wanted nothing else. He turned away long enough to find a stone, a good rugged piece of granite, and he drove it into the padlock half a dozen times, making a series of tiny, useless dents.

"Harder," she coached.

But he was tired, arms shaking and the stone tumbling out of his hands, missing his toes by nothing and rolling away from him. For a moment he thought he heard a motor, someone's boat out on the lake. But he couldn't see the water from there, the motor's purr dissolving into bird songs and the sound of the wind that made the tall pines nod with a calm dignity.

"I can't break it," he confessed, ashamed of his weakness.

"You need to be persistent, Jimmy." She waited for a moment, then said, "Climb the fence, if you would like."

He glanced at the barbed wire, whispering, "I couldn't."

"I have seen it climbed," she assured him.

"I'll get cut."

"Not too badly, I should think."

He decided to try the stone again, finding new strength and the practice helping his aim. The padlock jumped and jerked with the blows, its face peppered with dents. If he could keep at it all day, without pause, he might wear the lock down. Then the gate would open and he could reach the cabin, gladly living out the rest of his life—a few vivid hours of pleasure—and when Mr. Greasy arrived home Jimmy would be shot out of hand. Shot and his body disposed of in the usual way. Buried in the trash pile, perhaps. Or anchored with stones and dropped into the black glacial waters.

He despised the old man. Almost as much as he loved the woman, he despised *him*. When his arms tired, Jimmy imagined a new way to kill Mr. Greasy, fury making the stone light and his aim true. He pushed himself to exhaustion, then paused and gasped, dimly aware of a woman's voice. He didn't recognize it. She was nobody of consequence. Again he focused on the lock, lifting the granite, and his mother grabbed his wrist, shouting, "What, Jimmy, what? What are you doing?"

Her face was strange, bewildered and wild and startling. Why did she look so strange? For a slippery instant he didn't know where he was or what he was doing—

—And she asked, "Who's that woman?"

Jimmy couldn't see anyone. The cabin's door was shut tight.

"I saw her," Mom was telling herself. "I promised the girls a boat ride, and we came here . . . since he's gone . . . to see what's so secret . . ."

Jimmy dropped the stone again, arms burning.

"Who is she?"

"Mrs. Greasy," said Jimmy.

"And he's got her locked up in there," Mom said to herself, anger in the words. "That bastard. That son-of-a-bitch bastard."

Jimmy told Mom next to nothing. He had spoken to a woman, and yes, he was trying to break the lock. She assumed he wanted to free her, which was a good thing. The right thing. He mentioned the spare key under a rock, and Mom shouted at his sisters, telling them, "We're looking for a key. Roll over the rocks, girls. Between here and the dock."

The twins were still wearing their life jackets, as if expecting the island to submerge itself any moment. They made a game of the hunt, and Jimmy halfheartedly helped, sometimes pausing to look back at the tiny house, thinking how it seemed empty now and this wasn't what Mrs. Greasy wanted.

"I found it," said a sister.

"I did," said the other one.

"No, I did."

"Thank you, both of you," Mom said diplomatically. Then she tried it in the padlock, and Jimmy heard the click and saw the gate swing open. He felt excitement mixed with a powerful disappointment, wishing he were alone. Mom told his sisters to stay put and wait, then she looked at him, saying, "Imagine. Locking up your wife, in this day and age."

Jimmy said nothing.

She started for the house, mounting its simple plank stairs and smacking the door with her fist, waiting and trying again. A bolt was thrown. The door opened, Mrs. Greasy smiling out at them. Her face had changed again. She had aged, the platinum hair turning white and her features worn but not wrinkled. She could have been an old man's wife. She looked like a one-time movie star, smiling with perfect teeth and asking, "What may I do for you, miss?"

"I don't know how," Mom said. "Maybe we can hide you. For now. Then we can take you to the mainland tonight—"

"Why?"

"So you can escape." A slow astonishment spread across Mom's face. "Don't you want to escape?"

The old face said nothing.

"Or maybe we could call the authorities, if you want—"

"I can't leave." She was wearing the old housecoat again; the room behind her was dark save for the bluish glow of the television. "I'm very happy here, thank you."

"No," Mom protested. "You can't be, no."

Jimmy was behind Mom, and he started to move closer.

"I have everything I need here," said the old woman. "Why should I want to leave?"

"She can't leave," said Jimmy.

Mrs. Greasy looked at him and smiled. "Hello, darling. Darling Jimmy."

Mom was confused by the voice's affection.

"She has to stay here," he told Mom. Couldn't she understand that?

"But you're a prisoner," Mom maintained. "You're being held against your will."

"My will." Mrs. Greasy seemed intrigued. "My will?"

Mom moved, up the first step and grabbing at the old woman, getting a handful of housecoat and not pulling hard, shouting, "You poor thing." Then the housecoat fell on her, still buttoned up in front but nothing inside it. She gave a startled sound, quick and soft, then a loud moan when she saw Mrs. Greasy still standing in the doorway. Changed now. Her hair was young again. Her weight had moved on her bones. Suddenly she was Mom's age wearing a sheer nightgown; and Mom staggered backwards, striking Jimmy and him bracing her as she collapsed to the ground.

"What are you?" Mom was pale and nervous and stubborn, saying, "What's the trick?"

Jimmy said, "She's like a ghost."

Mrs. Greasy said nothing.

"What are you?" Mom repeated. "I won't leave until you tell me."

Smiling, the apparition motioned towards her television, reporting, "I know what ghosts are. I see programs, news reports . . . but I'm something else, I think."

Nobody spoke.

"I do love my television," she said. "There was a program about the universe, how most of it is made of darkness that can be felt but not seen. That is me. This body is something I fashion out of your ordinary stuff. This body is no more me than that old robe is."

Mom began to stand, legs wobbling.

"I am rooted here, miss. Whatever I am, I require nothing but devotion and love. Perhaps I belong to some species that consumes those emotions. Or perhaps I'm someone's bait, a fancy lure meant to hook male souls." A pause. "Honestly, I don't know. I can invent a thousand stories that might explain my existence, which means I can explain nothing."

"How old are you?" Mom muttered.

"I remember the weight of the glaciers," she replied. "This was a treeless island when I woke, and I seduced my first husband—"

"What, an Indian?"

"A wolverine," Mrs. Greasy replied. Then she shook her head, adding, "Wolverines are very poor husbands, I think."

Mom gave a nervous little laugh.

"I have possessed all kinds, and human males are best. Though far from perfect." She nodded with authority and a vague amusement. "To the Indians, I was an enchanting maiden. To the trappers, I was a witch. My island was famous, and feared, and I think you know how men can be, miss. Men fear *fear* so much, they will do anything in its face to prove themselves, if only to themselves."

"They do," Mom whispered, nodding.

"Bert, my Bert, came here to hunt. He wasn't twice your age, Jimmy." A wink. "His guide wouldn't step ashore, knowing the legends. But Bert came here and found this cabin, and he shot the bear living inside it. My last human husband had died several years before. I transformed this body for Bert. For forty years, I have kept him enthralled."

"He's an ugly man," Mom grumbled.

"Yet he is perfectly devoted to me." A wistful expression, and she said, "Bert built the lodge and cabins to make money in order to buy me gifts. I appreciate gifts. And in his youth, his prime, he could show his devotion every day, if you know what I mean."

Jimmy felt the longing, stark and intoxicating.

"Poor Bert," Mrs. Greasy continued. "Age diminishes him. I can't help but follow my nature, calling for suitors, and he has to deal with them as best he can—"

"Suitors?" said Mom.

"What is a lady to do?" The apparition sighed and said, "They come to me, sensing my needs, and Bert has to do what he does—"

"What does he do?"

She seemed to lose the thought, eyes focusing on Jimmy and winking again, flirting with him. Suddenly she was fifteen, very pretty, her painted toes curling over that top stair, and her soft voice was saying, "If you were older, I might. A young man could put the resort on its feet again, and he could build me a better house—"

Mom grabbed Jimmy's arm, squeezing it.

"—But you are too young, and I know he would kill you." Then she told his mother, "Take him home. It's too soon and too much, and I give him back to you. One woman to another." And then she closed the heavy door, throwing the bolt, Jimmy up the stairs and beating on it while crying and screaming and his mother pulling him back, halfway carrying him to the gate and past. Only then did the spell diminish to where he could see again, noticing his little sisters standing in the distance, eyes huge and something terrifying them and Jimmy honestly unsure why that terror should be.

Mr. Greasy brought Dad back at dusk. Everyone waited down by the dock, Mom relieved and scared in equal measures. As the boat pulled in, she warned her children to act perfectly normal. Mr. Greasy was already staring at Jimmy, judging the threat. Dad was oblivious, climbing from the boat with an enormous northern pike. "Caught him on a spoon," he announced. "Twenty-plus pounds. And you should have seen him fight!"

Jimmy wondered if Mr. Greasy would shoot him. He almost wanted to be shot, thinking that's what it would take to stop his intense longing.

"Get the camera," said Dad. "Take my picture, will you?"

"Later," Mom replied.

"Now. Before the light's gone."

Mr. Greasy looked at Mom, asking, "How's the boy? Did he sit on the crapper all day?"

"All day," she answered.

"Well," he said, "that's good. That's what he needed, huh?"

Dad seemed momentarily confused, but his satisfaction returned. He lifted the big dripping fish with both hands on the stringer, and he shouted at his son, "Come look. Proud of your old man now, are you?"

Jimmy came out onto the dock.

Mom said, "Stay there."

"Why?" asked Dad. "What's wrong?"

"Nothing," she snapped. Then she said, "He's still sick. I want him to take it easy."

The old man watched with caution and amusement.

Jimmy never looked at the fish. He came up and made a gun with his hand, pointing it at Mr. Greasy's head. Bang-bang.

Mr. Greasy gave a snort, then laughed. "Fuck you, you little shit. You don't fucking scare me."

"What?" said Dad.

"Go sit down," said Mom.

"You're a goddamn little kid," the old man warned. "Fish bait, that's all."

"Get out of here," Mom told Mr. Greasy. "Will you just leave us alone?"

Dad had no idea what was happening. He lowered his trophy to the wood planks, stepped back and muttered, "What's happened? What?"

Mr. Greasy spat on the dock—a great wet glob—and said, "I hope he stayed home. I hope his mom watched him." Then he revved the engine and pulled away, out of the cove and out of sight.

"Get in the skiff," said Mom. "Now. Please."

"He's still got my tackle," Dad was saying. "Damn. I'll have to get it back tomorrow—"

"*Get in the boat!*"

She had brought Jimmy and the twins back in the skiff, then loaded its red tank with fresh gasoline. Who knew what Mr. Greasy would do when he saw the battered lock? She pulled her husband closer, then spoke in a low, angry, and uncompromising voice, and when he tried to step back, she tugged harder and said, "Do this for me, please. Please."

Dad said, "What about our luggage?"

"We don't have room for it."

"My wallet?"

"Here. I brought it." Mom waved to the girls, saying, "Come on. Climb down in here, please."

Dad saw their expressions, then noticed Jimmy's for the first time, finding something worth worrying about.

The girls were ready, orange life jackets over warm clothes. Mom made Jimmy climb in between them, then she said, "If you love me, do this. Don't ask questions. Just do it."

Dad got in the front, his face uncomprehending. Baffled. Mom untied the skiff and jumped in and pulled the cord and opened the throttle, and Dad finally realized, "We forgot my fish!"

She ignored him. All that mattered was distance, crossing the rough, open water by memory, hoping they could find the right bay and their car and that the car would start, buying them more distance. Jimmy wasn't certain what they were fleeing. The old man, or the apparition? Sometimes Jimmy looked back at the island, and Mom would smack him on the arm, as a warning. "I don't understand," Dad kept saying. "What woman? What danger? This is all just crazy, crazy, crazy. . . ."

Jimmy shut his eyes, picturing Mrs. Greasy.

Over the sound of the outboard, Mom screamed, "What are you thinking?"

"I want my fish," Dad answered.

"Not you. Shut up." Then she leaned close to her son, asking, "What are you thinking, dear?"

"Nothing," Jimmy lied. "About nothing."

"Don't think of her," she warned. "She gave you back to me. Remember? You belong to me, Jimmy."

Maybe for now. But one day, in a very few years, he would be old enough to leave home and come back here. He wouldn't even need a boat if he came in the winter, walking across the ice with a rifle in hand, then putting a bullet into Mr. Greasy, freeing him of his soul.

"Here, Jimmy," said Dad, working something carefully out of his fishing-vest pocket. "This is what I used to catch it."

The boy found a red-and-white spoon in his hands, almost filling them. He imagined the lure moving in the water, enticing fish with its motions and speed, and the brilliant flashes of reflected light. If he were a fish, he thought, he would bite on such a thing. Even if he knew it wasn't food, he would take it into his mouth.

"It was some fish," said Dad. "And it was mine!"

If someone or something worked hard to entice you, thought Jimmy, *then they had to genuinely treasure you.*

You could be sure.

And now he dropped the spoon and touched himself, not caring who noticed, smiling and smiling as they moved across the endless black water.

Joyce Carol Oates

In addition to being a respected novelist, short story writer, playwright, poet, and essayist, Joyce Carol Oates is the Roger S. Berlind Distinguished Professor in the Humanities at Princeton University. She won the National Book Award for her novel *Them*, and is the 1994 recipient of the Bram Stoker Award for Life Achievement in Horror Fiction. She is the author, most recently, of *Zombie*, a short novel about a serial killer, *What I Lived For*, nominated for the Pen/Faulkner Award, and *First Love: A Gothic Tale*. She has published three collections of her dark fiction: *Night-Side, Demon and other tales*, and *Haunted: Tales of the Grotesque*. Her short stories have appeared in *Omni, Playboy, The New Yorker, Harper's Magazine*, and *The Atlantic*, as well as in literary magazines and in anthologies such as *Architecture of Fear, Dark Forces, Metahorror, Little Deaths*, and has had stories in *Prize Stories: The O. Henry Awards*, and in previous volumes of *The Year's Best Fantasy & Horror*.

▬▬▬▬▬▬▬▬ can be read literally and/or symbolically, but either way, it's quite full of terror. It is reprinted from *Fear Itself*, edited by Jeff Gelb.

—E.D.

It was the most beautiful house I had ever seen up close. Or was ever to enter. Three storys high, broad, and gleaming pale pink, made of sandstone, Uncle Rebhorn said, custom-designed and *his* design of course. They came to get me— Uncle Rebhorn, Aunt Elinor, my cousin Audrey, who was my age, and my cousin Darren who was three years older—one Sunday in July 1969. How excited I was, how special I felt, singled out for a visit to Uncle Rebhorn's house in Grosse Pointe Shores. I see the house shimmering before me and then I see emptiness, a strange rectangular blackness, and nothing.

For at the center of what happened on that Sunday many years ago is blackness.

I can remember what led to the blackness and what followed after it—not clearly, but to a degree, as, waking vague and stunned from a powerful dream, we retain shreds of the dream though we remain incapable of making them coalesce into a whole; nor can we "see" them as we'd seen them during the dream. So I can summon back a memory of the black rectangle and I can superimpose depth upon it—for it could not be flat, like a canvas—but I have to admit defeat, I can't "see" anything inside it. And this black rectangle is at the center of that Sunday in July 1969, and at the center of my girlhood.

Unless it was the end of my girlhood.

But how do I know, if I can't remember?

I was eleven years old. It was to be my first time ever—and it was to be the last time, too, though I didn't know it then—that I was brought by my father's older stepbrother, Uncle Rebhorn, to visit his new house and to go sailing on Lake St. Clair. Because of my cousin Audrey, who was like a sister of mine though I saw her rarely—I guessed this was why. Mommy told me, in a careful, neutral voice, that of course Audrey didn't have any friends, or Darren either. I asked why and Mommy said they just didn't, that's all. That's the price you pay for *moving up* too quickly in the world.

All our family lived in the Detroit suburb of Hamtramck and had lived there for a long time. Uncle Rebhorn too, until the age of eighteen when he left and now, how many years later, he was a rich man—president of Rebhorn Auto Supply, Inc., and he'd married a well-to-do Grosse Pointe woman—and built his big, beautiful new house on Lake St. Clair everybody in the family talked about but nobody had actually seen. (Unless they'd seen the house from the outside? Not my parents, who were too proud to stoop to such a maneuver, but other relatives were said to have driven all the way to Grosse Pointe Shores to gape at Uncle Rebhorn's pink mansion, as much as they could see of it from Buena Vista Drive. Uninvited, they dared not ring the buzzer at the wrought-iron gate, shut and presumably locked at the foot of the drive.) Uncle Rebhorn, whom I did not know at all, had left Hamtramck far behind and was said to "scorn" his upbringing and his own family. There was a good deal of jealousy of course, and envy, but since everybody hoped secretly to be remembered by him sometime, and invited to share in his amazing good fortune—imagine, a millionaire in the family!—they were always sending cards, wedding invitations, announcements of births and christenings and confirmations; sometimes even telegrams, since Uncle Rebhorn's telephone number was unlisted and even his brothers didn't know what it was. Daddy said, with that heavy, sullen droop to his voice we tried never to hear, "If he wants to keep to himself that's fine, I can respect that. We'll keep to ourselves, too."

Then, out of nowhere, the invitation came to *me*. Just a telephone call from Aunt Elinor.

Mommy, who'd taken the call, of course, and made the arrangements, didn't want me to stay overnight. Aunt Elinor had suggested this for it was a long drive, between forty-five minutes and an hour, and she'd said that Audrey would be disappointed, but Mommy said no and that was that.

So, that Sunday, how vividly I can remember!—Uncle Rebhorn, Aunt Elinor, Audrey, and Darren came to get me in Uncle Rebhorn's shiny black Lincoln Continental, which rolled like a hearse up our street of woodframe asphalt-sided bungalows and drew stares from our neighbors. Daddy was gone—Daddy was not going to hang around, he said, on the chance of saying hello and maybe getting to shake hands with his stepbrother—but Mommy was with me, waiting at the front door when Uncle Rebhorn pulled up; but there were no words exchanged between Mommy and the Rebhorns, for Uncle Rebhorn merely tapped the car horn to signal their arrival, and Aunt Elinor, though she waved and smiled at

Mommy, did not get out of the car, and made not the slightest gesture inviting Mommy to come out to speak with *her*. I ran breathless to the curb—I had a panicky vision of Uncle Rebhorn starting the big black car up and leaving me behind in Hamtramck—and climbed into the back seat, to sit beside Audrey. "Get in, hurry, we don't have all day," Uncle Rebhorn said in that gruff jovial cartoon voice some adults use with children, meant to be playful—or maybe not. Aunt Elinor cast me a frowning sort of smile over her shoulder and put her finger to her lips as if to indicate that I take Uncle Rebhorn's remark in silence, as naturally I would. My heart was hammering with excitement just to be in such a magnificent automobile!

How fascinating the drive from our familiar neighborhood into the city of Detroit where there were so many black people on the streets and many of them, glimpsing Uncle Rebhorn's Lincoln Continental, stared openly. We moved swiftly along Outer Drive and so to Eight Mile Road and east to Lake St. Clair where I had never been before, and I could not believe how beautiful everything was once we turned onto Lakeshore Drive. Now it was my turn to stare and stare. Such mansions on grassy hills facing the lake! So many tall trees, so much leafy space! So much sky! (The sky in Hamtramck was usually low and overcast and wrinkled like soiled laundry.) And Lake St. Clair, which was a deep rich aqua, like a painted lake! During most of the drive, Uncle Rebhorn was talking, pointing out the mansions of wealthy, famous people—I only remember "Ford"—"Dodge"—"Fisher"—"Wilson"—and Aunt Elinor was nodding and murmuring inaudibly, and in the back seat, silent and subdued, Audrey and Darren and I sat looking out the tinted windows. I was a little hurt and disappointed that Audrey seemed to be ignoring me, and sitting very stiffly beside me; though I guessed that, with Uncle Rebhorn talking continuously, and addressing his remarks to the entire car, Audrey did not want to seem to interrupt him. Nor did Darren say a word to anyone.

At last, in Grosse Pointe Shores, we turned off Lakeshore Drive onto a narrow, curving road called Buena Vista, where the mansions were smaller, though still mansions; Buena Vista led into a cul-de-sac bordered by tall, massive oaks and elms. At the very end, overlooking the lake, was Uncle Rebhorn's house—as I've said, the most beautiful house I had ever seen up close, or would ever enter. Made of that pale pink glimmering sandstone, with a graceful portico covered in English ivy, and four slender columns, and dozens of latticed windows reflecting the sun like smiles, the house looked like a storybook illustration. And beyond was the sky, a pure cobalt blue except for thin wisps of cloud. Uncle Rebhorn pressed a button in the dashboard of his car, and the wrought-iron gate swung open—like nothing I'd ever seen before in real life. The driveway too was like no driveway I knew, curving and dipping, and comprised of rosy-pink gravel, exquisite as miniature seashells. Tiny pebbles flew up beneath the car as Uncle Rebhorn drove in and the gate swung miraculously shut behind us.

How lucky Audrey was to live here, I thought, gnawing at my thumbnail as Mommy had told me a thousand times not to do. Oh I would die to live in such a house, I thought.

Uncle Rebhorn seemed to have heard me. "*We* think so, yes indeed," he said. To my embarrassment, he was watching me through the rearview mirror and seemed to be winking at me. His eyes glittered bright and teasing. Had I spoken out loud without meaning to?—I could feel my face burn.

Darren, squeezed against the farther armrest, made a sniggering, derisive noise. He had not so much as glanced at me when I climbed into the car and had been sulky during the drive so I felt that he did not like me. He was a fattish, flaccid-skinned boy who looked more like twelve than fourteen; he had Uncle Rebhorn's lard-colored complexion and full, drooping lips, but not Uncle Rebhorn's shrewd-glittering eyes; his were damp and close-set and mean. Whatever Darren meant by his snigger, Uncle Rebhorn heard it above the hum of the air conditioner—was there anything Uncle Rebhorn could not hear?—and said in a low, pleasant, warning voice, "Son, mind your manners! Or somebody else will mind them for you."

Darren protested, "I didn't say anything, sir. I—"

Quickly, Aunt Elinor intervened, "Darren."

"—I'm sorry, sir. I won't do it again."

Uncle Rebhorn chuckled as if he found this very funny and in some way preposterous. But by this time he had pulled the magnificent black car up in front of the portico of the house and switched off the ignition. "Here we are!"

But to enter Uncle Rebhorn's sandstone mansion, it was strange, and a little scary, how we had to crouch. And push and squeeze our shoulders through the doorway. Even Audrey and me, who were the smallest. As we approached the big front door which was made of carved wood, with a beautiful gleaming brass American eagle, its dimensions seemed to shrink; the closer we got, the smaller the door got, reversing the usual circumstances where of course as you approach an object it increases in size, or gives that illusion. "Girls, watch your heads," Uncle Rebhorn cautioned, wagging his forefinger. He had a brusque laughing way of speaking as if most subjects were jokes or could be made to seem so by laughing. But his eyes, bright as chips of glass, were watchful and without humor.

How could this be?—Uncle Rebhorn's house that was so spacious-seeming on the outside was so cramped, and dark, and scary on the inside?

"Come on, come on! It's Sunday, it's the Sabbath, we haven't got all day!" Uncle Rebhorn cried, clapping his hands.

We were in a kind of tunnel, crowded together. There was a strong smell of something sharp and hurtful like ammonia; at first I couldn't breathe, and started to choke. Nobody paid any attention to me except Audrey who tugged at my wrist, whispering, "This way, June—don't make Daddy mad." Uncle Rebhorn led the way, followed by Darren, then Aunt Elinor, Audrey, and me, walking on our haunches in a squatting position; the tunnel was too low for standing upright and you couldn't crawl on your hands and knees because the floor was littered with shards of glass. Why was it so dark? Where were the windows I'd seen from the outside? "Isn't this fun! We're so glad you could join us today, June!" Aunt Elinor murmured. How awkward it must have been for a woman like Aunt Elinor, so prettily dressed in a tulip-yellow summer knit suit, white high-heeled pumps, and stockings, to make her way on her haunches in such a cramped space!—yet she did it uncomplaining, and with a smile.

Strands of cobweb brushed against my face. I was breathing so hard and in such a choppy way it sounded like sobbing which scared me because I knew Uncle Rebhorn would be offended. Several times Audrey squeezed my wrist so hard it hurt, cautioning me to be quiet; Aunt Elinor poked at me, too. Uncle Rebhorn was saying, cheerfully, "Who's hungry?—I'm starving," and again, in a louder voice, "Who's hungry?" and Darren echoed, "I'm starving!" and Uncle Rebhorn repeated bright and brassy as a TV commercial, *"Who's hungry?"* and this time Aunt Elinor, Darren, Audrey, and I echoed in a chorus, *"I'm starving!"* Which was the correct reply, Uncle Rebhorn accepted it with a happy chuckle.

Now we were in a larger space, the tunnel had opened out onto a room crowded with cartons and barrels, stacks of lumber and tar pots, workmen's things scattered about. There were two windows in this room but they were small and square and crudely criss-crossed by strips of plywood; there were no windowpanes, only fluttering strips of cheap transparent plastic that blocked out most of the light. I could not stop shivering though Audrey pinched me hard, and cast me an anxious, angry look. Why, when it was a warm summer day outside, was it so cold inside Uncle Rebhorn's house? Needles of freezing air rose from the floorboards. The sharp ammonia odor was mixed with a smell of food cooking which made my stomach queasy. Uncle Rebhorn was criticizing Aunt Elinor in his joky angry way, saying she'd let things go a bit, hadn't she?—and Aunt Elinor was frightened, stammering and pressing her hand against her bosom, saying the interior decorator had promised everything would be in place by now. "Plenty of time for Christmas, eh?" Uncle Rebhorn said sarcastically. For some reason, both Darren and Audrey giggled.

Uncle Rebhorn had a thick, strong neck and his head swiveled alertly and his eyes swung onto you before you were prepared—those gleaming, glassy-glittering eyes. There was a glisten to the whites of Uncle Rebhorn's eyes I had never seen in anyone before and his pupils were dilated and very black. He was a stocky man; he panted and made a snuffling noise, his wide nostrils flattened with deep, impatient inhalations. His pale skin was flushed, especially in the cheeks; there was a livid, feverish look to his face. He was dressed for Sunday in a red-plaid sport coat that fitted him tightly in the shoulders, and a white shirt with a necktie, and navy blue linen trousers that had picked up some cobwebs on our way in. Uncle Rebhorn had a glowing bald spot at the crown of his head over which he had carefully combed wetted strands of hair; his cheeks were bunched like muscles as he smiled. And smiled. How hard it was to look at Uncle Rebhorn, his eyes so glittering, and his *smile*—! When I try to remember him now miniature slices of blindness skid toward me in my vision, I have to blink carefully to regain my full sight. And why am I shivering, I must put an end to such neurotic behavior, what other purpose to this memoir?—what other purpose to any effort of the retrieval of memory that gives such pain?

Uncle Rebhorn chuckled deep in his throat and wagged a forefinger at me, "Naughty girl, I know what *you're* thinking," he said, and at once my face burned, I could feel my freckles standing out like hot inflamed pimples, though I did not know what he meant. Audrey, beside me, giggled again nervously, and Uncle Rebhorn shook his forefinger at her, too, "And you, honeybunch,—for sure, Daddy knows *you.*" He made a sudden motion at us the way one might gesture at a cowering dog to further frighten it, or to mock its fear; when, clutching at each other, Audrey and I flinched away, Uncle Rebhorn roared with laughter, raising his bushy eyebrows as if he was puzzled, and hurt. "Mmmmm girls, you don't think I'm going to hit you, do you?"

Quickly Audrey stammered, "Oh no, Daddy—*no.*"

I was so frightened I could not speak at all. I tried to hide behind Audrey who was shivering as badly as I was.

"You *don't* think I'm going to hit you, eh?" Uncle Rebhorn said, more menacingly; he swung his fist playfully in my direction and a strand of hair caught in his signet ring and I squealed with pain which made him laugh, and relent a little. Watching me, Darren and Audrey and even Aunt Elinor laughed. Aunt Elinor tidied my hair and again pressed a finger to her lips as if in warning.

I am not a naughty girl I wanted to protest and now too *I am not to blame.*

For Sunday dinner we sat on packing cases and ate from planks balanced across two sawhorses. A dwarfish olive-skinned woman with a single fierce eyebrow waited on us, wearing a white rayon uniform and a hairnet. She set plates down before us sulkily, though, with Uncle Rebhorn, who kept up a steady teasing banter with her, calling her "honey" and "sweetheart," she did exchange a smile. Aunt Elinor pretended to notice nothing, encouraging Audrey and me to eat. The dwarf-woman glanced at me with a look of contempt, guessing I was a poor relation I suppose, her dark eyes raked me like a razor.

Uncle Rebhorn and Darren ate hungrily. Father and son hunched over the improvised table in the same posture, bringing their faces close to their plates and, chewing, turning their heads slightly to the sides, eyes moist with pleasure. "Mmmmm!—good," Uncle Rebhorn declared. And Darren echoed, "—*good.*" Aunt Elinor and Audrey were picking at their food, managing to eat some of it, but I was nauseated and terrified of being sick to my stomach. The food was lukewarm, served in plastic containers. There were coarse slabs of tough, bright pink meat curling at the edges and leaking blood, and puddles of corn pudding, corn kernels, and slices of onion and green pepper in a runny pale sauce like pus. Uncle Rebhorn gazed up from his plate, his eyes soft at first, then regaining some of their glassy glitter when he saw how little his wife and daughter and niece had eaten. "Say, what's up? 'Waste not, want not.' Remember"—here he reached over and jabbed my shoulder with his fork—"this is the Sabbath, and keep it holy. Eh?"

Aunt Elinor smiled encouragingly at me. Her lipstick was crimson pink and glossy, a permanent smile; her hair was a shining pale blond like a helmet. She wore pretty pale-pink pearls in her ears and a matching necklace around her neck. In the car, she had seemed younger than my mother, but now, close up, I could see hairline creases in her skin, or actual cracks, as in glazed pottery; there was something out of focus in her eyes though she was looking directly at me. "June, dear, there is a hunger beyond hunger," she said softly, "and this is the hunger that must be reached."

Uncle Rebhorn added, emphatically, "And we're Americans. Remember *that.*"

Somehow, I managed to eat what was on my plate. *I am not a naughty girl but a good girl: see!*

For dessert, the dwarf-woman dropped bowls in front of us containing a quivering amber jelly. I thought it might be apple jelly, apple jelly with cinnamon, and my mouth watered in anticipation. We were to eat with spoons but my spoon wasn't sharp enough to cut into the jelly; and the jelly quivered harder, and wriggled in my bowl. Seeing the look on my face, Uncle Rebhorn asked pleasantly, "What's wrong now, Junie?" and I mumbled, "I don't know, sir," and Uncle Rebhorn chuckled, and said, "Hmmmm! You don't think your dessert is a *jellyfish*, do you?"—roaring with delight, as the others laughed, less forcefully, with him.

For that was exactly what it was: a jellyfish. Each of us had one, in our bowls. Warm and pulsing with life and fear radiating from it like raw nerves. ▬▬▬▬▬▬ ▬▬▬▬▬▬▬▬▬ flicking toward me, slivers of blindness. Unless fissures in the air itself?—fibrillations like those at the onset of sleep the way dreams begin to skid toward you—at you—into you—and there is no escape for the dream *is* you.

Yes I would like to cease my memoir here. I am not accustomed to writing, to selecting words with such care. When I speak, I often stammer but there is a comfort in that—nobody knows, what comfort!—for you hold back what you must say, hold it back until it is fully your own and cannot surprise you. *I am not to blame, I am not deserving of hurt neither then nor now* but do I believe this, even if I cannot succeed in having you believe it.

How can an experience belong to you if you cannot remember it? That is the extent of what I wish to know. If I cannot remember it, how then can I summon it back to comprehend it, still less to change it. *And why am I shivering, when the sun today is poison-hot burning through the foliage dry and crackling as papier-mâché yet I keep shivering shivering shivering if there is a God in heaven please forgive me.*

After Sunday dinner we were to go sailing. Uncle Rebhorn had a beautiful white sailboat bobbing at the end of a dock, out there in the lake, which was a rich deep aqua blue scintillating with light. On Lake St. Clair on this breezy summer afternoon there were many sailboats, speedboats, yachts. I had stared at them in wondering admiration as we'd driven along the Lakeshore Drive. What a dazzling sight like nothing in Hamtramck!

First, though, we had to change our clothes. All of us, said Uncle Rebhorn, have to change into bathing suits.

Audrey and I changed in a dark cubbyhole beneath a stairway. This was Audrey's room and nobody was supposed to come inside to disturb us but the door was pushing inward and Audrey whimpered, "No, no Daddy," laughing nervously and trying to hold the door shut with her arm. I was a shy child; when I had to change for gym class at school I turned my back to the other girls and changed as quickly as I could. Even showing my panties to another girl was embarrassing to me, my face burned with a strange wild heat. Uncle Rebhorn was on the other side of the door, we could hear his harsh labored breathing. His voice was light, though, when he asked, "Hmmmm—d'you naughty little girls need any help getting your panties down? Or your bathing suits on?" "No, Daddy, please," Audrey said. Her eyes were wide and stark in her face and she seemed not aware of me any longer but in a space of her own, trembling, hunched over. I was scared, too, but thinking why don't we joke with Uncle Rebhorn, he wants us to joke with him, that's the kind of man he is, what harm could he do us?—the most any adult had ever done to me by the age of eleven was Grandpa tickling me a little too hard so I'd screamed with laughter and kicked but that was years ago when I'd been a baby practically, and while I had not liked being tickled it was nothing truly painful or scary—was it? I tried to joke with my uncle through the door, I was giggling saying, "No no no, you stay out of here, Uncle Rebhorn! We don't need your help no we don't!"

There was a moment's silence, then Uncle Rebhorn chuckled appreciatively, but there came then suddenly the sound of Aunt Elinor's raised voice, and we heard a sharp slap, and a cry, a female cry immediately cut off. And the door ceased its inward movement, and Audrey shoved me whispering, "Hurry up! You dumb dope, hurry up!" So quickly—safely—we changed into our bathing suits.

It was a surprise, how by chance Audrey's and my bathing suits looked alike, and us like twin sisters in them: both were pretty shades of pink, with elasticized tops that fitted tight over our tiny, flat breasts. Mine had emerald green seahorses sewn onto the bodice and Audrey's had little ruffles, the suggestion of a skirt.

Seeing my face, which must have shown hurt, Audrey hugged me with her thin, cold arms. I thought she would say how much she liked me, I was her favorite cousin, she was happy to see me—but she didn't say anything at all.

Beyond the door Uncle Rebhorn was shouting and clapping his hands.

"C'mon move your sweet little asses! Chop-chop! Time's a-wastin'! There'll be hell to pay if we've lost the sun!"

Audrey and I crept out in our bathing suits and Aunt Elinor grabbed us by the hands making an annoyed "tsking" sound and pulling us hurriedly along. We had to push our way out of a small doorway—no more than an opening, a hole, in the wall—and then we were outside, on the back lawn of Uncle Rebhorn's property. What had seemed like lush green grass from a distance was synthetic grass, the kind you see laid out in flat strips on pavement. The hill was steep down to the dock, as if a giant hand was lifting it behind us, making us scramble. Uncle Rebhorn and Darren were trotting ahead, in matching swim trunks—gold trimmed in blue. Aunt Elinor had changed into a single-piece white satin bathing suit that exposed her bony shoulders and sunken chest; it was shocking to see her. She called out to Uncle Rebhorn that she wasn't feeling well—the sun had given her a migraine headache—sailing would make the headache worse—could she be excused?—but Uncle Rebhorn shouted over his shoulder, "You're coming with us, goddamn you! Why did we buy this frigging sailboat except to enjoy it?" Aunt Elinor winced, and murmured, "Yes, dear," and Uncle Rebhorn said, snorting, with a wink at Audrey and me, "Hmmm! It better be 'yes, dear,' you stupid cow-cunt."

By the time we crawled out onto the deck of the sailboat a chill wind had come up, and in fact the sun was disappearing like something being sucked down a drain. It was more like November than July, the sky heavy with clouds like stained concrete. Uncle Rebhorn said suddenly, "—bought this frigging sailboat to enjoy it for God's sake—for the family and that means *all the family.*" The sailboat was lurching in the choppy water like a living, frantic thing as Uncle Rebhorn loosed us from the dock and set sail. "First mate! Look sharp! Where the hell are you, boy? Move your ass!"—Uncle Rebhorn kept up a constant barrage of commands at poor Darren who scampered to obey them, yanking at ropes that slipped from his fingers, trying to swing the heavy, sodden mainsail around. The wind seemed to come from several directions at once and the sails flapped and whipped helplessly. Darren did his best but he was clumsy and ill-coordinated and terrified of his father. His pudgy face had turned ashen, and his eyes darted wildly about; his gold swim trunks, which were made of a shiny material like rayon, fitted him so tightly a loose belt of fat protruded over the waistband and jiggled comically as, desperate to follow Uncle Rebhorn's instructions, Darren fell to one knee, pushed himself up, slipped and fell again, this time onto his belly on the slippery deck. Uncle

Rebhorn, naked but for his swimming trunks and a visored sailor's cap jammed onto his head, shouted mercilessly, "Son, get *up*. Get that frigging sail to the wind or it's *mutiny!*"

The sailboat was now about thirty feet from the safety of the dock, careening and lurching in the water, which was nothing like the painted aqua water I had seen from shore; it was dark, metallic gray, and greasy, and very cold. Winds howled about us. There was no cabin in the sailboat, all was exposed, and Uncle Rebhorn had taken the only seat. I was terrified the sailboat would sink, or I would be swept off to drown in the water by wild, frothy waves washing across the deck. I had never been in any boat except rowboats with my parents in the Hamtramck Park lagoon. "Isn't this fun? Isn't it! Sailing is the most exciting—" Aunt Elinor shouted at me, with her wide fixed smile, but Uncle Rebhorn, seeing my white, pinched face, interrupted, "Nobody's going to drown today, least of all *you*. Ungrateful little brat!"

Aunt Elinor poked me, and smiled, pressing a finger to her lips. Of course, Uncle Rebhorn was just teasing.

For a few minutes it seemed as if the winds were filling our sails in the right way for the boat moved in a single unswerving direction. Darren was holding for dear life to a rope, to keep the mainsail steady. Then suddenly a dazzling white yacht sped by us, three times the size of Uncle Rebhorn's boat, dreamlike out of the flying spray, and in its wake Uncle Rebhorn's boat shuddered and lurched; there was a piercing, derisive sound of a horn—too late; the prow of the sailboat went under, freezing waves washed across the deck, the boat rocked crazily. I'd lost sight of Audrey and Aunt Elinor and was clutching a length of frayed rope with both hands, to keep myself from being swept overboard. How I whimpered with fear and pain! *This is your punishment, now you know you must be bad.* Uncle Rebhorn crouched at the prow of the boat, his eyes glittering in his flushed face, screaming commands at Darren who couldn't move fast enough to prevent the mainsail from suddenly swinging around, skimming over my head, and knocking Darren into the water.

Uncle Rebhorn yelled, "Son! Son!" With a hook at the end of a long wooden pole he fished about in the sudsy waves for my cousin, who sank like a bundle of sodden laundry; then surfaced again as a wave struck him from beneath and buoyed him upward; then sank again, this time beneath the lurching boat, his arms and legs flailing. I stared aghast, clutching at my rope. Audrey and Aunt Elinor were somewhere behind me, crying, "Help! Help!" Uncle Rebhorn ignored them, cursing as he scrambled to the other side of the boat, and swiping with the hook in the water until he snagged something and, blood vessels prominent as angry worms in his face, hauled Darren out of the water and onto the swaying deck. The hook had caught my cousin in the armpit, and streams of blood ran down his side. Was Darren alive?—I stared, I could not tell. Aunt Elinor was screaming hysterically. With deft, rough hands Uncle Rebhorn laid his son on his back, like a fat, pale fish, and stretched the boy's arms and legs out, and straddled Darren's hips and began to rock in a quickened rhythmic movement and to squeeze his rib cage, *squeeze and release! squeeze and release!* until driblets of foamy water and vomit began to be expelled from Darren's mouth, and, gasping and choking, the boy was breathing again. Tears of rage and sorrow streaked Uncle Rebhorn's flushed face.

"You disappoint me, son! Son, you disappoint me! I, your dad who gave you life—you disappoint me!"

A sudden prankish gust of wind lifted Uncle Rebhorn's sailor cap off his head and sent it flying and spinning out into the misty depths of Lake St. Clair.

I have been counseled not to retrieve the past where it is ▬▬▬ blocked by ▬▬▬ like those frequent attacks of "visual impairment" (*not* blindness, the neurologist insists) but have I not a right to my own memories? to my own past? Why should that right be taken from me?

What are you frightened of, Mother, my children ask me, sometimes in merriment, what are *you* frightened of?—as if anything truly significant, truly frightening, could have happened, or could have been imagined to have happened, to me.

So I joke with them, I tease them saying, "Maybe—*you!*"

For in giving birth to them I suffered ▬▬▬ slivers of ▬▬▬ too, which for the most part I have forgotten ▬▬▬ as all wounds heal and pain is lost in time—isn't it?

What happened on that lost Sunday in July 1969 in Uncle Rebhorn's house in Grosse Pointe Shores is a true mystery never comprehended by the very person (myself) who experienced it. For at the center of it is an emptiness ▬▬▬ black rectangular emptiness ▬▬▬ skidding toward me like a fracturing of the air *and it is ticklish too, my shivering turns convulsive on the brink of wild leaping laughter.* I recall the relief that my cousin Darren did not drown and I recall the relief that we returned to the dock which was swaying and rotted but did not collapse, held firm as Uncle Rebhorn cast a rope noose to secure the boat. I know that we returned breathless and excited from our outing on Lake St. Clair and that Aunt Elinor said it was too bad no snapshots had been taken to commemorate my visit, and Uncle Rebhorn asked where the Polaroid camera was, why did Aunt Elinor never remember it for God's sake, their lives and happy times flying by and nobody recording them. I know that we entered the house and once again in the dark cubbyhole that was my cousin Audrey's room beneath the stairs we were changing frantically from our bathing suits which were soaking wet into our dry clothes and this time Aunt Elinor, still less Audrey, could not prevent the door from pushing open ▬▬▬ ▬▬▬ crying "Daddy, no!" and "No, please, Daddy!" until I was crying too and laughing screaming as a man's rough fingers ▬▬▬ ran over my bare ribs bruising ▬▬▬ the frizzy-wiry hairs of his chest and belly tickling my face ▬▬▬ until what was beneath us which I had believed to be a floor fell away suddenly ▬▬▬ dissolving like ▬▬▬ water *I was not crying, I was not fighting I was a good girl: see?* ▬▬▬

AFTERWORD

It's night. It has been night for a long time. Hours pass—yet it's the same hour. I can't sleep. My mind is fractured like broken glass. Or a broken mirror, shards reflecting shards. I am incapable of thinking but only of receiving, like a fine-meshed net strung tight, mere glimmerings of thought. Teasing fragments of "memory"—or is it "invented memory"?—rise and turn and fall and sift and scatter and rearrange themselves into arabesques of patterns on the verge of becoming coherent, yet do not become coherent. As in a childhood riddle never explained. As in one of those ingeniously intricate childhood puzzle-drawings in which shapes—faces, figures of animals—are superimposed upon one another, obscured by clouds, trees, natural objects. Something wants to speak—but what? This insomniac state is perhaps but the nighttime, and therefore the most obvious expression of a general fascinated bafflement of consciousness, for I have to acknowledge that occasionally—not frequently (which would be madness) but occasionally—such fugue states grip me by day, in public places; I am especially vulnerable while being introduced to give a lecture or a reading, for instance, or, on rarer occasions, while being cited for some honor or award. At such times one must sit gravely listening, one must not be seen to demur, still less to be assailed by gusts of wild hilarity, disbelief. Yes, I think ironically, as an enthusiastic stranger's voice extols the public achievements of the largely fictitious "Joyce Carol Oates," yes but no: you don't know *me*. If you knew me, you would not say such outlandish things.

What should be said in place of these "outlandish things," I have no idea.

Yesterday in Manhattan, on the twenty-third, penthouse floor of a Fifth Avenue office building facing Trump Tower, at a lavish luncheon in my honor, in the grip of a powerful fugue state I felt as if I were about to remember something—but could not, cannot. Wanting desperately to reread a certain passage from Pascal's *Pensées*, which I have virtually memorized yet can't trust my memory to replicate with the full dignity and gravity these famous words demand.

> This is our true state; this is what makes us incapable of certain knowledge and of absolute ignorance. We sail within a vast sphere, ever drifting in uncertainty, driven from end to end. When we try to attach ourselves to any point and to fasten to it, it wavers and leaves us; and if we follow it, it eludes our grasp, slips past us, and vanishes forever. Nothing stays for us. This is our natural condition, and yet most contrary to our inclination; we burn with desire to find solid ground and an ultimate sure foundation whereupon to build a tower reaching to the Infinite. But our whole groundwork cracks, and the earth opens to abysses.

Unless you are more protectively self-deluded than Pascal, this is true for you, too.

Certainly for me.

"Joyce Carol Oates"—more helpfully comprehended as an imagination and a writing process, and not an individual—very possibly feels little of this existential anxiety, except in and through her fictitious personae; but I, who encompass, yet am hardly identical with "JCO," am in the grip of this anxiety whenever the momentum of my life slows, and its surface distractions fade. At such times, like the narrator of my story ▄▄ (its title refers precisely to the "abyss" of which Pascal speaks: a kind of black hole of the spirit) I seem about to remember and to know something—but what?

The story in this anthology is but one of any number of fictions I've created to attempt to comprehend, even in the face of ceaseless failure, this abyss, and the mystery surrounding it. The story is *not* autobiographical, except emotionally; I stand in awe of the possibility that being hypnotized by ▄▄ is a key to my putative industry.

At the same time, I think I am probably representative of the legion of people, women perhaps more than men, yet surely there are many men in our ranks as well, who are both fascinated by the contents of the unconscious and in terror of their uncontrolled eruption. The sudden incursion of an unwanted memory in our lives: how can we assimilate it into what we want to believe of ourselves? We build personalities, like "fictions," to withstand the roiling waters. Or we build fictions, like "personalities."

THE PRINTER'S DAUGHTER
Delia Sherman

Delia Sherman won the Campbell Award for best new writer in the speculative fiction field; she has also won the Mythopoeic Society Award. Her first book, *Through a Brazen Mirror*, is a fantasy novel based on a British folk ballad. Her second novel, *The Porcelain Dove*, published as a mainstream title, is based on French fairy tales and set during the French Revolution. She has also published short fiction and poetry in various collections, and works as a consulting editor for Tor Books in New York. Sherman lives in Boston, Massachusetts.

"The Printer's Daughter" is a tour de force, one of the very best of the year. It is reprinted from *Ruby Slippers, Golden Tears*, an anthology of adult fairy tales.

—T.W.

On the morning of All Hallow's Eve, Hal Spurtle sat at the window of his shop and watched the children play. They were ragged children, as it was a ragged street, their faces and caps smudged with dirt and their petticoats and breeches tattered as old paper. Grave as judges, they linked hands and danced sunwise, chanting the while in their bird-shrill voices.

> *Thread the needle, thread the needle,*
> *Eye, eye, eye.*
> *Thread the needle, thread the needle,*
> *Eye, eye, eye.*
> *The tailor's blind and he can't see,*
> *So we must thread the needle.*

Hal remembered singing that rhyme himself. He'd taught it to his young sisters as they played on a Shoreditch street that differed from this not so much as milk from cream. As he watched little Rose and Ned Ashcroft, Anne and Katty and Jane Dunne winding up and down the cobbles, he told the rhyme over to himself, very soft.

The children laughed as they played. Hal sighed and turned his eyes back to the trays of type, the compositor's stick, and the manuscript pages stacked before them. The collected sermons of the good Dr. Beswick, passed by the queen's censor and writ down in the Register of the Company of Stationers. Dull as an old knife, but legal to print and to sell, making a change from the bawdy broadsides, the saucy quartos, the unblushingly filthy octavos that made up the greater part of his stock-in-trade. The great pornographer Arentino himself might have turned color at *The Cuckold's Mery Iest* and expired altogether of shame at *In Praise of Pudding-Pricks*. But it had been a matter of Pride the son riding before Caution the father, for on being made free of the Company of Stationers, Hal must needs set up shop for himself, though he could scarce afford a press and its furniture. And so Hal had learned to converse with scarcity and rogues, until, by chance, a country clergyman approached him with a manuscript of sermons and a purse to pay for their printing.

Hal's old master, John Day, would have done the job in a week, but John Day had two 'prentices to ink, cut pages, and distribute type, as well as compositors, pressmen, gatherers, folders, and binders to do the work. Hal, working man-alone, had been at the business two weeks already, with Dr. Beswick threatening to take his sermons and his ten pounds elsewhere, God take the thought from him; for his ten pounds were scattered like grain among Hal's creditors.

Furthermore, Hal himself was weak and weary with poor feeding, and as like to drop a line of type as bring it whole to the imposing-table. On All Hallow's Eve, he did that once or twice, and then he transposed two lines of type, the which cost him fifty sheets of best French Imperial, and overinked a plate with so free a hand that he must pour the piss-pot over it to clean it. Not three impressions later, he did it again, whereupon Hal consigned Dr. Beswick and his sermons to the most noisesome deep of Hell; viz., Satan's arsehole. For overinking was such a monkey's trick as he'd not been guilty of for fifteen years or more.

An apprentice would serve the present need, he thought; a likely, lively lad who was content to live upon pulp and printer's ink, a lad who never reversed lines nor set them arsy-versy. But Hal well knew that were there such a 'prentice in London, he'd never bind himself to a press where half the texts were unlicensed and the other half unlicensable. He looked mournfully at twists of paper from *In Praise of Pudding-Pricks* and Dr. Beswick's sermons, equally damned by their ill printing, piled in the corner where an apprentice might sleep. Seized by a sudden fancy, Hal gathered up sheets of piety and bawdry and twisted them into skinny arms and legs, wrapped scraps and wads into a lumpy head and carcass, and bound the whole with thread into a human shape. When it was done, he shook his head over the poor, blind face, and taking up ink and pen, carefully limned features: a button nose, doe's eyes, and a Cupid's mouth. He thought it favored his small sister Kate.

The wind, having risen with the moon, came hunting down the narrow street for mischief, the which it found in the shape of Hal's window shutter. Howling, it pounced upon the latch, tore it open, and slapped the wood to and fro against the glass. Hal laid his poppet upon a nest of paper and ran out-a-doors to catch it. He had put the shutter up and was going in again when a small, straddling fellow clawed him by the elbow and would not be put by.

"I seek Hal Spurtle the printer's," he said.

"I am Hal Spurtle," said Hal. "What would you with me?"

"To go within," said the man. "My business is not for the common street."

Loathe was Hal to oblige him, the hour being late and none save rogues likely to be abroad. Yet rogues were the chiefest part of his custom; and so he brought the stranger into the shop. In the lamplight, the man proved a veritable Methuselah, with a face like a shelled walnut and a back like the hoop of a cart. His hands and stump-trimmed beard were vilely stained, and there hung a stink about him of sulphur and brimstone. By which signs Hal understood the stranger to be an alchemist, the which he further understood to be a filthy trade and unlawful. So it was with faint courtesy that he demanded of the old man once again why he sought Hal Spurtle the printer?

"To give him a job of work," answered the alchemist, and poked and patted in his gown until he found a thick sheaf of vellum tied with tape, the which he handed to Hal, who took it as gingerly as may be.

"Untie it. 'Twill not eat thee," said the old man.

Slowly, Hal did so, uncovering a page writ margin to margin in secretary hand, damnably crabbed. Forty pages in quarto, or perhaps fifty, say two weeks to set and print if the edition were not large. He squinted at the tiny, curling letters.

> *Liquour conioynyth male with female*
> *wyfe,*
> *And causith dede thingis to resorte to*
> *lyfe.*

Hal dropped the manuscript hastily. "Your job of work would bring me to my neck verse, grandad."

"*In Praise of Pudding-Pricks* could lose thee thy right hand, or any of the bawdry thou dost use to print here. This goose is only a little more spiced, and lays golden eggs besides. An edition of thirteen copies, printed as accurate as may be, sewn for binding. Shall we say twenty crowns?"

Hal's teeth watered at the sum. Twenty crowns would rid him of his debts and buy him a new font of type, an apprentice, even a pressman who knew a platen from a frisket. Before he could gather his wits to say yea or nay, the old man said, "It must be done by Sunday moonrise, mind, or 'tis no good."

"Sunday moonrise! Why did you not come to me earlier, pray? I cannot set, proof, print, and sew thirteen copies in two days, not if I worked without stop or let from dawn to dawn. The thing's impossible. As well ask a cat to pull a cart."

"You have no apprentice?"

"I have not, sir. And had I the two apprentices the law allows, yea, and twenty journeymen, too, still the job would take a week or more. And I've another book promised and owing must take precedence."

The old man peered shortsightedly into the shadows. "Yet I thought I saw an apprentice as I came in—a lad sleeping on a pallet, there in the corner."

Hal followed the goodman's gaze to the poppet. It did look uncommonly like a sleeping child. "'Tis naught," he said shortly. "A pile of paper."

The old man heaved himself upright, took up the lamp, and hobbled over to see for himself. "An homunculus, as I am a man! You'd not said you dabbled in the Art, Master Spurtle."

Hal crossed himself. "God forbid, sir."

The old man fixed him with a crow-bright eye that pierced Hal's skull from brow to bald spot. "Art lonely, lad?"

"Aye," said Hal, surprised into honesty.

"And no sister or wife to keep thy house or warm thy bed?"

"My sisters will not forgive me my learning, an it go not hand-in-hand with wealth. And as for a wife, I've no stomach for the wooing, nor coin for the keeping when she's won."

"No matter," said the old man. "See here, Hal Spurtle. Should I find thee a 'prentice fit for the work, wilt undertake to print my book by Sunday moonrise?"

"He needs must be a prodigy of nature."

"As prodigious as thou wilt. 'Tis a bargain, then. Thy hand on it, Hal Spurtle. This purse will stay thy present need."

The purse contained five pounds in silver: a goodly earnest. Hal weighed it in his palm. "Why, if I'm a madman, you're another, and there's a pair on us. My hand on it, then."

They shook hands solemnly, and then the old gentleman took up his carven stick, hobbled to the door, and, without another word, was gone like the devil in the old play.

St. Martin's tolled midnight. Hal rubbed his cheeks wearily and picked up the lamp to light him to bed. Catching a movement in the corner of his eye—*a rat*, he thought, and had turned him away when a voice arrested him: a small, dry voice, like the rustling of pages.

"Sinner," it said. "Look thou to thine end."

The hair crept upon Hal's skin like lice. What had the old rogue left behind him?

"To each thing must thou pay heed," said the voice. "To thy comings-in and thy goings-out, to thy pleasures and thy pains, that they be pleasing unto the Lord."

Hal considered. Surely a demon would not speak as from a pulpit; though 'twas said the devil could quote scripture to the soul's confusion. "Back to hell with thee, demon," said Hal peevishly. "I've no wish to look upon thy hideous countenance."

There was a faint rustling from the corner. "The kingdom of God is of a fairness beyond the measure of man, and the tidings thereof are comfortable," said the voice at last, sad and something fearful, like Hal's sister Kate begging grace for some roguery. The memory softening his heart, he turned and beheld no horned devil, but a girl-child of six years' growth, sitting mother-naked in a nest of paper.

"Hallelujah, saith the angel, and the sons of man rejoice," she said firmly.

Hal squatted down before her and reached out one hand to touch her head. It was not bald, but covered with an uneven pelt, white mottled with black, like blurred print. Her face was likewise piebald and soft as old rags, her cheeks round as peaches, like Kate's or Ann's or any of the small sisters whom Hal had fed and dandled. Like them, she was as bony as a curpup, and as hollow eyed. Only her mouth was fair, a pure and innocent bow.

The fair mouth opened, and she spoke. "A groat will buy my hand, good sir, and a penny my cunt. But 'tis three pennies for my mouth, for washing the taste out after."

"Out upon thee for a froward wench," cried Hal, and struck her with his open hand so that she wailed aloud with the pain of it. As shocked as he'd been by her bawdry, still more was Hal grieved by her piteous cries. So he caught up a clout from a chair, bundled it around her naked, flailing arms and legs, and gathered her, howling, to his breast.

"There, now," he crooned over the piebald hair. "Hush thee, do. Thou'rt not so hurt as astonished, the which may be said of me as well."

The child quietened at his voice, and sniffled, and settled against him. "His yoke is easy and his burden is light," she said tearfully. "Wherefore dost thou grieve him with thy sinning?"

Hal rocked her silently for a moment, then asked, "Art hungered, sweeting? Shall I fetch thee a sop of milk and bread?"

"Flesh and ale's good meat to my belly, and swiving thereafter."

Hal looked stonily upon the lass; she showed small, crooked teeth in an imp's smile. "Thou shalt cry, 'Pardon, pardon,' and it will avail thee naught. For sin is stamped upon thy soul from thy mother's womb; thou art cast and molded of it."

" 'As prodigious as thou wilt,' " murmured Hal. "I begin to apprehend." He loosed his arms, and the girl-child stood upright on paper-twist limbs and made her ways to the composing-table, and began to distribute the scattered type into the cases, her arms spinning like flywheels. The clout dropped from her shoulders and she stood naked on the floor.

Hal slipped into the inner room, where he hunted out hose and a shirt only a little torn, and a rope to belt it with. These he carried into the shop and tossed upon the table where she could not choose but to see them.

She fetched up the clothing and held it this way and that against her body until Hal began to laugh, whereat she cocked her head, aggrieved. "So ask not, saying, how shall we eat, or how shall we drink, or wherewithal shall we be clothed; for after all these things do the Gentiles seek."

"Do them on nonetheless; the wind will not temper itself to a shorn lamb, and thou'rt prodigy enough in a clothed state. And thou'lt need a name. Textura? Roman? Bastarda?" The child blew a fart with her lips. Hal grinned. "Not Bastarda. Demy. Broadside." Gazing here and there in search of inspiration, his eye chanced to light upon the press, the frisket unfolded, the tympan empty. "Frisket," he said decidedly.

The child smiled at that, and uttered not a word, neither of bawdry nor of scripture, by which Hal understood that she was much moved, as, in truth, was Hal himself.

"'Gie thee good den, Frisket," said Hal. "Now to bed, under the press, as snug as a mouse. We'll up betimes and begin work."

When he entered his shop at cock-crow next morning, Hal half thought he'd wandered in his sleep to his master's printing-shop at Alder's Gate. The composing and imposing tables were scrubbed clean of ink stains, the floor swept and garnished, the ink balls washed and hung to dry, and the piebald girl was bent over the press, industriously greasing the tracks. She'd shot up in the night, mushroomlike, to a gawky girl of twelve or thereabouts, with her hair grown to rat's tails strewn across the back of Hal's shirt, and her bony arms black to the elbow with ink.

"Frisket," said Hal. "Is't thou in very sooth, lass?"

"When I was a child, I understood as a child; now I am become a man, I put away childish things."

"Thou'rt nigher heaven than thou wast, and something stouter." He glanced suspiciously at the cupboard. "Hast left me a sup?"

"Man doth not live by bread alone," said Frisket smugly. "Come kiss me, sweet chuck, and clip me close." And she gestured to the hearth, where ale was warming, and a half loaf of bread and a crust of cheese laid ready on a plate, to which Hal applied himself right heartily.

"There is a wanton will not want one, if place and person were agreeable to his desires."

Hal swallowed hard and said, "List thee, poppet. Before we make a start, I would say a word. Sermonizing I can bear. Bawdry ill befits thy tender years. Cleave to Dr. Beswick, an it pleaseth thee, and let *In Praise of Pudding-Pricks* be."

Frisket looked dumpish. "As the goose is sauced, so is the gander," she said.

"I'd think shame to read the knavery my poverty beds me withal," Hal said.

"Out upon thee, old juggler! Thy sparrow is dead 'i the nest, and will not rise up and sing, squeeze and kiss I never so cleverly."

Hal yielded the field, blushing, nor sought to engage again; but as they worked that day composing and printing the sheets, he made note that Frisket's tongue wagged less, and more upon a pedantical breeze than a bawdy. So the morning flowed into day and the evening into night like streams into a river, quiet and unmarked. But when St. Anthony's bell came tolling midnight, there were only three sheets made perfect, twenty-four pages out of fifty-two. Despairing, Hal sat him down for a brace of minutes to rest his aching back.

He woke to broad daylight and Frisket mixing ink.

"Wake thee, wake thee, sinner, for the bridegroom cometh," she caroled.

Hal started to his feet. Ten stacks of perfect sheets stood ranged upon the composing-table. He took one up and checked it, back and front. The inking was dark and even, the lines prettily justified, the text as sensible and correct as such a text might be.

"So thou shalt ask thyself; am I a sinner, or am I a righteous man?" said Frisket anxiously.

Hal looked up at her ink-blotched face in wonder. "A righteous man, beyond all doubt. In fact," he continued, "there's a question here, which of us is master and which 'prentice."

Frisket smiled to show her teeth—piebald as her skin and hair—and then he and she turned to collating the sheets, to folding and cutting them into books and sewing the signatures together. They worked in quiet amity, with the ease of long use and custom, the one giving the other a knife or thread at need, without a word exchanged. Now and again he'd glance from the sewing-frame to see her ink-drop eyes upon him, whereat they'd smile at one another and bend to their tasks again. Joy became a friend, who long had been a stranger to Hal's heart, and his mind began to wander in uncharted seas of poems and plays and philosophical tracts that might be registered and put for public sale in St. Paul's churchyard, and a little house in St. Martin's Lane, with a shop at the back and two journeymen to run the press, and Frisket, of course, properly bound and entered in the rolls of the apprentices. She'd need a better name than Frisket, too. Mary, he thought—the mother of Our Lord. Mary Spurtle, his elder brother's child, if anyone were to ask. But he and she would know she was Hal's own, the daughter of his heart.

Come moonrise, Hal and Frisket were grinning at one another across the hearth, with thirteen quarto alchemical ordinals stacked neatly on the composing-table behind them. The door latch rattled, and Frisket ran to open it.

"Behold, the bridegroom cometh, and upon his brow is righteousness," she said, flourishing a bow.

The alchemist beetled his brows at her, and at Hal, who sat laughing by the fire. "Thou art pleased to take thine ease," he said testily. "The silver I gave thee cost me something in the making. I trust thou hast not squandered it in liquor."

"Nay, nay, good Master Alchemist, I have not, nor so much as a moment in sleep or sup. There is your book as you required it, printed as fine, though I say it, as Caxton in his prime."

The alchemist took up the topmost book and leafed through its pages, hemming here and hawing there, looking up at last and nodding to Hal almost with courtesy. "Excellent," he said. "Excellent good, in very sooth. Thou hast labored mightily, thou and thy 'prentice, in bringing forth this text. And so I will ask thee, Hal Spurtle, whether thou wouldst take a copy in payment, that is the only true receipt for the making of gold and silver, or content thee with twenty crowns."

Hal laughed aloud. "I cry thee pardon, grandad, but I'd leifer have ink upon my hands than quicksilver. Twenty crowns, wisely spent, will bring me to twenty more as well as thy receipt, and with more surety. We'll do well enough, my 'prentice and I."

The alchemist shrugged his shoulders, and having dealt the books here and there about his person, took out a purse and gave it over to Hal's hand and prepared to go his ways. Upon reaching the door, a thought stopped him. "Thy apprentice," he said. "How dost thou like him?"

Hal, feeling Frisket shadowy at his side, drew her forward into his arm. "I like her very well," he said.

"Her," said the old man. "Curious."

When he was gone, Hal tossed the heavy purse aloft, jingling. "Here's a weighty matter, poppet, must be lightened ere it burst. We've need of meat, and ale, and bread, and women's weeds to clothe thee withal."

"Smock climb apace, that I may see my joys."

"Aye, a smock, and petticoats and a woolen skirt and a shawl against the winter wind, and leathern shoes." He kissed her lightly upon the head. "I'll warrant thee to make a bonny wench. We'll to market at daylight."

Overwatched, Hal slept almost until noon, by which time Frisket had finished printing Dr. Beswick's sermons, aye, and cut and sewn them, too. Hal crowed with joy, swung her under the arms, bundled the books with binding thread, and carried them to Dr. Beswick's lodgings, where he gave them into the gentleman's hand, full of apologies for the delay and thanks for his patience.

"Patience," piped Frisket, "is of the virtues the most cardinal; for all things come to him who waiteth upon the word of God."

Hal looked sharp to see whether the reverend gentleman be offended or no. "My new apprentice, sir, my brother's child. Touched by the finger of God, sir, but quick and good-hearted as may be."

"So I perceive," said Dr. Beswick. "My own words upon patience, pat as I writ 'em. 'Tis pity he's so ill-marked. Stay, now, here's another sovereign. I'd not thought to see my books this sennight."

Hal took the sovereign and thanked the reverend gentleman, and bore Frisket off to the old-clothes market at Cornhill. He bought a woolen gown and a shawl, two smocks, and after some hesitation, a petticoat of fine scarlet, lifted, no doubt, from some merchant's drying yard, and a linen cap. Home again, he pinned and laced her into her new array as tenderly as a mother, even to braiding her magpie hair down her back and tying her cap over it.

"Thou'rt a proper lass now," he told her, "and the apple of mine eye. I'm off now to St. Paul's to hear the news, see perhaps may I come by a pamphlet or a book of ABC to print and sell. No more Merry Jests, my Frisket, or Valentines or Harlot's Tricks for us. From this moment, the bishop of London himself will have no cause to blush for our work."

"Here lieth an alehouse, with chambers above, and beds in the chambers. Pray you, love, walk in with me."

"Nay, child, I'll take thee another time. Take thou thine ease at home or abroad, but see thou stay within call and stray not, and, as thou lovest me, temper thy tongue as thou mayst; for not all have the trick of thy speech. If any ask, thou art my brother's child, called Mary, Mary Spurtle, come to keep my house and learn my trade." He took his purse then, and finding therein some coppers and a silver piece, wrapped them in a clout and bade her tie them underneath her petticoat.

She looked at the little bundle with bemusement. "I swive for love, and not for base coin," she said doubtfully.

"The daughter of the house must have coin when she ventures abroad. And thou art the only daughter I am like to have. So take thy purse. Thou hast earned it."

So Hal went whistling towards St. Paul's and Frisket watched him down the street, her eyes bright and shy as a mouse's.

"Hey there, wench." A boy's sharp treble hailed her from Mistress Dunne's front window. "What makest thou at Hal Printer's?"

Frisket stepped out into the street and smiled, which brought Jane and Ann and Katty forth across the cobbled street to sniff about her skirts in the manner of pet dogs: cautious, but more apt to fawn than to bite.

"What's thy name?" inquired Ann, who was the eldest.

Frisket opened her mouth and closed it again. "Frisket" was nowhere printed on her body. Yet Hal had given her another name, a name found in both sermon and bawdry, so, "Mary," she said. "Come, play with me."

"What wouldst thou play?" asked Katty, ever generous. "Wildflowers and Old Roger and Thread the Needle's our favorites, but we'll play a new if thou'lt learn it us."

Frisket had knowledge of many plays, all of them new to Katty, and all of them from that part of her mind Hal disapproved of her speaking. Accordingly, she hoisted one skinny shoulder as one who defers to her hosts, and Jane said, "Let it be Lazy Mary, then. Dost know it?"

Frisket shook her head.

"Hast the cat a-hold of thy tongue, Mary?" taunted Jane; in response to which Frisket exhibited hers, catless, but mottled pink and black, whereat she laughed till Ann cuffed her ear and bade her mend her manners. Jane subsiding, Ann told her the words to the game, that were *Lazy Mary, will you get up, will you get up, will you get up? Lazy Mary, will you get up, will you get up today?*

"And then thou shalt answer," interrupted Jane, "that thou wilt not, whatever dainties we offer, until that we offer thee a nice young man."

So they laid Frisket down among them, with her apron over her face, and turned about her, singing. And when it was time for her to answer, Frisket frowned under her apron, opened her mouth, and sang.

> *My mistress is a cunny fine*
> *And of the finest skin*
> *And if you care to open her,*
> *The best part lies within.*
> *Yet in her cunny burrow may*
> *Two tumblers and a ferret play.*

Jane giggled; Ann blushed rose, then white, then rose again.

"Nay, now, Mary, prithee do not mock us," said Katty.

"The devils of hell mock the blessed," said Frisket, "for those very joys they are blessed withal."

"Art mad?" asked Ann. "We are not to play with mad folk."

"Sing again," said Jane, and Frisket sang again, by bad fortune just when Mistress Dunne was out at her door to see her children play. Now, Mistress Dunne was a God-fearing woman, a great enemy to oaths and tobacco and all manner of loose living; so that hearing Frisket's song, she screeched like unto a scalded cat, and pounced upon the girl, and boxed her ears until they rang like St. Paul's at noon.

Frisket put her hands to her ears wonderingly, as though she hardly understood the smart. "Well mayst thou look sullen," said Mistress Dunne. "Thou'rt overripe for a beating. Filthy girl. Dost not know so much as wash thy face?"

Frisket spat upon her hand and rubbed her cheek, then held her hand to Mistress Dunne to show it neither more black nor more white, but mottled as before, like the coat of a spotted dog. Mistress Dunne looked at the hand, and the face, and the thick, piebald plait lying over Frisket's shoulder, and made the sign of the cross in the air between them. "Devil's mark," she cried, and spat, and gathering her children to her, chivvyed them within, Frisket trailing after, saying:

"May not a sinner, being penitent, enter into the kingdom of heaven?"

"God save us, the child is mad," cried Mistress Dunne, and clapped to the door against Frisket's nose, whereat Frisket, showing a perfect devil's countenance of red and black, cast a flood of Billingsgate upon the unyielding wood, drenching it with such verbs, nouns, and adverbs that would have stunk, had they been incarnate, as three days' fish do stink. And then she turned and ran heedless among the lanes and alleys of East Cheape.

The force that drove her no man could tell, nor could Frisket neither. She did not think as men thought, did nor feel or know or hope as a child begotten of man and born of woman. The highest and most base exhalations of man's soul had gone into her making, and the words they gave her were all she knew. Neither piety or bawdry taught her to say, "There is no place for me here; I must return to that I was." Yet such was in her heart. And so she sought the alchemist where he lay, that he who had made her flesh might unflesh her again and return her to her former state of ink and pulp and fiber.

Hal came again unto his house when the bells of St. Martin's were ringing for Evensong. His feet spurned the mud, and his eyes dwelt on the wonders of being able to command a font of print, and to buy the right of a pamphlet upon the making of cheese and enter it upon the Register, and still have money and enough in his purse to do the same again.

"Frisket," he sang as he lifted the latch. "Frisket, heart of my heart, come hither, and thou shalt partake of roast fowl and sack at the Doublet and Hose as 'twere any lady. Frisket? Frisket, I say! Beshrew me, where is the wench?" And receiving no answer, Hal peered and pried through his two small chambers where a mouse could not lie hid, searching in rising panic for his paper 'prentice, who in two days' time was grown to him the very daughter of his heart.

Presently did Hal go out into the streets around, calling for Frisket up and down, and then, weary and sick with worry, to Mistress Dunne to entreat her whether she had seen his niece or no.

"His niece, quotha!" she exclaimed. "His trull, more like, and a good riddance to her and her slattern's tongue."

Hal, hoping for news, kept firm hold upon his temper. "She knows no better, God forgive my brother that it should be so," he said humbly. "I've hopes of teaching her better ways in time. She's a good lass at heart."

"A good lass would disdain to know such oaths, nor profane the purity of her lips with bawdry."

"She is as innocent of offense as of the true meaning of what she says."

Mistress Dunne patted Hal on the shoulder. "Thou'rt a kind man, Hal Spurtle, and simple as a newborn lamb. Never doubt thy self-called niece hath cozened thee finely. She's off with thy purse or thy linen, or some costly matter of thy trade, depend on't." And from this opinion she could not be turned.

So Hal took him home again to his empty shop, emptier now of one piebald, cheeky wench, and soon came out again, determined as Jason to find that moth-eaten golden fleece the ancient alchemist, to beg of him news of Frisket.

The while Hal was seeking her up and down, Frisket had won through the alleys of Cheape Ward to Fish Street, that was a broad street of fair houses, very busy with horses, and men in furred gowns and velvet caps, and women in farthingales and hooded cloaks. They jostled her as she stood, heeding her no more than the lean dogs nosing at the fish heads in the road, save for one young girl with a feathered hat perched on her bright hair, who pressed a penny in Frisket's hand and smiled pityingly upon her. For want of a better direction, Frisket followed her, losing her almost at once in the bustle that bore Frisket with it across a bridge cobbled like a street and lined with rich houses. On the further bank, Frisket turned aside from the high way to walk along the river, flowing gray and brown as porridge between slick, pewter banks. The sky was pewter too, tarnished and pitted with clouds, and the houses along the wharf leaned between them like beggars at an almshouse board.

One in three of those houses were marked like taverns, with signs painted bright above their doors, as the Cardinal's Cap, the Bird in the Bush, the Silent Woman, the Snake and Apple. Outside this last, a weaseling, minching fellow accosted Frisket, who gazed thoughtfully at the one-eyed snake of the blazon, that curled from Adam's loins toward the Apple held between Eve's plump thighs.

"Hey, thou ninny," he said. "What maketh thou here, walking so bold in Southwark?"

Frisket's ado with Mistress Dunne had taught her to stick to scripture. So she bethought her a moment and said, "The ways of the Lord are surpassing strange and beyond the wit of man to tell them."

The man drew closer, darted out his hand like Adam's snake and, clipping her by the wrist, held her fast. "A prating Puritan maid, by Cock," he snarled. "Marked like the Devil's own, and comely as a succubus withal. What are thy parents?"

"We have no father or mother, save that Heavenly Parent is Father and Mother to us all."

The man's eyes gleamed in his sharp face. "Art meat for my feeding, then."

Frisket, finding no apt response recorded in the tablets of her mind, met his eyes gravely, then at his fingers about her wrist, and back into his eyes, whereupon he dropped her arm to shield him with his hand from her gaze. "Go thy ways," he said. "Thou'rt safe from me. Yet the Southwark bawdy houses are an ill place for a maid to wander, even a maid touched by God."

Frisket nodded. "The way of righteousness is the way of truth, and much beset with thorns." Then she turned her about and made away from the river, leaving the bawd muttering and scratching his head.

Some things she did, that afternoon and evening of her flight, who can say why or wherefore: she bought a loaf with the young girl's penny and divided it among a man in the stocks, three beggars, and a starve-boned dog; she slipped into the Bear Garden to watch the baiting with ink-drop eyes, and when 'twas done, crept back to where the bears were kept tied in the straw, undid their muzzles with quick fingers, picked apart the heavy knots about their feet, and slipped away again, leaving the gate a little ajar behind her. Just at dusk, she passed a tall wooden building with cressets burning by the door, and a noise within like a giant's roaring, and bills without proclaiming that Mr. William Shak-spere, his *Tragedie of Cymbaline* was this day to be played. The bills were hastily run-up, and the inking over-heavy, so that the letters were spread and blurred; Frisket frowned ere she turned away.

Some little time later, she came to a tavern, and passed it not, but entered under its sign of The Swan and Cygnet. Within was noise and heat enough for a liberty of Hell, from trollops and cony-catchers and 'prentices and clerks and wharfmen, all calling for ale while tavernmaids and potboys scurried among them with tankards and trays and wooden bowls.

Frisket made like a hunting dog for the back of the house, where sat a young man drinking all among the kegs and barrels. He, like the man in the stocks, the bears, and the beggar, was in difficulties. The host stood glaring while he expostulated, pale as a ghost, showing a pair of strings across his palm that might have borne a purse, before they'd been cut.

"I'll leave the jewel from my ear in surety," he was saying. "An I come not again to pay you, it will bring you twenty times the price of the ale and meat."

"For all I know, 'tis base metal overlaid with brass, and worth no more than thy word. I'm minded to take thy two shillings out of thy hide, and set thee up for an exemplum of a liar and a thieving knave."

He raised one hand like a haunch of beef, and the young man sprang to his feet, caught between pride and fear whether he would flee the host or close with him. And at such a pass things stood when Frisket slipped between them and laid her hand upon the host's uplifted arm, and said, "I'll pay thy price, though it be an hundred pound."

The host shaking her away, she took her pocket and jingled it in his ear that would hear no other plea, and it spoke to him, and calmed him, and by and by he took the monies owed him, and a little over to buy a pottle of wine to soothe

the young man's nerves, and left them there together amongst the kegs and barrels in the quiet back of the tavern.

The young man smoothed his doublet that was worn and frayed at the cuffs, and then his beard, and having set himself to rights, handed Frisket onto a jointstool as it had been a chair of state and she the queen's own grace.

"Robert Blanke the poet thanks thee, fair maid," said he. "Without thy silver physic, I had been as dead as Lazarus, without hope of resurrection. How may I call thee?"

"Mary, sir, and withal the merriest Mary thou hast melled withal."

The young man eyed her in the uncertain light. "A harlot? Sure, I grow old, that jades look like fillies to me, and trollops like young maids."

"For I am thy savior, saith the Lord, and a present help in all thy trouble."

"Now the Lord help me indeed, for I bandy words with a madwoman. Yet the mad are touched by God, they say, and own a wisdom beyond the understanding of the wise." He reached out long fingers and, taking her by the chin, tilted her head gently to catch the light. What he saw was a girl on womanhood's threshold, her brow serene, her nose straight and fine, her eyes large and smooth-lidded, her lips clearcarved in a perfect Cupid's bow, her expression open and grave. Thus might an angel look, he thought, or a spirit of antiquity dressed in flesh and a patched woollen gown, were an angel's skin marred and mottled everywhere with flecks of black like blurred print. He released her chin and caressed his beard. "What are you?" he asked.

"I am," said Frisket, "none of your plain or garden whores; I can read and play the virginals. We are children of God, each one, and His angels have the keeping of the least of us no less than of the greatest."

"Sweet Jesu preserve us. A very sensible nonsense, as I live. I well can believe that you, like the phoenix, are alone of your kind, and I accept that you mean no harm. I am your debtor for your mere acquaintance, the more for your saving of me. And therefore I ask of you what you would of me?"

Blanke was a quick-witted man, and eager to unriddle her cypher. Still it took Frisket long and long to make him understand what she was and what she wanted, by which time the tavern was empty and the host hovering by with a broom and a scowl.

"Hark ye," said the poet. " 'Tis dawn, or very nigh, and my head is a tennis ball betwixt your sermons and your bawdries. Company me to my lodging and rest you there, and we'll take counsel of a new day."

So went they their ways through the waking streets, and when they reached the tenement where the poet lodged, he bowed her reverently through the door, saying, "I serve you in all honor, Mistress Mary; in token of which I will leave you my bed to rest upon, and sleep myself upon the floor."

For the first time Frisket smiled at him, showing even teeth as mottled as the rest of her. "For the eye of God sleepeth not," she said, "but watcheth ever over thy slumbers and wakings."

So Robert Blanke slept and Frisket watched, and Hal Spurtle came at last to the goal he had pursued throughout the long, sad night: the shop of the old alchemist, on Pardoner's Lane in Cripplegate, outside London wall.

When the old man opened the door, he knit his brows. "Too late," he said.

"The offer once refused will not be made again. Thou hast thy twenty crowns. Go thy ways."

Hal stuck his foot betwixt door and jamb. "And right content I am with them, I assure you. 'Tis my 'prentice, sir, the child you made from my poppet of paper."

"Hist," said the alchemist, and bundled Hal into the shop as quick as he'd been minded to bundle him out. "Hast no sense, man, to quack hidden things abroad in the public street? Thou'lt be the death of us both."

"And she's less sense than I, poor unbegotten mite, three days old, knows printing and naught else, not even her name, not the skill to ask her way home again. Here are ten crowns, the half of thy fee, to inquire of thy demons where she may be and how she may be faring." And Hal pressed his purse into the alchemist's greasy hand.

"Put up, man. I'll help thee for kindness' sake, or not at all. Now," he said when Hal had put the purse into his bosom again, "now. The tale of the paper 'prentice. Calmly and simply as may be." He listened, his sharp eyes hooded and his stained hands laced before his long nose, while Hal told him of Frisket's cleverness and her goodness and her speaking in phrases either from Dr. Beswick's sermons or from one of the bawdy pamphlets whose spoiled sheets he'd used in her making. And when Hal was done, the alchemist lipped at his fingers and hemmed once or twice, and nosed out a great clasped book, and found a page in it, and ran his finger down the page, and hemmed again, and peered out another that was small and black and powdery with age, and consulted that, and shut it, and closed his eyes, and munched his jaws. And just as Hal decided that the old gentleman had fallen asleep, he sat himself upright and said:

"Thine apprentice, called by thee Frisket, was lent thee for a space, to answer thy present need. Give thanks for the loan, and grieve not the loss. For she is not of this earth, nor is there a place for her therein."

The tears started to Hal's eyes, nor was he too proud to let them fall, but wept for the daughter of his heart. And the alchemist rose from his chair, and laid his hand upon his shoulder, and pressed it. "Be of good cheer, man. The joy thou hadst of her is real. And consider that all children grow and leave their father's house, and 'prentices become journeymen at last."

"Yea," said Hal. "And yet may their fathers mourn them."

"Even so," said the alchemist.

And Hal went from him to St. Paul's church, and knelt within, and prayed a space, and from thence among the bookstalls, inquiring for a journeyman to hire.

And it came to pass that Robert Blanke the poet woke to the sun's golden fingers laid upon his face and Frisket seated in the peaked window of his chamber, that was small and damp and high in the house.

Blanke sat up, scrubbed his hands in his eyes, and raked his hair seemly with his fingers. "Art up, old snorter?" Frisket inquired. "Or shall I lend a hand to raise thee?"

"Peace, good Mistress Mary, I prithee, peace. I am up, as you see, but in no wise awake. Give me an hour to learn to believe in you again, and to think what I may do with you."

So Frisket accompanied Blanke to a cookshop, where she bought him a mutton pie, and to a tavern, where she bought him a tankard of small ale, and watched him eat and drink the same, and then into St. George's church, where she sat in a bench while he took to his knees, and so back to his lodging again as the dusk drew her mantle across the sky.

" 'Twas less magic than desire birthed thee," Blanke said to her, "the printer's desire for company; the alchemist's desire for his grimoire. So logic would argue 'tis desire must send thee back to thy papery womb. And there, dear Mistress Mary, is the rub. For my desire is rather to keep thee whole and sensible than to see thee senseless rubbish."

"Beware the Last Days, when all men are come to Judgment, and the inmost secret thoughts of their hearts laid bare."

And each in his own manner pled his case, to and fro like lawyers, until Blanke threw up his hands and declared himself desirous, at least, of pleasing her who desired no other thing than to put off her dress of flesh, that chafed her as it had been a dress of fire.

"I have considered, and I have prayed, and I have invented a rite seems to answer your purpose." And he opened his mind and said what he purposed, whereat Frisket nodded and did off her clothes and laid her down upon his table, that he had cleared of his writing and his candle and his pens. The which persuaded him above all else that she was not of mankind.

"The Lord giveth," he said solemnly, "and the Lord taketh away. Even as it pleaseth the Lord, so cometh things to pass: blessed be the name of the Lord." And he took his quill pen into his hand, and pressed the inky tip of it to her breastbone, that fanned apart as he touched it into leaves of paper, close-woven and white as snow, printed small and even, the margins wide and straight. Thus he unfolded Frisket and sorted her, praying over her all the while the service for the burial of the dead, and when he'd made an end, he folded the great bundle of pages into her scarlet petticoat, that became a binding of scarlet leather stamped with gold on the cover and on the spine. And he lit a candle, for it had grown full dark, and turned the book to the light, and opened it.

The title page was plain and bare of ornament, bearing only the name of the book—*The Philosophy of the Senses:A Novel in Five Parts*—and the name of the author—Mary Spurtle. Blanke turned the page, crisp and white as a communion host, and read there, printed sharp and clear beyond all common type: "This book is dedicated to my father, Henry Spurtle, printer of East Cheape, and to Robert Blanke, poet and friend."

On the instant, Blanke started up from his chair and hied him to East Cheape, where he inquired high and low of one Henry Spurtle, printer, where his shop lay. And by and by he came to the lane behind St. Martin's church, and a low house that leaked out light and the heavy, wooden clacking of a printing press. Blanke knocked at the door, which was opened by a tall, sad-eyed man with a grandfather's lined cheeks under his nut-brown hair.

"I deal no more in curiosities," he said, and made to close the door.

"Stay, Hal Spurtle, an you would hear news of your daughter Mary."

A light came into Hal's dull eye, and he drew Blanke into his shop, that was all a-bustle with activity. A man sat at the composing-table, selecting and sliding type into a composing stick with the steady rhythm of a new-wound clock. A boy stood at the press, an inking ball in each hand, ready to apply them to the form when his master should be pleased to return to the press. Hal wiped inky hands on his leathern apron. "A pamphlet on cheese-making," he said, and bidding his new apprentice and his journeyman make all tidy 'gainst the morning's work, he gestured Blanke into the inner chamber, where the poet told him of Mistress Mary and all that had befallen her that he knew or guessed. And when he had done, he give Hal the book bound in red leather and said, "This is the book. I read the title and the letter dedicatory, and not one word more. For the book is yours, and no man else hath the right to read it."

Hal wiped his hands clean upon a clout, and took the book, and ran his thumb along the spine and along the gilded edges, and opened it, and gazed long and long upon the dedication to the author's father, Henry Spurtle, printer of East Cheape. As one who leaves a mourner to his grief, Blanke crept to the door; but when he lifted the latch, Hal raised his eyes and said, "I thank thee, Robert Blanke, poet and friend. I'd repay thee, an I could."

"Thy thanks suffice, and Mistress Mary's tale, more wonderful than Master Boccaccio's. And yet am I bold to beg the boon of thee to read the book and learn what she become."

"Beyond question thou shalt read her, aye, and dine with me before, if thou wilt. So much would any father do for the man who returned his daughter to him. Further, I had in mind to print an edition of thy poems, had thou enough to make two perfect sheets or three, cut into octavo and bound in boards, the profit to be split between us."

Blanke laughed aloud and clasped Hal's hand and pumped it as he'd pump water from his mouth. "Now am I fallen deeply in thy debt," he cried. "Yet why speak of debt betwixt close kin? For if thou art her father, then am I her godfather, and we two bound together by love of her who has no like on earth. Now, thou hast a great work here in hand, must be pursued i' the heat. Come Sunday next, I'll be your man, and we'll drink to Mistress Mary in good sack. In the meantime, I'll look out my poems and copy them fair."

Hal pressed his hand and took him to the door and latched it behind him and smiled at his journeyman, who was making his bed under the press, and at his new 'prentice, asleep already in the shadowed corner by the fire, and at the sheets of the pamphlet on cheese-making, all hung out neat to dry. And he went into his inner chamber and closed the door, and took *The Philosophy of the Senses* in his hands, and opened it, and began to read.

PRAYER

Nancy Willard

JACOB AND THE ANGEL

Jane Yolen

Nancy Willard is the author of two magical novels, *Sister Water* and *Things Invisible to See*, as well as short fiction, essay collections, and children's books. Her poetry collections include *Household Tales of Moon and Water* and *Water Walker*. She has received grants from NEA in fiction and poetry, and lectures at Vassar.

Jane Yolen is the author of three enchanting adult fantasy novels (*Briar Rose*, *White Jenna*, and *Sister Light, Sister Dark*) as well as nonfiction and children's books. Her poetry has been published in *Parabola*; *The Greycourt Review*; *Peregrine*; *Snow White, Blood Red*; and *The Armless Maiden*, among others. She has received the World Fantasy Award and many other honors.

"Prayer" by Nancy Willard and "Jacob and the Angel" by Jane Yolen are two of the works to be found in *Among Angels*: an exquisite volume of poems (on the subject of angels) which Yolen and Willard wrote back and forth to each other over several years. Illustrated with luminous art by S. Saelig Gallagher, *Among Angels* is highly recommended.

—T.W.

Prayer

Angel of lost spectacles
and hens' teeth,

angel of snow's breath
and the insomnia

of cats, angel
of snapshots fading

to infinity,
don't drop me—

shoeless,
wingless.

Defender of burrows,
carry me—

carry me
in your pocket of light.

Jacob and the Angel

The chandelier of stars
hung low above the field
when the angel closed on him.
He could not pry
porphyritic fingers
from his thigh,
nor break the granite hold.
Stone has no heart for pity.
He was lamed before night's end,
named before dawn;
shriven, driven, broken, repaired.
The angel could have gone on and on.
God asks much for little,
little for much.
We who have no choice must choose:
to win, to lose,
to wrestle with angels.

THE LION AND THE LARK
Patricia A. McKillip

Patricia A. McKillip, winner of the World Fantasy Award, is one of the very finest writers working in the field today. She has published many wonderful books, including *The Forgotten Beasts of Eld, Stepping from the Shadows, Fool's Run,* and *The Cygnet and the Firebird.* Her most recent works are *Something Rich and Strange* and *The Book of Atrix Wolfe,* both highly recommended. McKillip grew up in America, Germany, and England, and now lives in the Catskill Mountains of New York.

"The Lion and the Lark" is a literary fairy tale reminiscent of such old folktales as "Beauty and the Beast," "The Falcon King," or "East of the Sun, West of the Moon." It is a thoughtful and poetic story that poses the question: *How much can love stand?* The story is reprinted from *The Armless Maiden.*

—T.W.

There was once a merchant who lived in an ancient and magical city with his three daughters. They were all very fond of each other, and as happy as those with love and leisure and wealth can afford to be. The eldest, named Pearl, pretended domesticity. She made bread and forgot to let it rise before she baked it; she pricked her fingers sewing black satin garters; she inflicted such oddities as eggplant soup and barley muffins on her long-suffering family. She was very beautiful, though a trifle awkward and absent-minded, and she had suitors who risked their teeth on her hard, flat bread as boldly as knights of old slew dragons for the heart's sake. The second daughter, named Diamond, wore delicate, gold-rimmed spectacles, and was never without a book or a crossword puzzle at hand. She discoursed learnedly on the origins of the phoenix and the conjunctions of various astrological signs. She had an answer for everything, and was considered by all her suitors to be wondrously wise.

The youngest daughter, called Lark, sang a great deal but never spoke much. Because her voice was so like her mother's, her father doted on her. She was by no means the fairest of the three daughters; she did not shine with beauty or wit. She was pale and slight, with dark eyes, straight, serious brows, and dark braided hair. She had a loving and sensible heart, and she adored her family, though they worried her with their extravagances and foolishness. She wore Pearl's crooked garters, helped Diamond with her crossword puzzles, and heard odd questions arise from deep in her mind when she sang. "What is life?" she would wonder. "What is love? What is man?" This last gave her a good deal to ponder, as she watched her father shower his daughters with chocolates and taffeta gowns and gold bracelets. The young gentlemen who came calling seemed especially puzzling. They sat in their velvet shirts and their leather boots, nibbling burnt cakes and praising Diamond's mind, and all the while their eyes said other things. Now, their eyes said: Now. Then: Patience, patience. You are flowers, their mouths said, you are jewels, you are golden dreams. Their eyes said: I eat flowers, I burn with dreams, I have a tower without a door in my heart and I will keep you there. . . .

Her sisters seemed fearless in the face of this power—whether from innocence or design, Lark was uncertain. Since she was wary of men, and seldom spoke to them, she felt herself safe. She spoke mostly to her father, who only had a foolish, doting look in his eyes, and who of all men could make her smile.

One day their father left on a long journey to a distant city where he had lucrative business dealings. Before he left, he promised to bring his daughters whatever they asked for. Diamond, in a riddling mood, said merrily, "Bring us our names!"

"Oh, yes," Pearl pleaded, kissing his balding pate. "I do love pearls." She was wearing as many as she had, on her wrists, in her hair, on her shoes. "I always want more."

"But," their father said with an anxious glance at his youngest, who was listening with her grave, slightly perplexed expression, "does Lark love larks?"

Her face changed instantly, growing so bright she looked almost beautiful. "Oh, yes. Bring me my singing name, Father. I would rather have that than all the lifeless, deathless jewels in the world."

Her sisters laughed; they petted her and kissed her, and told her that she was still a child to hunger after worthless presents. Someday she would learn to ask for gifts that would outlast love, for when love had ceased, she would still possess what it had once been worth.

"But what is love?" she asked, confused. "Can it be bought like yardage?" But they only laughed harder and gave her no answers.

She was still puzzling ten days later when their father returned. Pearl was in the kitchen baking spinach tea cakes, and Diamond in the library, dozing over the philosophical writings of Lord Thiggut Moselby. Lark heard a knock at the door, and then the lovely, liquid singing of a lark. Laughing, she ran down the hall before the servants could come, and swung open the door to greet their father.

He stared at her. In his hands he held a little silver cage. Within the cage, the lark sang constantly, desperately, each note more beautiful than the last, as if, coaxing the rarest, finest song from itself, it might buy its freedom. As Lark reached for it, she saw the dark blood mount in her father's face, the veins throb in his temples. Before she could touch the cage, he lifted it high over his head, dashed it with all his might to the stone steps.

"No!" he shouted. The lark fluttered within the bent silver; his boot lifted over cage and bird, crushed both into the stones. "No!"

"No!" Lark screamed. And then she put both fists to her mouth and said nothing more, retreating as far as she could without moving from the sudden, incomprehensible violence. Dimly, she heard her father sobbing. He was on his knees, his face buried in her skirt. She moved finally, unclenched one hand, allowed it to touch his hair.

"What is it, Father?" she whispered. "Why have you killed the lark?"

He made a great, hollow sound, like the groan of a tree split to its heart. "Because I have killed you."

In the kitchen, Pearl arranged burnt tea cakes on a pretty plate. The maid who should have opened the door hummed as she dusted the parlor, and thought of the carriage driver's son. Upstairs, Diamond woke herself up midsnore, and stared dazedly at Lord Moselby's famous words and wondered, for just an instant, why they sounded so empty. That has nothing to do with life, she protested, and then went back to sleep. Lark sat down on the steps beside the mess of feathers and silver and blood, and listened to her father's broken words.

"On the way back . . . we drove through a wood . . . just today, it was . . . I had not found you a lark. I heard one singing. I sent the post boy looking one way, I searched another. I followed the lark's song, and saw it finally, resting on the head of a great stone lion." His face wrinkled and fought itself; words fell like stones, like the tread of a stone beast. "A long line of lions stretched up the steps of a huge castle. Vines covered it so thickly it seemed no light could pass through the windows. It looked abandoned. I gave it no thought. The lark had all my attention. I took off my hat and crept up to it. I had it, I had it . . . singing in my hat and trying to fly. . . . And then the lion turned its head to look at me."

Lark shuddered; she could not speak. She felt her father shudder.

"It said, 'You have stolen my lark.' Its tail began to twitch. It opened its stone mouth wide to show me its teeth. 'I will kill you for that.' And it gathered its body into a crouch. I babbled—I made promises—I am not a young man to run from lions. My heart nearly burst with fear. I wish it had . . . I promised—"

"What," she whispered, "did you promise?"

"Anything it wanted."

"And what did it want?"

"The first thing that met me when I arrived home from my journey." He hid his face against her, shaking her with his sobs. "I thought it would be the cat! It always suns itself at the gate! Or Columbine at worst—she always wants an excuse to leave her work. Why did you answer the door? Why?"

Her eyes filled with sudden tears. "Because I heard the lark."

Her father lifted his head. "You shall not go," he said fiercely. "I'll bar the doors. The lion will never find you. If it does, I'll shoot it, burn it—"

"How can you harm a stone lion? It could crash through the door and drag me into the street whenever it chooses." She stopped abruptly, for an odd, confused violence tangled her thoughts. She wanted to make sounds she had never heard from herself before. *You killed me for a bird!* she wanted to shout. *A father is nothing but a foolish old man!* Then she thought more calmly, *But I always knew that.* She stood up, gently pried his fingers from her skirt. "I'll go now. Perhaps I can make a bargain with this lion. If it's a lark it wants, I'll sing to it. Perhaps I can go and come home so quickly my sisters will not even know."

"They will never forgive me."

"Of course they will." She stepped over the crushed cage, started down the path without looking back. "I have."

But the sun had begun to set before she found the castle deep in the forest beyond the city. Even Pearl, gaily proffering tea cakes, must notice an insufficiency of Lark, and down in the pantry, Columbine would be whispering of the strange, bloody smear she had to clean off the porch. . . . The stone lion, of pale marble, snarling a warning on its pedestal, seemed to leap into her sight between the dark trees. To her horror, she saw behind it a long line of stone lions, one at each broad step leading up to the massive, barred doors of the castle.

"Oh," she breathed, cold with terror, and the first lion turned its ponderous head. A final ray of sunlight gilded its eye. It stared at her until the light faded. She heard it whisper,

"Who are you?"

"I am the lark," she said tremulously, "my father sent to replace the one he stole."

"Can you sing?"

She sang, blind and trembling, while the dark wood rustled around her, grew close. A hand slid over her mouth, a voice spoke into her ear. "Not very well, it seems."

She felt rough stubbled skin against her cheek, arms tense with muscle; the voice, husky and pleasant, murmured against her hair. She turned, amazed, alarmed for different reasons. "Not when I am so frightened," she said to the shadowy face above hers. "I expected to be eaten."

She saw a sudden glint of teeth. "If you wish."

"I would rather not be."

"Then I will leave that open to negotiation. You are very brave. And very honest to come here. I expected your father to send along the family cat or some little yapping powder puff of a dog."

"Why did you terrify him so?"

"He took my lark. Being stone by day, I have so few pleasures."

"Are you bewitched?"

He nodded at the castle. Candles and torches appeared on steps now. A row of men stood where the lions had been, waiting, while a line of pages carrying light trooped down the steps to guide them. "That is my castle. I have been under a spell so long I scarcely remember why. My memory has been turning to stone for some time, now . . . I am only human at night, and sunlight is dangerous to me." He touched her cheek with his hand; unused to being touched, she started. Then, unused to being touched, she took a step toward him. He was tall and lean, and if the mingling of fire and moonlight did not lie, his face was neither foolish nor cruel. He was unlike her sisters' suitors; there was a certain sadness in his voice, a hesitancy and humor that made her want to hear him speak. He did not touch her again when she drew closer, but she heard the pleased smile in his voice. "Will you have supper with me?" he asked. "And tell me the story of your life?"

"It has no story yet."

"You are here. There is a story in that." He took her hand, then, and drew it under his arm. He led her past the pages and the armed men, up the stairs to the open doors. His face, she found, was quite easy to look at. He had tawny hair and eyes, and rough, strong, graceful features that were young in expression and happier than their experience.

"Tell me your name," he asked, as she crossed his threshold.

"Lark," she answered, and he laughed.

His name, she discovered over asparagus soup, was Perrin. Over salmon and partridge and salad, she discovered that he was gentle and courteous to his servants, had an ear for his musicians' playing, and had lean, strong hands that moved easily among the jeweled goblets and gold-rimmed plates. Over port and nuts, she discovered that his hands, choosing walnuts and enclosing them to crack them, made her mouth go dry and her heart beat. When he opened her palm to put a nut into it, she felt something melt through her from throat to thigh, and for the first time in her life she wished she were beautiful. Over candlelight, as he led her to her room, she saw herself in his eyes. In his bed, astonished, she thought she discovered how simple life was.

And so they were married, under moonlight, by a priest who was bewitched by day and pontifical by night. Lark slept until dusk and sang until morning. She was, she wrote her sisters and her father, entirely happy. Divinely happy. No one could believe how happy. When wistful questions rose to the surface of her mind, she pushed them under again ruthlessly. Still they came—words bubbling up—stubborn, half coherent: Who cast this spell and is my love still in danger? How long can I so blissfully ignore the fact that by day I am married to a stone, and by night to a man who cannot bear the touch of sunlight? Should we not do something to break the spell? Why is even the priest, who preaches endlessly about the light of grace, content to live only in the dark? "We are used to it," Perrin said lightly, when she ventured these questions, and then he made her laugh, in the ways he had, so that she forgot to ask if living in the dark, and in a paradox, was something men inherently found more comfortable than women.

One day she received letters from both sisters saying that they were to be married in the same ceremony; and she must come, she could not refuse them, they absolutely refused to be married without her; and if their bridegrooms cast themselves disconsolately into a dozen mill ponds, or hung themselves from a hundred pear trees, not even that would move them to marry without her presence.

"I see I must go," she said with delight. She flung her arms around Perrin's neck. "Please come," she pleaded. "I don't want to leave you. Not for a night, nor for a single hour. You'll like my sisters—they're funny and foolish, and wiser, in their ways, than I am."

"I cannot," he whispered, loath to refuse her anything.

"Please."

"I dare not."

"Please."

"If I am touched by light as fine as thread, you will not see me again for seven years except in the shape of a dove."

"Seven years," she said numbly, terrified. Then she thought of lovely, clumsy Pearl and her burnt tea cakes, and of Diamond and her puzzles and earnest discourses on the similarities between the moon and a dragon's egg. She pushed her face against Perrin, torn between her various loves, gripping him in anguish. "Please," she begged. "I must see them. But I cannot leave you. But I must go to them. I promise: no light will find you, my night-love. No light, ever."

So her father sealed a room in his house so completely that by day it was dark as night, and by night as dark as death. By chance, or perhaps because, deep in the most secret regions of his mind he thought to free Lark from her strange, enchanted husband, and bring her back to light and into his life, he used a piece of unseasoned wood to make a shutter. While Lark busied herself hanging pearls on Pearl, diamonds on Diamond, and swathing them both in yards of lace, Sun opened a hair-fine crack in the green wood where Perrin waited.

The wedding was a sumptuous, decadent affair. Both brides were dressed in cloth-of-gold, and they carried huge languorous bouquets of calla lilies. So many lilies and white irises and white roses crowded the sides of the church that, in their windows and on their pedestals, the faces of the saints were hidden. Even the sun, which had so easily found Perrin in his darkness, had trouble finding its way into the church. But the guests, holding fat candles of beeswax, lit the church with stars instead. The bridegrooms wore suits of white and midnight blue; one wore pearl buttons and studs and buckles, the other diamonds. To Lark they looked very much alike, both tall and handsome, tweaking their mustaches straight, and dutifully assuming a serious expression as they listened to the priest, while their eyes said: at last, at last, I have waited so long, the trap is closing, the night is coming. . . . But their faces were at once so vain and tender and foolish that Lark's heart warmed to them. They did not seem to realize that one had been an ingredient in Pearl's recipes that she had stirred into her life, and the other a three-letter solution in Diamond's crossword puzzle. At the end of the ceremony, when the bridegrooms had searched through cascades of heavy lace to kiss their brides' faces, the guests blew out their candles.

In the sudden darkness a single hair-fine thread of light shone between two rose petals.

Lark dropped her candle. Panicked without knowing why, she stumbled through the church, out into light, where she forced a carriage driver to gallop madly through the streets of the city to her father's house. Not daring to let light through Perrin's door, she pounded on it.

She heard a gentle, mournful word she did not understand.

She pounded again. Again the sad voice spoke a single word.

The third time she pounded, she recognized the voice.

She flung open the door. A white dove sitting in a hair-fine thread of light fluttered into the air, and flew out the door.

"Oh, my love," she whispered, stunned. She felt something warm on her cheek that was not a tear, and touched it: a drop of blood. A small white feather floated out of the air, caught on the lace above her heart. "Oh," she said again, too grieved for tears, staring into the empty room, her empty life, and then down the empty hall, her empty future.

"Oh, why," she cried, wild with sorrow, "have I chosen to love a lion, a dove, an enchantment, instead of a fond foolish man with waxed mustaches whom nothing, neither light nor dark, can ever change? Someone who could never be snatched away by magic? Oh, my sweet dove, will I ever see you? How will I find you?"

Sunlight glittered at the end of the hall in a bright and ominous jewel. She went toward it thoughtlessly, trembling, barely able to walk. A drop of blood had fallen on the floor, and into the blood, a small white feather.

She heard Perrin's voice, as in a dream: *Seven years.* Beyond the open window on the flagstones another crimson jewel gleamed. Another feather fluttered, caught in it. On the garden wall she saw the dove turned to look at her.

Seven years.

This, its eyes said. *Or your father's house, where you are loved, and where there is no mystery in day or night. Stay. Or follow.*

Seven years.

By the end of the second year, she had learned to speak to animals and understand the mute, fleeting language of the butterflies. By the end of the third year, she had walked everywhere in the world. She had made herself a gown of soft white feathers stained with blood that grew longer and longer as she followed the dove. By the end of the fifth year, her face had grown familiar to the stars, and the moon kept its eye on her. By the end of the sixth year, the gown of feathers and her hair swept behind her, mingling light and dark, and she had become, to the world's eye, a figure of mystery and enchantment. In her own eyes she was simply Lark, who loved Perrin; all the enchantment lay in him.

At the end of the seventh year she lost him.

The jeweled path of blood, the moon-white feathers stopped. It left her stranded, bewildered, on a mountainside in some lonely part of the world. In disbelief, she searched frantically: stones, tree boughs, earth. Nothing told her which direction to go. One direction was as likely as another, and all, to her despairing heart, went nowhere. She threw herself on the ground finally and wept for the first time since her father had killed the lark.

"So close," she cried, pounding the earth in fury and sorrow. "So close—another step, another drop of blood—oh, but perhaps he is dead, my Perrin, after losing so much blood to show me the way. So many years, so much blood, so much silence, so much, too much, too much . . ." She fell silent finally, dazed and exhausted with grief. The wind whispered to her, comforting; the trees sighed for her, weeping leaves that caressed her face. Birds spoke.

Maybe the dove is not dead, they said. *We saw none of ours fall dying from the sky. Enchantments do not die, they are transformed . . . Light sees everything. Ask the sun. Who knows him better than the sun who changed him into a dove?*

"Do you know?" she whispered to the sun, and for an instant saw its face among the clouds.

No, it said in words of fire, and with fire, shaped something out of itself. *It's you I have watched, for seven years, as constant and faithful to your love as I am to the world. Take this. Open it when your need is greatest.*

She felt warm light in her hand. The light hardened into a tiny box with jeweled hinges and the sun's face on its lid. She turned her face away disconsolately; a box was not a bird. But she held it, and it kept her warm through dusk and nightfall as she lay unmoving on the cold ground.

She asked the full moon when it rose above the mountain, "Have you seen my white dove? For seven years you showed me each drop of blood, each white feather, even on the darkest night."

It was you I watched, the moon said. *More constant than the moon on the darkest night, for I hid then and you never faltered in your journey. I have not seen your dove.*

"Do you know," she whispered to the wind, and heard it question its four messengers, who blew everywhere in the world. *No*, they said, and *No*, and *No*, And then the sweet south wind blew against her cheek, smelling of roses and warm seas and endless summers. "*Yes.*"

She lifted her face from the ground. Twigs and dirt clung to her. Her long hair was full of leaves and spiders and the grandchildren of spiders. Full of webs, it looked as filmy as a bridal veil. Her face was moon pale; moonlight could have traced the bones through it. Her eyes were fiery with tears.

"My dove."

"He has become a lion again. The seven years are over. But the dove changed shape under the eyes of an enchanted dragon, and when the dragon saw lion, battle sparked. He is still fighting."

Lark sat up. "Where?"

"In a distant land, beside a southern sea. I brought you a nut from one of the trees there. It is no ordinary nut. Now listen. This is what you must do . . ."

So she followed the South Wind to the land beside the southern sea, where the sky flashed red with dragon fire, and its fierce roars blew down trees and tore the sails from every passing ship. The lion, no longer stone by daylight, was golden and as flecked with blood as Lark's gown of feathers. Lark never questioned the wind's advice, for she was desperate beyond the advice of mortals. She went to the seashore and found reeds broken in the battle, each singing a different, haunting note through its hollow throat. She counted. She picked the eleventh reed and waited. When the dragon bent low, curling around itself to roar rage and fire at the lion gnawing at its wing, she ran forward quickly, struck its throat with the reed.

Smoke hissed from its scales, as if the reed had seared it. It tried to roar; no sound came out, no fire. Its great neck sagged; scales darkened with blood and smoke. One eye closed. The lion leaped for its throat.

There was a flash, as if the sun had struck the earth. Lark crouched, covering her face. The world was suddenly very quiet. She heard bullfrogs among the reeds, the warm, slow waves fanning across the sand. She opened her eyes.

The dragon had fallen on its back, with the lion sprawled on top of it. A woman lay on her back, with Perrin on top of her. His eyes were closed, his face bloody; he drew deep, ragged breaths, one hand clutching the woman's shoulder, his open mouth against her neck. The woman's weary face, upturned to the sky above Perrin's shoulder, was also bloodstained; her free hand lifted weakly, fell again across Perrin's back. Her hair was as gold as the sun's little box; her face as pale and perfect as the moon's face. Lark stared. The waves grew full again, spilled with a languorous sigh across the sand. The woman drew a deep breath. Her eyes flickered open; they were as blue as the sky.

She turned her head, looked at Perrin. She lifted her hand from his back, touched her eyes delicately, her brows rising in silent question. Then she looked again at the blood on his face.

She stiffened, began pushing at him and talking at the same time. "I remember. I remember now. You were that monstrous lion that kept nipping at my wings." Her voice was low and sweet, amused as she tugged at Perrin. "You must get up. What if someone should see us? Oh, dear. You must be hurt." She shifted out from under him, made a hasty adjustment to her bodice, and caught sight of Lark. "Oh, my dear," she cried, "it's not what you think."

"I know," Lark whispered, still amazed at the woman's beauty, and at the sight of Perrin, whom she had not seen in seven years, and never in the light, lying golden-haired and slack against another woman's body. The woman bent over Perrin, turned him on his back.

"He is hurt. Is there water?" She glanced around vaguely, as if she expected a bullfrog to emerge in tie and tails, with water on a tray. But Lark had already fetched it in her hands, from a little rill of fresh water.

She moistened Perrin's face with it, let his lips wander over her hands, searching for more. The woman was gazing at Lark.

"You must be an enchantress or a witch," she exclaimed. "That explains your— unusual appearance. And the way we suddenly became ourselves again. I am— we are most grateful to you. My father is king of this desert, and he will reward you richly if you come to his court." She took a tattered piece of her hem, wiped a corner of Perrin's lips, then, in after-thought, her own.

"My name is Lark. This man is—"

"Yes," the princess said, musing. Her eyes were very wide, very blue; she was not listening to Lark. "He is, isn't he? Do you know, I think there was a kind of prophecy when I was born that I would marry a lion. I'm sure there was. Of course they kept it secret all these years, for fear I might actually meet a lion, but—here it is. He. A lion among men. Do you think I should explain to my father what he was, or do you think I should just—not exactly lie, but omit that part of his past? What do you think? Witches know these things."

"I think," Lark said unsteadily, brushing sand out of Perrin's hair, "that you are mistaken. I am—"

"So I should tell my father. Will you help me raise him? There is a griffin just beyond those rocks. Very nice; in fact we became friends before I had to fight the lion. I had no one else to talk to except bullfrogs. And you know what frogs are like. Very little small talk, and that they repeat incessantly." She hoisted Perrin up, brushing sand off his shoulders, his chest, his thighs. "I don't think my father will mind at all. About the lion part. Do you?" She put her fingers to her lips suddenly and gave a piercing whistle that silenced the frogs and brought the griffin, huge and flaming red, up over the rocks. "Come," she said to it. Lark clung to Perrin's arm.

"Wait," she said desperately, words coming slowly, clumsily, for she had scarcely spoken to mortals in seven years. "You don't understand. Wait until he wakes. I have been following him for seven years."

"Then how wonderful that you have found him. The griffin will fly us to my father's palace. It's the only one for miles, in the desert. You'll find it easily." She laid her hand on Lark's. "Please come. I'd take you with us, but it would tire the griffin—"

"But I have a magic nut for it to rest on, while we cross the sea—"

"But you see we are going across the desert, and anyway I think a nut might be a little small." She smiled brightly, but very wearily at Lark. "I feel I will never be able to thank you enough." She pushed the upright Perrin against the griffin's back, and he toppled face down between the bright, uplifted wings.

"Perrin!" Lark cried desperately, and the princess, clinging to the griffin's neck, looked down at her, startled, uncertain. But the thrust of the griffin's great wings tangled wind and sand together and choked Lark's voice. She coughed and spat sand while the princess, cheerful again, waved one hand and held Perrin tightly with the other.

"Good-bye . . ."

"No!" Lark screamed. No one heard her but the frogs.

She sat awake all night, a dove in speckled plumage, mourning with the singing reeds. When the sun rose, it barely recognized her, so pale and wild was her face, so blank with grief her eyes. Light touched her gently. She stirred finally, sighed, watching the glittering net of gold the sun cast across the sea. They should have been waking in a great tree growing out of the sea, she and Perrin and the griffin, a wondrous sight that passing sailors might have spun into tales for their grandchildren. Instead, here she was, abandoned among the bullfrogs, while her true love had flown away with the princess. What would he think when he woke and saw her golden hair, heard her sweet, amused voice telling him that she had been the dragon he had fought, and that at the battle's end, she had awakened in his arms? An enchantress—a strange, startling woman who wore a gown of bloodstained feathers, whose long black hair was bound with cobweb, whose face and eyes seemed more of a wild creature's than a human's—had wandered by at the right moment and freed them from their spells.

And so. And therefore. And of course what all this must mean was, beyond doubt, their destiny: the marriage of the dragon and the lion. And if they were very lucky—wouldn't it be splendid—the enchantress might come to see them married.

"Will he remember me?" Lark murmured to the bullfrogs. "If he saw me now, would he even recognize me?" She tried to see her face reflected in the waves—but of the faces gliding and breaking across the sand, none seemed to belong to her, and she asked desperately, "How will he recognize me if I cannot recognize myself?"

She stood up then, her hands to her mouth, staring at her faceless shadow in the sand. She whispered, her throat aching with grief, "What must I do? Where can I begin? To find my lost love and myself?"

"You know where he is," the sea murmured. "Go there."

"But she is so beautiful—and I have become so—"

"He is not here," the reeds sang in their soft, hollow voices. "Find him. He is again enchanted."

"Again! First a stone lion, and then a dove, and then a real lion—now what is he?"

"He is enchanted by his human form."

She was silent, still gazing at her morning shadow. "I never knew him fully human," she said at last. "And he never knew me. If we meet now by daylight, who is to say whether he will recognize Lark, or I will recognize Perrin? Those were names we left behind long ago."

"Love recognizes love," the reeds murmured. Her shadow whispered,

"I will guide you."

So she set her back to the sun and followed her shadow across the desert.

By day the sun was a roaring lion, by night the moon a pure white dove. Lion and dove accompanied her, showed her hidden springs of cool water among the barren stones, and trees that shook down dates and figs and nuts into her hands. Finally, climbing a rocky hill, she saw an enormous and beautiful palace, whose immense gates of bronze and gold lay open to welcome the richly dressed people riding horses and dromedaries and elegant palanquins into it.

She hurried to join them before the sun set and the gates were closed. Her bare feet were scraped and raw; she limped a little. Her feathers had grown frayed; her face was gaunt, streaked with dust and sorrow. She looked like a begger, she knew, but the people spoke to her kindly, and even tossed her a coin or two.

"We have come for the wedding of our princess and the Lion of the Desert, whom it is her destiny to wed."

"Who foretold such a destiny?" Lark asked, her voice trembling.

"Someone," they assured her. "The king's astrologer. A great sorceress disguised as a beggar, not unlike yourself. A bullfrog, who spoke with a human tongue at her birth. Her mother was frightened by a lion just before childbirth, and dreamed it. No one exactly remembers who, but someone did. Destiny or no, they will marry in three days, and never was there a more splendid couple than the princess and her lion."

Lark crept into the shadow of the gate. "Now what shall I do?" she murmured, her eyes wide, dark with urgency. "With his eyes full of her, he will never notice a beggar."

Sun slid a last gleam down the gold edge of the gate. She remembered its gift then and drew the little gold box out of her pocket. She opened it.

A light sprang out of it, swirled around her like a storm of gold dust, glittering, shimmering. It settled on her, turned the feathers into the finest silk and silk cloth of gold. It turned the cobwebs in her hair into a long sparkling net of diamonds and pearls. It turned the dust on her feet into soft golden leather and pearls. Light played over her face, hiding shadows of grief and despair. Seeing the wonderful dress, she laughed for the first time in seven years, and with wonder, she recognized Lark's voice.

As she walked down the streets, people stared at her, marveling. They made way for her. A man offered her his palanquin, a woman her sunshade. She shook her head at both, laughing again. "I will not be shut up in a box, nor will I shut out the sun." So she walked, and all the wedding guests slowed to accompany her to the inner courtyard.

Word of her had passed into the palace long before she did. The princess, dressed in fine flowing silks the color of her eyes, came out to meet the stranger who rivaled the sun. She saw the dress before she saw Lark's face.

"Oh, my dear," she breathed, hurrying down the steps. "Say this is a wedding gift for me. You cannot possibly wear this to my wedding—no one will look at me! Say you brought it for me. Or tell me what I can give you in return for it." She stepped back, half-laughing, still staring at the sun's creation. "Where are my manners? You came all the way from—from—and here all I can do is—where are you from, anyway? Who in the world are you?" She looked finally into Lark's eyes. She clapped her hands, laughing again, with a touch of relief in her voice. "Oh, it is the witch! You have come! Perrin will be so pleased to meet you. He is sleeping now; he is still weak from his wounds." She took Lark's hand in hers and led her up the steps. "Now tell me how I can persuade you to let me have that dress. Look how everyone stares at you. It will make me the most beautiful woman in the world on my wedding day. And you're a witch, you don't care how you look. Anyway, it's not necessary for you to look like this. People will think you're only human."

Lark, who had been thinking while the princess chattered, answered, "I will give you the dress for a price."

"Anything!"

Lark stopped short. "No—you must not say that!" she cried fiercely. "Ever! You could pay far more than you ever imagined for something as trivial as this dress!"

"All right," the princess said gently, patting her hand. "I will not give you just anything. Though I'd hardly call this dress trivial. But tell me what you want."

"I want a night alone with your bridegroom."

The princess's brows rose. She glanced around hastily to see if anyone were listening, then she took Lark's other hand. "We must observe a few proprieties," she said softly, smiling. "Not even I have had a whole night in my lion's bed—he had been too ill. I would not grant this to any woman. But you are a witch, and you helped us before, and I know you mean no harm. I assume you wish to tend him during the night with magic arts so that he can heal faster."

"If I can do that, I will. But—"

"Then you may. But I must have the dress first."

Lark was silent. So was the princess, who held her eyes until Lark bowed her head. *Then I have lost*, she thought, *for he will never even look at me without this dress.*

The princess said lightly, "You were gracious to refuse my first impulse to give you anything. I trust you, but in that dress you are very beautiful, and you know how men are. Or perhaps, being a witch, you don't. Anyway, there is no need at all for you to appear to him like this. And how can I surprise him on our wedding day with this dress if he sees you in it first?"

You are like my sisters, Lark thought. *Foolish and wiser than I am.* She yielded, knowing she wanted to see Perrin with all her heart, and the princess only wanted what dazzled her eyes. "You are right," she said. "You may tell people that I will stay with Perrin to heal him if I can. And that I brought the dress for you."

The princess kissed her cheek. "Thank you. I will find you something else to wear, and show you his room. I'm not insensitive—I fell in love with him myself the moment I looked at him. So I can hardly blame you for—and of course he is in love with me. But we hardly know each other, and I don't want to confuse him with possibilities at this delicate time. You understand."

"Perfectly."

"Good."

She took Lark to her own sumptuous rooms and had her maid dress Lark in something she called "refreshingly simple" but which Lark called "drab," and knew it belonged not even to the maid, but to someone much farther down the social strata, who stayed in shadows and was not allowed to wear lace.

I am more wren or sparrow than Lark, she thought sadly, as the princess brought her to Perrin's room.

"Till sunrise," she said; the tone of her voice added, *And not a moment after.*

"Yes," Lark said absently, gazing at her sleeping love. At last the puzzled princess closed the door, left Lark in the twilight.

Lark approached the bed. She saw Perrin's face in the light of a single candle beside the bed. It was bruised and scratched; there was a long weal from a dragon's claw down one bare shoulder. He looked older, weathered, his pale skin burned by the sun, which had scarcely touched it in years. The candlelight picked out a thread of silver here and there among the lion's gold of his hair. She reached out impulsively, touched the silver. "My poor Perrin," she said softly. "At least, as a dove, for seven years, you were faithful to me. You shed blood at every seventh step I took. And I took seven steps for every drop you shed. How strange to find you naked in this bed, waiting for a swan instead of Lark. At least I had you for a little while, and at long last you are unbewitched."

She bent over him, kissed his lips gently. He opened his eyes.

She turned away quickly before the loving expression in them changed to disappointment. But he moved more swiftly, reaching out to catch her hand before she left.

"Lark?" He gave a deep sigh as she turned again, and eased back into the pillows. "I heard your sweet voice in my dream. . . . I didn't want to wake and end the dream. But you kissed me awake. You are real, aren't you?" he asked anxiously, as she lingered in the shadows, and he pulled her out of darkness into light.

He looked at her for a long time, silently, until her eyes filled with tears. "I've changed," she said.

"Yes," he said. "You have been enchanted, too."

"And so have you, once again."

He shook his head. "You have set me free."

"And I will set you free again," she said softly, "to marry whom you choose."

He moved again, too abruptly, and winced. His hold tightened on her hand. "Have I lost all enchantment?" he asked sadly. "Did you love the spellbound man more than you can love the ordinary mortal? Is that why you left me?"

She stared at him. "I never left you—"

"You disappeared," he said wearily. "After seven long years of flying around in the shape of a dove, due to your father's appalling carelessness, I finally turned back into a lion, and you were gone. I thought you could not bear to stay with me through yet another enchantment. I didn't blame you. But it grieved me badly— I was glad when the dragon attacked me, because I thought it might kill me. Then I woke up in my own body, in a strange bed, with a princess beside me explaining that we were destined to be married."

"Did you tell her you were married?"

He sighed. "I thought it was just another way of being enchanted. A lion, a dove, marriage to a beautiful princess I don't love—what difference did anything make? You were gone. I didn't care any longer what happened to me." She swallowed, but could not speak. "Are you about to leave me again?" he asked painfully. "Is that why you'll come no closer?"

"No," she whispered. "I thought—I didn't think you still remembered me."

He closed his eyes. "For seven years I left you my heart's blood to follow. . . ."

"And for seven years I followed. And then on the last day of the seventh year, you disappeared. I couldn't find you anywhere. I asked the sun, the moon, the wind. I followed the south wind to find you. It told me how to break the spell over you. So I did—"

His eyes opened again. "You. You are the enchantress the princess talks about. You rescued both of us. And then—"

"She took you away from me before I could tell her—I tried—"

His face was growing peaceful in the candlelight. "She doesn't listen very well. But why did you think I had forgotten you?"

"I thought—she was so beautiful, I thought—and I have grown so worn, so strange—"

For the first time in seven years, she saw him smile. "You have walked the world, and spoken to the sun and wind . . . I have only been enchanted. You have become the enchantress." He pulled her closer, kissed her hand, and then her wrist. He added, as she began to smile, "What a poor opinion you must have of my human shape to think that after all these years I would prefer the peacock to the Lark."

He pulled her closer, kissed the crook of her elbow, and then her breast. And then she caught his lips and kissed him, one hand in his hair, the other in his hand.

And thus the princess found them, as she opened the door, speaking softly, "My dear, I forgot, if he wakes you must give him this potion—I mean, this tea of mild herbs to ease his pain a little—" She kicked the door shut and saw their surprised faces. "Well," she said frostily. "Really."

"This is my wife," Perrin said.

"Well, really." She flung the sleeping potion out the window, and folded her arms. "You might have told me."

"I never thought I would see her again."

"How extraordinarily careless of you both." She tapped her foot furiously for a moment, and then said, slowly, her face clearing a little, "That's why you were there to rescue us! Now I understand. And I snatched him away from you without even thinking—and after you had searched for him so long, I made you search— oh, my dear." She clasped her hands tightly. "What I said. About not spending a full night here. You must not think—"

"I understand."

"No, but really—tell her, Perrin."

"It doesn't matter," Perrin said gently. "You were kind to me. That's what Lark will remember."

But she remembered everything, as they flew on the griffin's back across the sea: her father's foolish bargain, the fearsome stone lion, the seven years when she followed a white dove beyond any human life, the battle between dragon and lion, and then the hopeless loss of him again. She turned the nut in her palm, and questions rose in her head: Can I truly stand more mysteries, the possibilities of more hardships, more enchanting princesses between us? Would it be better just to crack the nut and eat it? Then we would all fall into the sea, in this moment when our love is finally intact. He seems to live from spell to spell. Is it better to die now, before something worse can happen to him? How much can love stand?

Perrin caught her eyes and smiled at her. She heard the griffin's labored breathing, felt the weary catch in its mighty wings. She tossed the nut high into the air and watched it fall a long, long way before it hit the water. And then the great tree grew out of the sea, to the astonishment of passing sailors, who remembered it all their lives, and told their incredulous grandchildren of watching a griffin red as fire drop out of the blue to rest among its boughs.

Honorable Mentions
1995

Ackerman, Will, "Enough to Drive You Bats," *Thin Ice* XVII.
Ackroyd, Peter, "A Tale of the Expected," *The Guardian*, Dec. 22.
Adams, Benjamin, "The Frieze of Life," *Blood Muse*.
Alexis, André, "Five Stories of Ottawa," *Despair: and other stories of Ottawa*.
———, "Kuala Lumpur," Ibid.
———, "The Night Piece," Ibid.
———, "The Third Terrace," Ibid.
Allen, Lori Negridge, "Anorexic," *Tomorrow* No. 17, Oct.
Allison, Tim, "The Day Nothing Happened," *Weirdbook* 29.
Aniolowski, Scott David, "I Dream of Wires," *Made in Goatswood*.
Antczak, Steve, "Reality," *Adventures in the Twilight Zone*.
Antczak, Steve and Nicoll, Gregory, "The Coffin-Maker," *Deathrealm* #26.
Antieau, Kim, "A Leash of Lovers," *Tomorrow* No. 15, June.
Arceneaux, K. C., "The Glass," *Chicago Review*, Vol. 41, Number 1.
Armstrong, Douglas D., "The Vagrant," *Alfred Hitchcock Mystery Magazine*, March.
Arnzen, Michael A., "The Blood Ran Out," *100 Vicious Little Vampire Stories*.
———, "Piano Lessons," (poem) *Deathrealm* #24.
———, "While My Guitar Gently Weeps," *Dark Regions* Vol. 3, Number 1.
Ashley, Allen, "Theseus Rex," *The Third Alternative* 8.
Avery, Simon, "Blue Nothings," Ibid.
———, "November Flowers," *Cold Cuts III*.
Ayne, Blythe, "Djinneyah & Co.," *100 Wicked Little Witch Stories*.
Bailey, Dale, "Sheep's Clothing," *The Magazine of Fantasy & Science Fiction*, Oct./Nov.
Baird, Alison, "Dragon Pearl," *On Spec*, Winter 1994/95.
Baker, Mike, "The Swashbuckler and the Vampire," *Celebrity Vampires*.
Baker, Scott, "Full Fathom Deep," *Interzone* No. 99, Sept.
Ballantine, Lee, "Yves Tanguy Fear 1949," (poem) *Once Upon a Midnight . . .*
Beckert, Christine, "Scavenger Hunt," *Pirate Writings*, Summer.
Beecher, Dennis S., "One for the Hangman," *Rictus* Number 5.
———, "When Yesterday Bleeds," *White Knuckles*, Vol. 1, Number 3.
Behrendt, Fred, "Beauty," *Made in Goatswood*.
Beinhart, Larry, "Funny Story," *No Alibi*.
Bell, Marvin, "The Book of the Dead Man (#25)" (poem), *Shenandoah*, Spring.
———, "Mothballs," (poem) *Xanadu 3*.
Bennett, Nancy, "Flesh," (poem) *Transversions*, Vol. 1, Number 2.
———, "Pupation," (poem) *Transversions*, Vol. 1, Number 4.
Berman, Judith, "The Year in Storms," *Realms of Fantasy*, Feb.
Better, Cathy Drinkwater, "A Stone Madonna," (poem) *The Silver Web* #12.
Bird, Carmel, "Conservatory," *Dark House*.
———, "A Telephone Call for Genevieve Snow," *Strange Fruit*.
Bishop, Anne, "Match Girl," *Ruby Slippers, Golden Tears*.
Bishop, Michael, "Among the Handlers or The Mark 16 Hands On Assembly of Jesus Risen, Formerly Snake-O-Rama," *Dante's Disciples*.
———, "Spiritual Dysfunction and Counterangelic Longings; or, Sariela: A Case Study in One Act," *Heaven Sent*.

Bisson, Terry, "There Are No Dead," *Omni*, Jan.
Bittner, Robert, "The Light in Cordelia's Eyes," *Haunts* #29.
Blevins, Tippi N., "Raptorial Night," (poem) *Lore*, Vol. 1, Number 3, Winter.
———, "Las Malditas (the Accursed)," (poem) *The Silver Web* #12.
Blicker, Karen, "Bon Appetit," (poem) *Transversions*, Vol. 1, Number 2.
Bloch, Robert, "None Are So Blind," *More Phobias*.
Blumlein, Michael, "Hymenoptera," *Dark Love*.
Bohnhoff, Maya Kathryn, "The Sons of the Father," *Century* #3.
Bonansinga, Jay R., "Necrotica," *Grue* #17.
Borton, Douglas, "Fangs," *Vampire Detectives*.
Boston, Bruce, "The Last Existentialist," *The Year's Best Fantastic Fiction*.
Bowen, Gary, "Dream Eater," *Dead of Night* #13, Summer.
———, "The Final Pleasure," *Bloodsongs* #6.
Bowes, Richard, "At Darlington's," *F & SF*, Oct./Nov.
———, "Fountains in Summer," *Full Spectrum 5*.
Boyczuk, Robert, "Assassination and the New World Order," *Prairie Fire*, Summer.
Bradbury, Ray, "Another Fine Mess," *F & SF*, April.
———, "Quicker than the Eye," *David Copperfield's Tales of the Impossible*.
———, "The Witch Door," *Playboy*, Dec.
Brandner, Gary, "The Merry Go-Round Man," *Fear Itself*.
Brantingham, Juleen, "Burning in the Light," *100 Wicked Little Witch Stories*.
———, "Daughters," *100 Wicked Little Witch Stories*.
Braunbeck, Gary A., "Drowning with Others," *Tombs*.
———, "Some Touch of Pity," *Werewolves*.
Brennert, Alan, "Cradle," *F & SF*, Jan./*100 Vicious Little Vampire Stories*.
———, "The Man Who Loved the Sea," *F & SF*, Sept.
Brewster, Kent, "In the Pound, Near Breaktime," *Tomorrow* No. 17, Oct.
Bricker, Michael Scott, "The Darkness in Her Touch," *100 Vicious Little Vampire Stories*.
———, "Symphony for the Quiet Ones," *Blood Muse*.
Brite, Poppy Z., "Mussolini and the Axeman's Jazz," *Dark Destiny: Proprietors of Fate*.
Brooke, J., "Scorpion's Kiss," *Asimov's Science Fiction*, June.
Brooke, Keith, "Debbs is Back," *Peeping Tom* #20.
———, "Skin," *Peeping Tom* #17.
Brown, Carroll, "The Borderlands," *F & SF*, Dec.
Brown, Molly, "Feeding Julie," *Interzone* No. 100, Oct.
Brunner, John, "All Under Heaven," *Asimov's Science Fiction*, mid-Dec.
———, "Real Messengers," *Heaven Sent*.
Bryant, Edward, "Big Dogs, Strange Days," *Peter S. Beagle's Immortal Unicorn*.
———, "Calling the Lightning by Name," *High Fantastic*.
Buchanan, C. J., "The Prince," (poem) *The Chicago Review*, Vol. 41, Number 1.
Bukiet, Melvin Jules, "The Devil and the Dutchman," *While the Messiah Tarries*.
———, "The Golden Calf and the Red Heifer," Ibid.
———, "Himmler's Chickens," Ibid.
———, "The Library of Moloch," Ibid.
———, "Postscript to a Dead Language," Ibid.
Bull, S. Emerson, "Champion of Lost Causes," *Terminal Fright* #10.
Burke, Caitlin, "Windows," *High Fantastic*.
Burleson, Donald R., "Brownie," *Terminal Fright* #8.
———, "The Daemon-Sultan," *The Azathoth Cycle*.
———, "Sheets," *Lore* Vol. 1, Number 3, Winter.
Burns, Cliff, "The Goblins," *Das Grosse Lesebuch Der Fantasy*.

———, "While You Were Away," *Chelsea Hotel*, Summer.
Burt, Steve, "Garden Plot," *All Hallows* 8.
———, "Uncle Bando's Chimes," *Heliocentric Net*, Spring.
Butler, Robert Olen, "Jealous Husband Returns in Form of Parrot," *The New Yorker*, May 22.
Butterworth, Jack and Capullo, Greg, "All She Does is Eat," (graphic novel) *Taboo* #8.
Byers, Richard Lee, "The Powers Of Darkness," *Fear Itself*.
Byrne, Candyce, "The Death of Beatrix Potter," *Asimov's Science Fiction*, Aug.
Cacek, P. D., "Ancient One," (Paper Moon Press chapbook).
———, "Just a Little Bug," *David Copperfield's Tales of the Impossible*.
———, "Mime Games," *Pulphouse* issue 19.
———, "Yrena," *Blood Muse*.
Cadger, Rick, "A Breath of Not Belonging," *The Third Alternative* 5.
———, "House Calls," *Violent Spectres* #2.
Cadigan, Pat, "Sometimes Salvation," *Sisters of the Night*.
Cadnum, Michael, "Naked Little Men," *Ruby Slippers, Golden Tears*.
Campbell, Ramsey, "The Alternative," *Darklands Two*.
———, "The Body in the Window," *Stranger by Night: The Hot Blood Series*.
———, "Going Under," *Dark Love*.
———, "The Horror Under Warrendown," *Made in Goatswood*.
Cancilla, Dominick, "Dispassionate Muse," *The Urbanite* No. 5.
Cannon, Peter, "The Undercliffe Sentences," *Made in Goatswood*.
Carmody, Isobele, "A Splinter of Darkness," *Dark House*.
Carper, Steve, "The Changeling Variations," *Transversions*, Vol. 1, Number 2.
Carrabis, Joseph-David, "The Boy Who Loved Horses," *Pulphouse* issue 19.
Carroll, Jonathan, "The Fall Collection," (first English publication) *The Panic Hand*.
Carusone, Al, "The Stick People," *Don't Open the Door After the Sun Goes Down*.
———, "Whispered Around Lonesome Campfires," Ibid.
Casey, Alan, "Face Painting," *Psychotrope* 3.
Castle, Mort, "Dani's Story," *After Hours* #25, Winter.
Castro, Adam-Troy, "Baby Girl Diamond," *Adventures in the Twilight Zone*.
Cave, Hugh B., "Forever is a Long Long Time," *The Urbanite* No. 6.
Caves, Sally, "Ketamine," *F & SF*, March.
Ceder, D., "Something Forgotten," *Psychotrope* 3.
Charlton, Shearon, "Pumpkinskull," *Thin Ice* XVI.
Charon, Dan, "Fitting Ends," *TriQuarterly*, Fall.
Cherryh, C. J., and Fancher, Jane S., "Pot of Dreams," *Marion Zimmer Bradley's Fantasy Magazine*.
Chetwynd-Hayes, R., "The Bed-Sitting Room," *Shudders and Shivers*.
———, "The Cumberloo," Ibid.
———, "The Floaters," *After Hours* #25, Winter.
———, "The Intruders," *Thin Ice* XVI.
Chilson, Rob, "The Paranoia Theory," *Tomorrow* No. 18, Dec.
Clark, David Aaron, "Frank, On the Prowl," *Love Bites*.
Clark, Simon, "Acorns—A Bitter Substitute for Olives," *Cold Cuts III*.
———, "The Bike Ride Home," *Grotesque* #8.
———, "Man in Danger—A Video Self-Portrait," *Violent Spectres* #2.
———, "The Old Man at the Gate," *All Hallows* 9.
Clark, Simon and Laws, Stephen, "Annabel Says," (British Fantasy Society chapbook).
Clegg, Douglas, "Celeste, of the Chosen," *Deathrealm* #25.
———, "Coming of Age," *Forbidden Acts*.
———, "The Mysteries of Paris," *More Phobias*.

Coburn, Andrew, "A Woolfe in Vita's Clothing," *Ellery Queen's Mystery Magazine*, Dec.
Cody, Liza, "Love in Vain," *No Alibi*.
Collins, Max Allan, "The Night of Their Lives," *Vampire Detectives*.
———, "Traces of Red," *Celebrity Vampires*.
Collins, Nancy A., "Down in the Hole," *More Phobias*.
———, "The Land of the Reflected Ones," *Tombs*.
———, "Thin Walls," *Dark Love*.
Compton, Ian, "Absolutely Normal," *The Silver Web* #12.
Constantine, Storm, "Blue Flame of a Candle," *Tombs*.
———, "Return to Gehenna," *Dante's Disciples*.
Cook, John Paul, "Lairwatcher," *Haunts* #29.
Cooper, Louise, "His True and Only Wife," *Realms of Fantasy*, April.
Coppula, Kathleen A., "Wide Open," *Terminal Fright* #8.
Costello, Matthew, "The Last Vanish," *David Copperfield's Tales of the Impossible*.
Coulstock, Brett, "Ceilidh," *Eidolon* 19.
Coulter, Lynn, "Swamp Water," *F & SF*, Feb.
Couzens, Gary, "Four A.M.," *Peeping Tom* #20.
Cowan, Jim, "Alderley Edge," *Century* #1.
Coward, Mat, "No Night by Myself," *No Alibi*.
———, "Those Things," *Cold Cuts III*.
Cox, Deidre, "Footnotes," *Crossroads*, Vol. 4, Number 13.
Crawford, James, "Black and White and Bed All Over," *Seeds of Fear: The Hot Blood Series*.
Crawford, Stephen R., "Exorcism," *Not One of Us* #13.
Crew, Gary, "The Staircase," *Dark House*.
Crowther, Peter, "All We Know of Heaven," *Excalibur*.
———, "Beyond the Window," (poem) *The Third Alternative* 5.
———, "Bindlestiff," *Werewolves*.
———, "A Breeze from a Distant Shore," *Adventures in the Twilight Zone*.
———, "Cankerman," *Cold Cuts III*.
———, "Fallen Angel," *Kimota* Issue 3, Winter.
———, "Home Comforts," *Vampire Detectives*.
———, "A Time to Dance," *Dark Asylum 1*.
Cyr, Heidi, "Parlor Tricks You Can Play on Yourself," *EQMM*, Sep.
Daemon, Shira, "Crimes of Fashion," *Blood Muse*.
———, "Dairy Queen," *Xanadu 3*.
———, "While Visions of Sugarplums . . ." *Tomorrow* No. 18, Dec.
Dahme, Joanne, "Weeping Willows," *Out For Blood*.
Dalkey, Kara, "The Chrysanthemum Robe," *The Armless Maiden*.
Danehy-Oakes, Dan'l, "Outside the Walls," *Realms of Fantasy*, June.
Darlington, Andy, "The Lurker in the Room With a View," *Tales From Tartarus*.
Daum, G. L., "And After a While, There Came a Stillness . . ." *Tales of the Unanticipated* #14.
Day, Holly, "In Hiding," (poem) *Not One of Us* #14.
De Lint, Charles, "The Big Sky," *Heaven Sent*.
———, "Bird Bones and Wood Ash," *The Ivory and the Horn*.
———, "The Forever Trees," *Worlds of Fantasy & Horror* #2, Spring.
De Noux, O'Neil "A Heartbeat," *Dead of Night* #11, Winter.
Dean, David, "Falling Boy," *EQMM*, April.
Deaver, Jeffery, "Together," *EQMM*, Feb.
Dee, Ron, "Strawberry Fields Forever," *Eldritch Tales* 30.

Deja, Thomas, "How Does it Feel?" *Not One of Us* #14.
———, "The Running Reflex," *Rictus* Number 5.
DeWolf, David, "Massacre Summer," *Deathrealm* #25.
DiChario, Nicholas A., "Diddling with Grandmother's Iron Maiden," *Witch Fantastic*.
Disher, Gary, "Dead Set," *Dark House*.
Donahue, Suzanne, "The Looker," *Haunts* #29.
Donaldson, Stephen R. "The Kings of Tarshish Shall Bring Gifts," *The Book of Kings*.
Dorr, James S., "Flying," *Dead of Night* #13, Summer.
———, "The Hunt," *100 Wicked Little Witch Stories*.
———, "The Resurrection Man," (poem) *Once Upon a Midnight* . . .
Douglas, Carole Nelson, "Dracula on the Rocks," *Celebrity Vampires*.
Douglas, Conda V., "Cathedral Song," *Dark Regions* Vol. 3, Issue 1.
Doyle, Noreen, "The Chapter of Bringing a Boat Into Heaven," *Realms of Fantasy*, Feb.
Drummond, Mike, "The Helix," *New Mystery*, Spring.
Dumars, Denise, "In Jonah's City," (poem) *Dark Regions*, Vol. 3, Number 1.
Dunn, Dawn, "A Good Witch Is Hard to Find," *100 Wicked Little Witch Stories*.
Dunn, J. R., "Little Red," *Century* #1.
Dunn, Katherine, "Pieces," *The Barker*, Dec.
Dyson, Jeremy, "City Deep," *Tombs*.
D'Ammassa, Don, "The Dunwich Gate," *Terminal Fright* #10.
———, "Hair Apparent," *100 Wicked Little Witch Stories*.
———, "The Houseguest," *Terminal Fright* #7.
———, "Twisted Images," (Necronomicon Press chapbook).
D'Arcy, Danya, "Chain," (poem) *Lore*, Vol. 1, Number 3, Winter.
Edwards, Wayne, "A Siren's Kiss," *The Third Alternative* 5.
Effinger, George Alec, "Maureen Birnbaum at the Looming Awfulness," *F & SF*, March.
Ehinger, Matt, "March," *Aberrations* #33.
Eisenstein, Phyllis, "No Refunds," *Sisters in Fantasy*.
Elgin, Suzette Haden, "Only a Housewife," *F & SF*, Sept.
Ellison, Harlan, "Anywhere But Here, With Anyone But You," *Harlan Ellison's Dream Corridor* Issue 2.
———, "Chatting With Anubis," *Lore*, Vol. 1, Number 1, Summer.
———, "Keyboard," *F & SF*, Jan.
———, "Midnight in the Sunken Cathedral," *Eidolon* 17/18.
———, "Pulling Hard Time," *F & SF*, Oct./Nov.
Elrod, P. N., "You'll Catch Your Death," *Vampire Detectives*.
Emery, Lorin, "Pinch of Salt," *Substance*, Spring.
Emshwiller, Carol, "After Shock," *Century* #3.
Emswiler, Tim, "The Game of Kings," *Lore*, Vol. 1, Number 3, Winter.
Eskridge, Kelley, "Alien Jane," *Century* #1.
Etchemendy, Nancy, "Cooking With Rodents," *Rat Tales*.
———, "The Lily and the Weaver's Heart," *The Armless Maiden*.
———, "Mollusk Dreams," *Xanadu* 3.
Evans, Christopher, "House Call," *Heaven Sent*.
Evans, Kendall, "Homunculus," *Weirdbook* 29.
Evans, R. G., "Wishbone," *Eulogy* 9.
Evans, Sarah J., "Hands," *Grotesque* #7.
———, "Stale Madness," *Cold Cuts III*.
Faust, Christa, "Epiphany," *Splatterpunks II: Over the Edge*.
Feeley, Gregory, "In Fear of Little Nell," *Enchanted Forests*.

Feist, Raymond E., "Geroldo's Incredible Trick," *David Copperfield's Tales of the Impossible.*
Files, Gemma, "Ring of Fire," *Palace Corbie* #6.
———, "Skin City," *A Crimson Kind of Evil.*
Finch, Paul, "The Chasm," *All Hallows* #10.
Finch, Sheila, "Firstborn, Seaborn," *Sisters in Fantasy.*
Finnegan, Madeleine V., "Dancing Through the Wall," *Peeping Tom* #20.
———, "The Odalisque," *Peeping Tom* #18.
Fitch, Marina, "The Banks of the River," *Desire Burn.*
———, "Stampede of Light," *Peter S. Beagle's Immortal Unicorn.*
Flood, Julian, "Control," *Tomorrow* No. 15, June.
Floyd, Trevor, "Psycho on My Train," *Into the Darkness*, Vol. 1, Number 3.
Flynn, Michael F., "The Promise of God," *F & SF*, March.
Forbes, DeLoris Stanton, "Many a Pickle Makes a Mickle," *AHMM*, June.
Fowler, Christopher, "A Century and a Second," *Flesh Wounds.*
———, "Ginansia's Ravishment," *Tombs.*
———, "Jouissance de la Mort," *Flesh Wounds.*
———, "The Laundry Imp," *Dark Terrors.*
———, "The Most Boring Woman in the World," *Flesh Wounds.*
———, "The Unreliable History of Plaster City," Ibid.
———, "The Young Executives," Ibid.
Fowler, Karen Joy, "The Brew," *Peter S. Beagle's Immortal Unicorn.*
———, "Shimabara," *Full Spectrum 5.*
Fox, Chris, "One Noon in August," *Good News Bad News*, Oct.
Fox, Janet, "Garage Sale," *100 Wicked Little Witch Stories.*
———, "To Love the Dark," (poem) *Once Upon a Midnight . . .*
Frackelton, Alan S. "Making Something of Yourself," *Violent Spectres* #3.
Frasier, Carrie, "Man on the Tracks, Ralston Station," (poem) *High Fantastic.*
Frazier, Robert, "Points of Convergence," *Grue* #17.
Freimor, Jacqueline, "Strangle, Strangle," *AHMM*, June.
Freireich, Valerie J., "Convert," *Tomorrow* No. 13, Feb.
Friesner, Esther M., "A Birthday," *F & SF*, Aug.
———, "A Few Good Menehune," *Orphans of the Night.*
Frounfeller, Michael D., "The Framing," *Random Realities* #6.
Fuller, Thomas E., "Captain Royate Montgomery Writes Home," (poem) *Once Upon a Midnight . . .*
Gaiman, Neil, "Don't Ask Jack," *Fan Magazine* #3.
Gallagher, Stephen, "God's Bright Little Engine," *Tombs.*
———, "In Gethsemene," *Heaven Sent.*
Galloway, Patricia, "The Prince," *Truly Grim Tales.*
———, "The Good Mother," Ibid.
———, "The Name," Ibid.
Garland, Mark A. "Death's Door," *Bruce Coville's Book of Nightmares.*
Garnett, David, "Brute Skill," *Interzone* No. 93, Mar.
Geddes, Cindie, "Control," *Terminal Fright* #7.
Gilbert, Jeff, "The Thing is the Lake by My House," *Beer Fear.*
Gilliam, Richard, "Darkened Roads," *Adventures in the Twilight Zone.*
Gilman, Laura Anne, "Exposure," *Blood Muse.*
Glasby, John, "The Nameless Tower," *The Azathoth Cycle.*
Gluckman, Janet Berliner and Guthridge, George, "Inyanga," *100 Wicked Little Witch Stories.*
Goingback, Owl, "Grass Dancer," *Excalibur.*

Goldman, Ken, "The Snow Angel," *Heliocentric Net*, Spring.
Goldstein, Lisa, "A Game of Cards," *Sisters in Fantasy*.
Gordon, John, "Vampire in Venice," *Point Horror 13 Again*.
Gorman, Ed, "The Brasher Girl," *Cages*.
———, "Kinship," Ibid.
———, "The Morning of August 18th," Ibid.
———, "Out There in the Darkness," (Subterranean Press chapbook).
———, "Survival," *Cages*.
———, "Synandra," *Heaven Sent*.
Gramlich, Charles A., "Judas Nailed His Mouth Open," (poem) *Once Upon a Midnight . . .*
Greco, Jr., Ralph, "The Turning Too Far," *Eulogy* #8.
Greenberg, Joanne, "Fugue for Chant and Gregger," *Hadassah*.
Greenberg, Lawrence, "Sotto Voce," *Peter Straub's Ghosts*.
Greenland, Colin, "Grandma," *Point Horror 13 Again*.
———, "The Traveling Companion," *Strange Plasma* #8.
Gresh, Lois H., "Snip My Suckers," *100 Vicious Little Vampire Stories*.
Gresham, Stephen, "Once Upon A Darkness," *Fear Itself*.
Grindle, Lucretia W., "Hooves," *More Phobias*.
Griner, Paul, "Nails," *Glimmer Train* issue 16, Fall.
Gross, Philip, "Close Cut," *Point Horror 13 Again*.
Gust, Michael, "Siena Blue," *Deathrealm* #24.
Haber, Karen, "A Round of Cards with the General," *Wheel of Fortune*.
———, "The Vampire of the Opera," *Celebrity Vampires*.
———, "The King Who Would Fly," *The Book of Kings*.
Hahn, Mary Downing, "Give a Puppet a Hand," *Bruce Coville's Book of Nightmares*.
Hall, Melissa Mia and Winter, Douglas E., "Playing Dolls," *Forbidden Acts*.
Halligan, Marion, "Like a Kiss," *Dark House*.
Hambly, Barbara, "Madeleine," *Sisters of the Night*.
Hanson, Janice L., "Every Good Teacher," *Into the Darkness*, Vol. 1, Number 3.
Harbour, Katherine, "Fading," *Not One of Us* #13.
Hardin, Rob, "Interrogator Frames," *Forbidden Acts*.
Hardy, Melissa, "The Rose Girl," *The Malahat Review*, Fall.
Harrison, M. John, "Empty," *Sisters of the Night*.
Hautala, Rick, "The Back of My Hands," *More Phobias*.
———, "Silver Rings," *Northern Frights* 3.
Hembree, Amy, "Stonework," *Palace Corbie* #6.
Hemmingson, Michael, "Pain," *Nice Little Stories Jam-Packed With Depraved Sex & Violence*.
Hendee, J. C., "Necromorph Loves Black Cat (First Meeting)" (poem) *Not One of Us* #13.
Henderson, C. J., "Free the Old Ones," *Made in Goatswood*.
———, "Idiot Savant," *The Azathoth Cycle*.
Herber, Keith, "Doc," "Fortunes," *Made in Goatswood*.
Herron, Don, "Life After," *100 Vicious Little Vampire Stories*.
Hill, David W., "The Curtain Falls," *Green Echo*.
Hoar, Jere, "Prey, Don't Tell," *EQMM*, March.
Hoch, Edward D., "No Blood for a Vampire," *Vampire Detectives*.
Hodge, Brian, "Chronicles of a Couch Potato," *Phantasm*, Vol I, Number 2.
———, "Extinctions in Paradise," *Werewolves*.
———, "Godflesh," *Stranger by Night*.
———, "The Meat in the Machine," *Cyber-Psycho's A.O.D.* #6.

Hodgson, Pamela D., "Crumbs Under Thy Table," *100 Vicious Little Vampire Stories*.
Hodgson, Sheila, "The Boat Hook,"*Ghosts & Scholars* 19.
Hoffman, Nina Kiriki, "The Biting-a Hologram Blues," *100 Vicious Little Vampire Stories*.
———, "But Now Am Found," *F & SF*, Oct./Nov.
———, "Family History," *100 Vicious Little Vampire Stories*.
———, "Food Chain," *Sisters of the Night*.
———, "For Richer, for Stranger," *F & SF*, June.
———, "On Reflection," *The Urbanite* #5.
Holder, Nancy, "Dinner in the Hall of Mirrors," *The Splendour Falls*.
———, "Divine Right," *The Book of Kings*.
———, "Heat," *Desire Burn*.
———, "North of Soho," *After Hours* #25, Winter.
———, "Undercover," *Vampire Detectives*.
Holdstock, Robert, "Infantasm," *The Merlin Chronicles*.
Holmstrom, David, "A Bad Night in Kansas," *AHMM*, Jan.
Hood, Robert, "Peeking," *Strange Fruit*.
Hook, Andrew, "Slender Lois, Slow Doris," *The Third Alternative* 6.
Hopkins, Brian A., "Gaffed," *Something Haunts Us All*.
Hornbostel, Don, "Almost a Miracle," *Plot* #1.
Houarner, Gerard Daniel, "What Was Left," *Aberrations* 29.
———, "The Lost Mothers," *The End* 3.
Howard, Hilary, "Journey's End," *Peeping Tom* #18.
Howe, David J., "The Third Time," *Dark Asylum* 1.
Hoyt, Sarah Marques de Almedia, "Thirst," *Bloodsongs* #4.
Huff, Tanya, "This Town Ain't Big Enough," *Vampire Detectives*.
Hughes, Rhys H., "A Carpet Seldom Found," *Tales From Tartarus*.
———, "Cat O'Nine Tales," *Worming the Harpy and Other Bitter Pills*.
———, "The Chimney," *Tales From Tartarus*.
———, "Fallow," *All Hallows* #10.
———, "The Forest Chapel Bell," *Tales From Tartarus*.
———, "The Good News Grimoire," *Worming the Harpy* . . .
———, "The Man Who Mistook His Wife's Hat for the Mad Hatter's Wife," Ibid.
———, "One Man's Meat," *Tales From Tartarus*.
———, "Trombonhomie," *Psychotrope* 3.
———, "Velocity Oranges," *Tales From Tartarus*.
———, "What to Do When the Devil Comes Round to Tea," *Worming the Harpy* . . .
———, "Worming the Harpy," *Tales From Tartarus*.
Humphries, Dwight E., "One Crow, Many Graves," (poem) *Once Upon a Midnight* . . .
Husain, Shakrukh, "What Will Be Will Be," *Women Who Wear the Breeches: Delicious and Dangerous Tales*.
Indick, Ben P., "The Rose Cavalier," *100 Vicious Little Vampire Stories*.
Jacob, Charlee, "Scalpel Mouth," *Symphonie's Gift* #4.
———, "Spirit Wolves," *Into the Darkness*, Vol. 1, Number 4.
———, "Waiting for the Winter," *Crossroads*, Vol. 4, Number 13.
Jarman, Mark, "Unholy Sonnet 1," (poem) *The Southern Review*, Summer.
Jennings, Paul, "Clear as Mud," *Undone! More Bad Endings*.
———, "Nails," *Unbearable: More Bizarre Stories*.
———, "What a Woman!" *Undone! More Bad Endings*.
———, "You Be the Judge," Ibid.
Johnson, Calvin W., "Sisyphus," *Tomorrow* No. 17, Oct.

Johnson, Ken, "Pelican," *Terminal Fright* #8.
Johnson-Haddad, Barbara, "Hallow's After," (poem) *Crypt of Cthulhu* No. 89.
Jones, Bruce, "Home Movies," *Stranger by Night*.
Jones, Gwyneth, "The Grass Princess," *Seven Tales and a Fable*.
Jones, Heather Rose, "Skins," *Sword and Sorceress XII*.
Julian, Astrid, "The Hunter and the Stag," *Xanadu 3*.
Kadleková, Vilma, "The Goods," trans. M. Kledma and Bruce Sterling, *Interzone*, No. 91, Jan.
Kaminsky, Stuart, "Hidden," *Dark Love*.
Kaplan, Howard N., "Food for Monkey's Brain," *Grue* #17.
Karr, Phyllis Ann, "Merlin's Dark Mirror," *The Merlin Chronicles*.
Kasturi, Sandra, "The Changeling," (poem) *On Spec*, Winter.
———, "Five Cantos From the Prayer Book of Aphrodite," (poem) *Transversions*, Vol. 1, Number 2.
———, "Winter Aconite," (poem) *On Spec*, Fall.
Kauderer, Herb, "Survivor," (poem) *Not One of Us* #13.
Kaylan, Howard, "The Energy Pals," *Forbidden Acts*.
Kennett, Rick, "Bottle Green Dreams," *All Hallows* #8.
Kenworthy, Chris, "Landing in the Grass," *Peeping Tom* #19.
———, "The Pig's Nose," *Peeping Tom* #17.
Kernaghan, Eileen, "The Robber-Maiden's Story," *Transversions* #2.
Ketchum, Jack, "The Turning," *Vampire Detectives*.
Kidd, A. F., "Deck the Halls," *Ghosts & Scholars* #20.
Kiernan, Caitlín R., "The Comedy of St. Jehanne d'Arc," *Dark Destiny: Proprietors of Fate*.
———, "Hoar Isis," *The Urbanite* No. 6.
Kilpatrick, Nancy, "Snow Angel," *Northern Frights 3*.
Kilworth, Garry, "Cherub," *Heaven Sent*.
———, "Masterpiece," *Ruby Slippers, Golden Tears*.
King, Tappan, "Wolf's Heart," *The Armless Maiden*.
Kinney, Julie, "Charon's Wife," (poem) *Xanadu 3*.
Knight, Tracy, "Sand Boils," *Werewolves*.
Koja, Kathe, "DMZ," *Amazing Stories: The Anthology*.
———, "Jubilee," *Peter Straub's Ghosts*.
———"Waking the Prince," *Ruby Slippers, Golden Tears*.
Koja, Kathe and Malzberg, Barry N., "Girl's Night Out," *Vampire Detectives*.
———, "Mysterious Elisions, Riotous Thrusts," *Forbidden Acts*.
———, "The Unbolted," *Wheel of Fortune*.
———, "The Unchained," *Tombs*.
———, "The Witches of Delight," *Witch Fantastic*.
Koke, John Austin and Bond, Jonathan, "Tunnel Rats," *Rat Tales*.
Kolpak, Diana, "Bedtime Story," *The Urbanite* #6.
Kopaska-Merkel, David C. and Storm, Sue, "Twilight Weavers," *Night Songs*, Spring.
Kratts, Aimee, "The Laurel Lake Laser," *100 Wicked Little Witch Stories*.
Kreighbaum, Mark, "And by a Word, Immortal," *100 Vicious Little Vampire Stories*.
———, "Ars Brevis," *Blood Muse*.
Kreps, Robert W., "Not an Accident," *Aberrations* #29.
Kress, Nancy, "Fault Lines," (novella) *Asimov's Science Fiction*, Aug.
———, "Hard Drive," *Killing Me Softly*.
———, "Summer Wind," *Ruby Slippers, Golden Tears*.
Kushner, Ellen, "Now I Lay Me Down to Sleep," *The Armless Maiden*.
Lamb, Jean, "The Broom's Tale," *Deathrealm* #23.

Lamsley, Terry, "Someone to Dump On," *All Hallows* #8.
———, "The Toddler," *Ghosts & Scholars* #20.
Lane, Joel, "Every Form of Refuge," *Panurge 23: Water Baby*.
———, "Just Enough," *100 Vicious Little Vampire Stories*.
———, "The Outside World," *The Urbanite* #6.
Lannes, Roberta, "A Feast at Grief's Table," *Dark Terrors*.
Lansdale, Joe R., "Master of Misery," *Warriors of Blood and Dream*.
Lansdale, Joe R., Keith, and Kasey Jo, "The Companion," *Great Writers & Kids* . . .
Lau, Evelyn, "Pleasure," *Fresh Girls and Other Stories*.
Lawrence, Peter, "All the King's Men," *Dark House*.
Laws, Stephen, "The Fractured Man," *Cold Cuts III*.
Lear, Alan Webster, "Do Bats Eat Cats?" *Tales From Tartarus*.
Ledgerwood, Jo Etta, "Water Babies," *High Fantastic*.
Lee, Edward, "Header," (Necropublications chapbook).
Lee, Jeffrey A., "The Menhir," *Ghosts & Scholars* #20.
Lee, John, "Tricks of Memory," *Albedo 1* #7.
Lee, Mary Soon, "Ebb Tide," *F & SF*, May.
Lee, Mike, "High Heels from Hell," *Forbidden Acts*.
Lee, Tanith, "Age," *The Ultimate Dragon*.
———, "The Beast," *Ruby Slippers, Golden Tears*.
———, "The Champion," *Xanadu 3*.
———, "Edwige," *Asimov's Science Fiction*, July.
———, "Saxon Flaxen," *Ancient Enchantresses*.
———, "She Sleeps in a Tower," *The Armless Maiden*.
———, "These Beasts," *F & SF*, June.
Leech, Ben, "The Parasite," *Cold Cuts III*.
Leonard, Carol, "Medea," *Dark Angels: lesbian vampire stories*.
Lepovetsky, Lisa, "The Day of Hitler's Birth," (poem) *Once Upon a Midnight* . . .
———, "Here Be Monsters," *EQMM*, Oct.
LeRoss, D. E. and Janszoon, Josef P., "The Final Diary Entry of Kees Huijgens" (Necronomicon Press).
Lethem, Jonathan, "The Insipid Profession of Jonathan Hornebom," *Full Spectrum 5*.
Leuci, Bob, "All-American Boy," *EQMM*, June.
Levinthal, Marc and Skipp, John Mason, "The Punchline," (novella) *Dark Destiny: Proprietors of Fate*.
Lewis, D. F., "Clumsy Nirvana," *Transversions*, Vol. 1, Number 2.
———, "Gongoozler," *Psychotrope 3*.
Lewis, Paul, "When the Rose Blooms," *Cold Cuts III*.
Ligotti, Thomas, "The Bungalow House," *The Urbanite* #5.
Lillie, Brent, "Gag Reflex," *Eidolon* #16.
Linaweaver, Brad, "A Real Babe," *Peter Straub's Ghosts*.
Lindberg, Christine, "Frankenstein: A/Scent of Disgust," (poem) *Mattoid 48*.
Link, Kelly, "Water Off a Black Dog's Back," *Century* #3.
Linscott, Gillian, "The Big Five-O," *EQMM*, Oct.
Little, Bentley, "See Marilyn Monroe's Panties!," *Seeds of Fear*.
Lockley, Steve, "Moths," *Cold Cuts III*.
Logan, David, "Hell on Earth Street," *The Third Alternative* #6.
———, "The Little Red Car With L-Plates On," *Peeping Tom* #17.
Long, N. D., "Kangaroos in Nevada," *Premonitions* No. 4.
Love, Penelope, "Unseen," *Made in Goatswood*.
Lowder, James, "The Persistence of Vision," *City of Darkness: Unseen*.
Lucas, Tim and Lloyd, David, "The Disaster Area," (graphic novel) *Taboo* #8.

Lumley, Brian, "Back Row," *Stranger by Night*.
Lustbader, Eric, "The Devil on Myrtle Ave.," *Peter S. Beagle's Immortal Unicorn*.
———, "The Singing Tree," *David Copperfield's Tales of the Impossible*.
Luth, Michael, "The Walking Stick," *EQMM*, March.
Lynch, Richard, "The Mime of Still-life," *The New Renaissance*, Vol. IX, Number 2.
Lyons, Lynda, "Adam," *Deathrealm* #26.
MacCulloch, Simon, "The Nine Billion Names of Nosferatu," *100 Vicious Little Vampire Stories*.
MacGregor, Susan, "About Face," *On Spec*, Fall.
Mackey, Allen, "The Plague Jar," *The Azathoth Cycle*.
MacLeod, Ian R., "Ellen O'Hara," *Asimov's Science Fiction*, Feb.
———, "The Noonday Pool," *F & SF*, May.
———, "Tirkiluk," *F & SF*, Feb.
Macrae, Stuart L., "Carousel," (poem) *Footsteps* issue 1.
Mailander, Jane, "Wolf Enough," *Tomorrow* No. 13, Feb.
Malzberg, Barry N., "The Known Iniquities of Love," *Non-Stop Magazine* No 2, Winter.
Marcinko, Thomas, "The Dark Nightingale Returns," *100 Vicious Little Vampire Stories*.
Marcus, Ben, "Intercourse With Resuscitated Wife," *The Age of Wire and String*.
Mason, Lisa, "Every Mystery Unexplained," *David Copperfield's Tales of the Impossible*.
Massie, Elizabeth, "The Reclamation of Sweeney Todd," *After Hours* #25, Winter.
Masterton, Graham, "Egg," *Flights of Fear*.
———, "Evidence of Angels," *Point Horror 13 Again*.
———, "Fairy Story," *Faces of Fear*.
———, "The Gray Madonna," *Fear Itself*.
———, "Grief," *Faces of Fear*.
———, "The Hungry Moon," *Dark Terrors*.
———, "The Joujouka Penis-Beetle," *Stranger by Night*.
———, "Spirit-Jump," *Faces of Fear*.
Matheson, Richard Christian, "Bleed," *Dark Terrors*.
Matter, Holly Wade, "Martine's Room," *Century* #1.
———, "Mr. Pacifaker's House," *Asimov's Science Fiction*, July.
Matthews, Patricia, "Goatman," *F & SF*, May.
McAuley, Paul J., "The True History of Dr. Pretorius," *Interzone* No. 98, Aug.
McAuliffe, Mark A., "A Red Valentine," *Skintomb 6*.
McCafferty, Taylor, "Just a Thought," *AHMM*, April.
McCaffery, Simon, "Little Men," *Tomorrow* No. 13, Feb.
McCaffrey, Anne and Kennedy, Georgeanne, "Zeus: The Howling," *Great Writers & Kids* . . .
McClean, Peter G. "Lepidopteraphilia," *Albedo 1* #8.
McCoy, Robert Wayne and Monteleone, Thomas F., "The Stuff of Life to Knit You," *The Splendour Falls*.
McDermott, Kirstyn, "Running With the Gods," *Skintomb 6*.
McDevitt, Jack, "Ellie," *Asimov's Science Fiction*, May.
McGarry, Terry, "Fleadh de Deux," *Blood Muse*.
McGrath, Niall, "In the Mine," (poem) *Transversions*, Vol. 1, Number 3.
McHugh, Maureen F., "Learning to Breathe," *Tales of the Unanticipated* #15.
McInerny, Ralph, "Paradise," *EQMM*, Jan.
McIrvin, Michael, "Nothing on Earth Will Ever Be the Same," *Century* #2.
McKenzie, K. J., "Blind Seeking the Blind," *Eidolon* #17/18.
McLaughlin, Mark, "Regarding the Situation on Clove Street," *Argonaut Science Fiction* #20.

———, "Thousandskins," *Carnage Hall* #6.
———, "You Don't Want to Know," *Rictus* #5.
McMahan, Rick, "In the Den of Iniquity," *Into the Darkness*, Vol. 1, Number 3.
McMartin, Sean, "The Last Oasis," *AHMM*, Nov.
McNaughton, Brian, "The Conversion of St. Monocarp," *100 Wicked Little Witch Stories*.
———, "La fille aux yeux d'e'mail," *Flesh Fantastic*.
Meacham, Beth, "Coyote," *Sisters in Fantasy*.
Mecklam, Todd, "Mr. Keim Adrift," *Skintomb 6*.
Meikle, William, "The Flute and the Glen," *Kimota* issue 3, Winter.
———, "It'll Be a Long Hot Summer," *Threads 7*.
———, "The Sweller in the Dress Hold," *Footsteps* issue 1.
———, "The Watcher in the Dunes," *Grotesque* #7.
Messina, Marianne, "The Justicer," *Rictus* #6.
Metaxes, Eric, "Gretel's Skull Discovered!" *The New York Times Magazine*, April 23.
Meth, Clifford Lawrence, "Max," *Crib Death and Other Bedtime Stories*.
———, "Uncle Joe," Ibid.
Metzger, Th., "Pyre," *Fear Itself*.
Meyers, Linda Curtis, "Cinderella in Middle Age," *Peregrine, Annual Literary Journal of Amherst Writers and Artists*, 1995.
Meynard, Yves, "Nausicaä," *Tomorrow* No. 13, Feb.
Miller, James, "Gothic Blues," *Violent Spectres* #2.
———, "The Outpost," *The Third Alternative* #7.
Miller, Rex, "Black Casper," *Dark Destiny: Proprietors of Fate*.
Millitello, Deborah, "The Boy Who Cried Dragon," *Bruce Coville's Book of Nightmares*.
Milosevic, Mario, "Assistance," *Space & Time* #85, Spring.
Monteleone, Thomas F., "Looking for Mr. Flip," *Peter Straub's Ghosts*.
Moon, Elizabeth, "Aura," *F & SF*, Aug.
———, "Horse of Her Dreams," *Sisters in Fantasy*.
Moorcock, Michael, "No Ordinary Christian," *Tombs*.
Moore, Alan, "Light of Thy Countenance," *Forbidden Acts*.
Morgan, Jill M., "Grave Promises," *More Phobias*.
Moriarty, Morgan J., "Savior of the Sidewalk Life," *Dreams and Nightmares* #44.
Morlan, A. R., "Little Nips," *Symphonie's Gift* #2.
———, "River of Glass, Mirror of Water," *Symphonie's Gift* #5.
Morris, Mark, "The Chiseller's Reunion," *Close to the Bone*.
———, "Down to Earth," Ibid.
Morton, Gary Lynn, "Dust Devil," *The End* #3.
Morton, Lisa, "The Free Way" (Fool's Press chapbook).
———, "Love Eats," *Dark Terrors*.
Mosiman, Billie Sue, "The Anomaly of Mondays," *More Phobias*.
———, "Man of the Dead," *Blood Muse*.
———, "Technicolor Love," *Dead of Night* No. 12, Spring.
Mundt, Martin, "Hunger Gulag," *100 Wicked Little Witch Stories*.
Murphy, Boomer, "Road Eater," *Grue* #17.
Murphy, Kevin Andrew and Roche, Thomas S., "Headturner," *Splatterpunks II: Over the Edge*.
Murphy, Pat, "Points of Departure," *F & SF*, July.
Murphy, R. A., "Revamp," *Urges* No. 1, Sep.
Murray, Will, "The Mudang," *100 Wicked Little Witch Stories*.
Myers, Gary, "The Last Night of Earth," *The Azathoth Cycle*.
Nasir, Jamil, "Pine Needle Whiskey," *Tomorrow* No. 15, June.

Nasrin, Taslima, "Things Cheaply Had," (poem) *The New Yorker*, Oct. 9.
Navarro, Yvonne, "The Best Years of My Life," 100 *Vicious Little Vampire Stories*.
———, "The Nature of Death," *Phantasm* Vol. I, Number 2.
———, "Recall," *After Hours* No. 25, Winter.
———, "Touch Me," *Selling Venus*.
Neilson, Philip, "Rock and Roll Has to Die," *Dark House*.
Nelson, Dale J., "The Mandrakes," *Ghosts & Scholars* #19.
Newland, Emily, "Never Hurt Me," *Thin Ice* XVI.
Newman, Kim, "Where the Bodies Are Buried 3: Black and White and Red All Over," *Dark Terrors*.
Newton, Kurt, "The Birthday Ritual," *Not One of Us* #13.
———, "The Burning Man," *Not One of Us* #14.
———, "Containment," (poem) *Transversions*, Vol. 1, Number 2.
———, "Puppies for Sale," *Rictus* #5.
———, "Skins," *Crossroads*, Vol. 4, Number 12.
Nicastro, Kathleen, "Death's Day Off," *Dalhousie Review*, Spring.
Nichols, Lyn D., "Rhapsody," *Blood Muse*.
Nichols, Stan, "Picking Up the Tab," *Point Horror 13 Again*.
Nicholson, Jeff, "Cat Lover," (graphic novel) *Taboo* #8.
Nickels, Tim, "Airbabies," *The Third Alternative* #7.
Nickle, David, "The Summer Worms," *Northern Frights 3*.
Noble, Carol Trowbridge, "Strange Flowers," *Thin Ice* XVI.
Norris, Rafe, "Black as Night," *Peeping Tom* #18.
Novakovich, Josip, "Wool," *Yolk* (Graywolf Press).
Nowak, Julie A., "Blue Blood," *Tomorrow* No. 17, Oct.
Nutman, Philip, "Where There's Smoke," *The Splendour Falls*.
———, "Blackpool Rock," *Forbidden Acts*.
Nystrom, Jan, "A Young Lady Who Fell From A Star," *Chick-Lit On the Edge: New Women's Fiction*.
Oates, Joyce Carol, "The Hand-Puppet," *David Copperfield's Tales of the Impossible*.
———, "The Hands," *Epoch*, Vol. 44, Number 2.
———, "The Vision," *Michigan Quarterly Review*, Winter.
O'Hara, Clancy, "The Asylum Choir," *Pulphouse: A Fiction Magazine*, Winter.
Olson, Steven Paul, "Fatman," *Grue* #17.
Ormond, K. K., "Beecher Street," *Palace Corbie* #6.
O'Callaghan, Maxine and Apperson, Brandon, "Wuffs," *Great Writers & Kids* . . .
O'Driscoll, M. M., "Johnnie's Weddings," *Cold Cuts III*.
O'Driscoll, Mike, "The Ties That Blind," *The Third Alternative* #5.
O'Sullivan, G. F., "Etchitt's Hound," *White Knuckles*, Vol. 1, Number 1.
Page, Gerald W., "Shaken, Not Stirred," *Weirdbook* #29.
Palwick, Susan, "The Real Princess," *Ruby Slippers, Golden Tears*.
Partain, R. K., "A Matter of Honor," 100 *Wicked Little Witch Stories*.
Partridge, Norman, "The Bars on Satan's Jailhouse," (Roadkill Press chapbook).
———, "The Pack," *Werewolves*.
———, "Styx," *Peter Straub's Ghosts*.
———, "Undead Origami," *Celebrity Vampires*.
Partridge, Norman and Sallee, Wayne Allen, "How Naethen Learned to See," *Deathrealm* #26.
Paul, Barbara, "The Secret," *Vampire Detectives*.
Pausacker, Jenny, "The Princess in the Tower," *Dark House*.
Payne, Francis, "What the Stone of Ciparri Says," *Bloodsongs* #6.
Peake, Fabian, "Nevermore," (poem) *Carnage Hall* #6.
Pearce, Gerald, "Below Baghdad," *Century* #3.

Perez, Dan, "Gil," *Xanadu* 3.
Perkins, Gerald, "Grandfather's Briefcase," *The Ultimate Dragon*.
Petrie, Paul, "The Bow of Ulysses," (poem) *The Sewanee Review*, Summer.
Piccirilli, Tom, "Bury St. Edmonds," *Terminal Fright* #7.
———, "Eye-Biting and Other Displays of Affection," *Pentacle*.
———, "Gone," *Not One of Us* #14.
———, "The Hanging Man," *The Silver Web* #12.
———, "The Lean," *Deathrealm* #26.
———, "Like a Hell-Broth," *Terminal Fright* #10.
———, "Maleficia," *Terminal Fright* #8.
———, "Paindance," *Terminal Fright* #9.
———, "Sorrow Laughed," *100 Wicked Little Witch Stories*.
Pinn, Paul, "Fishbone Tanner," *Grotesque* #8.
———, "The Tides of Quiddity," *The Third Alternative* #7.
Platana, Janette, "Komodo Dragon," (poem) *Deathrealm* #25.
Playford, Nicholas, "Hinges," *The Prisoner Gains a Blurred Skin*.
Pollack, Rachel, "The Bead Woman," *Strange Plasma* #8.
Powell, David L., "Brothers in Arms," *Grue* #17.
Powell, Todd, "Flesh Floats," *White Knuckles*, Vol. 1, Number 1.
Preece, Jon, "As Gone as the Dead," *Tales From Tartarus*.
Pryor, Michael, "Hunter of Darkness, Hunter of Light," *Aurealis* #15.
Ptacek, Kathryn, "Pleasure Domes," *Love Bites*.
———, "Poppet," *100 Wicked Little Witch Stories*.
———, "Three, Four, Shut the Door," *More Phobias*.
Rainey, Stephen Mark, "Angels of the Mist," *100 Vicious Little Vampire Stories*.
———, "The Pit of the Shoggoths," *The Azathoth Cycle*.
———, "Somewhere My Love," *100 Wicked Little Witch Stories*.
Rajan, Lynda, "Trial by Teaspoon," *The Penguin Book of Modern Fantasy by Women*.
Randal, John W., "Suburbia," *Year 2000* issue 1.
Rathbone, Wendy, "Piper," (poem) *Tales of the Unanticipated* #14.
Recktenwalt, D. M., "The Sayanara Shoes," *Black Moon* #2.
Reed, Kit, "The Singing Marine," *F & SF*, Oct./Nov.
Reisman, Nancy, "House Fires," *Glimmer Train* #15.
Rendell, Ruth, "Burning End," *EQMM*, Dec.
———, "Lizzie's Lover," *EQMM*, mid-Dec.
———, "Unacceptable Levels," *EQMM*, March.
Resnick, Mike, "The Light that Binds, the Claws That Catch," *The Year's Best Fantastic Fiction*.
Resnick, Mike and Shwartz, Susan, "Bibi," *Asimov's Science Fiction*, Mid-Dec.
Rice, Jane, "The Sixth Dog," (Necronomicon Press chapbook).
Rich, Mark, "The Giver," *Palace Corbie* #6.
Richardson, Randal, "The Woman on the Beach," *Random Realities* #6.
Richerson, Carrie, "No End in Sight," *More Phobias*.
Riedel, Kate, "Chad," *Not One of Us* #14.
Robbins, Richard, "Coming Back to Life," *The North Atlantic Review*, May/June.
Roberts, John Maddox, "Pirates," *AHMM*, Jan.
Roberts, Keith, "Piper's Wait," *Worlds of Fantasy & Horror* #2, Spring.
Robertson, R. Garcia y, "Happy Hunting Ground," *F & SF*, Dec.
Robins, Madeleine E., "Abelard's Kiss," *F & SF*, Aug.
Roche, Thomas S., "Self-Portrait in Nightmares," *City of Darkness: Unseen*.
Rogers, Bruce Holland, "The Apple Golem," *Xanadu* 3.
———, "A Common Night," *Fantastic Alice*.
———, "An Eye for Acquisitions," *Witch Fantastic*.

———, "Heart of Shanodin," *Magic: The Gathering/Tapestries*.
———, "Page Turner," *Aberrations* #30.
———, "These Shoes Strangers Have Died of," *Enchanted Forests*.
———, "What the Wind Carries," *High Fantastic*.
Rogers, Steven, "The Killer Soul," *Worlds of Fantasy & Horror* #2, Spring.
Rose, Malcolm, "The Ultimate Assassin," *Point Horror 13 Again*.
Rosenblum, Mary, "The Gardener," *Killing Me Softly*.
Rowand, Richard, "Residual Flight," *Xanadu 3*.
Rowe, Michael, "Wild Things Live There," *Northern Frights 3*.
Royle, Nicholas, "Bethnal Green to Kensal Rise," *Night Dreams* #2.
———, "The Harvestman," *Dark Asylum*, April.
———, "The Lagoon," *Dark Terrors*.
———, "London Wall," *The Third Alternative* #8.
Rubenstein, Gillian, "The Dog at the Door," *Dark House*.
Rufer-Bach, Kimberly, "Daddy's Girl," *Adventures in the Twilight Zone*.
Rusch, Kristine Kathryn, "The Boy Who Needed Heroes," *The Armless Maiden*.
———, "Courting Rites,"*Sisters in Fantasy*.
———, "Scars," *AHMM*, mid-Dec.
———, "Spirit Guides," *F & SF*, June/*Heaven Sent*.
Russo, Patricia, "Knock, Knock," *White Knuckles*, Vol. 1, Issue 2.
Ryals, Davyne A., "Carapace," *Tomorrow* No. 18, Dec.
Ryan, Shawn, "The Laying of Hands," *More Phobias*.
Sallee, Wayne Allen, "A God in the Hand," *More Phobias*.
———, "Lullaby & Goodnight," *Seeds of Fear*.
Salmonson, Jessica Amanda, "Black Rainbow," (poem) *Deathrealm* #26.
———, "Namer of Beasts, Maker of Souls," *The Merlin Chronicles*.
———, "The Novitiate," *Weirdbook* #29.
———, "The Strangeness of Lovers," (poem) *Grue* #17.
———, "The Strange Voyage of Doctor Morbid," *Deathrealm* #23/*Angels of Darkness*.
———, "The Watcher," (poem) *Deathrealm* #24.
Sammarco, Diane, "The Queen," *Made in Goatswood*.
Sammon, Paul M., "Within You, Without You," *Splatterpunks II: Over the Edge*.
Samuels, Mark, "The Search For Kruptos," *Tales From Tartarus*.
Saplak, Charles M., "Backstage," *The Urbanite* #5.
———, "The Numismatist," *The Urbanite* #6.
Sarafin, James, "The Word for Breaking August Sky," *AHMM*, July.
Sargent, Pamela, "Erdeni's Tiger," *Ancient Enchantresses*.
Savage, Felicity, "Appreciate It," *Tomorrow* No. 18, Dec.
———, "La Charmante," *Century* #2.
Schimel, Lawrence, "In the Schwarzwald," (poem) *Once Upon a Midnight . . .*
Schwader, Ann K., "Don't Look Down," (poem) *Grue* #17.
Schweitzer, Darrell, "Climbing," *After Hours* #25, Winter.
———, "Each Evening, Emily Dreamed of the Grave," (poem) *Lore*, Vol. 1, Number 2, Autumn.
———, "Silkie Son," *Weirdbook* #29.
———, "The Witch of the World's End," *100 Wicked Little Witch Stories*.
Schweitzer, Darrell and Hollander, Jason Van, "The Magical Dilemma of Mondesir," *Century* #2.
Scofidio, M. R., "In the Bleak Mid-Winter, Long Ago," *The Urbanite* #6.
———, "The Road to Hell," *The Urbanite* #5.
Scotch, Cheri, "Children of the Night," *Werewolves*.
Segriff, Larry, "Seeds of Death," *The Book of Kings*.
Self, Will, "Inclusion," *Esquire*, Feb.

———, "Ward 9," *The Quantity Theory of Insanity.*
Shadle, Kevin, "Wolftail," *Into the Darkness,* Vol. 1, Number 4.
Shaw, Melissa Lee, "Harpbreak," *Writers of the Future XI.*
Shawl, Nisi, "The Rainses'," *Asimov's Science Fiction,* April.
Sheffield, Charles, "The Phantom of Dunwell Cove," *Asimov's Science Fiction,* Aug.
Shepard, Lucius, "Human History," World Fantasy Convention Program Book.
Shirley, John, "War And Peace," *Fear Itself.*
Shwartz, Susan, "The Monsters of Mill Creek Park," *Enchanted Forests.*
———, "The Tenth Worthy," *Peter S. Beagle's Immortal Unicorn.*
Sickafoose, Munro, "Knives," *The Armless Maiden.*
Silva, David B., "And He Who Mourns," *Peter Straub's Ghosts.*
———, "Black and White," *Eulogy #9.*
Silverberg, Robert, "The Second Shield," *Playboy,* Dec.
Simner, Janni Lee, "Drawing the Moon," *Bruce Coville's Book of Nightmares.*
———, "Virginia Woods," *Enchanted Forests.*
Slatton, T. Diane, "Fiddlesticks," *100 Wicked Little Witch Stories.*
Smeds, Dave, "The Eight of December," *David Copperfield's Tales of the Impossible.*
———, "Survivor," *Peter S. Beagle's Immortal Unicorn.*
Smith, Michael Marshall, "Missed Connection," Time Out Net Books (online).
Smith, Sarah, "When the Red Storm Comes: or The History of a Young Lady's . . ." *Tomorrow* No. 14, June.
Smith, Tim, "Not From Here," *Peter Straub's Ghosts.*
Snyder, Midori, "The Armless Maiden," *The Armless Maiden.*
Soderstrom, Martin R., "Forever Young," *100 Vicious Little Vampire Stories.*
Somtow, S. P., "Beloved Disciple," *Dark Destiny: Proprietors of Fate.*
———, "Diamonds Aren't Forever," *David Copperfield's Tales of the Impossible.*
———, "Jeffrey Dahmer," (poem) *Once Upon a Midnight . . .*
———, "A Thief in the Night," *Peter S. Beagle's Immortal Unicorn.*
Souto, Marcial, "The Man Who Put Out the Sun," *Winter Tales II.*
Spencer, William Browning, "The Death of the Novel," *Century #1.*
———, "The Oddskeeper's Daughter," *Wheel of Fortune.*
Spizzirri, Peter M., "Angels, Strange Angels," *100 Vicious Little Vampire Stories.*
Springer, Nancy, "Black Angel," *Orphans of the Night.*
Stableford, Brian, "The Devil's Men," *100 Wicked Little Witch Stories.*
———, "The Exploration of Inner Space," *100 Vicious Little Vampire Stories.*
———, "The Hunger and Ecstasy of Vampires," (novella) *Interzone* Nos. 91–92, Jan.–Feb.
———, "Rent," *The Velvet Vampyre* issue XXVI.
———, "The Road to Hell," *Interzone* No. 97, July.
———, "The Serpent," *Interzone* No. 99, Sept.
Staig, Laurence, "Angelica's Room," *Point Horror 13 Again.*
Stansfield, Frederick, "The Return of Yig," *Crypt of Cthulhu #89.*
Steiber, Ellen, "The Fox Wife," *Ruby Slippers, Golden Tears.*
Stephens, Lorina J., "For a Cup of Tea," *On Spec,* Winter.
Stevens, Bryce, "Bandages," *Bloodsongs #6.*
Stewart, W. G., "Walk With Monsters, Walk Alone," (poem) *Once Upon a Midnight . . .*
Stone, Jr., Del, "The Fear of Fear Itself," *More Phobias.*
———, "I Feel My Body Grow," *100 Wicked Little Witch Stories.*
———, "The Parasitorium," *Blood Muse.*
Storm, Sue, "Halfbreed," *Star Bones Weep the Blood of Angels.*
———, "Mexico Blue," Ibid.
———, "The Wolf-Girl's Song," Ibid.

——, "I Hug the Snow to My Chest," *Palace Corbie* #6.
Storm, Sue and Kopaska-Merkel, David, "Eye of Moon," (poem) *Not One of Us* #13.
Stratman, Thomas M. K., "The Bataan Gamble," *Wheel of Fortune*.
Straub, Peter, "Hunger: An Introduction," *Peter Straub's Ghosts*.
Straub, Peter and Straub, Benjamin, "In Transit," *Great Writers & Kids* . . .
Strickland, Brad, "They Know," *More Phobias*.
Suarez-Beard, Beverly, "The Ruby," *Realms of Fantasy*, Aug.
Sudburg, Micole, "Calliope," *Xanadu 3*.
Sussex, Lucy, "The Lady With the Ermine," *Strange Fruit*.
Sutton, David, "La Serenissima," *Beyond* #3.
Swanwick, Michael, "North of Diddy-Wah-Diddy," *Killing Me Softly*.
Szymanski, Michael G., "Random Access," *Made in Goatswood*.
Taff, John F. D., "The Dark Level," *Deathrealm* #25.
——, "Just a Phone Call Away," *Seeds of Fear*.
Tan, Amy, "Young Girl's Wish," *The New Yorker*, Oct. 2.
Tarr, Judith, "Dame à la Licorne," *Peter S. Beagle's Immortal Unicorn*.
Taylor, Lucy, "Convergence," Ibid.
——, "Heart Pains," *High Fantastic*.
——, "Love in the Age of Ice," *Flesh Fantastic*.
Tem, Melanie, "Intimates," *Splatterpunks II: Over the Edge*.
——, "Presence," *Dark Angels: lesbian vampire stories*.
——, "Wife of Fifty Years," *Desire Burn*.
Tem, Melanie and Tem, Joseph R., "House Full of Hearts," *Great Writers & Kids* . . .
Tem, Steve Rasnic, "After the Night," *After Hours* #25.
——, "The Dead Who Do Not Sleep Under Green Sheets," (poem) *Once Upon a Midnight* . . .
——, "Mouths," *100 Vicious Little Vampire Stories*.
——, "Presage," *All Hallows* #8.
——, "Sampled," *Dark Terrors*.
——, "Tall Skies," *High Fantastic*.
Tem, Steve Rasnic and Tem, Melanie, "Nvumbi," *Xanadu 3*.
Theriault, Mireille, "Forever Yours," *Psychosis*.
Thomas, Jeffrey, "The Boarded Window," *The Bones of the Old Ones*.
——, "The Bones of the Old Ones," Ibid.
——, "Book Worm," Ibid.
——, "Empathy," *Lore*, Vol. 1, Number 3, Winter.
——, "Fallen," *Green Echo*.
——, "The Ice Ship," (poem) *The Bones of the Old Ones*.
——, "The Red Spectacles," *Terminal Fright* #9.
——, "The Reflections of Ghosts," *The Silver Web* #12.
——, "A Woman's Scream," *The Urbanite* #6.
Thompson, Patrick, "The Stones," Net Books, Dec.
Thunder, Scott, "Loathe to Bend Over," *Terminal Fright* #9.
Tilton, Lois, "Bite Me," *Love Bites*.
——, "Small Workers," *100 Wicked Little Witch Stories*.
Timlett, Peter Valentine, "Pain," *Urges 1*, Sep.
——, "The Rite of Challenge," *The Merlin Chronicles*.
Totman, Brandon W., "The Daughter," (poem) *Not One of Us* #14.
——, "Elemental Conclusions," *Rictus* #5.
Travis, Julie, "The Guinea Worm," *The Third Alternative* #5.
Travis, Tia, "Shatter," *Fear Itself*.
Tremayne, Peter, "The Foxes of Fascoum," *Weirdbook* #29.
Tripp, William T., "Snowshifter," *Plot* #4.

Turville-Heitz, M., "Sing Heavenly Muse," *Blood Muse*.
Turzillo, Mary A., "Morgaine Mourns the Loss of Lancelot," (poem) *Once Upon a Midnight . . .*
Tuttle, Lisa, "Food Man," CRANK! Autumn 1994 (appeared 1995).
———, "The Ghost Trap," *Point Horror 13 Again*.
———, "In Jealousy," *Obsessions*.
———, "White Lady's Grave," *Tombs*.
Underwood, John, "Hymn to Night," (poem) *Eldritch Tales* #30.
Urban, Scott, "Victims," *Fear Itself*.
Vachss, Andrew, "Alibi," *EQMM*, April.
VanderMeer, Jeff, "At the Crossroads, Burying the Dog," *Dark Terrors*.
———, "The Bone-Carver's Tale," *Asimov's Science Fiction*, April.
Van de Wetering, Janwillem, "Happy Hermits," *EQMM*, mid-Dec.
Van Eekhout, Greg, "Down and Dirty With a Demon Muse," *The Radical Romantic*, Vol. 3, Number 4.
Van Pelt, James, "Eight Words," *Pulphouse* issue 19.
Van Wagoner, Robert Hodgson, "Letters to a Urologist," *The Carolina Quarterly*, Winter.
Vassallo, Marc, "The Three-Legged Man," *Ploughshares*, Fall.
Vincent, Peter, "Completion," *Tales From Tartarus*.
Vukcevich, Ray, "Group," *Pulphouse* issue 19.
Wade, Susan, "Intruders," *F & SF*, July.
Waggoner, Tim, "Hair of the . . .," *Thin Ice* XVI.
———, "Newcomer," *100 Wicked Little Witch Stories*.
Wagner, Karl Edward, "I've Come to Talk With You Again," *Dark Terrors*.
———, "The Picture of Jonathan Collins," *Forbidden Acts*.
Wagner-Hankins, Maggie, "The Body," *AHMM*, July.
Waldrop, Howard, "Occam's Ducks," *Omni*, Feb.
Walsh, Pat, "The Martinmas Pilgrim," *All Hallows* #9.
Wandrei, Howard, "Tis Claude," *Time Burial*.
Ward, C. E., "Brank's Folly," *Ghosts & Scholars* #20.
Ward, Clive, "Caveat Emptor," *All Hallows* #9.
Ward, Cynthia, "The Robbery," *100 Wicked Little Witch Stories*.
Ward, Frank, "Birdy," *Space & Time* #85, Spring.
Warren, Kaaron, "Skin Holes," *Strange Fruit*.
Wasylyk, Stephen, "Sticks and Stones and the Chocolate Shop," *AHMM*, Nov.
Watkins, Graham, "Here There Be Spyders," *Fear Itself*.
Watson, Ian, "The Amber Room," *Tombs*.
Watt-Evans, Lawrence, "Impostor Syndrome," *More Phobias*.
———, "The Cat Came Back," *Bruce Coville's Book of Nightmares*.
Webb, Don, "The Agony Man," *Forbidden Acts*.
———, "The Flower Man," *Interzone* No. 99, Sept.
———, "The Gold of the Vulgar," *High Fantastic*.
———, "Thirteen Lines," *Blood Muse*.
Webb, Wendy, "The Wall of the World," *Dark Destiny: Proprietors of Fate*.
Weissenborn, Frank, "The Crosses Upon the Moor," *The Lepers*.
———, "The Entropy of Paine (The Good Son)" Ibid.
———, "The Podium Moth," (A Narrative Screenplay) Ibid.
Welsh, Irvine, "The Shooter," *The Acid House*.
———, "Snuff," Ibid.
———, "Vat 96," Ibid.
Wentworth, K. D., "Under the Weather," *AHMM*, Oct.
Westlake, Donald E., "Skeeks," *Playboy*, June.

Wheeler, Deborah, "Transfusion," *Realms of Fantasy*, Aug.
Wilhelm, Kate, "All for One," (novella) *A Flush of Shadows*.
———, "Torch Song," (novella) Ibid.
Wilkinson, Michael, "Slate," (poem) *The Third Alternative* #7.
Williams, Conrad, "The Diminished," *Dark Asylum 1*.
———, "Inside Brian," Ibid.
———, "The Pocket," *Watchfire*.
Williams, Reade, "Heartbreak," *Tales of the Unanticipated* #14.
Williams, Sean, "A Map of the Mines of Barnath," *Eidolon* #16.
Williams, Tad, "Monsieur Vergalant's Canard," *F & SF*, Sept.
———, "Three Duets for Virgin and Nosehorn," *Peter S. Beagle's Immortal Unicorn*.
Williamson, Chet, "Coventry Carol," *Peter Straub's Ghosts*.
Williamson, J. N., "Origin of a Species," *Vampire Detectives*.
Williamson, Neil, "Cages," *The Third Alternative* #6.
Wiloch, Thomas, "Mechanism of the Secret Moon." (poem) *Once Upon a Midnight . . .*
———, "My Father's Business," *The Urbanite* #6.
———, "The Terrible Secret," *Grue* #17.
Wilson, David Niall, "Another Saturday Night," *100 Vicious Little Vampire Stories*.
———, "The Fall of the House of Escher," *The Fall of the House of Escher & Other Illusions*.
———, "On the Third Day," Ibid.
———, "A Taste of Blood and Roses," *Werewolves*.
Wilson, F. Paul, "XXX," *David Copperfield's Tales of the Impossible*.
Wilson, Gahan, "The Casino Mirago," *Wheel of Fortune*.
———, "Hansel and Grettel," *Ruby Slippers, Golden Tears*.
Wilson, Robert Charles, "The Perseids," *Northern Frights 3*.
Wimsatt, Alison, "Vampires," (poem) *Nova Express*, Spring/Summer.
Wisman, Ken, "The Homeless," *Frost on the Window*.
Wolfe, Gene, "Bed & Breakfast," *Dante's Disciples*.
———, "The Ziggurat," *Full Spectrum 5*.
Wolverton, Dave, "In the Teeth of Glory," *David Copperfield's Tales of the Impossible*.
Wood, Peter H., "Mary's Desk," *All Hallows* #8.
Worley, Jeff, "UFO Lands Near Beatrice, Nebraska; Dog Killed," (poem) *The Prairie Schooner*, Fall.
Yarbro, Chelsea Quinn, "Tin Lizzies," *The Ultimate Dragon*.
Yolen, Jane, "Allerleirauh," *The Armless Maiden*.
———, "The Elf King's Daughter," (poem) *Once Upon a Midnight . . .*
———, "Sister Death," *Sisters of the Night*.
———, "The Traveler and the Tale," *Ruby Slippers, Golden Tears*.
———, "Vamping the Muse," *Blood Muse*.
———, "When Raven Sang," (poem) *Peregrine, Annual Literary Journal of Amherst Writers and Artists*, 1995.
———, "The Witch's Ride," *Here There Be Witches*.
Yolen, Jane and Stemple, Heidi Elisabet Yolen, "Daffodils," *Great Writers & Kids . . .*
Yorke, Margaret, "A Little Dose of Friendship," *EQMM*, Jan.
Yourgrau, Barry, "Acrobats," *The Sadness of Sex*.
———, "The Horse," Ibid.
———, "Lioness," Ibid.
Zelencik, Linda M., "A Blue Moon in June," *AHMM*, Oct.
Zimmerman, Michael Ryan, "Dripping Crackers," *Splatterpunks II: Over the Edge*.

The People Behind the Book

Horror Editor ELLEN DATLOW has been fiction editor of *Omni* magazine for over a decade. She has edited a number of outstanding anthologies, including *Blood Is Not Enough*, *A Whisper of Blood*, *Alien Sex*, *The Omni Books of Science Fiction*, *Little Deaths*, *Off Limits*, and (with Terri Windling) *Snow White, Blood Red* and *Black Thorn, White Rose*. She lives in New York City.

Fantasy Editor TERRI WINDLING, five-time winner of the World Fantasy Award, developed the innovative Ace Fantasy line in the 1980s. She currently is a consulting editor for Tor Books' fantasy line and runs The Endicott Studio, a transatlantic company specializing in book publishing projects and art for exhibition. She created and packaged the ongoing *Adult Fairy Tales* series of novels (Tor), the *Borderland* "punk urban fantasy" series for teenagers (Tor & HB), and co-created the *Brian Froud's Faerielands* series (Bantam). She has published over a dozen fine anthologies, including the recent book, *The Armless Maiden* (Tor), has a novel forthcoming this year from Tor Books, and a TV film in development at Columbia pictures for NBC. She lives in Devon, England, and Tucson, Arizona.

Packager JAMES FRENKEL & ASSOCIATES is JAMES FRENKEL and JAMES MINZ. James Frenkel edited Dell's SF line in the 1970s, was the publisher of Bluejay Books and was consulting editor for the Collier-Nucleus SF/Fantasy reprint series. A consulting editor for Tor Books since 1986, he edits and packages a variety of science fiction, fantasy, horror, and mystery books from his base in Madison, Wisconsin. Mr. Minz presides over a legion of interns from the University of Wisconsin, who helped create various projects.

Media Critic EDWARD BRYANT is a major author of horror and science fiction, having won Hugo awards for his work. He reviews books for a number of major newspapers and magazines, and is also a radio personality. He lives with his rubber sharks in the Port of Denver, Colorado.

Artist THOMAS CANTY is one of the most distinguished artists working in fantasy. He has won World Fantasy awards for his distinctive book jacket and cover illustrations, and is a noted book designer working in diverse fields of book publishing; he has active projects with a number of publishers, including some with various small presses. He also created children's picturebook series for St. Martin's Press and Ariel Books. He lives in Massachusetts.

ALSO AVAILABLE FROM ST. MARTIN'S PRESS

		Quantity	Price
The Year's Best Fantasy: **First Annual Collection** ISBN: 0-312-01852-5 (paperback)	($12.95)	_____	_____
The Year's Best Fantasy: **Second Annual Collection** ISBN: 0-312-03007-X (paperback)	($13.95)	_____	_____
The Year's Best Fantasy and Horror: **Third Annual Collection** ISBN: 0-312-04450-X (paperback)	($14.95)	_____	_____
The Year's Best Fantasy and Horror: Fourth **Annual Collection** ISBN: 0-312-06007-6 (paperback) ISBN: 0-312-06005-X (hardcover—$27.95)	($15.95)	_____	_____
The Year's Best Fantasy and Horror: **Fifth Annual Collection** ISBN: 0-312-07888-9 (paperback) ISBN: 0-312-07887-0 (hardcover—$27.95)	($15.95)	_____	_____
The Year's Best Fantasy and Horror: **Sixth Annual Collection** ISBN: 0-312-09422-1 (paperback) ISBN: 0-312-09421-3 (hardcover—$27.95)	($16.95)	_____	_____
The Year's Best Fantasy and Horror: Seventh **Annual Collection** ISBN: 0-312-11102-9 (paperback) ISBN: 0-312-11103-7 (hardcover—$26.95)	($16.95)	_____	_____

Postage & Handling

(Books up to $15.00 - add $3.50;
books above $15.00, add $4.00—
plus $1.00 for each additional book) _____

New York State residents add applicable Sales Tax. _____

AMOUNT ENCLOSED: _____

Name _____

Address _____

City _____ State _____ Zip _____

Send this form with payment to:
Publishers Book & Audio, P.O. Box 070059, 5448 Arthur Kill Road, Staten Island, NY 10307. Telephone (800) 288-2131.
Please allow three weeks for delivery.

For bulk orders (10 copies or more) please contact:
St. Martin's Press Special Sales Department toll free at 800-221-7945 ext. 645 for information. In New York State call 212-674-5151.